Algernon Blackwood
Tales of Terror and Darkness

Algernon Blackwood
Tales of Terror and Darkness

Part One
Tales of the Uncanny and Supernatural
Part Two
Tales of the Mysterious and Macabre

SPRING BOOKS
London · New York · Sydney · Toronto

This edition first published 1977 by
The Hamlyn Publishing Group
London · New York · Sydney · Toronto
Astronaut House
Feltham, Middlesex

ISBN 0 600 30347 0

Reproduced by photo-lithography by
Butler & Tanner Ltd, Frome and London

Part One
Tales of the Uncanny and Supernatural

CONTENTS PAGE

The Doll	1
Running Wolf	36
The Little Beggar	56
The Occupant of the Room	61
The Man Whom the Trees Loved	71
The Valley of the Beasts	144
The South Wind	166
The Man Who Was Milligan	170
The Trod	181
The Terror of the Twins	213
The Deferred Appointment	221
Accessory Before the Fact	227
The Glamour of the Snow	234
The House of the Past	256
The Decoy	262
The Tradition	283
The Touch of Pan	289
Entrance and Exit	311
The Pikestaffe Case	316
The Empty Sleeve	349
Violence	366
The Lost Valley	374

THE DOLL

Some nights are merely dark, others are dark in a suggestive way as though something ominous, mysterious, is going to happen. In certain remote outlying suburbs, at anyrate, this seems true, where great spaces between the lamps go dead at night, where little happens, where a ring at the door is a summons almost, and people cry 'Let's go to town!' In the villa gardens the mangy cedars sigh in the wind, but the hedges stiffen, there is a muffling of spontaneous activity.

On this particular November night a moist breeze barely stirred the silver pine in the narrow drive leading to the 'Laurels' where Colonel Masters lived, Colonel Hymber Masters, late of an Indian regiment, with many distinguished letters after his name. The housemaid in the limited staff being out, it was the cook who answered the bell when it rang with a sudden, sharp clang soon after ten o'clock—and gave an audible gasp half of surprise, half of fear. The bell's sudden clangour was an unpleasant and unwelcome sound. Monica, the Colonel's adored yet rather neglected child, was asleep upstairs, but the cook was not frightened lest Monica be disturbed, nor because it seemed a bit late for the bell to ring so violently; she was frightened because when she opened the door to let the fine rain drive in she saw a black man standing on the steps. There, in the wind and the rain, stood a tall, slim nigger holding a parcel.

Dark-skinned, at any rate, he was, she reflected afterwards, whether negro, Hindu or Arab; the word 'nigger' describing any man not really white. Wearing a stained yellow mackintosh and dirty slouch hat, and 'looking like a devil, so help me, God', he shoved the little parcel at her out of the gloom, the light from the hall flaring red into his gleaming eyes. 'For Colonel Masters', he whispered rapidly, 'and very special into his own personal touch and no one else.' And he melted away into the night with his 'strange foreign accent, his eyes of fire, and his nasty hissing voice'.

He was gone, swallowed up in the wind and rain.

'But I saw his eyes,' swore the cook the next morning to the housemaid, 'his fiery eyes, and his nasty look, and his black hands and long thin fingers, and his nails all shiny pink, and he looked to me—if you know wot I mean—he looked like— death...'

Thus the cook, so far as she was intelligently articulate next day, but standing now against the closed door with the small brown paper parcel in her hands, impressed by the orders that it was to be given into his personal touch, she was relieved by the fact that Colonel Masters never returned till after midnight and that she need not act at once. The reflection brought a certain comfort that restored her equanimity a little, though she still stood there, holding the parcel gingerly in her grimy hands, reluctant, hesitating, uneasy. A parcel, even brought by a mysterious dark stranger, was not in itself frightening, yet frightened she certainly felt. Instinct and superstition worked perhaps; the wind, the rain, the fact of being alone in the house, the unexpected black man, these also contributed to her discomfort. A vague sense of horror touched her, her Irish blood stirred ancient dreams, so that she began to shake a little, as though the parcel contained something alive, explosive, poisonous, unholy almost, as though it moved, and, her fingers loosening their hold, the parcel—dropped. It fell on the tiled floor with a queer, sharp clack, but it lay motionless. She eyed it closely, cautiously, but, thank God, it did not move, an inert, brown-paper parcel. Brought by an errand boy in daylight, it might have been groceries, tobacco, even a mended shirt. She peeped and tinkered, that sharp clack puzzled her. Then, after a few minutes, remembering her duty, she picked it up gingerly even while she shivered. It was to be handed into the Colonel's 'personal touch'. She compromised, deciding to place it on his desk and to tell him about it in the morning; only Colonel Masters, with those mysterious years in the East behind him, his temper and his tyrannical orders, was not easy of direct approach at the best of times, in the morning least of all.

The cook left it at that—that is, she left it on the desk in his study, but left out all explanations about its arrival. She had decided to be vague about such unimportant details, for Mrs. O'Reilly was afraid of Colonel Masters, and only his professed love of Monica made her believe that he was quite human. He paid her well, oh yes, and sometimes he smiled, and he was a handsome man, if a bit too dark for her fancy, yet he also paid her an occasional compliment about her curry, and that soothed her for the moment. They suited one another, at any rate, and she stayed, robbing him comfortably, if cautiously.

'It ain't no good,' she assured the housemaid next day, 'wot with that "personal touch into his hands, and no one else", and that black man's eyes and that crack when it came away in my hands and fell on the floor. It ain't no good, not to us nor anybody. No man as black as he was means lucky stars to anybody. A parcel indeed—with those devil's eyes—'

'What did you do with it?' enquired the housemaid.

The cook looked her up and down. 'Put it in the fire o'course,' she replied. 'On the stove if you want to know exact.'

It was the housemaid's turn to look the cook up and down. 'I don't think,' she remarked.

The cook reflected, probably because she found no immediate answer.

'Well,' she puffed out presently, 'D'you know wot *I* think? You don't. So I'll tell you. It was something the master's afraid of, that's wot it was. He's afraid of something—ever since I been here I've known that. And that's wot it was. He done somebody wrong in India long ago and that lanky nigger brought wot's coming to him, and that's why I say I put it on the stove—see?' She dropped her voice. 'It was a bloody idol,' she whispered, 'that's wot it was, that parcel, and he— why, he's a bloody secret worshipper.' And she crossed herself. 'That's why I said I put it on the stove—see?'

The housemaid stared and gasped.

3

'And you mark my words, young Jane!' added the cook, turning to her dough.

And there the matter rested for a period, for the cook, being Irish, had more laughter in her than tears, and beyond admitting to the scared housemaid that she had not really burnt the parcel but had left it on the study table, she almost forgot the incident. It was not her job, in any case, to answer the front door. She had 'delivered' the parcel. Her conscience was quite clear.

Thus, nobody 'marked her words' apparently, for nothing untoward happened, as the way is in remote Suburbia, and Monica in her lonely play was happy, and Colonel Masters as tyrannical and grim as ever. The moist wintry wind blew through the silver pine, the rain beat against the bow window and no one called. For a week this lasted, a longish time in uneventful Suburbia.

But suddenly one morning Colonel Masters rang his study bell and, the housemaid being upstairs, it was the cook who answered. He held a brown paper parcel in his hands, half opened, the string dangling.

'I found this on my desk. I haven't been in my room for a week. Who brought it? And when did it come?' His face, yellow as usual, held a fiery tinge.

Mrs. O'Reilly replied, post-dating the arrival vaguely.

'I asked *who* brought it?' he insisted sharply.

'A stranger,' she fumbled. 'Not any one,' she added nervously, 'from hereabouts. No one I ever seen before. It was a man.'

'What did he look like?' The question came like a bullet.

Mrs. O'Reilly was rather taken by surprise. 'D-darkish,' she stumbled. 'Very darkish,' she added, 'if I saw him right. Only he came and went so quick I didn't get his face proper like, and...'

'Any message?' the Colonel cut her short.

She hesitated. 'There was no answer,' she began, remembering former occasions.

'Any *message,* I asked you!' he thundered.

'No message, sir, none at all. And he was gone before I could get his name and address, sir, but I think it was a sort of black man, or it may have been the darkness of the night—I couldn't reely say, sir...'

In another minute she would have burst into tears or dropped to the floor in a faint, such was her terror of her employer especially when she was lying blind. The Colonel, however, saved her both disasters by abruptly holding out the half opened parcel towards her. He neither cross-examined nor cursed her as she had expected. He spoke with the curtness that betrayed anger and anxiety, almost, it occurred to her, distress.

'Take it away and burn it,' he ordered in his army voice, passing it into her outstretched hands. 'Burn it,' he repeated it, 'or chuck the damned thing away.' He almost flung it at her as though he did not want to touch it. 'If the man comes back,' he ordered in a voice of steel, 'tell him it's been destroyed—and say it *didn't reach me,*' laying tremendous emphasis on the final words. 'You understand?' He almost chucked it at her.

'Yes, sir. Exactly, sir,' and she turned and stumbled out, holding the parcel gingerly in her arms rather than in her hands and fingers, as though it contained something that might bite or sting.

Yet her fear had somehow lessened, for if he, Colonel Masters, could treat the parcel so contemptuously, why should she feel afraid of it? And, once alone in her kitchen among her household gods, she opened it. Turning back the thick paper wrappings, she started, and to her rather disappointed amazement, she found herself staring at nothing but a fair, waxen faced doll that could be bought in any toy-shop for one shilling and sixpence. A commonplace little cheap doll! Its face was pallid, white, expressionless, its flaxen hair was dirty, its tiny ill-shaped hands and fingers lay motionless by its side, its mouth was closed, though somehow grinning, no teeth visible, its eyelashes ridiculously like a worn tooth brush, its entire presentment in its flimsy skirt, contemptible, harmless, even ugly.

A doll! She giggled to herself, all fear evaporated.

'Gawd!' she thought. 'The master must have a conscience like the floor of a parrot's cage! And worse than that!' She was too afraid of him to despise him, her feeling was probably more like pity. 'At any rate,' she reflected, 'he had the wind up pretty bad. It was something else he expected—not a two penny halfpenny doll!' Her warm heart felt almost sorry for him.

Instead of 'chucking the damned thing away or burning it,' however,—for it was quite a nice looking doll, she presented it to Monica, and Monica, having few new toys, instantly adored it, promising faithfully, as gravely warned by Mrs. O'Reilly, that she would never *never* let her father know she had it.

Her father, Colonel Hymber Masters, was, it seems, what's called a 'disappointed' man, a man whose fate forced him to live in surroundings he detested, disappointed in his career probably, possibly in love as well, Monica a love-child doubtless, and limited by his pension to face daily conditions that he loathed.

He was a silent, bitter sort of fellow, no more than that, and not so much disliked in the neighbourhood, as misunderstood. A sombre man they reckoned him, with his dark, furrowed face and silent ways. Yet 'dark' in the suburbs meant mysterious, and 'silent' invited female fantasy to fill the vacuum. It's the frank, corn-haired man who invites sympathy and generous comment. He enjoyed his Bridge, however, and was accepted as a first-class player. Thus, he went out nightly, and rarely came back before midnight. He was welcome among the gamblers evidently, while the fact that he had an adored child at home softened the picture of this 'mysterious' man. Monica, though rarely seen, appealed to the women of the neighbourhood, and 'whatever her origin' said the gossips, 'he loves her'.

To Monica, meanwhile, in her rather play-less, toy-less life, the doll, her new treasure, was a spot of gold. The fact that it was a 'secret' present from her father, added to its value. Many other presents had come to her like that; she thought nothing of it; only, he had never given her a doll before, and it spelt rapture.

THE DOLL

Never, never, would she betray her pleasure and delight; it should remain her secret and his; and that made her love it all the more. She loved her father too, his taciturn silence was something she vaguely respected and adored. 'That's just like father,' she always said, when a strange new present came, and she knew instinctively that she must never say *Thank you* for it, for that was part of the lovely game between them. But this doll was exceptionally marvellous.

'It's much more real and alive than my Teddy bears,' she told the cook, after examining it critically. 'What ever made him think of it? Why, it even talks to me!' and she cuddled and fondled the half misshapen toy. 'It's my baby,' she cried, taking it against her cheek.

For no Teddy bear could really be a child; cuddly bears were not offspring, whereas a doll was a potential baby. It brought sweetness, as both cook and governess realized, into a rather grim house, hope and tenderness, a maternal flavour almost, something anyhow that no young bear could possibly bring. A child, a human baby! And yet both cook and governess—for both were present at the actual delivery—recalled later that Monica opened the parcel and recognised the doll with a yell of wild delight that seemed almost a scream of pain. There was this too high note of delirious exultation as though some instinctive horror of revulsion were instantly smothered and obliterated in a whirl of overmastering joy. It was Madame Jodzka who recalled—long afterwards—this singular contradiction.

'I did think she shrieked at it a bit, now you ask me,' admitted Mrs. O'Reilly later, though at the actual moment all she said was 'Oh, lovely, darling, ain't it a pet!' While all Madame Jodzka said was a cautionary 'If you squash its mouth like that, Monica, it won't be able to breathe!'

While Monica, paying no attention to either of them, fell to cuddling the doll with ecstasy.

A cheap little flaxen-haired, waxen-faced doll.

That so strange a case should come to us at second hand is, admittedly, a pity; that so much of the information should reach us largely through a cook and housemaid and through a foreigner of questionable validity, is equally unfortunate. Where precisely the reported facts creep across the feathery frontier into the incredible and thence into the fantastic would need the spider's thread of the big telescopes to define. With the eye to the telescope, the thread of that New Zealand spider seems thick as a rope; but with the eye examining second-hand reports the thread becomes elusive gossamer.

The Polish governess, Madame Jodzka, left the house rather abruptly. Though adored by Monica and accepted by Colonel Masters, she left not long after the arrival of the doll. She was a comely, youngish widow of birth and breeding, tactful, discreet, understanding. She adored Monica, and Monica was happy with her; she feared her employer, yet perhaps secretly admired him as the strong, silent, dominating Englishman. He gave her great freedom, she never took liberties, everything went smoothly. The pay was good and she needed it. Then, suddenly she left. In the suddenness of her departure, as in the odd reason she gave for leaving, lie doubtless the first hints of this remarkable affair, creeping across that 'feathery frontier' into the incredible and fantastic. An understandable reason she gave for leaving was that she was too frightened to stay in the house another night. She left at twenty-four hours' notice. Her reason was absurd, even if understandable, because any woman might find herself so frightened in a certain building that it has become intolerable to her nerves. Foolish or otherwise, this is understandable. An *idée fixe*, an obsession, once lodged in the mind of a superstitious, therefore hysterically-favoured woman, cannot be dislodged by argument. It may be absurd, yet it is 'understandable'.

The story behind the reason for Madame Jodzka's sudden terror is another matter, and it is best given quite simply. It relates to the doll. She swears by all her gods that she saw the doll 'walking by itself'. It was walking in a disjointed, hoppity, hideous fashion across the bed in which Monica lay sleeping.

THE DOLL

In the gleam of the night-light, Madame Jodzka swears she saw this happen. She was half inside the opened door, peeping in, as her habit, and duty decreed, to see if all was well with the child before going up to bed herself. The light, if faint, was clear. A jerky movement on the counterpane first caught he attention, for a smallish object seemed blundering awkwardly across its slippery silken surface. Something rolling, possibly, some object Monica had left outside on falling asleep rolling mechanically as the child shifted or turned over.

After staring for some seconds, she then saw that it was not merely an 'object', since it had a living outline, nor was it rolling mechanically, or sliding, as she had first imagined. It was horribly taking steps, small but quite deliberate steps as though alive. It had a tiny, dreadful face, it had an expressionless tiny face, and the face had eyes—small, brightly shining eyes, and the eyes looked straight at Madame Jodzka.

She watched for a few seconds thunderstruck, and she suddenly realised with a shock of utter horror that this small, purposive monster was the doll, Monica's doll! And this doll was moving towards her across the tumbled surface of the counterpane. It was coming in her direction—straight at her.

Madame Jodzka gripped herself, physically and mentally, making a great effort, it seems, to deny the abnormal, the incredible. She denied the ice in her veins and down her spine. She prayed. She thought frantically of her priest in Warsaw. Making no audible sound, she screamed in her mind. But the doll, quickening its pace, came hobbling straight towards her, its glassy eyes fixed hard upon her own.

Then Madame Jodzka fainted.

That she was, in some ways, a remarkable woman, with a sense of values, is clear from the fact that she realised this story 'wouldn't wash', for she confided it only to the cook in cautious whispers, while giving her employer some more 'washable' tale about a family death that obliged her to hurry home to Warsaw. Nor was there the slightest attempt at embroidery, for on recovering consciousness she had recovered her courage, too—and done a remarkable thing: she had compelled herself to investigate. Aided and fortified by her religion, she compelled herself to make an examination. She had tiptoed further into the room, had made sure that Monica was sleeping peacefully, and that the doll lay—motionless—half way down the counterpane. She gave it a long, concentrated look. Its lidless eyes, fringed by hideously ridiculous black lashes, were fixed on space. Its expression was not so much innocent, as blankly stupid, idiotic, a mask of death that aped cheaply a pretence of life, where life could never be. Not ugly merely, it was revolting.

Madame Jodzka, however, did more than study this visage with concentration, for with admirable pluck she forced herself to touch the little horror. She actually picked it up. Her faith, her deep religious conviction, denied the former evidence of her senses. She had *not* seen movement. It was incredible, impossible. The fault lay somewhere in herself. This persuasion, at any rate, lasted long enough to enable her to touch the repulsive little toy, to pick it up, to lift it. She placed it steadily on the table near the bed between the bowl of flowers and the nightlight, where it lay on its back helpless, innocent, yet horrible, and only then on shaking legs did she leave the room and go up to her own bed. That her fingers remained ice-cold until eventually she fell asleep can be explained, of course, too easily and naturally to claim examination.

Whether imagined or actual, it must have been, none the less, a horrifying spectacle—a mechanical outline from a commercial factory walking like a living thing with a purpose. It holds the nightmare touch. To Madame Jodzka, protected since youth within cast-iron tenets, it came as a shock. And a shock dislocates. The sight smashed everything she knew as possible and real. The flow of her blood was interrupted, it froze, there came icy terror into her heart, her normal mechanism failed for a moment, she fainted. And fainting seemed a natural result. Yet it was the shock of the incredible masquerade that gave her the courage to act. She loved Monica, apart from any consideration of paid duty. The sight of this tiny monstrosity strutting across the counterpane not far from the child's sleeping face and folded hands—it was this that enabled her to pick it up with naked fingers and set it out of reach...

For hours, before falling asleep, she reviewed the incredible thing, alternately denying the facts, then accepting them, yet taking into sleep finally the assured conviction that her senses had not deceived her. There seems little, indeed, that in a court of law could have been advanced against her character for reliability, for sincerity, for the logic of her detailed account.

'I'm sorry,' said Colonel Masters quietly, referring to her bereavement. He looked searchingly at her. 'And Monica will miss you,' he added with one of his rare smiles. 'She needs you.' Then just as she turned away, he suddenly extended his hand. 'If perhaps later you can come back—do let me know. Your influence is—so helpful—and good.'

She mumbled some phrase with a promise in it, yet she left with a queer, deep impression that it was not merely, not chiefly perhaps, Monica who needed her. She wished he had not used quite those words. A sense of shame lay in her, almost as though she were running away from duty, or at least from a change to help that God had put in her way. 'Your influence is—so good.'

Already in the train and on the boat conscience attacked her, biting, scratching, gnawing. She had deserted a child she loved, a child who needed her, because she was scared out of her wits. No, that was a one-sided statement. She had left a house because the Devil had come into it. No, that was only partially true. When a hysterical temperament, engrained since early childhood in fixed dogmas, begins to sift facts and analyse reactions, logic and common sense themselves become confused. Thought led one way, emotion another, and no honest conclusion dawned on her mind.

She hurried on to Warsaw, to a stepfather, a retired General whose gay life had no place for her and who would not welcome her return. It was a derogatory prospect for this youngish widow who had taken a job in order to escape from his vulgar activities to return now empty-handed. Yet it was easier, perhaps, to face a step-father's selfish anger than to go and tell Colonel Masters her real reason for leaving his service. Her conscience, too, troubled her on another score as thoughts and memories travelled backwards and half-forgotten details emerged.

Those spots of blood, for instance, mentioned by Mrs. O'Reilly, the superstitious Irish cook. She had made it a rule to ignore Mrs. O'Reilly's silly fairy tales, yet now she recalled suddenly those ridiculous discussions about the laundry list and the foolish remarks that the cook and housemaid had let fall.

'But there ain't no paint in a doll, I tell you. It's all sawdust and wax and muck,' from the housemaid. 'I know red paint when I see it, and that ain't paint, it's blood.' And from Mrs. O'Reilly later: 'Mother o' God! Another red blob! She's biting her finger-nails—and that's not *my* job...!'

The red stains on sheets and pillow cases were puzzling certainly, but Madame Jodzka, hearing these remarks by chance as it were, had paid no particular attention to them at the moment. The laundry lists were hardly her affair. These ridiculous servants anyhow...! And yet, now in the train, those spots of red, be they paint or blood, crept back to trouble her.

Another thing, oddly enough, also troubled her—the ill-defined feeling that she was deserting a man who needed help, help that she could give. It was too vague to put into words. Was it based on his remark that her influence was 'good' perhaps? She could not say. It was an intuition, and few intuitions bear analysis. Supporting it, however, was a conviction she had felt since first she entered the service of Colonel Masters, the conviction, namely, that he had a past that frightened him. There was something he had done, something he regretted and was probably ashamed of, something at any rate, for which he feared retribution. A retribution, moreover, he expected; a punishment that would come like a thief in the night and seize him by the throat.

It was against this dreaded vengeance that her influence was 'good', a protective influence possibly that her religion supplied, something on the side of the angels, in any case, that her personality provided.

Her mind worked thus, it seems; and whether a concealed admiration for this sombre and mysterious man, an admiration and protective instinct never admitted even to her inmost self, existed below the surface, hidden yet urgent, remains the secret of her own heart.

It was naturally and according to human nature, at any rate, that after a few weeks of her step-father's outrageous behaviour in the house, his cruelty too, she decided to return. She prayed to her gods incessantly, also she found oppressive her sense of neglected duty and failure of self-respect. She returned to the soulless suburban villa. It was understandable; the welcome from Monica was also understandable, the relief and pleasure of Colonel Masters still more so. It was expressed, this latter, in a courteous message only, tactfully worded, as though she had merely left for brief necessity, for it was some days before she actually saw him to speak to. From cook and housemaid the welcome was voluble and—disquieting. There were no more inexplicable 'spots of red', but there were other unaccountable happenings even more distressing.

'She's missed you something terrible,' said Mrs. O'Reilly, 'though she's found something else to keep her quiet—if you like to put it that way.' And she made the sign of the cross.

'The doll?' asked Madame Jodzka with a start of shocked horror, forcing herself to come straight to the point and forcing herself also to speak lightly, casually.

'That's it, Madame. The bleeding doll.'

The governess had heard the strange adjective many times already, but did not know whether to take it figuratively or not. She chose the latter.

'Blood?' he asked in a lowered voice.

The cook's body gave an odd jerk. 'Well,' she explained. 'I

meant more the way it goes on. Like a thing of flesh and blood, if you get me. And the way *she* treats it and plays with it,' and her voice, while loud, had a hush of fear in it somewhere. She held her arms before her in a protective, shielding way, as though to ward off aggression.

'Scratches ain't proof of nothing,' interjected the housemaid scornfully.

'You mean,' asked Madame Jodzka gravely, 'there's a question of—of injury—to someone?' She suppressed an involuntary gasp, but paid no attention to the maid's interruption otherwise.

Mrs. O'Reilly seemed to mismanage her breath for a moment.

'It ain't Miss Monica it's after,' she announced in a defiant whisper as soon as she recovered herself, 'it's someone else. *That's* what I mean. And no man as black as *he* was,' she let herself go, 'ever brought no good into a house, not since I was born.'

'Someone else—?' repeated Madame Jodzka almost to herself, seizing the vital words.

'You and yer black man!' interjected the housemaid. 'Get along with yer! Thank God I ain't a Christian or anything like that! But I did 'ear them sort of jerky shuffling footseps one night, I admit, and the doll did look bigger—swollen like— when I peeked in an looked—'

'Stop it!' cried Mrs O'Reilly, 'for you ain't saying what's true or what you reely know.'

She turned to the governess.

'There's more talk what means nothing about this doll,' she said by way of apology, 'that all the fairy tales I was brought up with as a child in Mayo, and I—I wouldn't be believing anything of it.'

Turning her back contemptuously on the chattering housemaid, she came close to Madame Jodzka.

'There's no harm coming to Miss Monica, Madame,' she whispered vehemently, 'you can be quite sure about *her*. Any trouble there may be is for someone else.' And again she crossed herself.

THE DOLL

Madame Jodzka, in the privacy of her room, reflected between her prayers. She felt a deep, a dreadful uneasiness.

A doll! A cheap, tawdry little toy made in factories by the hundred, by the thousand, a manufactured article of commerce for children to play with... But...

'The way she treats it and plays with it...' rang on in her disturbed mind.

A doll! But for the maternal suggestion, a doll was a pathetic, even horrible plaything, yet to watch a child busy with it involved deep reflections, since here the future mother prophesied. The child fondles and caresses her doll with passionate love, cares for it, seeks its welfare, yet stuffs it down into the perambulator, its head and neck twisted, its limbs broken and contorted, leaving it atrociously upside down so that blood and breathing cannot possibly function, while she runs to the window to see if the rain has stopped or the sun has come out. A blind and hideous automatism dictated by the race, provided nothing of more immediate interest interferes, yet a herd-instinct that overcomes all obstacles, its vitality insuperable. The maternity instinct defies, even denies death. The doll, whether left upside down on the floor with broken teeth and ruined eyes, or lovingly arranged to be overlaid in the night, squashed, tortured, mutilated, survives all cruelties and disasters, and asserts finally its immortal qualities. It is unkillable. It is beyond death.

A child with her doll, reflected Madame Jodzka, is an epitome of nature's remorseless and unconquerable passion, of her dominant purpose—the survival of the race. ...

Such thoughts, influenced perhaps by her bitter subconscious grievance against nature for depriving her of a child of her own, were unable to hold that level for long; they soon dropped back to the concrete case that perplexed and frightened her—Monica and her flaxen haired, sightless, idiotic doll. In the middle of her prayers, falling asleep incontinently, she did not even dream of it, and she woke refreshed and vigorous, facing the fact that sooner or later, sooner probably, she would have to speak to her employer.

She watched and listened. She watched Monica; she watched the doll. All seemed as normal as in a thousand other homes. Her mind reviewed the position, and where mind and superstition clashed, the former held its own easily. During her evening off she enjoyed the local cinema, leaving the heated building with the conviction that coloured fantasy benumbed the faculties, and that ordinary life was in itself prosaic. Yet before she had covered the half-mile to the house, her deep, unaccountable uneasiness returned with overmastering power.

Mrs. O'Reilly had seen Monica to bed for her, and it was Mrs. O'Reilly who let her in. Her face was like the dead.

'It's been talking,' whispered the cook, even before she closed the door. She was white about the gills.

'Talking! *Who*'s been talking? What do you mean?'

Mrs. O'Reilly closed the door softly. 'Both,' she stated with dramatic emphasis, then sat down and wiped her face. She looked distraught with fear.

Madame took command, if only a command based on dreadful insecurity.

'Both?' she repeated, in a voice deliberately loud so as to counteract the other's whisper. 'What are you talking about?'

'They've *both* been talking—talking together,' stated the cook.

The governess kept silent for a moment, fighting to deny a shrinking heart.

'You've heard them talking together, you mean?' she asked presently in a shaking voice that tried to be ordinary.

Mrs. O'Reilly nodded, looking over her shoulder as she did so. Her nerves were, obviously, in rags. 'I thought you'd *never* come back,' she whimpered. 'I could hardly stay in the house.'

Madame looked intently into her frightened eyes.

'You *heard*...?' she asked quietly.

'I listened at the door. There were two voices. Different voices.'

Madame Jodzka did not insist or cross-examine, as though acute fear helped her to a greater wisdom.

'You mean, Mrs. O'Reilly,' she said in flat, quiet tones, 'that you heard Miss Monica talking to her doll as she always does,

THE DOLL

and herself inventing the doll's answers in a changed voice? Isn't that what you mean you heard?'

But Mrs. O'Reilly was not to be shaken. By way of answer she crossed herself and shook her head.

She spoke in a low whisper. 'Come up now and listen with me, Madame, and judge for yourself.'

Thus, soon after midnight, and Monica long since asleep, these two, the cook and governess in a suburban villa, took up their places in the dark corridor outside a child's bedroom door. It was a quiet windless night; Colonel Masters, whom they both feared, doubtless long since gone to his room in another corner of the ungainly villa. It must have been a long dreary wait before sounds in the child's bedroom first became audible—the low quiet sound of voices talking audibly—two voices. A hushed, secretive, unpleasant sound in the room where Monica slept peacefully with her beloved doll beside her. Yet two voices assuredly, it was.

Both women sat erect, both crossed themselves involuntarily, exchanging glances. Both were bewildered, terrified. Both sat aghast.

What lay in Mrs. O'Reilly's superstitious mind, only the gods of 'ould Oireland' can tell, but what the Polish woman's contained was clear as a bell; it was not two voices talking, it was only one. Her ear was pressed against the crack in the door. She listened intently; shaking to the bone, she listened. Voices in sleep-talking, she remembered, changed oddly.

'The child's talking to herself in sleep,' she whispered firmly, 'and that's all it is, Mrs. O'Reilly. She's just talking in her sleep,' she repeated with emphasis to the woman crowding against her shoulder as though in need of support. 'Can't you hear it,' she added loudly, half angrily, 'isn't it the same voice always? Listen carefully and you'll see I'm right.'

She listened herself more closely than before.

'Listen! Hark...!' she repeated in a breathless whisper, concentrating her mind upon the curious sound, 'isn't that the same voice—answering itself?'

Yet, as she listened, another sound disturbed her concentration, and this time it seemed a sound behind her—a faint, rustling, shuffling sound rather like footsteps hurrying away on tiptoe. She turned her head sharply and found that she had been whispering to no one. There was no one beside her. She was alone in the darkened corridor. Mrs. O'Reilly was gone. From the well of the house below a voice came up in a smothered cry beneath the darkened stairs: 'Mother o'God and all the Saints...' and more besides.

A gasp of surprise and alarm escaped her, doubtless at finding herself deserted and alone but in the same instant, exactly as in the story books, came another sound that caught her breath still more aghast—the rattle of a key in the front door below. Colonel Masters, after all, had not yet come in and gone to bed as expected: he was coming in now. Would Mrs. O'Reilly have time to slip across the hall before he caught her? More—and worse—would he come up and peep into Monica's bedroom on his way up to bed, as he rarely did? Madame Jodzka listened, her nerves in rags. She heard him fling down his coat. He was a man quick in such actions. The stick or umbrella was banged down noisily, hastily. The same instant his step sounded on the stairs. He was coming up. Another minute and he would start into the passage where she crouched against Monica's door.

He was mounting rapidly, two stairs at a time.

She, too, was quick in action and decision. She thought in a flash. To be caught crouching outside the door was ludicrous, but to be caught inside the door would be natural and explicable. She acted at once.

With a palpitating heart, she opened the bedroom door and stepped inside. A second later she heard Colonel Masters' tread, as he stumped along the corridor up to bed. He passed the door. He went on. She heard this with intense relief.

Now, inside the room, the door closed behind her, she saw the picture clearly.

Monica, sound asleep, was playing with her beloved doll, but in her sleep. She was indubitably in deep slumber. Her fingers, however, were roughing the doll this way and that, as though some dream perplexed her. The child was mumbling in her sleep, though no words were distinguishable. Muffled sighs and groans issued from her lips. Yet another sound there certainly was, though it could not have issued from the child's mouth. Whence, then, did it come?

Madame Jodzka paused, holding her breath, her heart panting. She watched and listened intently. She heard squeaks and grunts, but a moment's examination convinced her whence these noises came. They did not come from Monica's lips. They issued indubitably from the doll she clutched and twisted in her dream. The joints, as Monica twisted them emitted these odd sounds, as though the sawdust in knees and elbows wheezed and squeaked against the unnatural rubbing. Monica obviously was wholly unconscious of these noises. At the doll's neck screwed round, the material—wax, thread, sawdust—produced this curious grating sound that was almost like syllables of a word or words.

Madame Jodzka stared and listened. She felt icy cold. Seeking for a natural explanation she found none. Prayer and terror raced in her helter-skelter. Her skin began to sweat.

Then, suddenly Monica, her expression peaceful and composed, turned over in her sleep, and the dreadful doll, released from the dream-clutch, fell to one side on the bed and lay apparently lifeless and inert. In which moment, to Madame Jodzka's unbelieving yet horrified ears, it continued to squeak and utter. It went on mouthing by itself. Worse than that, the next instant it stood abruptly upright, rising on its twisted legs. It started moving. It began to move, walking crookedly, across the counterpane. Its glassy, sightless eyes, seemed to look straight at her. It presented an inhuman and appalling picture, a picture of the utterly incredible. With a queer, hoppity motion of its broken legs and joints, it came fumbling and tumbling across the rough unevenness of the slippery counterpane towards her. Its appearance was deliberate and aggressive. The sounds, as of syllables, came with it—strange, meaningless syllables that yet managed to convey anger. It stumbled towards her like a living thing. Its whole presentment conveyed attack.

Once again, this effect of a mere child's toy, aping the life of some awful monstrosity with purpose and passion in its hideous tiny outline, brought collapse to the plucky Polish governess. The rush of blood without control drained her heart, and a moment of unconsciousness supervened so that everything, as it were, turned black.

This time, however, the moment of dark unconsciousness passed instantly: it came and went, almost like a moment of forgetfulness in passion. Passionate it certainly was, for the reaction came upon her like a storm. With recovered consciousness a sudden rage rushed into her woman's heart—perhaps a coward's rage, an exaggerated fury against her own weakness? It rushed, in any case, to help her. She staggered, caught her breath, clutched violently at the cupboard next to her, and—recovered her self-control. A fury of resentment blazed through her, fury against this utterly incredible exhibition of a wax doll walking and squawking as though it were something intelligently alive that could utter syllables. Syllables, she felt convinced, in a language she did not know.

If the monstrous can paralyse, it also can affront. The sight and sound of this cheap factory toy behaving with a will and heart of its own stung her into an act of violence that became imperative. For it was more than she could stand. Irresistibly, she rushed forward. She hurled herself against it, her only avaible weapon the high-heeled shoe her foot kicked loose on the instant, determined to smash down the frightful apparition into fragments and annihilate it. Hysterical, no doubt, she was at the moment, and yet logical: the godless horror must be blotted out of visible existence. This one thing obsessed her—to destroy beyond all possibility of survival. It must be smashed into fragments, into dust.

They stood close, face to face, the glassy eyes staring into her own, her hand held high for the destruction she craved—but the hand did not fall. A stinging pain, sharp as a serpent's bite, darted suddenly through her fingers, wrist and arm, her grip was broken, the shoe spun sideways across the room, and in the flickering light of the candle, it seemed to her, the whole room quivered. Paralysed and helpless, she stood utterly aghast. What gods or saints could come to aid her? None. Her own will alone could help her. Some effort, at any rate, she made, trembling, on the edge of collapse: 'My God!' she heard her half whispering, strangled voice cry out. 'It is not true! You are a lie! My God denies you! I call upon my God...!'

Whereupon, to her added horror, the dreadful little doll, waving a broken arm, squawked back at her, as though in definite answer, the strange disjointed syllables she could not understand, syllables as though in another tongue. The same instant it collapsed abruptly on the counterpane like a toy balloon that had been pricked. It shrank down in a mutilated mess before her eyes, while Monica—added touch of horror—stirred uneasily in her sleep, turning over and stretching out her hands as though feeling blindly for something that she missed. And this sight of the innocently sleeping child fumbling instinctively towards an incomprehensibly evil and dangerous something that attracted her proved again too strong for the Polish woman to control.

The blackness intervened a second time.

It was undoubtedly a blur in memory that followed, emotion and superstition proving too much for common-sense to deal with. She just remembers violent, unreasoned action on her part before she came back to clearer consciousness in her own room, praying volubly on her knees against her own bed. The interval of transit down the corridor and upstairs remained a blank. Yet her shoe was with her, clutched tightly in her hand. And she remembered also having clutched an inert, waxen doll with frantic fingers, clutched and crushed and crumpled its awful little frame till the sawdust came spurting from its broken joints and its tiny body was mutilated beyond recognition, if not annihilated... then stuffing it down ruthlessly on a table far out of Monica's reach—Monica lying peacefully in deepest sleep.

She remembered that. She also saw the clear picture of the small monster lying upside down, grossly untidy, an obscene attitude in the disorder of its flimsy dress and exposed limbs, lying motionless, its eyes crookedly aglint, motionless, yet alive till, alive moreover with intense and malignant purpose.

No duration or intensity of prayer could obliterate the picture.

She knew now that a plain, face to face talk with her employer was essential; her conscience, her peace of mind, her sanity, her sense of duty all demanded this. Deliberately, and she was sure, rightly, she had never once risked a word with the child herself. Danger lay that way, the danger of emphasizing something in the child's mind that was best left ignored. But with Colonel Masters, who paid her for her services, believed in her integrity, trusted her, with him there must be an immediate explanation.

An interview was absurdly difficult; in the first place because he loathed and avoided such occasions; secondly because he was so exceedingly impervious to approach, being so rarely even visible at all. At night he came home late, in the mornings no one dared go near him. He expected the little household, its routine established, to run itself. The only inmate who dared beard him was Mrs. O'Reilly, who periodically, once every six months, walked straight into his study, gave notice, received an addition to her wages, and then left him alone for another six months.

Madame Jodzka, knowing his habits, waylaid him in the hall next morning while Monica was lying down before lunch, as usual. He was on his way out and she had been watching from the upper landing. She had hardly set eyes on him since her return from Warsaw. His lean, upright figure, his dark, emotionless face, she thought magnificent. He was the perfect expression of the soldier. Her heart fluttered as she raced downstairs. Her carefully prepared sentences, however, evaporated when he stopped and looked at her, a jumble of wild words pouring from her in confused English instead. He cut her rigmarole short, though he listened politely enough at first.

THE DOLL

'I'm so glad you were able to come back to us, as I told you. Monica missed you very much—'

'She has something now she plays with—'

'The very thing,' he interrupted. 'No doubt the kind of toy she needs... Your excellent judgment... Please tell me if there's anything else you think...' and he half turned as though to move away.

'But I didn't get it. It's a horrible—*horrible*—'

Colonel Masters uttered one of his rare laughs. 'Of course, all children's toys are horrible, but if she's pleased with it... I haven't seen it, I'm no judge... If you can buy something better—' and he shrugged his shoulders.

'I didn't buy it,' she cried desperately. 'It was brought. It makes sounds by itself—syllables. I've seen it move—move by itself. It's a doll.'

He turned from the front door which he had just reached as though he had been shot; the skin held a sudden pallor beneath the flush and something contradicted the blazing eyes, something that seemed to shrink.

'A doll,' he repeated in a very quiet voice. 'You said—a doll?'

But his eyes and face disconcerted her, so that she merely gave a fumbling account of a parcel that had been brought. His question about a parcel he had ordered strictly to be destroyed added to her confusion.

'Wasn't it?' he asked in a rasping whisper, as though a disobeyed order seemed incredible.

'It was thrown away, I believe,' she prevaricated, unable to meet his eyes, anxious to protect the cook as well. 'I think Monica—perhaps found it.' She despised her lack of courage, but his intensity scattered her wits; she was conscious, moreover, of a strange desire not to give him pain, as though his safety and happiness, not Monica's, were at stake. 'It—talks!—as well as *moves*,' she cried desperately, forcing herself at last to look at him.

Colonel Masters seemed to stiffen; his breath caught oddly.

'You say Monica has it? Plays with it? You've seen movement and heard sounds like syllables?' He asked the questions in a low voice, almost as though talking to himself. 'You've—listened?' he whispered.

Unable to find convincing words, she bowed her head, while some terror in him came across to her like a blast of icy wind. The man was afraid in his heart. Instead, however, of some explosive reply by way of blame or criticism, he spoke quietly, even calmly: 'You did right to come and tell me this—quite right,' adding then in so low a tone that she barely caught the ominous words, 'for I have been expecting something of the sort... sooner or later... it was bound to come...' the voice dying away into the handkerchief he put to his face.

And abruptly then, as though aware of an appeal for sympathy, an emotional reaction swept her fear away. Stepping closer, she looked her employer straight in the eyes.

'See the child for yourself,' she said with sudden firmness. 'Come and listen with me. Come into the bedroom.'

She saw him stagger. For a moment he said nothing.

'Who,' he then asked, the low voice unsteady, 'who brought that parcel?'

'A man, I believe.'

There was a pause that seemed like minutes before his next question.

'White,' he asked, 'or—black?'

'Dark,' she told him, 'very dark.'

He was shaking like a leaf, the skin of his face blanched; he leaned against the door, wilted, limp; unless she somehow took command there threatened a collapse she did not wish to witness.

'You shall come with me tonight,' she said firmly, 'and we shall listen together. Wait till I return now. I go for brandy,' and a minute later as she came back breathless and watched him gulp down half a tumbler full, she knew that she had done right in telling him. His obedience proved it, though it seemed strange that cowardice should borrow from its like to produce courage.

'Tonight,' she repeated, 'tonight after your Bridge. We meet in the corridor outside the bedroom. At half-past twelve.'

THE DOLL

He pulled himself into an upright position, staring at her fixedly, making a movement of his head, half bow, half nod. 'Twelve thirty,' he muttered, 'in the passage outside the bedroom door,' and using his stick rather heavily, he opened the door and passed out into the drive. She watched him go, aware that her fear had changed to pity, aware also that she watched the stumbling gait of a man too conscience-stricken to know a moment's peace, too frightened even to think of God.

Madame Jodzka kept the appointment; she had eaten no supper, but had stayed in her room—praying. She had first put Monica to bed.

'My doll,' the child pleaded, good as gold, after being tucked up. 'I must have my doll or else I'll never get to sleep,' and Madame Jodzka had brought it with reluctant fingers, placing it on the night-table beside the bed.

'She'll sleep quite comfortably here, Monica, darling. Why not leave her outside the sheets?' It had been carefully mended, she noticed, patched together with pins and stitches.

The child grabbed at it. 'I want her in bed beside me, close against me,' she said with a happy smile. 'We tell each other stories. If she's too far away I can't hear what she says.' And she seized it with a cuddling pleasure that made the woman's heart turn cold.

'Of course, darling—if it helps you to fall asleep quickly, you shall have it,' and Monica did not see the trembling fingers, nor notice the horror in the face and voice. Indeed, hardly was the doll against her cheek on the pillow, her fingers half stroking the flaxen hair and pink wax cheeks, than her eyes closed, a sigh of deep content breathed out, and Monica was asleep.

Madame Jodzka, fearful of looking behind her, tiptoed to the door, and left the room. In the passage she wiped a cold sweat from her forehead. 'God bless her and protect her,' her heart murmured, 'and may God forgive me if I've sinned.'

She kept the appointment; she knew Colonel Masters would keep it, too.

It had been a long wait from eight o'clock till after midnight.

With great determination she had kept away from the bedroom door, fearful lest she might hear a sound that would necessitate action on her part: she went to her room and stayed there. But praying exhausted itself, for it both excited and betrayed her. If her God could help, a brief request alone was needed. To go on praying for help hour by hour was not only an insult to her deity, but it also wore her out physically. She stopped, therefore, and read some pages of a Polish saint which she did not understand. Later she fell into a state of horrified nervous drowse. In due course, she slept...

A noise awoke her—steps going softly past her door. A glance at her watch showed eleven o'clock. The steps, though stealthy, were familiar. Mrs. O'Reilly was waddling up to bed. The sounds died away. Madame Jodzka, a trifle ashamed, though she hardly knew why, returned to her Polish saint, yet determined to keep her ears open. Then slept again...

What woke her a second time she could not tell. She was startled. She listened. The night was unpleasantly still, the house quiet as the grave. No casual traffic passed. No wind stirred the gloomy evergreens in the drive. The world outside was silent. And then, as she saw by her watch that it was some minutes after midnight, a sharp click became audible that acted like a pistol shot to her keyed-up nerves. It was the front door closing softly. Steps followed across the hall below, then up the stairs, unsteadily a little. Colonel Masters had come in. He was coming up slowly, unwillingly she felt, to keep the appointment. Madame Jodzka started from her chair, looked in the glass, mumbled a quick confused prayer, and opened her door into the dark passage.

She stiffened, physically and mentally. 'Now, he'll hear and perhaps see—for himself,' she thought. 'And God help him!'

She marched along the passage and reached the door of Monica's bedroom, listening with such intentness that she seemed to hear only the confused running murmur of her own blood. Having reached the appointed spot, she stood stock still and waited while his steps approached. A moment later

THE DOLL

his bulk blocked the passage, shown up as a dark shadow by the light in the hall below. This bulk came nearer, came right up to her. She believed she said 'Good evening', and that he mumbled something about 'I said I'd come... damned nonsense...' or words to that effect, whereupon the couple stood side by side in the darkened silence of the corridor, remote from the rest of the house, and waited without further words. They stood shoulder to shoulder outside the door of Monica's bedroom. Her heart was knocking against her side.

She heard his breathing, there came a whiff of spirits, of stale tobacco smoke, his outline seemed to shift against the wall unsteadily, he moved his feet; and a sudden, extraordinary wave of emotion swept over her, half of protective maternal yearning, half almost of sexual desire, so that for a passing instant she burned to take him in her arms and kiss him savagely, and at the same time shield him from some appalling danger his blunt ignorance laid him open to. With revulsion, pity, and a sense of sin and passion, she acknowledged this odd sudden weakness in herself, but the face of the Warsaw priest flashed across her fuddled mind the next instant. There was evil in the air. This meant the Devil. She felt herself trembling dreadfully, shaking in her shoes, losing her balance, her whole body leaning over, but leaning in his direction. A moment more and she must have fallen towards him, dropped into his arms.

A sound broke the silence, and she drew up just in time. It came from beyond the door, from inside the bedroom.

'Hark!' she whispered, her hand upon his arm, and while he made no movement, spoke no word, she saw his head and shoulders bend down toward the panel of the closed door. There was a noise, upon the other side, there were noises, Monica's voice distinctly recognisable, another slighter, shriller sound accompanying it, breaking in upon it, answering it. Two voices.

'Listen,' she repeated in a whisper scarcely audible, and felt his warm hand grip her own so fiercely that it hurt her.

No words were distinguishable at first, just these odd broken sounds of two separate voices in that dark corridor of the silent house—the voice of a child, and the other a strange, faint, hardly human sound, while yet a voice.

'*Que le bon Dieu*—' she began, then faltered, breath failing her, for she saw Colonel Masters stoop down suddenly and do the last thing that would have occurred to her as likely: he put his eye to the key-hole and kept it there steadily, for the best part of a minute, his hand still gripping her own firmly. He knelt on one knee to keep his balance.

The sounds had ceased, no movement now stirred inside the room. The night-light, she knew, would show him clearly the pillows of the bed, Monica's head, the doll in her arms. Colonel Masters must see clearly anything there was to see, and he yet gave no sign that he saw anything. She experienced a queer sensation for a few seconds—almost as though she had perhaps imagined everything and proved herself a consummate, idiotic, hysterical fool. For a few seconds this ghastly thought flashed over her, the odd silence emphasising it. Had she been, after all, just a crazy lunatic? Had her senses all decived her? Why should he see nothing, make no sign? Why had the voice, the voices, ceased? Not a murmur of any sort was audible in the room.

Then Colonel Masters, suddenly releasing his grip of her hand, shuffled on to both feet and stood up straight, while in the same instant she herself stiffened, trying to prepare for the angry scorn, the contemptuous abuse he was about to pour upon her. Protecting herself against this attack, expecting it, she was the more amazed at what she did hear:

'I saw it,' came in a strangled whisper. 'I saw it walk!'

She stood paralysed.

'It's watching me,' he added, scarcely audible. '*Me!*'

The revulsion of feeling at first left her speechles; it was the sheer terror in his strangled whisper that restored a measure of self possession to her. Yet it was he who found words first, awful whispered words, words spoken to himself, it seemed, more than to her.

'It's what I've always feared—I knew it must come some day—yet not like this. Not this way.'

Then immediately the voice in the room became audible, and it was a sweet and gentle voice, sincere and natural, with feeling in it—Monica's childish voice, pleading:

'Don't go, don't leave me! Come back into bed—please.'

An incomprehensible sound followed, as though by way of answer. There were syllables in that faint, creaky tone Madame Jodzka recognised, but syllables she could not comprehend. They seemed to enter her like points of ice. She froze. And facing her stood the motionless, inanimate bulk of him, his outline, then leaned over towards her, his lips so close to her own face that, as he spoke, she felt the breath upon her cheek.

'*Buth laga*...' she heard him repeat the syllables to himself again and again. '*Revenge*... in Hindustani...!' He drew a long, anguished breath. The sounds sank into her like drops of poison, the syllables she had heard several times already but had not understood. At last she understood their meaning. Revenge!

'I must go in, go in,' he was mumbling to himself. 'I must go in and face it.' Her intuition was justified: the danger was not for Monica but for himself. Her sudden protective maternal instinct found its explanation too. The lethal power concentrated in that hideous puppet was aimed at *him*. He began to edge impetuously past her.

'No!' she cried. 'I'll go! Let me go in!' pushing him aside with all her strength. But his hand was already on the knob and the next instant the door was open and he was inside the room. On the threshold they stood still a second, side by side, though she was slightly behind, struggling to shove past him and stand protectively in front.

She stared across his shoulder, her eyes so wide open that the intense strain to note everything at once threatened to defeat its own end. Sight, none the less, worked normally; she saw all there was to see, and that was—nothing; nothing unusual that is, nothing abnormal, nothing terrifying, so that this second time the threat of anti-climax rose to her mind. Had she worked herself up to this peak of horror merely to behold Monica lying sound asleep in a safe and quiet room? The flickering night-light revealed no more than a child in natural slumber without a toy of any sort against her pillow. There stood the glass of water beside the flowers in their saucer, the picture-book on the sill of the window within reach, the window opened a little at the bottom, and there also lay the calm face of Monica with eyes tight shut upon the pillow. Her breathing was deep and regular, no sign of disquiet anywhere, no hint of disturbance that might have accompanied that pleading sentence of two minutes ago, except that the bedclothes were perhaps somewhat tumbled. The counterpane humped itself in folds towards the foot of the bed, she noticed, as though Monica, finding it too warm, had tossed it away in sleep. No more than that.

In that first moment Colonel Masters and the governess took in this whole pretty picture complete. The room was so still that the child's breathing was distinctly audible. Their eyes roved all over. Nothing was anywhere in movement. Yet the same instant Madame Jodzka became aware that there *was* movement. Something stirred. The report came, perhaps, through her skin, for no sense announced it. It was undeniable; in that still, silent room there was movement somewhere, and with that unreported movement there was danger.

Certain, rightly or wrongly, that she herself was safe, also that the quietly sleeping child was safe, she was equally certain that Colonel Masters was the one in danger. She knew that in her very bones.

'Wait here by the door,' she said almost peremptorily, as she felt him pushing past her further into the quiet room. 'You saw it watching you. It's somewhere!—Take care!'

She clutched at him, but he was already beyond her.

'Damned nonsense,' he muttered and strode forward.

Never before in her whole life had she admired a man more than in this instant when she saw him moving towards what she knew to be physical and spiritual danger—never bevore, and

THE DOLL

never again, was such a hideous and dreadful sight to be repeatable in a woman's life. Pity and horror drowned her in a sea of passionate, futile longing. A man going to meet his fate, it flashed over her, was something none, without power to help, should witness. No human power can stay the course of the stars.

Her eye rested, as it were by chance, on the crumpled ridges and hollows of the discarded counterpane. These lay by the foot of the bed in shadow, confused a little in their contours and their masses. Had Monica not moved, they must have lain thus till morning. But Monica did move. At this particular moment she turned over in her sleep. She stretched her little legs before settling down in the new position, and this stretching squeezed and twisted the contours of the heavy counterpane at the foot of the bed. The tiny landscape altered thus a fraction, its immediate detail shifted. And an outline—a very small outline—emerged. Hitherto, it had lain concealed among the shadows. It emerged now with disconcerting rapidity, as though a spring released it. Out of its nest of darkness it seemed almost to leap forward. Fast it came, supernaturally fast, its velocity actually shocking, for a shock came with it. It was exceedingly small, it was exceedingly dreadful, its head erect and venomous and the movement of its legs and arms, as of its bitter, glittering eyes, aping humanity. Malignant evil, personified and aggressive, shaped itself in this otherwise ridiculous outline.

It was the doll.

Racing with incredible security across the slippery surface of the crumpled silk counterpane, it dived and climbed and shot forward with an appearance of complete control and deliberate purpose. That it had a definite aim was overwhelmingly obvious. Its fixed, glassy eyes were concentrated upon a point beyond and behind the terrified governess, the point precisely where Colonel Masters, her employer, stood against her shoulder.

A frantic, half protective movement on her part, seemed lost in the air...

She turned instinctively, putting an arm about his shoulders, which he instantly flung off.

'Let the bloody thing come,' he cried. 'I'll deal with it...!' He thrust her violently aside.

The doll came at him. The hinges of its diminutive broken arms and its jointed legs emitted a thin, creaking sound as it came darting—the syllables Madame Jodzka had already heard more than once. Syllables she had heard without understanding—'*buth laga*'—but syllables now packed with awful meaning: *Revenge*.

The sounds hissed and squeaked, yet clear as a bell as the beast advanced at this miraculous speed.

Before Colonel Masters could move an inch backwards or forwards in self protection, before he could command himself to any sort of action, or contrive the smallest measure of self defence, ir was off the bed and at him. It settled. Savagely, its little jaws of tiny make-believe were bitten deep into Colonel Masters' throat, fastened tightly.

In a flash this happened, in a flash it was over. In Madame Jodzka's memory it remained like the impression of a lightning flash, simultaneously etched in black and white. It had happened in the present as though it had no past. It came and was gone again. Her faculties, as after a vivid lightning, were momentarily paralysed, without past or present. She had witnessed these awful things, but had not realised them. It was this lack of realisation that struck her motionless and dumb.

Colonel Masters, on the other hand, stood beside her quietly as though nothing unusual had happened, wholly master of himself, calm, collected. At the moment of attack no sound had left his lips, there had been no gesture even of defence. Whatever had come, he had apparently accepted. The words that now fell from his lips were, thus, all the more dreadful in their appalling common-placeness.

'Hadn't you better put that counterpane straight a bit... perhaps?'

Common sense, as always, enables the gas of hysteria to escape.

THE DOLL

Madame Jodzka gasped, but she obeyed. Automatically she moved across to do his bidding, yet aware, even as she thus moved, that he flicked something from his neck, as though a wasp, a mosquito, or some poisonous insect, had tried to sting him. She remembered no more than that, for he, in his calmness, had contributed nothing else.

Fumbling with the folds of slippery counterpane she tried to straighten out, she was startled to find that Monica was sitting up in bed, awake.

'Oh, Doska—you here!' the child exclaimed innocently, straight out of sleep and using the affectionate nickname. 'And Daddy too! Oh, my goodness...!'

'Sm-moothing your bed, darling,' she stammered, hardly aware of what she said. 'You ought to be asleep. I just looked in to see...' She mumbled a few other automatic words.

'And Daddy with you!' repeated the child excitedly, sleep still about her, wondering what it all meant. 'Ooh! Ooh!' holding out her arms.

This brief exchange of spoken words, though it takes a minute to describe, occurred simultaneously with the action—perhaps ten seconds all told, for while the governess fumbled with the counterpane, Colonel Masters was in the act of brushing something from his neck. Nothing else was audible, nothing but his quick gasp and sudden intake of breath: but something else—she swears it on her Warsaw priest—was visible. Madame Jodzka maintains by all her gods she saw this other thing.

In moments of paralysing stress it is not the senses that act less speedily nor with less precision; their action, on the contrary, is intensified and speeded up: what takes longer is the registration of their reports. The numbed brain causes the apparent delay; realisation is slowed down.

Madame Jodzka thus only realised a fraction of a second later what her eyes had indubitably witnessed; a dark-skinned arm slanting in through the open window by the bed and snatching at a small object that lay on the floor after dropping from Colonel

Masters' throat, then withdrawing again at lightning speed into the darkness of the night outside.

No one but herself, apparently, had seen this—it was almost supernaturally swift.

'And now you'll be asleep again in two minutes, lucky Monica,' Colonel Masters was whispering over by the bed. 'I just peeped in to see that you were all right...' His voice was thin, dreadfully soundless.

Madame Jodzka, against the door, frozen, terrified, looded on and listened. 'Are you quite well, Daddy? Sure? I had a dream, but it's gone now.'

'Splendid. Never better in my life. But better still if I saw you sound asleep. Come now, I'll blow out this silly nightlight, for that's what woke you up, I'll be bound.'

He blew it out, he and the child blew it out together, the latter with sleepy laughter that then hushed. And Colonel Masters tiptoed to join Madame Jodzka at the door. 'A lot of damned fuss about nothing,' she heard him muttering in that same thin dreadful voice, and then, as they closed the door and stood a moment in the darkened passage, he did suddenly an unexpected thing. He took the Polish woman in his arms, held her fiercely to him for a second, kissed her vehemently, and flung her away.

'Bless you and thank you,' he said in a low, angry voice. 'You did your best. You made a great fight. But I got what I deserved. I've been waiting years for it.' And he was off down the stairs to his own quarters. Half way down he stopped and looked up to where she stood against the rails. 'Tell the doctor,' he whispered hoarsely, 'that I took a sleeping draught —an overdose.' And he was gone.

And this was, roughly, what she did tell the doctor next morning when a hurried telephone summons brought him to the bed whereon a dead man lay with a swollen, blackened tongue. She told the same tale at the inquest too and an emptied bottle of a powerful sleeping-draught supported her...

THE DOLL

And Monica, too young to realise grief beyond its trumpery meaning of a selfishly felt loss, never once—oddly enough—referred to the absence of the lovely doll that had comforted so many hours, proved such an intimate companion day and night in a life that held no other playmates. It seemed forgotten, expunged utterly from her memory, as though it had never existed at all. She stared blankly, stupidly, when a doll was mentioned: she preferred her worn-out Teddy bears. The slate of memory, in this particular, was wiped clean.

'They're so warm and comfy,' she described her bears, 'and they cuddle without tickling. Besides,' she added innocently, 'they don't squeak and try to slip away...'

Thus in the suburbs, where great spaces between the lamps go dead at night, where the moist wind comes whispering through the mournful branches of the silver-pines, where nothing happens and people cry 'Let's go to town!' there are occasional stirrings among the dead dry bones that hide behind respectable villa walls...

RUNNING WOLF

The man who enjoys an adventure outside the general experience of the race, and imparts it to others, must not be surprised if he is taken for either a liar or a fool, as Malcolm Hyde, hotel clerk on a holiday, discovered in due course. Nor is 'enjoy' the right word to use in describing his emotions; the word he chose was probably 'survive'.

When he first set eyes on Medicine Lake he was struck by its still, sparkling beauty, lying there in the vast Canadian backwoods; next, by its extreme loneliness; and, lastly—a good deal later, this—by its combination of beauty, loneliness, and singular atmosphere, due to the fact that it was the scene of his adventure.

'It's fairly stiff with big fish,' said Morton of the Montreal Sporting Club. 'Spend your holidays there—up Mattawa way, some fifteen miles west of Stony Creek. You'll have it all to yourself except for an old Indian who's got a shack there. Camp on the east side—if you'll take a tip from me.' He then talked for half an hour about the wonderful sport; yet he was not otherwise very communicative, and did not suffer questions gladly, Hyde noticed. Nor had he stayed there very long himself. If it was such a paradise as Morton, its discoverer and the most experienced rod in the province, claimed, why had he himself spent only three days there?

'Ran short of grub,' was the explanation offered; but to another friend he had mentioned briefly, 'flies' and to a third, so Hyde learned later, he gave the excuse that his half-breed 'took sick', necessitating a quick return to civilisation.

Hyde, however, cared little for the explanations; his interest in these came later. 'Stiff with fish' was the phrase he liked. He took the Canadian Pacific train to Mattawa, laid in his outfit at Stony Creek, and set off thence for the fifteen-mile canoe-trip without a care in the world.

Travelling light, the portages did not trouble him; the water was swift and easy, the rapids negotiable; everything came his way, as the saying is. Occasionally he saw big fish making for the deeper pools, and was sorely tempted to stop; but he resisted. He pushed on between the immense world of forests that stretched for hundreds of miles, known to deer, bear, moose, and wolf, but strange to any echo of human tread, a deserted and primeval wilderness. The autumn day was calm, the water sang and sparkled, the blue sky hung cloudless over all, ablaze with light. Toward evening he passed an old beaver-dam, rounded a little point, and had his first sight of Medicine Lake. He lifted his dripping paddle; the canoe shot with silent glide into calm water. He gave an exclamation of delight, for the loveliness caught his breath away.

Though primarily a sportsman, he was not insensible to beauty. The lake formed a crescent, perhaps four miles long, its width between a mile and half a mile. The slanting gold of sunset flooded it. No wind stirred its crystal surface. Here it had lain since the redskins' god first made it; here it would lie until he dried it up again. Towering spruce and hemlock trooped to its very edge, majestic cedars leaned down as if to drink, crimson sumachs shone in fiery patches, and maples gleamed orange and red beyond belief. The air was like wine, with the silence of a dream.

It was here the red men formerly 'made medicine', with all the wild ritual and tribal ceremony of an ancient day. But it was of Morton, rather than of Indians, that Hyde thought. If this lonely, hidden paradise was really stiff with big fish, he owed a lot to Morton for the information. Peace invaded him, but the excitement of the hunter lay below.

He looked about him with quick, practised eye for a camping-place before the sun sank below the forests and the half-lights came. The Indian's shack, lying in full sunshine on the eastern shore, he found at once; but the trees lay too thick about it for comfort, nor did he wish to be so close to its inhabitant. Upon the opposite side, however, an ideal clearing offered. This lay already in shadow, the huge forest darkening it toward evening; but the open space attracted. He paddled over quickly and examined it. The ground was hard and dry, he found, and a little brook ran tinkling down one side of it into the lake. This outfall, too, would be a good fishing spot. Also it was sheltered. A few low willows marked the mouth.

An experienced camper soon makes up his mind. It was a perfect site, and some charred logs, with traces of former fires, proved that he was not the first to think so. Hyde was delighted. Then, suddenly, disappointment came to tinge his pleasure. His kit was landed, and preparations for putting up the tent were begun, when he recalled a detail that excitement had so far kept in the background of his mind—Morton's advice. But not Morton's only, for the storekeeper at Stony Creek had reinforced it. The big fellow with straggling moustache and stooping shoulders, dressed in shirt and trousers, had handed him out a final sentence with the bacon, flour, condensed milk, and sugar. He had repeated Morton's half-forgotten words:

'Put yer tent on the east shore, I should,' he had said at parting.

He remembered Morton, too, apparently. 'A shortish fellow, brown as an Indian and fairly smelling of the woods. Travelling with Jake, the half-breed.' That assuredly was Morton. 'Didn't stay long, now, did he,' he added to himself in a reflective tone.

'Going Windy Lake way, are yer? Or Ten Mile Water, maybe?' he had first inquired of Hyde.

'Medicine Lake.'

'Is that so?' the man said, as though he doubted it for some obscure reason. He pulled at his ragged moustache a moment. 'Is that so, now?' he repeated. And the final words followed him down-stream after a considerable pause—the advice about the best shore on which to put his tent.

All this now suddenly flashed back upon Hyde's mind with a tinge of disappointment and annoyance, for when two experienced men agreed, their opinion was not to be lightly disregarded. He wished he had asked the storekeeper for more details. He looked about him, he reflected, he hesitated. His ideal camping ground lay certainly on the forbidden shore. What in the world, he wondered, could be the objection to it?

But the light was fading; he must decide quickly one way or the other. After staring at his unpacked dunnage, and the tent, already half erected, he made up his mind with a muttered expression that consigned both Morton and the storekeeper to less pleasant places. 'They must have *some* reason,' he growled to himself; 'fellows like that usually know what they're talking about. I guess I'd better shift over to the other side—for tonight, at any rate.'

He glanced across the water before actually reloading. No smoke rose from the Indian's shack. He had seen no sign of a canoe. The man, he decided, was away. Reluctantly, then, he left the good camping-ground and paddled across the lake, and half an hour later his tent was up, firewood collected, and two small trout were already caught for supper. But the bigger fish, he knew, lay waiting for him on the other side by the little outfall, and he fell asleep at length on his bed of balsam boughs, annoyed and disappointed, yet wondering how a mere sentence could have persuaded him so easily against his own better judgment. He slept like the dead; the sun was well up before he stirred.

But his morning mood was a very different one. The brilliant light, the peace, the intoxicating air, all this was too exhilarating for the mind to harbour foolish fancies, and he marvelled that he could have been so weak the night before. No hesitation lay in him anywhere. He struck camp immediately after breakfast, paddled back across the strip of shining water, and quickly settled in upon the forbidden shore, as he now called it, with a contemptuous grin. And the more he saw of the spot, the better he liked it. There was plenty of wood, running water to drink, an open space about the tent, and there were no flies. The fishing, moreover, was magnificent. Morton's description was fully justified, and 'stiff with big fish' for once was not an exaggeration.

The useless hours of the early afternoon he passed dozing in the sun, or wandering through the underbrush beyond the camp. He found no sign of anything unusual. He bathed in a cool, deep pool; he revelled in the lonely little paradise. Lonely it certainly was, but the loneliness was part of its charm; the stillnes, the peace, the isolation of this beautiful backwoods lake delighted him. The silence was divine. He was entirely satisfied.

After a brew of tea, he strolled toward evening along the shore, looking for the first sign of a rising fish. A faint ripple on the water, with the lengthening shadows, made good conditions. *Plop* followed *plop*, as the big fellows rose, snatched at their food, and vanished into the depths. He hurried back. Ten minutes later he had taken his rods and was gliding cautiously in the canoe through the quiet water.

So good was the sport, indeed, and so quickly did the big trout pile up in the bottom of the canoe, that despite the growing lateness, he found it hard to tear himself away. 'One more,' he said, 'and then I really will go.' He landed that 'one more', and was in the act of taking off the hook, when the deep silence of the evening was curiously disturbed. He became abruptly aware that some one watched him. A pair of eyes, it seemed, were fixed upon him from some point in the surrounding shadows.

Thus, at least, he interpreted the odd disturbance in his happy mood; for thus he felt it. The feeling stole over him without the slightest warning. He was not alone. The slippery big trout dropped from his fingers. He sat motionless, and stared about him.

Nothing stirred; the ripple on the lake had died away; there was no wind; the forest lay a single purple mass of shadow; the yellow sky, fast fading, threw reflections that troubled the eye and made distances uncertain. But there was no sound, no movement; he saw no figure anywhere. Yet he knew that some one watched him, and a wave of quite unreasoning terror gripped him. The nose of the canoe was against the bank. In a moment, and instinctively, he shoved it off and paddled into deeper water. The watcher, it came to him also instinctively, was quite close to him upon that bank. But where? And who? Was it the Indian?

Here, in deeper water, and some twenty yards from the shore, he paused and strained both sight and hearing to find some possible clue. He felt half ashamed, now that the first strange feeling passed a little. But the certainty remained. Absurd as it was, he felt positive that some one watched him with concentrated and intent regard. Every fibre in his being told him so; and though he could discover no figure, no new outline on the shore, he could even have sworn in which clump of willow bushes the hidden person crouched and stared. His attention seemed drawn to that particular clump.

The water dripped slowly from his paddle, now lying across the thwarts. There was no other sound. The canvas of his tent gleamed dimly. A star or two were out. He waited. Nothing happened.

Then, as suddenly as it had come, the feeling passed, and he knew that the person who had been watching him intently had gone. It was as if a current had been turned off; the normal world flowed back; the landscape emptied as if some one had left a room. The disagreeable feeling left him at the same time, so that he instantly turned the canoe in to the shore again, landed, and, paddle in hand, went over to examine the clump of willows he had singled out as the place of concealment. There was no one there, of course, nor any trace of recent human occupancy. No leaves, no branches stirred, nor was a single twig displaced; his keen and practised sight detected no sign of tracks upon the ground. Yet, for all that, he felt positive that a little time ago some one had crouched among these very leaves and watched him. He remained absolutely convinced of it. The watcher, whether Indian hunter, stray lumberman, or wandering half-breed, had now withdrawn, a search was useless, and dusk was falling. He returned to his little camp, more disturbed perhaps than he cared to acknowledge. He cooked his supper, hung up his catch on a string, so that no prowling animal could get at it during the night, and prepared to make himself comfortable until bedtime. Unconsciously, he built a bigger fire than usual, and found himself peering over his pipe into the deep shadows beyond the firelight, straining his ears to catch the slightest sound. He remained generally on the alert in a way that was new to him.

A man under such conditions and in such a place need not know discomfort until the sense of loneliness strikes him as too vivid a reality. Loneliness in a backwoods camp brings charm, pleasure, and a happy sense of calm until, and unless, it comes too near. It should remain an ingredient only among other conditions; it should not be directly, vividly noticed. Once it has crept within short range, however, it may easily cross the narrow line between comfort and discomfort, and darkness is an undesirable time for the transition. A curious dread may easily follow—the dread lest the loneliness suddenly be disturbed, and the solitary human feel himself open to attack.

For Hyde, now, this transition had been already accomplished; the too intimate sense of his loneliness had shifted abruptly into the worst condition of no longer being quite alone. It was an awkward moment, and the hotel clerk realised his position exactly. He did not quite like it. He sat there, with his back to the blazing logs, a very visible object in the light, while all about him the darkness of the forest lay like an impenetrable wall. He could not see a yard beyond the small circle of his camp-fire; the silence about him was like the silence of the dead. No leaf rustled, no wave lapped; he himself sat motionless as a log.

Then again he became suddenly aware that the person who watched him had returned, and that same intent and concentrated gaze as before was fixed upon him where he lay. There was no warning; he heard no stealthy tread or snapping of dry twigs, yet the owner of those steady eyes was very close to him, probably not a dozen feet away. This sense of proximity was overwhelming.

It is unquestionable that a shiver ran down his spine. This

time, moreover, he felt positive that the man crouched just beyond the firelight, the distance he himself could see being nicely calculated, and straight in front of him. For some minutes he sat without stirring a single muscle, yet with each muscle ready and alert, straining his eyes in vain to pierce the darkness, but only succeeding in dazzling his sight with the reflected light. Then, as he shifted his position slowly, cautiously, to obtain another angle of vision, his heart gave two big thumps against his ribs and the hair seemed to rise on his scalp with the sense of cold that gave him goose-flesh. In the darkness facing him he saw two small and greenish circles that were certainly a pair of eyes, yet not the eyes of Indian hunter, or of any human being. It was a pair of animal eyes that stared so fixedly at him out of the night. And this certainty had an immediate and natural effect upon him.

For, at the menace of those eyes, the fears of millions of long dead hunters since the dawn of time woke in him. Hotel clerk though he was, heredity surged through him in an automatic wave of instinct. His hand groped for a weapon. His fingers fell on the iron head of his small camp axe, and at once he was himself again. Confidence returned; the vague, superstitious dread was gone. This was a bear or wolf that smelt his catch and came to steal it. With beings of that sort he knew instinctively how to deal, yet admitting, by this very instinct, that his original dread had been of quite another kind.

'I'll damned quick find out what it is,' he exclaimed aloud, and snatching a burning brand from the fire, he hurled it with good aim straight at the eyes of the beast before him.

The bit of pitch-pine fell in a shower of sparks that lit the dry grass this side of the animal, flared up a moment, then died quickly down again. But in that instant of bright illumination he saw clearly what his unwelcome visitor was. A big timber wolf sat on its hindquarters, staring steadily at him through the firelight. He saw its legs and shoulders, he saw its hair, he saw also the big hemlock trunks lit up behind it, and the willow scrub on each side. It formed a vivid, clear-cut picture shown in clear detail by the momentary blaze. To his amazement, however, the wolf did not turn and bolt away from the burning log, but withdrew a few yards only, and sat there again on its haunches, staring, staring as before. Heavens, how it stared! He 'shoo-ed' it, but without effect; it did not budge. He did not waste another good log on it, for his fear was dissipated now; a timber wolf was a timber wolf, and it might sit there as long as it pleased, provided it did not try to steal his catch. No alarm was in him any more. He knew that wolves were harmless in the summer and autumn, and even when 'packed' in the winter, they would attack a man only when suffering desperate hunger. So he lay and watched the beast, threw bits of stick in its direction, even talked to it, wondering only that it never moved. 'You can stay there for ever, if you like,' he remarked to it aloud, 'for you cannot get at my fish, and the rest of the grub I shall take into the tent with me!'

The creature blinked its bright green eyes, but made no move.

Why, then, if his fear was gone, did he think of certain things as he rolled himself in the Hudson Bay blankets before going to sleep? The immobility of the animal was strange, its refusal to turn and bolt was still stranger. Never before had he known a wild creature that was not afraid of fire. Why did it sit and watch him, as with purpose in its gleaming eyes? How had he felt its presence earlier and instantly? A timber wolf, especially a solitary wolf, was a timid thing, yet this one feared neither man nor fire. Now, as he lay there wrapped in his blankets inside the cosy tent, it sat outside beneath the stars, beside the fading embers, the wind chilly in its fur, the ground cooling beneath its planted paws, watching him, steadily watching him, perhaps until the dawn.

It was unusual, it was strange. Having neither imagination nor tradition, he called upon no store of racial visions. Matter of fact, a hotel clerk on a fishing holiday, he lay there in his blankets, merely wondering and puzzled. A timber wolf was a timber wolf and nothing more. Yet this timber wolf—the idea haunted him—was different. In a word, the deeper part of his original uneasiness remained. He tossed about, he shivered sometimes in his broken sleep; he did not go out to see, but he woke early and unrefreshed.

Again with the sunshine and the morning wind, however, the incident of the night before was forgotten, almost unreal. His hunting zeal was uppermost. The tea and fish were delicious, his pipe had never tasted so good, the glory of this lonely lake amid primeval forests went to his head a little; he was a hunter before the Lord, and nothing else. He tried the edge of the lake, and in the excitement of playing a big fish, knew suddenly that *it*, the wolf, was there. He paused with the rod, exactly as if struck. He looked about him, he looked in a definite direction. The brilliant sunshine made every smallest detail clear and sharp—boulders of granite, burned stems, crimson sumach, pebbles along the shore in neat, separate detail—without revealing where the watcher hid. Then, his sight wandering farther inshore among the tangled undergrowth, he suddenly picked up the familiar, half-expected outline. The wolf was lying behind a granite boulder, so that only the head, the muzzle, and the eyes were visible. It merged in its background. Had he not known it was a wolf, he could never have separated it from the landscape. The eyes shone in the sunlight.

There it lay. He looked straight at it. Their eyes, in fact, actually met full and square. 'Great Scott!' he exclaimed aloud, 'why, it's like looking at a human being!'

From that moment, unwittingly, he established a singular personal relation with the beast. And what followed confirmed this undesirable impression, for the animal rose instantly and came down in leisurely fashion to the shore, where it stood looking back at him. It stood and stared into his eyes like some great wild dog, so that he was aware of a new and almost incredible sensation—that it courted recognition.

'Well! Well!' he exclaimed again, relieving his feelings by addressing it aloud, 'if this doesn't beat everything I ever saw! What d'you want, anyway?'

He examined it now more carefully. He had never seen a

wolf so big before; it was a tremendous beast, a nasty customer to tackle, he reflected, if it ever came to that. It stood there absolutely fearless, and ful of confidence. In the clear sunlight he took in every detail of it—a huge, shaggy, lean-flanked timber wolf, its wicked eyes staring straight into his own, almost with a kind of purpose in them. He saw its great jaws, its teeth, and its tongue hung out, dropping saliva a little. And yet the idea of its savagery, its fierceness, was very little in him.

He was amazed and puzzled beyond belief. He wished the Indian would come back. He did not understand this strange behaviour in an animal. Its eyes, the odd expression in them, gave him a queer, unusual, difficult feeling. Had his nerves gone wrong, he almost wondered.

The beast stood on the shore and looked at him. He wished for the first time that he had brought a rifle. With a resounding smack he brought his paddle down flat upon the water, using all his strength, till the echoes rang as from a pistol-shot that was audible from one end of the lake to the other. The wolf never stirred. He shouted, but the beast remained unmoved. He blinked his eyes, speaking as to a dog, a domestic animal, a creature accustomed to human ways. It blinked its eyes in return.

At length, increasing his distance from the shore, he continued fishing, and the excitement of the marvellous sport held his attention—his surface attention, at any rate. At times he almost forgot the attendant beast; yet whenever he looked up, he saw it there. And worse; when he slowly paddled home again, he observed it trotting along the shore as though to keep him company. Crossing a little bay, he spurted, hoping to reach the other point before his undesired and undesirable attendant. Instantly the brute broke into that rapid, tireless lope that, except on ice, can run down anything on four legs in the woods. When he reached the distant point, the wolf was waiting for him. He raised his paddle from the water, pausing a moment for reflection; for his very close attention—there were dusk and night yet to come—he certainly did not relish. His camp was near; he had to land; he felt uncomfortable even in the sunshine of broad day, when, to his keen relief, about half a mile from the tent, he saw the creature suddenly stop and sit down in the open. He waited a moment, then paddled on. It did not follow. There was no attempt to move; it merely sat and watched him. After a few hundred yards, he looked back. It was still sitting where he left it. And the absurd, yet significant, feeling came to him that the beast divined his thought, his anxiety, his dread, and was now showing him, as well as it could, that it entertained no hostile feeling and did not meditate attack.

He turned the canoe toward the shore; he landed; he cooked his supper in the dusk; the animal made no sign. Not far away it certainly lay and watched, but it did not advance. And to Hyde, observant now in a new way, came one sharp, vivid reminder of the strange atmosphere into which his commonplace personality had strayed: he suddenly recalled that his relations with the beast, already established, had progressed distinctly a stage further. This startled him, yet without the accompanying alarm he must certainly have felt twenty-four hours before. He had an understanding with the wolf. He was aware of friendly thoughts toward it. He even went so far as to set out a few big fish on the spot where he had first seen it sitting the previous night. 'If he comes,' he thought, 'he is welcome to them, I've got plenty, anyway.' He thought of it now as 'he'.

Yet the wolf made no appearance until he was in the act of entering his tent a good deal later. It was close on ten o'clock, whereas nine was his hour, and late at that, for turning in. He had, therefore, unconsciously been waiting for him. Then, as he was closing the flap, he saw the eyes close to where he had placed the fish. He waited, hiding himself, and expecting to hear sounds of munching jaws; but all was silence. Only the eyes glowed steadily out of the background of pitch darkness. He closed the flap. He had no slightest fear. In ten minutes he was sound asleep.

He could not have slept very long, for when he woke up he could see the shine of a faint red light through the canvas, and the fire had not died down completely. He rose and cautiously peeped out. The air was very cold, he saw his breath. But he also saw the wolf, for it had come in, and was sitting by the dying embers, not two yards away from where he crouched behind the flap. And this time, at these very close quarters, there was something in the attitude of the big wild thing that caught his attention with a vivid thrill of startled surprise and a sudden shock of cold that held him spellbound. He stared, unable to believe his eyes; for the wolf's attitude conveyed to him something familiar that at first he was unable to explain. Its pose reached him in the terms of another thing with which he was entirely at home. What was it? Did his senses betray him? Was he still asleep and dreaming?

Then, suddenly, with a start of uncanny recognition, he knew. Its attitude was that of a dog. Having found the clue, his mind then made an awful leap. For it was, after all, no dog its appearance aped, but something nearer to himself, and more familiar still. Good heavens! It sat there with the pose, the attitude, the gesture in repose of something almost human. And then, with a second shock of biting wonder, it came to him like a revelation. The wolf sat beside that camp-fire as a man might sit.

Before he could weigh his extraordinary discovery, before he could examine it in detail or with care, the animal, sitting in this ghastly fashion, seemed to feel his eyes fixed on it. It slowly turned and looked him in the face, and for the first time Hyde felt a fullblooded superstitious fear flood through his entire being. He seemed transfixed with that nameless terror that is said to attack human beings who suddenly face the dead, finding themselves bereft of speech and movement. This moment of paralysis certainly occurred. Its passing, however, was as singular as its advent. For almost at once he was aware of something beyond and above this mockery of human attitude and pose, something that ran along unaccustomed nerves and reached his feeling, even perhaps his heart. The revulsion was extraordinary, its result still more extraordinary and unexpected. Yet the fact remains. He was aware of another thing that had the effect of stilling his terror as soon as it was born. He was aware of appeal, silent, half expressed, yet vastly pathetic. He saw in the savage eyes a beseeching, even a yearning, expression that changed his mood as by magic from dread to natural sympathy. The great grey brute, symbol of cruel ferocity, sat there beside his dying fire and appealed for help.

The gulf betwixt animal and human seemed in that instant bridged. It was, of course, incredible. Hyde, sleep still possibly clinging to his inner being with the shades and half shapes of dream yet about his soul, acknowledged, how he knew not, the amazing fact. He found himself nodding to the brute in half consent, and instantly, without more ado, the lean grey shape rose like a wraith and trotted off swiftly, but with stealthy tread, into the background of the night.

When Hyde woke in the morning his first impression was that he must have dreamed the entire incident. His practical nature asserted itself. There was a bite in the fresh autumn air; the bright sun allowed no half lights anywhere; he felt brisk in mind and body. Reviewing what had happened, he came to the conclusion that it was utterly vain to speculate; no possible explanation of the animal's behaviour occurred to him: he was dealing with something entirely outside his experience. His fear, however, had completely left him. The odd sense of friendliness remained. The beast had a definite purpose, and he himself was included in that purpose. His sympathy held good.

But with the sympathy there was also an intense curiosity. 'If it shows itself again,' he told himself, 'I'll go up close and find out what it wants.' The fish laid out the night before had not been touched.

It must have been a full hour after breakfast when he next saw the brute; it was standing on the edge of the clearing, looking at him in the way now become familiar. Hyde immediately picked up his axe and advanced toward it boldly, keeping his eyes fixed straight upon its own. There was nervousness in him, but kept well under; nothing betrayed it; step by step he drew nearer until some ten yards separated them. The wolf had not stirred a muscle as yet. Its jaws hung open, its eyes observed him intently; it allowed him to approach without a sign of what its mood might be. Then, with these ten yards between them, it turned abruptly and moved slowly off, looking back first over one shoulder and then over the other, exactly as a dog might do, to see if he was following.

A singular journey it was they then made together, animal and man. The trees surrounded them at once, for they felt the lake behind them, entering the tangled bush beyond. The beast, Hyde noticed, obviously picked the easiest track for him to follow; for obstacles that meant nothing to the four-legged expert, yet were difficult for a man, were carefully avoided with an almost uncanny skill, while yet the general direction was accurately kept. Occasionally there were windfalls to be surmounted; but though the wolf bounded over these with ease, it was always waiting for the man on the other side after he had laboriously climbed over. Deeper and deeper into the heart of the lonely forest they penetrated in this singular fashion, cutting across the arc of the lake's crescent, it seemed to Hyde; for after two miles or so, he recognised the big rocky bluff that overhung the water at its northern end. This outstanding bluff he had seen from his camp, one side of it falling sheer into the water; it was probably the spot, he imagined, where the Indians held their medicine-making ceremonies, for it stood out in isolated fashion, and its top formed a private plateau not easy of access. And it was here, close to a big spruce at the foot of the bluff upon the forest side, that the wolf stopped suddenly and for the first time since its appearance gave audible expression to its feelings. It sat down on its haunches, lifted its muzzle with open jaws, and gave vent to a subdued and long-drawn howl that was more like the wail of a dog than the fierce barking cry associated with a wolf.

By this time Hyde had lost not only fear, but caution too; nor, oddly enough, did this warning howl, revive a sign of unwelcome emotion in him. In that curious sound he detected the same message that the eyes conveyed—appeal for help. He paused, nevertheless, a little startled, and while the wolf sat waiting for him, he looked about him quickly. There was young timber here; it had once been a small clearing, evidently. Axe and fire had done their work, but there was evidence to an experienced eye that it was Indians and not white men who had once been busy here. Some part of the medicine ritual, doubtless, took place in the little clearing, thought the man, as he advanced again towards his patient leader. The end of their queer journey, he felt, was close at hand.

He had not taken two steps before the animal got up and moved very slowly in the direction of some low bushes that formed a clump just beyond. It entered these, first looking back to make sure that its companion watched. The bushes hid it; a moment later it emerged again. Twice it performed this pantomime, each time, as it reappeared, standing still and staring at the man with as distinct an expression of appeal in the eyes as an animal may compass, probably. Its excitement, meanwhile, certainly increased, and this excitement was, with equal certainty, communicated to the man. Hyde made up his mind quickly. Gripping his axe tightly, and ready to use it at the first hint of malice, he moved slowly nearer to the bushes, wondering with something of a tremor what would happen.

If he expected to be startled, his expectation was at once fulfilled; but it was the behaviour of the beast that made him jump. It positively frisked about him like a happy dog. It frisked for joy. Its excitement was intense, yet from its open mouth no sound was audible. With a sudden leap, then, it bounded past him into the clump of bushes, against whose very edge he stood, and began scraping vigorously at the ground. Hyde stood and stared, amazement and interest now banishing all his nervousness, even when the beast, in its violent scraping, actually touched his body with its own. He had, perhaps, the feeling that he was in a dream, one of those fantastic dreams in which things may happen without involving an adequate surprise; for otherwise the manner of scraping and scratching at the ground must have seemed an impossible phenomenon. No wolf, no dog certainly, used its paws in the way those paws were working. Hyde had the odd, distressing sensation that it was hands, not paws, he watched. And yet, somehow, the natural, adequate surprise he should have felt was absent. The strange action seemed not entirely unnatural. In his heart some deep hidden spring of sympathy and pity stirred instead. He was aware of pathos.

The wolf stopped in its task and looked up into his face. Hyde acted without hesitation then. Afterwards he was wholly at a loss to explain his own conduct. It seemed he knew what to do, divined what was asked, expected of him. Between his mind and the dumb desire yearning through the savage animal there was intelligent and intelligible communication. He cut a stake and sharpened it, for the stones would blunt his axe-edge. He entered the clump of bushes to complete the digging his four-legged companion had begun. And while he worked, though he did not forget the close proximity of the wolf, he paid no attention to it; often his back was turned as he stooped over the laborious clearing away of the hard earth; no uneasiness or sense of danger was in him any more. The wolf sat outside the clump and watched the operations. Its concentrated attention, its patience, its intense eagerness, the gentleness and docility of the grey, fierce, and probably hungry brute, its obvious pleasure and satisfaction, too, at having won the human to its mysterious purpose—these were colours in the strange picture that Hyde thought of later when dealing with the human herd in his hotel again. At the moment he was aware chiefly of pathos and affection. The whole business was, of course, not to be believed, but that discovery came later, too, when telling it to others.

The digging continued for fully half an hour before his labour was rewarded by the discovery of a small whitish object. He picked it up and examined it—the finger-bone of a man. Other discoveries then followed quickly and in quantity. The *cache* was laid bare. He collected nearly the complete skeleton. The skull however, he found last, and might not have found at all but for the guidance of his strangely alert companion. It lay some few yards away from the central hole now dug, and the wolf stood nuzzling the ground with its nose before Hyde understood that he was meant to dig exactly in that spot for it. Between the beast's very paws his stake struck hard upon it. He scraped the earth from the bone and examined it carefully. It was perfect, save for the fact that some wild animal had gnawed it, the teeth-marks being still plainly visible. Close beside it lay the rusty iron head of a tomahawk. This and the smallness of the bones confirmed him in his judgment that it was the skeleton not of a white man, but of an Indian.

During the excitement of the discovery of the bones one by one, and finally of the skull, but, more especially, during the period of intense interest while Hyde was examining them, he had paid little if any attention to the wolf. He was aware that it sat and watched him, never moving its keen eyes for a single moment from the actual operations, but sign or movement it made none at all. He knew that it was pleased and satisfied, he knew also that he had now fulfilled its purpose in a great measure. The further intuition that now came to him, derived, he felt positive, from his companion's dumb desire, was perhaps the cream of the entire experience to him. Gathering the bones together in his coat, he carried them, together with the tomahawk, to the foot of the big spruce where the animal had first stopped. His leg actually touched the creature's muzzle as he passed. It turned its head to watch, but did not follow, nor did it move a muscle while he prepared the platform of boughs upon which he then laid the poor worn bones of an Indian who had been killed, doubtless, in sudden attack or ambush, and to whose remains had been denied the last grace of proper tribal burial. He wrapped the bones in bark; he laid the tomahawk beside the skull; he lit the circular fire round the pyre, and the blue smoke rose upward into the clear bright sunshine of the Canadian autumn morning till it was lost among the mighty trees far overhead.

In the moment before actually lighting the little fire he had turned to note what his companion did. It sat five yards away, he saw, gazing intently, and one of its front paws was raised a little from the ground. It made no sign of any kind. He finished the work, becoming so absorbed in it that he had eyes for nothing but the tending and guarding of his careful ceremonial fire. It was only when the platform of boughs collapsed, laying their charred burden gently on the fragrant earth among the soft wood ashes, that he turned again, as though to show the wolf what he had done, and seek, perhaps, some look of satisfaction in its curiously expressive eyes. But the place he searched was empty. The wolf had gone.

He did not see it again; it gave no sign of its presence anywhere; he was not watched. He fished as before, wandered through the bush about his camp, sat smoking round his fire after dark, and slept peacefully in his cosy little tent. He was not disturbed. No howl was ever audible in the distant forest, no twig snapped beneath a stealthy tread, he saw no eyes. The wolf that behaved like a man had gone for ever.

It was the day before he left that Hyde, noticing smoke rising from the shack across the lake, paddled over to exchange a word or two with the Indian, who had evidently now returned. The Redskin came down to meet him as he landed, but it was soon plain that he spoke very little English. He emitted the familiar grunts at first; then bit by bit Hyde stirred his limited vocabulary into action. The net result, however, was slight enough, though it was certainly direct:

'You camp there?' the man asked, pointing to the other side.
'Yes.'
'Wolf come?'
'Yes.'
'You see wolf?'
'Yes.'

The Indian stared at him fixedly a moment, a keen, wondering look upon his coppery, creased face.

'You 'fraid wolf?' he asked after a moment's pause.

'No,' replied Hyde, truthfully. He knew it was useless to ask questions of his own, though he was eager for information. The other would have told him nothing. It was sheer luck that the man had touched on the subject at all, and Hyde realised that his own best role was merely to answer, but to ask no questions. Then, suddenly, the Indian became comparatively voluble. There was awe in his voice and manner.

'Him no wolf. Him big medicine wolf. Him spirit wolf.'

Whereupon he drank the tea the other had brewed for him, closed his lips tightly, and said no more. His outline was discernible on the shore, rigid and motionless, an hour later, when Hyde's canoe turned the corner of the lake three miles away, and landed to make the portages up the first rapid of his homeward stream.

It was Morton who, after some persuasion, supplied further details of what he called the legend. Some hundred years before, the tribe that lived in the territory beyond the lake began their annual medicine-making ceremonies on the big rocky bluff at the northern end; but no medicine could be made. The spirits, declared the chief medicine man, would not answer. They were offended. An investigation followed. It was discovered that a young brave had recently killed a wolf, a thing strictly forbidden, since the wolf was the totem animal of the tribe. To make matters worse, the name of the guilty man was Running Wolf. The offence being unpardonable, the man was cursed and driven from the tribe:

'Go out. Wander alone among the woods, and if we see you we slay you. Your bones shall be scattered in the forest, and your spirit shall not enter the Happy Hunting Grounds till one of another race shall find and bury them.'

'Which meant,' explained Morton laconically, his only comment on the story, 'probably for ever.'

THE LITTLE BEGGAR

He was on his way from his bachelor flat to the club, a man of middle age with a slight stoop, and an expression of face firm yet gentle, the blue eyes with light and courage in them, and a faint hint of melancholy—or was it resignation?—about the strong mouth. It was early in April, a slight drizzle of warm rain falling through the coming dusk; but spring was in the air, a bird sang rapturously on a pavement tree. And the man's heart wakened at the sound, for it was the lift of the year, and low in the western sky above the London roofs there was a band of tender colour.

His way led him past one of the great terminal stations that open the gates of London seawards; the birds, the coloured clouds, and the thought of a sunny coast-line worked simultaneously in his heart. These messages of spring woke music in him. The music, however, found no expression, beyond a quiet sigh, so quiet that not even a child, had he carried one in his big arms, need have noticed it. His pace quickened, his figure straightened up, he lifted his eyes and there was a new light in them. Upon the wet pavement, where the street lamps already laid their network of faint gold, he saw, perhaps a dozen yards in front of him, the figure of a little boy.

The boy, for some reason, caught his attention and his interest vividly. He was dressed in Etons, the broad white collar badly rumpled, the pointed coat hitched grotesquely sideways, while, from beneath the rather grimy straw hat, his thick light hair escaped at various angles. This general air of effort and distress was due to the fact that the little fellow was struggling with a bag packed evidently to bursting point, too big and heavy for him to manage for more than ten yards at a time. He changed it from one hand to the other, resting it in the intervals upon the ground, each effort making it rub against his leg so that the trousers were hoisted considerably above the boot. He was a pathetic figure.

'I must help him,' said the man. 'He'll never get there at this rate. He'll miss his train to the sea.' For his destination was obvious, since a pair of wooden spades was tied clumsily and insecurely to the straps of the bursting bag.

Occasionally, too, the lad, who seemed about ten years old, looked about him to right and left, questionably, anxiously, as though he expected someone—someone to help, or perhaps to meet him. His behaviour even gave the impression that he was not quite sure of his way. The man hurried to overtake him.

'I really must give the little beggar a hand,' he repeated to himself, as he went. He smiled. The fatherly, protective side of him, naturally strong, was touched—touched a little more, perhaps, than the occasion seemed to warrant. The smile broadened into a jolly laugh, as he came up against the great stuffed bag, now resting on the pavement, its owner panting beside it, still looking to right and left alternately. At which instant, exactly, the boy, hearing his step, turned round, and for the first time looked him full in the face with a pair of big blue eyes that held unabashed and happy welcome in them.

'Oh, I say, sir, it's most awfully ripping of you,' he said in a confiding voice, before the man had time to speak. 'I hunted everywhere; but I never thought of looking *behind* me.'

But the man, standing dumb and astonished for a few seconds beside the little fellow, missed the latter sentence altogether, for there was in the clear blue eyes an expression so trustful, so frankly affectionate almost, and in the voice music of so natural a kind, that all the tenderness in him rose, like a sudden tide, and he yearned towards the boy as though he were his little son. Thought, born of some sudden revival of emotion, flashed back swiftly across a stretch of twelve blank years... and for an instant the lines of the mouth grew deeper, though in the eyes the light turned softer, brighter...

'It's too big for you, my boy,' he said, recovering himself with a jolly laugh; 'or, rather, you're not big enough—yet—for it— eh! Where to, now? Ah! the station, I suppose?' And he stooped to grasp the handles of the bulging bag, first poking the spades more securely in beneath the straps; but in doing so became aware that something the boy had said had given him pain. What was it? Why was it? This stray little stranger, met upon the London pavements! Yet so swift is thought that, even while he stooped and before his fingers actually touched the leather, he had found what hurt him—and smiled a little at himself. It was the mode of address the boy made use of, contradicting faintly the affectionate expression in the eyes. It was the word 'sir' that made him feel like a schoolmaster or a tutor; it made him feel old. It was not the word he needed, and—yes—had longed for, somehow almost expected. And there was such strange trouble in his mind and heart that, as he grasped the bag, he did not catch the boy's rejoinder to his question. But, of course, it must be the railway station; he was going to the seaside for Easter; his people would be at the ticket-office waiting for him. Bracing himself a little for the effort, he seized the leather handles and lifted the bag from the ground.

'Oh, thanks awfully, sir!' repeated the boy. He watched him with a true schoolboy grin of gratitude, as though it were great fun, yet also with a true urchin's sense that the proper thing had happened, since such jobs, of course, were for grown-up men. And this time, though he used the objectionable word again, the voice betrayed recognition of the fact that he somehow had a right to look to this particular man for help, and that this particular man only did the right and natural thing in giving help.

But the man, swaying sideways, nearly lost his balance. He had calculated automatically the probable energy necessary to lift the weight; he had put this energy forth. He received a shock as though he had been struck, for the bag had no weight at all; it was as light as a feather. It might have been of tissue-paper, a phantom bag. And the shock was mental as well as physical. His mind swayed with his body.

'By jove!' cried the boy, strutting merrily beside him, hands in his pockets. 'Thanks most awfully. This *is* jolly!'

THE LITTLE BEGGAR

The objectionable word was omitted, but the man scarcely heard the words at all. For a mist swam before his eyes, the street lamps grew blurred and distant, the drizzle thickened in the air. He still heard the wild, sweet song of the bird, still knew the west had gold upon its lips. It was the rest of the world about him that grew dim. Strange thoughts rose in a cloud. Reality and dream played games, the games of childhood, through his heart. Memories, robed flamingly, trooped past his inner sight, radiant, swift and as of yesterday, closing his eyelids for a moment to the outer world. Rossetti came to him, singing too sweetly a hidden pain in perfect words across those twelve blank years: 'The Hour that might have been, yet might not be, which man's and woman's heart conceived and bore, yet whereof time was barren...' In a second's flash the entire sonnet, 'Stillborn Love', passed on this inner screen 'with eyes where burning memory lights love home...'

Mingled with these—all in an instant of time—came practical thoughts as well. This boy! The ridiculous effort he made to carry this ridiculously light bag! The poignant tenderness, the awakened yearning! Was it a girl dressed up? The happy face, the innocent, confiding smile, the music in the voice, the dear soft blue eyes, and yet, at the same time, something that was *not* there—some indescribable, incalculable element that was lacking. He felt acutely this curious lack. What was it? Who was this merry youngster? He glanced down cautiously as they moved side by side. He felt shy, hopeful, marvellously tender. His heart yearned inexpressibly; the boy, looking elsewhere, did not notice the examination, did not notice, of course, that his companion caught his breath and walked uncertainly.

But the man was troubled. The face reminded him, as he gazed, of many children, of children he had loved and played with, both boys and girls, his Substitute Children, as he had always called them in his heart... Then, suddenly, the boy came closer and took his arm. They were close upon the station now. The sweet human perfume of a small, deeply loved, helpless and dependent little life rose past his face.

He suddenly blurted out: 'But, I say, this bag of yours—it weighs simply nothing!'

The boy laughed—a ring of true careless joy was in the sound. He looked up.

'Do you know what's in it? Shall I tell you?' He added in a whisper: 'I will, if you like.'

But the man was suddenly afraid and dared not ask.

'Brown paper probably,' he evaded laughingly; ,or birds' eggs. You've been up to some wicked lark or other.'

The little chap clasped both hands upon the supporting arm. He took a quick, dancing step or two, then stopped dead, and made the man stop with him. He stood on tiptoe to reach the distant ear. His face wore a lovely smile of truth and trust and delight.

'My future,' he whispered. And the man turned into ice.

They entered the great station. The last of the daylight was shut out. They reached the ticket-office. The crowds of hurrying people surged about them. The man set down the bag. For a moment or two the boy looked quickly about him to right and left, searching, then turned his big blue eyes upon the other with his radiant smile:

'She's in the waiting-room as usual,' he said. 'I'll go and fetch her—though she *ought* to know you're here.' He stood on tiptoe, his hands upon the other's shoulders, his face thrust close. 'Kiss me, father. I shan't be a second.'

'You little beggar!' said the man, in a voice he could not control; then, opening his big arms wide, saw only an empty space before him.

He turned and walked slowly back to his flat instead of to the club; and when he got home he read over for the thousandth time the letter—its ink a little faded during the twelve intervening years—in which she had accepted his love two short weeks before death took her.

THE OCCUPANT OF THE ROOM

He arrived late at night by the yellow *diligence*, stiff and cramped after the toilsome ascent of three slow hours. The village, a single mass of shadow, was already asleep. Only in front of the little hotel was there noise and light and bustle—for a moment. The horses, with tired, slouching gait, crossed the road and disappeared into the stable of their own accord, their harness trailing in the dust; and the lumbering *diligence* stood for the night where they had dragged it—the body of a great yellow-sided beetle with broken legs.

In spite of his physical weariness, the schoolmaster, revelling in the first hours of his ten-guinea holiday, felt exhilarated. For the high Alpine valley was marvellously still; stars twinkled over the torn ridges of the Dent du Midi where spectral snows gleamed against rocks that looked like ebony; and the keen air smelt of pine forests, dew-soaked pastures, and freshly sawn wood. He took it all in with a kind of bewildered delight for a few minutes, while the other three passengers gave directions about their luggage and went to their rooms. Then he turned and walked over the coarse matting into the glare of the hall, only just able to resist stopping to examine the big mountain map that hung upon the wall by the door.

And, with a sudden disagreeable shock, he came down from the ideal to the actual. For at the inn-the only inn—there was no vacant room. Even the available sofas were occupied...

How stupid he had been not to write! Yet it had been impossible, he remembered, for he had come to the decision suddenly that morning in Geneva, enticed by the brilliance of the weather after a week of rain.

They talked endlessly, this gold-braided porter and the hard-faced old woman—her face was hard, he noticed—gesticulating all the time, and pointing all about the village with suggestions that he ill understood, for his French was limited and their *patois* was fearful.

'*There!*'—he might find a room, 'or *there!* But we are, *hélas,* full—more full than we care about. To-morrow, perhaps—if So-and-So give up their rooms——!' And then, with much shrugging of shoulders, the hard-faced old woman stared at the gold-braided porter, and the porter stared sleepily at the schoolmaster.

At length, however, by some process of hope he did not himself understand, and following directions given by the old woman that were utterly unintelligible, he went out into the street and walked towards a dark group of houses she had pointed out to him. He only knew that he meant to thunder at a door and ask for a room. He was too weary to think out details. The porter half made to go with him, but turned back at the last moment to speak with the old woman. The houses sketched themselves dimly in the general blackness. The air was cold. The whole valley was filled with the rush and thunder of falling water. He was thinking vaguely that the dawn could not be very far away, and that he might even spend the night wandering in the woods, when there was a sharp noise behind him and he turned to see a figure hurrying after him. It was the porter—running.

And in the little hall of the inn there began again a confused three-cornered conversation, with frequent muttered colloquy and whispered asides in *patois* between the woman and the porter—the net result of which was that, 'If Monsieur did not object—there *was* a room, after all, on the first floor—only it was in a sense "engaged". That is to say——'

But the schoolmaster took the room without inquiring too closely into the puzzle that had somehow provided it so suddenly. The ethics of hotel-keeping had nothing to do with him. If the woman offered him quarters it was not for him to argue with her whether the said quarters were legitimately hers to offer.

But the porter, evidently a little thrilled, accompanied the

THE OCCUPANT OF THE ROOM

guest up to the room and supplied in a mixture of French and English details omitted by the landlady—and Minturn, the schoolmaster, soon shared the thrill with him, and found himself in the atmosphere of a possible tragedy.

All who know the peculiar excitement that belongs to lofty mountain valleys where dangerous climbing is a chief feature of the attractions, will understand a certain faint element of high alarm that goes with the picture. One looks up at the desolate, soaring ridges and thinks involuntarily of the men who find their pleasure for days and nights together scaling perilous summits among the clouds, and conquering inch by inch the icy peaks that for ever shake their dark terror in the sky. The atmosphere of adventure, spiced with the possible horror of a very grim order of tragedy, is inseparable from any imaginative contemplation of the scene: and the idea Minturn gleaned from the half-frightened porter lost nothing by his ignorance of the language. This Englishwoman, the real occupant of the room, had insisted on going without a guide. She had left just before daybreak two days before—the porter had seen her start—and ... she had not returned! The route was difficult and dangerous, yet not impossible for a skilled climber, even a solitary one. And the Englishwoman was an experienced mountaineer. Also, she was self-willed, careless of advice, bored by warnings, self-confident to a degree. Queer, moreover; for she kept entirely to herself, and sometimes remained in her room with locked doors, admitting no one, for days together; a 'crank', evidently, of the first water.

This much Minturn gathered clearly enough from the porter's talk while his luggage was brought in and the room set to rights; further, too, that the search party had gone out and *might*, of course, return at any moment. In which case——. Thus the room was empty, yet still hers. 'If Monsieur did not object—if the risk he ran of having to turn out suddenly in the night——' It was the loquacious porter who furnished the details that made the transaction questionable; and Minturn dismissed the loquacious porter as soon as possible, and prepared to get into the hastily arranged bed and snatch all the hours of sleep he could before he was turned out.

At first, it must be admitted, he felt uncomfortable—distinctly uncomfortable. He was in some one else's room. He had really no right to be there. It was in the nature of an unwarrantable intrusion; and while he unpacked he kept looking over his shoulder as though some one were watching him from the corners. Any moment, it seemed, he would hear a step in the passage, a knock would come at the door, the door would open, and there he would see this vigorous Englishwoman looking him up and down with anger. Worse still—he would hear her voice asking him what he was doing in her room—her bedroom. Of course, he had an adequate explanation, but still——!

Then, reflecting that he was already half undressed, the humour of it flashed for a second across his mind, and he laughed—*guietly*. And at once, after that laughter, under his breath, came the sudden sense of tragedy he had felt before. Perhaps, even while he smiled, her body lay broken and cold upon those awful heights, the wind of snow playing over her hair, her glazed eyes staring sightless up to the stars... It made him shudder. The sense of this woman whom he had never seen, whose name even he did not know, became extraordinarily real. Almost he could imagine that she was somewhere in the room with him, hidden, observing all he did.

He opened the door softly to put his boots outside, and when he closed it again he turned the key. Then he finished unpacking and distributed his few things about the room. It was soon done; for, in the first place, he had only a small Gladstone and a knapsack, and secondly, the only place where he could spread his clothes was the sofa. There was no chest of drawers, and the cupboard, an unusually large and solid one, was locked. The Englishwoman's things had evidently been hastily put away in it. The only sign of her recent presence was a bunch of faded *Alpenrosen* standing in a glass jar upon the washhand stand. This, and a certain faint perfume, were all that remained. In spite, however, of these very slight evidences, the whole room

THE OCCUPANT OF THE ROOM

was pervaded with a curious sense of occupancy that he found exceedingly distasteful. One moment the atmosphere seemed subtly charged with a 'just left' feeling; the next it was a queer awareness of 'still here' that made him turn and look hurriedly behind him.

Altogether, the room inspired him with a singular aversion, and the strength of this aversion seemed the only excuse for his tossing the faded flowers out of the window, and then hanging his mackintosh upon the cupboard door in such a way as to screen it as much as possible from view. For the sight of that big, ugly cupboard, filled with the clothing of a woman who might then be beyond any further need of covering—thus his imagination insisted on picturing it—touched in him a startled sense of the incongruous that did not stop there, but crept through his mind gradually till it merged somehow into a sense of a rather grotesque horror. At any rate, the sight of that cupboard was offensive, and he covered it almost instinctively. Then, turning out the electric light, he got into bed.

But the instant the room was dark he realised that it was more than he could stand; for, with the blackness, there came a sudden rush of cold that he found it hard to explain. And the odd thing was that, when he lit the candle beside his bed, he noticed that his hand trembled.

This, of course, was too much. His imagination was taking liberties and must be called to heel. Yet the way he called it to order was significant, and its very deliberateness betrayed a mind that has already admitted fear. And fear, once in, is difficult to dislodge. He lay there upon his elbow in bed and carefully took note of all the objects in the room—with the intention, as it were, of taking an inventory of everything his senses perceived, then drawing a line, adding them up finally, and saying with decision, 'That's all the room contains! I've counted every single thing. There is nothing more. *Now*—I may sleep in peace!'

And it was during this absurd process of enumerating the furniture of the room that the dreadful sense of distressing lassitude came over him that made it difficult even to finish counting. It came swiftly, yet with an amazing kind of violence that overwhelmed him softly and easily with a sensation of enervating weariness hard to describe. And its first effect was to banish fear. He no longer possessed enough energy to feel really afraid or nervous. The cold remained, but the alarm vanished. And into every corner of his usually vigorous personality crept the insidious poison of a *muscular* fatigue—at first—that in a few seconds, it seemed, translated itself into *spiritual* inertia. A sudden consciousness of the foolishness, the crass futility of life, of effort, of fighting—of all that makes life worth living, oozed into every fibre of his being, and left him utterly weak. A spirit of black pessimism, that was not even vigorous enough to assert itself, invaded the secret chambers of his heart...

Every picture that presented itself to his mind came dressed in grey shadows; those bored and sweating horses toiling up the ascent to—nothing! That hard-faced landlady taking so much trouble to let her desire for gain conquer her sense of morality—for a few francs! That gold-braided porter, so talkative, fussy, energetic, and so anxious to tell all he knew! What was the use of them all? And for himself, what in the world was the good of all the labour and drudgery he went through in that preparatory school where he was junior master? What could it lead to? Wherein lay the value of so much uncertain toil, when the ultimate secrets of life were hidden and no one knew the final goal? How foolish was effort, discipline, work! How vain was pleasure! How trivial the noblest life!...

With a jump that nearly upset the candle Minturn challenged this weak mood. Such vicious thoughts were usually so remote from his normal character that the sudden vile invasion produced a swift reaction. Yet, only for a moment. Instantly, again, the depression descended upon him like a wave. His work—it could lead to nothing but the dreary labour of a small headmastership after all—seemed as vain and foolish as his holiday in the Alps. What an idiot he had been, to be sure, to come out with a knapsack merely to work himself into a state of exhaustion climbing over toilsome mountains that led to nowhere—resulted in nothing. A dreariness of the grave possessed him. Life was a ghastly fraud! Religion a childish humbug! Everything was merely a trap—a trap of death; a coloured toy that Nature used as a decoy! But a decoy for what? For nothing! There was no meaning in anything. The only *real* thing was—DEATH. And the happiest people were those who found it soonest.

Then why wait for it to come?

He sprang out of bed, thoroughly frightened. This was horrible. Surely mere physical fatigue could not produce a world so black, an outlook so dismal, a cowardice that struck with such sudden hopelessness at the very roots of life? For, normally, he was cheerful and strong, full of the tides of healthy living; and this appalling lassitude swept the very basis of his personality into nothingness and the desire for death. It was like the development of a Secondary Personality. He had read, of course, how certain persons who suffered shocks developed thereafter entirely different characteristics, memory, tastes, and so forth. It had all rather frightened him. Though scientific men vouched for it, it was hardly to be believed. Yet here was a similar thing taking place in his own consciousness. He was, beyond question, experiencing all the mental variations of—*someone else*! It was un-moral. It was awful. It was—well, after all, at the same time, it was uncommonly interesting.

And this interest he began to feel was the first sign of his returned normal Self. For to feel interest is to live, and to love life.

He sprang into the middle of the room—then switched on the electric light. And the first thing that struck his eye was—the big cupboard.

'Hallo! There's that—beastly cupboard!' he exclaimed to himself, involuntarily, yet aloud. It held all the clothes, the swinging skirts and coats and summer blouses of the dead woman. For he knew now—somehow or other—that she *was* dead...

At that moment, through the open windows, rushed the sound

of falling water, bringing with it a vivid realisation of the desolate, snow-swept heights. He saw her—positively *saw* her!—lying where she had fallen, the frost upon her cheeks, the snow-dust eddying about her hair and eyes, her broken limbs pushing against the lumps of ice. For a moment the sense of spiritual lassitude—of the emptiness of life—vanished before this picture of broken effort—of a small human force battling pluckily, yet in vain, against the impersonal and pitiless potencies of inanimate nature—and he found himself again his normal self. Then instantly, returned again that terrible sense of cold, nothingness, emptiness...

And he found himself standing opposite the big cupboard where her clothes were. He suddenly wanted to see those clothes—things she had used and worn. Quite close he stood, almost touching it. The next second he had touched it. His knuckles struck upon the wood.

Why he knocked is hard to say. It was an instinctive movement probably. Something in his deepest self dictated it—ordered it. He knocked at the door. And the dull sound upon the wood into the stillness of that room brought—horror. Why it should have done so he found it as hard to explain to himself as why he should have felt impelled to knock. The fact remains that when he heard the faint reverberation inside the cupboard, it brought with it so vivid a realisation of the woman's presence that he stood there shivering upon the floor with a dreadful sense of anticipation; he almost expected to hear an answering knock from within—the rustling of the hanging skirts perhaps—or, worse still, to see the locked door slowly open towards him.

And from that moment, he declares that in some way or other he must have partially lost control of himself, or at least of his better judgment; for he became possessed by such an over-mastering desire to tear open that cupboard door and see the clothes within, that he tried every key in the room in the vain effort to unlock it, and then, finally, before he quite realised what he was doing—rang the bell!

But, having rung the bell for no obvious or intelligent reason at two o'clock in the morning, he then stood waiting in the middle of the floor for the servant to come, conscious for the first time that something outside his ordinary self had pushed him towards the act. It was almost like an internal voice that directed him... and thus, when at last steps came down the passage and he faced the cross and sleepy chambermaid, amazed at being summoned at such an hour, he found no difficulty in the matter of what he should say. For the same power that insisted he should open the cupboard door also impelled him to utter words over which he apparently had no control.

'It's not *you* I rang for!' he said with decision and impatience. 'I want a man. Wake the porter and send him up to me at once —hurry! I tell you, hurry——!'

And when the girl had gone, frightened at his earnestness, Minturn realised that the words surprised himself as much as they surprised her. Until they were out of his mouth he had not known what exactly he was saying. But now he understood that some force, foreign to his own personality, was using his mind and organs. The black depression that had possessed him a few moments before was also part of it. The powerful mood of this vanished woman had somehow momentarily taken possession of him—communicated, possibly, by the atmosphere of things in the room still belonging to her. But even now, when the porter, without coat or collar, stood beside him in the room, he did not understand why he insisted, with a positive fury admitting no denial, that the key of that cupboard must be found and the door instantly opened.

The scene was a curious one. After some perplexed whispering with the chambermaid at the end of the passage, the porter managed to find and produce the key in question. Neither he nor the girl knew clearly what this excited Englishman was up to, or why he was so passionately intent upon opening the cupboard at two o'clock in the morning. They watched him with an air of wondering what was going to happen next. But something of his curious earnestness, even of his late fear, communicated itself to them, and the sound of the key grating in the lock made them both jump.

They held their breath as the creaking door swung slowly open. All heard the clatter of that other key as it fell against the wooden floor—within. The cupboard had been locked *from the inside*. But it was the scared housemaid, from her position in the corridor, who first saw—and with a wild scream fell crashing against the banisters.

The porter made no attempt to save her. The schoolmaster and himself made a simultaneous rush towards the door, now wide open. They, too, had seen.

There were no clothes, skirts or blouses on the pegs, but they saw the body of the Englishwoman suspended in mid-air, the head bent forward. Jarred by the movement of unlocking, the body swung slowly round to face them... Pinned upon the inside of the door was a hotel envelope with the following words pencilled in straggling writing:

'Tired—unhappy—hopelessly depressed... I cannot face life any longer... All is black. I must put an end to it.... I meant to do it on the mountains, but was afraid. I slipped back to my room unobserved. This way is easiest and best. ...'

THE MAN WHOM THE TREES LOVED

I

He painted trees as by some special divining instinct of their essential qualities. He understood them. He knew why in an oak forest, for instance, each individual was utterly distinct from its fellows, and why no two beeches in the whole world were alike. People asked him down to paint a favourite lime or silver birch, for he caught the individuality of a tree as some catch the individuality of a horse. How he managed it was something of a puzzle, for he never had painting lessons, his drawing was often wildly inaccurate, and, while his perception of a Tree Personality was true and vivid, his rendering of it might almost approach the ludicrous. Yet the character and personality of that particular tree stood there alive beneath his brush—shining, frowning, dreaming, as the case might be, friendly or hostile, good or evil. It emerged.

There was nothing else in the wide world that he could paint; flowers and landscapes he only muddled away into a smudge; with people he was helpless and hopeless; also with animals. Skies he could sometimes manage, or effects of wind in foliage, but as a rule he left these all severely alone. He kept to trees, wisely following an instinct that was guided by love. It was quite arresting, this way he had of making a tree look almost like a being—alive. It approached the uncanny.

'Yes, Sanderson knows what he's doing when he paints a tree!' thought old David Bittacy, C. B., late of the Woods and Forests. 'Why, you can almost hear it rustle. You can smell the thing. You can hear the rain drip through its leaves. You can almost see the branches move. It grows.' For in this way somewhat he expressed his satisfaction, half to persuade himself that the twenty guineas were well spent (since his wife thought otherwise), and half to explain this uncanny reality of life that lay in the fine old cedar framed above his study table.

Yet in the general view the mind of Mr. Bittacy was held to be austere, not to say morose. Few divined in him the secretly tenacious love of nature that had been fostered by years spent in the forests and jungles of the eastern world. It was odd for an Englishman, due possibly to that Eurasian ancestor. Surreptitiously, as though half ashamed of it, he had kept alive a sense of beauty that hardly belonged to his type, and was unusual for its vitality. Trees, in particular, nourished it. He, also, understood trees, felt a subtle sense of communion with them, born perhaps of those years he had lived in caring for them, guarding, protecting, nursing, years of solitude among their great shadowy presences. He kept it largely to himself, of course, because he knew the world he lived in. He also kept it from his wife—to some extent. He knew it came between them, knew that she feared it, was opposed. But what he did not know, or realise at any rate, was the extent to which she grasped the power which they wielded over his life. Her fear, he judged, was simply due to those years in India, when for weeks at a time his calling took him away from her into the jungle forests, while she remained at home dreading all manner of evils that might befall him. This, of course, explained her instinctive opposition to the passion for woods that still influenced and clung to him. It was a natural survival of those anxious days of waiting in solitude for his safe return.

For Mrs. Bittacy, daughter of an evangelical clergyman, was a self-sacrificing woman, who in most things found a happy duty in sharing her husband's joys and sorrows to the point of self-obliteration. Only in this matter of the trees she was less successful than in others. It remained a problem difficult of compromise.

He knew, for instance, that what she objected to in this portrait of the cedar on their lawn was really not the price he had given for it, but the unpleasant way in which the transaction emphasised this breach between their common interests—the only one they had, but deep.

Sanderson, the artist, earned little enough money by his strange talent; such cheques were few and far between. The owners of fine or interesting trees who cared to have them painted singly were rare indeed; and the 'studies' that he made for his own delight he also kept for his own delight. Even were there buyers, he would not sell them. Only a few, and these peculiarly intimate friends, might even see them, for he disliked to hear the undiscerning criticism of those who did not understand. Not that he minded laughter at his craftmanship—he admitted it with scorn—but that remarks about the personality of the tree itself could easily wound or anger him. He resented slighting observations concerning them, as though insults offered to personal friends who could not answer for themselves. He was instantly up in arms.

'It really *is* extraordinary', said a Woman who Understood, 'that you can make that cypress seem an individual, when in reality all cypresses are so *exactly* alike.'

And though the bit of calculated flattery had come so near to saying the right, true thing, Sanderson flushed as though she had slighted a friend beneath his very nose. Abruptly he passed in front of her and turned the picture to the wall.

'Almost as queer,' he answered rudely, copying her silly emphasis, 'as that *you* should have imagined individuality in your husband, Madame, when in reality all men are so *exactly* alike!'

Since the only thing that differentiated her husband from the mob was the money for which she had married him, Sanderson's relations with that particular family terminated on the spot, chance of prospective 'orders' with it. His sensitiveness, perhaps, was morbid. At any rate the way to reach his heart lay through his trees. He might be said to love trees. He certainly drew a splendid inspiration from them, and the source of a man's inspiration, be it music, religion, or a woman, is never a safe thing to criticise.

'I do think, perhaps, it was just a little extravagant, dear,' said

Mrs. Bittacy, referring to the cedar cheque, 'when we want a lawn-mower so badly too. But, as it gives you such pleasure——'

'It reminds me of a certain day, Sophia,' replied the old gentleman, looking first proudly at herself, then fondly at the picture, 'now long gone by. It reminds me of another tree—that Kentish lawn in the spring, birds singing in the lilacs, and someone in a muslin frock waiting patiently beneath a certain cedar—not the one in the picture, I know, but——'

'I was not waiting,' she said indignantly, 'I was picking fir-cones for the schoolroom fire——'

'Fir-cones, my dear, do not grow on cedars, and schoolroom fires were not made in June in my young days.'

'And anyhow it isn't the same cedar.'

'It has made me fond of all cedars for its sake,' he answered, 'and it reminds me that you are the same young girl still——'

She crossed the room to his side, and together they looked out of the window where, upon the lawn of their Hampshire cottage, a ragged Lebanon stood in solitary state.

'You're as full of dreams as ever,' she said gently, 'and I don't regret the cheque a bit—really. Only it would have been more real if it had been the original tree, wouldn't it?'

'That was blown down long ago. I passed the place last year, and there's not a sign of it left,' he replied tenderly. And presently, when he released her from his side, she went up to the wall and carefully dusted the picture Sanderson had made of the cedar on their present lawn. She went all round the frame with her tiny handkerchief, standing on tiptoe to reach the top rim.

'What I like about it,' said the old fellow to himself when his wife had left the room, 'is the way he has made it live. All trees have it, of course, but a cedar taught it to me first—the 'something' trees possess that makes them know I'm there when I stand close and watch. I suppose I felt it then because I was in love, and love reveals life everywhere.' He glanced a moment at the Lebanon looming gaunt and sombre through the gathering dusk. A curious wistful expression danced a moment through his eyes. 'Yes, Sanderson has seen it as it is,' he murmured, 'solemnly dreaming there, its dim hidden life against the Forest edge, and as different from that other tree in Kent as I am from—from the vicar, say. It's quite a stranger, too. I don't know anything about it really. That other cedar I loved; this old fellow I respect. Friendly though—yes, on the whole quite friendly. He's painted the friendliness right enough. He saw that. I'd like to know that man better,' he added. 'I'd like to ask him how he saw so clearly that it stands there between this cottage and the Forest—yet somehow more in sympathy with us than with the mass of woods behind—a sort of go-between.' *That* I never noticed before. I see it now—through his eyes. It stands there like a sentinel—protective rather.'

He turned away abruptly to look through the window. He saw the great encircling mass of gloom that was the Forest, fringing their little lawn. It pressed up closer in the darkness. The prim garden with its formal beds of flowers seemed an impertinence almost—some little coloured insect that sought to settle on a sleeping monster—some gaudy fly that danced impudently down the edge of a great river that could engulf it with a toss of its smallest wave. That Forest with its thousand years of growth and its deep spreading being was some such slumbering monster, yes. Their cottage and garden stood too near its running lip. When the winds were strong and lifted its shadowy skirts of black and purple.... He loved this feeling of the Forest Personality; he had always loved it.

'Queer,' he reflected, 'awfully queer, that trees should bring me such a sense of dim, vast living! I used to feel it particularly, I remember, in India; in Canadian woods as well; but never in little English woods till here. And Sanderson's the only man I ever knew who felt it too. He's never said so, but there's the proof,' and he turned again to the picture that he loved. A thrill of unaccustomed life ran through him as he looked. 'I wonder, by Jove, I wonder,' his thoughts ran on, 'whether a tree—er—in any lawful meaning of the term can be—alive. I remember some writing fellow telling me long ago that trees had once been moving things, animal organisms of some sort, that had stood so long feeding, sleeping, dreaming, or something, in the same place, that they had lost the power to get away...!'

Fancies flew pell-mell about his mind, and, lighting a cheroot, he dropped into an armchair beside the open window and let them play. Outside the blackbirds whistled in the shrubberies across the lawn. He smelt the earth and trees and flowers, the perfume of mown grass, and the bits of open heath-land far away in the heart of the woods. The summer wind stirred very faintly through the leaves. But the great New Forest hardly raised her sweeping skirts of black and purple shadow.

Mr. Bittacy, however, knew intimately every detail of that wilderness of trees within. He knew all the purple coombs splashed with yellow waves of gorse; sweet with juniper and myrtle, and gleaming with clear and dark-eyed pools that watched the sky. There hawks hovered, circling hour by hour, and the flicker of the peewit's flight, its melancholy, petulant cry, deepened the sense of stillness. He knew the solitary pines, dwarfed, tufted, vigorous, that sang to every lost wind, travellers like the gipsies who pitched their bush-like tents beneath them; he knew the shaggy ponies, with foals like baby centaurs; the chattering jays, the milky call of cuckoos in the spring, and the boom of the bittern from the lonely marches. The undergrowth of watching hollies, he knew too, strange and mysterious, with their dark, suggestive beauty, and the yellow shimmer of their pale dropped leaves.

Here all the Forest lived and breathed in safety, secure from mutilation. No terror of the axe could haunt the peace of its vast subconscious life, no terror of devastating Man afflict it with the dread of premature death. It knew itself supreme; it spread and preened itself without concealment. It set no spires to carry warnings, for no wind brought messages of alarm as it bulged outwards to the sun and stars.

But, once its leafy portals left behind, the trees of the countryside were otherwise. The houses threatened then; they knew themselves in danger. The roads were no longer glades of silent turf, but noisy, cruel ways by which men came to attack them. They were civilised, cared for—but cared for in order that some day they might be put to death. Even in the villages, where the solemn and immemorial repose of giant chestnuts aped security, the tossing of a silver birch against their mass, impatient in the littlest wind, brought warning. Dust clogged their leaves. The inner humming of their quiet life became inaudible beneath the scream and shriek of clattering traffic. They longed and prayed to enter the great Peace of the Forest yonder, but they could not move. They, knew, moreover, that the Forest with its august, deep splendour, despised and pitied them. They were a thing of artificial gardens, and belonged to beds of flowers all forced to grow one way....

'I'd like to know that artist fellow better,' was the thought upon which he returned at length to the things of practical liffe. 'I wonder if Sophia would mind him here for a bit—?' He rose with the sound of the gong, brushing the ashes from his speckled waistcoat. He pulled the waistcoat down. He was slim and spare in figure, active in his movements. In the dim light, but for that silvery moustache, he might easily have passed for a man of forty.

'I'll suggest it to her anyhow,' he decided on his way upstairs to dress. His thought really was that Sanderson could probably explain this world of things he had always felt about—trees. A man who could paint the soul of a cedar in that way must know it all.

'Why not?' she gave her verdict later over the bread-and-butter puddings; 'unless you think he'd find it dull without companions.'

'He would paint all day in the Forest, dear. I'd like to pick his brains a bit, too, if I could manage it.'

'You can manage anything, David,' was what she answered, for this elderly childless couple used an affectionate politeness long since deemed old-fashioned. The remark, however, displeased her, making her feel uneasy, and she did not notice his rejoinder, smiling his pleasure and content—'Except yourself and our bank account, my dear.' This passion of his for trees was of old a bone of contention, though very mild contention. It frightened her. That was the truth. The Bible, her Baedeker for earth and heaven, did not mention it. Her husband, while humouring her, could never alter that instinctive dread she had. He soothed, but never changed her. She liked the woods, perhaps as spots for shade and picnics, but she could not, as he did, love them.

And after dinner, with a lamp beside the open window, he read aloud from *The Times* the evening post had brought, such fragments as he thought might interest her. The custom was invariable, except on Sundays, when, to please his wife, he dozed over Tennyson or Farrar as their mood might be. She knitted while he read, asked gentle questions, told him his voice was a 'lovely reading voice', and enjoyed the little discussions that occasions prompted because he always let her win them with 'Ah, Sophia, I had never thought of it quite in *that* way before; but now you mention it I must say I think there's something in it....'

For David Bittacy was wise. It was long after marriage, during his months of loneliness spent with trees and forests in India, his wife waiting at home in the Bungalow, that his other, deeper side had developed the strange passion that she could not understand. And after one or two serious attempts to let her share it with him, he had given up and learned to hide it from her. He learned, that is, to speak of it only casually; for since she knew it was there, to keep silence altogether would only increase her pain. So from time to time he skimmed the surface just to let her show him where he was wrong and think she won the day. It remained a debatable land of compromise. He listened with patience to her criticism, her excursions and alarms, knowing that while it gave her satisfaction, it could not change himself. The thing lay in him too deep and true for change. But, for peace's sake, some meeting-place was desirable, and he found it thus.

It was her one fault in his eyes, this religious mania carried over from her up-bringing, and it did no serious harm. Great emotion could shake it sometimes out of her. She clung to it because her father taught it her and not because she had thought it out for herself. Indeed, like many women, she never really *thought* at all, but merely reflected the images of others' thinking which she had learned to see. So, wise in his knowledge of human nature, old David Bittacy accepted the pain of being obliged to keep a portion of his inner life shut off from the woman he deeply loved. He regarded her little biblical phrases as oddities that still clung to a rather fine, big soul—like horns and little useless things some animals have not yet lost in the course of evolution while they have outgrown their use.

'My dear, what is it? You frightened me!' She asked it suddenly, sitting up so abruptly that her cap dropped sideways almost to her ear. For David Bittacy behind his crackling paper had uttered a sharp exclamation of surprise. He had lowered the sheet and was staring at her over the tops of his gold glasses.

'Listen to this, if you please,' he said, a note of eagerness in his voice, 'listen to this, my dear Sophia. It's from an address by Francis Darwin before the Royal Society. He is president, you know, and son of the great Darwin. Listen carefully, I beg you. It is *most* significant.'

'I *am* listening, David,' she said with some astonishment, looking up. She stopped her knitting. For a second she glanced behind her. Something had suddenly changed in the room, and it made her feel wide awake, though before she had been almost dozing. Her husband's voice and manner had introduced this new thing. Her instincts rose in warning. '*Do* read it, dear.' He took a deep breath, looking first again over the rims of his glasses to make quite sure of her attention. He had evidently come across something of genuine interest, although herself she often found the passages from these 'Addresses' somewhat heavy.

In a deep, emphatic voice he read aloud:

'It is impossible to know whether or not plants are conscious; but it is consistent with the doctrine of continuity that in all living things there is something psychic, and if we accept this point of view——'

'*If*,' she interrupted, scenting danger.

He ignored the interruption as a thing of slight value he was accustomed to.

'If we accept this point of view,' he continued, 'we must believe that in plants there exists a faint copy of *what we know as consciousness in ourselves.*'

He laid the paper down and steadily stared at her. Their eyes met. He had italicised the last phrase.

For a minute or two his wife made no reply or comment. They stared at one another in silence. He waited for the meaning of the words to reach her understanding with full import. Then he turned and read them again in part, while she, released from that curious driving look in his eyes, instinctively again glanced over her shoulder round the room. It was almost as if she felt some one had come in to them unnoticed.

'We must believe that in plants there exists a faint copy of what we know as consciousness in ourselves.'

'*If*,' she repeated lamely, feeling before the stare of those questioning eyes she must say something, but not yet having gathered her wits together quite.

'*Consciousness*,' he rejoined. And then he added gravely: 'That, my dear, is the statement of a scientific man of the Twentieth Century.'

Mrs. Bittacy sat forward in her chair so that her silk flounces crackled louder than the newspaper. She made a characteristic little sound between sniffing and snorting. She put her shoes closely together, with her hands upon her knees.

'David,' she said quietly, 'I think these scientific men are simply losing their heads. There is nothing in the Bible that I can remember about any such thing whatsoever.'

'Nothing, Sophia, that I can remember either,' he answered patiently. Then, after a pause, he added, half to himself perhaps more than to her: 'And, now that I come to think about it, it seems that Sanderson once said something to me that was similar.'

'Then Mr. Sanderson is a wise and thoughtful man, and a safe man,' she quickly took him up, 'if he said that.'

For she thought her husband referred to her remark about the Bible, and not to her judgment of the scientific men. And he did not correct her mistake.

'And plants, you see, dear, are not the same thing as trees,' she drove her advantage home, 'not quite, that is.'

'I agree,' said David quietly; 'but both belong to the great vegetable kingdom.'

There was a moment's pause before she answered.

'Pah! the vegetable kingdom, indeed!' She tossed her pretty old head. And into the words she put a degree of contempt that, could the vegetable kingdom have heard it, might have made it feel ashamed for covering a third of the world with its wonderful tangled network of roots and branches, delicate shaking leaves, and its millions of spires that caught the sun and wind and rain. Its very right to existence seemed in question.

II

Sanderson accordingly came down, and on the whole his short visit was a success. Why he came at all was a mystery to those who heard of it, for he never paid visits and was certainly not the kind of man to court a customer. There must have been something in Bittacy he liked.

Mrs. Bittacy was glad when he left. He brought no dress-suit for one thing, not even a dinner-jacket, and he wore very low collars with big balloon ties like a Frenchman, and let his hair grow longer than was nice, she felt. Not that these things were important, but that she considered them symptoms of something a little disordered. The ties were unnecessarily flowing.

For all that he was an interesting man, and, in spite of his eccentricities of dress and so forth, a gentleman. 'Perhaps,' she reflected in her genuinely charitable heart, 'he had other uses for the twenty guineas, an invalid sister or an old mother to support! She had no notion of the cost of brushes, frames, paints and canvases. Also she forgave him much for the sake of his beautiful eyes and his eager enthusiasm of manner. So many men of thirty were already blasé.

Still, when the visit was over, she felt relieved. She said nothing about his coming a second time, and her husband, she was glad to notice, had likewise made no suggestion. For, truth to tell, the way the younger man engrossed the older, keeping him out for hours in the Forest, talking on the lawn in the blazing sun, and in the evenings when the damp of dusk came creeping out from the surrounding woods, all regardless of his age and usual habits, was not quite to her taste. Of course, Mr. Sanderson did not know how easily those attacks of Indian fever came back, but David surely might have told him.

They talked trees from morning till night. It stirred in her the old subconscious trail of dread, a trail that led ever into the darkness of big woods; and such feelings, as her early evangelical training taught her, were tempting. To regard them in any other ways was to play with danger.

Her mind, as she watched these two, was charged with curious thoughts of dread she could not understand, yet feared the more on that account. The way they studied that old mangy cedar was a trifle unnecessary, unwise, she felt. It was disregarding the sense of proportion which deity had set upon the world for men's safe guidance.

Even after dinner they smoked their cigars upon the low branches that swept down and touched the lawn, until at length she insisted on their coming in. Cedars, she had somewhere heard, were not safe after sundown; it was not wholesome to be too near them; to sleep beneath them was even dangerous, though what the precise danger was she had forgotten. The upas was the tree she really meant.

At any rate she summoned David in, and Sanderson came presently after him.

For a long time, before deciding on this peremptory step, she had watched them surreptitiously from the drawing-room window—her husband and her guest. The dusk enveloped them with its damp veil of gauze. She saw the glowing tips of their cigars, and heard the drone of voices. Bats flitted overhead, and big, silent moths whirred softly over the rhododendron blossoms. And it came suddenly to her, while she watched, that her husband had somehow altered these last few days—since Mr. Sanderson's arrival in fact. A change had come over him, though what it was she could not say. She hesitated, indeed, to search. That was the instinctive dread operating in her. Provided it passed she would rather not know. Small things, of course, she noticed; small outward signs. He had neglected *The Times* for one thing, left off his speckled waistcoats for another. He was absent-minded sometimes; showed vagueness in practical details where hitherto he showed decision. And—he had begun to talk in his sleep again.

These and a dozen other small peculiarities came suddenly upon her with the rush of a combined attack. They brought with them a faint distress that made her shiver. Momentarily her mind was startled, then confused, as her eyes picked out the shadowy figures in the dusk, the cedar covering them, the Forest close at their backs. And then, before she could think, or seek internal guidance as her habit was, this whisper, muffled and very hurried, ran across her brain: 'It's Mr. Sanderson. Call David in at once!'

And she had done so. Her shrill voice crossed the lawn and died away into the Forest, quickly smothered. No echo followed it. The sound fell dead against the rampart of a thousand listening trees.

'The damp is so very penetrating, even in summer,' she murmured when they came obediently. She was half surprised at her own audacity, half repentant. They came so meekly at her call. 'And my husband is sensitive to fever from the East. No, *please* do not throw away your cigars. We can sit by the open window and enjoy the evening while you smoke.'

She was very talkative for a moment; subconscious excitement was the cause.

'It is so still—so wonderfully still,' she went on, as no one spoke, 'so peaceful, and the air so very sweet... and God is always near to those who need His aid.' The words slipped out before she realised quite what she was saying, yet fortunately, in time to lower her voice, for no one heard them. They were, perhaps, an instinctive expression of relief. It flustered her that she could have said the thing at all.

Sanderson brought her shawl and helped to arrange the chairs; she thanked him in her old-fashioned, gentle way, declining the lamps which he had offered to light. 'They attract the moths and insects so, I think!'

The three of them sat there in the gloaming, Mr. Bittacy's white moustache and his wife's yellow shawl gleaming at their end of the little horseshoe, Sanderson with his wild black hair and shining eyes midway between them. The painter went on talking softly, continuing evidently the conversation begun with his host beneath the cedar. Mrs. Bittacy, on her guard, listened—uneasily.

'For trees, you see, rather conceal themselves in daylight. They reveal themselves fully only after sunset. I never *knew* a tree,' he bowed here slightly towards the lady as though to apologise for something he felt she would not quite understand or like, 'until I've seen it in the night. Your cedar, for instance,' looking towards her husband again so that Mrs. Bittacy caught the gleaming of his turned eyes. 'I failed with badly at first, because I did it in the morning. You shall see to-morrow what I mean—that first sketch is upstairs in my portfolio; it's quite another tree to the one you bought. That view'—he leaned forward, lowering his voice—'I caught one morning about two o'clock in very faint moonlight and the stars. I saw the naked being of the thing——'

'You mean that you went out, Mr. Sanderson, at that hour?' the old lady asked with astonishment and mild rebuke. She did not care particularly for his choice of adjectives either.

'I fear it was rather a liberty to take in another's house, perhaps,' he answered courteously. 'But, having chanced to wake,

I saw the tree from my window, and made my way downstairs.'

'It's a wonder Boxer didn't bite you; he sleeps loose in the hall,' she said.

'On the contrary. The dog came out with me. I hope,' he added, 'the noise didn't disturb you, though it's rather late to say so. I feel quite guilty.' His white teeth showed in the dusk as he smiled. A smell of earth and flowers stole in through the window on a breath of wandering air.

Mrs. Bittacy said nothing at the moment. 'We both sleep like tops,' put in her husband, laughing. 'You're a courageous man, though, Sanderson; and, by Jove, the picture justifies you. Few artists would have taken so much trouble, though I read once that Holman Hunt, Rossetti, or some one of that lot, painted all night in his orchard to get an effect of moonlight that he wanted.'

He chattered on. His wife was glad to hear his voice; it made her feel more easy in her mind. But presently the other held the floor again, and her thoughts grew darkened and afraid. Instinctively she feared the influence on her husband. The Mystery and wonder that lie in woods, in forests, in great gatherings of trees everywhere, seemed so real and present while he talked.

'The Night transfigures all things in a way,' he was saying; 'dut nothing so searchingly as trees. From behind a veil that sunlight hangs before them in the day they emerge and show themselves. Even buildings do that—in a measure—but trees particularly. In the daytime they sleep; at night they wake, they manifest, turn active—live. You remember,' turning politely again in the direction of his hostess, 'how clearly Henley understood that?'

'That socialist person, you mean?' asked the lady. Her tone and accent made the substantive sound criminal. It almost hissed, the way she uttered it.

'The poet, yes,' replied the artist tactfully, 'the friend of Stewenson, you remember, Stevenson who wrote those charming children's verses.'

He quoted in a low voice the lines he meant. It was, for once, the time, the place, and the setting all together. The words floated out across the lawn towards the wall of blue darkness where the big Forest swept the little garden with its league-long curve that was like the shore-line of a sea. A wave of distant sound that was like surf accompanied his voice, as though the wind was fain to listen too:

> Not to the staring Day,
> For all the importunate questionings he pursues
> In his big, violent voice,
> Shall those mild things of bulk and multitude,
> The trees—God's sentinels . . .
> Yield of their huge, unutterable selves.
>
> . . . .
>
> But at the word
> Of the ancient, sacerdotal Nigth,
> Night of the many secrets, whose effect—
> Transfiguring, hierophantic, dread—
> Themselves alone may fully apprehend,
> They tremble and are changed:
> In each the uncouth, individual soul
> Looms forth and glooms
> Essential, and, their bodily presences
> Touched with inordinate significance,
> Wearing the darkness like a livery
> Of some mysterious and tremendous guild,
> The brood—they menace—they appal.

The voice of Mrs. Bittacy presently broke the silence that followed.

'I like that part about God's sentinels,' she murmured. There was no sharpness in her tone; it was hushed and quiet. The truth, so musically uttered, muted her shrill objections though it had not lessened her alarm. Her husband made no comment; his cigar, she noticed, had gone out.

'And old trees in particular,' continued the artist, as though to himself, 'have very definite personalities. You can offend, wound, please them; the moment you stand within their shade you feel whether they come out to you, or whether they withdraw.' He turned abruptly towards his host. 'You know that singular essay of Prentice Mulford's no doubt "God in the Trees"

—extravagant perhaps, but yet with a fine true beauty in it? You've never read it, no?' he asked.

But it was Mrs. Bittacy who answered; her husband keeping his curious deep silence.

'I never did!' It fell like a drip of cold water from the face muffled in the yellow shawl; even a child could have supplied the remainder of the unspoken thought.

'Ah,' said Sanderson gently, 'but there *is* 'God' in the trees, God in a very subtle aspect and sometimes—I have known the trees express it too—that which is *not* God—dark and terrible. Have you ever noticed, too, how clearly trees show what they want—choose their companions, at least? How beeches, for instance, allow no life too near them—birds or squirrels in their boughs, nor any growth beneath? The silence in the beech wood is quite terrifying often! And how pines like bilberry bushes at their feet and sometimes little oaks—all trees making a clear, deliberate choice, and holding firmly to it? Some trees obviously—it's very strange and marked—seem to prefer the human.'

The old lady sat up crackling, for this was more than she could permit. Her stiff silk dress emitted little sharp reports.

'We know,' she answered, 'that He was said to have walked in the garden in the cool of the evening'—the gulp betrayed the effort that it cost her—'but we are nowhere told that He hid in the trees, or anything like that. Trees, after all, we must remember, are only large vegetables.'

'True,' was the soft answer, 'but in everything that grows, has life, that is, there's mystery past all finding out. The wonder that lies hidden in our own souls lies also hidden, I venture to assert, in the stupidity and silence of a mere potato.'

The observation was not meant to be amusing. It was *not* amusing. No one laughed. On the contrary, the words conveyed in too literal a sense the feeling that haunted all that conversation. Each one in his own way realised—with beauty, with wonder, with alarm—that the talk had somehow brought the whole vegetable kingdom nearer to that of man. Some link had been established between the two. It was not wise, with that great Forest listening at their very doors, to speak so plainly. The Forest edged up closer while they did so.

And Mrs. Bittacy, anxious to interrupt the horrid spell, broke suddenly in upon it with a matter-of-fact suggestion. She did not like her husband's prolonged silence, stillness. He seemed so negative—so changed.

'David,' she said, raising her voice, 'I think you're feeling the dampness. It's grown chilly. The fever comes so suddenly, you know, and it might be wise to take the tincture. I'll go and get it, dear, at once. It's better.' And before he could object she had left the room to bring the homoeopathic dose that she believed in, and that, to please her, he swallowed by the tumbler-full from week to week.

And the moment the door closed behind her, Sanderson began again, though now in quite a different tone. Mr. Bittacy sat up in his chair. The two men obviously resumed the conversation—the real conversation interrupted beneath the cedar—and left aside the sham one which was so much dust merely thrown in the old lady's eyes.

'Trees love you, that's the fact,' he said earnestly. 'Your service to them all these years abroad has made them know you.'

'Know me?'

'Made them, yes,'—he paused a moment, then added,—'made them *aware of your presence*; aware of a force outside themselves that deliberately seeks their welfare, don't you see?'

'By Jove, Sanderson—!' This put into plain language actual sensations he had felt, yet had never dared to phrase in words before. 'They get into touch with me, as it were?' he ventured, laughing at his own sentence, yet laughing only with his lips.

'Exactly,' was the quick, emphatic reply. 'They seek to blend with something they feel instinctively to be good for them, helpful to their essential beings, encouraging to their best expression—their life.'

'Good Lord, Sir!' Bittacy heard himself saying, 'but you're

putting my own thoughts into words. D'you know, I've felt something like that for years. As though—' he looked round to make sure his wife was not there, then finished the sentence—'as though the trees were after me!'

'"Amalgamate" seems the best word, perhaps,' said Sanderson slowly. 'They would draw you to themselves. Good forces, you see, always seek to merge; evil to separate; that's why Good in the end must always win the day—everywhere. The accumulation in the long run becomes overwhelming. Evil tends to separation, dissolution, death. The comradeship of trees, their instinct to run together, is a vital symbol. Trees in a mass are good; alone, you may take it generally, are—well, dangerous. Look at a monkey-puzzler, or better still a holly. Look at it, watch it, understand it. Did you ever see more plainly an evil thought made visible? They're wicked. Beautiful too, oh yes! There's a strange, miscalculated beauty often in evil——'

'That cedar, then——?'

'Not evil, no; but alien, rather. Cedars grow in forests all-together. The poor thing has drifted, that is all.'

They were getting rather deep. Sanderson, talking against time, spoke so fast. It was too condensed. Bittacy hardly followed that last bit. His mind floundered among his own less definite, less sorted thoughts, till presently another sentence from the artist startled him into attention again.

'That cedar will protect you here, though, because you both have humanised it by your thinking so lovingly of its presence. The others can't get past it, as it were.'

'Protect me!' he exclaimed. 'Protect me from their love?'

Sanderson laughed. 'We're getting rather mixed,' he said; 'we're talking of one thing in the terms of another really. But what I mean is—you see—that their love for you, their "awareness" of your personality and presence involves the idea of winning you—across the border—into themselves—into their world of living. It means, in a way, taking you over.'

The ideas the artist started in his mind ran furious wild races to and fro. It was like a maze sprung suddenly into movement. The whirling of the intricate lines bewildered him. They went so fast, leaving but half-an explanation of their goal. He followed first one, then another, but a new one always dashed across to intercept before he could get anywhere.

'But India,' he said, presently in a lower voice, 'India is so far away—from this little English forest. The trees, too, are utterly different for one thing.'

The rustle of skirts warned of Mrs. Bittacy's approach. This was a sentence he could turn round another way in case she came up and pressed for explanation.

'There is communion among trees all the world over,' was the strange quick reply. 'They always know.'

'They always know! You think then——?'

'The winds, you see—the great, swift carriers! They have their ancient rights of way about the world. An easterly wind, for instance, carrying on stage by stage as it were—linking dropped messages and meanings from land to land like the birds—an easterly wind——'

Mrs. Bittacy swept in upon them with the tumbler—

'There, David,' she said, 'that will ward off any beginnings of attack. Just a spoonful, dear. Oh, oh! not *all*!' for he had swallowed half the contents at a single gulp as usual; 'another dose before you go to bed, and the balance in the morning, first thing when you wake.'

She turned to her guest, who put the tumbler down for her upon a table at his elbow. She had heard them speak of the east wind. She emphasised the warning she had misinterpreted. The private part of the conversation came to an abrupt end.

'It is the one thing that upsets him more than any other—an east wind,' she said, 'and I am glad, Mr. Sanderson, to hear you think so too.'

III

A deep hush followed, in the middle of which an owl was heard calling its muffled note in the forest. A big moth whirred with a soft collision against one of the windows. Mrs. Bittacy started slightly, but no one spoke. Above the trees the stars were faintly visible. From the distance came the barking of a dog.

Bittacy, relighting his cigar, broke the little spell of silence that had caught all three.

'It's rather a comforting thought,' he said, throwing the match out of the window, 'that life is about us everywhere, and that there is really no dividing line between what we call organic and inorganic.'

'The universe, yes,' said Sanderson, 'is all one, really. We're puzzled by the gaps we cannot see across, but as a fact, I suppose, there are no gaps at all.'

Mrs. Bittacy rustled ominously, holding her peace meanwhile. She feared long words she did not understand. Beelzebub lay hid among too many syllables.

'In trees and plants especially, there dreams an exquisite life that no one yet has proved unconscious.'

'Or conscious either, Mr. Sanderson,' she neatly interjected. 'It's only man that was made after His image, not shrubberies and things...'

Her husband interposed without delay.

'It is not necessary,' he explained suavely, 'to say that they're alive in the sense that we are alive. At the same time,' with an eye to his wife, 'I see no harm in holding, dear, that all created things contain some measure of His life Who made them. It's only beautiful to hold that He created nothing dead. We are not pantheists for all that!' he added soothingly.

'Oh, no! Not that, I hope!' The word alarmed her. It was worse than hope. Through her puzzled mind stole a stealthy, dangerous thing... like a panther.

'I like to think that even in decay there's life,' the painter murmured. 'The falling apart of rotten wood breeds sentiency; there's force and motion in the falling of a dying leaf, in the breaking up and crumbling of everything indeed. And take an inert stone: it's crammed with heat and weight and potencies of all sorts. What holds its particles together indeed? We understand it as little as gravity or why a needle always turns to the "North". Both things may be a mode of life...'

'You think a compass has a soul, Mr. Sanderson?' exclaimed the lady with a crackling of her silk flounces that conveyed a sense of outrage even more plainly than her tone. The artist smiled to himself in the darkness, but it was Bittacy who hastened to reply.

'Our friend merely suggests that these mysterious agencies,' he said quietly, 'may be due to some kind of life we cannot understand. Why should water only run downhill? Why should trees grow at right angles to the surface of the ground, and towards the sun? Why should the worlds spin for ever on their axes? Why should fire change the form of everything it touches without really destroying them? To say these things follow the law of their being explains nothing. Mr. Sanderson merely suggests—poetically, my dear, of course—that these may be manifestations of life, though life at a different stage to ours.'

'The "*breath* of life," we read, "He breathed into them". These things do not breathe.' She said it with triumph.

Then Sanderson put in a word. But he spoke rather to himself or to his host than by way of serious rejoinder to the ruffled lady.

'But plants do breathe too, you know,' he said. 'They breathe, they eat, they digest, they move about, and they adapt themselves to their environment as men and animals do. They have a nervous system too... at least a complex system of nuclei which have some of the qualities of nerve cells. They may have memory too. Certainly, they know definite action in response to stimulus. And though this may be physiological, no one has proved that it is only that, and not—psychological.'

He did not notice, apparently, the little gasp that was audible behind the yellow shawl. Bittacy cleared his throat, threw his extinguished cigar upon the lawn, crossed and recrossed his legs.

'And in trees,' continued the other, 'behind a great forest, for instance,' pointing towards the woods, 'may stand a rather splendid Entity that manifests through all the thousand individual trees—some huge collective life, quite as minutely and delicately organised as our own. It might merge and blend with ours under certain conditions, so that we could understand it by *being* it, for a time at least. It might even engulf human vitality into the immense whirlpool of its own vast dreaming life. The pull of a big forest on a man can be tremendous and utterly overwhelming.'

The mouth of Mrs. Bittacy was heard to close with a snap. Her shawl, and particularly her crackling dress, exhaled the protest that burned within her like a pain. She was too distressed to be overawed, but at the same time too confused 'mid the litter of words and meanings half understood, to find immediate phrases she could use. Whatever the actual meaning of his language might be, however, and whatever subtle dangers lay concealed behind them meanwhile, they certainly wove a kind of gentle spell with the glimmering darkness that held all three delicately enmeshed there by that open window. The odours of dewy lawn, flowers, trees, and earth formed part of it.

'The moods,' he continued, 'that people waken in us are due to their hidden life affecting our own. Deep calls to deep. A person, for instance, joins you in an empty room: you both instantly change. The new arrival, though in silence, has caused a change of mood. May not the moods of Nature touch and stir us in virtue of a similar prerogative? The sea, the hills, the desert, wake passion, joy, terror, as the case may be; for a few, perhaps,' he glanced significantly at his host so that Mrs. Bittacy again caught the turning of his eyes, 'emotions of a curious, flaming splendour that are quite nameless. Well... whence come these powers? Surely from nothing that is... dead! Does not the influence of a forest, its sway and strange ascendancy over certain minds, betray a direct manifestation of life? It lies otherwise beyond all explanation, this mysterious emanation of big woods. Some natures, of course, deliberately invite it. The authority of a host of trees,—his voice grew almost solemn as he said the words 'is something not to be denied. One feels it here, I think, particularly.'

There was considerable tension in the air as he ceased speaking. Mr. Bittacy had not intended that the talk should go so far. They had drifted. He did not wish to see his wife unhappy or afraid, and he was aware—acutely so—that her feelings were stirred to a point he did not care about. Something in her, as he put it, was 'working up' towards explosion.

He sought to generalise the conversation, diluting this accumulated emotion by spreading it.

'The sea is His and He made it,' he suggested vaguely, hoping Sanderson would take the hint, 'and with the trees it is the same...'

'The whole gigantic vegetable kingdom, yes,' the artist took him up, 'all at the service of man, for food, for shelter and for a thousand purposes of his daily life. Is it not striking what a lot of the globe they cover... exquisitely organised life, yet stationary, always ready to our hand when we want them, never running away? But the taking them, for all that, not so easy. One man shrinks from picking flowers, another from cutting down trees. And, it's curious that most of the forest tales and legends are dark, mysterious, and somewhat ill-omened. The forest-beings are rarely gay and harmless. The forest life was felt as terrible. Tree-worship still survives to-day. Wood-cutters...those who take the life of trees... you see, a race of haunted men...'

He stopped abruptly, a singular catch in his voice. Bittacy felt something even before the sentences were over. His wife, he knew, felt it still more strongly. For it was in the middle of the heavy silence following upon these last remarks, that Mrs. Bittacy, rising with a violent abruptness from her chair, drew the attention of the others to something moving towards them across the lawn. It came silently. In outline it was large and curiously spread. It rose high, too, for the sky above the shrubberies, still pale gold from the sunset, was dimmed by its passage. She declared afterwards that it moved in 'looping circles', but what she perhaps meant to convey was 'spirals'.

She screamed faintly. 'It's come at last! And it's you that brought it!'

She turned excitedly, half afraid, half angry, to Sanderson. With a breathless sort of gasp she said it, politeness all forgotten. 'I knew it... if you went on. I knew it. Oh! Oh!' And she cried again, 'Your talking has brought it out!' The terror that shook her voice was rather dreadful.

But the confusion of her vehement words passed unnoticed in the first surprise they caused. For a moment nothing happened.

'What is it you think you see, my dear?' asked her husband, startled. Sanderson said nothing. All three leaned forward, the men still sitting, but Mrs. Bittacy had rushed hurriedly to the window, placing herself of a purpose, as it seemed, between her husband and the lawn. She pointed. Her little hand made a silhouette against the sky, the yellow shawl hanging from the arm like a cloud.

'Beyond the cedar—between it and the lilacs.' The voice had lost its shrillness; it was thin and hushed. 'There... now you see it going round upon itself again—going back, thank God! .... going back to the Forest.' It sank to a whisper, shaking. She repeated, with a great dropping sigh of relief—'Thank God! I thought ... at first... it was coming here ... to us!... David... to *you*!'

She stepped back from the window, her movements confused, feeling in the darkness for the support of a chair, and finding her husband's outstretched hand instead. 'Hold me, dear, hold me, please... tight. Do not let me go.' She was in what he called afterwards 'a regular state'. He drew her firmly down upon her chair again.

'Smoke, Sophie, my dear,' he said quickly, trying to make his voice calm and natural. 'I see it, yes. It's smoke blowing over from the gardener's cottage...'

'But, David,'—and there was new horror in her whisper now—'it made a noise. It makes it still. I hear it swishing.' Some such word she used—swishing, sishing, rushing, or something of the kind. 'David, I'm very frightened. It's something awful! That man has called it out...!'

'Hush, hush,' whispered her husband. He stroked her trembling hand beside him.

'It is in the wind,' said Sanderson, speaking for the first time, very quietly. The expression on his face was not visible in the gloom, but his voice was soft and unafraid. At the sound of it, Mrs. Bittacy started violently again. Bittacy drew his chair a little forward to obstruct her view of him. He felt bewildered himself, a little, hardly knowing quite what to say or do. It was all so very curious and sudden.

But Mrs. Bittacy was badly frightened. It seemed to her that what she saw came from the enveloping forest just beyond their little garden. It emerged in a sort of secret way, moving towards them as with a purpose, stealthily difficultly. Then something stopped it. It could not advance beyond the cedar. The cedar—this impression remained with her afterwards too—prevented, kept it back. Like a rising sea the Forest had surged a moment in their direction through the covering darkness, and this visible movement was its first wave Thus to her mind it seemed... like that mysterious turn of the tide that used to frighten and mystify her in childhood on the sands. The outward surge of some enormous Power was what she felt.. something to which every instinct in her being rose in opposition because it threatened her and hers. In that moment she realised the Personality of the Forest... menacing.

In the stumbling movement that she made away from the window and towards the bell she barely caught the sentence Sanderson—or was it her husband?—murmured to himself: 'It came because we talked of it; our thinking made it aware of us and brought it out. But the cedar stops it. It cannot cross the lawn, you see...'

All three were standing now, and her husband's voice broke in with authority while his wife's fingers touched the bell.

'My dear, I should *not* say anything to Thompson.' The anxiety he felt was manifest in his voice, but his outward composure had returned. 'The gardener can go...'

Then Sanderson cut him short. 'Allow me,' he said quickly.

'I'll see if anything's wrong.' And before either of them could answer or object, he was gone, leaping out by the open window. They saw his figure vanish with a run across the lawn into the darkness.

A moment later the maid entered, in answer to the bell, and with her came the loud barking of the terrier from the hall.

'The lamps,' said her master shortly, and as she softly closed the door behind her, they heard the wind pass with a mournful sound of singing round the outer walls. A rustle of foliage from the distance passed within it.

'You see, the wind *is* rising. It *was* the wind!' He put a comforting arm about her, distressed to feel that she was trembling. But he knew that he was trembling too, though with a kind of odd elation rather than alarm. 'And it *was* smoke that you saw coming from Stride's cottage, or from the rubbish heaps he's been burning in the kitchen garden. The noise we heard was the branches rustling in the wind. Why should you be so nervous?'

A thin whispering voice answered him:

'I was afraid for *you*, dear. Something frightened me for *you*. That man makes me feel so uneasy and uncomfortable for his influence upon you. It's very foolish, I know. I think... I'm tired; I feel so overwrought and restless.' The words poured out in a hurried jumble and she kept turning to the window while she spoke.

'The strain of having a visitor,' he said soothingly, 'has taxed you. We're so unused to having people in the house. He goes to-morrow.' He warmed her cold hands between his own, stroking them tenderly. More, for the life of him, he could not say or do. The joy of a strange, internal excitement made his heart beat faster. He knew not what it was. He knew only, perhaps, whence it came.

She peered close into his face through the gloom, and said a curious thing. 'I thought, David, for a moment... you seemed... different. My nerves are all on edge to-night.' She made no further reference to her husband's visitor.

A sound of footsteps from the lawn warned of Sanderson's return, as he answered quickly in a lowered tone—'There's no need to be afraid on my account, dear girl. There's nothing wrong with me, I assure you; I never felt so well and happy in my life.'

Thompson came in with the lamps and brightness, and scarcely had she gone again when Sanderson in turn was seen climbing through the window.

'There's nothing,' he said lightly, as he closed it behind him. 'Somebody's been burning leaves, and the smoke is drifting a little through the trees. The wind,' he added, glancing at his host a moment significantly, but in so discreet a way that Mrs. Bittacy did not observe it, 'the wind, too, has begun to roar... in the Forest... further out.'

But Mrs. Bittacy noticed about him two things which increased her uneasiness. She noticed the shining of his eyes, because a similar light had suddenly come into her husband's; and she noticed, too, the apparent depth of meaning he put into those simple words that 'the wind had begun to roar in the Forest... further out.' Her mind retained the disagreeable impression that he meant more than he said. In his tone lay quite another implication. It was not actually 'wind' he spoke of, and it would not reman 'further out'... rather, it was coming in. Another impresion she got too—still more unwelcome—was that her husbansiunderstood his hidden meaning.

IV

'David, dear,' she observed gently as soon as they were alone upstairs, 'I have a horrible uneasy feeling about that man. I cannot get rid of it.' The tremor in her voice caught all his tenderness.

He turned to look at her. 'Of what kind, my dear? You're so imaginative sometimes, aren't you?'

'I think,' she hesitated, stammering a little, confused, still frightened, 'I mean—isn't he a hypnotist, or full of those theosofical ideas, or something of the sort? You know what I mean—'

He was too accustomed to her little confused alarms to explain them away seriously as a rule, or to correct her verbal inaccuracies, but to-night he felt she needed careful, tender treatment. He soothed her as best he could.

'But there's no harm in that, even if he is,' he answered quietly. 'Those are only new names for very old ideas, you know, dear.' There was no trace of impatience in his voice.

'That's what I mean,' she replied, the texts he dreaded rising in an unuttered crowd behind the words. 'He's one of those things that we are warned would come—one of the Latter-Day things.' For her mind still bristled with the bogeys of Antichrist and Prophecy, and she had only escaped the Number of the Beast, as it were, by the skin of her teeth. The Pope drew most of her fire usually, because she could understand him; the target was plain and she could shoot. But this tree-and-forest business was so vague and horrible. It terrified her. 'He makes me think,' she went on, 'of Principalities and Powers in high places, and of things that walk in darkness. I did *not* like the way he spoke of trees getting alive in the night, and all that; it made me think of wolves in sheep's clothing. And when I saw that awful thing in the sky above the lawn—'

But he interrupted her at once, for that was something he had decided it was best to leave unmentioned. Certainly it was better not discussed.

'He only meant, I think, Sophie,' he put in gravely, yet with a little smile, 'that trees may have a measure of conscious life—rather a nice idea on the whole, surely,—something like that bit we read in the *Times* the other night, you remember—and that a big forest may possess a sort of Collective Personality. Remember, he's an artist, and poetical.'

'It's dangerous,' she said emphatically. 'I feel it's playing with fire, unwise, unsafe—'

'Yet all to the glory of God,' he urged gently. 'We must not shut our ears and eyes to knowledge—of any kind, must we?'

'With you, David, the wish is always farther than the thought,' she rejoined. For, like the child who thought that 'suffered under Pontius Pilate' was 'suffered under a bunch of violets,' she heard her proverbs phonetically and reproduced them thus. She hoped to convey her warning in the quotation. 'And we must always try the spirits whether they be of God,' she added tentatively.

'Certainly, dear, we can always do that,' he assented, getting into bed.

But, after a little pause, during which she blew the light out, David Bittacy settling down to sleep with an excitement in his blood that was new and bewilderingly delightful, realised that perhaps he had not said quite enough to comfort her. She was lying awake by his side, still frightened. He put his head up in the darkness.

'Sophie,' he said softly, 'you must remember, too, that in any case between us and—and all that sort of thing—there is a great gulf fixed, a gulf that cannot be crossed—er—while we are still in the body.'

And hearing no reply, he satisfied himself that she was already asleep and happy. But Mrs. Bittacy was not asleep. She heard the sentence, only she said nothing because she felt her thought was better unexpressed. She was afraid to hear the words in the darkness. The Forest outside was listening and might hear them too—the Forest that was 'roaring further out'.

And the thought was this: That gulf, of course, existed, but Sanderson had somehow bridged it.

It was much later that night when she awoke out of troubled, uneasy dreams and heard a sound that twisted her very nerves with fear. It passed immediately with full waking, for, listen as she might, there was nothing audible but the inarticulate murmur of the night. It was in her dreams she heard it, and the dreams had vanished with it. But the sound was recognisable, for it was that rushing noise that had come across the lawn; only this time closer. Just above her face while she slept had passed this murmur as of rustling branches in the very room, a sound of foliage whispering. 'A going in the tops of the mulberry trees,' ran through her mind. She had dreamed that she lay beneath a spreading tree somewhere, a tree that whispered with ten thousand soft lips of green; and the dream continued for a moment even after waking.

She sat up in bed and stared about her. The window was open at the top; she saw the stars; the door, she remembered, was locked as usual; the room, of course, was empty. The deep hush of the summer night lay over all, broken only by another sound that now issued from the shadows close beside the bed, a human sound, yet unnatural, a sound that seized the fear with which she had waked and instantly increased it. And, although it was one she recognised as familiar, at first she could not name it. Some seconds certainly passed—and they were very long ones—before she understood that it was her husband talking in his sleep.

The direction of the voice confused and puzzled her, moreover, for it was not, as she first supposed, beside her. There was distance in it. The next minute, by the light of the sinking candle flame, she saw his white figure standing out in the middle of the room, half-way towards the window. The candle-light slowly grew. She saw him move then nearer to the window, with arms outstretched. His speech was low and mumbled, the words running together too much to be distinguishable.

And she shivered. To her, sleep-talking was uncanny to the point of horror; it was like the talking of the dead, mere parody of a living voice, unnatural.

'David!' she whispered, dreading the sound of her own voice, and half afraid to interrupt him and see his face. She could not bear the sight of the wide-opened eyes. 'David, you're walking in your sleep. Do—come back to bed, dear, *please!*'

Her whisper seemed so dreadfully loud in the still darkness. At the sound of her voice he paused, then turned slowly round to face her. His widely-opened eyes stared into her own without recognition; they looked through her into something beyond; it was as though he knew the direction of the sound, yet could not see her. They were shining, she noticed, as the eyes of Sanderson had shone several hours ago; and his face was flushed, distraught. Anxiety was written upon every feature. And, instantly, recognising that the fever was upon him, she forgot her terror temporarily in practical considerations. He came back to bed without waking. She closed his eyelids. Presently he composed himself quietly to sleep, or rather to deeper sleep. She contrived to make him swallow something from the tumbler beside the bed.

Then she rose very quietly to close the window, feeling the night air blow in too fresh and keen. She put the candle where it could not reach him. The sight of the big Baxter Bible beside it comforted her a little, but all through her underbeing ran the warnings of a curious alarm. And it was while in the act of fastening the catch with one hand and pulling the string of the blind with the other, that her husband sat up again in bed, and spoke in words this time that were distinctly audible. The eyes had opened wide again. He pointed. She stood stock still and listened, her shadow distorted on the blind. He did not come out towards her as at first she feared.

The whispering voice was very clear, horrible, too, beyond all she had ever known.

'They are roaring in the Forest further out... and I... must go and see.' He stared beyond her as he said it, to the woods. 'They are needing me. They sent for me...' Then his eyes wandering back again to things within the room, he lay down, his purpose suddenly changed. And that change was horrible as well, more horrible, perhaps, because of its revelation of another detailed world he moved in far away from her.

The singular phrase chilled her blood; for a moment she was utterly terrified. That tone of the somnambulist, differing so slightly yet so distressingly from normal, waking speech, seemed to her somehow wicked. Evil and danger lay waiting thick behind it. She leaned against the window-sill, shaking in every limb. She had an awful feeling for a moment that something was coming in to fetch him.

'Not yet, then,' she heard in a much lower voice from the bed, 'but later. It will be better so... I shall go later...'

The words expressed some fringe of these alarms that had haunted her so long, and that the arrival and presence of Sanderson seemed to have brought to the very edge of a climax she could not even dare to think about. They gave it form; they brought it closer; they sent her thoughts to her Deity in a wild, deep prayer for help and guidance. For here was a direct, unconscious betrayal of a world of inner purposes and claims her husband recognised while he kept them almost wholly to himself.

By the time she reached his side and knew the comfort of his touch, the eyes had closed again, this time of their own accord, and the head lay calmly back upon the pillows. She gently straightened the bed clothes. She watched him for some minutes, shading the candle carefully with one hand. There was a smile of strangest peace upon the face.

Then, blowing out the candle, she knelt down and prayed before getting back into bed. But no sleep came to her. She lay awake all night thinking, wondering, praying, until at length with the chorus of the birds and the glimmer of the dawn upon the green blind, she fell into a slumber of complete exhaustion.

But while she slept the wind continued roaring in the Forest further out. The sound came closer—sometimes very close indeed.

V

With the departure of Sanderson the significance of the curious incidents waned, because the moods that had pruced them passed away. Mrs. Bittacy soon afterwards came to regard them as some growth of disproportion that had been very largely, perhaps, in her own mind. It did not strike her that this change was sudden, for it came about quite naturally. For one thing her husband never spoke of the matter, and for another she remembered how many things in life that had seemed inexplicable and singular at the time turned out later to have been quite commonplace.

Most of it, certainly, she put down to the presence of the artist and to his wild, suggestive talk. With his walcome removal, the world turned ordinary again and safe. The fever, though it lasted as usual a short time only, had not allowed of her husband's getting up to say good-bye, and she had conveyed his regrets and adieux. In the morning Mr. Sanderson had seemed ordinary enough. In his town hat and gloves, as she saw him go, he seemed tame and unalarming.

'After all,' she thought as she watched the pony-cart bear him off, 'he's only an artist!' What she had thought he might be otherwise her slim imagination did not venture to disclose. Her change of feeling was wholesome and refreshing. She felt a little ashamed of her behaviour. She gave him a smile—genuine because the relief she felt was genuine—as he bent over her hand and kissed it, but she did not suggest a second visit, and her husband, she noted with satisfaction and relief, had said nothing either.

The little household fell again into the normal and sleepy routine to which it was accustomed. The name of Arthur Sanderson was rarely if ever mentioned. Nor, for her part, did she mention to her husband the incident of his walking in his sleep and the wild words he used. But to forget it was equally impossible. Thus it lay buried deep within her like a centre of some unknown disease of which it was a mysterious symptom, waiting to spread at the first favourable opportunity. She prayed against it every night and morning: prayed that she might forget it—that God would keep her husband safe from harm.

For in spite of much surface foolishness that many might have read as weakness, Mrs. Bittacy had balance, sanity, and a fine deep faith. She was greater than she knew. Her love for her husband and her God were somehow one, an achievement only possible to a single-hearted nobility of soul.

There followed a summer of great violence and beauty; of beauty, because the refreshing rains at night prolonged the glory of the spring and spread it all across July, keeping the foliage young and sweet; of violence, because the winds thatt tore about the south of England brushed the whole country into dancing movement. They swept the woods magnificently, and kept them roaring with a perpetual grand voice. Their deepest notes seemed never to leave the sky. They sang and souted, and torn leaves raced and fluttered through the air long before their usually appointed time. Many a tree, after days of this roaring and dancing, fell exhausted to the ground. The cedar on the lawn gave up two limbs that fell upon successive days, at the same hour too—just before dusk. The wind often makes its most boisterous effort at that time, before it drops with the sun, and these two huge branches lay in dark ruin covering half the lawn. They spread across it and towards the house. They left an ugly gaping space upon the tree, so that the Lebanon looked unfinished, half destroyed, a monster shorn of its old-time comeliness and splendour. Far more of the Forest was now visible than before; it peered through the breach of the broken defences. They could see from the windows of the house now—especially from the drawing-room and bedroom windows—straight out into the glades and depths beyond.

Mrs. Bittacy's niece and nephew, who were staying on a visit at the time, enjoyed themselves immensely helping the gardeners carry off the fragments. It took two days to do this, for Mr. Bittacy insisted on the branches being moved entire. He would not allow them to be chopped; also, he would not consent to their use as firewood. Under his superintendence the unwieldy masses were dragged to the edge of the garden and arranged upon the frontier line between the Forest and the lawn. The children were delighted with the scheme. They entered into it with enthusiasm. At all costs this defence against the inroads of the Forest must be made secure. They caught their uncle's earnestness, felt even something of a hidden motive that he had, and the visit, usually rather dreaded, became the visit of their lives instead. It vas Aunt Sophia this time who seemed discouraging and dull.

'She's got so old and funny,' opined Stephen.

But Alice, who felt in the silent displeasure of her aunt something that half alarmed her, said:

'I think she's afraid of the woods. She never comes into them with us, you see.'

'All the more reason then for making this wall impreg—all fat and thick and solid,' he concluded, unable to manage the longer word. 'Then nothing—simply *nothing*—can get through. Can it, Uncle David?' And Mr. Bittacy, jacket discarded and working in his speckled waistcoat, went puffing to their aid, arranging the massive limb of the cedar like a hedge.

'Come on,' he said, 'whatever happens, you know, we must finish before it's dark. Already the wind is roaring in the Forest further out.' And Alice caught the phrase and instantly echoed it. 'Stevie,' she cried below her breath, 'look sharp, you lazy lump. Didn't you hear what Uncle David said? It'll come in and catch us before we've done!'

They worked like Trojans, and, sitting beneath the wistaria tree that climbed the southern wall of the cottage, Mrs. Bittacy with her knitting watched them, calling from time to time insignificant messages of counsel and advice. The messages passed, of course, unheeded. Mostly, indeed, they were unheard, for the workers were too absorbed. She warned her husband not to get too hot, Alice not to tear her dress, Stephen not to strain his back with pulling. Her mind hovered between the homoeopathic medicine-chest upstairs and her anxiety to see the business finished.

For this breaking up of the cedar had stirred again her slumbering alarms. It revived memories of the visit of Mr. Sanderson that had been sinking into oblivion; she recalled his queer and odious way of talking, and many things she hoped forgotten drew their heads up from that subconscious region to which all forgetting is impossible. They looked at her and nodded. They were full of life; they had no intention of being pushed aside and buried permanently. 'Now look!' they whispered, 'didn't we tell you so?' They had been merely waiting the right moment to assert their presence. And all her former vague distress crept over her. Anxiety, uneasiness returned. That dreadful sinking of the heart came too.

This incident of the cedar's breaking up was actually so unimportant, and yet her husband's attitude towards it made it so significant. There was nothing that he said in particular, or did, or left undone that frightened her, but his general air of earnestness seemed so unwarranted. She felt that he deemed the thing important. He was so exercised about it. This evidence of sudden concern and interest, buried all the summer from her sight and knowledge, she realised now had been buried purposely; he had kept it intentionally concealed. Deeply submerged in him there ran this tide of other thoughts, desires, hopes. What were they? Whither did they lead? The accident to the tree betrayed it most unpleasantly; and, doubtless, more than he was aware.

She watched his grave and serious face as he worked there with the children, and as she watched she felt afraid. It vexed her that the children worked so eagerly. They unconsciously supported him. The thing she feared she would not even name. But it was waiting.

Moreover, as far as her puzzled mind could deal with a dread so vague and incoherent, the collapse of the cedar somehow brought it nearer. The fact that, all so ill-explained and formless, the thing yet lay in her consciousness, out of reach but moving and alive, filled her with a kind of puzzled, dreadful wonder. Its presence was so very real, its power so gripping, its partial concealment so abominable. Then, out of the dim confusion, she grasped one thought and saw it stand quite clear before her eyes. She found difficulty in clothing it in words, but its meaning perhaps was this: that cedar stood in their life for something friendly; its downfall meant disaster; a sense of some protective influence about the cottage, and about her husband in particular, was thereby weakened.

'Why do you fear the big winds so?' he had asked her several days before, after a particularly boisterous day; and the answer she gave surprised her while she gave it. One of those heads poked up unconsciously, and let slip the truth:

'Because, David, I feel they—bring the Forest with them,' she faltered. 'They blow something from the trees—into the mind —into the house.'

He looked at her keenly for a moment.

'That must be why I love them then,' he answered. 'They blow the souls of the trees about the sky like clouds.'

The conversation dropped. She had never heard him talk in quite that way before.

And another time, when he had coaxed her to go with him down one of the nearer glades, she asked why he took the small hand-axe with him, and what he wanted it for.

'To cut the ivy that clings to the trunks and takes their life away,' he said.

'But can't the verdurers do that?' she asked. 'That's what they're paid for, isn't it?'

Whereupon he explained that ivy was a parasite the trees knew not how to fight alone, and that the verdurers were careless and did not do it thoroughly. They gave a chop here and there, leaving the tree to do the rest for itself if it could.

'Besides, I like to do it for them. I love to help them and protect,' he added, the foliage rustling all about his quiet words as they went.

And these stray remarks, as his attitude towards the broken cedar, betrayed this curious, subtle change that was going forward in his personality. Slowly and surely all the summer it had increased.

It was growing—the thought startled her horribly—just as a tree grows, the outer evidence from day to day so slight as to be unnoticeable, yet the rising tide so deep and irresistible. The alteration spread all through and over him, was in both mind and actions, sometimes almost in his face as well. Occasionally, thus, it stood up straight outside himself and frightened her.

His life was somehow becoming linked so intimately with trees, and with all that trees signified. His interests became more and more their interests, his activity combined with theirs, his thoughts and feelings theirs, his purpose, hope, desire, his fate——

His fate! The darkness of some vague, enormous terror dropped its shadow on her when she thought of it. Some instinct in her heart she dreaded infinitely more than death—for death meant sweet translation for his soul—came gradually to associate the thought of him with the thought of trees, in particular with these Forest trees. Sometimes, before she could face the thing, argue it away, or pray it into silence, she found the thought of him running swiftly through her mind like a thought of the Forest itself, the two most intimately linked and joined together, each a part and complement of the other, one being.

The idea was too dim for her to see it face to face. Its mere possibility dissolved the instant she focussed it to get the truth behind it. It was too utterly elusive, mad, protean. Under the attack of even a minute's concentration the very meaning of it vanished, melted away. The idea lay really behind any words that she could ever find, beyond the touch of definite thought. Her mind was unable to grapple with it. But, while it vanished the trail of its approach and disappearance flickered a moment before her shaking vision. The horror certainly remained.

Reduced to the simple human statement that her temperament sought instinctively it stood perhaps at this: her husband loved her, and he loved the trees as well; but the trees came first, claimed parts of him she did not know. *She* loved her God and him. *He* loved the trees and her.

Thus, in guise of some faint, distressing compromise, the matter shaped itself for her perplexed mind in the terms of conflict. A silent, hidden battle raged, but as yet raged far away. The breaking of the cedar was a visible outward fragment of a distant and mysterious encounter that was coming daily closer to them both. The wind, instead of roaring in the

Forest further out, now came nearer, booming in fitful gusts cout its edge and frontiers.

Meanwhile the summer dimmed. The autumn winds went sighing through the woods; leaves turned to golden red, and the evenings were drawing in with cosy shadows before the first sign of anything seriously untoward made its appearance. It came then with a flat, decided kind of violence that indicated mature preparation beforehand. It was not impulsive nor ill-considered. In a fashion it seemed expected, and indeed inevitable. For within a fortnight of their annual change to the little village of Seillans above St. Raphael—a change so regular for the past ten years that it was not even discussed between them—David Bittacy abruptly refused to go.

Thompson had laid the tea-table, prepared the spirit lamp beneath the urn, pulled down the blinds in that swift and silent way she had, and left the room. The lamps were still unlit. The fire-light shone on the chintz armchairs, and Boxer lay asleep on the black horse-hair rug. Upon the walls the gilt picture frames gleamed faintly, the pictures themselves indistinguishable. Mrs. Bittacy had warmed the tea-pot and was in the act of pouring the water in to heat the cups when her husband, looking up from his chair across the hearth, made the abrupt announcement:

'My dear,' he said, as though following a train of thought of which she only heard this final phrase, 'it's really quite impossible for me to go.'

And so abrupt, inconsequent, it sounded that she at first misunderstood. She thought he meant go out into the garden or the woods. But her heart leaped all the same. The tone of his voice was ominous.

'Of course not', she answered, 'it would be *most* unwise. Why should you——?' She referred to the mist that always spread on autumn nights upon the lawn; but before she finished the sentence she knew that *he* referred to something else. And her heart than gave its second horrible leap.

'David! You mean abroad?' she gasped.

'I mean abroad, dear, yes.'

It reminded her of the tone used when saying good-bye years ago before one of those jungle expeditions she dreaded. His voice then was so serious, so final. It was serious and final now. For several moments she could think of nothing to say. She busied herself with the tea-pot. She had filled one cup with hot water till it overflowed, and she emptied it slowly into the slop-basin, trying with all her might not to let him see the trembling of her hand. The firelight and the dimness of the room both helped her. But in any case he would hardly have noticed it. His thoughts were far away. ...

VI

Mrs. Bittacy had never liked their present home. She preferred a flat, more open country that left approaches clear. She liked to see things coming. This cottage on the very edge of the old hunting grounds of William the Conqueror had never satisfied her ideal of a safe and pleasant place to settle down in. The sea-coast, with treeless downs behind and a clear horizon in front, as at Eastbourne, say, was her ideal of a proper home.

It was curious, this instinctive aversion she felt to being shut in—by trees especially; a kind of claustrophobia almost; probably due, as has been said, to the days in India when the trees took her husband off and surrounded him with dangers. In those weeks of solitude the feeling had matured. She had fought it in her fashion, but never conquered it. Apparently routed, it had a way of creeping back in other forms. In this particular case, yielding to his strong desire, she thought the battle won, but the terror of the trees came back before the first month had passed. They laughed in her face.

She never lost knowledge of the fact that the leagues of forest lay about their cottage like a mighty wall, a crowding, watching, listening presence that shut them in from freedom and escape. Far from morbid naturally, she did her best to deny the thought, and so simple and unartificial was her type of mind that for weeks together she would wholly lose it. Then, suddenly it would return upon her with a rush of bleak reality. It was not only in her mind; it existed apart from any mere mood; a separate fear that walked alone; it came and went, yet when it went—went only to watch her from another point of view. It was in abeyance—hidden round the corner.

The Forest never let her go completely. It was ever ready to encroach. All the branches, she sometimes fancied, stretched one way—towards their tiny cottage and garden, as though it sought to draw them in and merge them in itself. Its great, deep-breathing soul resented the mockery, the insolence, the irritation of the prim garden at its very gates. It would absorb and smother them if it could. And every wind that blew its thundering message over the huge sounding-board of the million, shaking trees conveyed the purpose that it had. They had angered its great soul. At its heart was this deep, incessant roaring.

All this she never framed in words; the subtleties of language lay far beyond her reach. But instinctively she felt it; and more besides. It troubled her profoundly. Chiefly, moreover, for her husband. Merely for herself, the nightmare might have left her cold. It was David's peculiar interest in the trees that gave the special invitation.

Jealousy, then, in its most subtle aspect came to strengthen this aversion and dislike, for it came in a form that no reasonable wife could possibly object to. Her husband's passion, she reflected, was natural and inborn. It had decided his vocation, fed his ambition, nourished his dreams, desires, hopes. All his best years of active life had been spent in the care and guardianship of trees. He knew them, understood their secret life and nature, 'managed' them intuitively as other men 'managed' dogs and horses. He could not live for long away from them without a strange, acute nostalgia that stole his peace of mind and consequently his strength of body. A forest made him happy and at peace; it nursed and fed and soothed his deepest moods. Trees influenced the sources of his life, lowered or raised the very heart-beat in him. Cut off from them he languished as a lover of the sea can droop inland, or a mountaineer may pine in the flat monotony of the plains.

This she could understand, in a fashion at least, and make allowances for. She had yielded gently, even sweetly, to his choice of their English home; for in the little island there is nothing that suggests the woods of wilder countries so nearly as the New Forest. It has the genuine air and mystery, the depth and splendour, the loneliness, and here and there the strong, untamable quality of old-time forests as Bittacy of the Department knew them.

In a single detail only had he yielded to her wishes. He consented to a cottage on the edge, instead of in the heart of it. And for a dozen years now they had dwelt in peace and happiness at the lips of this great spreading thing that covered so many leagues with its tangle of swamps and moors and splendid ancient trees.

Only with the last two years or so—with his own increasing age, and physical decline perhaps—had come this marked growth of passionate interest in the welfare of the Forest. She had watched it grow, at first had laughed at it, then talked sympathetically so far as sincerity permitted, then had argued mildly, finally come to realise that its treatment lay altogether beyond her powers, and so had come to fear it with all her heart.

The six weeks they annually spent away from their English home, each regarded very differently of course. For her husband it meant a painful exile that did his health no good; he yearned for his trees—the sight and sound and smell of them; but for herself it meant release from a haunting dread—escape. To renounce those six weeks by the sea on the sunny, shining coast of France, was almost more than this little woman, even with her unselfishness, could face.

After the first shock of the announcement, she reflected as deeply as her nature permitted, prayed, wept in secret—and made up her mind. Duty, she felt clearly, pointed to renunciation.

The discipline would certainly be severe—she did not dream at the moment how severe!—but this fine, consistent little Christian saw it plain; she accepted it, too, without any sighing of the martyr, though the courage she showed was of the martyr order. Her husband should never know the cost. In all but this one passion his unselfishness was ever as great as her own. The love she had borne him all these years, like the love she bore her anthropomorphic deity, was deep and real. She loved to suffer for them both. Besides, the way her husband had put it to her was singular. It did not take the form of a mere selfish predilection. Something higher than two wills in conflict seeking compromise was in it from the beginning.

'I feel, Sophia, it would be really more than I could manage,' he said slowly, gazing into the fire over the tops of his stretched-out muddy boots. 'My duty and my happiness lie here with the Forest and with you. My life is deeply rooted in this place. Something I can't define connects my inner being with these trees, and separation would make me ill—might even kill me. My hold on life would weaken; here is my source of supply. I cannot explain it better than that.' He looked up steadily into her face across the table so that she saw the gravity of his expression and the shining of his steady eyes.

'David, you feel it as strongly as that!' she said, forgetting the tea things altogether.

'Yes,' he replied, 'I do. And it's not of the body only; I feel it in my soul.'

The reality of what he hinted at crept into that shadow-covered room like an actual Presence and stood beside them. It came not by the windows of the door, but it filled the entire space between the walls and ceiling. It took the heat from the fire before her face. She felt suddenly cold, confused a little, frightened. She almost felt the rush of foliage in the wind. It stood between them.

'There are things—some things,' she faltered, 'we are not intended to know, I think.' The words expresssed her general attitude to life, not alone to this particular incident.

And after a pause of several minutes, disregarding the criticism as though he had not heard it—'I cannot explain it better than that, you see,' his grave voice answered. 'There *is* this deep, tremendous link,—some secret power they emanate that keeps me well and happy and—alive. If you cannot understand, I feel at least you may be able to—forgive.' His tone grew tender, gentle, soft. 'My selfishness, I know, must seem quite unforgivable. I cannot help it somehow; these trees, this ancient Forest, both seem knitted into all that makes me live, and if I go——'

There was a little sound of collapse in his voice. He stopped abruptly, and sank back in his chair. And, at that, a distinct lump came up into her throat which she had great difficulty in managing while she went over and put her arms about him.

'My dear,' she murmured, 'God will direct. We will accept His guidance. He has always shown the way before.'

'My selfishness afflicts me—' he began, but she would not let him finish.

'David, He will direct. Nothing shall harm you. You've never once been selfish, and I cannot bear to hear you say such things. The way will open that is best for you—for both of us.' She kissed him; she would not let him speak; her heart was in her throat, and she felt for him far more than for herself.

And then he had suggested that she should go alone perhaps for a shorter time, and stay in her brother's villa with the children, Alice and Stephen. It was always open to her as she well knew.

'You need the change,' he said, when the lamps had been lit and the servant had gone out again 'you need it as much as I dread it. I could manage somehow till you returned, and should feel happier that way if you went. I cannot leave this Forest that I love so well. I even feel, Sophie dear'—he sat up straight and faced her as he half whispered it—'that I can *never* leave it again. My life and happiness lie here together.'

And even while scorning the idea that she could leave him alone with the influence of the Forest all about him to have its unimpeded way, she felt the pangs of that subtle jealousy bite keen and close. He loved the Forest better than herself, for he placed it first. Behind the words, moreover, hid the unuttered thought that made her so uneasy. The terror Sanderson had brought revived and shook its wings before her very eyes. For the whole conversation, of which this was a fragment, conveyed the unutterable implication that while he could not spare the trees, they equally could not spare him. The vividness with which he managed to conceal and yet betray the fact brought a profound distress that crossed the border between presentiment and warning into positive alarm.

He clearly felt that the trees would miss him—the trees he tended, guarded, watched over, loved.

'David, I shall stay here with you. I think you need me, really,—don't you?' Eagerly, with a touch of heart-felt passion the words poured out.

'Now more than ever, dear. God bless you for your sweet unselfishness. And your sacrifice,' he added, 'is all the greater because you cannot understand the thing that makes it necessary for me to sty.'

'Perhaps in the spring instead——' she said, with a tremor in the voice.

'In the spring—perhaps,' he answered gently, almost beneath his breath. 'For they will not need me then. All the world can love them in the spring. It's in the winter that they're lonely and neglected. I wish to say with them particularly then. I even feel I ought to—and I must.'

And in this way, without further speech, the decision was made. Mrs. Bittacy, at least asked no more questions. Yet she could not bring herself to show more sympathy than was necessary. She felt, for one thing, that if she did, it might lead him to speak freely, and to tell her things she could not possibly bear to know. And she dared not take the risk of that.

VII

This was at the end of summer, but the autumn followed close. The conversation really marked the threshold between the two seasons, and marked at the same time the line between her husband's negative and aggressive state. She almost felt she had done wrong to yield, he grew so bold, concealment all discarded. He went, that is, quite openly to the woods, forgetting all his duties, all his former occupations. He even sought to coax her to go with him. The hidden thing blazed out without disguise. And, while she trembled at his energy, she admired the virile passion he displayed. Her jealousy had long ago retired before her fear, accepting the second place, one desire now was to protect. The wife turned wholly mother.

He said so little, but—he hated to come in. From morning to night he wandered in the Forest; often he went out after dinner; his mind was charged with trees—their foliage, growth, development; their wonder, beauty, strength; their loneliness in isolation, their power in a herded mass. He knew the effect of every wind upon them; the danger from the boisterous north, the glory from the west, the eastern dryness, and the soft, moist tenderness that a south wind left upon their thinning boughs. He spoke all day of their sensations; how they drank the fading sunshine, dreamed in the moonlight, thrilled to the kiss of stars. The dew could bring them half the passion of the night, but frost sent them plunging beneath the ground to dwell with hopes of a later coming softness in their roots. They nursed the life they carried—insects, larvae, chrysalis—and when the skies above them melted, he spoke of them standing 'motionless in an ecstasy of rain', or in the noon of sunshine 'self-poised upon their prodigy of shade'.

And once in the middle of the night she woke at the sound of his voice, and heard him—wide awake, not talking in his sleep—but talking towards the window where the shadow of the cedar fell at noon:

> O art thou sighing for Lebanon
> In the long breeze that streams to thy delicious East?
> Sighing for Lebanon,
> Dark cedar;

and, when, half charmed, half terrified, she turned and called to him by name, he merely said—

'My dear, I felt the loneliness—suddenly realised it—the alien desolation of that tree, set here upon our little lawn in England when all her Eastern brothers call to her in sleep.' And the answer seemed so queer, so 'un-evangelical', that she waited in silence till he slept again. The poetry passed her by. It seemed unnecessary and out of place. It made her ache with suspicion, fear, jealousy.

The fear, however, seemed somehow all lapped up and banished soon afterwards by her unwilling admiration of the rushing splendour of her husband's state. Her anxiety, at any rate, shifted from the religious to the medical. She thought he might be losing his steadiness of mind a little. How often in her prayers she offered thanks for the guidance that made her stay with him to help and watch is impossible to say. It certainly was twice a day.

She even went so far once, when Mr. Mortimer, the vicar, called, and brought with him a more or less distinguished doctor —as to tell the professional man privately some symptoms of her husband's queerness. And his answer that there was 'nothing he could prescribe for' added not a little to her sense of unholy bewilderment. No doubt Sir James had never been 'consulted' under such unorthodox conditions before. His sense of what was becoming naturally overrode his acquired instincts as a skilled instrument that might help the race.

'No fever, you think?' she asked insistently with hurry, determined to get something from him.

'Nothing that *I* can deal with, as I told you, Madam,' was the reply.

Evidently he did not care about being invited to examine patients in this surreptitious way before a tea-pot on the lawn, chance of a fee most problematical. He liked to see a tongue and feel a thumping pulse; to know the pedigree and bank account of his questioner as well. It was most unusual, in abominable taste besides. Of course it was. But the drowning woman seized the only straw she could.

For now the aggressive attitude of her husband overcame her

to the point where she found it difficult even to question him. Yet in the house he was so kind and gentle, doing all he could to make her sacrifice as easy as possible.

'David, you really *are* unwise to go out now. The night is damp and very chilly. The ground is soaked in dew. You'll catch your death of cold.'

His face lightened. 'Won't you come with me, dear,—just for once? I'm only going to the corner of the hollies to see the beech that stands so lonely by itself.'

She had been out with him in the short dark afternoon, and they had passed that evil group of hollies where the gipsies camped. Nothing else would grow there, but the hollies throve upon the stony soil.

'David, the beech is all right and safe.' She had learned his phraseology a little, made clever out of due season by her love. 'There's no wind to-night.'

'But it's rising,' he answered, 'rising in the east. I heard it in the bare and hungry larches. They need the sun and dew, and always cry out when wind's upon them from the east.'

She sent a short unspoken prayer most swiftly to her deity as she heard him say it. For every time now, when he spoke in this familiar, intimate way of the life of the trees, she felt a sheet of cold fasten tight against her very skin and flesh. She shivered. How *could* he possibly know such things?

Yet, in all else, and in the relations of his daily life, he was sane and reasonable, loving, kind and tender. It was only on the subject of the trees he seemed unhinged and queer. Most curiously it seemed that, since the collapse of the cedar they both loved, though in different fashion, his departure from the normal had increased. Why else did he watch them as a man might watch a sickly child? Why did he linger especially in the dusk to catch their 'mood of night' as he called it? Why think so carefully upon them when the frost was threatening of the wind appeared to rise?

As she put it so frequently now to herself—How could he possibly *know* such things?

He went. As she closed the front door after him she heard the distant roaring in the Forest. ...

And then it suddenly struck her: How could she know them too?

It dropped upon her like a blow that she felt at once all over, upon body, heart and mind. The discovery rushed out from its ambush to overwhelm. The truth of it, making all arguing futile, numbed her faculties. But though at first it deadened her, she soon revived, and her being rose into aggressive opposition. A wild yet calculated courage like that which animates the leaders of splendid forlorn hopes flamed in her little person—flamed grandly, and invincible. While knowing herself insignificant and weak, she knew at the same time that power at her back which moves the worlds. The faith that filled her was the weapon in her hands, and the right by which she claimed it; but the spirit of utter, selfless sacrifice that characterised her life was the means by which she mastered its immediate use. For a kind of white and faultless intuition guided her to the attack. Behind her stood her Bible and her God.

How so magnificent a divination came to her at all may well be a matter for astonishment, though some clue of explanation lies, perhaps, in the very simpleness of her nature. At any rate, she saw quite clearly certain things; saw them in moments only— after prayer, in the still silence of the night, or when left alone those long hours in the house with her knitting and her thoughts —and the guidance which then flashed into her remained, even after the manner of its coming was forgotten.

They came to her, these things she saw, formless, wordless; she could not put them into any kind of language; but by the very fact of being uncaught in sentence they retained their original clear vigour.

Hours of patient waiting brought the first, and the others followed easily afterwards, by degrees, on subsequent days, a little and a little. Her husband had been gone since early morning, and had taken his luncheon with him. She was sitting by the tea things, the cups and tea-pot warmed, the muffins in the fender keeping hot, all ready for his return, when she realised quite abruptly that this thing which took him off, which kept him out so many hours day after day, this that was against her own little will and instinct—was enormous as the sea. It was no mere prettiness of single Trees, but something massed and mountainous. About her rose the wall of its huge opposition to the sky, its scale gigantic, it power utterly prodigious. What she knew of it hitherto as green and delicate forms waving and rustling in the winds was but, as it were, the spray of foam that broke into sight upon the nearer edge of viewless depths far, far away. The trees, indeed, were sentinels set visibly about the limits of a camp that itself remained invisible. The awful hum and murmur of the main body in the distance passed into that still room about her with the firelight and hissing kettle. Out yonder—in the Forest further out—the thing that was ever roaring at the centre was dreadfully increasing.

The sense of definite battle, too—battle between herself and the Forest for his soul—came with it. Its presentment was as clear as though Thompson had come into the room and quietly told her that the cottage was surrounded. 'Please, ma'am, there are trees come up about the house,' she might have suddenly announced. And equally might have heard her own answer: 'It's all right, Thompson. The main body is still far away.'

Immediately upon its heels, then, came another truth, with a close reality that shocked her. She saw that jealousy was not confined to the human and animal world alone, but ran through all creation. The Vegetable Kingdom knew in too. So-called inanimate nature shared it with the rest. Trees felt it. This Forest just beyond the window—standing there in the silence of the autumn evening across the little lawn—this Forest understood it equally. The remorseless, branching power that sought to keep exclusively for itself the thing it loved and needed, spread like a running desire through all its million leaves and stems and roots. In humans, of course, it was consciously directed; in animals it acted with frank instinctiveness; but in trees this jealousy rose in some blind tide of impersonal and unconscious wrath that would sweep opposition from its path as the wind sweeps powdered snow from the surface of the ice. Their number was a host with endless reinforcements, and once it realised its passion was returned the power increased. Her husband loved the trees... They had become aware of it. ... They would take him from her in the end. ... For, equally, the trees loved him.

Then, while she heard his footsteps in the hall and the closing of the front door, she saw a third thing clearly—realised the widening of the gap between herself and him. This other love had made it. All these weeks of the summer when she felt so close to him, now especially when she had made the biggest sacrifice of her life to stay by his side and help him, he had been slowly, surely—drawing away. The estrangement was here and now—a fact accomplished. It had been all this time maturing; there yawned this broad deep space between them. Across the empty distance she saw the change in merciless perspective. It revealed his face and figure, dearly-loved, once fondly worshipped, far on the other side in shadowy distance, small, the back turned from her, and moving while she watched—moving away from her.

They had their tea in silence then. She asked no questions, he volunteered no information of this day. The heart was big within her, the terrible loneliness of age spread through her like a rising icy mist. She watched him, filling all his wants. His hair was untidy and his boots were caked with blackish mud. He moved with a restless, swaying motion that somehow blanched her cheek and sent a miserable shivering down her back. It reminded her of trees. His eyes were very bright.

He brought in with him an odour of the earth and forest that seemed to choke her and make it difficult to breathe; and—what she noticed with a climax of almost uncontrollable alarm—upon his face beneath the lamplight shone traces of a mild, faint glory that made her think of moonlight falling upon a wood through speckled shadows. It was his new-found happiness that shone there, a happiness uncaused by her and in which she had no part.

In his coat was a spray of faded yellow beach leaves. 'I brought this from the Forest for you,' he said, with all the air that belonged to his little acts of devotion long ago. And she took the spray of leaves mechanically with a smile and a murmured 'thank you, dear,' as though he had unknowingly put into her hands the weapon for her own destruction and she had accepted it.

And when the tea was over and he left the room, he did not go to his study, or to change his clothes. She heard the front door softly shut behind him as he again went out towards the Forest.

A moment later she was in her room upstairs, kneeling beside the bed—the side he slept on—and praying wildly through a flood of tears that God would save and keep him to her. Wind brushed the window panes behind her while she knelt.

VIII

One sunny November morning, when the strain had reached a pitch that made repression almost unmanageable, she came to an impulsive decision, and obeyed it. Her husband had again gone out with luncheon for the day. She took adventure in her hands and followed him. The power of clear-seeing was strong upon her, forcing her up to some unnatural level of understanding. To stay indoors and wait inactive for his return seemed suddenly impossible. She meant to know what he knew, feel what he felt, put herself in his place. She would dare the fascination of the Forest—share it with him. It was greatly daring; but it would give her greater understanding how to help and save him and therefore greater Power. She went upstairs a moment first to pray.

In a thick, warm skirt, and wearing heavy boots—those walking boots she used with him upon the mountains about Seillans —she left the cottage by the back way and turned towards the

Forest. She could not actually follow him, for he had started off an hour before and she knew not exactly his direction. What was so urgent in her was the wish to be with him in the woods, to walk beneath the leafless branches just as he did: to be there when he was there, even though not together. For it had come to her that she might thus share with him for once this horrible mighty life and breathing of the trees he loved. In winter, he had said, they needed him particularly; and winter now was coming. Her love *must* bring her something of what he felt himself—the huge attraction, the suction and the pull of all the trees. Thus, in some vicarious fashion, she might share, though unknown to himself, this very thing that was taking him away from her. She might thus even lessen its attack upon himself.

The impulse came to her clairvoyantly, and she obeyed without a sign of hesitation. Deeper comprehension would come to her of the whole awful puzzle. And come it did, yet not in the way she imagined and expected.

The air was very still, the sky a cold pale blue, but cloudless. The entire Forest stood silent, at attention. It knew perfectly well that she had come. It knew the moment when she entered; watched and followed her; and behind her something dropped without a sound and shut her in. Her feet upon the glades of mossy grass fell silently, as the oaks and beeches shifted past in rows and took up their positions at her back. It was not pleasant, this way they grew so dense behind her the instant she had passed. She realised that they gathered in an ever-growing army, massed, herded, trooped, between her and the cottage, shutting off escape. They let her pass so easily, but to get out again she would know them differently—thick, crowded, branches all drawn and hostile. Already their increasing numbers bewildered her. In front, they looked so sparse and scattered, with open spaces where the sunshine fell; but when she turned it seemed they stood so close together, a serried army, darkening the sunlight. They blocked the day, collected all the shadows, stood with their leafless and forbidding rampart like the night. They swallowed down into themselves the very glade by which she came. For when she glanced behind her—rarely—the way she had come was shadowy and lost.

Yet the morning sparkled overhead, and a glance of excitement ran quivering through the entire day. It was what she always knew as 'children's weather', so clear and harmless, without a sign of danger, nothing ominous to threaten or alarm. Steadfast in her purpose, looking back as little as she dared, Sophia Bittacy marched slowly and deliberately into the heart of the silent woods, deeper, ever deeper. ...

And then, abruptly, in an open space where the sunshine fell unhindered, she stopped. It was one of the breathing-places of the forest. Dead, withered bracken lay in patches of unsightly grey. There were bits of heather too. All round the trees stood looking on—oak, beech, holly, ash, pine, larch, with here and there small groups of juniper. On the lips of this breathing-space of the woods she stopped to rest, disobeying her instinct for the first time. For the other instinct in her was to go on. She did not really want to rest.

This was the little act that brought it to her—the wireless message from a vast Emitter.

'I've been stopped,' she thought to herself with a horrid qualm.

She looked about her in this quiet, ancient place. Nothing stirred. There was no life nor sign of life; no birds sang; no rabbits scuttled off at her approach. The stillness was bewildering, and gravity hung down upon it like a heavy curtain. It hushed the heart in her. Could this be part of what her husband felt—this sense of thick entanglement with stems, boughs, roots, and foliage?

'This has always been as it is now,' she thought, yet not knowing why she thought it. 'Ever since the Forest grew it has been still and secret here. It has never changed.' The curtain of silence drew closer while she said it, thickening round her. 'For a thousand years—I'm here with a thousand years. And behind this place stand all the forests of the world!'

So foreign to her temperament were such thoughts, and so

alien to all she had been taught to look for in Nature, that she strove against them. She made an effort to oppose. But they clung and haunted just the same; they refused to be dispersed. The curtain hung dense and heavy as though its texture thickened. The air with difficulty came through.

And then she thought that curtain stirred. There was movement somewhere. That obscure dim thing which ever broods behind the visible appearance of trees came nearer to her. She caught her breath and stared about her, listening intently. The trees, perhaps because she saw them more in detail now, it seemed to her had changed. A vague, faint alteration spread over them, at first so slight she scarcely would admit it, then growing steadily, though still obscurely, outwards. 'They tremble and are changed,' flashed through her mind the horrid line that Sanderson had quoted. Yet the change was graceful for all the uncouthness attendant upon the size of so vast a movement. They had turned in her direction. That was it. *They saw her*.

In this way the change expressed itself in her groping, terrified thought. Till now it had been otherwise: she had looked at them from her own point of view; now they looked at her from theirs. They stared her in the face and eyes; they stared at her all over. In some unkind, resentful, hostile way, they watched her. Hitherto in life she had watched them variously, in superficial ways, reading into them what her own mind suggested. Now they read into her the things they actually *were*, and not merely another's interpretation of them.

They seemed in their motionless silence there instinct with life, a life, moreover, that breathed about her a species of terrible soft enchantment that bewitched. It branched all through her, climbing to the brain. The Forest held her with its huge and giant fascination. In this secluded breathing-spot that the centuries had left untouched, she had stepped close against the hidden pulse of the whole collective mass of them. They were aware of her and had turned to gaze with their myriad, vast sight upon the intruder. They shouted at her in the silence. For she wanted to look back at them, but it was like staring at a crowd, and her glance merely shifted from one tree to another, hurriedly, finding in none the one she sought. They saw her so easily, each and all. The rows that stood behind her also stared. But she could not return the gaze. Her husband, she realised, could. And their steady stare shocked her as though in some sense she knew that she was naked. They saw so much of her: she saw of them—so little.

Her efforts to return their gaze were pitiful. The constant shifting increased her bewilderment. Conscious of this awful and enormous sight all over her, she let her eyes first rest upon the ground; and then she closed them altogether. She kept the lids as tight together as ever they would go.

But the sight of the trees came even into that inner darkness behind the fastened lids, for there was no escaping it. Outside, in the light, she still knew that the leaves of the hollies glittered smoothly, that the dead foliage of the oaks hung crisp in the air above her, that the needles of the little junipers were pointing all one way. The spread perception of the Forest was focussed on herself, and no mere shutting of the eyes could hide its scattered yet concentrated stare—the all-inclusive vision of great woods.

There was no wind, yet here and there a single leaf hanging by its dried-up stalk shook all alone with great rapidity—rattling. It was the sentry drawing attention to her presence. And then, again, as once long weeks before, she felt their Being as a tide about her. The tide had turned. That memory of her childhood sands came back, when the nurse said, 'The tide has turned now; we must go in,' and she saw the mass of piled-up waters, green and heaped to the horizon, and realised that it was slowly coming in. The gigantic mass of it, too vast for hurry, loaded with massive purpose, she used to feel, was moving towards herself. The fluid body of the sea was creeping along beneath the sky to the very spot upon the yellow sands where she stood and played. The sight and thought of it had always overwhelmed her with a sense of awe—as though her puny self were the object of the whole sea's advance. 'The tide has turned; we had better now go in.'

This was happening now about her—the same thing was happening in the woods—slow, sure, and steady, and its motion as little discernible as the sea's. The tide had turned. The small human presence that had ventured among its green and mountainous depths, moreover, was its objective.

That all was clear within her while she sat and waited with tight-shut lids. But the next moment she opened her eyes with a sudden realisation of something more. The presence that it sought was after all not hers. It was the presence of some one other than herself. And then she understood. Her eyes had opened with a click, it seemed; but the sound, in reality, was outside herself. Across the clearing where her sunshine lay so calm and still, she saw the figure of her husband moving among the trees—a man, like a tree, walking.

With hands behind his back, and head uplifted, he moved quite slowly, as though absorbed in his own thoughts. Hardly fifty paces separated them, but he had no inkling of her presence there so near. With mind intent and senses all turned inwards, he marched past her like a figure in a dream, and like a figure in a dream she saw him go. Love, yearning, pity rose in a storm within her, but as in nightmare she found no words or movement possible. She sat and watched him go—go from her—go into the deeper reaches of the green enveloping woods. Desire to save, to bid him stop and turn, ran in a passion through her being, but there was nothing she could do. She saw him go away from her, go of his own accord and willingly beyond her; she saw the branches drop about his steps and hide him. His figure faded out among the speckled shade and sunlight. The trees covered him. The tide just took him, all unresisting and content to go. Upon the bosom of the green soft sea he floated away beyond her reach of vision. Her eyes could follow him no longer. He was gone.

And then for the first time she realised, even at that distance, that the look upon his face was one of peace and happiness—

rapt, and caught away in joy, a look of youth. That expression now he never showed to her. But she *had* known it. Years ago, in the early days of their married life, she had seen it on his face. Now it no longer obeyed the summons of her presence and her love. The woods alone could call it forth; it answered to the trees; the Forest had taken every part of him—from her —his very heart and soul. ...

Her sight that had plunged inwards to the fields of faded memory now came back to outer things again. She looked about her, and her love, returning empty-handed and unsatisfied, left her open to the invading of the bleakest terror she had ever known. That such things could be real and happen found her utterly helpless. Terror invaded the quietest corners of her heart, that had never yet known quailing. She could not—for moments at any rate—reach either her Bible or her God. Desolate in an empty world of fear she sat with eyes too dry and hot for tears, yet with a coldness as of ice upon her very flesh. She stared, unseeing, about her. That horror which stalks in the stillness of the noonday, when the glare of an artificial sunshine lights up the motionless trees, moved all about her. In front and behind she was aware of it. Beyond this stealthy silence, just within the edge of it, the things of another world were passing. But she could not know them. Her husband knew them, knew their beauty and their awe, yes, but for her they were out of reach. She might not share with him the very least of them. It seemed that behind and through the glare of this wintry noonday in the heart of the woods there brooded another universe of life and passion, for her all unexpressed. The silence veiled it, the stillness hid it; but he moved with it all and understood. His love interpreted it.

She rose to her feet, tottered feebly, and collapsed again upon the moss. Yet for herself she felt no terror; no little personal fear could touch her whose anguish and deep longing streamed all out to him whom she bravely loved. In this time of utter self-forgetfulness, when she realised that the battle was hopeless, thinking she had lost even her God, she found Him again quite close beside her like a little Presence in this terrible heart of the hostile Forest. But at first she did not recognise that He was there; she did not know Him in that strangely unacceptable guise. For He stood so very close, so very intimate, so very sweet and comforting, and yet so hard to understand—as Resignation.

Once more she struggled to her feet, and this time turned successfully and slowly made her way along the mossy glade by which she came. And at first she marvelled, though only for a moment, at the ease with which she found the path. For a moment only, because almost at once she saw the truth. The trees were glad that she should go. They helped her on her way. The Forest did not want her.
The tide was coming in, indeed, yet not for her.
And so, in another of those flashes of clear vision that of late had lifted life above the normal level, she saw and understood the whole terrible thing complete.
Till now, though unexpressed in thought or language, her fear had been that the woods her husband loved would somehow take him from her—to merge his life in theirs—even to kill him in some mysterious way. This time she saw her deep mistake, and so seeing, let in upon herself the fuller agony of horror. For their jealousy was not the petty jealousy of animals or humans. They wanted him because they loved him, but they did not want him dead. Full charged with his splendid life and enthusiasm they wanted him. They wanted him—alive.
It was she who stood in their way, and it was she whom they intended to remove.
This was what brought the sense of abject helplessness. She stood upon the sands against an entire ocean slowly rolling in against her. For, as all the forces of a human being combine unconsciously to eject a grain of sand that has crept beneath the skin to cause discomfort, so the entire mass of what Sanderson had called the Collective Consciousness of the Forest strove to eject this human atom that stood across the path of its desire.

Loving her husband, she had crept beneath its skin. It was her they would eject and take away; it was her they would destroy, not him. Him, whom they loved and needed, they would keep alive. They meant to take him living.

She reached the house in safety, though she never remembered how she found her way. It was made all simple for her. The branches almost urged her out.

But behind her, as she left the shadowed precincts, she felt as though some towering Angel of the Woods let fall across the threshold the flaming sword of a countless multitude of leaves that formed behind her a barrier, green, shimmering, and impassable. Into the Forest she never walked again.

. . . .

And she went about her daily duties with a calm and quietness that was a perpetual astonishment even to herself, for it hardly seemed of this world at all. She talked to her husband when he came in for tea—after dark. Resignation brings a curious large courage—when there is nothing more to lose. The soul takes risks, and dares. Is it a curious short-cut sometimes to the heights?

'David, I went into the Forest, too, this morning; soon after you I went. I saw you there.'

'Wasn't it wonderful?' he answered simply, inclining his head a little. There was no surprise or annoyance in his look; a mild and gentle *ennui* rather. He asked no real question. She thought of some garden tree the wind attacks too suddenly, bending it over when it does not want to bend—the mild unwillingness with which it yields. She often saw him this way now, in the terms of trees.

'It was very wonderful indeed, dear, yes,' she replied low, her voice not faltering though indistinct. 'But for me it was too—too strange and big.'

The passion of tears lay just below the quiet voice all unbetrayed. Somehow she kept them back.

There was a pause, and then he added:

'I find it more and more so every day.' His voice passed through the lamp-lit room like a murmur of the wind in branches. The look of youth and happiness she had caught upon his face out there had wholly gone, and an expression of weariness was in its place, as of a man distressed vaguely at finding himself in uncongenial surroundings where he is slightly ill at ease. It was the house he hated—coming back to rooms and walls and furniture. The ceilings and closed windows confined him. Yet, in it, no suggestion that he found *her* irksome. Her presence seemed of no account at all; indeed, he hardly noticed her. For whole long periods he lost her, did not know that she was there. He had no need of her. He lived alone. Each lived alone.

The outward signs by which she recognised that the awful battle was against her and the terms of surrender accepted were pathetic. She put the medicine-chest away upon the shelf; she gave the orders for his pocket-luncheon before he asked; she went to bed alone and early, leaving the front door unlocked, with milk and bread and butter in the hall beside the lamp—all concessions that she felt impelled to make. For more and more, unless the weather was too violent, he went out after dinner even, staying for hours in the woods. But she never slept until she heard the front door close below, and knew soon afterwards his careful step come creeping up the stairs and into the room so softly. Until she heard his regular deep breathing close beside her, she lay awake. All strength or desire to resist had gone for good. The thing against her was too huge and powerful. Capitulation was complete, a fact accomplished. She dated it from the day she followed him to the Forest.

Moreover, the time for evacuation—her own evacuation—seemed approaching. It came stealthily ever nearer, surely and slowly as the rising tide she used to dread. At the high-water mark she stood waiting calmly—waiting to be swept away. Across the lawn all those terrible days of early winter the encircling Forest watched it come, guiding its silent swell and currents towards her feet. Only she never once gave up her Bible or her praying. This complete resignation, moreover, had somehow brought to her a strange great understanding, and if she could not share her husband's horrible abandonment to powers outside himself, she could, and did, in some half-groping way grasp at shadowy meanings that might make such abandonment—possible, yes, but more than merely possible—in some extraordinary sense not evil.

Hitherto she had divided the beyond-world into two sharp halves—spirits good or spirits evil. But thoughts came to her now, on soft and very tentative feet, like the footsteps of the gods which are on wool, that besides these definite classes, there might be other Powers as well, belonging definitely to neither one nor the other. Her thought stopped dead at that. But the big idea found lodgment in her little mind, and, owing to the largeness of her heart, remained there unejected. It even brought a certain solace with it.

The failure—or unwillingness, as she preferred to state it—of her God to interfere and help, that also she came in a measure to understand. For here, she found it more and more possible to imagine, was perhaps no positive evil at work, but only something that usually stands away from humankind, something alien and not commonly recognised. There *was* a gulf fixed between the two, and Mr. Sanderson *had* bridged it, by his talk, his explanations, his attitude of mind. Through these her husband had found the way into it. His temperament and natural passion for the woods had prepared the soul in him, and the moment he saw the way to go he took it—the line of least resistance. Life was, of course, open to all, and her husband had the right to choose it where he would. He had chosen it—away from her, away from other men, but not necessarily away from God. This was an enormous concession that she skirted, never really faced; it was too revolutionary to face. But its possibility peeped into her bewildered mind. It might delay his progress, or it might advence it. Who could know? And why should God, who ordered all things with such magnificent detail, from the pathway of a sun to the falling of a sparrow, object to his free choice, or interfere to hinder him and stop?

She came to realise resignation, that is, in another aspect. It gave her comfort, if not peace. She fought against all belittling of her God. It was, perhaps, enough that He—knew.

'You are not alone, dear, in the trees out there?' she ventured one night, as he crept on tiptoe into the room not far from midnight. 'God is with you?'

'Magnificently,' was the immediate answer, given with enthusiasm, 'for He is everywhere. And I only wish that you——'

But she stuffed the clothes against her ears. That invitation on his lips was more than she could bear to hear. It seemed like asking her to hurry to her own execution. She buried her face among the sheets and blankets, shaking all over like a leaf.

IX

And so the thought that she was the one to go remained and grew. It was, perhaps, the first sign of that weakening of the mind which indicated the singular manner of her going. For it was her mental opposition, the trees felt, that stood in their way. Once that was overcome, obliterated, her physical presence did not matter. She would be harmless.

Having accepted defeat, because she had come to feel that his obsession was not actually evil, she accepted at the same time the conditions of an atrocious loneliness. She stood now from her husband farther than from the moon. They had no visitors. Callers were few and far between, and less encouraged than before. The empty dark of winter was before them. Among the neighbours was none in whom, without disloyalty to her husband, she could confide. Mr. Mortimer, had he been single, might have helped her in this desert of solitude that preyed upon her mind, but his wife was there the obstacle; for Mrs. Mortimer wore sandals, believed that nuts were the complete food of man, and indulged in other idiosyncrasies that classed her inevitably among the 'latter signs' which Mrs. Bittacy had been taught to dread as dangerous. She stood most desolately alone.

Solitude, therefore, in which the mind unhindered feeds upon its own delusions, was the assignable cause of her gradual mental disruption and collapse.

With the definite arrival of the colder weather her husband gave up his rambles after dark; evenings were spent together over the fire; he read *The Times;* they even talked about their postponed visit abroad in the coming spring. No restlessness was on him at the change; he seemed content and easy in his mind; spoke little of the trees and woods; enjoyed far better health than if there had been change of scene, and to herself was tender, kind, solicitous over trifles, as in the distant days of their first honeymoon.

But this deep calm could not deceive her; it meant, she fully understood, that he felt sure of himself, sure of her, and sure of the trees as well. It all lay buried in the depths of him, too secure and deep, too intimately established in his central being to permit of those surface fluctuations which betray disharmony within. His life was hid with trees. Even the fever, so dreaded in the damp of winter, left him free. She now knew why. The fever was due to their efforts to obtain him, his efforts to respond and go—physical results of a fierce unrest he had never understood till Sanderson came with his wicked explanations. Now it was otherwise. The bridge was made. And—he had gone.

And she, brave, loyal, and consistent soul, found herself utterly alone, even trying to make his passage easy. It seemed that she stood at the bottom of some huge ravine that opened in her mind, the walls whereof instead of rock were trees that reached enormous to the sky, engulfing her. God alone knew that she was there. He watched, permitted, even perhaps approved. At any rate—He knew.

During those quiet evenings in the house, moreover, while they sat over the fire listening to the roaming winds about the house her husband knew continual access to the world his alien love had furnished for him. Never for a single instant was he cut off from it. She gazed at the newspaper spread before his face and knees, saw the smoke of his cheroot curl up above the edge, noticed the little hole in his evening socks, and listened to the paragraphs he read aloud as of old. But this was all a veil he spread about himself of purpose. Behind it—he escaped. It was the conjurer's trick to divert the sight to unimportant details while the essential thing went forward unobserved. He managed wonderfully; she loved him for the pains he took to spare her distress; but all the while she knew that the body lolling in that armchair before her eyes contained the merest fragment of his actual self. It was little better than a corpse. It was an empty shell. The essential soul of him was out yonder with the Forest—farther out near that ever-roaring heart of it.

And, with the dark, the Forest came up boldly and pressed against the very walls and windows, peering in upon them, joining hands above the slates and chimneys. The winds were always walking on the lawn and gravel paths; steps came and went and came again; some one seemed always talking in the woods, some one was in the building too. She passed them on the stairs, or running soft and muffled, very large and gentle, down the passages and landings after dusk, as though loose fragments of the Day had broken off and stayed there caught among the shadows, trying to get out. They blundered silently all about the house. They waited till she passed, then made a run for it. And her husband always knew. She saw him more than once deliberately avoid them because—*she* was there. More than once, too, she saw him stand and listen when he thought she was not near, then heard herself the long bounding stride of their approach across the silent garden. Already *he* had heard them in the windy distance of the night, far, far away. They sped, she well knew, along that glade of mossy turf by which she last came out; it cushioned their tread exactly as it had cushioned her own.

It seemed to her the trees were always in the house with him, and in their very bedroom. He welcomed them, unaware that she also knew, and trembled.

One night in their bedroom it caught her unawares. She

THE MAN WHOM THE TREES LOVED

woke out of deep sleep and it came upon her before she could gather her forces for control.

The day had been wildly boisterous, but now the wind had dropped; only its rags went fluttering through the night. The rays of the full moon fell in a shower between the branches. Overhead still raced the scud and wrack, shaped like hurrying monsters; but below the earth was quiet. Still and dripping stood the hosts of trees. Their trunks gleamed wet and sparkling where the moon caught them. There was a strong smell of mould and fallen leaves. The air was sharp—heavy with odour.

And she knew all this the instant that she woke; for it seemed to her that she had been elsewhere—following her husband—as though she had been *out*! There was no dream at all, merely this definite, haunting certainty. It dived away, lost, buried in the night. She sat upright in bed. She had come back.

The room shone pale in the moonlight reflected through the windows, for the blinds were up, and she saw her husband's form beside her, motionless in deep sleep. But what caught her unawares was the horrid thing that by this fact of sudden, unexpected waking she had surprised these other things in the room, beside the very bed, gathered close about him while he slept. It was their dreadful boldness—herself of no account as it were—that terrified her into screaming before she could collect her powers to prevent. She screamed before she realised what she did — a long, high shriek of terror that filled the room, yet made so little actual sound. For wet and shimmering presences stood grouped all round that bed. She saw their outline underneath the ceiling, the green, spread bulk of them, their vague extension over walls and furniture. They shifted to and fro, massed yet traslucent, mild yet thick, moving and turning within themselves to a hushed noise of multitudinous soft rustling. In their sound was something very sweet and winning that fell into her with a spell of horrible enchantment. They were so mild, each one alone, yet so terrific in their combination. Cold seized her. The sheets against her body turned to ice.

She screamed a second time, though the sound hardly issued from her throat. The spell sank deeper, reaching to the heart; for it softened all the currents of her blood and took life from her in a stream—towards themselves. Resistance in that moment seemed impossible.

Her husband then stirred in his sleep, and woke. And, instantly, the forms drew up, erect, and gathered themselves in some amazing way together. They lessened in extent—then scattered through the air like an effect of light when shadows seek to smother it. It was tremendous, yet most exquisite. A sheet of pale-green shadow that yet had form and substance filled the room. There was a rush of silent movement, as the Presences drew past her through the air—and then were gone.

But, clearest of all, she saw the manner of their going; for she recognised in their tumult of escape by the window open at the top, the same wide 'looping circles'—spirals it seemed—that she had seen upon the lawn those weeks ago when Sanderson had talked. The room once more was empty.

In the collapse that followed, she heard her husband's voice, as though coming from some great distance. Her own replies she heard as well. Both were so strange and unlike their normal speech, the very words unnatural:

'What is it, dear? Why do you wake me *now*?' And his voice whispered it with a sighing sound, like wind in pine boughs.

'A moment since something went past me through the air of the room. Back to the night outside it went.' Her voice, too, held the same note as of wind entangled among too many leaves.

'My dear, it *was* the wind.'

'But it called, David. It was calling *you*—by name!'

'The stir of the branches, dear, was what you heard. Now, sleep again, I beg you, sleep.'

'It had a crowd of eyes all through and over it—before and behind——' Her voice grew louder. But his own in reply sank lower, far away, and oddly hushed.

'The moonlight, dear, upon the sea of twigs and boughs in the rain, was what you saw.'

'But it frightened me. I've lost my God—and you—I'm cold as death!'

'My dear, it is the cold of the early morning hours. The whole world sleeps. Now sleep again yourself.'

He whispered close to her ear. She felt his hand stroking her. His voice was soft and very soothing. But only a part of him was there; only a part of him was speaking; it was a half-emptied body that lay beside her and uttered these strange sentences, even forcing her own singular choice of words. The horrible, dim enchantment of the trees was close about them in the room—gnarled, ancient, lonely trees of winter, whispering round the human life they loved.

'And let me sleep again,' she heard him murmur as he settled down among the clothes, 'sleep back into that deep, delicious peace from which you called me. ...'

His dreamy, happy tone, and that look of youth and joy she discerned upon his features even in the filtered moonlight, touched her again as with the spell of those shining, mild green presences. It sank down into her. She felt sleep grope for her. On the threshold of slumber one of those strange vagrant voices that loss of consciousness lets loose cried faintly in her heart—

'There is joy in the Forest over one sinner that——'

Then sleep took her before she had time to realise even that she was vilely parodying one of her most precious texts, and that the irreverence was ghastly. ...

And though she quickly slept again, her sleep was not as usual, dreamless. It was not woods and trees she dreamed of, but a small and curious dream that kept coming again and again upon her: that she stood upon a wee, bare rock in the sea, and that the tide was rising. The water first came to her feet, then to her knees, then to her waist. Each time the dream returned, the tide seemed higher. Once it rose to her neck, once even to her mouth, covering her lips for a moment so that she could not breathe. She did not wake between the dreams; a period of drab and dreamless slumber intervened. But, finally, the water rose above her eyes and face, completely covering her head.

And then came explanation—the sort of explanation dreams bring. She understood. For, beneath the water, she had seen the world of seaweed rising from the bottom of the sea like a forest of dense green—long, sinuous stems, immense thick branches, millions of feelers spreading through the darkened watery depths the power of their ocean foliage. The Vegetable Kingdom was even in the sea. It was everywhere. Earth, air, and water helped it, way of escape there was none.

And even underneath the sea she heard that terrible sound of roaring—was it surf or wind or voices?—further out, yet coming steadily towards her.

And so, in the loneliness of that drab English winter, the mind of Mrs. Bittacy, preying upon itself, and fed by constant dread, went lost in disproportion. Dreariness filled the weeks with dismal, sunless skies and a clinging moisture that knew no wholesome tonic of keen frosts. Alone with her thoughts, both her husband and her God withdrawn into distance, she counted the days to Spring. She groped her way, stumbling down the long dark tunnel. Through the arch at the far end lay a brilliant picture of the violet sea sparkling on the coast of France. There lay safety and escape for both of them, could she but hold on. Behind her the trees blocked up the other entrance. She never once looked back.

She drooped. Vitality passed from her, drawn out and away as by some steady suction. Immense and incessant was this sensation of her powers draining off. The taps were all turned on. Her personality, as it were, streamed steadily away, coaxed outwards by this Power that never wearied and seemed inexhaustible. It won her as the full moon wins the tide. She waned; she faded; she obeyed.

At first she watched the process, and recognised exactly what was going on. Her physical life, and that balance of the mind which depends on physical well-being, were being slowly undermined. She saw that clearly. Only the soul, dwelling like a star apart from these and independent of them, lay safe somewhere—with her distant God. That she knew—tranquilly. The spiritual love that linked her to her husband was safe from all attack. Later, in His good time, they would merge together again because of it. But, meanwhile, all of her that had kinship with the earth was slowly going. This separation was being remorselessly accomplished. Every part of her the trees could touch was being steadily drained from her. She was being—removed.

After a time, however, even this power of realisation went so that she no longer 'watched the process' or knew exactly what was going on. The one satisfaction she had known—the feeling that it was sweet to suffer for his sake—went with it. She stood utterly alone with this terror of the trees... mid the ruins of her broken and disordered mind.

She slept badly; woke in the morning with hot and tired eyes; her head ached dully; she grew confused in thought and lost the clues of daily life in the most feeble fashion. At the same time she lost sight, too, of that brilliant picture at the exit of the tunnel; it faded away into a tiny semicircle of pale light, the violet sea and the sunshine the merest point of white, remote as a star and equally inaccessible. She knew now that she could never reach it. And through the darkness that stretched behind, the power of the trees came close and caught her, twining about her feet and arms, climbing to her very lips. She woke at night, finding it difficult to breathe. There seemed wet leaves pressed against her mouth, and soft green tendrils clinging to her neck. Her feet were heavy, half rooted, as it were, in deep, thick earth. Huge creepers stretched along the whole of that black tunnel, feeling about her person for points where they might fasten well, as ivy or the giant parasites of the Vegetable Kingdom settle down on the trees themselves to sap their life and kill them.

Slowly and surely the morbid growth possessed her life and held her. She feared those very winds that ran about the wintry forest. They were in league with it. They helped it everywhere.

'Why don't you sleep, dear?' It was her husband now who played the role of nurse, tending her little wants with an honest care that at least aped the services of love. He was so utterly unconscious of the raging battle he had caused. 'What is it that keeps you so wide awake and restless?'

'The winds,' she whispered in the dark. For hours she had lain watching the tossing of the trees through the blindless windows. 'They go walking and talking everywhere to-night, keeping me awake. And all the time they call so loudly to you.'

And this strange whispered answer appalled her for a moment until the meaning of it faded and left her in a dark confusion of the mind that was now becoming almost permanent.

'The trees excite them in the night. The winds are the great swift carriers. Go with them, dear—and not against. You'll find sleep that way if you do.'

'The storm is rising,' she began, hardly knowing what she said.

'All the more then—go with them. Don't resist. They'll take you to the trees, that's all.'

Resist! The word touched on the button of some text that once had helped her.

'Resist the devil and he will flee from you,' she heard her whispered answer, and the same second had buried her face beneath the clothes in a flood of hysterical weeping.

But her husband did not seem disturbed. Perhaps he did not hear it, for the wind ran just then against the windows with a booming shout, and the roaring of the Forest farther out came behind the blow, surging into the room. Perhaps, too, he was already asleep again. She slowly regained a sort of dull composure. Her face emerged from the tangle of sheets and blankets. With a growing terror over her—she listened. The storm was rising. It came with a sudden and impetuous rush that made all further sleep for her impossible.

Alone in a shaking world, it seemed, she lay and listened. That storm interpreted for her mind the climax. The Forest bellowed out its victory to the winds; the winds in turn proclaimed it to the Night. The whole world knew of her complete defeat, her loss, her little human pain. This was the roar and shout of victory that she listened to.

For, unmistakably, the trees were shouting in the dark. There were sounds, too, like the flapping of great sails, a thousand at a time, and sometimes reports that resembled more than anything else the distant booming of enormous drums. The trees stood up—the whole beleaguering host of them stood up—and with the uproar of their million branches drummed the thundering message out across the night. It seemed as if they all had broken loose. Their roots swept trailing over field and hedge and roof. They tossed their bushy heads beneath the clouds with a wild, delighted shuffling of great boughs. With trunks upright they raced leaping through the sky. There was upheaval and adventure in the awful sound they made, and their cry was like the cry of a sea that has broken through its gates and poured loose upon the world. ...

Through it all her husband slept peacefully as though he heard it not. It was, as she well knew, the sleep of the semi-dead. For he was out with all that clamouring turmoil. The part of him hat she had lost was there. The form that slept so calmly at her side was but the shell, half emptied. ...

And when the winter's morning stole upon the scene at length, with a pale, washed sunshine that followed the departing tempest, the first thing she saw, as she crept to the window and looked out, was the ruined cedar lying on the lawn. Only the gaunt and crippled trunk of it remained. The single giant bough that had been left to it lay dark upon the grass, sucked endways towards the Forest by a great wind eddy. It lay there like a mass of driftwood from a wreck, left by the ebbing of a high spring-tide upon the sands—remnant of some friendly, splendid vessel that once had sheltered men.

And in the distance she heard the roaring of the Forest further out. Her husband's voice was in it.

THE VALLEY OF THE BEASTS

I

As they emerged suddenly from the dense forest the Indian halted, and Grimwood, his employer, stood beside him, gazing into the beautiful wooded valley that lay spread below them in the blaze of a golden sunset. Both men leaned upon their rifles, caught by the enchantment of the unexpected scene.

'We camp here,' said Tooshalli abruptly, after a careful survey. 'To-morrow we make a plan.'

He spoke excellent English. The note of decision, almost of authority, in his voice was noticeable, but Grimwood set it down to the natural excitement of the moment. Every track they had followed during the last two days, but one track in particular as well, had headed straight for this remote and hidden valley, and the sport promised to be unusual.

'That's so,' he replied, in the tone of one giving an order. 'You can make camp ready at once.' And he sat down on a fallen hemlock to take off his moccasin boots and grease his feet that ached from the arduous day now drawing to a close. Though under ordinary circumstances he would have pushed on for another hour or two he was not averse to a night here, for exhaustion had come upon him during the last bit of rough going, his eye and muscles were no longer steady, and it was doubtful if he could have shot straight enough to kill. He did not mean to miss a second time.

With his Canadian friend, Iredale, the latter's half-breed, and his own Indian, Tooshalli, the party had set out three weeks ago to find the 'wonderful big moose' the Indians reported were travelling in the Snow River country. They soon found that the tale was true; tracks were abundant; they saw fine animals nearly every day, but though carrying good heads, the hunters expected better still and left them alone. Pushing up the river to a chain of small lakes near its source, they then separated into two parties, each with its nine-foot bark canoe, and packed in for three days after the yet bigger animals the Indians agreed would be found in the deeper woods beyond. Excitement was keen, expectation keener still. The day before they separated, Iredale shot the biggest moose of his life, and its head, bigger even than the grand Alaskan heads, hangs in his house to-day. Grimwood's hunting blood was fairly up. His blood was of the fiery, not to say ferocious, quality. It almost seemed he liked killing for its own sake.

Four days after the party broke into two he came upon a gigantic track, whose measurements and length of stride keyed every nerve he possessed to its highest tension.

Tooshalli examined the tracks for some minutes with care. 'It is the biggest moose in the world,' he said at length, a new expression on his inscrutable red visage.

Following it all that day, they yet got no sight of the big fellow that seemed to be frequenting a little marshy dip of country, too small to be called valley, where willow and undergrowth abounded. He had not yet scented his pursuers. They were after him again at dawn. Towards the evening of the second day Grimwood caught a sudden glimpse of the monster among a thick clump of willows, and the sight of the magnificent head that easily beat all records set his heart beating like a hammer with excitement. He aimed and fired. But the moose, instead of crashing, went thundering away throught the farther scrub and disappeared, the sound of his plunging canter presently dying away. Grimwood had missed, even if he had wounded.

They camped, and all next day, leaving the canoe behind, they followed the huge track, but though finding signs of blood, these were not plentiful, and the shot had evidently only grazed the animal. The travelling was of the hardest. Towards evening, utterly exhausted, the spoor led them to the ridge they now stood upon, gazing down into the enchanting valley that opened at their feet. The giant moose had gone down into this valley. He would consider himself safe there. Grimwood agreed with the Indian's judgment. They would camp for the night and continue at dawn the wild hunt after 'the biggest moose in the world'.

Supper was over, the small fire used for cooking dying down, when Grimwood became first aware that the Indian was not behaving quite as usual. What particular detail drew his attention is hard to say. He was a slow-witted, heavy man, full-blooded, unobservant; a fact had to hurt him through his comfort, through his pleasure, before he noticed it. Yet anyone else must have observed the changed mood of the Redskin long ago. Tooshalli had made the fire, fried the bacon, served the tea, and was arranging the blankets, his own and his employer's, before the latter remarked upon his—silence. Tooshalli had not uttered a word for over an hour and a half, since he had first set eyes upon the new valley, to be exact. And his employer now noticed the unaccustomed silence, because after food he liked to listen to wood talk and hunting lore.

'Tired out, aren't you?' said big Grimwood, looking into the dark face across the firelight. He resented the absence of conversation, now that he noticed it. He was over-weary himself, he felt more irritable than usual, though his temper was always vile.

'Lost your tongue, eh?' he went on with a growl, as the Indian returned his stare with solemn, expressionless face. That dark inscrutable look got on his nerves a bit. 'Speak up, man!' he exclaimed sharply. 'What's it all about?'

The Englishman had at last realised that there was something to 'speak up' about. The discovery, in his present state, annoyed him further. Tooshalli stared gravely, but made no reply. The silence was prolonged almost into minutes. Presently the head turned sideways, as though the man listened. The other watched him very closely, anger growing in him.

But it was the way the Redskin turned his head, keeping his body rigid, that gave the jerk to Grimwood's nerves, providing him with a sensation he had never known in his life before—it gave him what is generally called 'the goose-flesh'. It seemed to jangle his entire system, yet at the same time made him cautious. He did not like it, this combination of emotions puzzled him.

'Say something, I tell you,' he repeated in a harsher tone, raising his voice. He sat up, drawing his great body closer to the fire. 'Say something, damn it!'

His voice fell dead against the surrounding trees, making the silence of the forest unpleasantly noticeable. Very still the great woods stood about them: there was no wind, no stir of branches; only the crackle of a snapping twig was audible from time to time, as the night-life moved unwarily sometimes, watching the humans round their little fire. The October air had a frosty touch that nipped.

The Redskin did not answer. No muscle of his neck nor of his stiffened body moved. He seemed all ears.

'Well?' repeated the Englishman, lowering his voice this time instinctively. 'What d'you hear, God damn it!' The touch of odd nervousness that made his anger grow betrayed itself in his language.

Tooshalli slowly turned his head back again to its normal position, the body rigid as before.

'I hear nothing, Mr. Grimwood,' he said, gazing with quiet dignity into his employer's eyes.

This was too much for the other, a man of savage temper at the best of times. He was the type of Englishman who he'd strong views as to the right way of treating 'inferior' races.

'That's a lie, Tooshalli, and I won't have you lie to me. Now what was it? Tell me at once!'

'I hear nothing,' repeated the other. 'I only think.'

'And what is it you're pleased to think?' Impatience made a nasty expression round the mouth.

'I go not,' was the abrupt reply, unalterable decision in the voice.

The man's rejoinder was so unexpected that Grimwood found

nothing to say at first. For a moment he did not take its meaning; his mind, always slow, was confused by impatience, also by what he considered the foolishness of the little scene. Then in a flash he understood; but he also understood the immovable obstinacy of the race he had to deal with. Tooshalli was informing him that he refused to go into the valley where the big moose had vanished. And his astonishment was so great at first that he merely sat and stared. No words came to him.

'It is——' said the Indian, but used a native term.

'What's that mean?' Grimwood found his tongue, but his quiet tone was ominous.

'Mr. Grimwood, it mean the "Valley of the Beasts",' was the reply in a tone quieter still.

The Englishman made a great, a genuine effort at self-control. He was dealing, he forced himself to remember, with a superstitious Redskin. He knew the stubbornness of the type. If the man left him his sport was irretrievably spoilt, for he could not hunt in this wilderness alone, and even if he got the coveted head, he could never, never get it out alone. His native selfishness seconded his effort. Persuasion, if only he could keep back his rising anger, was his role to play.

'The Valley of the Beasts,' he said, a smile on his lips rather than in his darkening eyes; 'but that's just what we want. It's beasts we're after, isn't it?' His voice had a false cheery ring that could not have deceived a child. 'But what d'you mean, anyhow—the Valley of the Beasts?' He asked it with a dull attempt at sympathy.

'It belong to Ishtot, Mr. Grimwood.' The man looked him full in the face, no flinching in the eyes.

'My—our—big moose is there,' said the other, who recognised the name of the Indian Hunting God, and understanding better, felt confident he would soon persuade his man. Tooshalli, he remembered, too, was nominally a Christian. 'We'll follow him at dawn and get the biggest head the world has ever seen. You will be famous,' he added, his temper better in hand again. 'Your tribe will honour you. And the white hunters wil pay you much money.'

'He go there to save himself. I go not.'

The other's anger revived with a leap at this stupid obstinacy. But, in spite of it, he noticed the old choice of words. He began to realise that nothing now would move the man. At the same time he also realised that violence on his part must prove worse than useless. Yet violence was natural to his 'dominant' type.

'That brute Grimwood' was the way most men spoke of him.

'Back at the settlement you're a Christian, remember,' he tried, in his clumsy way, another line. 'And disobedience means hell-fire. You know that!'

'I a Christian—at the post,' was the reply, 'but out here the Red God rule. Ishtot keep that valley for himself. No Indian hunt there.' It was as though a granite boulder spoke.

The savage temper of the Englishman, enforced by the long difficult suppression, rose wickedly into sudden flame. He stood up, kicking his blankets aside. He strode across the dying fire to the Indian's side. Tooshalli also rose. They faced each other, two humans alone in the wilderness, watched by countless invisible forest eyes.

Tooshalli stood motionless, yet as though he expected violence from the foolish, ignorant white-face. 'You go alone, Mr. Grimwood.' There was no fear in him.

Grimwood choked with rage. His words came forth with difficulty, though he roared them into the silence of the forest:

'I pay you, don't I? You'll do what *I* say, not what *you* say!' His voice woke the echoes.

The Indian, arms hanging by his side, gave the old reply.

'I go not,' he repeated firmly.

It stung the other into uncontrollable fury.

The beast then came uppermost; it came out. 'You've said that once too often, Tooshalli!' and he struck him brutally in the face. The Indian fell, rose to his knees again, collapsed sideways beside the fire, then struggled back into a sitting position. He never once took his eyes from the white man's face.

Beside himself with anger, Grimwood stood over him. 'Is that enough? Will you obey me now?' he shouted.

'I go not,' came the thick reply, blood streaming from his mouth. The eyes had no flinching in them. 'That valley Ishtot keep. Ishtot see us now. *He see you.*' The last words he uttered with strange, almost uncanny emphasis.

Grimwood, arm raised, fist clenched, about to repeat his terrible assault, paused suddenly. His arm sank to his side. What exactly stopped him he could never say. For one thing he feared his own anger, feared that if he let himself go he would not stop till he had killed—committed murder. He knew his own fearful temper and stood afraid of it. Yet it was not only that. The calm firmness of the Redskin, his courage under pain, and something in the fixed and burning eyes arrested him. Was it also something in the words he had used—'Ishtot see *you*'— that stung him into a queer caution midway in his violence?

He could not say. He only knew that a momentary sense of awe came over him. He became unpleasantly aware of the enveloping forest, so still, listening in a kind of impenetrable, remorseless silence. This lonely wilderness, looking silently upon what might easily prove murder, laid a faint, inexplicable chill upon his raging blood. The hand dropped slowly to his side again, the fist unclenched itself, his breath came more evenly.

'Look you here,' he said, adopting without knowing it the local way of speech. 'I ain't a bad man, though your going-on do make a man damned tired. I'll give you another chance.' His voice was sullen, but a new note in it surprised even himself. 'I'll do that. You can have the night to think it over, Tooshalli —see? Talk it over with your——'

He did not finish the sentence. Somehow the name of the Redskin God refused to pass his lips. He turned away, flung himself into his blankets, and in less than ten minutes, exhausted as much by his anger as by the day's hard going, he was sound asleep.

The Indian, crouching beside the dying fire, had said nothing.

THE VALLEY OF THE BEASTS

Night held the woods, the sky was thick with stars, the life of the forest went about its business quietly, with that wondrous skill which millions of years have perfected. The Redskin, so close to this skill that he instinctively used and borrowed from it, was silent, alert and wise, his outline as inconspicuous as though he merged, like his four-footed teachers, into the mass of the surrounding bush.

He moved perhaps, yet nothing knew he moved. His wisdom, derived from that eternal, ancient mother who from infinite experience makes no mistakes, did not fail him. His soft tread made no sound; his breathing, as his weight, was calculated. The stars observed him, but they did not tell; the light air knew his whereabouts, yet without betrayal. ...

The chill dawn gleamed at length between the trees, lighting the pale ashes of an extinguished fire, also of a bulky, obvious form beneath a blanket. The form moved clumsily. The cold was penetrating.

And that bulky form moved because a dream had come to trouble it. A dark figure stole across its confused field of vision. The form started, but it did not wake. The figure spoke: 'Take this,' it whispered, handing a little stick, curiously carved. 'It is the totem of great Ishtot. In the valley all memory of the White Gods will leave you. Call upon Ishtot. ... Call on Him if you dare'; and the dark figure glided away out of the dream and out of all remembrance. ...

II

The first thing Grimwood noticed when he woke was that Tooshalli was not there. No fire burned, no tea was ready. He felt exceedingly annoyed. He glared about him, then got up with a curse to make the fire. His mind seemed confused and troubled. At first he only realised one thing clearly—his guide had left him in the night.

It was very cold. He lit the wood with difficulty and made his tea, and the actual world came gradually back to him. The Red

Indian had gone; perhaps the blow, perhaps the superstitious terror, perhaps both, had driven him away. He was alone, that was the outstanding fact. For anything beyond outstanding facts, Grimwood felt little interest. Imaginative speculation was beyond his compass. Close to the brute creation, it seemed, his nature lay.

It was while packing his blankets—he did it automatically, a dull, vicious resentment in him—that his fingers struck a bit of wood that he was about to throw away when its unusual shape caught his attention suddenly. His odd dream came back then. But was it a dream? The bit of wood was undoubtedly a totem stick. He examined it. He paid it more attention than he meant to, wished to. Yes, it was unquestionably a totem stick. The dream, then, was not a dream. Tooshalli had quit, but, following with Redskin faithfulness some code of his own, hap left him the means of safety. He chuckled sourly, but thrust the stick inside his belt. 'One never knows,' he mumbled to himself.

He faced the situation squarely. He was alone in the wilderness. His capable, experienced woodsman had deserted him. The situation was serious. What should he do? A weakling would certainly retrace his steps, following the track they had made, afraid to be left alone in this vast hinterland of pathless forest. But Grimwood was of another build. Alarmed he might be, but he would not give in. He had the defects of his own qualities. The brutality of his nature argued force. He was determined and a sportsman. He would go on. And ten minutes after breakfast, having first made a *cache* of what provisions were left over, he was on his way—down across the ridge and into the mysterious valley, the Valley of the Beasts.

It looked, in the morning sunlight, entrancing. The trees closed in behind him, but he did not notice. It led him on. ...

He followed the track of the gigantic moose he meant to kill, and the sweet, delicious sunshine helped him. The air was like wine, the seductive spoor of the great beast, with here and there a faint splash of blood on leaves or ground, lay for ever just before his eyes. He found the valley, though the actual word did not occur to him, enticing; more and more he noticed the beauty, the desolate grandeur of the mighty spruce and hemlock, the splendour of the granite bluffs which in places rose above the forest and caught the sun. ... The valley was deeper, vaster than he had imagined. He felt safe, at home in it, though, again, these actual terms did not occur to him. ... Here he could hide for ever and find peace. ... He became aware of a new quality in the deep loneliness. The scenery for the first time in his life appealed to him, and the form of the appeal was curious—he felt the comfort of it.

For a man of his habit, this was odd, yet the new sensations stole over him so gently, their approach so gradual, that they were first recognised by his consciousness indirectly. They had already established themselves in him before he noticed them; and the indirectness took this form—that the passion of the chase gave place to an interest in the valley itself. The lust of the hunt, the fierce desire to find and kill, the keen wish, in a word, to see his quarry within range, to aim, to fire, to witness the natural consummation of the long expedition—these had all become measurably less, while the effect of the valley upon him had increased in strength. There was a welcome about it that he did not understand.

The change was singular, yet, oddly enough, it did not occur to him as singular; it was unnatural, yet it did not strike him so. To a dull mind of his unobservant, unanalytical type, a change had to be marked and dramatic before he noticed it; something in the nature of a shock must accompany it for him to recognise it had happened. And there had been no shock. The spoor of the great moose was much clearer, now that he caught up with the animal that made it; the blood more frequent; he had noticed the spot where it had rested, its huge body leaving a marked imprint on the soft ground; where it had reached up to eat the leaves of saplings here and there was also visible; he had come undoubtedly very near to it, and any minute now might see its great bulk within range of an easy shot. Yet his ardour had somehow lessened.

He first realised this change in himself when it suddenly occurred to him that the animal itself had grown less cautious. It must scent him easily now, since a moose, its sight being indifferent, depends chiefly for its safety upon its unusually keen sense of smell, and the wind came from behind him. This now struck him as decidedly uncommon: the moose itself was obviously careless of his close approach. It felt no fear.

It was this inexplicable alteration in the animal's behaviour that made him recognise, at last, the alteration in his own. He had followed it now for a couple of hours and had descended some eight hundred to a thousand feet; the trees were thinner and more sparsely placed; there were open park-like places where silver birch, sumach and maple splashed their blazing colours; and a crystal stream, broken by many waterfalls, foamed past towards the bed of the great valley, yet another thousand feet below. By a quiet pool against some over-arching rocks, the moose had evidently paused to drink, paused at its leisure, moreover. Grimwood, rising from a close examination of the direction the creature had taken after drinking—the hoofmarks were fresh and very distinct in the marshy ground about the pool—looked suddenly straight into the great creature's eyes. It was not twenty yards from where he stood, yet he had been standing on that spot for at least ten minutes, caught by the wonder and loneliness of the scene. The moose, therefore, had been close beside him all this time. It had been calmly drinking, undisturbed by his presence, unafraid.

The shock came now, the shock that woke his heavy nature into realisation. For some seconds, probably for minutes, he stood rooted to the ground, motionless, hardly breathing. He stared as though he saw a vision. The animal's head was lowered, but turned obliquely somewhat, so that the eyes, placed sideways in its great head, could see him properly; its immense proboscis hung as though stuffed upon an English wall; he saw the fore-feet planted wide apart, the slope of the enormous shoulders dropping back towards the fine hind-quarters and lean flanks. It was a magnificent bull. The horns and head justified his wildest expectations, they were superb, a record specimen, and a phrase—where had he heard it?—ran vaguely, as from far distance, through his mind: 'the biggest moose in the world'.

There was the extraordinary fact, however, that he did not shoot; nor feel the wish to shoot. The familiar instinct, so strongly hitherto in his blood, made no sign; the desire to kill apparently had left him. To raise his rifle, aim and fire had become suddenly an absolute impossibility.

He did not move. The animal and the human stared into each other's eyes for a length of time whose interval he could not measure. Then came a soft noise close beside him: the rifle had slipped from his grasp and fallen with a thud into the mossy earth at his feet. And the moose, for the first time now, was moving. With slow, easy stride, its great weight causing a squelching sound as the feet drew out of the moist ground, it came towards him, the bulk of the shoulders giving it an appearance of swaying like a ship at sea. It reached his side, it almost touched him, the magnificent head bent low, the spread of the gigantic horns lay beneath his very eyes. He could have patted, stroked it. He saw, with a touch of pity, that blood trickled from a sore in its left shoulder, matting the thick hair. It sniffed the fallen rifle.

Then, lifting its head and shoulders again, it sniffed the air, this time with an audible sound that shook from Grimwood's mind the last possibility that he witnessed a vision or dreamed a dream. One moment it gazed into his face, its big brown eyes shining and unafraid, then turned abruptly, and swung away at a speed ever rapidly increasing across the park-like spaces till it was lost finally in the dark tangle of undergrowth beyond. And the Englishman's muscles turned to paper, his paralysis passed, his legs refused to support his weight, and he sank heavily to the ground.

III

It seems he slept, slept long and heavily; he sat up, stretched himself, yawned and rubbed his eyes. The sun had moved across the sky, for the shadows, he saw, now ran from west to east, and they were long shadows. He had slept evidently for hours, and evening was drawing in. He was aware that he felt hungry. In his pouch-like pockets he had dried meat, sugar, matches, tea, and the little billy that never left him. He would make a fire, boil some tea and eat.

But he took no steps to carry out his purpose, he felt disinclined to move, he sat thinking, thinking ... What was he thinking about? He did not know, he could not say exactly; it was more like fugitive pictures that passed across his mind. Who, and where, was he! This was the Valley of the Beasts, that he knew; he felt sure of nothing else. How long had he been here, and where had he come from, and why? The questions did not linger for their answers, almost as though his interest in them was merely automatic. He felt happy, peaceful, unafraid.

He looked about him, and the spell of this virgin forest came upon him like a charm; only the sound of falling water, the murmur of wind sighing among innumerable branches, broke the enveloping silence. Overhead, beyond the crests of the towering trees, a cloudless evening sky was palling into transparent orange, opal, mother of pearl. He saw buzzards soaring lazily. A scarlet tanager flashed by. Soon would the owls begin to call and the darkness fall like a sweet black veil and hide all detail, while the stars sparkled in their countless thousands ...

A glint of something that shone upon the ground caught his eye—a smooth, polished strip of rounded metal: his rifle. And he started to his feet impulsively, yet not knowing exactly what he meant to do. At the sight of the weapon, something had leaped to life in him, then faded out, died down, and was gone again.

'I'm—I'm——' he began muttering to himself, but could not finish what he was about to say. His name had disappeared com-

THE VALLEY OF THE BEASTS

pletely. 'I'm in the Valley of the Beasts,' he repeated in place of what he sought but could not find.

This fact, that he was in the Valley of the Beasts, seemed the only positive item of knowledge that he had. About the name something known and familiar clung, though the sequence that led up to it he could not trace. Presently, newertheless, he rose to his feet, advanced a few steps, stooped and picked up the shining metal thing, his rifle. He examined it a moment, a feeling of dread and loathing rising in him, a sensation of almost horror that made him tremble, then, with a convulsive movement that betrayed an intense reaction of some sort he could not comprehend, he flung the thing far from him into the foaming torrent. He saw the splash it made, he also saw that same instant a large grizzly bear swing heavily along the bank not a dozen yards from where he stood. It, too, heard the splash, for it started, turned, paused a second, then changed its direction and came towards him. It came up close. Its fur brushed his body. It examined him leisurely, as the moose had done, sniffed, half rose upon its terrible hind legs, opened its mouth so that red tongue and gleaming teeth were plainly visible, then flopped back upon all fours again with a deep growl that yet had no anger in it, and swung off at a quick trot back to the bank of the torrent. He had felt its hot breath upon his face, but he had felt no fear. The monster was puzzled but not hostile. It disappeared.

'They know not——' he sought for the word 'man', but could not find it. 'They have never been hunted.'

The words ran through his mind, if perhaps he was not entirely certain of their meaning; they rose, as it were, automatically; a familiar sound lay in them somewhere. At the same time there rose feelings in him that were equally, though in another way, familiar and quite natural, feelings he had once known intimately but long since laid aside.

What were they? What was their origin? They seemed distant as the stars, yet were actually in his body, in his blood and nerves, part and parcel of his flesh. Long, long ago ... Oh, how long, how long?

Thinking was difficult; feeling was what he most easily and naturally managed. He could not think for long; feeling rose up and drowned the effort quickly.

That huge and awful bear—not a nerve, not a muscle quivered in him as its acrid smell rose to his nostrils, its fur brushed down his legs. Yet he was aware that somewhere there was danger, though not here. Somewhere there was attack, hostility, wicked and calculated plans against him—as against that splendid, roaming animal that had sniffed, examined, then gone its own way, satisfied. Yes, active attack, hostility and careful, cruel plans against his safety, but—not here. Here he was safe, secure, at peace; here he was happy; here he could roam at will, no eye cast sideways into forest depths, no ear pricked high to catch sounds not explained, no nostrils quivering to scent alarm. He felt this, but he did not think it. He felt hungry, thirsty too.

Something prompted him now at last to act. His billy lay at his feet, and he picked it up; the matches—he carried them in a metal case whose screw top kept out all moisture—were in his hand. Gathering a few dry twigs, he stooped to light them, then suddenly drew back with the first touch of fear he had yet known.

Fire! What *was* fire? The idea was repugnant to him, it was impossible, he was afraid of fire. He flung the metal case after the rifle and saw it gleam in the last rays of sunset, then sink with a little splash beneath the water. Glancing down at his billy, he realised next that he could not make use of it either, nor of the dark dry dusty stuff he had meant to boil in water. He felt no repugnance, certainly no fear, in connection with these things, only he could not handle them, he did not need them, he had forgotten, yes, 'forgotten', what they meant exactly. This strange forgetfulness was increasing in him rapidly, becoming more and more complete with every minute. Yet his thirst must be quenched.

The next moment he found himself at the water's edge; he stooped to fill his billy; paused, hesitated, examined the rushing water, then abruptly moved a few feet higher up the stream, leaving the metal can behind him. His handling of it had been oddly clumsy, his gestures awkward, even unnatural. He now flung himself down with an easy, simple motion of his entire body, lowered his face to a quiet pool he had found, and drank his fill of the cool, refreshing liquid. But, though unaware of the fact, he did not drink. He lapped.

Then, crouching where he was, he ate the meat and sugar from his pockets, lapped more water, moved back a short distance again into the dry ground beneath the trees, but moved this time without rising to his feet, curled his body into a comfortable position and closed his eyes again to sleep ... No single question now raised its head in him. He felt contentment, satisfaction only...

He stirred, shook himself, opened half an eye and saw, as he had felt already in slumber, that he was not alone. In the parklike spaces in front of him, as in the shadowed fringe of the trees at his back, there was sound and movement, the sound of stealthy feet, the movement of innumerable dark bodies. There was the pad and tread of animals, the stir of backs, of smooth and shaggy beasts, in countless numbers. Upon this host fell the light of a half moon sailing high in a cloudless sky; the gleam of stars, sparkling in the clear night air like diamonds, shone reflected in hundreds of ever-shifting eyes, most of them but a few feet above the ground. The whole valley was alive.

He sat upon his haunches, staring, staring, but staring in wonder, not in fear, though the foremost of the great host were so near that he could have stretched an arm and touched them. It was an ever-moving, ever-shifting throng he gazed at, spellbound, in the pale light of moon and stars, now fading slowly towards the approaching dawn. And the smell of the forest itself was not sweeter to him in that moment than the mingled perfume, raw, pungent, acrid, of this furry host of beautiful wild animals that moved like a sea, with a strange murmuring, too, like sea, as the myriad feet and bodies passed to and fro together. Nor was the gleam of the starry, phosphorescent eyes less pleasantly friendly than those happy lamps that light home-lost wanderers to cosy rooms and safety. Through the wild army, in a word, poured to him the deep comfort of the entire valley, a comfort which held both the sweetness of invitation and the welcome of some magical home-coming.

No thoughts came to him, but feeling rose in a tide of wonder and acceptance. He was in his rightful place. His nature had come home. There was this dim, vague consciousness in him that after long, futile straying in another place where uncongenil conditions had forced him to be unnatural and therefore terrible, he had returned at last where he belonged. Here, in the Valley of the Beasts, he had found peace, security and happiness. He would be—he was at last—himself.

It was a marvellous, even a magical, scene he watched, his nerves at highest tension yet quite steady, his senses exquisitely alert, yet no uneasiness in the full accurate reports they furnished. Strong as some deep flood-tide, yet dim, as with untold time and distance, rose over him the spell of long-forgotten memory of a state where he was content and happy, where he was *natural*. The outlines, as it were, of mighty, primitive pictures, flashed before him, yet were gone again before the detail was filled in.

He watched the great army of the animals, they were all about him now; he crouched upon his haunches in the centre of an ever-moving circle of wild forest life. Great timber wolves he saw pass to and fro, loping past him with long stride and graceful swing; their red tongues lolling out; they swarmed in hundreds. Behind, yet mingling freely with them, rolled the huge grizzlies, not clumsy as their uncouth bodies promised, but swiftly, lightly, easily, their half tumbling gait masking agility and speed. They gambolled, sometimes they rose and stood half upright, they were comely in their mass and power, they rolled past him so close that he could touch them. And the black bear and the brown went with them, bears beyond counting, monsters and little ones, a splendid multitude. Beyond them, yet only a little farther back, where the park-like spaces made free movement easier, rose a sea of horns and antlers like a miniature forest in the silvery moonlight.

The immense tribe of deer gathered in vast throngs beneath

THE VALLEY OF THE BEASTS

the starlit sky. Moose and caribou, he saw, the mighty wapiti, and the smaller deer in their crowding thousands. He heard the sound of meeting horns, the tread of innumerable hoofs, the occasional pawing of the ground as the bigger creatures manoeuvred for more space about them. A wolf, he saw, was licking gently at the shoulder of a great bull-moose that had been injured. And the tide receded, advanced again, once more receded, rising and falling like a living sea whose waves were animal shapes, the inhabitants of the Valley of the Beasts.

Beneath the quiet moonlight they swayed to and fro before him. They watched him, knew him, recognised him. They made him welcome.

He was aware, moreover, of a world of smaller life that formed an under-sea, as it were, numerous under-currents rather, running in and out between the great upright legs of the larger creatures. These, though he could not see them clearly, covered the earth, he was aware, in enormous numbers, darting hither and thither, now hiding, now reappearing, too intent upon their busy purposes to pay him attention like their huger comrades, yet ever and anon tumbling against his back, cannoning from his sides, scampering across his legs even, then gone again with a scuttering sound of rapid little feet, and rushing back in to the general host beyond. And with this smaller world also he felt at home.

How long he sat gazing, happy in himself, secure, satisfied, contented, natural, he could not say, but it was long enough for the desire to mingle with what he saw, to know closer contact, to become one with them all—long enough for this deep blind desire to assert itself, so that at length he began to move from his mossy seat towards them, to move, moreover, as they moved, and not upright on two feet.

The moon was lower now, just sinking behind a towering cedar whose ragged crest broke its light into silvery spray. The stars were a little paler too. A line of faint red was visible beyond the heights at the valley's eastern end.

He paused and looked about him, as he advanced slowly,

aware that the host already made an opening in their ranks and that the bear even nosed the earth in front, as though to show the way that was easiest to follow. Then, suddenly, a lynx leaped past him into the low branches of a hemlock, and he lifted his head to admire its perfect poise. He saw in the same instant the arrival of the birds, the army of the eagles, hawks and buzzards, birds of prey—the awakening flight that just precedes the dawn. He saw the flock and streaming lines, hiding the whitening stars a moment as they passed with a prodigious whirr of wings. There came the hooting of an owl from the tree immediately overhead where the lynx now crouched, but not maliciously, along its branch.

He started. He half rose to an upright position. He knew not why he did so, knew not exactly why he started. But in the attempt to find his new, and, as it now seemed, his unaccustomed balance, one hand fell against his side and came in contact with a hard straight thing that projected awkwardly from his clothing. He pulled it out, feeling it all over with his fingers. It was a little stick. He raised it nearer to his eyes, examined it in the light of dawn now growing swiftly, remembered, or half remembered what it was—and stood stock still.

'The totem stick,' he mumbled to himself, yet audibly, finding his speech, and finding another thing—a glint of peering memory—for the first time since entering the valley.

A shock of fire ran through his body; he straightened himself, aware that a moment before he had been crawling upon his hands and knees; it seemed that something broke in his brain, lifting a veil, flinging a shutter free. And Memory peered dreadfully through the widening gap.

'I'm—I'm Grimwood,' his voice uttered, though below his breath. 'Tooshalli's left me. I'm alone...!'

He was aware of a sudden change in the animals surrounding him. A big, grey wolf sat three feet away, glaring into his face; at its side an enormous grizzly swayed itself from one foot to the other; behind it, as if looking over its shoulder, loomed a gigantic wapiti, its horns merged in the shadows of the drooping cedar boughs. But the northern dawn was nearer, the sun already close to the horizon. He saw details with sharp distinctness now. The great bear rose, balancing a moment on its massive hindquarters, then took a step towards him, its front paws spread like arms. Its wicked head lolled horribly, as a huge bull-moose, lowering its horns as if about to charge, came up with a couple of long strides and joined it. A sudden excitement ran quivering over the entire host; the distant ranks moved in a new, unpleasant way; a thousand heads were lifted, ears were pricked, a forest of ugly muzzles pointed up to the wind. And the Englishman, beside himself suddenly with a sense of ultimate terror that saw no possible escape, stiffened and stood rigid. The horror of his position petrified him. Motionless and silent he faced the awful army of his enemies, while the white light of breaking day added fresh ghastliness to the scene which was the setting for his cruel death in the Valley of the Beasts.

Above him crouched the hideous lynx, ready to spring the instant he sought safety in the tree; above it again, he was aware of a thousand talons of steel, fierce hooked beaks of iron, and the angry beating of prodigious wings.

He reeled, for the grizzly touched his body with its outstretched paw; the wolf crouched just before its deadly spring; in another second, he would have been torn to pieces, crushed, devoured, when terror, operating naturally as ever, released the muscles of his throat and tongue. He shouted with what he believed was his last breath on earth. He called aloud in his frenzy. It was a prayer to whatever gods there be, it was an anguished cry for help to heaven.

'Ishtot! Great Ishtot, help me!' his voice rang out, while his hand still clutched the forgotten totem stick.

And the Red Heaven heard him.

Grimwood that same instant was aware of a presence that, but for his terror of the beasts, must have frightened him into sheer unconsciousness. A gigantic Red Indian stood before him. Yet, while the figure rose close in front of him, causing the birds to settle and the wild animals to crouch quietly where they stood, it rose also from a great distance, for it seemed to fill the entire valley with its influence, its power, its amazing majesty. In some way, moreover, that he could not understand, its vast appearance included the actual valley itself with all its trees, its running streams, its open spaces and its rocky bluffs. These marked its outline, as it were, the outline of a superhuman shape. There was a mighty bow, there was a quiver of enormous arrows, there was this Redskin figure to whom they belonged.

Yet the appearance, the outline, the face and figure too—these *were* the valley; and when the voice became audible, it was the valley itself that uttered the appalling words. It was the voice of trees and wind, and of running, falling water that woke the echoes in the Valley of the Beasts, as, in that same moment, the sun topped the ridge and filled the scene, the outline of the majestic figure too, with a flood of dazzling light:

'You have shed blood in this my valley... *I will not save*...!'

The figure melted away into the sunlit forest, merging with the new-born day. But Grimwood saw close against his face the shining teeth, hot fetid breath passed over his cheeks, a power enveloped his whole body as though a mountain crushed him. He closed his eyes. He fell. A sharp, crackling sound passed through his brain, but already unconscious, he did not hear it.

* * *

His eyes opened again, and the first thing they took in was fire. He shrank back instinctively.

'It's all right, old man. We'll bring you round. Nothing to be frightened about.' He saw the face of Iredale looking down into his own. Behind Iredale stood Tooshalli. His face was swollen. Grimwood remembered the blow. The big man began to cry.

'Painful still, is it?' Iredale said sympathetically. 'Here, swallow a little more of this. It'll set you right in no time.'

Grimwood gulped down the spirit. He made a violent effort to control himself, but was unable to keep the tears back. He felt no pain. It was his heart that ached, though why or wherefore, he had no idea.

'I'm all to pieces,' he mumbled, ashamed yet somehow not ashamed. 'My nerves are rotten. What's happened?' There was as yet no memory in him.

'You've been hugged by a bear, old man. But no bones broken. Tooshalli saved you. He fired in the nick of time—a brave shot, for he might easily have hit you instead of the brute.'

'The other brute,' whispered Grimwood, as the whisky worked in him and memory came slowly back.

'Where are we?' he asked presently, looking about him.

He saw a lake, canoes drawn up on the shore, two tents, and figures moving. Iredale explained matters briefly, then left him to sleep a bit. Tooshalli, it appeared, travelling without rest, had reached Iredale's camping ground twenty-four hours after leaving his employer. He found it deserted, Iredale and his Indian being on the hunt. When they returned at nightfall, he had explained his presence in his brief native fashion: 'He struck me and I quit. He hunt now alone in Ishtot's Valley of the Beasts. He is dead, I think. I come to tell you.'

Iredale and his guide, with Tooshalli as leader, started off then and there, but Grimwood had covered a considerable distance, though leaving an easy track to follow. It was the moose tracks and the blood that chiefly guided them. They came up with him suddenly enough—in the grip of an enormous bear.

It was Tooshalli that fired.

* * *

The Indian lives now in easy circumstances, all his needs cared for, while Grimwood, his benefactor but no longer his employer, had given up hunting. He is a quiet, easy-tempered, almost gentle sort of fellow, and people wonder rather why he hasn't married. 'Just the fellow to make a good father,' is what they say; 'so kind, good-natured and affectionate.' Among his pipes, in a glass case over the mantelpiece, hangs a totem stick. He declares it saved his soul, but what he means by the expression he has never quite explained.

THE SOUTH WIND

It is impossible to say through which sense, or combination of senses, I knew that Someone was approaching—was already near; but most probably it was the deep underlying 'mother-sense' including them all that conveyed the delicate warning. At any rate, the scene-shifters of my moods knew it too, for very swiftly they prepared the stage; then, ever soft-footed and invisible, stood aside to wait.

As I went down the village street on my way to bed after midnight, the high Alpine valley lay silent in its frozen stillness. For days it had now lain thus, even the mouths of its cataracts stopped with ice; and for days, too, the dry, tight cold had drawn up the nerves of the humans in it to a sharp, thin pitch of exhilaration that at last began to call for the gentler comfort of relaxation. The key had been a little too high, the inner tautness too prolonged. The tension of that implacable north-east wind, the *bise noire,* had drawn its twisted wires too long through our very entrails. We all sighed for some loosening of the bands—the comforting touch of something damp, soft, less penetratingly acute.

And now, as I turned, midway in the little journey from the inn to my room above La Poste, this sudden warning that Someone was approaching repeated its silent wireless message, and I paused to listen and to watch.

Yet at first I searched in vain. The village street lay empty—a white ribbon between the black walls of the big-roofed chalets; there were no lights in any of the houses; the hotels stood gaunt and ugly with their myriad shuttered windows; and the church, topped by the Crown of Savoy in stone, was so engulfed by the shadows of the mountains that it seemed almost a part of them.

Beyond, reared the immense buttresses of the Dent du Midi, terrible and stalwart against the sky, their feet resting among the crowding pines, their streaked precipices tilting up at violent angles towards the stars. The bands of snow, belting their enormous flanks, stretched for miles, faintly gleaming, like Saturn's rings. To the right I could just make out the pinnacles of the Dents Blanches, cruelly pointed; and, still farther, the Dent de Bonnaveau, as of iron and crystal, running up its gaunt and dreadful pyramid into relentless depths of night. Everywhere in the hard, black sparkling air was the rigid spell of winter. It seemed as if this valley could never melt again, never know currents of warm wind, never taste the sun, nor yield its million flowers.

And now, dipping down behind me out of the reaches of the darkness, the New Comer moved close, heralded by this subtle yet compelling admonition that had arrested me in my very tracks. For, just as I turned in at the door, kicking the crunched snow from my boots against the granite step, I *knew* that, from the heart of all this tightly frozen winter's night, the 'Someone' whose message had travelled so delicately in advance was now, quite suddenly, at my very heels. And while my eyes lifted to sift their way between the darkness and the snow I became aware that It was already coming down the village street. It ran on feathered feet, pressing close against the enclosing walls, yet at the same time spreading from side to side, brushing the windowpanes, rustling against the doors, and even including the shingled roofs in its enveloping advent. It came, too—*against the wind*...

It flew up close and passed me, very faintly singing, running down between the chalets and the church, very swift, very soft, neither man nor animal, neither woman, girl, nor child, turning the corner of the snowy road beyond the *Curé's* house with a rushing cantering motion, that made me think of a Body of water —something of fluid and generous shape, too mighty to be confined in common forms. And, as it passed, is touched me— touched me through all skin and flesh upon the naked nerves, loosening, relieving, setting free the congealed sources of life which the *bise* so long had mercilessly bound, so that magic currents, flowing and released, washed down all the secret byways of the spirit and flooded again with full tide into a thousand dried-up cisterns of the heart.

The thrill I experienced is quite incommunicable in words. I ran upstairs and opened all my windows wide, knowing that soon the Messenger would return with a million others—only to find that already it had been there before me. Its taste was in the air, fragrant and alive; in my very mouth—and all the currents of the inner life ran sweet again, and full. Nothing in the whole village was quite the same as it had been before. The deeply slumbering peasants, even behind their shuttered windows and barred doors; the *Curé*, the servants at the inn, the consumptive man opposite, the children in the house behind the church, the horde of tourists in the caravanserai—all knew— more or less, according to the delicacy of their receiving apparatus—that Something charged with fresh and living force ha swept on viewless feet down the village street, passed noiselessly between the cracks of doors and windows, touched nerves and eyelids, and—set them free. In response to the great Order of Release that the messenger had left everywhere behind her, even the dreams of the sleepers had shifted into softer and more flowing keys...

And the Valley—the Valley also knew! For, as I watched from my window, something loosened about the trees and stones and boulders; about the massed snows on the great slopes; about the roots of the hanging icicles that fringed and sheeted the dark cliffs; and down in the deepest beds of the killed and silent streams. Far overhead, across those desolate bleak shoulders of the mountains, ran some sudden softness like the rush of awakening life... and was gone. A touch, lithe yet dewy, as of silk and water mixed, dropped softly over all... and, silently, without resistance, the *bise noire,* utterly routed, went back to the icy caverns of the north and east, where it sleeps, hated of men, and dreams its keen black dreams of death and desolation...

... And some five hours later, when I woke and looked

towards the sunrise, I saw those strips of pearly grey, just tinged with red, the Messenger had been to summon... charged with the warm moisture that brings relief. On the wings of a rising South Wind they came down hurriedly to cap the mountains and to unbind the captive forces of life; then moved with flying streamers up our own valley, sponging from the thirsty woods their richest perfume...

And farther down, in soft, wet fields, stood the leafless poplars, with little pools of water gemming the grass between and pouring their musical overflow through runnels of dark and sodden leaves to join the rapidly increasing torrents descending from the mountains. For across the entire valley ran magically that sweet and welcome message of relief which Job knew when he put the whole delicious tenderness and passion of it into less than a dozen words: '*He comforteth the earth with the south wind.*'

THE MAN WHO WAS MILLIGAN

Milligan looked round the dingy rooms with an appraising air, while the landlady stood behind him, wondering whether he would decide to take them. She stood with her arms crossed; her eye was observant. She, in her turn, was appraising Milligan, of course. He was a clerk in a tourist agency, and in his spare time he wrote stories for the cinema. What attracted him just now in the very ordinary lodgings was the big folding-doors. All he really needed was a bed-sitting-room, with breakfast, but he suddenly saw himself sitting in that front room writing his scenarios—successfuly at last. It was rather tempting. He would be a literary man—with a study! 'Your price seems a trifle high, Mrs.—er—?' he opened the bargain.

'Bostock, sir, Mrs. Bostock,' she informed him, then recited her tale of woe about the high cost of living. It was an unnecessary recitation, for Milligan was not listening, having already decided in his mind to take the rooms.

While Mrs. Bostock droned monotonously on, his eye fell casually upon a picture that hung above the plush mantelpiece—a Chinese scene showing a man in a boat upon a little lake. He glanced at it, no more than that. It was better than glancing at Mrs. Bostock. The landlady, however, instantly caught that glance and noticed its direction.

'Me'usband'—she switched off her main theme—'brought it 'ome from China. From Hong-Kong, I *should* say.' And the way she aspirated the 'H' in Hong made Milligan smile. He perceived that she was proud of the picture evidently.

'It's wonderful,' he said. 'Probably it's worth something, too, These Chinese drawings—some of 'em—are very rare, I believe.'

The little picture was worth perhaps two shillings, and he knew it; but he had found his way to Mrs. Bostock's heart, and, incidentally, had persuaded her to take a shilling off the rent.

THE MAN WHO WAS MILLIGAN

The picture, he felt sure, had been stolen by her late husband, a sea captain. To her it was a kind of nest-egg. If she ever found herself in difficulties, it would fetch money. Milligan, by chance, had stumbled upon what he called a 'good line'.

Being an honest creature, he had no wish to use his knowledge, but every week thereafter, almost every day, indeed, some remark concerning the Chinese drawing passed between them; with the natural result that, while it bored him a good deal, he cultivated the theme, and in so doing gazed much and often at the Chinaman. That Celestial, sitting in the boat with his back to the room, rowing, rowing eternally across the placid lake without advancing, he came to know in every detail.

Every time Mrs. Bostock chatted with him, his eye wandered from her grimy visage to the drawing. He used it to end the chat with.

'I like your picture so much,' he observed. 'It's nice to live with.' He put it straight, he flicked dust from the frame with his handkerchief. 'It's so much better than these modern things. It's worth a bit—I dare say——'

It chanced, at the time, that Lafcadio Hearn, the writer about Japan, was in his mind. He had once arranged a successful trip to Japan for a client of his firm, and the client had made him a present of one of Hearn's strange and wonderful books. It was hardly in the line of Milligan's reading, for it had no 'film value', and he had sold the book—a collection of Chinese stories—to a secondhand bookseller for a shilling. But he had glanced at it first, and a story in it had remained sharply in his mind: a story about a picture of a man in a boat. An observer, watching the picture, had seen the man move. The man actually began to row. Finally, the man rowed right out of the picture and into the place—a temple—where the observer stood.

Milligan thought it foolish, yet his memory retained the details vividly. They stuck in his head. The graphic description was realistic. Milligan caught himself thinking of it every time he met a Chinaman in the street, every time he sold a ticket to China or Japan. It rose, it flitted by, it vanished. The memory persisted. And the moment his eye first saw Mrs. Bostock's treasure over the plush mantelpiece, this vivid memory of Hearn's story had again risen, flitted by, and vanished. It betrayed its vitality, at any rate. Wonderful chap, that Hearn, thought Milligan.

All this was natural enough, without mystery, without a hint of anything queer or out of the ordinary. What was a little queer—it struck Milligan so, at any rate—was an idea that began to grow in him from the very first week of his tenancy.

'That *might* be the very drawing the fellow wrote about,' occurred to him one night as he laboured at a lurid scenario which was to make his fortune. 'Not impossible at all. It's an old picture probably. Exactly what Hearn described, too. I wonder! Why not?'

Why not, indeed? A fellow—especially a literary fellow—should use his imagination. Milligan used his. Sometimes he used it in prolonged labour till the early hours. The gas-light flickered across his pages, across that lake in China, across the boat, across the back and arms and pigtail of that diminutive Ching who rowed eternally over a placid Chinese lake without advancing an inch. The scenario of the moment brought in China, aptly enough. A glance at the picture, he found, was not unhelpful in the way of stimulating a flagging imagination.

Milligan glanced often. The gas-light was always flickering. Shadows were for ever shifting to and fro across Mrs. Bostock's worthless nest-egg. It was easy to imagine that the boat, the water, even the figure moved. Those dancing shadows! How they played about the arms, the back, the outline of the boat, the oars!

And when it was two in the morning, and the London streets lay hushed, and a great stillness blanketed the whole city, Milligan felt even a little thrilled. It was, he thought, 'imaginative', to catch these slight, elusive movements in the drawing. He imagined the fellow rowing about, changing his position, landing. It helped his own mood, his incidents, his atmosphere. He had read Thomas Burke, of course. His scenarios always referred to Chinamen as 'Chinks'.

THE MAN WHO WAS MILLIGAN

'That Chink's alive!' he whispered to himself. 'By Jove! He moves in the picture. His place changes. It's an inspiration. I must use it somehow——!' And imagination, eerily stimulated in the deep silence of the sleeping city, was at work again.

This was the beginning of the strange adventure which befell the literary Milligan, whose imagination worked in the stillness of the small hours, but whose scenarios were never used.

'For why write scenarios,' he said to me, 'when you can *live* them?'

In Peking, ten or twelve years later, he said this to me, and I am probably the only person to whom this scenario he 'lived' was ever confided.

In Peking his name was not Milligan at all. He was not working in a tourist agency. He was a rich man, aged thirty-eight, a 'figure' in the English community there, a man of influence and position. But all that does not matter. What matters is the story of how he came to be in China at all—and this he does not know. He does not know how he came to be in China at all. There is no recollection of the journey even. Nor can he state precisely how he began the speculations and enterprises that made him prosperous, beyond that he suddenly found himself concerned in big, fortunate undertakings in the Chinese city.

There is this deep gap in the years.

'Loss of memory, I suppose they call it,' he mentioned, after our chance acquaintanceship had grown into a friendship that gave me his confidence. What he *could* tell he told me frankly and without reserve, glad to talk of it, I think, to someone who did not mock, and making no condition of secrecy, moreover.

There was some link, apparently, between myself and the man who had been Milligan. Chance, that some call destiny, revealed it. And, as I listened to his amazing tale, I swore that on my return to London I would visit Mrs. Bostock and buy the picture. I wanted that Chinese drawing badly. I wanted to examine it myself. Her nest-egg at last should be worth something, as Milligan, ten years before, had told her.

What happened was, apparently, as follows: Milligan, first of all, discovered in himself, somewhat suddenly it seemed, a new interest in China and things Chinese. If the birth of this interest was abrupt, its growth was extremely rapid. China fairly leapt at him. He read books, talked with travellers, studied the map, the history, the civilisation of China. The psychology of the Celestial race absorbed him. The subject obsessed him. He longed to go to China. It became a yearning that left him no peace day or night. In practical terms of time, money and opportunity, the journey was, of course, impossible. He lived on in London, but actually he lived already in China, for where a man's thought is there shall his consciousness be also.

All this I could readily understand, for others, similarly, have felt the call and spell of countries like Egypt, Africa, the desert. There was nothing incomprehensible nor peculiar in the fascination China exercised upon the imaginative Milligan. It was his business, moreover, to sell exciting tickets to travellers, and China happened to have fired his particular temperament. Natural enough!

Natural enough, too, that, through this, the picture in his lodgings should have acquired more meaning for him, and that he should have studied it more closely and more frequently. It was the only Chinese object he had within constant reach, and he told me at wearisome length how he knew every tiniest detail of the drawing, and how it became for him a kind of symbol, almost a kind of sacred symbol, upon which he focussed his intense desires—frustrated desires. Wearisome, yes, until he reached a point in his story that suddenly galvanised my interest, so that I began to listen with uncommon, if a rather creepy, curiosity.

The picture, he informed me, altered. There was movement among its details that he already knew by heart.

'*Movement!*' he half-whispered to me, his eyes shining, a faint shudder running through his big body.

The sincerity of deep conviction with which he described what happened left a lasting impression on my mind. His words, his manner, conveyed the truth of a genuine experience. Hitherto only the back of the Chink's head had been visible. Then, one night, Milligan saw his profile. The face was turned. It now looked a little over the shoulder, and towards the room.

From this moment, though he never detected actual movement when it occurred, the alteration in the drawing was marked and rapid. The face retained its new position; the angle of the profile did not widen, but the position of oars and boat, the attitude of arms and back, their size as well, these now changed from day to day.

There was a dreadful rapidity about these changes. The figure of the Chink grew bigger; the boat grew bigger too. They were coming nearer. 'I had the awful conviction,' whispered the man who had been Milligan, 'that they were coming—to fetch me. I used to get all of a sweat each time I saw the size and nearness grow. It was appalling, but also it was delightful somehow——'

I permitted myself a question: 'Did your landlady notice it too?' I enquired, concealing my scepticism.

'Mrs. Bostock was ill in bed the whole time. She never came into the room once.'

'The servant?' I persisted. 'Or any of your friends?'

He hesitated. 'The girl who did the room,' he said honestly, 'observed nothing. She gave notice suddenly without a reason. So did the next girl. I never asked them anything. As for my friends'—he smiled faintly—'I was too scared—to bring them in.'

'You were afraid they might *not* see what you saw?'

He shrugged his shoulders. 'It scared me,' he repeated, looking past me towards the shuttered windows of his study where we sat.

The account he gave of it all made my flesh creep even in that bright Peking sunshine. He certainly described what he saw, or believed he saw, as, day after day, night after night, that Chink rowed his boat slowly, slowly, surely, surely, very gradually, but with remorseless purpose, nearer, nearer—and nearer. The lodger watched. He also waited.

'The man,' he whispered, 'was rowing into the room. It was his purpose to row into the room. He was *coming to fetch me.*' And he mopped his forehead at the thought of what had happened ten years ago.

Suddenly he leant forward.

'In the end,' his thin voice rattled almost against my face, 'he —did fetch me. I'm in that picture with him now. I'm not in China, as *you* think I am. This'—he tapped his chest, the chest of a successful business man—'is not me. I'm not Milligan. Milligan is in that picture with the Chink. He's in that boat. Sitting beside that Chink. Motionless. Being stared at by a succession of lodgers. Sitting in that stiff little boat. Very tiny. Not dead, but captive. Sitting without breath. Without feeling. Painted, yet alive. Caught on the surface of that placid Chinese lake until time or death dissolve the drawing——'

I thought he was going to faint, but, oddly enough, I did *not* think him merely mad. His mood, his crawling horror, his intense sincerity took me bodily into his own deep nightmare. He recovered quickly. He was a man who had himself always well in hand. He told me the end at once.

He had been to a dance and he came home tired, sober, having well enjoyed himself, it seems, about four in the morning. The time was early spring, and dawn was just giving faint signs of breaking, but the hall and passage of the house were still dark.

He entered his room and lit the gas, going at once to the mirror to have a look at himself. This was the first thing he did, he assured me, and in the mirror he saw, behind himself, the boat and the Chinaman, both of them—gigantic.

Gigantic was the word he used, though he used it, of course, relatively. The Chinaman was standing in the room. He was in the lake in front of the plush mantelpiece. The wall was gone—there was a sort of hazy space. Close at the Chinaman's heels lay the boat, both oars resting sideways on the water, their heads still in the rowlocks. Water was up to his feet, to Milligan's feet, for he not only felt his shoes soaked through, but he also heard the lapping sound of diminutive wavelets on the 'shore'.

He gave a great sigh. No cry, either of terror or surprise, he said, escaped him. His only sound was this great sigh—of acceptance, of resignation, of a mind benumbed and yet secretly delighted. The big Chink beckoned, smiled, nodded his yellow face, retreating very slowly as he did so. And Milligan obeyed. He followed. He stepped into the boat. The Chink took up the oars, and rowed him slowly, very slowly, across the placid lake, into the picture and out of his familiar, known surroundings, rowed him slowly, very slowly, into the land of his heart's deep desire.

* * *

All the way home to England in the steamer this strangest of strange narratives haunted me. I still saw the man who was Milligan sitting in the study of his big, expensive house as he told it to me. His shrewd business brain had built that house; the fortune he had made provided the good lunch and cigars we had enjoyed together. From the moment of entering the boat his memory had remained a blank. Continuity of personality though still, it seemed to me, rather uncertain somewhere, had revived only when he was already a rich man who had spent years in China. This big gap in the years remains.

In my mind lay every detail of the story; in my pocket-book lay the address of Mrs. Bostock's rooms. I prayed heaven she might still be living, even if aged and crumpled by ten more English winters.

I had arranged to cable 'Milligan' at once; we had selected the very words I was to use: 'Two figures in boat,' or 'One figure in boat.' He asked for the message in these words. Fortune favoured me; I found the rooms; Mrs. Bostock was alive; the rooms were unoccupied; I looked over them; I saw—the picture.

Before visiting Mrs. Bostock's however, I had visited the newspaper files in the British Museum, and the 'Disappearance of James Milligan' was there for all to read. Millions had evidently read it. It had been *the* news of the day. Columns of space were devoted to it; dozens of false clues were started; crime was suggested, of course. His disappearance was complete. Milligan was a case of 'sunk without trace', with a vengeance.

It was in the dingy front room that I experienced what was perhaps the most vivid thrill of wonder life has ever given me. I stood, appraising the room as a would-be lodger. Behind me, her arms crossed, appraising me in turn just as she had appraised her former lodger of ten years ago, stood Mrs. Bostock. Probably I looked more prosperous than he had looked; her attitude, at any rate, was attentive to a fault. Why I should have trembled a little is hard to say, but self-control was certainly not as full as it might hade been, for my voice shook a trifle as, at length, I drew her attention with calculated purpose to the picture above the plush mantelpiece. I praised it.

'Me 'usband brought it back from Hong-Kong,' I heard her say.

My breath caught a little, so that there was a slight pause before I said the next thing. My voice went slightly husky.

'I have a collection of Chinese drawings,' I mentioned. 'If you cared to sell, perhaps——'

'Oh, many 'as wanted to buy it,' she lied easily, hoping to increase its value.

I mentioned five pounds. I mentioned another figure too—the figure in the boat.

'That single figure,' I explained in as calm a tone as I could muster, 'is so good, you see. The Chinese artists never overcrowded their paintings. Now, if—instead of that single figure—there were two'—I moved closer to the picture, hoping she would follow—'the value,' I went on, 'would, of course, be less.'

Mrs. Bostock had followed me. I had tempted her greed; I had tested her truth as well. We stood side by side immediately beneath the drawing. We examined it together.

At the mention of five pounds the woman had given a little gasp, jerking her body at the same time. Now, at such close quarters with the thing she hoped to sell me, her voice was dumb at first. At first. For a moment later a strange sound escaped her lips, a sound that was meant to be a cry, but only succeeded in being a wheezy struggle to get her breath. Her mouth opened wide, her eyes popped almost from her face. She staggered, recovered her balance by putting a hand on my arm for support, she stepped still nearer to the mantelpiece and thrust her head and shoulders close against the drawing. Her blind eyes peered. Her skin was already white.

'Two of 'em!' she exclaimed in a terrified whisper. 'Two of 'em, so 'elp me, Gawd! And the other's *him*!'

I was ready to support. I had expected her to collapse perhaps. I felt rather like collapsing myself. She swayed, turning her horror-stricken countenance to mine.

'Mr. Milligan!' she screamed aloud, then, her voice returning in full volume: 'It's Mr. Milligan. All this time that's where 'e's been. And I never noticed it till now!'

She swooned away.

The second figure faced the room, for the boat was in the position of being pushed by the oars, not rowed. The features were unmistakable. ... Half an hour later I sent a cable to Peking: '*Two figures in boat.*'

The real climax, I think, came three days later, when, with the picture safely in my rooms, I had arranged for 'specialists' to call and examine it. A chemist, an experienced dealer, and a sort of expert psychic investigator were already upstairs when I reached my flat.

The picture was in my bedroom. I had examined it myself—examined Milligan's face and figure—hour after hour, my flesh crawling, my hair almost rising, as I did so. My guests were in the sitting-room, the servant informed me, handing me a telegram as I hurried up in the lift. My three friends were already known to each other, and, after apologising for the delay, I brought in the drawing and laid it before them on the small table. I intended to tell them the story after their examination; the psychic investigator I meant to keep when the other two had left. Setting the drawing in front of them, I looked over their shoulders at it.

There was only one figure—the Chink. He sat alone in the little boat. He was rowing, not pushing; his back was to the room.

The dealer said the drawing was worth a shilling; the chemist said nothing; I, too, said nothing; but the psychic investigator turned sharply and complained that I was hurting him. My hand, it seems, had clutched the shoulder nearest to me, and it happened to be his. I allowed him to leave when the other two left. ...

I was alone. I remembered the telegram. More to steady my mind than for any interest I felt in it, my fingers tore it open. It was a cablegram from—Peking, signed by a friend of Milligan and myself:

'Milligan died heart failure yesterday.'

THE TROD

Young Norman was being whirled in one of the newest streamlined expresses towards the north. He leaned back in his first-class Smoker and lit a cigarette. On the rack in front of him was his gun-case with the pair of guns he never willingly allowed out of his sight, his magazine with over a thousand cartridges beside it, and the rest of his luggage, he knew, was safely in the van. He was looking forward to a really good week's shooting at Greystones, one of the best moors in England.

He realised that he was uncommonly lucky to have been invited at all. Yet a question mark lay in him. Why precisely, he wondered, had he been asked? For one thing, he knew his host, Sir Hiram Digby, very slightly. He had met him once or twice at various shoots in Norfolk, and while he had acquitted himself well when standing near him, he could not honestly think this was the reason for the invitation. There had been too many good shots present, and far better shots, for him to have been specially picked out. There was another reason, he was certain. His thoughts, as he puffed his cigarette reflectively, turned easily enough in another direction—towards Diana Travers, Sir Hiram Digby's niece.

The wish, he remembered, is often father to the thought, yet he clung to it obstinately, and with lingering enjoyment. It was Diana Travers who had suggested his name; it well might be, it probably was, and the more he thought it over, the more positive he felt. It explained the invitation, at any rate.

A curious thrill of excitement and delight ran through him as memory went backwards and played about her. A curious being, he saw her, quite unlike the usual run of girls, but curious, in the way that he himself perhaps was curious, for he was just old enough to have discovered that he was curious, standing apart somehow from the young men of his age and station.

Well born, rich, sporting and all the rest, he yet did not quite belong to his time in certain ways. He could drink, revel, go wild, enjoy himself with his companions, but up to a point only—when he withdrew unsatisfied. There were 'other things' that claimed him with some terrible inner power; and the two could not mix. These other things he could not quite explain even to himself, but to his boon companions—never. Were they things of the spirit? He could not say. Wild, pagan things belonging to an older day. He knew not. They were of unspeakable loveliness and power, drawing him away from ordinary modern life—*that* he knew. He could not define them to himself, much less speak of them to others.

And then he met Diana Travers and knew, though he did not dare put his discovery into actual words, that she felt something similar.

He came across her first at a dance in town, he remembered, remembering also how bored he had been until the casual introduction, and after it, how happy, enchanted, satisfied. It was assuredly not that he had fallen suddenly in love, nor that she was wildly beautiful—a tall, fair girl with a radiant, yet not lovely face, soft voice, graceful movements—for there were thousands, Norman knew, who excelled her in all these qualities. No, it was not the usual love attack, the mating fever, the herd-instinct that she might be *his* girl, but the old conviction, rather, that there lay concealed in her the same nameless, mysterious longings that lay also in himsel—the terrible and lovely power that drew him from his human kind towards unknown 'other things'.

As they stood together on the balcony, where they had escaped from the heat and clamour of the ball-room, he acknowledged to himself, yet without utterance, this overpowering, strange conviction that their fates were in some way linked together. He could not explain it at the time, he could not explain it now—while he thought it over in the railway carriage, and his conscious mind rejected it as imagination. Yet it remained. Their talk, indeed, had been ordinary enough, nor was he conscious of the slightest desire to flirt or make love; it was just that, as the saying is, they 'clicked' and that each felt delightfully easy in the other's company, happy and at home. It was almost, he reflected, as though they shared some rather wonderful deep secret that had no need of words, a secret that lay, indeed, beyond the reach of words altogether.

They had met several times since, and on each occasion he had been aware of the same feeling; and once when he ran across her by chance in the park they walked together for over an hour and she had talked more freely. Talked suddenly about herself, moreover, openly and naturally, as though she knew he would understand. In the open air, it struck him, she was more spontaneous than in the artificial surroundings of walls and furniture. It was not so much that she said anything significant, but rather the voice and manner and gestures that she used.

She had been admitting how she disliked London and all its works, loathing especially the Season with its glittering routine of so-called gaiety, adding that she always longed to get back to Marston, Sir Hiram's place in Essex. 'There are the marshes,' she said, with quiet enthusiasm, 'and the sea, and I go with my uncle duck-flighting in the twilight, or in the dawn when the sun comes up like a red ball out of the sea, and the mists over the marshes drift away ... and things, you know, may happen...'

He had been watching her movements with admiration as she spoke, thinking the name of huntress was well chosen, and now there was a note of strange passion in her voice that he heard for the first time. Her whole being, moreover, conveyed the sense that he would understand some emotional yearning in her that her actual words omitted.

He stopped and stared at her.

'That's to be alive,' she added with a laugh that made her eyes shine. 'The wind and the rain blowing in your face and the ducks streaming by. You feel yourself part of nature. Gates open, as it were. It was how we were meant to live, I'm sure.'

Such phrases from any other girl must have made him feel shy and embarrassed, from her they were merely natural and true. He had not taken her up, however, beyond confessing that he agreed with her, and the conversation had passed on to other things. Yet the reason he had not become enthusiastic or taken up the little clue she offered, was because his inmost heart knew what she meant.

Her confession, not striking in itself, concealed, while it revealed, a whole region of significant, mysterious 'other things' best left alone in words. 'You and I think alike,' was what she had really said. 'You and I share this strange, unearthly longing, only for God's sake, don't let us talk about it...!'

'A queer girl, anyhow,' he now smiled to himself, as the train rushed northwards, and then asked himself what exactly he knew about her? Very little, practically nothing, beyond that, both parents being dead, she lived with her elderly bachelor uncle and was doing the London Season. 'A thoroughbred anyhow,' he told himself, 'lovely as a nymph into the bargain...' and his thoughts went dreaming rather foolishly. Then suddenly, as he lit another cigarette, a much more definite thought emerged. It gave him something of a start, for it sprang up abruptly out of his mood of reverie in the way that a true judgment sometimes leaps to recognition in the state between sleeping and waking.

'She *knows*. Knows about these other lovely and mysterious things that have always haunted me. She has—yes, experienced them. She can explain them to me. She wants to share them with me. ...'

Norman sat up with a jerk, as though something had scared him. He had been dreaming, these ideas were the phantasmagoria of a dream. Yet his heart, he noticed, was beating rather rapidly, as though a deep inner excitement had touched him in his condition of half-dream.

He looked up at his gun-cases and cartridges in the rack, then shaded his eyes and gazed out of the window. The train was doing at least sixty. The character of the country it rushed through was changing. The hedges of the midlands had gone, and stone walls were beginning to take their place. The country was getting wilder, lonelier, less inhabited. He drew unconsciously a deep breath of satisfaction. He must actually have slept for a considerable time, he realised, for his watch told him that in a few minutes he would reach the junction where he had to change. Bracendale, the local station for Greystones, he remembered, was on a little branch line that wandered away among the hills. And some fifteen minutes later he found himself, luggage and all, in the creaky, grunting train that would land him at Bracendale towards five o'clock. The dusk had fallen when, with great effort apparently, the struggling engine deposited him with his precious guns and cartridges on the deserted platform amid swirling mists a damp wind prepared for his reception. To his considerable relief a car was there to carry him the remaining ten miles to the Lodge, and he was soon comfortably installed among its luxurious rugs for the drive across the hills.

He settled back comfortably to enjoy the keen mountain air.

After leaving the station, the car followed a road up a narrow valley for a time; a small beck fell tumbling from the hills on the left, where occasionally dark plantations of fir trooped down to the side of the road; but what struck him chiefly was the air of desolation and loneliness that hung over all the countryside. The landscape seemed to him wilder and less inhabited even than the Scottish Highlands. Not a house, not a croft, was to be seen. A sense of desertion, due partly to the dusk no doubt, hung brooding over everything, as though human influence was not welcomed here, perhaps not possible. Bleak and inhospitable it looked certainly, though for himself this loneliness held a thrill of wild beauty that appealed to him.

A few black-faced sheep strung occasionally across the road, and once they passed a bearded shepherd hurrying downhill with his dog. They vanished into the mist like wraiths. It seemed impossible to Norman that the country could be so desolate and uninhabited when he knew that only a few score miles away lay the large manufacturing towns of Lancashire. The car, meanwhile, was steadily climbing up the valley and presently they came to more open country and passed a few scattered farmhouses with an occasional field of oats beside them.

Norman asked the chauffeur if many people lived hereabouts, and the man was clearly delighted to be spoken to.

'No, sir,' he said, 'it's a right desolate spot at the best of times, and I'm glad enough,' he added, 'when it's time for us to go back south again.' It had been a wonderful season for the grouse, and there was every promise of a record year.

Norman noticed an odd thing about the farmhouses they passed, for many of them, if not all, had a large cross carved over the lintel of the doors, and even some of the gates leading from the road into the fields had a smaller cross cut into the top bar. The car's flash-light picked them out. It reminded him of the shrines and crosses scattered over the countryside in Catholic countries abroad, but seemed a little incongruous in England. He asked the chauffeur if most of the people hereabout were Catholics, and the man's answer, given with emphasis, touched his curiosity.

'Oh, no, I don't think so,' was the reply. 'In fact, sir, if you ask me, the people round here are about as heathen as you could find in any Christian country.'

Norman drew his attention to the crosses everywhere, asking him how he accounted for them if the inhabitants were heathen, and the man hesitated a moment before replying, as though, glad to talk otherwise, the subject was not wholly to his liking.

'Well, sir,' he said at length, watching the road carefully in front of him, 'they don't tell *me* much about what they think, counting me for a foreigner like, as I come from the south. But they're a rum lot to my way of thinking. What I'm told,' he added after a further pause, 'is that they carve these crosses to protect themselves.'

'Protect themselves!' exclaimed Norman a little startled. 'Protect themselves from—what?'

THE TROD

'At, there, sir,' said the man after hesitating again, 'that's more than I can say. I've heard of a haunted house before now, but never a haunted countryside. Yet that's what they believe, I take it. It's all haunted, sir—everywhere. It's the devil of a job to get any of them to turn out after dark, as I know well, and even in the daytime they won't stir far without a crucifix hung round their nec. Even the men won't.'

The car had put on speed while he spoke and Norman had to ask him to ease up a bit; the man, he felt sure, was prey to a touch of superstitious fear as they raced along the darkening road, yet glad enough to talk, provided he was not laughed at. After his last burst of speech he had drawn a deep breath, as though glad to have got it off his chest.

'What you tell me is most interesting,' Norman commented invitingly. 'I've come across that sort of thing abroad, but never yet in England. There's something in it, you know,' he added persuasively, 'if we only knew what. I wish I knew the reason, for I'm sure it's a mistake just to laugh it all away.' He lit a cigarette, handing one also to his companion, and making him slow down while they lighted them. 'You're an observant fellow, I see,' he went on, 'and I'll be bound you've come across some queer things. I wish I had your opportunity. It interests me very much.'

'You're right, sir,' the chauffeur agreed, as they drove on again, 'and it can't be laughed away, not *all* of it. There's something about the whole place 'ere that ain't right, as you might say. It "got" me a bit when I first came 'ere some years ago, but now I'm kind of used to it.'

'I don't think I should ever get *quite* used to it,' said Norman, 'till I'd got to the bottom of it. Do tell me anything you've noticed. I'd like to know—and I'll keep it to myself.'

Feeling sure the man had interesting things to tell and having now won his confidence, he begged him to drive more slowly; he was afraid they would reach the house before there had been time to tell more, possibly even some personal experiences.

'There's a funny sort of road, or track rather, you may be

seeing out shooting,' the chauffeur went on eagerly enough, yet half nervously. 'It leads across the moor, and no man or woman will set foot on it to save their lives, not even in the daytime, let alone at night.'

Norman said eagerly that he would like to see it, asking its whereabouts, but of course the directions only puzzled him.

'You'll be seeing it, sir, one of these days out shooting and if you watch the natives, you'll find I'm telling you right.'

'What's wrong with it?' Norman asked. 'Haunted—eh?'

'That's it, sir,' the man admitted, after a longish pause. 'But a queer kind of 'aunting. They do say it's just too lovely to look at—and keep your senses.'

It was the other's turn to hesitate, for something in him trembled.

Now, young Norman was aware of two things very clearly: first, that it wasn't quite the thing to pump his host's employee in this way; second, that what the man told him held an extraordinary, almost alarming interest for him. All folk-lore interested him intensely, legends and local superstitions included. Was this, perhaps a 'fairy-ridden' stretch of country, he asked himself? Yet he was not in Ireland, where it would have been natural, but in stolid, matter-of-fact England. The chauffeur was obviously an observant, commonplace southerner, and yet he had become impressed, even a little scared, by what he had noticed. That lay beyond question: the man was relieved to talk to someone who would not laugh at him, while at the same time he was obviously a bit frightened.

A third question rose in his mind as well: this talk of haunted country, of bogies, fairies and the rest, fantastic though it was, perhaps, stirred a queer, yet delicious feeling in him—in his heart, doubtless—that his host's niece, Diana, had a link with it somewhere. The origin of a deep intuition is hardly discoverable. He made no attempt to probe it. This was Diana's country, she must know all the chauffeur hinted, and more besides. There must be something in the atmosphere that attracted her. She had been instrumental in making her uncle invite him. She wanted him to come, she wanted him to taste and share things, 'other things', that to her were vital.

These thoughts flashed across him with an elaboration of detail impossible to describe. That the wish was, again, father to the thoughts, doubtless operated, yet the conviction persistently remained and the intuitive flash provided, apparently, inspiration, so that he plied the chauffeur with further questions that produced valuable results. He referred even to the Little People, the Fairies, without exciting contempt or laughter—with the result that the man gave him finally a somewhat dangerous confidence. Solemnly warning his passenger that 'Sir Hiram mustn't hear of it' or he'd lose his job, the man described a remarkable incident that had happened, so to speak, under his own eyes. Sir Hiram's sister was lost on the moors some years ago and was never found...and the local talk and belief had it that she had been 'carried off'. Yet not carried off against her will: she had wanted to go.

'Would that be Mrs. Travers?' Norman asked.

'That's who it was, sir, exactly, seeing as 'ow you know the family. And it was the strangest disappearance that ever came *my* way.' He gave a slight shudder and, if not quite to his listener's surprise, suddenly crossed himself.

Diana's mother!

A pause followed the extraordinary story, and then, for once, Norman used words first spoken (to Horatio) to a man who had never heard them before and received them with appropriate satisfaction.

'Yes, sir,' he went on, 'and now he's got her up here for the first time since it happened years ago—in the very country where her mother was taken—and I'm told his idea is that he 'opes it will put her right—'

'Put her right?'

'I should say—cure her, sir. She's supposed to have the same—the same—' he fumbled for a word—'unbalance as wot her mother had.' A strange rush of hope and terror swept across Norman's heart and mind, but he made a great effort and denied them both, so that his companion little guessed this raging storm. Changing the subject as best he could, controlling his voice with difficulty so as to make it sound normal, he asked casually:

'Do other people—I mean, *have* other people disappeared here?'

'They do say so, sir,' was the reply. 'I've heard many a tale, though I couldn't say as I proved anything. Natives, according to the talk, 'ave disappeared, nor no trace of them ever found. Children mostly. But the people round here won't speak of it and it's difficult to find out, as they never go to the Police and keep it dark among themselves—'

'Couldn't they have fallen into potholes, or something like that?' Norman interrupted, to which the man replied that there was only one pothole in the whole district and the danger spot most carefully fenced round. 'It's the place itself, sir,' he added finally with conviction, as though he could tell of a first-hand personal experience if he dared, 'it's the whole country that's so strange.'

Norman risked the direct question.

'And what you've seen yourself, with your own eyes,' he asked, 'did it—sort of frighten you? I mean, you observe so carefully that anything you reported would be valuable.'

'Well, sir,' came the reply after a little hesitation, 'I can't say "frightened" exactly, though—if you ask me—I didn't like it. It made me feel queer all over, and I ain't a religious man—'

'Do tell me,' Norman pressed, feeling the house was now not far away and time was short. 'I shall keep it to myself—and I shall believe you. I've had odd experiences myself.'

The man needed no urging, however: he seemed glad to tell his tale.

'It's not really very much,' he said lowering his voice. 'It was like this, you see, sir. The garage and my rooms lie down at an old farmhouse about a quarter-mile from the Lodge, and from my bedroom window I can see across the moor quite a way. It takes in that trail I was speaking of before, and along that track exactly I sometimes saw lights moving in a sort of wavering line. A bit faint, they were, and sort of dancing about and going out and coming on again, and at first I took them for marsh lights—I've seen marsh lights down at our marshes at home—marsh gas we call it. That's what I thought at first, but I know better now.'

'You never went out to examine them closer?'

'No, sir, I did *not*,' came the emphatic reply.

'Or asked any of the natives what they thought?'

The chauffeur gave a curious little laugh; it was a half shy, half embarrassed laugh. Yes, he had once got a native who was willing to say something, but it was only with difficulty that Norman persuaded him to repeat it.

'Well, sir, what he told me'—again that embarrassed little laugh—'the words *he* used were "It was the Gay People changing their hunting grounds." That's what *he* said and crossed himself as he said it. They always changed their grounds at what he called the Equinox.'

'The Gay People... the Equinox. ...'

The odd phrases were not new to Norman, but he heard them now as though for the first time, they had meaning. The equinox, the solstice, he knew naturally what the words meant, but the 'Gay People' belonged to some inner phantasmagoria of his own he had hitherto thought of only imaginatively. It pertained, that is, to some private 'imaginative creed' he believed in when he had been reading Yeats, James Stephens, A.E., or when he was trying to write poetry of his own.

Now, side by side with this burly chauffeur from the sceptical South, he came up against it—bang. And he admitted frankly to himself, it gave him a half-incredible thrill of wonder, delight and passion.

'The Gay People,' he repeated, half to himself, half to the driver. 'The fellow called them *that*?'

'That's wot he called them,' repeated the matter-of-fact chauffeur. 'And they were passing,' he added, almost defiantly, as though he expected to be called a liar and deserved, it 'passing in a stream of dancing lights along the Trod.'

'The Trod,' murmured Norman under his breath.

'The Trod,' repeated the man in a whisper, 'that track I spoke of—' and the car swerved, as though the touch on the wheel was unsteady for a second, though it instantly recovered itself as they swung into the drive.

The Lodge flew past, carying a cross, Norman noticed, like all the other buildings; and a few minutes later the grey stone shooting-box, small and unpretentious, came in sight. Diana herself was on the step to welcome him, to his great delight.

'What a picture,' he thought, as he saw her in her tweeds, her retriever beside her, the hall lamp blazing on her golden hair, one hand shading her eyes. Radiant, intoxicating, delicious, unearthly—he could not find the words—and he knew in that sudden instant that he loved her far beyond all that language could express. The dark background of the grey stone building, with the dim, mysterious moors behind, was exactly right. She stood there, framed in the wonder of two worlds—his girl!

Yet her reception chilled him to the bone. Excited, bubbling over as he was, his words of pleasure ready to tumble about each other, his heart primed with fairy tales and wonder, she had nothing to say except that tea was waiting, and that she hoped he had had a good journey. Response to his own inner convulsions there was none: she was polite, genial, cordial even, but beyond that—nothing. They exchanged commonplaces and she mentioned that the grouse were plentiful, that her uncle had got some of the best 'guns' in England—which pleased his vanity for a moment—and that she hoped he would enjoy himself.

Her leaden reaction left him speechless. He felt convicted of boyish, idiotic fantasy.

'I asked particularly for you to come,' she admitted frankly, as they crossed the hall. 'I had an idea somehow you'd like to be here.'

He thanked her, but betrayed nothing of his first delight, now chilled and rendered voiceless.

THE TROD

'It's your sort of country,' she added, turning towards him with a swish of her skirts. 'At least, I think it is.'

'If *you* like it,' he returned quietly, 'I certainly shall like it too.'

She stopped a moment and looked hard at him. 'But of course I like it,' she said with conviction. 'And it's much lovelier than those Essex marshes.'

Remembering her first description of those Essex marshes, he thought of a hundred answers, but before the right one came to him he found himself in the drawing-room chatting to his hostess, Lady Digby. The rest of the house-party were still out on the moor.

'Diana will show you the garden before the darkness comes,' Lady Digby suggested presently. 'It's quite a pretty view.'

The 'pretty view' thrilled Norman with its wild beauty, for the moor beyond stretched right down to the sea at Saltbeck, and in the other direction the hills ran away, fold upon fold, into a dim blue distance. The Lodge and its garden seemed an oasis in a wilderness of primeval loveliness, unkempt and wild as when God first made it. He was aware of its intense, seductive loveliness that appealed to all the strange, unearthly side of him, but at the same time he felt the powerful, enticing human seductiveness of the girl who was showing him round. And the two conflicted violently in his soul. The conflict left him puzzled, distraught, stupid, since first one, then the other, took the upper hand. What saved him from a sudden tumultuous confession of his imagined passion, probably, was the girls' calm, almost cold, indifference. Obviously without response she felt nothing of the tumult that possessed him.

Exchanging commonplaces, they admired the 'pretty view' together, then turned back in due course to the house. 'I catch their voices,' remarked Diana. 'Let's go in and hear all about it and how many birds they got.' And it was on the door of the french window that she suddenly amazed—and, truth to tell—almost frightened him.

'Dick,' she said, using his first name, to his utter bewilderment and delight, and grasping his hand tightly in both of her own, 'I may need your help.' She spoke with a fiery intensity. Her eyes went blazing suddenly. 'It was here, you know, that mother—went. And I think—I'm certain of it—they're *after me, too*. And I don't know which is right—to go or to stay. All this'—she swept her arm to include the house, the chattering room, the garden—'is such rubbish—cheap, nasty, worthless. The other is so satisfying—its eternal loveliness, and yet—' her voice dropped to a whisper—'*soulless,* without hope or future. You may help me.' Her eyes turned upon him with a sudden amazing fire. 'That's why I asked you here.'

She kissed him on the eyes—an impersonal, passionless kiss, and the next minute they were in the room, crowded, with the 'guns' from a large shooting brake which had just arrived.

How Norman staggered in among the noisy throng and played his part as a fellow guest, he never understood. He managed it somehow, while in his heart sang the wild music of the Irish Fairy's enticing whisper: 'I kiss you and the world begins to fade.' A queer feeling came to him that he was going lost to life as he knew it, that Diana with her sweet passionless kiss had sealed his fate, that the known world must fade and die because she knew the way to another, lovelier region where nothing could ever pass or die because it was literally everlasting—the state of evolution belonging to fairyland, the land of the deathless Gay People. ...

Sir Hiram welcomed him cordially, then introduced him to the others, upon which followed the usual description by the guns of the day's sport. They drank their whiskies and sodas, in due course they went up to dress for dinner, but after dinner there was no carousing, for their host bundled them all off to an early bed. The next day they were going to shoot the best beat on the moor and clear eyes and steady hands were important. The two drives for which Greystones was celebrated were to be taken—Telegraph Hill and Silvermine—both well known wherever shooting men congregated so that anticipation and exitement were understandable. An early bed was a small

THE TROD

price to pay and Norman, keen and eager as any of them, was glad enough to get to his room when the others trooped upstairs. To be included as a crack shot among all these famous guns was, naturally, a great event to him. He longed to justify himself.

Yet his heart was heavy and dissatisfied, a strange uneasiness gnawed at him despite all his efforts to think only of the morrow's thrill. For Diana had not come down to dinner, nor had he set eyes on her the whole evening. His polite enquiry about her was met by his host's cheery laugh: 'Oh, she's all right, Norman, thank ee; she keeps to herself a bit when a shoot's on. Shooting, you see, ain't her line exactly, but she may come out with us to-morrow.' He brushed her tastes aside. 'Try and persuade her, if you can. The air'll do her good.'

Once in his room, his thoughts and emotions tried in vain to sort themselves out satisfactorily: there was a strange confusion in his mind, an uneasy sense of excitement that was half delight, half fearful anticipation, yet anticipation of he knew not exactly what. That sudden use of his familiar first name, the extraordinary kiss, establishing an unprepared intimacy, deep if passionless, had left him the entire evening in a state of hungry expectancy with nerves on edge. If only she had made an appearance at dinner, if only he could have had a further word with her! He wondered how he would ever get to sleep with this inner turmoil in his brain, and if he slept badly he would shoot badly.

It was this reflection about shooting badly that convinced him abruptly that his sudden 'love' was not of the ordinary accepted kind; had he been humanly 'in love', no consideration of that sort could have entered his head for a moment. His queer uneasiness, half mixed with delight as it was, increased. The tie was surely of another sort.

Turning out the electric light, he looked from his window across the moor, wondering if he might see the strange lights the chauffeur had told him about. He saw only the dim carpet of the rolling moorland fading into darkness where a moon hid behind fleecy, drifting clouds. A soft, sweet, fragrant air went past him; there was a murmur of falling water. It was intoxicating; he drew in a deep delicious breath. For a second he imagined a golden-haired Diana, with flying hair and flaming eyes, pursuing her lost mother midway between the silvery clouds and shadowy moor... then turned back into his room and flooded it with light... in which instant he saw something concrete lying on his pillow—a scrap of paper—no, an envelope. He tore it open.

'Always wear this when you go out. I wear one too. They cannot come up with you unless you wish, if you wear it. Mother...'

The word 'mother', full of imaginative suggestion, was crossed out; the signature was 'Diana'. With a faint musical tinkle, a little silver crucifix slipped from the pencilled note and fell to the floor.

As Norman stood beside the bed with the note in his hand, and before he stooped to recover the crucifix, there fell upon him with an amazing certainty the eerie conviction that all this had happened before. As a rule this odd sensation is too fleeting to be retained for analysis; yet he held it now for several seconds without effort. Startled, he saw quite clearly that it was not passing in ordinary time, but somewhere outside ordinary time as he knew it. It had happened 'before' because it was happening 'always'. He had caught it in the act.

For a flashing instant he understood; the crucifix symbolised security among known conditions, and if he held to it he would be protected, mentally and spiritually, against a terrific draw into unknown conditions. It meant no more than that—a support to the mind.

That antagonistic 'draw' of terrific power, involved the nameless, secret yearnings of his fundamental nature. Diana, aware of this inner conflict, shared the terror and the joy. Her mother, whence she derived the opportunity, had yielded—and had disappeared from life as humans know it. Diana herself was now tempted and afraid. She sked his help. Both he and she together, in some condition outside ordinary time, had met this conflict many times already. He had experienced all this before—the incident of the crucifix, its appeal for help, the delight, the joy, the fear involved. And even as he realised all this, the strange, eerie sensation vanished and was gone, as though it never had been. It became unseizable, lost beyond recapture. It left him with a sensation of loss, of cold, of isolation, a realisation of homelessness, yet of intense attraction towards a world unrealised.

He stooped, picked up the small silver crucifix, re-read the pencilled note letter by letter, kissed the paper that her hand had touched, then sat down on the bed and smiled with a sudden gush of human relief and happiness. The eerie sensation had gone its way beyond recovery. That Diana had thought about him was all that mattered. This little superstition about wearing the crucifix was sweet and touching, and of course he would wear the thing against his heart. And see that she came out tomorrow with him too! His relief was sincere. Now he could sleep. And tomorrow he might not shoot too badly. But before he climbed into bed, he looked in his diary to find out when the equinox was due, and found to his astonishment that it was on the 23rd of September, and that tonight was the 21st! The discovery gave him something of a turn, but he soon fell asleep with the letter against his cheek and the little silver crucifix hung round his neck.

He woke next morning when he was called to find the sun streaming into his room, promising perfect shooting weather. In broad daylight the normal reactions followed as they usually do; the incidents of the day before now seemed slightly ridiculous—his talk with Diana, the crucifix, the chauffeur's fairy-tales above all. He had stumbled upon a nest of hysterical delusions, born of a mysterious disappearance many years ago. It was natural he thought, as he shaved himself, that his host disliked all reference to the subject and its aftermath. For all that, as he went down to breakfast, he felt secretly comforted that he had hung the little silver crucifix round his neck. No one, at any rate, he reflected, could see it.

He had done full justice to the well stocked sideboard and was just finishing his coffee when Diana came into the empty room, and his mind, now charged with the prosaic prospects of the coming shoot, acknowledged a shock. Fact and imagination clashed. The girl was white and drawn. Before he could rise to greet her, she came straight across to the chair beside him.

'Dick,' she began at once, 'have you got it on?'

He produced the crucifix after a moment's fumbling.

'Of course I have,' he said. 'You asked me to wear it.' Remembering the hesitation in his bedroom, he felt rather foolish. He felt foolish anyhow, wearing a superstitious crucifix on a day's shooting.

Her next words dispelled the feeling of incongruity.

'I was out early,' she said in a tense, low voice, 'and I heard mother's voice calling me on the moor. It was unmistakeable. Close in my ear, then far away. I was with the dog and the dog heard it too and ran for shelter. His hair was up.'

'What did you hear?' Norman asked gently, taking her hand.

'My pet name—"Dis",' she told him, 'the name only mother used.'

'What words did you hear?' he asked, trembling in spite of himself.

'Quite distinctly—in that distant muffled voice—I heard her call: "Come to me, Dis, oh, come to me quickly!"'

For a moment Norman made no answer. He felt her hand trembling in his. Then he turned and looked straight into her eyes.

'Did you *want* to go?' he asked.

There was a pause before she replied. 'Dick,' she said, 'when I heard that voice, *nothing else in the world seemed to matter*—!' at which moment her uncle's figure, bursting in through the door, shouted that the cars were ready and waiting, and the conversation came to an abrupt end.

This abrupt interruption at the moment of deepest interest left

Norman, as may be imagined, excusably and dreadfully disturbed. A word from his host on this particular shooting party was, of course, a command. He dared not keep these great 'guns' waiting. Diana, too, shot out as though a bullet had hit her. But her last words went on ringing in his ears, in his heart as well: 'Nothing else in the world seemed to matter.' He understood in his deepest being what she meant. There was a 'call' away from human things, a call into some unimaginable state of bliss no words described, and she had heard it, heard it in her *mother's* voice—the strongest tie humanity knows. Her mother, having left the world, sent back a message.

Norman, trembling unaccountably, hurried to fetch his gun and join the car, and Diana, obeying the orders of her uncle, was shoved into the Ford with her retriever. She had just time to whisper to him 'Keep off the Trod—don't put a foot on it,' and the two cars whisked off and separated them.

The 'shoot' took place, nevertheless, ordinarily, so far as Norman was concerned, for the hunter's passion was too strong in him to be smothered. If his mind was mystical, his body was primitive. He was by nature a hunter before the Lord. The imaginative, mystical view of life, as with peasants and woodsmen, lay deep below, the first birds put an end to all reflection. He was soon too busy to bother about anything else but firing as fast as he could and changing his guns swiftly and smoothly. Breaking through this practical excitement, none the less, flashed swift, haunting thoughts and fancies—Diana's face and voice and eyes, her mother's supernatural call, his own secret yearnings, and, above all, her warning about the Trod. Both sides of his mixed nature operated furiously. Apparently, he shot well, but how he managed it, heaven only knew.

The drive in due course was over and the pick-up completed. Sir Hiram came over and asked if he would mind taking the outside butt at the next drive.

'You see', he explained courteously, 'I always ask the youngest of the party to take the outside, as it's a devil of a walk for the old 'uns. Probably,' he added, 'you'll get more shooting than anyone, as the birds slip away over yonder butt down a little gully. So you'll find it worth the extra swot!'

Norman and his loader set off on their long tramp, while the rest of the guns made their way down to the road where the cars would carry them as far as the track allowed. After nearly a mile's detour Norman was puzzled by his loader striking across the heather instead of following the obvious path. He himself, naturally, kept to the smooth track. He had not gone ten yards along the track before the loader's startled voice shouted at him:

'For the love of God, sir, come off! You're walking on the Trod!'

'It's a good path,' cried Norman. 'What's wrong with it?'

The man eyed him a moment. 'It's the Trod, sir,' he said gravely, as though that were enough. 'We don't walk on it—not at this time o'year especially.' He crossed himself. 'Come off it, sir, into the heather.'

The two men stood facing one another for a minute.

'If you don't believe me, sir, just watch them sheep,' said the man in a voice full of excitement and emotion. 'You'll see they won't put foot on it. Nor any other animal either.'

Norman watched a band of black-faced sheep move hesitatingly down the moorland slope. He was impatient to get on, half angry. For the moment he had forgotten all about Diana's warning. Fuming and annoyed, he watched. To his amazement, the little band of black-faced sheep, on reaching the obvious path, jumped clear over it. They jumped the Trod. Not one of them would touch it. It was an astonishing sight. Each animal leapt across, as though the Trod might burn or injure them. They went their way across the rough heather and disappeared from sight.

Norman, remembering the warning uncomfortably, paused and lit a cigarette.

'That's odd,' he said. 'It's the easiest way.'

'Maybe,' replied the loader. 'But the easiest way may not be the best—or safest.'

'The safest?'

'I've got children of me own,' said the loader.

It was a significant statement. It made Norman reflect a moment.

'Safest,' he repeated, remembering all he had heard, yet longing eagerly to hear more. 'You mean, children especially are in danger? Young folks—eh?—is that it?' A moment later, he added, 'I can quite believe it, you know, it's a queer bit of country—to my way of thinking.'

The understanding sympathy won the man's confidence, as it was meant to do.

'And it's equinox time, isn't it?' Norman ventured further.

The man responded quickly enough, finding a 'gun' who wouldn't laugh at him. As with the chauffeur, he was evidently relieved to give some kind of utterance to fears and superstitions he was at heart ashamed of and yet believed in.

'I don't mind for myself, sir,' he broke out, obviously glad to talk, 'for I'm leaving these parts as soon as the grouse shooting's over, but I've two little'uns up here just now, and I want to keep 'em. Too many young'uns get lost on the moor for my liking. I'm sending 'em tomorrow down to my aunt at Crossways—'

'Good for you,' put in Norman. 'It's the equinox just now, isn't it? And that's the dangerous time, they say.'

The loader eyed him cautiously a moment, weighing perhaps his value as a recipient of private fears, beliefs, fancies and the rest, yet deciding finally that Norman was worthy of his confidences.

'That's what my father always said,' he agreed.

'Your father? It's always wise to listen to what a father tells,' the other suggested. 'No doubt he'd seen something—worth seeing.'

A silence fell between them. Norman felt he had been, perhaps, too eager to draw the man out; yet the loader was reflecting merely. There was something he yearned to tell.

'Worth seeing,' the man repeated, 'well—that's as may be. But not of this world, and wonderful, it certainly was. It put ice into his bones, that's all I can swear to. And he wasn't the sort to be fooled easy, let me tell you. It was on his daying bed he told me—and a man doesn't lie with death in his eyes.'

That Norman was standing idly on this important shoot was sufficient proof of his tremendous interest, and the man beyond question was aware of it.

'In daylight,' Norman asked quietly, assuming the truth of what he hoped to hear.

'It was just at nightfall,' the other said, 'and he was coming from a sick friend at a farm beyond the Garage. The doctor had frightened him, I take it, so it was abit late when he started for home across the moor and, without realising that it was equinox time, he found himself on the Trod before he knew it. And, to his terror, the whole place was lit up, and he saw a column of figures moving down it towards him. They was all bright and lovely, he described 'em, gay and terrible, laughing and singing and crying, and jewels shining in their hair, and—worst of all— he swears he saw young children who had gone lost on the moor years before, and a girl he had loved these twenty years back, no older than when he saw her last, and as gay and happy and laughing as though the passing years was nothing—'

'They called to him?' asked Norman, strangely moved. 'They asked him to join them?'

'The girl did,' replied the man. 'The girl, he said, with no years to her back, drew him something terrible. "Come with us," he swears she sang to him, "come with us and be happy and young forever," and, if my father hadn't clutched hold of his crucifix in time—my God—he would have gone—'

The loader stopped, embarrassed lest he had told too much.

'If he'd gone, he'd have lost his soul,' put in Norman, guided by a horrible intuition of his own.

'That's what they say, sir,' agreed the man, obviously relieved.

Simultaneously, they hurried on, Sir Hiram's practical world breaking in upon this strange interlude. A big shoot was in progress. They must not be late at their appointed place.

'And where does the Trod start?' Norman asked presently, and the man described the little cave of the Black Waters whence the beck, dark with the peat, ran thence towards the sea across the bleak moors. The scenery provided an admirable setting for the 'fairy-tale' he had just listened to; yet his thoughts, as they ploughed forward through the heather, went back to the lovely, fascinating tale, to the superstitious dream of the 'Gay People' changing their hunting grounds along that unholy Trod when the equinox flamed with unearthly blazing, when the human young, unsatisfied with earthly pleasures, might be invited to join another ageless evolution that, if it knew no hope, shared at least an unstained, eternal, happy present. Diana's temptation, her mother's incredible disappearance, his own heart-searing yearnings in the balance to boot, took strange shape as practical possibilities.

The cumulative effect of all he had heard, from chauffeur, loader, and from the girl herself, began, it may be, to operate, sence the human mind, especially the imaginative human mind, is ever open to attack along the line of least resistance.

He stumbled on, holding his gun firmly, as though a modern weapon of destruction helped to steady his feet, to say nothing of his mind, now full of seething dreams. They reached the appointed butt. And hardly had they settled themselves in it than the first birds began to come, and all conversation was impossible. This was the celebrated 'Silvermine Drive', and Norman had never in his life seen so many grouse as he now saw. His guns got too hot to hold, yet still the grouse poured over. ...

The Drive finished in due course, and after a hurried lunch came the equally famous Telegraph Hill Drive, where there were even more birds than before, and when this came to an end Norman found that his shoulder was sore from the recoil and that he had developed a slight gun-headache, so that he was glad enough to climb into the car that took him back to the Lodge and tea. The excitement, naturally, had been great, the nervous hope that he had shot well enough to justify his inclusion in the great shoot had also played upon his vitality. He found himself exhausted, and after tea he was relieved to slip up to his bedroom for a quiet hour or two.

Lying comfortably on his sofa with a cigarette, thinking over the fire and fury of the recent hours, his thoughts turned gradually aside to other things. The hunter, it seemed, withdrew; the dreamer, never wholly submerged, re-appeared. His mind reviewed the tales he had heard from the chauffeur and the loader, while the story of Diana's mother, the strange words of the girl herself, took possession of his thoughts. Too weary to be critical, he remembered them. His own natural leaning enforced their possible truth, while fatigue made analysis too difficult to bother about, so that imagination cast its spell of glamour undefied. ... He burned to know the truth. In the end he made up his mind to creep out the following night and watch the Trod. It would be the night of the equinox. That ought to settle things one way or the other—proof or disproof. Only he must examine it in the daylight first.

It was disturbing at dinner to find that the girl was absent, had in fact, according to Sir Hiram, gone away for a day or so to see an old school-friend in a neighbouring town. She would be back, however, for the final shoot, he added, an explanation which Norman interpreted to mean that her uncle had deliberately sent her out of danger. He felt positive he was right. Sir Hiram might scorn such 'rubbishy tales', but he was taking no chances. It was at the equinox that his sister had mysteriously disappeared. The girl was best elsewhere. Nor could all the pleasant compliments about Norman's good shooting on the two Drives conceal his host's genuine uneasiness. Diana was 'best elsewhere'.

Norman fell asleep with the firm determination that he must explore the Trod next day in good light, making sure of his landmarks and then creep out at night when the household was quiet, and see what happened.

There was no shooting next day. His task was easy. Keepers and dogs went out to pick up any birds that had been left from the previous day. After breakfast he slipped off across the waste of heather and soon found it—a deep smooth groove running through occasional hollows where no water lay, nor any faintest

THE TROD

track of man or beast upon its soft, black peaty surface. Obviously, it was a track through the deep heather no one—neither man nor animal—used. He again noted the landmarks carefully, and felt sure he could find it again in the darkness... and, in due course, the day passed along its normal course, the 'guns' after dinner discussed the next day's beat, and all turned in early in pleasurable anticipation of the shoot to come.

Norman went up to bed with a beating heart, for his plan to slip out of the sleeping house later and explore the moorland with its 'haunted Trod', was not exactly what a host expected of a guest. The absence of Diana, moreover, deliberately planned, added to his deep uneasiness. Her sudden disappearance to visit 'an old school friend' was not convincing. Nor had she even left a line of explanation. It came to him that others besides the chauffeur and the loader took these fantastic fairy-tales seriously. His thoughts flew buzzing like bees outside a bee-hive...

From his window he looked out upon the night. The moon, in her second quarter, shone brightly at moments, then became hidden behind fleecy clouds. Higher up, evidently, a raging wind was driving, but below over the moorland a deathly stillness reigned. This stillness touched his nerves, and the dogs, howling in their kennels, added to a sense of superstitious uneasiness in his blood. The deep stillness seemed to hide a busy activity behind the silence. Something was stirring in the night, something out on the moor.

He turned back from the window and saw the lighted room, its cosy comfort, its well-lit luxury, its delicious bed waiting for weary limbs. He hesitated. The two sides of his nature clashed ... but in the end the strange absence of Diana, her words, her abrupt sensational kiss, her odd silence... the quixotic feeling that he *might* help—these finally decided him.

Changing quickly into his shooting clothes, and making sure that the lights in all the bedroom windows he could see were out, he crept down in stockinged feet to the front door, carrying a pair of tennis shoes in his hand. The front door was unlocked, opening without noise, so that he slipped quietly across the gravel drive on to the grass, and thence, having now put on his shoes, on to the moor beyond.

The house faded behind him, patches of silvery moonlight shone through thin racing clouds, the taste of the night air was intoxicating. How could he ever have hesitated? The wonder and mystery of the wild country-side, haunted or otherwise, caught him by the throat. As he climbed the railings leading from the cultivated garden to the moor, there came a faint odd whispering sound behind him, so that he paused and listened for a moment. Was it wind or footsteps? It was neither—merely the flap of his open coat trailing across the fence. Bah! his nerves were jumpy. He laughed—almost laughed aloud, such was the exhilaration in him—and moved on quickly through the weird half lights. And for some reason his spirits rose, his blood went racing: here was an adventure the other side of his nature delighted in, yet his 'other side' now took ominously the upper hand.

How primitive, after all, these 'shooting parties' were! For men of brains and character, the best that England could produce, to spend all this time and money, hunting as the cave-men hunted! The fox, the deer, the bird—earlier men needed these for food, yet thousands of years later the finest males of the twentieth century—sportsmen all—spent millions on superior weapons, which gave the hunted animal no chance, to bring them down. Not to be a 'sportsman' was to be an inferior Englishman...! The 'sportsman' was the flower of the race. It struck him, not for the first time, as a grim, a cheap, ideal. Was there no other climax of chivalric achievement more desirable?

This flashed across his mind as a hundred times before, while yet he himself, admittedly, was a 'sportsman' born. Against it, at the same time, rose some strange glamour of eternal, deathless things that took no account of killing, things that caught his soul away in ecstasy. Fairy tales, of course, were fairy tales, yet they enshrined the undying truths of life and human nature within their golden 'nonsense', catching at the skirts of radiant wonder, whispering ageless secrets of the soul, giving hints of ineffable glories that lay outside the normal scales of space and time as accepted by the reasoning mind. And this attitude now rose upon him like a wild ungovernable wind of spring, fragrant, delicious, intoxicating. Fairies, the Little People, the 'Gay People', happy dwellers in some non-human state...

Diana's mother had disappeared, yearning with secret, surreptitious calls for her daughter to come and join her. The girl herself acknowledged the call and was afraid, while yet her practical, hard-boiled uncle took particular trouble to keep her out of the way. Even for him, typical 'sportsman', the time of the equinox was dangerous. These reflections, tumbling about his mind and heart, flooded Norman's being, while his yearning and desire for the girl came over him like a flame.

The moor, meanwhile, easy enough to walk on in the daytime, seemed unexpectedly difficult at night, the heather longer, the ground very uneven. He was always putting his legs into little hollows that he could not see, and he was relieved when at last he could make out the loom of the garage which was one of his landmarks. He knew that he had not much further to go before he reached the Trod.

The turmoil in his mind had been such that he had paid little attention to the occasional slight sounds he heard as though somebody were at his heels, but now, on reaching the Trod, he became uneasily convinced that someone was not far behind him. So certain, indeed, was he of someone else that he let himself down silently into the deep heather and waited.

He listened intently, breathing very softly. The same instant he knew that he was right. Those sounds were not imagination. Footsteps were at his heels. The swish through the heather of a moving body was unmistakable. He caught distinct footsteps then. The footsteps came to a pause quite near to where he crouched. At which moment exactly, the clouds raced past the moon, letting down a clear space of silvery light, so that he saw the 'follower' brilliantly defined.

It was Diana.

'I knew it,' he said half aloud, 'I was sure of it long ago,' while his heart, faced with a yearning hope and fear, both half fulfilled, yet gave no leap of relief or pleasure. A shiver ran up and down his spine. Crouching there deep among the heather on the edge of the Trod, he knew more of terror than of happiness. It was all too clear for misunderstanding. She had been drawn irresistibly on the night of the equinox to the danger zone where her mother had so mysteriously 'disappeared'.

'I'm here,' he added with a great effort in the same low whisper. 'You asked my help. I'm here to meet you... dear...'

The words, even if he actually uttered them, died on his lips. The girl, he saw, stood still a moment, gazing in a dazed way, as though puzzled by something that obstructed her passage. Like a sleep walker, she stared about her, beautiful as a dream, yet only half conscious of her surroundings. Her eyes shone in the moonlight, her hands were half outstretched, yet not towards himself.

'Diana,' he heard himself crying, 'can you see me? Do you see who I am? Don't you recognise me? I've come to help—to save—you!'

It was plain she neither heard nor saw him standing there in front of her. She was aware of an obstructing presence, no more than that. Her glazed, shining eyes looked far beyond him—along the Trod. And a terror clutched him that, unless he quickly did the right thing, she would be lost to him for ever.

He sprang to his feet and went towards her, but with the extraordinary sensation that he at once came up against some intervening wall of resistance that made normal movement difficult. It was almost like forcing his way through moving water or a drift of wind, and it was with an effort that he reached her side and stood now close against her.

'Diana!' he cried, 'Dis—Dis,' using the name her mother used. 'Can't you see who I am? Don't you know me? I've come to save you—' and he stretched his hands towards her.

There was no response; she made no sign.

THE TROD

'I've come to lead you back—to lead you home—for God's sake, answer me, look into my eyes!'

She turned her head in his direction, as though to look into his face, but her eyes went past him towards the moonlit moor beyond. He noticed only, while she stared with those unseeing eyes, that her left hand fumbled weakly at a tiny crucifix that hung on a thin silver chain about her neck. He put out his hand and seized her by the arm, but the instant he touched her he found himself suddenly powerless to move. There came this strange arrest. And at the same instant, the whole Trod became startlingly lit up with a kind of unearthly radiance, and a strange greenish light shone upon the track right across the moor beyond where they stood. A deep terror for himself as well as for her rose over him simultaneously. It came to him, with a shock of ice, that his own soul as well as hers, lay in sudden danger.

His eyes turned irresistibly towards the Trod, so strangely shining in the night. Though his hand still touched the girl, his mind was caught away in phantasmal possibilities. For two passions seized and fought within him: the fierce desire to possess her in the world of men and women, or to go with her headlong, recklessly, and share some ineffable ecstasy of happiness beyond the familiar world where ordinary time and space held sway. Her own nature already held the key and knew the danger. ... His whole being rocked.

The two incompatible passions gored the very heart in him. In a flash he realised his alternative—the dreary desolation of human progress with its grinding future, the joy and glory of a soulless happiness that reason denied and yet the heart welcomed as an ultimate truth. These two!

Yet of what value and meaning could she ever be to him as wife and mother if she were now drawn away—away to where her mother now eternally passed her golden, time-less life? How could he face this daily exile of her soul, this hourly isolation, this rape of her normal being his earthly nature held so dear and precious? While—should he save her, keeping her safe against the *human* hearth—how should he hold her to him, he himself tainted with the golden poison...?

Norman saw both sides with remorseless clarity in that swift instant while the Trod took on its shining radiance. His reasoning mind, he knew, ad sunk away; his heart, wildly beating, was uppermost. With a supreme effort he kept his touch upon Diana's arm. His fingers clutched at the rough tweed of her sleeve. His entire being seemed rapt in some incredible ecstasy. He stood, he stared, he wondered, lost in an ineffable dream of beauty. One link only with the normal he held to like a vice—his touch upon her tough tweed sleeve, and, in his fading memory, the picture of a crucifix her weakening fingers weakly fumbled.

Figures were now moving fast and furious along the Trod; he could see them approaching from the distance. It was an inspiring, an intoxicating vision, and yet quite credible, with no foolish phantasmagoria of any childish sort. He saw everything as plainly as though he watched a parade in Whitehall, or a procession at some southern Battle of Flowers. Yet lovely, happy, radiant—and irresistibly enticing. As the figures came nearer, the light increased, so that it was obvious *they* emanated light of their own against the dark moorland. Nor were the individual figures particularly striking, least of all sensational. They seemed 'natural', yet natural only because they were true and justified.

In the lead, as they drew nearer, Norman saw a tall dark man riding a white horse, close behind him a fair shining woman in a green dress, her long, golden hair falling to her waist. On her head he saw a circlet of gold in which was set a red stone that shone and glowed like burning flame. Beside her was another woman, dark and beautiful, with white stones sparkling in her hair as diamonds or crystals sparkle. It was a gorgeous and a radiant sight. Their faces shone with the ecstasy of youth. In some indescribable way they all spread happiness and joy about them, their eyes blazing with a peace and beneficence he had never seen in any human eyes.

THE TROD

These passed, and more and more poured by, some riding, some walking, young and old and children, men with hunting spears and unstrung bows, then youthful figures with harps and lyres, and one and all making friendly gestures of invitation to come and join them, as they flowed past silently. Silently, yes, silently, without a sound of footsteps or of rustling heather, silently along the illuminated Trod, and yet, silent though their passing was, there came to him an impression of singing, laughter, even an air of dancing. Such figures, he realised, could not move without rhythm, rhythm of sound and gesture, for it was as essential to them as breathing. Happy, radiant, gay they were for ever from the grinding effort and struggle of the world's strenuous evolutionary battles—free, if soulless. The 'Gay People' as the natives called them. And the sight wrenched at the deepest roots of his own mixed being. To go with them and share their soulless bliss forever... or to stay and face the grim battle of Humanity's terrific—noble, yes— but almost hopeless, evolution?

That he was torn in two seemed an understatement. The pain seared and burned him in his very vitals. Diana, the girl, drew him as with some power of the stars themselves, and his hand still felt the tweed of her cloth beneath his fingers. His mind and heart, his nerves, his straining muscles, seemed fused in a fury of contradictions and acceptances. The glorious procession flowed streaming by, as though the stars had touched the common moorland earth, dripping their lavish gold in quiet glory—when suddenly Diana wrenched herself away and ran headlong towards them.

A golden-haired woman, he saw, had stepped out of the actual Trod, and had come to a halt directly in front of where he stood. Radiant and wonderful, she stood for a moment poised.

'Dis... Dis...' he heard in tones like music. 'Come... come to me. Come and join us! The way is always open. There are no regrets...!'

The girl was half way to her mother before he could break the awful spell that held him motionless. But the rough cloth of her sleeve held clutched between his fingers, and with it the broken chain that caught her little crucifix. The silver cross swung and dangled a moment, then dropped among the heather.

It was as he stooped frantically to recover in that Fate played that strange, unusual card she keeps in reserve for moments when the world seems lost; for, as he fell, his own chain and crucifix, to which he had not once given a thought, flicked up and caught him on the lip. Thinking it was a broken edge of torn heather that stung him into pain, he dashed it aside—only to find it was the foolish metal symbol Diana had made him promise to wear, in his own safety. It was the sharp stab of pain, not the superstitious mental reaction, that roused immediate action in him.

In a second he was on his feet again, and a second later he had overtaken the striding girl and had both arms possessingly round her figure. An instant afterwards his lips were on her own, her head and shoulders torn backwards against his breast.

'Dis!' he cried wildly, 'we must stay here together! You belong to me. I hold you tight—forever... here!'

What else he cried he hardly knows. He felt her weight sink back into his arms. It seems he carried her. He felt her convulsive weeping sobs against his heart. Her arms clung tightly round him.

In the distance he saw the line of moving figures die fading off into the enveloping moorland, dipping down into the curving dimness. Clouds raced back across the moon. There was no sound, the wind lay still, no tumbling beck was audible, the peewits slept.

Putting his own coat about her, he carried her home... and in due course he married her; he married Diana, he married Dis as well, a queer, lovely girl, but a girl without a soul, almost without a mind—a girl as commonplace as the radiant nonentity pictured with shining teeth on the cover of a popular magazine —a standardised creature whose essence had 'gone elsewhere'.

THE TERROR OF THE TWINS

That the man's hopes had built upon a son to inherit his name and estates—a single son, that is—was to be expected; but no one could have foreseen the depth and bitterness of his disappointment, the cold, implacable fury, when there arrived instead—twins. For, though the elder legally must inherit, that other ran him so deadly close. A daughter would have been a more reasonable defeat. But twins——! To miss his dream by so feeble a device——!

The complete frustration of a hope deeply cherished for years may easily result in strange fevers of the soul, but the violence of the father's hatred, existing as it did side by side with a love he could not deny, was something to set psychologists thinking. More than unnatural, it was positively uncanny. Being a man of rigid self-control, however, it operated inwardly, and doubtless along some morbid line of weakness little suspected even by those nearest to him, preying upon his thought to such dreadful extent that finally the mind gave way. The suppressed rage and bitterness deprived him, so the family decided, of his reason, and he spent the last years of his life under restraint. He was possessed naturally of immense forces—of will, feeling, desire; his dynamic value truly tremendous, driving through life like a great engine; and the intensity of this concentrated and buried hatred was guessed by few. The twins themselves, however, knew it. They divined it, at least, for it operated ceaselessly against them side by side with the genuine soft love that occasionally sweetened it, to their great perplexity. They spoke of it only to each other, though.

'At twenty-one,' Edward, the elder, would remark sometimes, unhappily, 'we shall know more.' 'Too much,' Ernest would reply, with a rush of unreasoning terror the thought never failed to evoke—*in him*. 'Things father said always happened—in life.' And they paled perceptibly. For the hatred, thus compressed into a veritable bomb of psychic energy, had found at the last a singular expression in the cry of the father's distraught mind. On the occasion of their final visit to the asylum, preceding his death by a few hours only, very calmly, but with an intensity that drove the words into their hearts like points of burning metal, he had spoken. In the presence of the attendant, at the door of the dreadful padded cell, he said it: 'You are not two, but *one*. I still regard you as one. And at the coming of age, by h——, you shall find it out!'

The lads perhaps had never fully divined that icy hatred which lay so well concealed against them, but that this final sentence was a curse, backed by all the man's terrific force, they quite well realised; and accordingly, almost unknown to each other, they had come to dread the day inexpressibly. On the morning of that twenty-first birthday—their father gone these five years into the Unknown, yet still sometimes so strangely close to them—they shared the same biting, inner terror, just as they shared all other emotions of their life—intimately, without speech. During the daytime they managed to keep it at a distance, but when the dusk fell about the old house they knew the stealthy approach of a kind of panic sense. Their self-respect weakened swiftly... and they persuaded their old friend, and once tutor, the vicar, to sit up with them till midnight. ... He had humoured them to that extent, willing to forgo his sleep, and at the same time more than a little interested in their singular belief—that before the day was out, before midnight struck, that is, the curse of that terrible man would somehow come into operation against them.

Festivities over and the guests departed, they sat up in the library, the room usually occupied by their father, and little used since. Mr. Curtice, a robust man of fifty-five, and a firm believer in spiritual principalities and powers, dark as well as good, affected (for their own good) to regard the youths' obsession with a kindly cynicism. 'I do not think it likely for one moment,' he said gravely, 'that such a thing would be permitted. All spirits are in the hands of God, and the violent ones more especially.' To which Edward made the extraordinary reply: 'Even if father does not come himself he will—*send*!' And Ernest agreed: 'All this time he's been making preparations for this very day. We've both known it for a long time—by odd things that have happened, by our dreams, by nasty little dark hints of various kinds, and by these persistent attacks of terror that come from nowhere, especially of late. Haven't we, Edward?' Edward assenting with a shudder. 'Father has been *at us* of late with renewed violence. To-night it will be a regular assault upon our lives, or minds, or souls!'

'Strong personalities *may* possibly leave behind them forces that continue to act,' observed Mr. Curtice with caution, while the brothers replied almost in the same breath: 'That's exactly what we feel so curiously. Though—nothing has actually happened yet, you know, and it's a good many years now since——'

This was the way the twins spoke of it all. And it was their profound conviction that had touched their old friend's sense of duty. The experiment should justify itself—and cure them. Meanwhile none of the family knew. Everything was planned secretly.

The library was the quietest room in the house. It had shuttered bow-windows, thick carpets, heavy doors. Books lined the walls, and there was a capacious open fireplace of brick in which the woodlogs blazed and roared, for the autumn night was chilly. Round this the three of them were grouped, the clergyman reading aloud from the Book of Job in low tones; Edward and Ernest, in dinner-jackets, occupying deep leather arm-chairs, listening. They looked exactly what they were—Cambridge 'undergrads', their faces pale against their dark hair, and alike as two peas. A shaded lamp behind the clergyman threw the rest of the room into shadow. The reading voice was steady, even monotonous, but something in it betrayed an underlying anxiety, and although the eyes rarely left the printed page, they took in every movement of the young men opposite, and noted every change upon their faces. It was his aim to produce an unexciting atmosphere, yet to miss nothing; if anything did occur to see it from the very beginning. Not to be taken by surprise was his main idea. ... And thus, upon this falsely peaceful scene, the minutes passed the hour of eleven and slipped rapidly along towards midnight.

The novel element in his account of this distressing and dreadful occurrence seems to be that what happened—happened without the slightest warning or preparation. There was no gradual presentiment of any horror; no strange blast of cold air; no dwindling of heat or light; no shaking of windows or mysterious tapping upon furniture. Without preliminaries it fell with its black trappings of terror upon the scene.

The clergyman had been reading aloud for some considerable time, one or other of the twins—Ernest usually—making occasional remarks, which proved that his sense of dread was disappearing. As the time grew short and nothing happened they grew more at their ease. Edward, indeed, actually nodded, dozed, and finally fell asleep. It was a few minutes before midnight. Ernest, slightly yawning, was stretching himself in the big chair. 'Nothing's going to happen,' he said aloud, in a pause. 'Your good influence has prevented it.' He even laughed now. 'What superstitious asses we've been, sir; haven't we——?'

Curtice, then, dropping his Bible, looked hard at him under the lamp. For in that second, even while the words sounded, there had come about a most abrupt and dreadful change; and so swiftly that the clergyman, in spite of himself, was taken utterly by surprise and had no time to think. There had swooped down upon the quiet library—so he puts it—an immense hushing silence, so profound that the peace already reigning there seemed clamour by comparison; and out of this enveloping stillness there rose through the space about them a living and abominable Invasion—soft, motionless, terrific. It was as though vast engines, working at full speed and pressure, yet too swift and delicate to be appreciable to any definite sense, had suddenly dropped down upon them—from nowhere. 'It made me think,' the vicar used to say afterwards, 'of the *Mauretania* machinery compressed into a nutshell, yet losing none of its awful power.'

'... haven't we?' repeated Ernest, still laughing. And Curtice, making no audible reply, heard the true answer in his heart: 'Because everything has *already happened*—even as you feared.'

Yet, to the vicar's supreme astonishment, Ernest still noticed —nothing!

'Look,' the boy added, 'Eddy's sound asleep—sleeping like a pig. Doesn't say much for your reading, you know, sir!' And he laughed again—lightly, even foolishly. But that laughter jarred, for the clergyman understood now that the sleep of the elder twin was either feigned—or *unnatural*.

And while the easy words fell so lightly from his lips, the monstrous engines worked and pulsed against him and against his sleeping brother, all their huge energy concentrated down into points fine as Suggestion, delicate as Thought. The Invasion affected everything. The very objects in the room altered incredibly, revealing suddenly behind their normal exteriors horrid little hearts of darkness. It was truly amazing, this vile metamorphosis. Books, chairs, pictures, all yielded up their pleasant aspect, and betrayed, as with silent mocking laughter, their inner soul of blackness—their *decay*. This is how Curtice tries to body forth in words what he actually witnessed. ... And Ernest, yawning, talking lightly, half foolishly —still noticed nothing!

For all this, as described, came about in something like ten seconds; and with it swept into the clergyman's mind, like a blow, the memory of that sinister phrase used more than once by Edward: 'If father doesn't come, he will certainly—*send*.' And Curtice understood that he had done both—both sent and come himself. ... That violent mind, released from its spell of madness in the body, yet still retaining the old implacable hatred, was now directing the terrible, unseen assault. This silent room, so hushed and still, was charged to the brim. The horror of it, as he said later, 'seemed to peel the very skin from my back.' ... And, while Ernest noticed nothing, Edward slept!... The soul of the clergyman, strong with the desire to help or save, yet realising that he was alone against a Legion, poured out in wordless prayer to his Deity. The clock just then, whirring before it struck, made itself audible.

'By Jove! It's all right, you see!' exclaimed Ernest, his voice oddly fainter and lower than before. 'There's midnight—and nothing's happened. Bally nonsense, all of it!' His voice had dwindled curiously in volume. 'I'll get the whisky and soda from the hall.' His relief was great and his manner showed it. But in him somewhere was a singular change. His voice, manner, gestures, his very tread as he moved over the thick carpet toward the door, all showed it. He seemed less *real,* less alive, reduced somehow to littleness, the voice without timbre or quality, the appearance of him diminished in some fashion quite ghastly. His presence, if not actually shrivelled, was at least impaired. Ernest had suffered a singular and horrible *decrease.* ...

The clock was still whirring before the strike. One heard the chain running up softly. Then the hammer fell upon the first stroke of midnight.

'I'm off,' he laughed faintly from the door; 'it's all been pure funk—on my part, at least...!' He passed out of sight into the hall. *The Power that throbbed so mightily about the room followed him out*. Almost at the same moment Edward woke up. But he woke with a tearing and indescribable cry of pain and anguish on his lips: 'Oh, oh, oh! But it hurts! It hurts! I can't hold you; leave me. It's breaking me asunder——'

The clergyman had sprung to his feet, but in the same instant everything had become normal once more—the room as it was before, the horror gone. There was nothing he could do or say, for there was no longer anything to put right, to defend, or to attack. Edward was speaking; his voice, deep and full as it never had been before: 'By Jove, how that sleep has refreshed me! I feel twice the chap I was before—twice the chap. I feel quite splendid. Your voice, sir, must have hypnotised me to sleep. ...' He crossed the room with great vigour. 'Where's—er—where's—Ernie, by the bye?' he asked casually, hesitating—almost searching—for the name. And a shadow as of a vanished memory crossed his face and was gone. The tone conveyed the most complete indifference where once the least word or movement of his twin had wakened solicitude, love. 'Gone away, I suppose—gone to bed, I mean, of course.'

Curtice has never been able to describe the dreadful conviction that overwhelmed him as he stood there staring, his heart in his mouth—the conviction, the positive certainty, that Edward had changed interiorly, had suffered an incredible accession to his existing personality. But he *knew* it as he watched. His mind, spirit, soul had most wonderfully increased. Something that hitherto the lad had known from the outside only, or by the magic of loving sympathy, had now passed, to be incorporated with his own being. And, being himself, it required no expression. Yet this visible increase was somehow terrible. Curtice shrank back from him. The instinct—he has never grasped the profound psychology of *that*, nor why it turned his soul dizzy with a kind of nausea—the instinct to strike him where he stood, passed, and a plaintive sound from the hall, stealing softly into the room between them, sent all that was left to him of self-possession into his feet. He turned and ran. Edward foolowed him—very leisurely.

They found Ernest, or what had been Ernest, crouching behind the table in the hall, weeping foolishly to himself. On his face lay blackness. The mouth was open, the jaw dropped; he dribbled hopelessly; and from the face had passed all signs of intelligence—of spirit.

For a few weeks he lingered on, regaining no sign of spiritual or mental life before the poor body, hopelessly disorganised, released what was left of him, from pure inertia—from complete and utter loss of vitality.

And the horrible thing—so the distressed family thought, at least—was that all those weeks Edward showed an indifference that was singularly brutal and complete. He rarely even went to visit him. I believe, too, it is true that he only once spoke of him by name; and that was when he said—

'Ernie? Oh, but Ernie is much better and happier where he is——!'

THE DEFERRED APPOINTMENT

The little 'Photographic Studio' in the side-street beyond Shepherd's Bush had done no business all day, for the light had been uninviting to even the vainest sitter, and the murky sky that foreboded snow had hung over London without a break since dawn. Pedestrians went hurrying and shivering along the pavements disappearing into the gloom of countless ugly little houses the moment they passed beyond the glare of the big electric standards that lit the thundering motor-buses in the main street. The first flakes of snow, indeed, were already falling slowly, as though they shrank from settling in the grime. The wind moaned and sang dismally, catching the ears and lifting the shabby coat-tails of Mr. Mortimer Jenkyn, 'Photographic Artist', as he stood outside and put the shutters up with his own cold hands in despair of further trade. It was five minutes to six.

With a lingering glance at the enlarged portrait of a fat man in masonic regalia who was the pride and glory of his window-front, he fixed the last hook of the shutter, and turned to go indoors. There was developing and framing to be done upstairs, not very remunerative work, but better, at any rate, than waiting in an empty studio for customers who did not come—wasting the heat of two oil-stoves into the bargain. And it was then, in the act of closing the street-door behind him, that he saw a man standing in the shadows of the narrow passage, staring fixedly into his face.

Mr. Jenkyn admits that he jumped. The man was so very close, yet he had not seen him come in; and in the eyes was such a curiously sad and appealing expression. He had already sent his assistant home, and there was no other occupant of the little two-storey house. The man must have slipped past him from the dark street while his back was turned. Who in the world could he be, and what could he want? Was he beggar, customer, or rogue?

'Good evening,' Mr. Jenkyn said, washing his hands, but using only half the oily politeness of tone with which he favoured sitters. He was just going to add 'sir', feeling it wiser to be on the safe side, when the stranger shifted his position so that the light fell directly upon his face, and Mr. Jenkyn was aware that he—recognised him. Unless he was greatly mistaken, it was the second-hand bookseller in the main street.

'Ah, it's you, Mr. Wilson!' he stammered, making half a question of it, as though not quite convinced. 'Pardon me; I did not quite catch your face—er—I was just shutting up.' The other bowed his head in reply. 'Won't you come in? Do, please.'

Mr. Jenkyn led the way. He wondered what was the matter. The visitor was not among his customers; indeed, he could hardly claim to know him, having only seen him occasionally when calling at the shop for slight purchases of paper and what not. The man, he now realised, looked fearfully ill and wasted, his face pale and haggard. It upset him rather, this sudden, abrupt call. He felt sorry, pained. He felt uneasy.

Into the studio they passed, the visitor going first as though he knew the way, Mr. Jenkyn noticing through his flurry that he was in his 'Sunday best'. Evidently he had come with a definite purpose. It was odd. Still without speaking, he moved straight across the room and posed himself in front of the dingy back-ground of painted trees, facing the camera. The studio was brightly lit. He seated himself in the faded armchair, crossed his legs, drew up the little round table with the artificial roses upon it in a tall, thin vase, and struck an attitude. He meant to be photographed. His eyes, staring straight into the lens, draped as it was with the black velvet curtain, seemed, however, to take no account of the Photographic Artist. But Mr. Jenkyn, standing still beside the door, felt a cold air playing over his face that was not merely the winter cold from the street. He felt his hair rise. A slight shiver ran down his back. In that pale, drawn face,

THE DEFERRED APPOINTMENT

and in those staring eyes across the room that gazed so fixedly into the draped camera, he read the signature of illness that no longer knows hope. It was Death that he saw.

In a flash the impression came and went—less than a second. The whole business, indeed, had not occupied two minutes. Mr. Jenkyn pulled himself together with a strong effort, dismissed his foolish obsession, and came sharply to practical considerations. 'Forgive me,' he said, a trifle thickly, confusedly, 'but I—er—did not quite realise. You desire to sit for your portrait, of course. I've had such a busy day, and—'ardly looked for a customer so late.' The clock, as he spoke, struck six. But he did not notice the sound. Through his mind ran another reflection: 'A man shouldn't 'ave his picture taken when he's ill and next door to dying. Lord! He'll want a lot of touching-up and finishin', too!'

He began discussing the size, price, and length—the usual rigmarole of his 'profession', and the other, sitting there, still vouchsafed no comment or reply. He simply made the impression of a man in a great hurry, who wished to finish a disagreeable business without unnecessary talk. Many men, reflected the photographer, were the same; being photographed was worse to them than going to the dentist. Mr. Jenkyn filled the pauses with his professional running talk and patter, while the sitter, fixed and motionless, kept his first position and stared at the camera. The photographer rather prided himself upon his ability to make sitters look bright and pleasant; but this man was hopeless. It was only afterwards Mr. Jenkyn recalled the singular fact that he never once touched him—that, in fact, something connected possibly with his frail appearance of deadly illness had prevented his going close to arrange the details of the hastily assumed pose.

'It must be a flashlight, of course, Mr. Wilson,' he said, fidgeting at length with the camera-stand, shifting it slightly nearer; while the other moved his head gently yet impatiently in agreement. Mr. Jenkyn longed to suggest his coming another time when he looked better, to speak with sympathy of his illness; to say something, in fact, that might establish a personal relation. But his tongue in this respect seemed utterly tied. It was just this personal relation which seemed impossible to approach—absolutely and peremptorily impossible. There seemed a barrier between the two. He could only chatter the usual professional commonplaces. To tell the truth, Mr. Jenkyn thinks he felt a little dazed the whole time—not quite his usual self. And, meanwhile, his uneasiness oddly increased. He hurried. He too, wanted the matter done with and his visitor gone.

At length everything was ready, only the flashlight waiting to be turned on, when stooping, he covered his head with the velvet cloth and peered through the lens—at no one! When he says 'at no one', however, he qualifies it thus: 'There was a quick flash of brilliant white light and a face in the middle of it —my gracious Heaven! But such a face—'*im*, yet not '*im*— like a sudden rushing glory of a face! It shot off like lightning out of the camera's field of vision. It left me blinded, I assure you, 'alf blinded, and that's a fac'. It was sheer dazzling!'

It seems Mr. Jenkyn remained entangled a moment in the cloth, eyes closed, breath coming in gasps, for when he got clear and straightened up again, staring once more at his customer over the top of the camera, he stared for the second time at—no one. And the cap that he held in his left hand he clapped feverishly over the uncovered lens. Mr. Jenkyn staggered... looked hurriedly round the empty studio, then ran, knocking a chair over as he went, into the passage. The hall was deserted, the front door closed. His vistor had disappeared 'almost as though he hadn't never been there at all'—thus he described it to himself in a terrified whisper. And again he felt the hair rise on his scalp; his skin crawled a little, and something put back the ice against his spine.

After a moment he returned to the studio and somewhat feverishly examined it. There stood the chair against the dingy background of trees; and there, close beside it, was the round table with the flower vase. Less than a minute ago Mr. Thomas Wilson, looking like death, had been sitting in that very chair.

THE DEFERRED APPOINTMENT

'It wasn't *all* a sort of dreamin', then,' ran through his disordered and frightened mind. 'I did see something...!' He remembered vaguely stories he had read in the newspapers, stories of queer warnings that saved people from disasters, apparitions, faces seen in dream, and so forth. 'Maybe,' he thought with confusion, 'something's going to 'appen to *me*!' Further than that he could not get for some little time, as he stood there staring about him, almost expecting that Mr. Wilson might reappear as strangely as he had disappeared. He went over the whole scene again and again, reconstructing it in minutest detail. And only then for the first time, did he plainly realise two things which somehow or other he had not thought strange before, but now thought very strange. For his visitor, he remembered, had not uttered a single word, nor had he, Mr. Jenkyn, once touched his person... And, thereupon, without more ado, he put on his hat and coat and went round to the little shop in the main street to buy some ink and stationery, which he did not in the least require.

The shop seemed all as usual, though Mr. Wilson himself was not visible behind the littered desk. A tall gentleman was talking in low tones to the partner. Mr. Jenkyn bowed as he went in, then stood examining a case of cheap stylographic pens, waiting for the others to finish. It was impossible to avoid overhearing. Besides, the little shop had distinguished customers sometimes, he had heard, and this evidently was one of them. He only understood part of the conversation, but he remembers all of it. 'Singular, yes, these last words of dying men,' the tall man was saying, 'very singular. You remember Newman's: "More light", wasn't it?' The bookseller nodded. 'Fine,' he said, 'fine, that!' There was a pause. Mr. Jenkyn stooped lower over the pens. 'This, too, was fine in its way,' the gentleman added, straightening up to go; 'the old promise, you see, unfulfilled but not forgotten. Cropped up suddenly out of the delirium. Curious, very curious! A good, conscientious man to the last. In all the twenty years I've known him he never broke his word...'

A motor-bus drowned a sentence, and then was heard in the

bookseller's voice, as he moved towards the door: '... You see, he was half-way down the stairs before they found him, always repeating the same thing, "I promised the wife, I promised the wife." And it was a job, I'm told, getting him back again... he struggled so. That's what finished him so quick, I suppose. Fifteen minutes later he was gone, and his last words were always the same, "I promised the wife"...'

The tall man was gone, and Mr. Jenkyn forgot about his purchases. 'When did it 'appen?' he heard himself asking in a voice he hardly recognised as his own. And the reply roared and thundered in his ears as he went down the street a minute later to his house: 'Close on six o'clock—a few minutes before the hour. Been ill for weeks, yes. Caught him out of bed with high fewer on his way to your place, Mr. Jenkyn, calling at the top of his voice that he'd forgotten to see you about his picture being taken. Yes, very sad, very sad indeed.'

But Mr. Jenkyn did not return to his studio. He left the light burning there all night. He went to the little room where he slept out, and next day gave the plate to be developed by his assistant. 'Defective plate, sir,' was the report in duae ourse; 'shows nothing but a flash of light—uncommonly brillinct.'

'Make a print of it all the same,' was the reply. Six months later, when he examined the plate and print, Mr. Jenkyn found that the singular streaks of light had disappeared from both. The uncommon brilliance had faded out completely as though it had never been there.

ACCESSORY BEFORE THE FACT

At the moorland cross-roads Martin stood examining the sign-post for several minutes in some bewilderment. The names on the four arms were not what he expected, distances were not given, and his map, he concluded with impatience, must be hopelessly out of date. Spreading it against the post, he stooped to study it more closely. The wind blew the corners flapping against his face. The small print was almost indecipherable in the fading light. It appeared, however—as well as he could make out—that two miles back he must have taken the wrong turning.

He remembered that turning. The path had looked inviting; he had hesitated a moment, then followed it, caught by the usual lure of walkers that it 'might prove a short cut'. The short-cut snare is old as human nature. For some minutes he studied the sign-post and the map alternately. Dusk was falling, and his knapsack had grown heavy. He could not make the two guides tally, however, and a feeling of uncertainty crept over his mind. He felt oddly baffled, frustrated. His thought grew thick. Decision was most difficult. 'I'm muddled,' he thought; 'I must be tired,' as at length he chose the most likely arm. 'Sooner or later it will bring me to an inn, though not the one I intended.' He accepted his walker's luck, and started briskly. The arm read, 'Over Litacy Hill' in small, fine letters that danced and shifted every time he looked at them; but the name was not discoverable on the map. It was, however, inviting like the short-cut. A similar impulse again directed his choice. Only this time it seemed more insistent, almost urgent.

And he became aware, then, of the exceeding loneliness of the country about him. The road for a hundred yards went straight, then curved like a white river running into space; the deep blue-green of heather lined the banks, spreading upwards through the twilight; and occasional small pines stood solitary here and there, all unexplained. The curious adjective, having made its appearance, haunted him. So many things that afternoon were similarly—unexplained: the short cut, the darkened map, the names on the sign-post, his own erratic impulses, and the growing strange confusion that crept upon his spirit. The entire country-side needed explanation, though perhaps 'interpretation' was the truer word. Those little lonely trees had made him see it. Why had he lost his way so easily? Why did he suffer vague impressions to influence his direction? Why was he here—exactly *here*? And why did he go now 'over Litacy Hill'?

Then, by a green field that shone like a thought of day-light amid the darkness of the moor, he saw a figure lying in the grass. It was a blot upon the landscape, a mere huddled patch of dirty rags, yet with a certain horrid picturesqueness too; and his mind—though his German was of the schoolroom order—at once picked out the German equivalents as against the English. *Lump* and *Lumpen* flashed across his brain most oddly. They seemed in that moment right, and so expressive, almost like onomatopoeic words, if that were possible of sight. Neither 'rags' nor 'rascal' would have fitted what he saw. The adequate description was in German.

Here was a clue tossed up by the part of him that did not reason. But it seems he missed it. And the next minute the tramp rose to a sitting posture and asked the time of evening. In German he asked it. And Martin, answering without a second's hesitation, gave it, also in German, '*halb sieben*'—half-past six. The instinctive guess was accurate. A glance at his watch when he looked a moment later proved it. He heard the man say, with the covert insolence of tramps, 'T'ank you; much opliged.' For Martin had not shown his watch—another intuition subconsciously obeyed.

He quickened his pace along that lonely road, a curious jumble of thoughts and feelings surging through him. He had somehow known the question would come, and come in German. Yet it flustered and dismayed him. Another thing had also flustered and dismayed him. He had expected it in the same queer fashion:

ACCESSORY BEFORE THE FACT

it was right. For when the ragged brown thing rose to ask the question, a part of it remained lying on the grass—another brown, dirty thing. There were two tramps. And he saw both faces clearly. Behind the untidy beards, and below the slouch hats, he caught the look of unpleasant, clever faces that watched him closely while he passed. The eyes followed him. For a second he looked straight into those eyes, so that he could not fail to know them. And he understood, quite horridly, that both faces were too sleek, refined, and cunning for those of ordinary tramps. The men were not really tramps at all. They were disguised.

'How covertly they watched me!' was his thought, as he hurried along the darkening road, in dead earnestness now aware of the loneliness and desolation of the moorland all about him.

Uneasy and distressed, he increased his pace. Midway in thinking what an unnecessarily clanking noise his nailed boots made upon the hard white road, there came upon him with a rush together the company of these things that haunted him as 'unexplained'. They brought a single definite message: That all this business was not really meant for him at all, and hence his confusion and bewilderment; that he had intruded into someone else's scenery, and was trespassing upon another's map of life. By some wrong *inner* turning he had interpolated his person into a group of foreign forces which operated in the little world of someone else. Unwittingly, somewhere, he had crossed the threshold, and now was fairly in—a trespasser, an eavesdropper, a Peeping Tom. He was listening, peeping; overhearing things he had no right to know, because they were intended for another. Like a ship at sea he was intercepting wireless messages he could not properly interpret, because his Receiver was not accurately tuned to their reception. And more—these messages were warnings!

Then fear dropped upon him like the night. He was caught in a net of delicate, deep forces he could not manage, knowing neither their origin nor purpose. He had walked into some huge psychic trap elaborately planned and baited, yet calculated for another than himself. Something had lured him in, something in the landscape, the time of day, his mood. Owing to some undiscovered weakness in himself he had been easily caught. His fear slipped easily into terror.

What happened next happened with such speed and concentration that it all seemed crammed into a moment. At once and in a heap it happened. It was quite inevitable. Down the white road to meet him a man came swaying from side to side in drunkenness quite obviously feigned—a tramp; and while Martin made room for him to pass, the lurch changed in a second to attack, and the fellow was upon him. The blow was sudden and terrific, yet even while it fell Martin was aware that behind him rushed a second man, who caught his legs from under him and bore him with a thud and crash to the ground. Blows rained then; he saw a gleam of something shining; a sudden deadly nausea plunged him into utter weakness where resistance was impossible. Something of fire entered his throat, and from his mouth poured a thick sweet thing that choked him. The world sank far away into darkness... Yet through all the horror and confusion ran the trail of two clear thoughts: he realised that the first tramp had sneaked at a fast double through the heather and so come to meet him; and that something heavy was torn from fastenings that clipped it tight and close beneath his clothes against his body...

Abruptly then the darkness lifted, passed utterly away. He found himself peering into the map against the sign-post. The wind was flapping the corners against his cheek, and he was poring over names that now he saw quite clear. Upon the arms of the sign-post above were those he had expected to find, and the map recorded them quite faithfully. All was accurate again and as it should be. He read the name of the village he had meant to make—it was plainly visible in the dusk, two miles the distance given. Bewildered, shaken, unable to think of anything, he stuffed the map into his pocket unfolded, and hurried forward like a man who has just wakened from an awful dream that had compressed into a single second all the detailed misery of some prolonged, oppressive nightmare.

He broke into a steady trot that soon became a run; the perspiration poured from him; his legs felt weak, and his breath was difficult to manage. He was only conscious of the overpowering desire to get away as fast as possible from the sign-post at the cross-roads where the dreadful vision had flashed upon him. For Martin, accountant on a holiday, had never dreamed of any world of psychic possibilities. The entire thing was torture. It was worse than a 'cooked' balance of the books that some conspiracy of clerks and directors proved at his innocent door. He raced as though the country-side ran crying at his heels. And always still ran with him the incredible conviction that none of this was really meant for himself at all. He had overheard the secrets of another. He had taken the warning for another into himself, and so altered its direction. He had thereby prevented its right delivery. It all shocked him beyond words. It dislocated the machinery of his just and accurate soul. The warning was intended for another, who could not—would not—now receive it.

The physical exertion, however, brought at length a more comfortable reaction and some measure of composure. With the lights in sight, he slowed down and entered the village at a reasonable pace. The inn was reached, a bedroom inspected and engaged, and supper ordered with the solid comfort of a large Bass to satisfy an unholy thirst and complete the restoration of balance. The unusual sensations largely passed away, and the odd feeling that anything in his simple, wholesome world required explanation was no longer present. Still with a vague uneasiness about him, though actual fear quite gone, he went into the bar to smoke an after-supper pipe and chat with the natives, as his pleasure was upon a holiday, and so saw two men leaning upon the counter at the far end with their backs towards him. He saw their faces instantly in the glass, and the pipe nearly slipped from between his teeth. Clean-shaven, sleek clever faces—and he caught a word or two as they talked over their drinks—German words. Well dressed they were, both men, with nothing about them calling for particular attention; they might have been two tourists holiday-making like himself in tweeds and walking-boots. And they presently paid for their drinks and went out. He never saw them face to face at all; but the sweat broke out afresh all over him, a feverish rush of heat and ice together ran about his body; beyond question he recognised the two tramps, this time not disguised—*not yet* disguised.

He remained in his corner without moving, puffing violently at an extinguished pipe, gripped helplessly by the return of that first vile terror. It came again to him with an absolute clarity of certainty that it was not with himself they had to do, these men, and, further, that he had no right in the world to interfere. He had no *locus standi* at all; it would be immoral... even if the opportunity came. And the opportunity, he felt, would come. He had been an eavesdropper, and had come upon private information of a secret kind that he had no right to make use of, even that good might come—even to save life. He sat on in his corner, terrified and silent, waiting for the thing that should happen next.

But night came without explanation. Nothing happened. He slept soundly. There was no other guest at the inn but an elderly man, apparently a tourist like himself. He wore gold-rimmed glasses, and in the morning Martin overheard him asking the landlord what direction he should take for Litacy Hill. His teeth began then to chatter and a weakness came into his knees. 'You turn to the left at the cross-roads,' Martin broke in before the landlord could reply; 'you'll see the sign-post about two miles from here, and after that it's a matter of four miles more.' How in the world did he know, flashed horribly through him. 'I'm going that way myself,' he was saying next; 'I'll go with you for a bit—if you don't mind!' The words came out impulsively and ill-considered; of their own accord they came. For his own direction was exactly opposite. *He did not want the man to go alone.* The stranger, however, easily evaded his offer of companionship.

ACCESSORY BEFORE THE FACT

He thanked him with the remark that he was starting later in the day... They were standing, all three, beside the horse-trough in front of the inn, when at that very moment a tramp, slouching along the road, looked up and asked the time of day. And it was the man with the gold-rimmed glasses who told him.

'T'ank you; much opliged,' the tramp replied, passing on with his slow, slouching gait, while the landlord, a talkative fellow, proceeded to remark upon the number of Germans that lived in England and were ready to swell the Teutonic invasion which *he*, for his part, deemed imminent.

But Martin heard it not. Before he had gone a mile upon his way he went into the woods to fight his conscience all alone. His feebleness, his cowardice were surely criminal. Real anguish tortured him. A dozen times he decided to go back upon his steps, and a dozen times the singular authority that whispered he had no right to interfere prevented him. How could he act upon knowledge gained by eavesdropping? How interfere in the private business of another's hidden life merely because he had overheard, as at the telephone, its secret dangers? Some inner confusion prevented straight thinking altogether. The stranger would merely think him mad. He had no 'fact' to go upon... He smothered a hundred impulses... and finally went on his way with a shaking, troubled heart.

The last two days of his holiday were ruined by doubts and questions and alarms—all justified later when he read of the murder of a tourist upon Litacy Hill. The man wore gold-rimmed glasses, and carried in a belt about his person a large sum of money. His throat was cut. And the police were hard upon the trail of a mysterious pair of tramps, said to be—Germans.

THE GLAMOUR OF THE SNOW

I

Hibbert, always conscious of two worlds, was in this mountain village conscious of three. It lay on the slopes of the Valais Alps, and he had taken a room in the little post office, where he could be at peace to write his book, yet at the same time enjoy the winter sports and find companionship in the hotels when he wanted it.

The three worlds that met and mingled here seemed to his imaginative temperament very obvious, though it is doubtful if another mind less intuitively equipped would have seen them so well-defined. There was the world of tourist English, civilised, quasi-educated, to which he belonged by birth, at any rate; there was the world of peasants to which he felt himself drawn by sympathy—for he loved and admired their toiling, simple life; and there was this other—which he could only call the world of Nature. To this last, however, in virtue of a vehement poetic imagination, and a tumultuous pagan instinct fed by his very blood, he felt that most of him belonged. The others borrowed from it, as it were, for visits. Here, with the soul of Nature, hid his central life.

Between all three was conflict—potential conflict. On the skating-rink each Sunday the tourists regarded the natives as intruders; in the church the peasants plainly questioned: 'Why do you come? We are here to worship; you to stare and whisper!' For neither of these two worlds accepted the other. And neither did Nature accept the tourists, for it took advantage of their least mistakes, and indeed, even of the peasant-world 'accepted' only those who were strong and bold enough to invade her savage domain with sufficient skill to protect themselves from several forms of—death.

Now Hibbert was keenly aware of this potential conflict and

want of harmony; he felt outside, yet caught by it—torn in the three directions because he was partly of each world, but wholly in only one. There grew in him a constant, subtle effort—or, at least, desire—to unify them and decide positively to which he should belong and live in. The attempt, of course, was largely subconscious. It was the natural instinct of a richly imaginative nature seeking the point of equilibrium, so that the mind could feel at peace and his brain be free to do good work.

Among the guests no one especially claimed his interest. The men were nice but undistinguished—athletic schoolmasters, doctors snatching a holiday, good fellows all; the women, equally various—the clever, the would-be-fast, the dare-to-be-dull, the women 'who understood', and the usual pack of jolly dancing girls and 'flappers'. And Hibbert, with his forty odd years of thick experience behind him, got on well with the lot; he understood them all; they belonged to definite, predigested types that are the same the world over, and that he had met the world over long ago.

But to none of them did he belong. His nature was too 'multiple' to subscribe to the set of shibboleths of any one class. And, since all liked him, and felt that somehow he seemed outside of them—spectator, looker-on—all sought to claim him.

In a sense, therefore, the three worlds fought for him: natives, tourists, Nature...

It was thus began the singular conflict for the soul of Hibbert. *In* his own soul, however, it took place. Neither the peasants nor the tourists were conscious that they fought for anything. And Nature, they say, is merely blind and automatic.

The assault upon him of the peasants may be left out of account, for it is obvious that they stood no chance of success. The tourist world, however, made a gallant effort to subdue him to themselves. But the evenings in the hotel, when dancing was not in order, were—English. The provincial imagination was set upon a throne and worshipped heavily through incense of the stupidest conventions possible. Hibbert used to go back early to his room in the post office to work.

'It is a mistake on my part to have *realised* that there is any conflict at all,' he thought, as he crunched home over the snow at midnight after one of the dances. 'It would have been better to have kept outside it all and done my work. Better,' he added, looking back down the silent village street to the church tower, 'and—safer.'

The adjective slipped from his mind before he was aware of it. He turned with an involuntary start and looked about him. He knew perfectly well what it meant—this thought that had thrust its head up from the instinctive region. He understood, without being able to express it fully, the meaning that betrayed itself in the choice of the adjective. For if he had ignored the existence of this conflict he would at the same time have remained outside the arena. Whereas now he had entered the lists. Now this battle for his soul must have issue. And he knew that the spell of Nature was greater for him than all other spells in the world combined—greater than love, revelry, pleasure, greater even than study. He had always been afraid to let himself go. His pagan soul dreaded her terrific powers of witchery even while he worshipped.

The little village already slept. The world lay smothered in snow. The chalet roofs shone white beneath the moon, and pitch-black shadows gathered against the walls of the church. His eye rested a moment on the square stone tower with its frosted cross that pointed to the sky: then travelled with a leap of many thousand feet to the enormous mountains that brushed the brilliant stars. Like a forest rose the huge peaks above the slumbering village, measuring the night and heavens. They beckoned him. And something born of the snowy desolation, born of the midnight and the silent grandeur, born of the great listening hollows of the night, something that lay 'twixt terror and wonder, dropped from the vast wintry spaces down into his heart—and called him. Very softly, unrecorded in any word or thought his brain could compass, it laid its spell upon him. Fingers of snow brushed the surface of his heart. The power and quiet majesty of the winter's night appalled him...

THE GLAMOUR OF THE SNOW

Fumbling a moment with the big unwieldy key, he let himself in and went upstairs to bed. Two thoughts went with him—apparently quite ordinary and sensible ones:

'What fools these peasants are to sleep through such a night!' And the other:

'Those dances tire me. I'll never go again. My work only suffers in the morning.' The claims of peasants and tourists upon him seemed thus in a single instant weakened.

The clash of battle troubled half his dreams. Nature had sent her Beauty of the Night and won the first assault. The others, routed and dismayed, fled far away.

II

'Don't go back to your dreary old post office. We're going to have supper in my room—something hot. Come and join us. Hurry up!'

There had been an ice carnival, and the last party, trailing up the snow-slope to the hotel, called him. The Chinese lanterns smoked and sputtered on the wires; the band had long since gone. The cold was bitter and the moon came only momentarily between high, driving clouds. From the shed where the people changed from skates to snow-boots he shouted something to the effect that he was 'following'; but no answer came; the moving shadows of those who had called were already merged high up against the village darkness. The voice died away. Doors slammed. Hibbert found himself alone on the deserted rink.

And it was then, quite suddenly, the impulse came to—stay and skate alone. The thought of the stuffy hotel room, and of those noisy people with their obvious jokes and laughter, oppressed him. He felt a longing to be alone with the night, to taste her wonder all by himself there beneath the stars, gliding over the ice. It was not yet midnight, and he could skate for half an hour. That supper party, if they noticed his absence at all, would merely think he had changed his mind and gone to bed.

It was an impulse, yes, and not an unnatural one; yet even at the time it struck him that something more than impulse lay concealed behind it. More than invitation, yet certainly less than command, there was a vague queer feeling that he stayed because he had to, almost as though there was something he had forgotten, overlooked, left undone. Imaginative temperaments are often thus; and impulse is ever weakness. For with such ill-considered opening of the doors to hasty action may come an invasion of other forces at the same time—forces merely waiting their opportunity perhaps!

He caught the fugitive warning even while he dismissed it as absurd, and the next minute he was whirling over the smooth ice in delightful curves and loops beneath the moon. There was no fear of collision. He could take his own speed and space as he willed. The shadows of the towering mountains fell across the rink, and a wind of ice came from the forests, where the snow lay ten feet deep. The hotel lights winked and went out. The village slept. The high wire netting could not keep out the wonder of the winter night that grew about him like a presence. He skated on and on, keen exhilarating pleasure in his tingling blood, and weariness all forgotten.

And then, midway in the delight of rushing movement, he saw a figure gliding behind the wire netting, watching him. With a start that almost made him lose his balance—for the abruptness of the new arrival was so unlooked for—he paused and stared. Although the light was dim he made out that it was the figure of a woman and that she was feeling her way along the netting, trying to get in. Against the white background of the snow-field he watched her rather stealthy efforts as she passed with a silent step over the banked-up snow. She was tall and slim and graceful; he could see that even in the dark. And then, of course, he understood. It was another adventurous skater like himself, stolen down unawares from hotel or chalet, and searching for the opening. At once, making a sign and pointing with one hand, he turned swiftly and skated over to the little entrance on the other side.

But, even before he got there, there was a sound on the ice behind him, and with an exclamation of amazement he could not suppress, he turned to see her swerving up to his side across the width of the rink. She had somehow found another way in.

Hibbert, as a rule, was punctilious, and in these free-and-easy places, perhaps, especially so. If only for his own protection he did not seek to make advances unless some kind of introduction paved the way. But for these two to skate together in the semi-darkness without speech, often of necessity brushing shoulders almost, was too absurd to think of. Accordingly he raised his cap and spoke. His actual words he seems unable to recall, nor what the girl said in reply, except that she answered him in accented English with some common place about doing figures at midnight on an empty rink. Quite natural it was, and right. She wore grey clothes of some kind, though not the customary long gloves or sweater, for indeed her hands were bare, and presently when he skated with her, he wondered with something like astonishment at their dry and icy coldness.

And she was delicious to skate with—supple, sure, and light, fast as a man yet with the freedom of a child, sinuous and steady at the same time. Her flexibility made him wonder, and when he asked where she had learned she murmured—he caught the breath against his ear and recalled later that it was singularly cold—that she could hardly tell, for she had been accustomed to the ice ever since she could remember.

But her face he never properly saw. A muffler of white fur buried her neck to the ears, and her cap came over the eyes. He only saw that she was young. Nor could he gather her hotel or chalet, for she pointed vaguely, when he asked her, up the slopes. 'Just over there——' she said, quickly taking his hand again. He did not press her; no doubt she wished to hide her escapade. And the touch of her hand thrilled him more than anything he could remember; even through his thick glove he felt the softness of that cold and delicate softness.

The clouds thickened over the mountains. It grew darker.

They talked very little, and did not always skate together. Often they separated, curving about in corners by themselves, but always coming together again in the centre of the rink; and when she left him thus Hibbert was conscious of—yes, of missing her. He found a peculiar satisfaction, almost a fascination, in skating by her side. It was quite an adventure—these two strangers with the ice and snow and night!

Midnight had long since sounded from the old church tower before they parted. She gave the sign, and he skated quickly to the shed, meaning to find a seat and help her take her skates off. Yet when he turned—she had already gone. He saw her slim figure gliding away across the snow... and hurrying for the last time round the rink alone he searched in vain for the opening she had twice used in this curious way.

'How very queer!' he thought, referring to the wire netting. 'She must have lifted it and wriggled under... !'

Wondering how in the world she managed it, what in the world had possessed him to be so free with her, and who in the world she was, he went up the steep slope to the post office and so to bed, her promise to come again another night still ringing delightfully in his ears. And curious were the thoughts and sensations that accompanied him. Most of all, perhaps, was the half suggestion of some dim memory that he had known this girl before, had met her somewhere, more—that she knew him. For in her voice—a low, soft, windy little voice it was, tender and soothing for all its quiet coldness—there lay some faint reminder of two others he had known, both long since gone; the voice of the woman he had loved, and—the voice of his mother.

But this time through his dreams there ran no clash of battle. He was conscious, rather, of something cold and clinging that made him think of sifting snowflakes climbing slowly with entangling touch and thickness round his feet. The snow, coming without noise, each flake so light and tiny none can mark the spot whereon it settles, yet the mass of it able to smother whole villages, wove through the very texture of his mind—cold, bewildering, deadening effort with its clinging network of the million feathery touches.

III

In the morning Hibbert realised he had done, perhaps, a foolish thing. The brilliant sunshine that drenched the valley made him see this, and the sight of his work-table with its typewriter, books, papers, and the rest, brought additional conviction. To have skated with a girl alone at midnight, no matter how innocently the thing had come about, was unwise—unfair, especially to her. Gossip in these little winter resorts was worse than in a provincial town. He hoped no one had seen them. Luckily the night had been dark. Most likely none had heard the ring of skates.

Deciding that in future he would be more careful, he plunged into work and sought to dismiss the matter from his mind.

But in his times of leisure the memory returned persistently to haunt him. When he 'ski-d', 'luged', or danced in the evenings, and especially when he skated on the little rink, he was aware that the eyes of his mind forever sought this strange companion of the night. A hundred times he fancied that he saw her, but always sight deceived him. Her face he might not know, but he could hardly fail to recognise her figure. Yet nowhere among the others did he catch a glimpse of that slim young creature he had skated with alone beneath the clouded stars. He searched in vain. Even his inquiries as to the occupants of the private chalets brought no results. He had lost her. But the queer thing was that he felt as though she were somewhere close; he *knew* she had not really gone. While people came and left with every day, it never once occurred to him that she had left. On the contrary, he felt assured that they would meet again.

This thought he never quite acknowledged. Perhaps it was the wish that fathered it only. And, even when he did meet her, it was a question how he would speak and claim acquaintance, or whether *she* would recognise himself. It might be awkward. He almost came to dread a meeting, though 'dread', of course, was far too strong a word to describe an emotion that was half delight, half wondering anticipation.

Meanwhile the season was in full swing. Hibbert felt in perfect health, worked hard, ski-d, skated, luged, and at night danced fairly often—in spite of his decision. This dancing was, however, an act of subconscious surrender; it really meant he hoped to find her among the whirling couples. He was searching for her without quite acknowledging it to himself; and the hotel-world, meanwhile, thinking it had won him over, teased and chaffed him. He made excuses in a similar vein; but all the time he watched and searched and—waited.

For several days the sky held clear and bright and frosty, bitterly cold, everything crisp and sparkling in the sun; but there was no sign of fresh snow, and the skiers began to grumble. On the mountains was an icy crust that made 'running' dangerous; they wanted the frozen, dry, and powdery snow that makes for speed, renders steering easier and falling less severe. But the keen east wind showed no signs of changing for a whole ten days. Then, suddenly, there came a touch of softer air and the weather-wise began to prophesy.

Hibbert, who was delicately sensitive to the least change in earth or sky, was perhaps the first to feel it. Only he did not prophesy. He knew through every nerve in his body that moisture had crept into the air, was accumulating, and that presently a fall would come. For he responded to the moods of Nature like a fine barometer.

And the knowledge, this time, brought into his heart a strange little wayward motion that was hard to account for—a feeling of unexplained uneasiness and disquieting joy. For behind it, woven through it rather, ran a faint exhilaration that connected remotely somewhere with that touch of delicious alarm, that tiny anticipating 'dread', that so puzzled him when he thought of his next meeting with his skating companion of the night. It lay beyond all words, all telling, this queer relationship between the two; but somehow the girl and snow ran in a pair across his mind.

Perhaps for imaginative writing-men, more than for other workers, the smallest change of mood betrays itself at once. His work at any rate revealed this slight shifting of emotional values in his soul. Not that his writing suffered, but that it altered, subtly as those changes of sky or sea or landscape that come with the passing of afternoon into evening—imperceptibly. A subconscious excitement sought to push outwards and express itself... and, knowing the uneven effect such moods produced in his work, he laid his pen aside and took instead to reading what he had to do.

Meanwhile the brilliance passed form the sunshine, the sky grew slowly overcast; by dusk the mountain tops came singularly close and sharp; the distant valley rose into absurdly near perspective. The moisture increased, rapidly approaching saturation point, when it must fall in snow. Hibbert watched and waited.

And in the morning the world lay smothered beneath its fresh white carpet. It snowed heavily till noon, thickly, incessantly, chokingly, a foot or more; then the sky cleared, the sun came out in splendour, the wind shifted back to the east, and frost came down upon the mountains with its keenest and most biting tooth. The drop in the temperature was tremendous, but the skiers were jubilant. Next day the 'running' would be fast and perfect. Already the mass was settling, and the surface freezing into those moss-like, powdery crystals that make the ski run almost of their own accord with the faint 'sishing' as of a bird's wings through the air.

IV

That night there was excitement in the little hotel-world, first because there was a *bal costumé*, but chiefly because the new snow had come. And Hibbert went—felt drawn to go; he did not go in costume, but he wanted to talk about the slopes and skiing with the other men, and at the same time...

Ah, there was the truth, the deeper necessity that called. For the singular connection between the stranger and the snow again betrayed itself, utterly beyond explanation as before, but vital and insistent. Some hidden instinct in his pagan soul—heaven knows how he phrased it even to himself, if the phrased it at all—whispered that with the snow the girl would be somewhere about, would emerge from her hiding place, would even look for him.

Absolutely unwarranted it was. He laughed while he stood before the little glass and trimmed his moustache, tried to make his black tie sit straight, and shook down his dinner jacket so that it should lie upon the shoulders without a crease. His brown eyes were very bright. 'I look younger than I usually do,' he thought. It was unusual, even significant, in a man who had no vanity about his appearance and certainly never questioned his age or tried to look younger than he was. Affairs of the heart, with one tumultuous exception, that left no fuel for lesser subsequent fires, had never troubled him. The forces of his soul and mind not called upon for 'work' and obvious duties, all went to Nature. The desolate, wild places of the earth were what he loved; night, and the beauty of the stars and snow. And this evening he felt their claims upon him mightily stirring. A rising wildness caught his blood, quickened his pulse, woke longing and passion too. But chiefly snow. The snow whirred softly through his thoughts like white, seductive dreams... For the snow had come; and She, it seemed, had somehow come with it—into his mind.

And yet he stood before that twisted mirror and pulled his tie and coat askew a dozen times, as though it mattered. 'What in the world is up with me?' he thought. Then, laughing a little, he turned before leaving the room to put his private papers in order. The green morocco desk that held them he took down from the shelf and laid upon the table. Tied to the lid was the visiting card with his brother's London address 'in case of accident'. On the way down to the hotel he wondered why he had done this, for though imaginative, he was not the kind of man who dealt in presentiments. Moods with him were strong, but ever held in leash.

'It's almost like a warning,' he thought, smiling. He drew his thick coat tightly round the throat as the freezing air bit at him. 'These warnings one reads of in stories sometimes...!'

A delicious happiness was in his blood. Over the edge of the hills across the valley rose the moon. He saw her silver sheet the world of snow. Snow covered all. It smothered sound and distance. It smothered houses, streets, and human beings. It smothered—life.

V

In the hall there was light and bustle; people were already arriving from the other hotels and chalets, their costumes hidden beneath many wraps. Groups of men in evening dress stood about smoking, talking 'snow' and 'skiing'. The band was tuning up. The claims of the hotel-world clashed about him faintly as of old. At the big glass windows of the verandah, peasants stopped a moment on their way home from the *café* to peer. Hibbert thought laughingly of that conflict he used to imagine. He laughed because it suddenly seemed so unreal. He belonged so utterly to Nature and the mountains, and especially to those desolate slopes where now the snow lay thick and fresh and sweet, that there was no question of a conflict at all. The power of the newly fallen snow had caught him, proving it without effort. Out there, upon those lonely reaches of the moonlit ridges, the snow lay ready—masses and masses of it—cool, soft, inviting. He longed for it. It awaited him. He thought of the intoxicating delight of skiing in the moonlight. ...

Thus, somehow, in vivid flashing vision, he thought of it while he stood there smoking with the other men and talking all the 'shop' of skiing.

And, ever mysteriously blended with this power of the snow, poured also through his inner being the power of the girl. He could not disabuse his mind of the insinuating presence of the two together. He remembered that queer skating-impulse of ten days ago, the impulse that had let her in. That any mind, even an imaginative one, could pass beneath the sway of such a fancy was strange enough; and Hibbert, while fully aware of the disorder, yet found curious joy in yielding to it. This insubordinate centre that drew him towards old pagan beliefs had assumed command. With a kind of sensuous pleasure he let himself be conquered.

And snow that night seemed in everybody's thoughts. The dancing couples talked of it; the hotel proprietors congratulated one another; it meant good sport and satisfied their guests; every one was planning trips and expeditions, talking of slopes and telemarks, of flying speed and distance, of drifts and crust and frost. Vitality and enthusiasm pulsed in the very air; all were alert and active, positive, radiating currents of creative life even into the stuffy atmosphere of that crowded ball-room. And the snow had caused it, the snow had brought it; all this discharge of eager sparkling energy was due primarily to the—Snow.

But in the mind of Hibbert, by some swift alchemy of his pagan yearnings, this energy became transmuted. It rarefied itself, gleaming in white and crystal currents of passionate anticipation which he transferred, as by a species of electrical imagination into the personality of the girl—the Girl of the Snow. She somewhere was waiting for him, expecting him, calling to him softly from those leagues of moonlit mountain. He remembered the touch of that cool, dry hand; the soft and icy breath against his cheek; the hush and softness of her presence in the way she came and the way she had gone again—like a flurry of snow the wind sent gliding up the slopes. She, like himself, belonged out there. He fancied that he heard her little windy voice come sifting to him through the snowy branches of the trees, calling his name... that haunting little voice that dived straight to the centre of his life as once, long years ago, two other voices used to do. ...

But nowhere among the costumed dancers did he see her slender figure. He danced with one and all, distrait and absent, a stupid partner as each girl discovered, his eyes ever turning towards the door and windows, hoping to catch the luring face, the vision that did not come... and at length, hoping even against hope. For the ball-room thinned; groups left one by one, going home to their hotels and chalets; the band tired obviously; people sat drinking lemon-squashes at the little tables, the men mopping their foreheads, everybody ready for bed.

It was close on midnight. As Hibbert passed through the hall to get his overcoat and snow-boots, he saw men in the passage by the 'sport-room', greasing their ski against an early start. Knapsack luncheons were being ordered by the kitchen swing doors. He sighed. Lighting a cigarette a friend offered him, he returned a confused reply to some question as to whether he could join their party in the morning. It seemed he did not hear it properly. He passed through the outer vestibule between the double glass doors, and went into the night.

The man who asked the question watched him go, an expression of anxiety momentarily in his eyes.

'Don't think he heard you,' said another, laughing. 'You've got to shout to Hibbert, his mind's so full of his work.'

'He works too hard,' suggested the first, 'full of queer ideas and dreams.'

But Hibbert's silence was not rudeness. He had not caught the invitation, that was all. The call of the hotel world had faded. He no longer heard it. Another wilder call was sounding in his ears.

For up the street he had seen a little figure moving. Close against the shadows of the baker's shop it glided—white, slim, enticing.

VI

And at once into his mind passed the hush and softness of the snow—yet with it a searching, crying wildness for the heights. He knew by some incalculable, swift instinct she would not meet him in the village street. It was not there, amid crowding houses, she would speak to him. Indeed, already she had disappeared, melted from view up the white vista of the moonlit road. Yonder, he divined, she waited where the highway narrowed abruptly into the mountain path beyond the chalets.

It did not even occur to him to hesitate; mad though it seemed, and was—this sudden craving for the heights with her, at least for open spaces where the snow lay thick and fresh—it was too imperious to be denied. He does not remember going up to his room putting the sweater over his evening clothes, and getting into the fur gauntlet gloves and the helmet cap of wool. Most certainly he has no recollection of fastening on his skis; he must have done it automatically. Some faculty of normal observation was in abeyance, as it were. His mind was out beyond the village—out with the snowy mountains and the moon.

Henri Défago, putting up the shutters over his *café* windows, saw him pass, and wondered mildly: 'Un monsieur qui fait du ski a cette heure! Il est Anglais, donc...!' He shrugged his shoulders, as though a man had the right to choose his own way of death. And Marthe Perotti, the hunchback wife of the shoemaker, looking by chance from her window, caught his figure moving swiftly up the road. She had other thoughts, for she knew and believed the old traditions of the witches and snow-beings that steal the souls of men. She had even heard, 'twas said, the dreaded 'synagogue' pass roaring down the street at night and now, as then, she hid her eyes. 'They've called to him... and he must go,' she murmured, making the sign of the cross.

But no one sought to stop him. Hibbert recalls only a single incident until he found himself beyond the houses, searching for her along the fringe of forest where the moonlight met the snow in a bewildering frieze of fantastic shadows. And the incident was simply this—that he remembered passing the church. Catching the outline of this tower against the stars, he was aware of a faint sense of hesitation. A vague uneasiness came and went—jarred unpleasantly across the flow of his excited feelings, chilling exhilaration. He caught the instant's discord, dismissed it, and —passed on. The seduction of the snow smothered the mind before he realised that it had brushed the skirts of warning.

And then he saw her. She stood there waiting in a little clear space of shining snow, dressed all in white, part of the moonlight and the glistening background, her slender figure just discernible.

'I waited, for I knew you would come,' the silvery little voice of windy beauty floated down to him. 'You *had* to come.'

'I'm ready,' he answered, 'I knew it too.'

The world of Nature caught him to its heart in those few words—the wonder and the glory of the night and snow. Life leaped within him. The passion of his pagan soul exulted, rose in joy, flowed out to her. He neither reflected nor considered, but let himself go like the veriest schoolboy in the wildness of first love.

'Give me your hand,' he cried, 'I'm coming...!'

'A little farther on, a little higher,' came her delicious answer. 'Here it is too near the village—and the church.'

And the words seemed wholly right and natural; he did not dream of questioning them; he understood that, with this little touch of civilisation in sight, the familiarity he suggested was impossible. Once out upon the open mountains, 'mid the freedom of huge slopes and towering peaks, the stars and moon to witness and the wilderness of snow to watch, they could taste an innocence of happy intercourse free from the dead conventions that imprison liberal minds.

He urged his pace, yet did not quite overtake her. The girl kept always just a little bit ahead of his best efforts.... And soon they left the trees behind and passed on to the enormous slopes of the sea of snow that rolled in mountainous terror and beauty to the stars. The wonder of the white world caught him away. Under the steady moonlight it was more than haunting. It was a living, white, bewildering power that deliciously confused the senses and laid a spell of wild perplexity upon the heart. It was a personality that cloaked, and yet revealed, itself through all this sheeted whiteness of snow. It rose, went with him, fled before, and followed after. Slowly it dropped lithe, gleaming arms about his neck, gathering him in. ...

Certainly some soft persuasion coaxed his very soul, urging him ever forwards, upwards, on towards the higher icy slopes. Judgment and reason left their throne, it seemed, completely, as in the madness of intoxication. The girl, slim and seductive, kept always just ahead, so that he never quite came up with her. He saw the white enchantment of her face and figure, something that streamed about her neck flying like a wreath of snow in the wind, and heard the alluring accents of her whispering voice that called from time to time: 'A little farther on, a little higher. ... Then we'll run home together!'

Sometimes he saw her hand stretched out to find his own, but each time, just as he came up with her, he saw her still in front, the hand and arm withdrawn. They took a gentle angle of ascent. The toil seemed nothing. In this crystal, wine-like air fatigue vanished. The sishing of the skis through the powdery surface of the snow was the only sound that broke the stillness; this, with his breathing and the rustle of her skirts, was all he heard. Cold moonshine, snow, and silence held the world. The sky was black and the peaks beyond cut into it like frosted wedges of iron and steel. Far below the valley slept the village long since hidden out of sight. He felt that he could never tire. ... The sound of the church clock rose from time to time faintly through the air—more and more distant.

'Give me your hand. It's time now to turn back.'

'Just one more slope,' she laughed. 'That ridge above us. Then we'll make for home.' And her low voice mingled pleasantly with the purring of their skis. His own seemed harsh and ugly by comparison.

'But I have never come so high before. It's glorious! This world of silent snow and moonlight—and *you*. You're a child of the snow, I swear. Let me come up—closer—to see your face—and touch your little hand.'

Her laughter answered him.

'Come on! A little higher. Here we're quite alone together.'

'It's magnificent,' he cried. 'But why did you hide away so long? I've looked and searched for you in vain ever since we skated——' he was going to say 'ten days ago', but the accurate memory of time had gone from him; he was not sure whether it was days or years or minutes. His thoughts of earth were scattered and confused.

THE GLAMOUR OF THE SNOW

'You looked for me in the wrong places,' he heard her murmur just above him. 'You looked in places where I never go. Hotels and houses kill me. I avoid them.' She laughed—a fine, shrill, windy little laugh.

'I loathe them too——'

He stopped. The girl had suddenly come quite close. A breath of ice passed through his very soul. She had touched him.

'But this awful cold!' he cried out sharply, 'this freezing cold that takes me. The wind is rising; it's a wind of ice. Come, let us turn...!'

But when he plunged forward to hold her, or at least to look, the girl was gone again. And something in the way she stood there a few feet beyond, and stared down into his eyes so steadfastly in silence, made him shiver. The moonlight was behind her, but in some odd way he could not focus sight upon her face, although so close. The gleam of eyes he caught, but all the rest seemed white and snowy as though he looked beyond her—out into space...

The sound of the church bell came up faintly from the valley far below, and he counted the strokes—five. A sudden, curious weakness seized him as he listened. Deep within it was, deadly yet somehow sweet, and hard to resist. He felt like sinking down upon the snow and lying there. ... They had been climbing for five hours. ... It was, of course, the warning of complete exhaustion.

With a great effort he fought and overcame it. It passed away as suddenly as it came.

'We'll turn,' he said with a decision he hardly felt. 'It will be dawn before we reach the village again. Come at once. It's time for home.'

The sense of exhilaration had utterly left him. An emotion that was akin to fear swept coldly through him. But her whispering answer turned it instantly to terror—a terror that gripped him horribly and turned him weak and unresisting.

'Our home is—*here*!' A burst of wild, high laughter, loud and shrill, accompanied the words. It was like a whistling wind.

The wind *had* risen, and clouds obscured the moon. 'A little higher—where we cannot hear the wicked bells,' she cried, and for the first time seized him deliberately by the hand. She moved, was suddenly close against his face. Again she touched him.

And Hibbert tried to turn away in escape, and so trying, found for the first time that the power of the snow—that other power which does not exhilarate but deadens effort—was upon him. The suffocating weakness that it brings to exhausted men, luring them to the sleep of death in her clinging soft embrace, lulling the will and conquering all desire for life—this was awfully upon him. His feet were heavy and entangled. He could not turn or move.

The girl stood in front of him, very near; he felt her chilly breath upon his cheeks; her hair passed blindingly across his eyes; and that icy wind came with her. He saw her whiteness close; again, it seemed, his sight passed through her into space as though she had no face. Her arms were round his neck. She drew him softly downwards to his knees. He sank; he yielded utterly; he obeyed. Her weight was upon him, smothering, delicious. The snow was to his waist. ... She kissed him softly on the lips, the eyes, all over his face. And then she spoke his name in that voice of love and wonder, the voice that held the accent of two others—both taken over long ago by Death—the voice of his mother, and of the woman he had loved.

He made one more feeble effort to resist. Then, realising even while he struggled that this soft weight about his heart was sweeter than anything life could ever bring, he let his muscles relax, and sank back into the soft oblivion of the covering snow. Her wentry kisses bore him into sleep.

VII

They say that men who know the sleep of exhaustion in the snow find no awakening on the hither side of death. ... The hours passed and the moon sank down below the white world's rim. Then, suddenly, there came a little crash upon his breast and neck, and Hibbert—woke.

He slowly turned bewildered, heavy eyes upon the desolate mountains, stared dizzily about him, tried to rise. At first his muscles would not act; a numbing, aching pain possessed him. He uttered a long, thin cry for help, and heard its faintness swallowed by the wind. And then he understood vaguely why he was only warm—not dead. For this very wind that took his cry had built up a sheltering mound of driven snow against his body while he slept. Like a curving wave it ran beside him. It was the breaking of its over-toppling edge that caused the crash, and the coldness of the mass against his neck that woke him.

Dawn kissed the eastern sky; pale gleams of gold shot every peak with splendour; but ice was in the air, and the dry and frozen snow blew like powder from the surface of the slopes. He saw the points of his skis projecting just below him. Then he—remembered. It seems he had just strength enough to realise that, could he but rise and stand, he might fly with terrific impetus towards the woods and village far beneath. The skis would carry him. But if he failed and fell...!

How he contrived it Hibbert never knew; this fear of death somehow called out his whole available reserve force. He rose slowly, balanced a moment, then, taking the angle of an immense zigzag, started down the awful slopes like an arrow from a bow. And automatically the splendid muscles of the practised skier and athlete saved and guided him, for he was hardly conscious of controlling either speed or direction. The snow stung face and eyes like fine steel shot; ridge after ridge flew past; the summits raced across the sky; the valley leaped up with bounds to meet him. He scarcely felt the ground beneath his feet as the huge slopes and distance melted before the lightning speed of that descent from death to life.

He took it in four mile-long zigzags, and it was the turning at each corner that nearly finished him, for then the strain of balancing taxed to the verge of collapse the remnants of his strength.

Slopes that have taken hours to climb can be descended in a

short half-hour on skis, but Hibbert had lost all count of time. Quite other thoughts and feelings mastered him in that wild, swift dropping through the air that was like the flight of a bird. For ever close upon his heels came following forms and voice with the whirling snow-dust. He heard that little silvery voice of death and laughter at his back. Shrill and wild, with the whistling of the wind past his ears, he caught its pursuing tones; but in anger now, no longer soft and coaxing. And it was accompanied; she did not follow alone. It seemed a host of these flying figures of the snow chased madly just behind him. He felt them furiously smite his neck and cheeks, snatch at his hands and try to entangle his feet and skis in drifts. His eyes they blinded, and they caught his breath away.

The terror of the heights and snow and winter desolation urged him forward in the maddest race with death a human being ever knew; and so terrific was the speed that before the gold and crimson had left the summits to touch the ice-lips of the lower glaciers, he saw the friendly forest far beneath swing up and welcome him.

And it was then, moving slowly along the edge of the woods, he saw a light. A man was carrying it. A procession of human figures was passing in a dark line laboriously through the snow. And—he heard the sound of chanting.

Instinctively, without a second's hesitation, he changed his course. No longer flying at an angle as before, he pointed his skis straight down the mountain-side. The dreadful steepness did not frighten him. He knew full well it meant a crashing tumble at the bottom, but he also knew it meant a doubling of his speed—with safety at the end. For, though no definite thought passed through his mind, he understood that it was the village *curé* who carried that little gleaming lantern in the dawn, and that he was taking the Host to a chalet on the lower slopes—to some peasant *in extremis*. He remembered her terror of the church and bells. She feared the holy symbols.

There was one last wild cry in his ears as he started, a shriek of the wind before his face, and a rush of stinging snow against closed eyelids—and then he dropped through empty space. Speed took sight from him. It seemed he flew off the surface of the world.

* * *

Indistinctly he recalls the murmur of men's voices, the touch of strong arms that lifted him, and the shooting pains as the skis were unfastened from the twisted ankle... for when he opened his eyes again to normal life he found himself lying in his bed at the post office with the doctor at his side. But for years to come the story of 'mad Hibbert's' skiing at night is recounted in that mountain village. He went, it seems, up slopes, and to a height that no man in his senses ever tried before. The tourists were agog about it for the rest of the season, and the very same day two of the bolder men went over the actual ground and photographed the slopes. Later Hibbert saw these photographs. He noticed one curious thing about them—though he did not mention it to any one:

There was only a single track.

THE HOUSE OF THE PAST

One night a Dream came to me and brought with her an old and rusty key. She led me across fields and sweet smelling lanes, where the hedges were already whispering to one another in the dark of the spring, till we came to a huge, gaunt house with staring windows and lofty roof half hidden in the shadows of very early morning. I noticed that the blinds were of heavy black, and that the house seemed wrapped in absolute stillness.

'This,' she whispered in my ear, 'is the House of the Past. Come with me and we will go through some of its rooms and passages; but quickly, for I have not the key for long, and the night is very nearly over. Yet, perchance, you shall remember!'

The key made a dreadful noise as she turned it in the lock, and when the great door swung open into an empty hall and we went in, I heard sounds of whispering and weeping, and the rustling of clothes, as of people moving in their sleep and about to wake. Then, instantly, a spirit of intense sadness came over me, drenching me to the soul; my eyes began to burn and smart, and in my heart I became aware of a strange sensation as of the uncoiling of something that had been asleep for ages. My whole being, unable to resist, at once surrendered itself to the spirit of deepest melancholy, and the pain of my heart, as the Things moved and woke, became in a moment of time too strong for words...

As we advanced, the faint voices and sobbings fled away before us into the interior of the House, and I became conscious that the air was full of hands held aloft, of swaying garments, of drooping tresses, and of eyes so sad and wistful that the tears, which were already brimming in my own, held back for wonder at the sight of such intolerable yearning.

'Do not allow all this sadness to overwhelm you,' whispered the Dream at my side. 'It is not often They wake. They sleep for years and years and years. The chambers are all full, and unless visitors such as we come to disturb them, they will never wake of their own accord. But, when one stirs, the sleep of the others is troubled, and they too awake, till the motion is communicated from one room to another and thus finally throughout the whole House... Then, sometimes, the sadness is too great to be borne, and the mind weakens. For this reason Memory gives to them the sweetest and deepest sleep she has, and she keeps this old key rusty from little use. But, listen now,' she added, holding up her hand: 'do you not hear all through the House that trembling of the air like the distant murmur of falling water? And do you not now... perhaps... *remember*?'

Even before she spoke, I had already caught faintly the beginning of a new sound; and, now, deep in the cellars beneath our feet, and from the upper regions of the great House as well, I heard the whispering, and the rustling and the inward stirring of the sleeping Shadows. It rose like a chord swept softly from huge unseen strings stretched somewhere among the foundations of the House, and its tremblings ran gently through its walls and ceilings. And I knew that I heard the slow awakening of the Ghosts of the Past.

Ah, me, with what terrible inrushing of sadness I stood with brimming eyes and listened to the faint dead voices of the long ago... For, indeed, the whole House was awakening; and there presently rose to my nostrils the subtle, penetrating perfume of age: of letters, long preserved, with ink faded and ribbons pale; of scented tresses, golden and brown, laid away, ah, how tenderly! among pressed flowers that still held the inmost delicacy of their forgotten fragrance; the scented presence of lost memories—the intoxicating incense of the past. My eyes o'erflowed, my heart tightened and expanded, as I yielded myself up without reserve to these old, old influences of sound and smell. These Ghosts of the Past—forgotten in the tumult of more recent memories—thronged round me, took my hands in theirs, and, ever whispering of what I had so long forgot, ever sighing, shaking from their hair and garments the ineffable odours of the dead ages, led me through the vast House, from room to room, from floor to floor.

And the Ghosts—were not all equally clear to me. Some had indeed but the faintest life, and stirred me so little that they left only an indistinct, blurred impression in the air; while others gazed half reproachfully at me out of faded, colourless eyes, as if longing to recall themselves to my recollection; and then, seeing they were not recognised, floated back gently into the shadows of their room, to sleep again undisturbed till the Final Day, when I should not fail to know them.

'Many of them have slept so long,' said the Dream beside me, 'that they wake only with the greatest difficulty. Once awake, however, they know and remember *you* even though you fail to remember them. For it is the rule in this House of the Past that, unless you recall them distinctly, remembering precisely when you knew them and with what particular causes in your past evolution they were associated, they cannot stay awake. Unless you remember them when your eyes meet, unless their look of recognition is returned by you, they are obliged to go back to their sleep, silent and sorrowful, their hands unpressed, their voices unheard, to sleep and dream, deathless and patient, till...'

At this moment, her words died away suddenly into the distance, and I became conscious of an overpowering sensation of delight and happiness. Something had touched me on the lips, and a strong, sweet fire flashed down into my heart and sent blood rushing tumultuously through my veins. My pulses beat wildly, my skin glowed, my eyes grew tender, and the terrible sadness of the place was instantly dispelled as if by magic. Turning with a cry of joy, that was at once swallowed up in the chorus of weeping and sighing round me, I looked... and instinctively stretched forth my arms in a rapture of happiness towards... towards a vision of a Face... hair, lips, eyes; a cloth of gold lay about the fair neck, and the old, old perfume of the East—ye stars, how long ago—was in her breath. Her lips were again on mine; her hair over my eyes; her arms about my neck, and the love of her ancient soul pouring into mine out of eyes still

THE HOUSE OF THE PAST

starry and undimmed. Oh, the fierce tumult, the untold wonder, if I could only remember!... That subtle, mist-dispelling odour of many ages ago, once so familiar... before the Hills of Atlantis were above the blue sea, or the sands had begun to form the bed of the Sphinx. Yet wait; it comes back; I begin to remember. Curtain upon curtain rises in my soul, and I can almost see beyond. But that hideous stretch of the years, awful and sinister, thousands upon thousands... My heart shakes, and I am afraid. Another curtain rises and a new vista, farther than the others, comes into view, interminable, running to a point among thick mists. Lo, they too are moving, rising, lightening. At last, I shall see... already I begin to recall... the dusky skin... the Eastern grace, the wondrous eyes that held the knowledge of Buddha and the wisdom of Christ before these had even dreamed of attainment. As a dream within a dream, it steals over me again, taking compelling possession of my whole being... the slender form... the stars in that magical Eastern sky... the whispering winds among the palm trees... the murmur of the river's waves and the music of the reeds where they bend and sigh in the shallows on the golden sand. Thousands of years ago in some aeonian distance. It fades a little and begins to pass; then seems again to rise. Ah me, that smile of the shining teeth... those lace-veined lids. Oh, who will help me to recall, for it is too far away, too dim, and I cannot wholly remember; though my lips are still tingling, and my arms still outstretched, it again begins to fade. Already there is a look of sadness too deep for words, as she realises that she is unrecognised... she, whose mere presence could once extinguish for me the entire universe... and she goes back slowly, mournfully, silently to her dim, tremendous sleep, to dream and dream of the day when I *must* remember her and she *must* come where she belongs...

She peers at me from the end of the room where the Shadows already cover her and win her back with outstretched arms to her age-long sleep in the House of the Past.

Trembling all over, with the strange odour still in my nostrils and the fire in my heart, I turned away and followed my Dream up a broad staircase into another part of the House.

As we entered the upper corridors I heard the wind pass singing over the roof. Its music took possession of me until I felt as though my whole body were a single heart, aching, straining, throbbing as if it would break; and all because I heard the wind singing round this House of the Past.

'But, remember,' whispered the Dream, answering my unspoken wonder, 'that you are listening to the song it has sung for untold ages into untold myriad ears. It carries back so appallingly far; and in that simple dirge, profound in its terrible monotony, are the associations and recollections, of the joys, griefs, and struggles of all your previous existence. The wind, like the sea, speaks to the inmost memory,' she added, 'and that is why its voice is one of such deep spiritual sadness. It is the song of things for ever incomplete, unfinished, unsatisfying.'

As we passed through the vaulted rooms, I noticed that no one stirred. There was no actual sound, only a general impression of deep, collective breathing, like the heave of a muffled ocean. But the rooms, I knew at once, were full to the walls, crowded, rows upon rows... And, from the floors below, rose ever the murmur of the weeping Shadows as they returned to their sleep, and settled down again in the silence, the darkness, and the dust. The dust... Ah, the dust that floated in this House of the Past, so thick, so penetrating; so fine, it filled the throat and eyes without pain; so fragrant, it soothed the senses and stilled the aching of the heart; so soft, it parched the tongue, without offence; yet so silently falling, gathering, settling over everything, that the air held it like a fine mist and the sleeping Shadows wore it for their shrouds.

'And these are the oldest,' said my Dream, 'the longest asleep,' pointing to the crowded rows of silent sleepers. 'None here have wakened for ages too many to count; and even if they woke, you would not know them. They are, like the others, all your own, but they are the memories of your earliest stages along the great Path of Evolution. Some day, though, they will awake, and you

THE HOUSE OF THE PAST

must know them, and answer their questions, for they cannot die till they have exhausted themselves again through you who gave them birth.'

'Ah me,' I thought, only half listening to or understanding these last words, 'what mothers, fathers, brothers may then be asleep in this room; what faithful lovers, what true friends, what ancient enemies! And to think that some day they will step forth and confront me, and I shall meet their eyes again, claim them, know them, forgive, and be forgiven... the memories of all my Past...'

I turned to speak to the Dream at my side, but she was already fading into dimness, and, as I looked again, the whole House melted away into the flush of the eastern sky, and I heard the birds singing and saw the clouds overhead veiling the stars in the light of coming day.

THE DECOY

It belonged to the category of unlovely houses about which an ugly superstition clings, one reason being, perhaps, its inability to inspire interest in itself without assistance. It seemed too ordinary to possess individuality, much less to exert an influence. Solid and ungainly, its huge bulk dwarfing the park timber, its best claim to notice was a negative one—it was unpretentious.

From the little hill its expressionless windows stared across the Kentish Weald, indifferent to weather, dreary in winter, bleak in spring, unblessed in summer. Some colossal hand had tossed it down, then let it starve to death, a country mansion that might well strain the adjectives of advertisers and find inheritors with difficulty. Its soul had fled, said some; it had committed suicide, thought others; and it was an inheritor, before he killed himself in the library, who thought this latter, yielding, apparently, to an hereditary taint in the family. For two other inheritors followed suit, with an interval of twenty years between them, and there was no clear reason to explain the three disasters. Only the first owner, indeed, lived permanently in the house, the others using it in the summer months and then deserting it with relief. Hence, when John Burley, present inheritor, assumed possession, he entered a house about which clung an ugly superstition, based, nevertheless, upon a series of undeniably ugly facts.

This century deals harshly with superstitious folk, deeming them fools or charlatans; but John Burley, robust, contemptuous of half lights, did not deal harshly with them, because he did not deal with them at all. He was hardly aware of their existence. He ignored them as he ignored, say, the Esquimaux, poets, and other human aspects that did not touch his scheme of life. A successful business man, he concentrated on what was real; he dealt with business people. His philanthropy, on a big scale, was also real; yet, though he would have denied it vehemently, he had his superstition as well. No man exists without some taint of superstition in his blood; the racial heritage is too rich to be escaped entirely. Burley's took this form—that unless he gave his tithe to the poor he would not prosper. This ugly mansion, he decided, would make an ideal Convalescent Home.

'Only cowards or lunatics kill themselves,' he declared flatly, when his use of the house was criticised. 'I'm neither one nor t'other.' He let out his gusty, boisterous laugh. In his invigorating atmosphere such weakness seemed contemptible, just as superstition in his presence seemed feeblest ignorance. Even its picturesqueness faded. 'I can't conceive,' he boomed, 'can't even imagine to myself,' he added emphatically, 'the state of mind in which a man can *think* of suicide, much less do it.' He threw his chest out with a challenging air. 'I tell you, Nancy, it's either cowardice or mania. And I've no use for either.'

Yet he was easy-going and good-humoured in his denunciation. He admitted his limitations with a hearty laugh his wife called noisy. Thus he made allowances for the fairy fears of sailorfolk, and had even been known to mention haunted ships his Companies owned. But he did so in the terms of tonnage and £ s. d. His scope was big; details were made for clerks.

His consent to pass a night in the mansion was the consent of a practical business man and philanthropist who dealt condescendingly with foolish human nature. It was based on the common-sense of tonnage and £ s. d. The local newspapers had revived the silly story of the suicides, calling attention to the effect of the superstition upon the fortunes of the house, and so, possibly, upon the fortunes of its present owner. But the mansion, otherwise a white elephant, was precisely ideal for his purpose, and so trivial a matter as spending a night in it should not stand in the way. 'We must take people as we find them, Nancy.'

His young wife had her motive, of course, in making the proposal, and, if she was amused by what she called 'spook-hunting', he saw no reason to refuse her the indulgence. He loved her, and took her as he found her—late in life. To allay the superstitions of prospective staff and patients and supporters, all, in fact, whose goodwill was necessary to success, he faced this boredom of a night in the building before its opening was announced. 'You see, John, if you, the owner, do this, it will nip damaging talk in the bud. If anything went wrong later it would only be put down to this suicide idea, this haunting influence. The Home will have a bad name from the start. There'll be endless trouble. It will be a failure.'

'You think my spending a night there will stop the nonsense?' he enquired.

'According to the old legend it breaks the spell,' she replied. 'That's the condition, anyhow.'

'But somebody's sure to die there sooner or later,' he objected. 'We can't prevent that.'

'We can prevent people whispering that they died unnaturally.' She explained the working of the public mind.

'I see,' he replied, his lip curling, yet quick to gauge the truth of what she told him about collective instinct.

'Unless *you* take poison in the hall,' she added laughingly, 'or elect to hang yourself with your braces from the hat peg.'

'I'll do it,' he agreed, after a moment's thought. 'I'll sit up with you. It will be like a honeymoon over again, you and I on the spree—eh?' He was even interested now; the boyish side of him was touched perhaps; but his enthusiasm was less when she explained that three was a better number than two on such an expedition.

'I've often done it before, John. We were always three.'

'Who?' he asked bluntly. He looked wonderingly at her, but she answered that if anything went wrong a party of three provided a better margin for help. It was sufficiently obvious. He listened and agreed. 'I'll get young Mortimer,' he suggested. 'Will he do?'

She hesitated. 'Well—he's cheery; he'll be interested, too. Yes, he's as good as another.' She seemed indifferent.

'And he'll make the time pass with his stories,' added her husband.

THE DECOY

So Captain Mortimer, late officer on a T.B.D., a 'cheery lad', afraid of nothing, cousin of Mrs. Burley, and now filling a good post in the company's London offices, was engaged as third hand in the expedition. But Captain Mortimer was young and ardent, and Mrs. Burley was young and pretty and ill-mated, and John Burley was a neglectful and self-satisfied husband.

Fate laid the trap with cunning, and John Burley, blind-eyed, careless of detail, floundered into it. He also floundered out again, though in a fashion none could have expected of him.

The night agreed upon eventually was as near to the shortest in the year as John Burley could contrive—June 18th—when the sun set at 8.18 and rose about a quarter to four. There would be barely three hours of true darkness. 'You're the expert,' he admitted, as she explained that sitting through the actual darkness only was required, not necessarily from sunset to sunrise. 'We'll do the thing properly. Mortimer's not very keen, he had a dance or something,' he added, noticing the look of annoyance that flashed swiftly in her eyes; 'but he got out of it. He's coming.' The pouting expression of the spoilt woman amused him. 'Oh, no, he didn't need much persuading really,' he assured her. 'Some girl or other, of course. He's young, remember.' To which no comment was forthcoming, though the implied comparison made her flush.

They motored from South Audley Street after an early tea, in due course passing Sevenoaks and entering the Kentish Weald; and, in order that the necessary advertisement should be given, the chauffeur, warned strictly to keep their purpose quiet, was to put up at the country inn and fetch them an hour after sunrise; they would breakfast in London. 'He'll tell everybody,' said his practical and cynical master; 'the local newspaper will have it all next day. A few hours' discomfort is worth while if it ends the nonsense. We'll read and smoke, and Mortimer shall tell us yarns about the sea.' He went with the driver into the house to superintend the arrangement of the room, the lights, the hampers of food, and so forth, leaving the pair upon the lawn.

'Four hours isn't much, but it's something,' whispered Mortimer, alone with her for the first time since they started. 'It's simply ripping of you to have got me in. You look divine to-night. You're the most wonderful woman in the world.' His blue eyes shone with the hungry desire he mistook for love. He looked as if he had blown in from the sea, for his skin was tanned and his light hair bleached a little by the sun. He took her hand, drawing her out of the slanting sunlight towards the rhododendrons.

'I didn't, you silly boy. It was John suggested your coming.' She released her hand with an affected effort. 'Besides, you overdid it—pretending you had a dance.'

'You could have objected,' he said eagerly, 'and didn't. Oh, you're too lovely, you're delicious!' He kissed her suddenly with passion. There was a tiny struggle, in which she yielded too easily, he thought.

'Harry, you're an idiot!' she cried breathlessly, when he let her go. 'I really don't know how you dare! And John's your friend. Besides, you know'—she glanced round quickly— 'it isn't safe here.' Her eyes shone happily, her cheeks were flaming. She looked what she was, a pretty, young, lustful animal, false to ideals, true to selfish passion only. 'Luckily,' she added, 'he trusts me too fully to think anything.'

The young man, worship in his eyes, laughed gaily. 'There's no harm in a kiss,' he said. 'You're a child to him, he never thinks of you as a woman. Anyhow, his head's full of ships and kings and sealing-wax,' he comforted her, while respecting her sudden instinct which warned him not to touch her again, 'and he never sees anything. Why, even at ten yards——'

From twenty yards away a big voice interrupted him, as John Burley came round a corner of the house and across the lawn towards them. The chauffeur, he announced, had left the hampers in the room on the first floor and gone back to the inn. 'Let's take a walk round,' he added, joining them, 'and see the garden. Five minutes before sunset we'll go in and feed.' He laughed. 'We must do the thing faithfully, you know, mustn't we, Nancy? Dark to dark, remember. Come on, Mortimer'—he took the young man's arm—'a last look round before we go in and hang ourselves from adjoining hooks in the matron's room!' He reached out his free hand towards his wife.

'Oh, hush, John!' she said quickly. 'I don't like—especially now the dusk is coming.' She shivered, as though it were a genuine little shiver, pursing her lips deliciously as she did so; whereupon he drew her forcibly to him, saying he was sorry, and kissed her exactly where she had been kissed two minutes before, while young Mortimer looked on. 'We'll take care of you between us,' he said. Behind a broad back the pair exchanged a swift but meaning glance, for there was that in his tone which enjoined wariness, and perhaps after all he was not so blind as he appeared. They had their code, these two. 'All's well,' was signalled; 'but another time be more careful!'

There still remained some minutes' sunlight before the huge red ball of fire would sink behind the wooded hills, and the trio, talking idly, a flutter of excitement in two hearts certainly, walked among the roses. It was a perfect evening, windless, perfumed, warm. Headless shadows preceded them gigantically across the lawn as they moved, and one side of the great building lay already dark; bats were flitting, moths darted to and fro above the azalea and rhododendron clumps. The talk turned chiefly on the uses of the mansion as a Convalescent Home, its probable running cost, suitable staff, and so forth.

'Come along,' John Burley said presently, breaking off and turning abruptly, 'we must be inside, actually inside, before the sun's gone. We must fulfil the conditions faithfully,' he repeated as though fond of the phrase. He was in earnest over everything in life, big or little, once he set his hand to it.

They entered, this incongruous trio of ghost-hunters, no one of them really intent upon the business in hand, and went slowly upstairs to the great room where the hampers lay. Already in the hall it was dark enough for three electric torches to flash usefully and help their steps as they moved with caution, lighting one corner after another. The air inside was chill and damp. 'Like an unused museum,' said Mortimer. 'I can smell the specimens.' They looked about them, sniffing. 'That's humanity,' declared his host, employer, friend, 'with cement and whitewash to flavour it'; and all three laughed as Mrs. Burley said she wished they had picked some roses and brought them in. Her husband was again in front on the broad staircase, Mortimer just behind him, when she called out. 'I don't like being last,' she exclaimed. 'It's so black behind me in the hall. I'll come between you two,' and the sailor took her outstretched hand, squeezing it, as he passed her up. 'There's a figure, remember,' she said hurriedly turning to gain her husband's attention, as when she touched wood at home. 'A figure is seen; that's part of the story. The figure of a man.' She gave a tiny shiver of pleasure, half-imagined alarm as she took his arm.

'I hope we shall see it,' he mentioned prosaically.

'I hope we shan't,' she replied with emphasis. 'It's only seen before—something happens.' Her husband said nothing, while Mortimer remarked facetiously that it would be a pity if they had their trouble for nothing. 'Something can hardly happen to all three of us,' he said lightly, as they entered a large room where the paper-hangers had conveniently left a rough table of bare planks. Mrs. Burley, busy with her own thoughts, began to unpack the sandwiches and wine. Her husband strolled over to the window. He seemed restless.

'So this'—his deep voice startled her—'is where one of us' —he looked round him—' is to——'

'John!' She stopped him sharply, with impatience. 'Several times already I've begged you.' Her voice rang rather shrill and querulous in the empty room, a new note in it. She was beginning to feel the atmosphere of the place, perhaps. On the sunny lawn it had not touched her, but now, with the fall of night, she was aware of it, as shadow called to shadow and the kingdom of darkness gathered power. Like a great whispering gallery, the whole house listened.

'Upon my word, Nancy,' he said with contrition, as he came and sat down beside her, 'I quite forgot again. Only I cannot take it seriously. It's utterly unthinkable to me that a man——'

'But why evoke the idea at all?' she insisted in a lowered voice, that snapped despite its faintness. 'Men, after all, don't do such things for nothing.'

'We don't know everything in the universe, do we?' Mortimer put in, trying clumsily to support her. 'All I know just now is that I'm famished and this veal and ham pie is delicious.' He was very busy with his knife and fork. His foot rested lightly on her own beneath the table; he could not keep his eyes off her face; he was continually passing new edibles to her.

'No,' agreed John Burley, 'not everything. You're right there.'

She kicked the younger man gently, flashing a warning with her eyes as well, while her husband, emptying his glass, his head thrown back, looked straight at them over the rim, apparently seeing nothing. They smoked their cigarettes round the table, Burley lighting a big cigar. 'Tell us about the figure, Nancy?' he inquired. 'At least there's no harm in that. It's new to me. I hadn't heard about a figure.' And she did so willingly, turning her chair sideways from the dangerous, reckless feet. Mortimer could now no longer touch her. 'I know very little,' she confessed; 'only what the paper said. It's a man... And he changes.'

'How changes?' asked her husband. 'Clothes, you mean, or what?'

Mrs. Burley laughed, as though she was glad to laugh. Then the answered: 'According to the story he shows himself each sime to the man——'

'The man who——?'

'Yes, yes, of course. He appears to the man who dies—as himself.'

'H'm,' grunted her husband, naturally puzzled. He stared at her.

'Each time the chap saw his own double'— Mortimer came this time usefully to the rescue—'before he did it.'

Considerable explanation followed, involving much psychic

jargon from Mrs. Burley, which fascinated and impressed the sailor, who thought her as wonderful as she was lovely, showing it in his eyes for all to see. John Burley's attention wandered. He moved over to the window, leaving them to finish the discussion between them; he took no part in it, made no comment even, merely listening idly and watching them with an air of absent-mindedness through the cloud of cigar smoke round his head. He moved from window to window, ensconcing himself in turn in each deep embrasure, examining the fastenings, measuring the thickness of the stonework with his handkerchief. He seemed restless, bored, obviously out of place in this ridiculous expedition. On his big massive face lay a quiet, resigned expression his wife had never seen before. She noticed it now as, the discussion ended, the pair tidied away the *débris* of dinner, lit the spirit lamp for coffee and laid out a supper which would be very welcome with the dawn. A draught passed through the room, making the papers flutter on the table. Mortimer turned down the smoking lamps with care.

'Wind's getting up a bit—from the south,' observed Burley from his niche, closing one-half of the casement window as he said it. To do this, he turned his back a moment, fumbling for several seconds with the latch, while Mortimer, noting it, seized his sudden opportunity with the foolish abandon of his age and temperament. Neither he nor his victim perceived that, against the outside darkness, the interior of the room was plainly reflected in the window-pane. One reckless, the other terrified, they snatched the fearful joy, which might, after all, have been lengthened by another full half-minute, for the head they feared, followed by the shoulders, pushed through the side of the casement still open, and remained outside, taking in the night.

'A grand air,' said his deep voice, as the head drew in again. 'I'd like to be at sea a night like this.' He left the casement open and came across the room towards them. 'Now,' he said cheerfully, arranging a seat for himself, 'let's get comfortable for the night. Mortimer, we expect stories from you without ceasing, until dawn or the ghost arrives. Horrible stories of

THE DECOY

chains and headless men, remember. Make it a night we shan't forget in a hurry.' He produced his gust of laughter.

They arranged their chairs, with other chairs to put their feet on, and Mortimer contrived a footstool by means of a hamper for the smallest feet; the air grew thick with tobacco smoke; eyes flashed and answered, watched perhaps as well; ears listened and perhaps grew wise; occasionally, as a window shook, they started and looked round; there were sounds about the house from time to time, when the entering wind, using broken or open windows, set loose objects rattling.

But Mrs. Burley vetoed horrible stories with decision. A big, empty mansion, lonely in the country, and even with the comfort of John Burley and a lover in it, has its atmosphere. Furnished rooms are far less ghostly. This atmosphere now came creeping everywhere, through spacious halls and sighing corridors, silent, invisible, but all-pervading, John Burley alone impervious to it, unaware of its soft attack upon the nerves. It entered possibly with the summer night wind, but possibly it was always there... And Mrs. Burley looked often at her husband, sitting near her at an angle; the light fell on his fine strong face; she felt that, though apparently so calm and quiet, he was really very restless; something about him was a little different; she could not define it; his mouth seemed set as with an effort; he looked, she thought curiously to herself, patient and very dignified; he was rather a dear after all. Why did she think the face inscrutable? Her thoughts wandered vaguely, unease, discomfort among them somewhere, while the heated blood—she had taken her share of wine—seethed in her.

Burley turned to the sailor for more stories. 'Sea and wind in them,' he asked. 'No horrors, remember!' And Mortimer told a tale about the shortage of rooms at a Welsh seaside place where spare rooms fetched fabulous prices, and one man alone refused to let—a retired captain of a South Seas trader, very poor, a bit crazy apparently. He had two furnished rooms in his house worth twenty guineas a week. The rooms faced south; he kept them full of flowers; but he would not let. An explanation of his unworldly obstinacy was not forthcoming until Mortimer—they fished together—gained his confidence. 'The South Wind lives in them,' the old fellow told him. 'I keep them free for her.'

'For *her*?'

'It was on the South Wind my love came to me,' said the other softly; 'and it was on the South Wind that she left——'

It was an odd tale to tell in such company, but he told it well.

'Beautiful,' thought Mrs. Burley. Aloud she said a quiet, 'Thank you. By "left" I suppose he meant she died or ran away?'

John Burley looked up with a certain surprise. 'We ask for a story,' he said, 'and you give us a poem.' He laughed. 'You're in love, Mortimer,' he informed him, 'and with my wife, probably.'

'Of course I am, sir,' replied the young man gallantly. 'A sailor's heart, you know,' while the face of the woman turned pink, then white. She knew her husband more intimately than Mortimer did, and there was something in his tone, his eyes, his words, she did not like. Harry was an idiot to choose such a tale. An irritated annoyance stirred in her, close upon dislike. 'Anyhow, it's better than horrors,' she said hurriedly.

'Well,' put in her husband, letting forth a minor gust of laughter, 'it's possible, at any rate. Though one's as crazy as the other.' His meaning was not wholly clear. 'If a man really loved,' he added in his blunt fashion, 'and was tricked by her, I could almost conceive his——'

'Oh, don't preach, John, for Heaven's sake. You're so dull in the pulpit.' But the interruption only served to emphasise the sentence which, otherwise, might have been passed over.

'Could conceive his finding life so worthless,' persisted the other, 'that——' He hesitated. 'But there, now, I promised I wouldn't,' he went on, laughing good-humouredly. Then, suddenly, as though in spite of himself, driven it seemed: 'Still, under such conditions, he might show his contempt for human nature and for life by——'

It was a tiny stifled scream that stopped him this time.

'John, I hate, I loathe you, when you talk like that. And you've broken your word again.' She was more than petulant; a nervous anger sounded in her voice. It was the way he had said it, looking from them towards the window, that made her quiver. She felt him suddenly as a man; she felt afraid of him.

Her husband made no reply; he rose and looked at his watch, leaning sideways towards the lamp, so that the expression of his face was shaded. 'Two o'clock,' he remarked. 'I think I'll take a turn through the house. I may find a workman asleep or something. Anyhow, the light will soon come now.' He laughed; the expression of his face, his tone of voice, relieved her momentarily. He went out. They heard his heavy tread echoing down the carpetless long corridor.

Mortimer began at once. 'Did he mean anything?' he asked breathlessly. 'He doesn't love you the least little bit, anyhow. He never did. I do. You're wasted on him. You belong to me.' The words poured out. He covered her face with kisses. 'Oh. I didn't mean *that*,' he caught between the kisses.

The sailor released her, staring. 'What then?' he whispered. 'Do you think he saw us on the lawn?' He paused a moment, as she made no reply. The steps were audible in the distance still. 'I know!' he exclaimed suddenly. 'It's the blessed house he feels. That's what it is. He doesn't like it.'

A wind sighed through the room, making the papers flutter; something rattled; and Mrs. Burley started. A loose end of rope swinging from the paperhanger's ladder caught her eye. She shivered slightly.

'He's different,' she replied in a low voice, nestling very close again, 'and so restless. Didn't you notice what he said just now —that under certain conditions he could understand a man'— she hesitated—'doing it,' she concluded, a sudden drop in her voice. 'Harry,' she looked full into his eyes, 'that's not like him. He didn't say that for nothing.'

'Nonsense! He's bored to tears, that's all. And the house is getting on your nerves, too.' He kissed her tenderly. Then, as she responded, he drew her nearer still and held her passionately, mumbling incoherent words, among which 'nothing to be afraid of' was distinguishable. Meanwhile, the steps were coming nearer. She pushed him away. 'You must behave yourself. I insist. You shall, Harry.' Then buried herself in his arms, her face hidden against his neck—only to disentagle herself the next instant and stand clear of him. 'I hate you, Harry,' she exclaimed sharply, a look of angry annoyance flashing across her face. 'And I *hate* myself. Why do you treat me——?' She broke off as the steps came closer, patted her hair straight, and stalked over to the open window.

'I believe after all you're only playing with me,' he said viciously. He stared in surprised disappointment, watching her. 'It's him you really love,' he added jealously. He looked and spoke like a petulant spoilt boy.

She did not turn her head. 'He's always been fair to me, kind and generous. He never blames me for anything. Give me a cigarette, and don't play the stage hero. My nerves are on edge, to tell you the truth.' Her voice jarred harshly, and as he lit her cigarette he noticed that her lips were trembling; his own hand trembled too. He was still holding the match, standing beside her at the window-sill, when the steps crossed the threshold and John Burley came into the room. He went straight up to the table and turned the lamp down. 'It was smoking,' he remarked. 'Didn't you see?'

'I'm sorry, sir.' And Mortimer sprang forward too late to help him. 'It was the draught as you pushed the door open.' The big man said, 'Ah!' and drew a chair over, facing them. 'It's just *the* very house,' he told them. 'I've been through every room in this floor. It will make a splendid Home, with very little alteration, too'. He turned round in his creaking wicker chair and looked up at his wife, who sat swinging her legs and smoking in the window embrasure. 'Lives will be saved inside these old walls. It's a good investment,' he went on, talking rather to himself it seemed. 'People will die here, too——'

'Hark!' Mrs. Burley interrupted him. 'That noise—what is it?' A faint thudding sound in the corridor or in the adjoining room was audible, making all three look round quickly, listening for a repetition, which did not come. The papers fluttered on the table, the lamps smoked an instant.

'Wind,' observed Burley calmly, 'our little friend, the South Wind. Something blown over again, that's all.' But, curiously, the three of them stood up. 'I'll go and see', he continued. 'Doors and windows are all open to let the paint dry.' Yet he did not move; he stood there watching a white moth that dashed round and round the lamp, flopping heavily now and again upon the bare deal table.

'Let me go, sir,' put in Mortimer eagerly. He was glad of the chance; for the first time he, too, felt uncomfortable. But there was another, who, apparently, suffered a discomfort greater than his own and was accordingly even more glad to get away. 'I'll go,' Mrs. Burley announced, with decision. 'I'd like to. I haven't been out of this room since we came. I'm not an atom afraid.'

It was strange that for a moment she did not make a move either; it seemed as if she waited for something. For perhaps fifteen seconds no one stirred or spoke. She knew by the look in her lover's eyes that he had now become aware of the slight, indefinite change in her husband's manner, and was alarmed by it. The fear in him woke her contempt; she suddenly despised the youth, and was conscious of a new, strange yearning towards her husband; against her worked nameless pressure, troubling her being. There was an alteration in the room, she thought; something had come in. The trio stood listening to the gentle wind outside, waiting for the sound to be repeated; two careless, passionate young lovers and a man stood waiting, listening, watching in that room; yet it seemed there were five persons altogether and not three, for two guilty consciences stood apart and separate from their owners. John Burley broke the silence.

'Yes, you go, Nancy. Nothing to be afraid of—there. It's only wind.' He spoke as though he meant it.

Mortimer bit his lips. 'I'll come with you,' he said instantly. He was confused. 'Let's all three go. I don't think we ought to be separated.' But Mrs. Burley was already at the door. 'I insist,' she said, with a forced laugh. 'I'll call if I'm frightened,' while her husband, saying nothing, watched her from the table.

'Take this,' said the sailor, flashing his electric torch as he went over to her. 'Two are better than one.' He saw her figure exquisitely silhouetted against the black corridor beyond; it was clear she wanted to go; any nervousness in her was mastered by a stronger emotion still; she was glad to be out of their presence for a bit. He had hoped to snatch a word of explanation in the corridor, but her manner stopped him. Something else stopped him, too.

'First door on the left,' he called out, his voice echoing down the empty length. 'That's the room where the noise came from. Shout if you want us.'

He watched her moving away, the light held steadily in front of her, but she made no answer, and he turned back to see John Burley lighting his cigar at the lamp chimney, his face thrust forward as he did so. He stood a second, watching him, as the lips sucked hard at the cigar to make it draw; the strenght of the features was emphasised to sternness. He had meant to stand by the door and listen for the least sound from the adjoining room, but now found his whole attention focussed on the face above the lamp. In that minute he realised that Burley had wished—had meant—his wife to go. In that minute also he forgot his love, his shameless, selfish little mistress, his worthless, caddish little self. For John Burley looked up. He straightened slowly, puffing hard and quickly to make sure his cigar was lit, and faced him. Mortimer moved forward into the room, self-conscious, embarrassed, cold.

'Of course it was only wind,' he said lightly, his one desire being to fill the interval while they were alone with common-places. He did not wish the other to speak. 'Dawn wind, probably.' He glanced at his wrist-watch. 'It's half-past two already and the sun gets up at a quarter to four. It's light by now, I expect. The shortest night is never quite dark.' He rambled on confusedly, for the others steady, silent stare embarrassed him.

A faint sound of Mrs. Burley moving in the next room made him stop a moment. He turned instinctively to the door, eager for an excuse to go.

'That's nothing,' said Burley, speaking at last and in a firm quiet voice. 'Only my wife, glad to be alone—my young and pretty wife. She's all right. I know her better than you do. Come in and shut the door.'

Mortimer obeyed. He closed the door and came close to the table, facing the other, who at once continued.

'If I thought,' he said, in that quiet deep voice, 'that you two were serious'—he uttered his words very slowly, with emphasis, with intense severity—'do you know what I should do? I will tell you, Mortimer. I should like one of us two—you or myself—to remain in this house, dead.'

His teeth gripped his cigar tightly; his hands were clenched; he went on through a half-closed mouth. His eyes blazed steadily.

'I trust her so absolutely—understand me?—that my belief in women, in human beings, would go. And with it the desire to live. Understand me?'

Each word to the young careless fool was a blow in the face, yet it was the softest blow, the flash of a big deep heart, that hurt the most. A dozen answers—denial, explanation, confession, taking all guilt upon himself—crowded his mind, only to be dismissed. He stood motionless and silent, staring hard into the other's eyes. No word passed his lips; there was no time in any case. It was in this position that Mrs. Burley, entering at that moment, found them. She saw her husband's face; the other man stood with his back to her. She came in with a little nervous laugh. 'A bell-rope swinging in the wind and hitting a sheet of metal before the fireplace,' she informed them. And all three laughed together then, though each laugh had a different sound. 'But I hate this house,' she added. 'I wish we had never come.'

'The moment there's light in the sky,' remarked her husband quietly, 'we can leave. That's the contract; let's see it through. Another half-hour will do it. Sit down, Nancy, and have a bit of something.' He got up and placed a chair for her. 'I think I'll take another look round.' He moved slowly to the door. 'I may go out on to the lawn a bit, and see what the sky is doing.'

It did not take half a minute to say the words, yet to Mortimer it seemed as though the voice would never end. His mind was confused and troubled. He loathed himself, he loathed the woman through whom he had got into this awkward mess.

The situation had suddenly become extremely painful; he had never imagined such a thing; the man he had thought blind had after all seen everything—known it all along, watched them, waited. And the woman, he was now certain, loved her husband; she had fooled him, Mortimer, all along, amusing herself.

'I'll come with you, sir. Do let me,' he said suddenly. Mrs. Burley stood pale and uncertain between them. She looked scared. What has happened, she was clearly wondering.

'No, no, Harry'—he called him 'Harry' for the first time— 'I'll be back in five minutes at most. My wife mustn't be alone either.' And he went out.

The young man waited till the footsteps sounded some distance down the corridor, then turned, but he did not move forward; for the first time he let pass unused what he called 'an opportunity'. His passion had left him; his love, as he once thought it, was gone. He looked at the pretty woman near him, wondering blankly what he had ever seen there to attract him so wildly. He wished to Heaven he was out of it all. He wished he were dead. John Burley's words suddenly appalled him.

One thing he saw plainly—she was frightened. This opened his lips.

'What's the matter?' he asked, and his hushed voice shirked the familiar Christian name. 'Did you see anything?' He nodded his head in the direction of the adjoining room. It was the sound of his own voice addressing her coldly that made him abruptly see himself as he really was, but it was her reply, honestly given, in a faint even voice, that told him she saw her own self too with similar clarity. God, he thought, how revealing a tone, a single word can be!

'I saw—nothing. Only I feel uneasy—dear.' That 'dear' was a call for help.

'Look here,' he cried, so loud that she held up a warning finger, 'I'm—I've been a damned fool, a cad! I'm most frightfully ashamed. I'll do anything—*anything* to get it right.' He felt cold, naked, his worthlessness laid bare; she felt, he knew, the same. Each revolted suddenly from the other. Yet he knew not quite how or wherefore this great change had thus abruptly come about, especially on her side. He felt that a bigger, deeper emotion than he could understand was working on them, making mere physical relationships seem empty, trivial, cheap and vulgar. His cold increased in face of this utter ignorance.

'Uneasy?' he repeated, perhaps hardly knowing exactly why he said it. 'Good Lord, but he can take care of himself——'

'Oh, *he* is a man,' she interrupted; 'yes.'

Steps were heard, firm, heavy steps, coming back along the corridor. It seemed to Mortimer that he had listened to this sound of steps all night, and would listen to them till he died. He crossed to the lamp and lit a cigarette, carefully this time, turning the wick down afterwards. Mrs. Burley also rose, moving over towards the door, away from him. They listened a moment to these firm and heavy steps, the tread of a man, John Burley. A man... and a philanderer, flashed across Mortimer's brain like fire, contrasting the two with fierce contempt for himself. The tread became less audible. There was distance in it. It had turned in somewhere.

'There!' she exclaimed in a hushed tone. 'He's gone in.'

'Nonsense! It passed us. He's going out on to the lawn.'

The pair listened breathlessly for a moment, when the sound of steps came distinctly from the adjoining room, walking across the boards, apparently towards the window.

'There!' she repeated. 'He did go in.'

Silence of perhaps a minute followed, in which they heard each other's breathing. 'I don't like being alone—in there,' Mrs. Burley said in a thin faltering voice, and moved as though to go out. Her hand was already on the knob of the door, when Mortimer stopped her with a violent gesture.

'Don't! For God's sake, don't!' he cried, before she could turn it. He darted forward. As he laid a hand upon her arm a thud was audible through the wall. It was a heavy sound, and this time there was no wind to cause it.

It's only that loose swinging thing,' he whispered thickly, a dreadful confusion blotting out clear thought and speech.

'There was no loose swaying thing at all,' she said in a failing voice, then reeled and swayed against him. 'I invented that. There was nothing.' As he caught her, staring helplessly, it seemed to him that a face with lifted lids rushed up a him. He saw two terrified eyes in a patch of ghastly white. Her whisper followed, as she sank into his arms. 'It's John, he's——'

At which instant, with terror at its climax, the sound of steps suddenly became audible once more—the firm and heavy tread of John Burley coming out again into the corridor. Such was their amazement and relief that they neither moved nor spoke. The steps drew nearer. The pair seemed petrified; Mortimer did not remove his arms, nor did Mrs. Burley attempt to release herself. They stared at the door and waited. It was pushed wider the next second, and John Burley stood beside them. He was so close he almost touched them—there in each other's arms.

'Jack, dear!' cried his wife, with a searching tenderness that made her voice seem strange.

He gazed a second at each in turn. 'I'm going out on to the lawn for a moment,' he said quietly. There was no expression on his face; he did not smile, he did not frown; he showed no feeling, no emotion—just looked into their eyes, and then withdrew round the edge of the door before either could utter a word in answer. The door swung to behind him. He was gone.

'He's going to the lawn. He said so.' It was Mortimer speaking, but his voice shook and stammered. Mrs. Burley had released herself. She stood now by the table, silent, gazing with fixed eyes at nothing, her lips parted, her expression vacant. Again she was aware of an alteration in the room: something had gone out. ... He watched her a second, uncertain what to say or do. It was the face of a drowned person, occurred to him. Something intangible, yet almost visible stood between them in that narrow space. Something had ended, there before his eyes, definitely ended. The barrier between them rose higher, denser. Through this barrier her words came to him with an odd whispering remoteness.

'Harry. ... You saw? You noticed?'

'What d'you mean?' he said gruffly. He tried to feel angry, contemptuous, but his breath caught absurdly.

'Harry—he was different. The eyes, the hair, the'—her face grew like death—'the twist in his face——'

'What on earth are you saying? Pull yourself together.' He saw that she was trembling down the whole length of her body, as she leaned against the table for support. His own legs shook. He stared hard at her.

'Altered, Harry ... altered.' Her horrified whisper came at him like a knife. For it was true. He, too, had noticed something about the husband's appearance that was not quite normal. Yet, even while they talked, they heard him going down the carpetless stairs; the sounds ceased as he crossed the hall; then came the noise of the front door banging, the reverberation even shaking the room a little where they stood.

Mortimer went over to her side. He walked unevenly.

'My dear! For God's sake—this is sheer nonsense. Don't let yourself go like this. I'll put it straight with him—it's all my fault.' He saw by her face that she did not understand his words; he was saying the wrong thing altogether; her mind was utterly elsewhere. 'He's all right,' he went on hurriedly. 'He's not on the lawn now——'

He broke off at sight of her. The horror that fastened on her brain plastered her face with deathly whiteness.

'That was not John at all,' she cried, a wail of misery and terror in her voice. She rushed to the window and he followed. To his immense relief a figure moving below was plainly visible. It was John Burley. They saw him in the faint grey of the dawn, as he crossed the lawn, going away from the house. He disappeared.

'There you are! See?' whispered Mortimer reassuringly. 'He'll be back in——' when a sound in the adjoining room, heavier, louder than before, cut appallingly across his words, and Mrs. Burley, with that wailing scream, fell back into his arms. He caught her only just in time, for he stiffened into ice, daft with the uncomprehended terror of it all, and helpless as a child.

'Darling, my darling—oh, God!' He bent, kissing her face wildly. He was utterly distraught.

'Harry! Jack—oh, oh!' she wailed in her anguish. 'It took on his likeness. It deceived us... to give him time. He's done it.'

She sat up suddenly. 'Go,' she said, pointing to the room beyond, then sank fainting, a dead weight in his arms.

He carried her unconscious body to a chair, then entering the adjoining room he flashed his torch upon the body of her husband hanging from a bracket in the wall. He cut it down five minutes too late.

THE TRADITION

The noises outside the little flat at first were very disconcerting after living in the country. They made sleep difficult. At the cottage in Sussex where the family had lived, night brought deep, comfortable silence, unless the wind was high, when the pine trees round the duck-pond made a sound like surf, or, if the gale was from the south-west, the orchard roared a bit unpleasantly.

But in London it was very different; sleep was easier in the daytime than at night. For, after nightfall, the rumble of the traffic became spasmodic instead of continuous; the motor-horns startled like warnings of alarm; after comparative silence the furious rushing of a taxicab touched the nerves. From dinner till eleven o'clock the streets subsided gradually; then came the army from theatres, parties, and late dinners, hurrying home to bed. The motor-horns during this hour were lively and incessant, like bugles of a regiment moving into battle. The parents rarely retired until this attack was over. If quick about it, sleep was possible then before the flying of the night-birds—an uncertain squadron—screamed half the street awake again. But, these finally disposed of, a delightful hush settled down upon the neighbourhood, profounder far than any peace of the countryside. The deep rumble of the produce wagons, coming in to the big London markets from the farms—generally about three a. m.—held no disturbing quality.

But sometimes in the stillness of very early morning, when streets were empty and pavements all deserted, there was a sound of another kind that was startling and unwelcome. For it was ominous. It came with a clattering violence that made nerves quiver and forced the heart to pause and listen. A strange resonance was in it, a volume of sound, moreover, that was hardly justified by its cause. For it was hoofs. A horse swept hurrying up the deserted street, and was close upon the building in a moment. It was audible suddenly, no gradual approach from a distance, but as though it turned a corner from soft ground that muffled the hoofs, on to the echoing, hard paving that emphasised the dreadful clatter. Nor did it die away again when once the house was reached. It ceased as abruptly as it came. The hoofs did not go away.

It was the mother who heard them first, and drew her husband's attention to their disagreeable quality.

'It is the mail-vans, dear,' he answered. 'They go at four a.m. to catch the early trains in to the country.'

She looked up sharply, as though something in his tone surprised her.

'But there's no sound of wheels,' she said. And then, as he did not reply, she added gravely, 'You have heard it too, John. I can tell.'

'I have,' he said. 'I have heard it—twice.'

And they looked at one another searchingly, each trying to read the other's mind. She did not question him; he did not propose writing to complain in a newspaper; both understood something that neither of them quite believed.

'I heard it first,' she then said softly, 'the night before Jack got the fever. And, as I listened, I heard him crying. But when I went in to see he was asleep. The noise stopped just outside the building.' There was a shadow in her eyes as she said this, and a hush crept in between her words. 'I did not hear it *go*.' She said this almost beneath her breath.

He looked a moment at the ground; then, coming towards her, he took her in his arms and kissed her. And she clung very tightly to him.

'Sometimes,' he said in a quiet voice, 'a mounted policeman passes down the street, I think.'

'It is a horse,' she answered. But whether it was a question or mere corroboration he did not ask, for at that moment the doctor arrived, and the question of little Jack's health became

THE TRADITION

the paramount matter of immediate interest. The great man's verdict was uncommonly disquieting.

All that night they sat up in the sick room. It was strangely still, as though by one accord the traffic avoided the house where a little boy hung between life and death. The motor-horns even had a muffled sound, and heavy drays and wagons used the side streets; there were fewer taxicabs about, or else they flew by noiselessly. Yet no straw was down, the expense prohibited that. And towards morning, very early, the mother decided to watch alone. She had been a trained nurse before her marriage, accustomed when she was younger to long vigils. 'You go down, dear, and get a little sleep,' she urged in a whisper. 'He's quiet now. At five o'clock I'll come for you to take my place.'

'You'll fetch me at once,' he whispered, 'if—' then hesitated—as though breath failed him. A moment he stood there staring from her face to the bed. 'If you hear anything,' he finished. She nodded, and he went downstairs to his study, not to his bedroom. He left the door ajar. He sat in darkness, listening. Mother, he knew, was listening, too, beside the bed. His heart was very full, for he did not believe the boy could live till morning. The picture of the room was all the time before his eyes—the shaded lamp, the table with the medicines, the little wasted figure beneath the blankets, and mother close beside it, listening. He sat alert, ready to fly upstairs at the smallest cry.

But no sound broke the stillness; the entire neighbourhood was silent; all London slept. He heard the clock strike three in the dining-room at the end of the corridor. It was still enough for that. There was not even the heavy rumble of a single produce wagon, though usually they passed about this time on their way to Smithfield and Covent Garden markets. He waited, far too anxious to close his eyes. ... At four o'clock he would go up and relieve her vigil. Four, he knew, was the time when life sinks to its lowest ebb. ... Then, in the middle of his reflections, thought stopped dead, and it seemed his heart stopped too.

Far away, but coming nearer with extraordinary rapidity, a

sharp, clear sound broke out of the surrounding stillness—a horse's hoofs. At first it was so distant that it might have been almost on the high roads of the country, but the amazing speed with which it came closer, and the sudden increase of the beating sound was such, that by the time he turned his head it seemed to have entered the street outside. It was within a hundred yards of the building. The next second it was before the very door. And something in him blenched. He knew a moment's complete paralysis. The abrupt cessation of the heavy clatter was strangest of all. It came like lightning, it struck, it paused. It did not go away again. Yet the sound of it was still beating in his ears as he dashed upstairs three steps at a time. It seemed in the house as well, on the stairs behind him, in the little passage-way, *inside the very bedroom*. It was an appalling sound. Yet he entered a room that was quiet, orderly, and calm. It was silent. Beside the bed his wife sat, holding Jack's hand, stroking it. She was soothing him; her face was very peaceful. No sound but her gentle whisper was audible.

He controlled himself by a tremendous effort, but his face betrayed his consternation and distress. 'Hush,' she said beneath her breath, 'he's sleeping much more calmly now. The crisis, bless God, is over, I do believe. I dared not leave him.'

He saw in a moment that she was right, and an untellable relief passed over him. He sat down beside her, very cold, yet perspiring with heat.

'You heard——?' he asked after a pause.

'Nothing,' she replied quickly, 'except his pitiful, wild words when the delirium was on him. It's passed. It lasted but a moment, or I'd have called you.'

He stared closely into her tired eyes. 'And his words?' he asked in a whisper. Whereupon she told him quietly that the little chap had sat up with wide-opened eyes and talked excitedly about a 'great, great horse' he heard, but that was not 'coming for him.' 'He laughed and said he would not go with it because he 'was not ready yet'. 'Some scrap of talk he had overheard from us,' she added, 'when we discussed the traffic once. ...'

'But *you* heard nothing?' he repeated almost impatiently.

No, she had heard nothing. After all, then, he *had* dozed a moment in his chair. ...

Four weeks later Jack, entirely convalescent, was playing a restricted game of hide-and-seek with his sister in the flat. It was really a forbidden joy, owing to noise and risk of breakages, but he had unusual privileges after his grave illness. It was dusk. The lamps in the street were being lit. 'Quietly, remember; your mother's resting in her room,' were the father's orders. She had just returned from a week by the sea, recuperating from the strain of nursing for so many nights. The traffic rolled and boomed along the streets below.

'Jack! Do come on and hide. It's your turn. I hid last.'

But the boy was standing spellbound by the window, staring hard at something on the pavement. Sybil called and tugged in vain. Tears threatened. Jack would not budge. He declared he saw something.

'Oh, you're always seeing something. I wish you'd go and hide. It's only because you can't think of a good place, really.'

'Look!' he cried in a voice of wonder. And as he said it his father rose quickly from his chair before the fire.

'Look,' the child repeated with delight and excitement. 'It's a great, great horse. And it's perfectly white all over.' His sister joined him at the window. 'Where? Where? I can't see it. Oh, *do* show me!'

Their father was standing close behind them now. 'I heard it,' he was whispering, but so low the childern did not notice him. His face was very pale.

'Straight in front of our door, stupid! Can't you see it? Oh, I do wish it had come for me. It's *such* a beauty!' And he clapped his hands with pleasure and excitement. 'Quick, quick! I can hear it. It's going away again!'

But, while the children stood half squabbling by the window their father leaned over a sofa in the adjoining room above a figure whose heart in sleep had quietly stopped its beating. The great, great horse had come. But this time he had not only heard its wonderful arrival. He had also heard it go. It seemed he heard the awful hoofs beat down the sky, far far away, and very swiftly, dying into silence, finally up among the stars.

THE TOUCH OF PAN

I

An idiot, Heber understood, was a person in whom intelligence had been arrested—instinct acted, but not reason. A lunatic, on the other hand, was someone whose reason had gone awry—the mechanism of the brain was injured. The lunatic was out of relation with his environment; the idiot had merely been delayed *en route*.

Be that as it might, he knew at any rate that a lunatic was not to be listened to, whereas an idiot—well, the one he fell in love with, certainly had the secret of some instinctual knowledge that was not only joy, but a kind of sheer natural joy. Probably it was that sheer natural joy of living that reason argues to be untaught, degraded. In any case—at thirty—he married her instead of the daughter of a duchess he was engaged to. They lead to-day that happy, natural, vagabond life called idiotic, unmindful of that world the majority of reasonable people live only to remember.

Though born into an artificial social clique that made it difficult, Heber had always loved the simple things. Nature, especially, meant much to him. He would rather see a woodland misty with bluebells than all the châteaux on the Loire; the thought of a mountain valley in the dawn made his feet lonely in the grandest houses. Yet in these very houses was his home established. Not that he under-estimated worldly things—their value was too obvious—but that it was another thing he wanted. Only he did not know precisely *what* he wanted until this particular idiot made it plain.

Her case was a mild one, possibly; the title bestowed by implication rather than by specific mention. Her family did not say that she was imbecile or half-witted, but that she was 'not all there' they probably did say. Perhaps she saw men as trees walking, perhaps she saw through a glass darkly. ... Heber, who had met her once or twice, though never yet to speak to, did not analyse her degree of sight, for in him, personally, she woke a secret joy and wonder that almost involved a touch of awe. The part of her that was 'not all there' dwelt in an 'elsewhere' that he longed to know about. He wanted to share it with her. She seemed aware of certain happy and desirable things that reason and too much thinking hid.

He just felt this instinctively without analysis. The values they set upon the prizes of life were similar. Money to her was just stamped metal, fame a loud noise of sorts, position nothing. Of people she was aware as a dog or bird might be aware—they were kind or unkind. Her parents, having collected much metal and achieved position, proceeded to make a loud noise of sorts with some success; and since she did not contribute, either by her appearance or her tastes, to their ambitions, they neglected her and made excuses. They were ashamed of her existence. Her father in particular justified Nietzsche's shrewd remark that no one with a loud voice can listen to subtle thoughts.

She was, perhaps, sixteen; for, though she did not look it, eighteen or nineteen was probably more in accord with her birth certificate. Her mother was content, however, that she should dress the lesser age, preferring to tell strangers that she was childish, rather than admit that she was backward.

'You'll never marry at all, child, much less marry as you might,' she said, 'if you go about with that rabbit expression on your face. That's not the way to catch a nice young man of the sort we get down to stay with us now. Many a chorus-girl with less than you've got has caught them easily enough. Your sister's done well. Why not do the same? There's nothing to be shy or frightened about.'

'But I'm not shy or frightened, mother. I'm bored. I mean *they* bore me.'

It made no difference to the girl; she was herself. The bored expression in the eyes—the rabbit, not-all-there expression—gave place sometimes to another look. Yet not often, nor with anybody. It was this other look that stirred the strange joy in the man who fell in love with her. It is not to be easily described. It was very wonderful. Whether sixteen or nineteen, she then looked—a thousand.

* * *

The house-party was of that up-to-date kind prevalent in Heber's world. Husbands and wives were not asked together. There was a cynical disregard of the decent (not the stupid) conventions that savoured of abandon, perhaps of decadence. He only went himself in the hope of seeing the backward daughter once again. Her millionaire parents afflicted him, the smart folk tired him. Their peculiar affection of a special language, their strange belief that they were of importance, their treatment of the servants, their calculated self-indulgence, all jarred upon him more than usual. At bottom he heartily despised the whole vapid set. He felt uncomfortable and out of place. Though not a prig, he abhorred the way these folk believed themselves the climax of fine living. Their open immorality disgusted him, their indiscriminate love-making was merely rather nasty; he watched the very girl he was at last to settle down with behaving as the tone of the clique expected over her final fling—and bored by the strain of so much 'modernity', he tried to get away. Tea was long over, the sunset interval invited, he felt hungry for trees and fields that were not self-conscious—and he escaped. The flaming June day was turning chill. Dusk hovered over the ancient house, veiling the pretentious new wing that had been added. And he came across the idiot girl at the bend of the drive, where the birch trees shivered in the evening wind. His heart gave a sudden leap.

She was leaning against one of the dreadful statues—it was a satyr—that sprinkled the lawn. Her back was to him; she gazed at a group of broken pine trees in the park beyond. He paused an instant, then went on quickly, while his mind scurried, to recall her name. They were within easy speaking range.

'Miss Elizabeth!' he cried, yet not too loudly, lest she might vanish as suddenly as she had appeared. She turned at once.

Her eyes and lips were smiling welcome at him without pretence. She showed no surprise.

'You're the first one of the lot who's said it properly,' she exclaimed, as he came up. 'Everybody calls me Elizabeth instead of Elspeth. It's idiotic. They don't even take the trouble to get a name right.'

'It is,' he agreed, 'quite idiotic.' He did not correct her. Possibly he had said Elspeth after all—the names were similar. Her perfectly natural voice was grateful to his ear, and soothing. He looked at her all over with an open admiration that she noticed and, without concealment, liked. She was very untidy, the grey stockings on her slim, vigorous legs were torn, her short skirt was spattered with mud. Her nut-brown hair, glossy and plentiful, flew loose about neck and shoulders. In place of the usual belt she had tied a coloured handkerchief round her waist. She wore no hat. What she had been doing to get in such a state, while her parents entertained a 'distinguished' party, he did not know, but it was not difficult to guess. Climbing trees or riding bareback and astride was probably the truth. Yet her dishevelled state became her well, and the welcome in her face delighted him. She remembered him, she was glad. He, too, was glad, and a sense both happy and reckless stirred in his heart. 'Like a wild animal,' he said, 'you come out in the dusk——'

'To play with my kind,' she answered in a flash, throwing him a glance of invitation that made his blood go dancing.

He leaned against the statue a moment, asking himself why this young Cinderella of a parvenu family delighted him when all the London beauties left him cold. There was a lift through his whole being as he watched her, slim and supple, grace shining through the untidy modern garb—almost as though she wore no clothes. He thought of a panther standing upright. Her poise was so alert—one arm upon the marble ledge, one leg bent across the other, the hip-line showing like a bird's curved wing. Wild animal or bird flashed across his mind; something untamed and natural. Another second and she might leap away—or spring into his arms.

It was a deep, delicious sensation in him that produced the mental picture. 'Pure and natural,' a voice whispered with it in his heart, 'as surely as *they* are just the other thing!' And the thrill struck with unerring aim at the very root of that unrest he had always known in the state of life to which he was called. She made the natural clean and pure. This girl and himself were somehow kin. The primitive thing broke loose in him.

In two seconds, while he stood with her beside the vulgar statue, these thoughts passed through his mind. But he did not at first, give utterance to any of them. He spoke more formally, although laughter, due to his happiness, lay close behind.

'They haven't asked you to the party, then? Or you don't care about it? Which is it?'

'Both,' she said, looking fearlessly into his face. 'But I've been waiting here ten minutes already. Why were you so long?'

This outspoken honesty was hardly what he expected, yet in another sense he was not surprised. Her eyes were very penetrating, very innocent, very frank. He felt her as clean and sweet as some young fawn that asks plainly to be stroked and fondled. He told the truth: 'I couldn't get away before. I had to play about and——' when she interrupted with impatience:

'*They* don't want you,' she exclaimed scornfully. 'I do.'

And, before he could choose one out of the several answers that rushed into his mind, she nudged him with her foot, holding it out a little so that he saw the shoelace was unfastened. She nodded her head towards it, and pulled her skirt up half an inch as he at once stooped down.

'And, anyhow,' she went on as he fumbled with the lace, touching her ankle with his hand, 'you're going to marry one of them. I read it in the paper. You'll be miserable. It's idiotic.'

The blood rushed to his head, but whether owing to his stooping or to something else, he could not say.

'I only came—I only accepted,' he said quickly, 'because I wanted to see you again.'

'Of course. I made mother ask you.'

He did an impulsive thing. Kneeling as he was, he bent his

head a little lower and suddenly kissed the soft grey stocking—then stood up and looked her in the face. She was laughing happily, no sign of embarrassment in her anywhere, no trace of outraged modesty. She only looked very pleased.

'I've tied a knot that won't come undone in a hurry——' he began, then stopped dead. For as he said it, gazing into her smiling face, another expression looked forth at him from the two big eyes of hazel. Something rushed from his heart to meet it. It may have been that playful kiss, it may have been the way she took it; but, at any rate, there was a strength in the new emotion that made him unsure of who he was and of whom he looked at. He forgot the place, the time, his own identity and hers. ... The lawn swept from beneath his feet, the English sunset with it. He forgot his host and hostess, his fellow guests, even his father's name and his own into the bargain. He was carried away upon a great tide, the girl always beside him. He left the shore-line in the distance, already half forgotten, the shore-line of his education, learning, manners, social point of view—everything to which his father had most carefully brought him up as the scion of an old established English family. This girl had torn up the anchor. Only the anchor had previously been loosened a little, perhaps, by his own unconscious and restless efforts. ...

Where was she taking him to? Upon what island would they land...?

'I'm younger than you—a good deal,' she broke in upon his rushing mood. 'But that doesn't matter a bit, does it? We're about the same age really.'

With the happy sound of her voice the extraordinary sensation passed—or, rather, it became normal. But that it lasted an appreciable time was proved by the fact that they had left the statue on the lawn, the house was no longer visible behind them, and they were now walking side by side between the massive rhododendron clumps. They brought up against a five-barred gate into the park. They leaned upon the topmost bar, and he felt her shoulder touching his—edging into it—as they looked across to the grove of pines.

THE TOUCH OF PAN

'I feel absurdly young,' he said without a sign of affectation, 'and yet I've been looking for you a thousand years and more.'

The afterglow lit up her face; it fell on her loose hair and tumbled blouse, turning them amber red. She looked not only soft and comely, but extraordinarily beautiful. The strange expression haunted the deep eyes again, the lips were a little parted, the young breast heaving slightly, joy and excitement in her whole presentment. And as he watched her he knew that all he had just felt was due to her close presence, her atmosphere, her perfume, her physical warmth and vigour. It had emanated directly from her being.

'Of course,' she said, and laughed so that he felt her breath upon his face. He bent lower to bring his own on a level, gazing straight into her eyes that were still fixed upon the field beyond. They were clear and luminous as pools of water, and in their centre, sharp as a photograph, he saw the reflection of the pine grove, perhaps a hundred yards away. With detailed accuracy he saw it, empty and motionless in the glimmering June dusk.

Then something caught his eye. He examined the picture more closely. He drew slightly nearer. He almost touched her face with his own, forgetting for a moment whose were the eyes that served him for a mirror. For, looking intently thus, it seemed to him that there was movement, a passing to and fro, a stirring as of figures among the trees... Then suddenly the entire picture was obliterated. She had dropped her lids. He heard her speaking—the warm breath was again upon his face:

'*In the heart of that wood dwell I*'.

His heart gave another leap—more violent than the first—for the sentence caught him like a spell. There was a lilt and rhythm in the words, a wonder and a beauty, that made it poetry. She laid emphasis upon the pronoun and the nouns. It seemed the last line of some delicious runic verse:

'In the *heart* of that *wood*—dwell *I*...'

And it flashed across him: that living, moving, inhabited pine wood was her thought. It was thus she thought it, saw it. Her nature flung back to a life she understood, a life that needed, claimed her. The ostentatious and artificial values that surrounded her she denied, even as the distinguished house-party of her ambitious, masquerading family neglected her. Of course she was unnoticed by them—just as a swallow or a wild-rose were unnoticed.

He knew her secret then, for she had told it to him. It was his own secret too. They were akin, as the birds and animals were akin. They belonged together in some free and open life, natural, wild, untamed. That unhampered life was flowing about them now, rising, beating with delicious tumult in her veins and his, yet innocent as the sunlight and the wind—because it was as freely recognised.

'Elspeth!' he cried, 'come, take me with you! We'll go at once. Come—hurry—before we forget to be happy, or remember to be wise again——!'

His words stopped half-way towards completion, for a perfume floated past him, born of the summer dusk, perhaps, yet sweet with a penetrating magic that made his senses reel with some remembered joy. No flower, no scented garden-bush delivered it. It was the perfume of young, spendthrift life, sweet with the purity that season had not yet stained. The girl moved closer. Gathering her loose hair between her fingers, she brushed his cheeks and eyes with it, her slim, warm body pressing against him as she leaned over laughingly.

'*In the darkness,*' she whispered in his ear; '*when the moon puts the house upon the statue!*'

And he understood. Her world lay behind the vulgar, staring bay. He turned. He heard the flutter of skirts—just caught the grey stockings, swift and light, and they flew behind the rhododendron masses. And she was gone.

He stood a long time, leaning upon that five-barred gate... It was the dressing-gong that recalled him at length to what seemed the present. By the conservatory door, as he went slowly in, he met his distinguished cousin—who was helping the girl he himself was to marry to enjoy her 'final fling'. He looked at his cousin. He realised suddenly that he was merely vicious. There was no sun and wind, no flowers—there was depravity only, lust instead of laughter, excitement in place of happiness. It was calculated, not spontaneous. His mind was in it. Without joy it was. He was not natural.

'Not a girl in the whole lot fit to look at,' his cousin exclaimed with peevish boredom, excusing himself stupidly for his illicit conduct. 'I'm off in the morning.' He shrugged his blue-blooded shoulders. 'These millionaires! Their shooting's all right, but their mixum-gatherum week-ends—bah!' His gesture completed all he had to say about this one in particular. He glanced sharply, nastily, at his companion. '*You* look as if you'd found something!' he added, with a suggestive grin. 'Or have you seen the ghost that was paid for with the house?' And he guffawed and let his eye-glass drop. 'Lady Hermione will be asking for an explanation—eh?'

'Idiot!' replied Heber, and ran upstairs to dress for dinner.

But the word was wrong, he remembered, as he closed his door. It was lunatic he had meant to say, yet something more as well. He saw the smart, modern philanderer somehow as a beast.

II

It was nearly midnight when he went up to bed, after an evening of intolerable amusement. The abandoned moral attitude, the common rudeness, the contempt of all others but themselves, the ugly jests, the horseplay of tasteless minds that passed for gaiety, above all the shamelessness of the women that behind the cover of fine breeding aped emancipation, afflicted him to a boredom that touched desperation.

He understood now with a clarity unknown before. As with his cousin, so with these. They took life, he saw, with a brazen effrontery they thought was freedom, while yet it was life that they denied. He felt vampired and degraded; spontaneity went out of him. The fact that the geography of bedrooms was studied openly seemed an affirmation of vice that sickened him. Their ways were nauseous merely. He escaped—unnoticed.

He locked his door, went to the open window, and looked out into the night—then started. For silver dressed the lawn and park, the shadow of the building lay dark across the elaborate garden, and the moon, he noticed, was just high enough to put the house upon the statue. The chimney-stacks edged the pedestal precisely.

'Odd!' he exclaimed. 'Odd that I should come at the very moment——!' then smiled as he realised how his proposed adventure would be misinterpreted, its natural innocence and spirit ruined—if he were seen. 'And someone would be sure to see me on a night like this. There are couples still hanging about in the garden.' And he glanced at the shrubberies and secret paths that seemed to float upon the warm June air like islands.

He stood for a moment framed in the glare of the electric light, then turned back into the room; and at that instant a low sound like a bird-call rose from the lawn below. It was soft and flutey, as though someone played two notes upon a reed, a piping sound. He had been seen, and she was waiting for him. Before he knew it, he had made an answering call, of oddly similar kind, then switched the light out.

Three minutes later, dressed in simpler clothes, with a cap pulled over his eyes, he reached the back lawn by means of the conservatory and billiard-room. He paused a moment to look about him. There was no one, although the lights were still ablaze. 'I am an idiot,' he chuckled to himself. 'I'm acting on instinct!' He ran.

The sweet night air bathed him from head to foot; there was strength and cleansing in it. The lawn shone wet with dew. He could almost smell the perfume of the stars. The fumes of wine, cigars and artificial scent were left behind, the atmosphere exhaled by civilisation, by heavy thoughts, by bodies overdressed, unwisely stimulated—all, all forgotten. He passed into a world of magical enchantment. The hush of the open sky came down. In black and white the garden lay, brimmed full with beauty, shot by the ancient silver of the moon, spangled with the stars' old-gold. And the night wind rustled in the rhododendron masses as he flew between them.

In a moment he was beside the statue, engulfed now by the shadow of the building, and the girl detached herself silently from the blur of darkness. Two arms were flung about his neck, a shower of soft hair fell on his cheek with a heady scent of earth and leaves and grass, and the same instant they were away together at full speed—towards the pine wood. Their feet were soundless on the soaking grass. They went so swiftly that they made a whir of following wind that blew her hair across his eyes.

And the sudden contrast caused a shock that put a blank, perhaps, upon his mind, so that he lost the standard of remembered things. For it was no longer merely a particular adventure; it seemed a habit and a natural joy resumed.

It was not new. He realised the momentum of an accustomed happiness, mislaid, it may be, but certainly familiar. They sped across the gravel paths that intersected the well-groomed lawn, they leaped the flower-beds, so laboriously shaped in mockery, they clambered over the ornamental iron railings, scorning the easier five-barred gate into the park. The longer grass then shook the dew in soaking showers against his knees. He stooped, as though in some foolish effort to turn up some thing, then realised that his legs, of course, were bare. *Her* garment was already high and free, for she, too, was barelegged like himself. He saw her little ankles, wet and shining in the moonlight, and flinging himself down, he kissed them happily, plunging his face into the dripping, perfumed grass. Her ringing laughter mingled with his own, as she stooped beside him the same instant; her hair hung in a silver cloud; her eyes gleamed through its curtain into his; then, suddenly, she soaked her hands in the heavy dew and passed them over his face with a softness that was like the touch of some scented southern wind.

'Now you are anointed with the Night,' she cried. 'No one will know you. You are forgotten of the world. Kiss me!'

'We'll play for ever and ever,' he cried, 'the eternal game that was old when still the world was young,' and lifting her in his arms he kissed her eyes and lips. There was some natural bliss of song and dance laughter in his heart, an elemental bliss that caught them together as wind and sunlight catch the branches of a tree. She leaped from the ground to meet his swinging arms, and in an instant was upon his shoulders. He ran with her, then tossed her off and caught her neatly as she fell. Evading a second capture, she danced ahead, holding out one shining arm that he might follow. Hand in hand they raced on together through the clean summer moonlight. Yet there remained a smooth softness as of fur against his neck and shoulders, and he saw then that she wore skins of tawny colour that clung to her body closely, that he wore them too, and that her skin, like his own, was of a sweet dusky brown.

Then, pulling her towards him, he stared into her face. She suffered the close gaze a second, but no longer, for with a burst of sparkling laughter again she leaped into his arms, and before he shook her free she had pulled and tweaked the two small horns that hid in the thick curly hair behind, and just above, the ears.

And that wilful tweaking turned him wild and reckless. That touch ran down him deep into the mothering earth. He leaped and ran and sang with a great laughing sound. The wine of eternal youth flushed all his veins with joy, and the old, old world was young again with every impulse of natural happiness intensified with the Earth's own foaming tide of life.

From head to foot he tingled with the delight of Spring, prodigal with creative power. Of course he could fly the bushes and fling wild across the open! Of course the wind and moonlight fitted close and soft about him like a skin! Of course he had youth and beauty for playmates, with dancing, laughter, singing, and a thousand kisses! For he and she were natural once again. They were free together of those long-forgotten days when 'Pan leaped through the roses in the month of June...!'

With the girl swaying this way and that upon his shoulders, tweaking his horns with mischief and desire, hanging her flying

THE TOUCH OF PAN

hair before his eyes, then bending swiftly over again to lift it, he danced to join the rest of their companions in the little moonlit grove of pines beyond...

III

They rose somewhat pointed, perhaps, against the moonlight, those English pines—more with the shape of cypresses, some might have thought. A stream gushed down between their roots, there were mossy ferns, and rough grey boulders with lichen on them. But there was no dimness, for the silver of the moon sprinkled freely through the branches like the faint sunlight that it really was, and the air ran out to meet them with a heady fragrance that was wiser far than wine.

The girl, in an instant, was whirled from her perch on his shoulders and caught by a dozen arms that bore her into the heart of the merry, careless throng. Whisht! Whew! Whir! She was gone, but another, fairer still, was in her place, with skins as soft and knees that clung as tightly. Her eyes were liquid amber, grapes hung between her little breasts, her arms entwined about him, smoother than marble, and as cool. She had a crystal laugh.

But he flung her off, so that she fell plump among a group of bigger figures lolling against a twisted root and roaring with a jollity that boomed like wind through the chorus of a song. They seized her, kissed her, then sent her flying. They were happier, after all, with their glad singing. They held stone goblets, red and foaming in their broad-palmed hands.

'The mountains lie behind us!' cried someone dancing past. 'We are come at last into our valley of delight. Grapec, breasts, and rich red lips! Ho! Ho! It is time to press thesm that the juice of life may run!' The figure waved a cluster of ferns across the air and vanished amid a cloud of song and laughter.

'It is ours. Use it!' answered a deep, ringing voice. 'The valleys are our own. No climbing now!' And a wind of echoing cries gave answer from all sides. 'Life! Life! Life! Abundans, flowing over—use it, use it!'

A troop of nymphs rushed forth, escaped from clustering arms and lips they yet openly desired. He chased them in and out among the waving branches, while she who had brought him ever followed, and sped past him and away again. He caught three gleaming soft brown bodies, then fell beneath them, smothered, bubbling with joyous laughter—next freed himself and, while they sought to drag him captive again, escaped and raced with a leap upon a slimmer, sweeter outline that swung up—only just in time upon a lower bough, whence she leaned down above him with hanging net of hair and merry eyes. A few feet beyond his reach, she laughed and teased him—the one who had brought him in, the one he ever sought, and who for ever sought him too...

It became a riotous glory of wild children who romped and played with an impassioned glee beneath the moon. For the world was young and they, her happy offspring, glowed with the life she poured so freely into them. All intermingled, the laughing voices rose into a foam of song that broke against the stars. The difficult mountains had been climbed and were forgotten. Good! Then, enjoy the luxuriant, fruitful valley and be glad! And glad they were, brimful with spontaneous energy, natural as birds and animals that obeyed the big, deep rhythm of a simpler age—natural as wind and innocent as sunshine.

Yet, for all the untamed riot, there was a lift of beauty pulsing underneath. Even when the wildest abandon approached the heat of orgy, when the recklessness appeared excess—there hid that marvellous touch of loveliness which makes the natural sacred. There was coherence, purpose, the fulfilling of an exquisite law: and—there was worship. The form it took, haply, was strange as well as riotous, yet in its strangeness dreamed innocence and purity, and in its very riot flamed that spirit which is divine.

For he found himself at length beside her once again; breathless and panting, her sweet brown limbs aglow from the excitement of escape denied; eyes shining like a blaze of stars, and pulses beating with tumultuous life—helpless and yielding against the strength that pinned her down between the roots.

THE TOUCH OF PAN

His eyes put mastery on her own. She looked up into his face, obedient, happy, soft with love, surrendering with the same delicious abandon that had swept her for a moment into other arms. 'You caught me in the end,' she sighed. 'I only played awhile.'

'I hold you for ever,' he replied, half wondering at the rough power in his voice.

It was here the hush of worship stole upon her little face, into her obedient eyes, about her parted lips. She ceased her wilful struggling.

'Listen!' she whispered. 'I hear a step upon the glades beyond. The iris and the lily open; the earth is ready, waiting; we must be ready too! *He* is coming!'

He released her and sprang up; the entire company rose too. All stood, all bowed the head. There was an instant's subtle panic, but it was the panic of reverent awe that preludes a descent of deity. For a wind passed through the branches with a sound that is the oldest in the world and so the youngest. Above it there rose the shrill, faint piping of a little reed...

Only the first, true sounds were audible—wind and water: the tinkling of the dewdrops as they fell, the murmur of the trees against the air. This was the piping that they heard. And in the hush the stars bent down to hear, the riot paused, the orgy passed and died. The figures waited, kneeling then with one accord. They listened with—the Earth.

'He comes... He comes...' the valley breathed about them.

A footfall from far away came treading across a world unruined and unstained. It fell with the wind and water, sweetening the valley into life as it approached. Across the rivers and forests it came gently, tenderly, but swiftly and with a power that knew majesty.

'He comes... He comes...!' rose with the murmur of the wind and water from the host of lowered heads.

The footfall came nearer, treading a world grown soft with worship. It reached the grove. It entered. There was a sense of intolerable loveliness, of brimming life, of rapture. The thousand faces lifted like a cloud. They heard the piping close... And so He came.

But He came with blessing. With the stupendous Presence there was joy, the joy of abundant, natural life, pure as the sunlight and the wind. He passed among them. There was great movement—as of a forest shaking, as of deep water falling, as of a cornfield swaying to the wind, gentle as of harebell shedding its burden of dew that it has held too long because of love. He passed among them, touching every head. The great hand swept with tenderness each face, lingered a moment on each beating heart. There was sweetness, peace, and loveliness; but above all, there was—life. He sanctioned every natural joy in them and blessed each passion with his power of creation... Yet each one saw him differently: some as a wife or maiden desired with fire, some as a youth or stalwart husband, others as a figure veiled with stars or cloaked in luminous mist, hardly attainable; others, again—the fewest these, not more than two or three—as that mysterious wonder which tempts the heart away from known familiar sweetness into a wilderness of undecipherable magic without flesh and blood.

To two, in particular, He came so near that they could feel his breath of hills and fields upon their eyes. He touched them with both mighty hands. He stroked the marble breasts, He felt the little hidden horns... and, as they bent lower so that their lips met together for an instant, He took her arms and twined them about the curved, brown neck that she might hold him closer still...

Again a footfall sounded far away upon an unruined world... and He was gone—back into the wind and water whence He came. The thousand faces lifted; all stood up; the hush of worship still among them. There was a quiet as of the dawn. The piping floated over woods and fields, fading into silence. All looked at one another... And then once more the laughter and the play broke loose.

THE TOUCH OF PAN

IV

'We'll go,' she cried, 'and peep upon that other world where life hangs like a prison on their eyes!'

And, in a moment, they were across the soaking grass, the lawn and flower-beds, and close to the walls of the heavy mansion. He peered in through a window, lifting her up to peer in with him. He recognised the world to which he outwardly belonged; he understood; a little gasp escaped him; and a slight shiver ran down the girl's body into his own. She turned her eyes away. 'See,' she murmured in his ear, 'it's ugly, it's not natural. They feel guilty and ashamed. There is no innocence!' She saw the men; it was the women that he saw chiefly.

Lolling ungracefully, with a kind of boldness that asserted independence, the women smoked their cigarettes with an air of invitation they sought to conceal and yet plainly showed. He saw his familiar world in nakedness. Their backs were bare, for all the elaborate clothes they wore; they hung their breasts uncleanly; in their eyes shone light that had never known the open sun. Hoping they were alluring and desirable, they feigned a guilty ignorance of that hope. They all pretended. Instead of wind and dew upon their hair, he saw flowers grown artificially to ape wild beauty, tresses without lustre borrowed from the slums of city factories. He watched them manoeuvring with the men; heard dark sentences; caught gestures half delivered whose meaning should just convey that glimpse of guilt they deemed to increase pleasure. The women were calculating, but nowhere glad; the men experienced, but nowhere joyous. Pretended innocence lay cloaked with a veil of something that whispered secretly, clandestine, ashamed, yet with a brazen air that laid mockery instead of sunshine in their smiles. Vice masqueraded in the ugly shape of pleasure; beauty was degraded into calculated tricks. They were not natural. They knew not joy.

'The forward ones, the civilised!' she laughed in his ear, tweaking his horns with energy. '*We* are the backward!'

'Unclean,' he muttered, recalling a catchword of the world he gazed upon.

They were the civilised! They were refined and educated—advanced. Generations of careful breeding, mate cautiously selecting mate, laid the polish of caste upon their hands and faces where gleamed ridiculous, untaught jewels—rings, bracelets, necklaces hanging absurdly from every possible angle.

'But—they are dressed up—for fun,' he exclaimed, more to himself than to the girl in skins who clung to his shoulder with her naked arms.

'Undressed!' she answered, putting her brown hand in play across his eyes. 'Only they have forgotten even that!' And another shiver passed through her into him. He turned and hid his face against the soft skins that touched his cheek. He kissed her body. Seizing his horns, she pressed him to her, laughing happily.

'Look!' she whispered, raising her head again; 'they're coming out.' And he saw that two of them, a man and a girl, with an interchange of secret glances, had stolen from the room and were already by the door of the conservatory that led into the garden. It was his wife to be—and his distinguished cousin.

'Oh, Pan!' she cried in mischief. The girl sprang from his arms and pointed. 'We will follow them. We will put natural life into their little veins!'

'Or panic terror,' he answered, catching the yellow panther skin and following her swiftly round the building. He kept in the shadow, though she ran full into the blaze of moonlight. 'But they can't see us,' she called, looking over her shoulder a moment. 'They can only feel our presence, perhaps.' And, as she danced across the lawn, it seemed a moonbeam slipped from a sapling birch tree that the wind curved earthwards, then tossed back against the sky.

Keeping just ahead, they led the pair, by methods known instinctively to elemental blood yet not translatable—led them towards the little grove of waiting pines. The night wind murmured in the branches; a bird woke into a sudden burst of song.

These sounds were plainly audible. But four little pointed ears caught other, wilder, notes behind the wind and music of the bird—the cries and ringing laughter, the leaping footsteps and the happy singing of their merry kin within the wood.

And the throng paused then amid the revels to watch the 'civilised' draw near. They presently reached the trees, halted, looked about them, hesitated a moment—then, with a hurried movement as of shame and fear lest they be caught, entered the zone of shadow.

'Let's go in here,' said the man, without music in his voice. 'It's dry on the pine needles, and we can't be seen.' He led the way; she picked up her skirts and followed over the strip of long wet grass. 'Here's a log all ready for us,' he added, sat down, and drew her into his arms with a sigh of satisfaction. 'Sit on my knee; it's warmer for your pretty figure.' He chuckled; evidently they were on familiar terms, for though she hesitated there was no real resistance in her, and she allowed the ungraceful roughness. 'But are we *quite* safe? Are you sure?' she asked between his kisses.

'What does it matter, even if we're not?' he replied, establishing her more securely on his knees. 'But, as a matter of fact, we're safer here than in my own house.' He kissed her hungrily. 'By Jove, Hermione, but you're divine,' he cried passionately, 'divinely beautiful, I love you with every atom of my being—with my very soul.'

'Yes, dear, I know—I mean, I know you do, but——'

'But what?' he asked impatiently.

'Those horrid detectives——'

He laughed. Yet it seemed to annoy him. 'My wife *is* a beast, isn't she?—to have me watched like that,' he said quickly.

'They're everywhere,' she replied, a sudden hush in her tone. She looked at the encircling trees a moment, then added bitterly: 'I hate her, simply *hate* her for it.'

'I love you,' he cried, crushing her to him, 'that's all that matters now. Don't let's waste time talking about the rest.'

She contrived to shudder, and hid her face against his coat, while he showered kisses on her neck and hair.

And the solemn pine trees watched them, the silvery moonlight fell on their faces, the scent of new-mown hay went floating past.

'I love you with my very soul,' he repeated with intense conviction. 'I'd do anything, give up anything, bear anything—just to give you a moment's happiness. I swear it—before God!'

There was a faint sound among the trees behind them, and the girl sat up, alert. She would have scrambled to her feet, but that he held her tight.

'What the devil's the matter with you to-night?' he asked in a different tone, his vexation plainly audible. 'You're as nervy as if *you* were being watched, instead of me.'

She paused before she answered, her finger on her lip. Then she spoke slowly, hushing her voice a little:

'Watched!' she repeated. 'That's exactly what I did feel. I've felt it ever since we came into the wood.'

'Nonsense, Hermione. It's too many cigarettes.' He drew her back into his arms, forcing her head up so that he could kiss her better.

'I suppose it is nonsense,' she said, smiling. 'It's gone now, anyhow.'

He began admiring her hair, her dress, her shoes, her pretty ankles, while she resisted in a way that proved her practice. 'It's not *me* you love,' she pouted, yet drinking in his praise. She listened to his repeated assurance that he loved her with his 'soul' and was prepared for any sacrifice.

'I feel so safe with you,' she murmured, knowing the moves in the game as well as he did. She looked up guiltily into his face, while he looked down with a passion that he thought perhaps was joy.

'You'll be married before the summer's out,' he said, 'and all the thrill and excitement will be over. Poor Hermione!' She lay back in his arms, drawing his face down with both hands, and kissing him on the lips. 'You'll have more of him than you can do with—eh? As much as you care about, anyhow.'

'I shall be much more free,' she whispered. 'Things will be easier. And I've got to marry someone——'

She broke off with another start. There was a sound again behind them. The man heard nothing. The blood in his temples pulsed too loudly, doubtless.

'Well, what is it this time?' he asked sharply.

She was peering into the wood, where the patches of dark shadow and moonlit spaces made odd, irregular patterns in the air. A low branch near them waved slightly in the wind.

'Did you hear?' she asked nervously.

'Wind,' he replied, annoyed that her change of mood disturbed his pleasure.

'But something moved——'

'Only a branch. We're quite alone, quite safe, I tell you,' and there was a rasping sound in his voice as he said it. 'Don't be so imaginative. I can take care of you.'

She sprang up. The moonlight caught her figure, revealing its exquisite young curves beneath the smother of the costly clothing. Her hair had dropped a little in the struggle. The man eyed her eagerly, making a quick, impatient gesture towards her, then stopped abruptly. He saw the terror in her eyes.

'Oh, hark! What's that?' she whispered in a startled voice. She put her finger up. 'Oh, let's go back. I don't like this wood. I'm frightened.'

'Rubbish,' he said, and tried to catch her by the waist.

'It's safer in the house—my room—or yours——' she broke off again. 'There it is—don't you hear? It's a footstep!' Her face was whiter than the moon.

'I tell you it's the wind in the branches,' he repeated gruffly. 'Oh, come on, *do*. We were just getting jolly together. There's nothing to be afraid of. Can't you believe me?' He tried to pull her down upon his knee again with force. His face wore an unpleasant expression that was half leer, half grin.

But the girl stood away from him. She continued to peer nervously about her. She listened intently.

'You give me the creeps,' he exclaimed crossly, clawing at her waist again with passionate eagerness that now betrayed exasperation. His disappointment turned him coarse.

The girl made a quick movement of escape, turning so as to look in every direction. She gave a little scream.

'That *was* a step. Oh, oh, it's close behind us. I heard it. We're being watched!' she cried in terror. She darted towards him, then shrank back. He did not try to touch her this time.

'Moonshine!' he growled. 'You've spoilt my—spoilt our chance with your silly nerves.'

But she did not hear him apparently. She stood there shivering as with sudden cold.

'There! I saw it again. I'm sure of it. Something went past me through the air.'

And the man, still thinking only of his own pleasure frustrated, got up heavily, something like anger in his eyes. 'All right,' he said testily; 'if you're going to make a fuss, we'd better go. The house *is* safer, possibly, as you say. You know my room. Come along!' Even that risk he would not take. He loved her with his 'soul'.

They crept stealthily out of the wood, the girl slightly in front of him, casting frightened backward glances. Afraid, guilty, ashamed, with an air as though they had been detected, they stole back towards the garden and the house, and disappeared from view.

And a wind rose suddenly with a rushing sound, poured through the wood as though to cleanse it, swept out the artificial scent and trace of shame, and brought back again the song, the laughter, and the happy revels. It roared across the park, it shook the windows of the house, then sank away as quickly as it came. The trees stood motionless again, guarding their secret in the clean, sweet moonlight that held the world in dream until the dawn stole up, and sunshine took the earth again with joy.

ENTRANCE AND EXIT

These three—the old physicist, the girl, and the young Anglican parson who was engaged to her—stood by the window of the country house. The blinds were not yet drawn. They could see the dark clump of pines in the field, with crests silhouetted against the pale wintry sky of the February afternoon. Snow, freshly fallen, lay upon lawn and hill. A big moon was already lighting up.

'Yes, that's the wood,' the old man said, 'and it was this very day fifty years ago—February 13—the man disappeared from its shadows; swept in this extraordinary, incredible fashion into invisibility—into *some other place*. Can you wonder the grove is haunted?' A strange impressiveness of manner belied the laugh following the words.

'Oh, please tell us,' the girl whispered; 'we're all alone now.' Curiosity triumphed; yet a vague alarm betrayed itself in the questioning glance she cast for protection at her younger companion, whose fine face, on the other hand, wore an expression that was grave and singularly rapt. He was listening keenly.

'As though Nature,' the physicist went on, half to himself, 'here and there concealed vacuums, gaps, holes in space (his mind was always speculative; more than speculative, some said), in fact, at right angles to three known ones— "higher space", through which a man might drop invisibly—a new direction, as Boyle, Gauss, and Hinton might call it; and what you, with your mystical turn'—looking toward the young priest—'might consider a spiritual change of condition, into a region where space and time do not exist, and where all dimensions are possible—because they are *one*.'

'But, *please*, the story,' the girl begged, not understanding these dark sayings, 'although I'm not sure that Arthur ought to hear it. He's much too interested in such queer things as it is!'

Smiling, yet uneasy, she stood closer to his side, as though her body might protect his soul.

'Very briefly, then, you shall hear what I remember of this haunting, for I was barely ten years old at the time. It was evening—clear and cold like this, with snow and moonlight—when someone reported to my father that a peculiar sound, variously described as crying, wailing, was being heard in the grove. He paid no attention until my sister heard it too, and was frightened. Then he sent a groom to investigate. Though the night was brilliant the man took a lantern. We watched from this very window till we lost his figure against the trees, and the lantern stopped swinging suddenly, as if he had put it down. It remained motionless. We waited half an hour, and then my father, curiously excited, I remember, went out quickly, and I, utterly terrified, went after him. We followed his tracks, which came to an end beside the lantern, the last step being a stride almost impossible for a man to have made. All around the snow was unbroken by a single mark, but the man himself had vanished. Then we heard him calling for help—above, behind, beyond us; from all directions at once, yet from none, came the sound of his voice; but though we called back he made no answer, and gradually his cries grew fainter and fainter, as if going into tremendous distance, and at last died away altogether.'

'And the man himself?' asked both listeners.

'Never returned—from that day to this had never been seen... At intervals for weeks and months afterwards reports came in that he was still heard crying, always crying for help. With time, even these reports ceased—for most of us,' he added under his breath; 'and that is all I know. A mere outline, as you see.'

The girl did not quite like the story, for the old man's manner made it too convincing. She was half disappointed, half frightened.

'See! there are the others coming home,' she exclaimed, with a note of relief, pointing to a group of figures moving over the snow near the pine trees. 'Now we can think of tea!' She crossed the room to budy herself with the friendly tray as the servant approached to fasten the shutters. The young priest, however, deeply interested, talked on with their host, though in a voice almost too low for her to hear. Only the final sentences reached her, making her uneasy—absurdly so, she thought—till afterwards.

'——for matter, as we know, interpenetrates matter,' she heard, 'and two objects may conceivably occupy the same space. The odd thing really is that one should hear, but not see; that air-waves should bring the voice, yet ether-waves fail to bring the picture.'

And then the older man: '——as if certain places in Nature, yes, invited the change—places where these extraordinary forces stir from the earth as from the surface of a living Being with organs—places like islands, mountain-tops, pine-woods, especially pines isolated from their kind. You know the queer results of digging absolutely virgin soil, of course—and that theory of the earth's being *alive*——' The voice dropped again.

'States of mind also helping the forces of the place,' she caught the priest's reply in part; 'such as conditions induced by music, by intense listening, by certain moments in the Mass even—by ecstasy or——'

'I say, what *do* you think?' cried a girl's voice, as the others came in with welcome chatter and odours of tweeds and open fields. 'As we passed your old haunted pine-wood we heard *such* a queer noise. Like someone wailing or crying. Caesar howled and ran; and Harry refused to go in and investigate. He positively funked it!' They all laughed. 'More like a rabbit in a trap than a person crying,' explained Harry, a blush kindly concealing his startling pallor. 'I wanted my tea too much to bother about an old rabbit.'

It was some time after tea when the girl became aware that the priest had disappeared, and putting two and two together, ran in alarm to her host's study. Quite easily, from the hastily opened shutters, they saw his figure moving across the snow. The moon was very bright over the world, yet he carried a lantern that shone pale yellow against the white brilliance.

'Oh, for God's sake, quick!' she cried, pale with fear. 'Quick! or we're too late! Arthur's simply wild about such things. Oh, I might have known—I might have guessed. And this is the very night. I'm terrified!'

By the time he had found his overcoat and slipped round the house with her from the back door, the lantern, they saw, was already swinging close to the pine-wood. The night was still as ice, bitterly cold. Breathlessly they ran, following the tracks. Half-way his steps diverged, and were plainly visible in the virgin snow by themselves. They heard the whispering of the branches ahead of them, for pines cry even when no airs stir. 'Follow me close,' said the old man sternly. The lantern, he already saw, lay upon the ground unattended; no human figure was anywhere visible.

'See! The steps come to an end here,' he whispered, stooping down as soon as they reached the lantern. The tracks, hitherto so regular, showed an odd wavering—the snow curiously disturbed. Quite suddenly they stopped. The final step was a very long one—a stride, almost immense, 'as though he was pushed forward from behind,' muttered the old man, too low to be overheard, 'or sucked forward from in front—as in a fall.'

The girl would have dashed forward but for his strong restraining grasp. She clutched him, uttering a sudden dreadful cry. 'Hark! I hear his voice!' she almost sobbed. They stood still to listen. A mystery that was more than the mystery of night closed about their hearts—a mystery that is beyond life and death, that only great awe and terror can summon from the deeps of the soul. Out of the heart of the trees, fifty feet away, issued a crying voice, half wailing, half singing, very faint. 'Help! help!' it sounded through the still night; 'for the love of God, pray for me!'

The melancholy rustling of the pines followed; and then again the singular crying voice shot past above their heads, now in front of them, now once more behind. It sounded everywhere. It grew fainter and fainter, fading away, it seemed, into distance that somehow was appalling... The grove, however, was empty of all but the sighing wind; the snow unbroken by any tread. The moon threw inky shadows; the cold bit; it was a terror of ice and death and this awful singing cry...

'But why *pray*?' screamed the girl, distracted, frantic with her bewildered terror. 'Why *pray*? Let us *do* something to help—*do* something...!' She swung round in a circle, nearly falling to the ground. Suddenly she perceived that the old man had dropped to his knees in the snow beside her and was—praying.

'Because the forces of prayer, of thought, of the will to help, alone can reach and succour him where he now is,' was all the answer she got. And a moment later both figures were kneeling in the snow, praying, so to speak, their very heart's life out...

The search may be imagined—the steps taken by police, friends, newspapers, by the whole country in fact... But the most curious part of this queer 'Higher Space' adventure is the end of it—at least, the 'end' so far as at present known. For after three weeks, when the winds of March were a-roar about the land, there crept over the fields towards the house the small dark figure of a man. He was thin, pallid as a ghost, worn and fearfully emaciated, but upon his face and in his eyes were traces of an astonishing radiance—a glory unlike anything ever seen... It may, of course, have been deliberate, or it may have been a genuine loss of memory only; none could say—least of all the girl whom his return snatched from the gates of death; but, at any rate, what had come to pass during the interval of his amazing disappearance he has never yet been able to reveal.

'And you must never ask me,' he would say to her—and repeat even after his complete and speedy restoration to bodily health '—for I simply cannot tell. I know no language, you see, that could express it. I was near you all the time. But I was also—elsewhere and otherwise...'

THE PIKESTAFFE CASE

I

The vitality of old governesses deserves an explanatory memorandum by a good physiologist. It is remarkable. They tend to survive the grown-up married men and women they once taught as children. They hang on for ever, as a man might put it crudely, a man, that is, who, taught by one of them in his earliest schoolroom days, would answer enquiries fifty years later without enthusiasm: 'Oh, we keep her going, yes. She doesn't want for anything!'

Miss Helena Speke had taught the children of a distinguished family, and these distinguished children, with expensive progeny of their own now, still kept her going. They had clubbed together, seeing that Miss Speke retained her wonderful health, and had established her in a nice little house where she could take respectable lodgers—men for preference—giving them the three B's—bed, bath, and breakfast. Being a capable woman, Miss Speke more than made both ends meet. She wanted for nothing. She kept going.

Applicants for her rooms, especially for the first-floor suite, had to be recommended. She had a stern face for those who rang the bell without a letter in their pockets. She never advertised. Indeed, there was no need to do so. The two upper floors had been occupied by the same tenants for many years—a chief clerk in a branch bank and a retired clergyman respectively. It was only the best suite that sometimes 'happened to be vacant at the moment'. From two guineas inclusive before the war, her price for this had been raised, naturally, to four, the tenant paying his gas-stove, light, and bath extra. Breakfast—she prided herself legitimately on her good breakfast—was included.

For a long time now this first-floor suite had been unoccupied. The cost of living worried Miss Speke, as it worried most other people. Her servant was cheap but incompetent, and once she could let the suite she meant to engage a better one. The distinguished children were scattered out of reach about the world; the eldest had been killed in the war; a married one, a woman, lived in India; another married one was in the throes of divorce —an expensive business; and the fourth, the most generous and last, found himself in the Bankruptcy Court, and so was unable to help.

It was in these conditions that Miss Speke, her vitality impaired, decided to advertise. Although she inserted the words 'references essential,' she meant in her heart to use her own judgment, and if a likely gentleman presented himself and agreed to pay her price, she might accept him. The clergyman and the bank official upstairs were a protection, she felt. She invariably mentioned them to applicants: 'I have a clergyman of the Church of England on the top floor. He's been with me for eleven years. And a banker has the floor below. Mine is a very quiet house, you see.' These words formed part of the ritual she recited in the hall, facing her proposed tenants on the linoleum by the hat-rack; and it was these words she addressed to the tall, thin, pale-faced man with scanty hair and spotless linen, who informed her that he was a tutor, a teacher of higher mathematics to the sons of various families—he mentioned some first-class names where references could be obtained—a student besides and something of an author in his leisure hours. His pupils he taught, of course, in their respective houses, one being in Belgrave Square, another in The Albany; it was only after tea, or in the evenings, that he did his own work. All this he explained briefly, but with great courtesy of manner.

Mr. Thorley was well spoken, with a gentle voice, kind, far-seeing eyes, and an air of being lonely and uncared-for that touched some forgotten, dried-up spring in Miss Speke's otherwise rather cautious heart. He looked every inch a scholar—'and a gentleman,' as she explained afterwards to everybody who was interested in him, these being numerous, of unexpected kinds and all very close, not to say unpleasantly close, questioners indeed. But what chiefly influenced her in his favour was the fact, elicited in conversation, that years ago he had been a caller at the house in Portman Square where she was governess to the distinguished family. She did not exactly remember him, but he had certainly known Lady Araminta, the mother of her charges.

Thus it was that Mr. Thorley—John Laking Thorley, M.A., of Jesus College, Cambridge—was accepted by Miss Speke as tenant of her best suite on the first floor at the price mentioned, breakfast included, winning her confidence so fully that she never went to the trouble even of taking up the references he gave her. She liked him, she felt safe with him, she pitied him. He had not bargained, nor tried to beat her down. He just reflected a moment, then agreed. He proved, indeed, an exemplary lodger, early to bed and not too early to rise, of regular habits, thoughtful of the expensive new servant, careful with towels, electric light, and inkstains, prompt in his payments, and never once troubling her with complaints or requests, as other lodgers did, not excepting the banker and the clergyman. Moreover, he was a tidy man, who never lost anything, because he invariably put everything in its proper place and thus knew exactly where to look for it. She noticed this tidiness at once.

Miss Speke, especially in the first days of his tenancy, studied him, as she studied all her lodgers. She studied his room when he was out 'of a morning'. At her leisure she did this, knowing he would never break in and disturb her unexpectedly. She was neither prying nor inquisitive, she assured herself, but she *was* curious. 'I have a right to know something about the gentlemen who sleep under my roof with me,' was the way she put it in her own mind. His clothes, she found, were ample, including evening dress, white gloves, and an opera hat. He had plenty of boots and shoes. His linen was good. His wardrobe, indeed, though a trifle uncared-for, especially his socks, was a gentleman's wardrobe. Only one thing puzzled her. The full-length mirror standing on mahogany legs—a present from the generous 'child', now in the Bankruptcy Court, and, a handsome thing, a special attraction in the best suite—this fine mirror Mr. Thorley evidently did not like. The second or third morning he was with her she went to his bedroom before the servant had done it up, and saw, to her surprise, that this full-length glass stood with its back to the room. It had been placed close against the wall in a corner, its unattractive back turned outward.

'It gave me quite a shock to see it,' as she said afterwards. 'And such a handsome piece, too!'

Her first thought, indeed, sent a cold chill down her energetic spine. 'He's cracked it!' But it was not cracked. She paused in some amazement, wondering why her new lodger had done this thing; then she turned the mirror again into its proper position, and left the room. Next morning she found it again with its face close against the wall. The following day it was the same—she turned it round, only to find it the next morning again with its back to the room.

She asked the servant, but the servant knew nothing about it.

'He likes it that way, I suppose, mum,' was all Sarah said. 'I never laid a 'and on it once.'

Miss Speke, after much puzzled consideration, decided it must be something to do with the light. Mr. Thorley, she remembered, wore horn-rimmed spectacles for reading. She scented a mystery. It caused her a slight—oh, a very slight—feeling of discomfort. Well, if he did not like the handsome mirror, she could perhaps use it in her own room. To see it neglected hurt her a little. Not many furnished rooms could boast a full-length glass, she reflected. A few days later, meeting Mr. Thorley on the linoleum before the hat-rack, she enquired if he was quite comfortable, and if the breakfast was to his liking. He was polite and even cordial. Everything was perfect, he assured her. He had never been so well looked after. And the house was so quiet.

'And the bed, Mr. Thorley? You sleep well, I hope.' She drew nearer to the subject of the mirror, but with caution. For some reason she found a difficulty in actually broaching it. It suddenly dawned upon her that there was something queer about his treatment of that full-length glass. She was by no means fanciful, Miss Speke, retired governess; only the faintest suspicion of something odd brushed her mind and vanished. But she did feel something. She found it impossible to mention the handsome thing outright.

'There's nothing you would like changed in the room, or altered?' she enquired with a smile, 'or—in any way put different—perhaps?'

Mr. Thorley hesitated for a moment. A curious expression, half sad, half yearning, she thought, lit on his thoughtful face for one second and was gone. The idea of moving anything seemed distasteful to him.

'Nothing, Miss Speke, I thank you,' he replied courteously, but without delay. 'Everything is really *just* as I like it.' Then, with a little bow, he asked: 'I trust my typewriter disturbs nobody. Please let me know if it does.'

Miss Speke assured him that nobody minded the typewriter in the least, nor even heard it, and, with another charming little bow and a smile, Mr. Thorley went out to give his lessons in the higher mathematics.

'There!' she reflected, 'and I never even asked him!' It had been impossible.

From the window she watched him going down the street, his head bent, evidently in deep thought, his books beneath his arm, looking, she thought, every inch the gentleman and the scholar that he undoubtedly was. His personality left a very strong impression on her mind. She found herself rather wondering about him. As he turned the corner Miss Speke owned to two things that rose simultaneously in her mind: first, the relief that the lodger was out for the day and could be counted upon not to return unexpectedly; secondly, that it would interest her to slip up and see what kind of books he read. A minute later she was in his sitting-room. It was already swept and dusted, the breakfast cleared away, and the books, she saw, lay partly on the table where he had just left them and partly on the broad mantelpiece he used as a shelf. She was alone, the servant was downstairs in the kitchen. She examined Mr. Thorley's books.

The examination left her bewildered and uninspired. 'I couldn't make them out at all,' she put it. But they were evidently what she called costly volumes, and that she liked. 'Something to do with his work, I suppose—mathematics, and all that,' she decided, after turning over pages covered with some kind of hieroglyphics, symbols being a word she did not know in that connection. There was no writing, there were no sentences, there was nothing she could lay hold of, and the diagrams she thought perhaps were Euclid, or possibly astronomical. Most of the names were odd and quite unknown to her. Gauss! Minowski! Lobatchewski! And it affronted her that some of these were German. A writer named Einstein was popular with her lodger, and that, she felt, was a pity, as well as a mistake in taste. It all alarmed her a little; or, rather she felt that touch of respect, almost of awe, pertaining to some world entirely beyond her ken. She was rather glad when the search—it was a duty—ended.

'There's nothing there,' she reflected, meaning there was nothing that explained his dislike of the full-length mirror. And disappointed, yet with a faint relief, she turned to his private papers. These, since he was a tidy man, were in a drawer. Mr. Thorley never left anything lying about. Now, a letter Miss Speke would not have thought of reading, but papers, especially learned papers, were another matter. Conscience, nevertheless, did prick her faintly as she cautiously turned over sheaf after sheaf of large white foolscap, covered with designs, and curves, and diagrams in ink, the ink he never spilt, and assuredly in his recent handwriting. And it was among these foolscap sheets that she suddenly came upon one sheet in particular that caught her attention and even startled her. In the centre, surrounded by scriggly hieroglyphics, numbers, curves and lines meaningless to her, she saw a drawing of the full-length mirror. Some of the curves ran into it and through it, emerging on the other side. She knew it was *the* mirror because its exact measurements were indicated in red ink.

This, as mentioned, startled her. What could it mean? She asked herself, staring intently at the curious sheet, as though it must somehow yield its secret to prolonged even if unintelligent enquiry. 'It looks like an experiment or something,' was the furthest her mind could probe into the mystery, though this, she admitted, was not very far. Holding the paper at various angles, even upside down, she examined it with puzzled curiosity, then slowly laid it down again in the exact place whence she had taken it. That faint breath of alarm had again suddenly brushed her soul, as though she approached a mystery she had better leave unsolved.

'It's very strange——' she began, carefully closing the drawer, but unable to complete the sentence even in her mind. 'I don't think I like it—quite,' and she turned to go out. It was just then that something touched her face, tickling one cheek, something fine as a cobweb, something in the air. She picked it away. It was a thread of silk, extremely fine, so fine, indeed, that it might almost have been a spider's web of gossamer such as one sees floating over the garden lawn on a sunny morning. Miss Speke brushed it away, giving it no further thought, and went about her usual daily duties.

II

But in her mind was established now a vague uneasiness, though so vague that at first she did not recognise it. Her thought would suddenly pause. 'Now, what is it?' she would ask herself. 'Something's on my mind. What is it I've forgotten?' The picture of her first-floor lodger appeared, and she knew at once. 'Oh, yes, it's that mirror and the diagrams, of course.' Some taut wire of alarm was quivering at the back of her mind. It was akin to those childhood alarms that pertain to the big unexplained mysteries no parent can elucidate because no parent knows. 'Only God can tell that,' says the parent evading the insoluble problem. 'I'd better not think about it,' was the analogous conclusion reached by Miss Speke. Meanwhile the impression the new lodger's personality made upon her mind perceptibly deepened. He seemed to her full of power, above little things, a man of intense and mysterious mental life. He was constantly and somewhat possessingly in her thoughts. The mere thought of him, she found, stimulated her.

It was just before luncheon, as she returned from her morning marketing, that the servant drew her attention to certain marks upon the carpet of Mr. Thorley's sitting-room. She had discovered them as she handled the vacuum cleaner—faint, short lines drawn by dark chalk or crayons, in shape like the top or bottom right-angle of a square bracket, and sometimes with a tiny arrow shown as well. There were occasional other marks, too, that Miss Speke recognised as the hieroglyphics she called squiggles. Mistress and servant examined them together in a stooping position. They found others on the bedroom carpet, too, only these were not straight; they were small curved lines; and about the feet of the full-length mirror they clustered in a quantity, segments of circles, some large, some small. They looked as if someone had snipped off curly hair, or pared his finger-nails with sharp scissors, only considerably larger, and they were so faint that they were only visible when the sunlight fell upon them.

'I knew they was drawn on,' said Sarah, puzzled, yet proud that she had found them, 'because they didn't come up with the dust and fluff.'

'I'll—speak to Mr. Thorley,' was the only comment Miss Speke made. 'I'll tell him.' Her voice was not quite steady, but the girl apparently noticed nothing.

'There's all this too, please, mum.' She pointed to a number of fine silk threads she had collected upon a bit of newspaper, preparatory to the dust-bin. 'They was stuck on the cupboard door and the walls, stretched all across the room, but rather 'igh up. I only saw them by chance. One caught on my face.'

Miss Speke stared, touched, examined for some seconds without speaking. She remembered the thread that had tickled her own cheek. She looked enquiringly round the room, and the servant, following her suggestion, indicated where the threads had been attached to walls and furniture. No marks, however, were left, there was no damage done.

'I'll mention it to Mr. Thorley,' said her mistress briefly, unwilling to discuss the matter with the new servant, much less to admit that she was uncomfortably at sea. 'Mr. Thorley,' she added, as though there was nothing unusual, 'is a high mathematician. He makes—measurements and—calculations of that sort.' She had not sufficient control of her voice to be more explicit, and she went from the room aware that, unaccountably, she was trembling. She had first gathered up the threads, meaning to show them to her lodger when she demanded an explanation. But the explanation was delayed, for—to state it bluntly—she was afraid to ask him for it. She put it off till the following morning, then till the day after, and, finally, she decided to say nothing about the matter at all. 'I'd better leave it, perhaps, after all,' she persuaded herself. 'There's no damage done, anyhow. I'd better not enquire.' All the same she did not like it. By the end of the week, however, she was able to pride herself upon her restraint and tact; the marks on the carpet, rubbed out by the girl, were not renewed, and the fine threads of silk were never again found stretching through the air from wall to furniture. Mr. Thorley had evidently noticed their removal and had discontinued what he had observed was an undesirable performance. He was a scholar and a gentleman. But he was more. He was frank and straight-dealing. One morning he asked to see his landlady and told her all about it himself.

'Oh,' he said in his pleasantest, easiest manner when she came into the room, 'I wanted to tell you, Miss Speke—indeed, I meant to do so long before this—about the marks I made on your carpets'—he smiled apologetically—'and the silk threads I stretched. I use them for measurements—for problems I set my pupils, and one morning I left them by mistake. The marks easily rub out. But I will use scraps of paper instead another time. I can pin these on—if you will kindly tell your excellent servant not to touch them—er—they're rather important to me.' He smiled again charmingly, and his face wore the wistful, rather yearning expression that had already appealed to her. The eyes, it struck her, were very brilliant. 'Any damage,' he added—

'though, I assure you, none is possible really—I would, of course, make good to you, Miss Speke.'

'Thank you, Mr. Thorley,' was all Miss Speke could find to say, so confused was her mind by troubling thoughts and questions she dared not express. 'Of course—this *is* my best suite, you see.'

It was all most amicable and pleasant between them.

'I wonder—have my books come?' he asked, as he went out. 'Ah, there they are, I do believe!' he exclaimed, for through the open front door a van was seen discharging a very large packing-case.

'Your books, Mr. Thorley——?' Miss Speke murmured, noting the size of the package with dismay. 'But I'm afraid—you'll hardly find space to put them in,' she stammered. 'The rooms—er'—she did not wish to disparage them—'are so small, aren't they?'

Mr. Thorley smiled delightfully. 'Oh, please do not trouble on that account,' he said. 'I shall find space all right, I assure you. It's merely a question of knowing where and how to put them,' and he proceeded to give the man instructions.

A few days later a second case arrived.

'I'm expecting some instruments, too,' he mentioned casually, 'mathematical instruments,' and he again assured her with his confident smile that she need have no anxiety on the score of space. Nor would he dent the walls or scrape the furniture the least little bit. There was always room, he reminded her gently again, provided one knew how to stow things away. Both books and instruments were necessary to his work. Miss Speke need feel no anxiety at all.

But Miss Speke felt more than anxiety, she felt uneasiness, she felt a singular growing dread. There lay in her a seed of distress that began to sprout rapidly. Everything arrived as Mr. Thorley has announced, case upon case was unpacked in his room by his own hands. The straw and wood she used for firing purposes, there was no mess, no litter, no untidiness, nor were walls and furniture injured in any way. What caused her dread to deepen into something bordering upon actual alarm was the fact that, on searching Mr. Thorley's rooms when he was out, she could discover no trace of any of the things that had arrived. There was no sign of either books or instruments. Where had he stored them? Where could they lie concealed? She asked herself innumerable questions, but found no answer to them. These stores, enough to choke and block the room, had been brought in through the sitting-room door. They could not possibly have been taken out again. They had *not* been taken out. Yet no trace of them was anywhere to be seen. It was very strange, she thought; indeed, it was more than strange. She felt excited. She felt a touch of hysterical alarm.

Meanwhile, thin strips of white paper, straight, angled, curved, were pinned upon the carpet; threads of finest silk again stretched overhead connecting the top of the door lintel with the window, the high cupboard with the curtain rods—yet too high to be brushed away merely by the head of anyone moving in the room. And the full-length mirror still stood with its face close against the wall.

The mystery of these aerial entanglements increased Miss Speke's alarm considerably. What could their purpose be? 'Thank God,' she thought, 'this isn't war time!' She knew enough to realise their meaning was not 'wireless'. That they bore some relation to the lines on the carpet and to the diagrams and curves upon the paper, she grasped vaguely. But what it all meant baffled her and made her feel quite stupid. Where all the books and instruments had disappeared added to her bewilderment. She felt more and more perturbed. A vague, uncertain fear was worse than something definite she could face and deal with. Her fear increased. Then, suddenly, yet with a reasonable enough excuse, Sarah gave notice.

For some reason Miss Speke did not argue with the girl. She preferred to let the real meaning of her leaving remain unexpressed. She just let her go. But the fact disturbed her extraordinarily. Sarah had given every satisfaction, there had been no sign of a grievance, no complaint, the work was not hard, the pay was good. It was simply that the girl preferred to leave. Miss Speke attributed it to Mr. Thorley. She became more and more disturbed in mind. Also she found herself, more and more, avoiding her lodger, whose regular habits made such avoidance an easy matter. Knowing his hours of exit and entrance, she took care to be out of the way. At the mere sound of his step she flew to cover. The new servant, a stupid, yet not inefficient country girl, betrayed no reaction of any sort, no unfavourable reaction at any rate. Having received her instructions, Lizzie did her work without complaint from either side. She did not remove the paper and the thread, nor did she mention them. She seemed just the country clod she was. Miss Speke, however, began to have restless nights. She contracted an unpleasant habit: she lay awake—listening.

III

As the result of one of these sleepless nights she came to the abrupt conclusion that she would be happier without Mr. Thorley in the house—only she had not the courage to ask him to leave. The truth was she had not the courage to speak to him at all, much less to give him notice, however nicely.

After much cogitation she hit upon a plan that promised well: she sent him a carefully worded letter explaining that, owing to increased cost of living, she found herself compelled to raise his terms. The 'raise' was more than considerable, it was unreasonable, but he paid what she demanded, sending down a cheque for three months in advance with his best compliments. The letter somehow made her tremble. It was at this stage she first became aware of the existence in her of other feelings than discomfort, uneasiness, and alarm. These other feelings, being in contradiction of her dread, were difficult to describe, but their result was plain—she did not really wish Mr. Thorley to go after all. His friendly 'compliments', his refusal of her hint, caused her a secret pleasure. It was not the cheque at the increased rate that pleased her—it was simply the fact that her lodger meant to stay.

It might be supposed that some delayed sense of romance had been stirred in her, but this really was not the case at all. Her pleasure was due to another source, but to a source uncommonly obscure and very strange. She feared him, feared his presence, above all, feared going into his room, while yet there was something about the mere idea of Mr. Thorley that entranced her. Another thing may as well be told at once—she herself faced it boldly—she would enter his dreaded room, when he was out, and would deliberately linger there. There was an odd feeling in the room that gave her pleasure, and more than pleasure—happiness. Surrounded by the enigmas of his personality, by the lines and curves of white paper pinned upon her carpet, by the tangle of silken threads above her head, by the mysterious books, the more than mysterious diagrams in his drawer—yet all these, even the dark perplexity of the rejected mirror and the vanished objects, were forgotten in the curious sense of happiness she derived from merely sitting in his room. Her fear contained this other remarkable ingredient—an uncommon sense of joy, of liberty, of freedom. She felt *exaltée*.

She could not explain it, she did not attempt to do so. She would go shaking and trembling into his room, and a few minutes later this sense of uncommon happiness—of release, almost of escape, she felt it—would steal over her as though in her dried-up frozen soul spring had burst upon midwinter, as though something that crawled had suddenly most gloriously found wings. An indescribable exhilaration caught her.

Under this influence the dingy street turned somehow radiant, and the front door of her poor lodging-house opened upon blue seas, yellow sands, and mountains carpeted with flowers. Her whole life, painfully repressed and crushed down in the dull service of conventional nonentities, flashed into colour, movement, and adventure. Nothing confined her. She was no longer limited. She knew advance in all possible directions. She knew the stars. She knew escape!

An attempt has been made to describe for her what she never could have described herself.

The reaction, upon coming out again, was painful. Her life in the past as a governess, little better than a servant; her life in the present as lodging-house keeper; her struggle with servants, with taxes, with daily expenses; her knowledge that no future but a mere 'living' lay in front of her until the grave was reached—these overwhelmed her with an intense depression that the contrast rendered almost insupportable. Whereas in *his* room she had perfume, freedom, liberty, and wonder—the wonder of some entirely new existence.

Thus, briefly, while Miss Speke longed for Mr. Thorley to leave her house, she became obsessed with the fear that one day he really *would* go. Her mind, it is seen, became uncommonly disturbed; her lodger's presence being undoubtedly the cause. Her nights were now more than restless, they were sleepless. Whence came, she asked herself repeatedly in the dark watches, her fear? Whence came, too, her strange enchantment?

It was at this juncture, then, that a further item of perplexity was added to her mind. Miss Speke, as has been seen, was honourably disposed; she respected the rights of others, their property as well. Yet, included in the odd mood of elation the room and its atmosphere caused her, was also a vagrant, elusive feeling that the intimate, the personal—above all, the personal—had lost their original rigidity. Small individual privacies, secrecy, no longer held their familiar meaning quite. The idea that most things in life were to be shared slipped into her. A 'secret', to this expensive mood, was a childish attitude.

At any rate, it was while lingering in her lodger's attractive room one day—a habit now—that she did something that caused her surprise, yet did not shock her. She saw an open letter lying on his table—and she read it.

Rather than an actual letter, however, it seemed a note, a memorandum. It began 'To J. L. T'.

In a boyish writing, the meaning of the language escaped her entirely. She understood the strange words as little as she understood the phases of the moon, while yet she derived from their perusal a feeling of mysterious beauty, similar to the emotions the changes of that lovely satellite stirred in her:

'To J. L. T.
'I followed your instructions, though with intense effort and difficulty. I woke at 4 o'clock. About ten minutes later, as you said might happen, I woke a *second time*. The change into the second state was as great as the change from sleeping to waking, in the ordinary meaning of these words. But I could not remain 'awake'. I fell asleep again in about a minute—back into the usual waking state, I mean. Description in words is impossible, as you know. What I felt was too terrific to feel for long. The new energy must presently have *burned me up*. It frightened me— as you warned me it would. And this fear, no doubt, was the cause of my 'falling asleep' again so quickly.
'Cannot we arrange a Call for Help for similar occasions in future?

G. P.'

Against this note Mr. Thorley had written various strangest 'squiggles'; higher mathematics, Miss Speke supposed. In the opposite margin, also in her lodger's writing, were these words:
'We must agree on a word to use when frightened. *Help,* or *Help me,* seems the best. To be uttered with the whole being.'
Mr. Thorley had added a few other notes. She read them without the faintest prick of conscience. Though she understood no single sentence, a thrill of deep delight ran through her:
'It amounts, of course, to a new direction; a direction at right angles to all we know, a new direction in oneself, a new direction—in living. But it can, perhaps, be translated into mathematical terms by the intellect. This, however, only a simile at best, Cannot be experienced that way. Actual experience possible only to *changed consciousness*. But good to become mathematically accustomed to it. The mathematical experiments are worth it. They induce the mind, at any rate, to dwell upon the new direction. This helps. ...'

Miss Speke laid down the letter exactly where she had found it. No shame was in her. 'G. P.' she knew, meant Gerald Pikestaffe; he was one of her lodger's best pupils, the one in Belgrave Square. Her feeling of mysterious elation, as already mentioned, seemed above all such matters as small secrecies or petty personal privacies. She had read a 'private' letter without remorse. One feeling only caused in her a certain commonplace emotion: the feeling that, while she read the letter, her lodger was present, watching her. He seemed close behind her, looking over her shoulder almost, observing her acts, her mood, her very thoughts —yet not objecting. He was aware, at any rate, of what she did...

It was under these circumstances that she bethought herself of her old tenant, the retired clergyman on the top floor, and sought his aid. The consolation of talking to another would be something, yet when the interview began all she could manage to say was that her mind was troubled and her heart not quite as it should be, and that she 'didn't know what to do about it all'. For the life of her she could not find more definite words. To mention Mr. Thorley she found suddenly utterly impossible.

'Prayer,' the old man interrupted her half-way, 'prayer, my dear lady. Prayer, I find,' he repeated smoothly, 'is always the best course in all one's troubles and perplexities. Leave it to God. He knows. And in His good time He will answer.' He advised her to read the Bible and Longfellow. She added Florence Barclay to the list and followed his advice. The books, however, comforted her very little.

After some hesitation she then tried her other tenant. But the 'banker' stopped her even sooner than the clergyman had done. MacPherson was very prompt:

'I can give you another ten shillings or maybe half a guinea,' he said briskly. 'Times are difficult, I know. But I can't do more. If that's sufficient I shall be delighted to stay on——' and, with a nod and a quick smile that settled the matter then and there, he was through the door and down the steps on the way to his office.

It was evident that Miss Speke must face her troubles alone, a fact, for the rest, life had already taught her. The loyal, courageous spirit in her accepted the situation. The alternate moods of happiness and depression, meanwhile, began to wear her out. 'If only Mr. Thorley would go! If only Mr. Thorley will not go!' For some weeks now she had successfully avoided him. He made no requests nor complaints. His habits were as regular as sunrise, his payments likewise. Not even the servant mentioned him. He became a shadow in the house.

Then, with the advent of summer-time, he came home, as it were, an hour earlier than usual. He invariably worked from 5.30 to 7.30, when he went out for his dinner. Tea he always had at a pupil's house. It was a light evening, caused by the advance of the clock, and Miss Speke, mending her underwear at the window, suddenly perceived his figure coming down the street.

She watched, fascinated. Of two instincts—to hide herself, or to wait there and catch his eye—she obeyed the latter. She had not seen him for several weeks, and a deep thrill of happiness ran through her. His walk was peculiar, she noticed at once; he did not walk in a straight line. His tall, thin outline flowed down the pavement in long, sweeping curves, yet quite steadily. He was not drunk. He came nearer; he was not twenty feet away; at ten feet she saw his face clearly, and received a shock. It was worn, and thin, and wasted, but a light of happiness, of something more than happiness indeed, shone in it. He reached the area railings. He looked up. His face seemed ablaze. Their eyes met, his with no start of recognition, hers with a steady stare of wonder. She ran into the passage, and before Mr. Thorley had time to use his latch-key she had opened the door for him herself. Little she knew, as she stood there trembling, that she stood also upon the threshold of an amazing adventure.

Face to face with him her presence of mind deserted her. She could only look up into that worn and wasted face, into those happy, severe, and brilliant eyes, where yet burned a strange expression of wistful yearning, of uncommon wonder, of something that seemed not of this world quite. Such an expression she had never seen before upon any human countenance. Its light dazzled her. There was uncommon fire in the eyes. It enthralled her. The same instant, as she stood there gazing at him without a single word, either of welcome or enquiry, it flashed across her that he needed something from her. He needed help, her help. It was a far-fetched notion, she was well aware, but it came to her irresistibly. The conviction was close to her, closer than her skin.

It was this knowledge, doubtless, that enabled her to hear without resentment the strange words he at once made use of:

'Ah, I thank you, Miss Speke, I thank you,' the thin lips parting in a smile, the shining eyes lit with an emotion of more than ordinary welcome. 'You cannot know what a relief it is to me to see you. You are so sound, so wholesome, so ordinary, so—forgive me, I beg—so commonplace.'

He was gone past her and upstairs into his sitting-room. She heard the key turn softly. She was aware that she had not shut the front door. She did so, then went back, trembling, happy, frightened, into her own room. She had a curious, rushing feeling, both frightful and bewildering, that the room did not contain her. ... She was still sitting there two hours later, when she heard Mr. Thorley's step come down the stairs and leave the house. She was still sitting there when she heard him return, open the door with his key, and go up to his sitting-room. The interval might have been two minutes or two weeks, instead of two hours merely. And all this time she had the wondrous sensation that the room did not contain her. The walls and ceilings did not shut her in. She was out of the room. Escape had come very close to her. She was out of the house ... out of herself as well....

IV

She went early to bed, taking this time the Bible with her. Her strange sensations had passed, they had left her gradually. She had made herself a cup of tea and had eaten a soft-boiled egg and some bread-and-butter. She felt more normal again, but her nerves were unusually sensitive. It was a comfort to know there were two men in the house with her, two worthy men, a clergyman and a banker. The Bible, the banker, the clergyman, with Mrs. Barclay and Longfellow not far from her bed, were certainly a source of comfort to her.

The traffic died away, the rumbling of the distant motor-buses ceased, and, with the passing of the hours, the night became intensely still.

It was April. Her window was opened at the top and she could smell the cool, damp air of coming spring. Soothed by the books she began to feel drowsy. She glanced at the clock—it was just on two—then blew out the candle and prepared to sleep. Her thoughts turned automatically to Mr. Thorley, lying asleep on the floor above, his threads and paper strips and mysterious diagrams all about him—when, suddenly, a voice broke through the silence with a cry for help. It was a man's voice, and it sounded a lond way off. But she recognised it instantly, and she sprang out of bed without a trace of fear. It was Mr. Thorley calling, and in the voice was anguish.

'He's in trouble? In danger! He needs help? I knew it!' ran rapidly through her mind, as she lit the candle with fingers that did not tremble. The clock showed three. She had slept a full hour. She opened the door and peered into the passage, but saw no one there; the stairs, too, were empty. The call was not repeated.

'Mr. Thorley!' she cried aloud. 'Mr. Thorley! Do you want anything?' And by the sound of her voice she realised how distant and muffled his own had been. 'I'm coming!'

She stood there waiting, but no answer came. There was no sound. She realised the uncommon stillness of the night.

'Did you call me?' she tried again, but with less confidence. 'Can I do anything for you?'

Again there was no answer; nothing stirred; the house was silent as the grave. The linoleum felt cold against her bare feet, and she stole back to get her slippers and a dressing-gown, while a hundred possibilities flashed through her mind at once. Oddly enough, she never once thought of burglars, nor of fire, nor, indeed, of any ordinary situation that required ordinary help. Why this was so she could not say. No ordinary fear, at any rate, assailed her in that moment, nor did she feel the smallest touch of nervousness about her own safety.

'Was it—I wonder—a dream?' she asked herself as she pulled the dressing-gown about her. 'Did I dream that voice——?' when the thrilling cry broke forth again, startling her so that she nearly dropped the candle:

'Help! Help! Help me!'

Very distinct, yet muffled as by distance, it was beyond all question the voice of Mr. Thorley. What she had taken for anguish in it she now recognised was terror. It sounded on the floor above, it was the closed door doubtless that gave the muffled effect of distance.

Miss Speke ran along the passage instantly, and with extraordinary speed for an elderly woman; she was half-way up the stairs in a moment, when, just as she reached the first little landing by the bathroom and turned to begin the second flight, the voice came again: 'Help! Help' but this time with a difference that, truth to tell, did set her nerves unpleasantly aquiver. For there were two voices instead of one, and they were not upstairs at all. Both were below her in the passage she had just that moment left. Close they were behind her. One, moreover, was not the voice of Mr. Thorley. It was a boy's clear soprano. Both called for help together, and both held a note of terror that made her heart shake.

Under these conditions it may be forgiven to Miss Speke that she lost her balance and reeled against the wall, clutching the banisters for a moment's support. Yet her courage did not fail her. She turned instantly and quickly went downstairs again—to find the passage empty of any living figure. There was no one visible. There was only silence, a motionless hat-rack, the door of her own room slightly ajar, and shadows.

'Mr. Thorley!' she called. 'Mr. Thorley!' her voice not quite so loud and confident as before. It had a whisper in it. No answer came. She repeated the words, her tone with still less volume. Only faint echoes that seemed to linger unduly came in response. Peering into her own room she found it exactly as she had left it. The dining-room, facing it, was likewise empty. Yet a moment before she had plainly heard two voices calling for help within a few yards of where she stood. Two voices! What could it mean? She noticed now for the first time a peculiar freshness in the air, a sharpness, almost a perfume, as though all the windows were wide open and the air of coming spring was in the house.

Terror, though close, had not yet actually gripped her. That she had gone crazy occurred to her, but only to be dismissed. She was quite sane and self-possessed. The changing direction of the sounds lay beyond all explanation, but an explanation, she was positive, there must be. The odd freshness in the air was heartening, and seemed to brace her. No, terror had not yet really gripped her. Ideas of summoning the servant, the clergyman, the banker, these she equally dismissed. It was no ordinary help that was needed, not theirs at any rate. She went boldly upstairs again and knocked at Mr. Thorley's bedroom door. She knocked again and again, loud enough to waken him, if he had perchance called out in sleep, but not loud enough to disturb her other tenants. No answer came. There was no sound within. No light shone through the cracks. With his sitting-room the same conditions held.

It was the strangeness of the second voice that now stole over her with a deadly fear. She found herself cold and shivering. As she, at length, went slowly downstairs again the cries were suddenly audible once more. She heard both voices: 'Help! Help! Help me!' Then silence. They were fainter this time. Far away, they sounded, withdrawn curiously into some remote distance, yet ever with the same anguish, the same terror in them as before. The direction, however, this time she could not tell at all. In a sense they seemed both close and far, both above her and below; they seemed—it was the only way she could describe the astounding thing—in any direction, or in all directions.

Miss Speke was really terrified at last. The strange, full horror of it gripped her, turning her heart suddenly to ice. The two voices, the terror in them, the extraordinary impression that they had withdrawn further into some astounding distance—this overcame her. She became appalled. Staggering into her room, she reached the bed and fell upon it in a senseless heap. She had fainted.

V

She slept late, owing probably to exhausted nerves. Though usually up and about by 7.30, it was after nine when the servant woke her. She sprawled half in the bed, half out; the candle, which luckily had extinguished itself in falling, lay upon the carpet. The events of the night came slowly back to her as she watched the servant's face. The girl was white and shaking.

'Are you ill, mum?' Lizzie asked anxiously in a whisper; then, without waiting for an answer, blurted out what she had really come in to say: 'Mr. Thorley, mum! I can't get into his room. There's no answer.' The girl was very frightened.

Mr. Thorley invariably had breakfast at 8 o'clock, and was out of the house punctually at 8.45.

'Was he ill in the night—perhaps—do you think?' Miss Speke said. It was the nearest she could get to asking if the girl had heard the voices. She had admirable control of herself by this time. She got up, still in her dressing-gown and slippers.

'Not that I know of, mum,' was the reply.

'Come,' said her mistress firmly. 'We'll go in.' And they went upstairs together.

The bedroom door, as the girl had said, was closed, but the sitting-room was open. Miss Speke led the way. The freshness of the night before lay still in the air, she noticed, though the windows were all closed tightly. There was an exhilarating sharpness, a delightful tang as of open space. She particularly mentions this. On the carpet, as usual, lay the strips of white paper, fastened with small pins, and the silk threads, also as usual, stretched across from lintel to cupboard, from window to bracket. Miss Speke brushed several of them from her face.

The door into the bedroom she opened, and went boldly in, followed more cautiously by the girl. 'There's nothing to be afraid of,' said her mistress firmly. The bed, she saw, had not been slept in. Everything was neat and tidy. The long mirror stood close against the wall, showing its ugly back as usual, while about its four feet clustered the curved strips of paper Miss Speke had grown accustomed to.

'Pull the blinds up, Lizzie,' she said in a quiet voice.

The light now enabled her to see everything quite clearly. There were silken threads, she noticed distinctly, stretching from bed to window, and though both windows were closed there was this strange sweetness in the air as of a flowering spring garden. She sniffed it with a curious feeling of pleasure, of freedom, of release, though Lizzie, apparently, noticed nothing of all this.

'There's his 'at and mackintosh,' the girl whispered in a frightened voice, pointing to the hooks on the door. 'And the umbrella in the corner. But I don't see 'is boots, mum. They weren't put out to be cleaned.'

Miss Speke turned and looked at her, voice and manner under full command. 'What do you mean?' she asked.

'Mr. Thorley ain't gone out, mum,' was the reply in a tremulous tone.

At that very moment a faint, distant cry was audible in a man's voice: 'Help! Help!' Immediately after it a soprano, fainter still, called from what seemed even greater distance: 'Help me!' The direction was not ascertainable. It seemed both in the room, yet far away outside in space above the roofs. A glance at the girl convinced Miss Speke that she had heard nothing.

'Mr. Thorley is not *here*,' whispered Miss Speke, one hand upon the brass bed-rail for support.

The room was undeniably empty.

'Leave everything exactly as it is,' ordered her mistress as they went out. Tears in her eyes, she lingered a moment on the threshold, but the sounds were not repeated. 'Exactly as it is,' she repeated, closing the bedroom and then the sitting-room door behind her. She locked the latter, putting the key in her pocket. Two days later, as Mr. Thorley had not returned, she informed the police. But Mr. Thorley never returned. He had disappeared completely. He left no trace. He was never heard of again, though—once—he was seen.

Yet, this is not entirely accurate perhaps, for he was seen twice, in the sense that he was seen by two persons, and though he was not 'heard of', he was certainly heard. Miss Speke heard his voice from time to time. She heard it in the daytime and at night; calling for help and always with the same words she had first heard: 'Help! Help! Help me!' It sounded very far away, withdrawn into immense distance, the distance ever increasing. Occasionally she heard the boy's voice with it; they called together sometimes; she never heard the soprano voice alone. But the anguish and terror she had first noticed were no longer present. Alarm had gone out of them. It was more like an echo that she heard. Through all the hubbub, confusion and distressing annoyance of the police search and enquiry, the voice and woices came to her, though she never mentioned them to a single living soul, not even to her old tenants, the clergyman and the banker. They kept their rooms on—which was about all she could have asked of them. The best suite was never let again. It was kept locked and empty. The dust accumulated. The mirror remained untouched, its face against the wall.

The voices, meanwhile, grew more and more faint; the distance seemed to increase; soon the voice of the boy was no longer heard at all, only the cry of Mr. Thorley, her mysterious but perfect lodger, sang distantly from time to time, both in the sunshine and in the still darkness of the night hours. The direction whence it came, too, remained, as before, undeterminable. It came from anywhere and everywhere—from above, below, on all sides. It had become, too, a pleasant, even a happy sound; no dread belonged to it any more. The intervals grew longer then; days first, then weeks passed without a sound; and invariably, after these increasing intervals, the voice had become fainter, weaker, withdrawn into ever greater and greater distance. With the coming of the warm spring days it grew almost inaudible. Finally, with the great summer heats, it died away completely.

VI

The disappearance of Mr. Thorley, however, had caused no public disturbance on its own account, not until it was bracketed with another disappearance, that of one of his pupils, Sir Mark Pikestaffe's son. The Pikestaffe Case then became a daily mystery that filled the papers. Mr. Thorley was of no consequence, whereas Sir Mark was a figure in the public eye.

Mr. Thorley's life, as enquiry proved, held no mystery. He had left everything in order. He did not owe a penny. He owned, indeed, considerable property, both in land and securities, and teaching mathematics, especially to promising pupils, seemed to have been a hobby merely. A half-brother called eventually to take away his few possessions, but the books and instruments he had brought into the lodging-house were never traced. He was a scholar and a gentleman to the last, a man, too, it appeared, of immense attainments and uncommon ability, one of the greatest mathematical brains, if the modest obituaries were to be believed, the world has ever known. His name now passed into oblivion. He left no record of his researches or achievements. Out of some mysterious sense of loyalty and protection Miss Speke never mentioned his peculiar personal habits. The strips of paper, as the silken threads, she had carefully removed and destroyed long before the police came to make their search of his rooms...

But the disappearance of young Gerald Pikestaffe raised a tremendous hubbub. It was some days before the two disappearances were connected, both having occurred on the same night, it was then proved. The boy, a lad of great talent, promising a brilliant future, and the favourite pupil of the older man, his tutor, had not even left the house. His room was empty—and that was all. He left no clue, no trace. Terrible hints and suggestions were, of course, spread far and wide, but there was not a scrap of evidence forthcoming to support them. Gerald Pikestaffe and Mr. Thorley, at the same moment of the same night, vanished from the face of the earth and were no more seen. The matter ended there. The one link between them appeared to have been an amazing, an exceptional gift for higher mathematics. The Pikestaffe Case merely added one more to the insoluble mysteries with which commonplace daily life is sprinkled.

It was some six weeks to a month after the event that Miss Speke received a letter from one of her former charges, the most generous one, now satisfactorily finished with the Bankruptcy Court. He had honourably discharged his obligations; he was doing well; he wrote and asked Miss Speke to put him up for a week or two. 'And do *please* give me Mr. Thorley's room,' he asked. 'The case thrilled me, and I should like to sleep in that room. I always loved mysteries, you remember... There's something *very* mysterious about this thing. Besides, I knew the P. boy a little—an astounding genius, if ever there was one.'

Though it cost her much effort and still more hesitation, she consented finally. She prepared the rooms herself. There was a new servant, Lizzie having given notice the day after the disappearance, and the older woman who now waited upon the clergyman and the banker was not quite to be trusted with the delicate job. Miss Speke, entering the empty rooms on tiptoe, a strange trepidation in her heart, but that same heart firm with courage, drew up the blinds, swept the floors, dusted the furniture, and made the bed. All she did with her own hands. Only the full-length mirror she did not touch. What terror still was in her clung to that handsome piece. It was haunted by memories. For her it was still both wonderful and somehow awful. The ghost of her strange experience hid invisibly in its polished, if now unseen, depths. She dared not handle it, far less move it from the resting-place where it rested in peace. *His* hands had placed it there. To her it was sacred.

It had been given to her by Colonel Lyle, who would now occupy the room, stand on the wondrous carpet, move through the air where once the mysterious silks had floated, sleep in the very bed itself. All this he could do, but the mirror he must not touch.

'I'll explain to him a little. I'll beg him not to move it. He's very understanding,' she said to herself, as she went out to buy some flowers for the sitting-room. Colonel Lyle was expected that very afternoon. Lilac, she remembered, was what he always liked. It took her longer than she expected to find really fresh bunches, of the colour that he preferred, and when she got back it was time to be thinking about his tea. The sun's rays fell slanting down the dingy street, touching it with happy gold. This, with thoughts of the tea-kettle and what vase would suit the flowers best, filled her mind as she passed along the linoleum in the narrow hall—then noticed suddenly a new hat and coat hanging on the usually empty pegs. Colonel Lyle had arrived before his time.

'He's already come,' she said to herself with a little gasp. A heavy dread settled instantly on her spirit. She stood a moment motionless in the passage, the lilac blossoms in her hand. She was listening.

'The gentleman's come, mum,' she heard the servant say, and at the same moment saw her at the top of the kitchen stairs in the hall. 'He went up to his room, mum.'

Miss Speke held out the flowers. With an effort to make her voice sound ordinary she gave an order about them. 'Put them in water, Mary, please. The double vase will do.' She watched the woman take them slowly, oh, so slowly, from her. But her mind was elsewhere. It was still listening. And after the woman had gone down to the kitchen again slowly, oh, so slowly, she stood motionless for some minutes, listening, still intently listening. But no sound broke the quiet of the afternoon. She heard only the blundering noises made by the woman in the kitchen below. On the floor above was—silence.

Miss Speke then turned and went upstairs.

Now, Miss Speke admits frankly that she was 'in a state', meaning thereby, doubtless, that her nerves were tightly strung. Her heart was thumping, her ears and eyes strained to their utmost capacity; her hands, she remembers, felt a little cold, and her legs moved uncertainly. She denies, however, that her 'state', though it may be described as nervous, could have betrayed her into either invention or delusion. What she saw she saw, and nothing can shake her conviction. Colonel Lyle, besides, is there to support her in the main outline, and Colonel Lyle, when first he had entered the room, was certainly not 'in a state', whatever excuses he may have offered later to comfort her. Moreover, to counteract her trepidation, she says that, as she pushed the door wide open—it was already ajar—the original mood of elation met her in the face with its lift of wonder and release. This modified her dread. She declares that joy rushed upon her, and that her 'nerves' were on the instant entirely forgotten.

'What I saw, I saw,' remains her emphatic and unshakable verdict. 'I saw—everything.'

The first thing she saw admitted certainly of no doubt. Colonel Lyle lay huddled up against the further wall, half upon the carpet and half-leaning on the wainscoting. He was unconscious. One arm was stretched towards the mirror, the hand still clutching one of its mahogany feet. And the mirror had been moved. It turned now slightly more towards the room.

The picture, indeed, told its own story, a story Colonel Lyle himself repeated afterwards when he had recovered. He was surprised to find the mirror—his mirror—with its face to the wall; he went forward to put in it its proper position; in doing this he looked into it; he saw something, and—the next thing he knew—Miss Speke was bringing him round.

She explains, further, that her overmastering curiosity to look into the mirror, as Colonel Lyle had evidently looked himself, prevented her from immediately rendering first-aid to that gentleman, as she unquestionably should have done. Instead, she crossed the room, stepped over his huddled form, turned the mirror a little further round towards her, and looked straight into it.

The eye, apparently, takes in a great deal more than the mind is consciously aware of having 'seen' at the moment. Miss Speke saw everything, she claims. But details certainly came back to her later, details she had not been aware of at the time. At the moment, however, her impressions, though extremely vivid, were limited to certain outstanding items. These items were—that her own reflection was not visible, no picture of herself being there; that Mr. Thorley and a boy—she recognised the Pikestaffe lad from the newspaper photographs she had seen—were plainly there, and that books and instruments in great quantity filled all the nearer space, blocking up the foreground. Beyond, behind, stretching in all directions, she affirms, was empty space that produced upon her the effect of the infinite heavens as seen in a clear night sky. This space was prodigious, yet in some way not alarming. It did not terrify; rather it comforted, and, in a sense, uplifted. A diffused soft light pervaded the huge panorama. There were no shadows, there were no high lights.

Curiously enough, however, the absence of any reproduction of herself did not at first strike her as at all out of the way; she noticed the fact, no more than that; it was, perhaps, naturally, the deep shock of seeing Mr. Thorley and the boy that held her absolutely spell-bound, arresting her faculties as though they had been frozen.

Mr. Thorley was moving to and fro, his body bent, his hand thrown forward. He looked as natural as in life. He moved steadily, as with a purpose, now nearer, now further, but his figure always bent as though he were intent upon something in his hands. The boy moved, too, but with a more gentle, less vigorous, motion that suggested floating. He followed the larger figure, keeping close, his face raised from time to time as though his companion spoke to him. The expression that he wore was quiet, peaceful, happy, and intent. He was absorbed in what he was doing at the moment. Then, suddenly, Mr. Thorley straightened himself up. He turned. Miss Speke saw his face for the first time. He looked into her eyes. The face blazed with light. The gaze was straight, and full, and clear. It betrayed recognition. Mr. Thorley smiled at her.

In a very few seconds she was aware of all this, of its main outlines, at any rate. She saw the moving, living figures in the midst of this stupendous and amazing space. The overwhelming surprise it caused her prevented, apparently, the lesser emotion of personal alarm; fear she certainly did not feel at first. It was when Mr. Thorley looked at her with his brilliant eyes and blazing smile that her heart gave its violent jump, missed a beat or two, then began hammering against her ribs like released machinery that has gone beyond control. She was aware of the happy glory in the face, a face that was thin to emaciation, almost transparent, yet wearing an expression that was no longer earthly. Then, as he smiled, he came towards her; he beckoned; he stretched both hands out, while the boy looked up and watched.

Mr. Thorley's advance, however, had two distracting peculiarities—that as he drew nearer he moved not in a straight line, but in a curve. As a skater performing 'edges', though on both feet instead of on one, he swept gracefully and with incredible speed in her direction. The other peculiarity was that with each step nearer his figure grew smaller. It lessened in height. He seemed, indeed, to be moving in two directions at once. He became diminutive.

The sight ought by rights to have paralysed her, yet it produced again, instead of terror, an effect of exhilaration she could not possibly account for. There came once again that fine elation to her mind. Not only did all desire to resist die away almost before it was born, but more, she felt its opposite—an overpowering wish to join him. The tiny hands were still stretched out to greet her, to draw her in, to welcome her; the smile upon the diminutive face, as it came nearer and nearer, was enchanting. She heard his voice then:

'Come, come to us! Here reality is nearer, and there is liberty...!'

The voice was very close and loud as in life, but it was not in front. It was behind her. Against her very ear it sounded in the air behind her back. She moved one foot forward; she raised her arms. She felt herself being sucked in—into that glorious space. There was an indescribable change in her whole being.

The cumulative effect of so many amazing happenings, all of them contrary to nature, should have been destructive to her reason. Their combined shock should have dislocated her system somewhere and have laid her low. But with every individual, it seems, the breaking-point is different. Her system, indeed, was dislocated, and a moment later and she was certainly laid low, yet it was not the effect of the figure, the voice, the gliding approach of Mr. Thorley that produced this. It was the flaw of little human egoism that brought her down. For it was in this instant that she first *realised* the absence of her own reflection in the mirror. The fact, though noticed before, had not entered her consciousness as such. It now definitely did so. The arms she lifted in greeting had no reflected counterpart. Her figure, she realised with a shock of terror, was not there. She dropped, then, like a stricken animal, one outstretched hand clutching the frame of the mirror as she did so.

'Gracious God!' she heard herself scream as she collapsed. She heard, too, the crash of the falling mirror which she overturned and brought down with her.

Whether the noise brought Colonel Lyle round, or whether it was the combined weight of Miss Speke and the handsome piece upon his legs that roused him, is of no consequence. He stirred, opened his eyes, disentangled himself and proceeded, not without astonishment, to render first-aid to the unconscious lady.

The explanations that followed are, equally, of little consequence. His own attack, he considered, was chiefly due to fatigue, to violent indigestion, and to the after-effects of his protracted bankruptcy proceedings. Thus, at any rate, he assured Miss Speke. He added, however, that he had received rather a shock from the handsome piece, for, surprised at finding it turned to the wall, he had replaced it and looked into it, but had not seen himself reflected. This had amazed him a good deal, yet what amazed him still more was that he had seen something moving in the depths of the glass. 'I saw a face, and it was a face I knew. It was Gerald Pikestaffe. Behind him was another figure, the figure of a man, whose face I could not see.' A mist rose before his eyes, his head swam a bit, and he evidently swayed for some unaccountable reason. It was a blow received in falling that stunned him momentarily.

He stood over her, while he fanned her face; her swoon was of brief duration; she recovered quickly; she listened to his story with a quiet mind. The after-effect of too great wonder leaves no room for pettier emotions, and traces of the exhilaration she had experienced were still about her heart and soul.

'Is it smashed?' was the first thing she asked, to which Colonel Lyle made no answer at first, merely pointing to the carpet where the frame of the long mirror lay in broken fragments.

'There was no glass, you see,' he said presently. He, too, was quiet, his manner very earnest; his voice, though subdued as by a hint of awe, betrayed the glow of some intense inner excitement that lit fire in his eyes as well. 'He had cut it out long ago, of course. He used the empty framework, merely.'

'Eh?' said Miss Speke, looking down incredulously, but finding no sign of splinters on the floor.

Her companion smiled. 'We shall find it about somewhere if we look,' he said calmly, which, indeed, proved later true— lying flat beneath the carpet under the bed. 'His measurements and alculations led—probably by chance—towards the mirror' —he seemed speaking to himself more than to his bewildered listener—'perhaps by chance, perhaps by knowledge,' he continued, 'up to the mirror—and then *through* it.' He looked down at Miss Speke and laughed a little. 'So, like Alice, he went through it, too, taking his books and instruments, the boy as well, all with him. The boy, that is, had the knowledge too.'

'I only know one thing,' said Miss Speke, unable to follow

him or find meaning in his words, 'I shall never let these rooms again. I shall lock them up.'

Her companion collected the broken pieces and made a little heap of them.

'And I shall pray for him,' added Miss Speke, as he led her presently downstairs to her own quarters. 'I shall never cease to pray for him as long as I live.'

'He hardly needs that,' murmured Colonel Lyle, but to himself. 'The first terror has long since left him. He's found the new direction—and moved along it.'

THE EMPTY SLEEVE

I

The Gilmer brothers were a couple of fussy and pernickety old bachelors of a rather retiring, not to say timid, disposition. There was grey in the pointed beard of John, the elder, and if any hair had remained to William it would also certainly have been of the same shade. They had private means. Their main interest in life was the collection of violins, for which they had the instinctive *flair* of true connoisseurs. Neither John nor William, however, could play a single note. They could only pluck the open strings. The production of tone, so necessary before the purchase, was done vicariously for them by another.

The only objection they had to the big building in which they occupied the roomy top floor was that Morgan, liftman and caretaker, insisted on wearing a billycock with his uniform after six o'clock in the evening, with a result disastrous to the beauty of the universe. For 'Mr. Morgan', as they called him between themselves, had a round and pasty face on the top of a round and conical body. In view, however, of the man's other rare qualities—including his devotion to themselves—this objection was not serious.

He had another peculiarity that amused them. On being found fault with, he explained nothing, but merely repeated the words of the complaint.

'Water in the bath wasn't really hot this morning, Morgan!'
'Water in the bath reely 'ot, wasn't it, sir?'
Or, from William, who was something of a faddist:
'My jar of sour milk came up late yesterday, Morgan.'
'Your jar sour milk come up late, sir, yesterday?'
Since, however, the statement of a complaint invariably

resulted in its remedy, the brothers had learned to look for no further explanation. Next morning the bath *was* hot, the sour milk *was* 'brortup' punctually. The uniform and billycock hat, though, remained an eyesore and source of oppression.

On this particular night John Gilmer, the elder, returning from a Masonic rehearsal, stepped into the lift and found Mr. Morgan with his hand ready on the iron rope.

'Fog's very thick outside,' said Mr. John pleasantly; and the lift was a third of the way up before Morgan had completed his customary repetition: 'Fog very thick outside, yes, sir.' And Mr. Gilmer then asked casually if his brother were alone, and received the reply that Mr. Hyman had called and had not yet gone away.

Now this Mr. Hyman was a Hebrew, and, like themselves, a connoisseur in violins, but, unlike themselves, who only kept their specimens to look at, he was a skilful and exquisite player. He was the only person they ever permitted to handle their pedigree instruments, to take them from the glass cases where they reposed in silent splendour, and to draw the sound out of their wondrous painted hearts of golden varnish. The brothers loathed to see his fingers touch them, yet loved to hear their singing voices in the room, for the latter confirmed their sound judgment as collectors, and made them certain their money had been well spent. Hyman, however, made no attempt to conceal his contempt and hatred for the mere collector. The atmosphere of the room fairly pulsed with these opposing forces of silent emotion when Hyman played and the Gilmers, alternately writhing and admiring, listened. The occasions, however, were not frequent. The Hebrew only came by invitation, and both brothers made a point of being in. It was a very formal proceeding—something of a sacred rite almost.

John Gilmer, therefore, was considerably surprised by the information Morgan had supplied. For one thing, Hyman, he had understood, was away on the Continent.

'Still in there, you say?' he repeated, after a moment's reflection.

'Still in there, Mr. John, sir.' Then, concealing his surprise from the liftman, he fell back upon his usual mild habit of complaining about the billycock hat and the uniform.

'You really should try and remember, Morgan,' he said, though kindly. 'That hat does not go well with that uniform!'

Morgan's pasty countenance betrayed no vestige of expression.

''At don't go well with the yewniform, sir,' he repeated, hanging up the disreputable bowler and replacing it with a gold-braided cap from the peg. 'No, sir, it don't, do it?' he added cryptically, smiling at the transformation thus effected.

And the lift then halted with an abrupt jerk at the top floor. By somebody's carelessness the landing was in darkness, and, to make things worse, Morgan, clumsily pulling the iron rope, happened to knock the billycock from its peg so that his sleeve, as he stooped to catch it, struck the switch and plunged the scene in a moment's complete obscurity.

And it was then, in the act of stepping out before the light was turned on again, that John Gilmer stumbled against something that shot along the landing past the open door. First he thought it must be a child, then a man, then—an animal. Its movement was rapid yet stealthy. Starting backwards instinctively to allow it room to pass, Gilmer collided in the darkness with Morgan, and Morgan incontinently screamed. There was a moment of stupid confusion. The heavy framework of the lift shook a little, as though something had stepped into it and then as quickly jumped out again. A rushing sound followed that resembled footsteps, yet at the same time was more like gliding—someone in soft slippers or stockinged feet, greatly hurrying. Then came silence again. Morgan sprang to the landing and turned up the electric light. Mr. Gilmer, at the same moment, did likewise to the switch in the lift. Light flooded the scene. Nothing was visible.

'Dog or cat, or something, I suppose, wasn't it?' exclaimed Gilmer, following the man out and looking round with bewildered amazement upon a deserted landing. He knew quite well, even while he spoke, that the words were foolish.

'Dog or cat, yes, sir, or—something,' echoed Morgan, his eyes narrowed to pin-points, then growing large, but his face stolid.

'The light should have been on,' Mr. Gilmer spoke with a touch of severity. The little occurrence had curiously disturbed his equanimity. He felt annoyed, upset, uneasy.

For a perceptible pause the liftman made no reply, and his employer, looking up, saw that, besides being flustered, he was white about the jaws. His voice, when he spoke, was without its normal assurance. This time he did not merely repeat. He explained.

'The light *was* on, sir, when last *I* come up!' he said, with emphasis, obviously speaking the truth. 'Only a moment ago,' he added.

Mr. Gilmer, for some reason, felt disinclined to press for explanations. He decided to ignore the matter.

Then the lift plunged down again into the depths like a diving-bell into water; and John Gilmer, pausing a moment first to reflect, let himself in softly with his latchkey, and, after hanging up hat and coat in the hall, entered the big sitting-room he and his brother shared in common.

The December fog that covered London like a dirty blanket had penetrated, he saw, into the room. The objects in it were half shrouded in the familiar yellowish haze.

II

In his dressing-gown and slippers, William Gilmer, almost invisible in his armchair by the gas-stove across the room, spoke at once. Through the thick atmosphere his face gleamed, showing an extinguished pipe hanging from his lips. His tone of voice conveyed emotion, an emotion he sought to suppress, of a quality, however, not easy to define.

'Hyman's been here,' he announced abruptly. 'You must have met him. He's this very instant gone out.'

It was quite easy to see that something had happened, for 'scenes' leave disturbance behind them in the atmosphere. But John made no immediate reference to this. He replied that he had seen no one—which was strictly true—and his brother thereupon, sitting bolt upright in the chair, turned quickly and faced him. His skin, in the foggy air, seemed paler than before.

'That's odd,' he said nervously.

'What's odd?' asked John.

'That you didn't see—anything. You ought to have run into one another on the doorstep.' His eyes went peering about the room. He was distinctly ill at ease. 'You're positive you saw no one? Did Morgan take him down before you came? Did Morgan see him?' He asked several questions at once.

'On the contrary, Morgan told me he was still here with you. Hyman probably walked down, and didn't take the lift at all,' he replied. 'That accounts for neither of us seeing him.' He decided to say nothing about the occurrence in the lift, for his brother's nerves, he saw plainly, were on edge.

William then stood up out of his chair, and the skin of his face changed its hue, for whereas a moment ago it was merely pale, it had now altered to a tint that lay somewhere between white and a livid grey. The man was fighting internal terror. For a moment these two brothers of middle age looked each other straight in the eye. Then John spoke:

'What's wrong, Billy?' he asked quietly. 'Something's upset you. What brought Hyman in this way—unexpectedly? I thought he was still in Germany.'

The brothers, affectionate and sympathetic, understood one another perfectly. They had no secrets. Yet for several minutes the younger one made no reply. It seemed difficult to choose his words apparently.

'Hyman played, I suppose—on the fiddles?' John helped him, wondering uneasily what was coming. He did not care much for the individual in question, though his talent was of such great use to them.

The other nodded in the affirmative, then plunged into rapid speech, talking under his breath as though he feared someone might overhear. Glancing over his shoulder down the foggy room, he drew his brother close.

'Hyman came,' he began, 'unexpectedly. He hand't written, and I hadn't asked him. You hadn't either, I suppose?'

John shook his head.

'When I came in from the dining-room I found him in the passage. The servant was taking away the dishes, and he had let himself in while the front door was ajar. Pretty col, wasn't it?'

'He's ana original,' said John, shrugging his shoulders. 'And you welcomed him?' he asked.

'I asked him in, of course. He explained he had something glorious for me to hear. Silenski had played it in the afternoon, and he had bought the music since. But Silenski's "Strad" hadn't the power—it's thin on the upper string, you remember, unequal, patchy—and he said no instrument in the world could do it justice but our "Joseph"—the small Guarnerius, you know, which he swears is the most perfect in the world.'

'And what was it? Did he play it?' asked John, growing more uneasy as he grew more interested. With relief he glanced round and saw the matchless little instrument lying there safe and sound in its glass case near the door.

'He played it—divinely: a Zigeuner Lullaby, a fine, passionate, rushing bit of inspiration, oddly misnamed "lullaby". And fancy, the fellow had memorised it already! He walked about the room on tiptoe while he played it, complaining of the light——'

'Complaining of the light?'

'Said the thing was crepuscular, and needed dusk for its full effect. I turned the lights out one by one, till finally there was only the glow of the gas logs. He insisted. You know that way he has with him? And then he got me in another matter: insisted on using some special strings he had brought with him, and put them on, too, himself—thicker than the A and E *we* use.'

For though neither Gilmer could produce a note, it was their pride that they kept their precious instruments in perfect condition for playing, choosing the exact thickness and quality of strings that suited the temperament of each violin; and the little Guarnerius in question always 'sang' best, they held, with thin strings.

'Infernal insolence,' exclaimed the listening brother, wondering what was coming next. 'Played it well, though, didn't he, this Lullaby thing?' he added, seeing that William hesitated. As he spoke he went nearer, sitting down close beside him in a leather chair.

'Magnificent! Pure fire of genius!' was the reply with enthusiasm, the voice at the same time dropping lower. 'Staccato like a silver hammer; harmonics like flutes, clear, soft, ringing; and the tone—well, the G string was a baritone, and the upper registers creamy and mellow as a boy's voice. John,' he added, 'that Guarnerius is the very pick of the period and'—again he hesitated—'Hyman loves it. He'd give his soul to have it.'

The more John heard, the more uncomfortable it made him. He had always disliked this gifted Hebrew, for in his secret heart he knew that he had always feared and distrusted him. Sometimes he had felt half afraid of him; the man's very forcible personality was too insistent to be pleasant. His type was of the dakr and sinister kind, and he possessed a violent will that rarely failed of accomplishing its desire.

'Wish I'd heard the fellow play,' he said at length, ignoring his brother's last remark, and going on to speak of the most matter-of-fact details he could think of. 'Did he use the Dodd bow, or the Tourte? That Dodd I picked up last month, you know, is the most perfectly balanced I have ever——'

He stopped abruptly, for William had suddenly got upon his feet and was standing there, searching the room with his eyes. A chill ran down John's spine as he watched him.

'What is it, Billy?' he asked sharply. 'Hear anything?'

William continued to peer about him through the thick air. 'Oh, nothing, probably,' he said, an odd catch in his voice; 'only——I keep feeling as if there was somebody listening. Do you think, perhaps'—he glanced over his shoulder—'there is someone at the door? I wisch—I wish you'd have a look, John.'

John obeyed, though without great eagerness. Crossing the room slowly, he opened the door, then switched on the light. The passage leading past the bathroom towards the bedrooms beyond was empty. The coats hung motionless from their pegs.

'No one, of course,' he said, as he closed the door and came back to the stove. He left the light burning in the passage. It was curious the way both brothers had this impression that they were not alone, thoug only one of them spoke of it.

'Used the Dodd or the Tourte, Bill—which?' continued John in the most natural voice he could assume.

But at that very same instant the water started to his eyes. His brother, he saw, was close upon the thing he really had to tell. But he had stuck fast.

III

By a great effort John Gilmer composed himself and remained in his chair. With detailed elaboration he lit a cigarette, staring hard at his brother over the flaring match while he did so. There he sat in his dressing-gown and slippers by the fireplace, eyes downcast, fingers playing idly with the red tassel. The electric light cast heavy shadows across the face. In a flash then, since emotion may sometimes express itself in attitude even better then in speech, the elder brother understood that Billy was about to tel him an unutterable thing.

By instinct he moved over to his side so that the same view of the room confronted him.

'Out with it, old man,' he said, with an effort to be natural. 'Tell me what you saw.'

Billy shuffled slowly round and the two sat side by side, facing the fog-draped chamber.

'It was like this,' he began softly, 'only I was standing instead of sitting, looking over to that door as you and I do now. Hyman moved to and fro in the faint glow of the gas logs against the far wall, plying that "crepuscular" thing in his most inspired sort of way, so that the music seemed to issue from himself rather than from the shining bit of wood under his chin, when—I noticed something coming over me that was'—he hesitated, searching for words—'that wasn't *all* due to the music,' he finished abruptly.

'His personality put a bit of hypnotism on you, eh?'

William shrugged his shoulders.

'The air was thickish with fog and the light was dim, cast upwards upon him from the stove,' he continued. 'I admit all that. But there wasn't light enough to throw shadows, you see, and——'

'Hyman looked queer?' the other helped him quickly.

Billy nodded hos head without turning.

'Changed there before my very eyes——' he whispered it—'turned animal——'

'Animal?' John felt his hair rising.

'That's the only way I can put it. His face and hands and body turned otherwise than usual. I lost the sound of his feet. When the bow-hand or the fingers on the strings passed in to the light, they were'—he uttered a soft, shuddering little laugh—'furry, oddly divided, the fingers massed together. And he paced stealthily. I thought every instant the fiddle would drop with a crash and he would spring at me across the room.

'My dear chap——'

'He moved with those big, lithe, striding steps one sees'—John held his breath in the little pause, listening keenly—'one sees those big brutes make in the cages when their desire is aflame for food or escape, or—or fierce passionate desire for anything they want with their whole nature——'

'The big felines!' John whistled softly.

'And every minute getting nearer and nearer to the door, as though he meant to make a sudden rush for it and get out.'

'With the violin! Of course you stopped him?'

'In the end. But for a long time, I swear to you, I found it difficult to know what to do, even to move. I couldn't get my voice for words of any kind; it was like a spell.'

'It *was* a spell,' suggested John firmly.

'Then, as he moved, still playing,' continued the other, 'he seemed to grow smaller; to shrink down below the line of the gas. I thought I should lose sight of him altogether. I turned the light up suddenly. There he was over by the door—crouching.'

'Playing on his knees, you mean?'

William closed his eyes in an effort to visualise it again.

'Crouching,' he repeated, at length, 'close to the floor. At least, I think so. It all happened so quickly, and I felt so bewildered, it was hard to see straight. But at first I could have sworn he was half his natural size. I called to him, I think I swore at him—I forget exactly, but I know he straightened up at once and stood before me down there in the light'—he pointed across the room to the door—'eyes gleaming, face white as chalk, perspiring like midsummer, and gradually filling out, straightening up, whatever you like to call it, to his natural size and appearance again. It was the most horrid thing I've ever seen.'

'As an—animal, you saw him still?'

'No; human again. Only much smaller.'

'What did he say?'

Billy reflected a moment.

'Nothing that I can remember,' he replied. 'You see, it was all over in a few seconds. In the full light, I felt so foolish, and nonplussed at first. To see him normal again baffled me. And, before I could collect myself, he had let himself out into the passage, and I heard the front door slam. A minute later—the same second almost, it seemed—you came in. I only remember grabbing the violin and getting it back safely under the glass case. The strings were still vibrating.'

The accoung was over. John asked no further questions. Nor did he say a single word about the lift, Morgan, or the extinguished light on the landing. There fell a longisch silence between the two men; and then, while they helped themselves to a generous supply of whisky-and-soda before going to bed, John looked up and spoke:

'If you agree, Billy,' he said quietly, 'I think I might write and suggest to Hyman that we shall no longer have need for his services.'

And Billy, acquiescing, added a sentence that expressed something of the singular dread lying but half-concealed in the atmosphere of the room, if not in their minds as well:

'Putting it, however, in a way that need not offend him.'
'Of course. There's no need to be rude, is there?'

Accordingly, next morning the letter was written; and John, saying nothing to his brother, took it round himself by hand to the Hebrew's rooms near Euston. The answer he dreaded was forthcoming:

'Mr. Hyman's still away abroad,' he was told. 'But we're forwarding letters; yes. Or I can give you 'is address if you'll prefer it.'. The letter went, therefore, to the number in Königstrasse, Munich, thus obtained.

Then, on his way back from the insurance company where he went to increase the sum that protected the small Guarnierius from loss by fire, accident, or theft, John Gilmer called at the offices of certain musical agents and ascertained that Silenski, the violinist, was performing at the time in Munich. It was only some days later, though, by diligent inquiry, he made certain that at a concert on a certain date the famous virtuoso had played a Zigeuner Lullaby of his own composition—the very date, it turned out, on which he himself had been to the Masonic rehearsal at Mark Masons' Hall.

John, however, said nothing of these discoveries to his brother William.

IV

It was about a week later when a reply to the letter came from Munich—a letter couched in somewhat offensive terms, though it contained neither words nor phrases that could actually be found fault with. Isidore Hyman was hurt and angry. On his return to London a month or so later, he proposed to call and talk the matter over. The offensive part of the letter, lay, perhaps, in his definite assumption that he could persuade the brothers to resume the old relations. John, however, wrote a brief reply to the effect that they had decided to buy no new fiddles; their collection being complete, there would be no occasion for them to invite his services as performer. This was final. No answer came, and the matter seemed to drop. Never for one moment, though, did it leave the consciousness of John Gilmer. Hyman had said that he would come, and come assuredly he would. He secretly gave Morgan instructions that he and his brother for the future were always 'out' when the Hebrew presented himself.

'He must have gone back to Germany, you see, almost at once after his visit here that night,' observed William—John however, making no reply.

One night towards the middle of January the two brothers came home together from a concert in Queen's Hall, and sat up later than usual in their sitting-room discussing over their whisky and tobacco the merits of the pieces and performers. It must have been past one o'clock when they turned out the lights in the passage and retired to bed. The air was still and frosty; moonlight over the roofs—one those sharp and dry winter nights that now seem to visit London rarely.

'Like the old-fashioned days when we were boys,' remarked William, pausing a moment by the passage window and looking out across the miles of silvery, sparkling roofs.

'Yes,' added John; 'the ponds freezing hard in the fields, rime on the nursery windows, and the sound of a horse's hoofs coming down the road in the distance, eh?' They smiled at the memory, then said good night, and separated. Their rooms were at opposite ends of the corridor; in between were the bathroom, dining-room, and sitting-room. It was a long, straggling flat. Half an hour later both brothers were sound alseep, the flat silent, only a dull murmur rising from the great city outside, and the moon sinking slowly to the level of the chimneys.

Perhaps two hours passed, perhaps three, when John Gilmer, sitting up in bed with a start, wide-awake and frightened, knew that someone was moving about in one of the three rooms that lay between him and his brother. He had absolutely no idea why he should have been frightened, for there was no dream or nightmare-memory that he brought over from unconsciousness, and yet he realised plainly that the fear he felt was by no means a foolish and unreasoning fear. It had a cause and a reason.

THE EMPTY SLEEVE

Also—which made it worse—it was fully warranted. Something in his sleep, forgotten in the instant of waking, had happened that set every nerve in his body on the watch. He was positive only of two things—first, that it was the entrance of this person, moving so quietly there in the flat, that sent chills down his spine; and, secondly, that this person was *not* his brother William.

John Gilmer was a timid man. The sight of a burglar, his eyes black-masked, suddenly confronting him in the passage, would most likely have deprived him of all power of decision—until the burglar had either shot him or escaped. But on this occasion some instinct told him that it was no burglar, and that the acute distress he experienced was not due to any message of ordinary physical fear. The thing that had gained access to his flat while he slept had first come—he felt sure of it—into his room, and had passed very close to his own bed, before going on. It had then doubtless gone to his brother's room, visiting them both stealthily to make sure they slept. And its mere passage through his room had been enough to wake him and set these drops of cold perspiration upon his skin. For it was—he felt it in every fibre of his body—something hostile.

The thought that it might at that very moment be in the room of his brother, however, brought him to his feet on the cold floor and set him moving with all the determination he could summon towards the door. He looked cautiously down an utterly dark passage; then crept on tiptoe along it. On the wall were old-fashioned weapons that had belonged to his father; and feeling a curved, sheathless sword that had come from some Turkish campaign of years gone by, his fingers closed tightly round it, and lifted it silently from the three hooks whereon it lay. He passed the doors of the bathroom and dining-room, making instinctively for the big sitting-room where the violins were kept in their glass cases. The cold nipped him. His eyes smarted with the effort to see in the darkness. Outside the closed door he hesitated.

Putting his ear to the crack, he listened. From within came a faint sound of someone moving. The same instant there rose the sharp, delicate 'ping' of a violin-string being plucked; and John Gilmer, with nerves that shook like the vibrations of that very string, opened the door wide with a fling and turned on the light at the same moment. The plucked string still echoed faintly in the air.

The sensation that met him on the threshold was the well-known one that things had been going on in the room which his unexpected arrival had that instant put a stop to. A second earlier and he would have discovered it all in the act. The atmosphere still held the feeling of rushing, silent movement with which the things had raced back to their normal, motionless positions. The immobility of the furniture was a mere attitude hurriedly assumed, and the moment his back was turned the whole business, whatever it might be, would begin again. With this presentment of the room—however—a purely imaginative one—came another, swiftly on its heels.

For one of the objects, less swift than the rest, had not quite regained its 'attitude' of repose. It still moved. Below the window curtains on the right, not far from the shelf that bore the violins in their glass cases, he made it out, slowly gliding along the floor. Then, even as his eye caught it, it came to rest.

And, while the cold perspiration broke out all over him afresh, he knew that this still moving item was the cause both of his waking and of his terror. This was the disturbance whose presence he had divined in the flat without actual hearing, and whose passage through his room, while he yet slept, had touched every nerve in his body as with ice. Clutching his Turkish sword tightly, he drew back with the utmost caution against the wall and watched, for the singular impression came to him that the movement was not that of a human being crouching, but rather of something that pertained to the animal world. He remembered, flash-like, the movements of reptiles, the stealth of the larger felines, the undulating glide of great snakes. For the moment, however, it did not move, and they faced one another.

The other side of the room was but dimly lighted, and the noise he made clicking up another electric lamp brought the thing flying forward again—towards himself. At such a moment it seemed absurd to think of so small a detail, but he remembered his bare feet, and, genuinely frightened, he leaped upon a chair and swished with his sword through the air about him. From this better point of view, with the increased light to aid him, he then saw two things—first, that the glass case usually covering the Guarnerius violin had been shifted; and, secondly, that the moving object was slowly elongating itself into an upright position. Semi-erect, yet most oddly, too, like a creature on its hind legs, it was coming swiftly towards him. It was making for the door—and escape.

The confusion of ghostly fear was somehow upon him so that he was too bewildered to see clearly, but he had sufficient control it seemed, to recover a certain power of action; for the moment the advancing figure was near enough for him to strike, that curved scimitar flashed and whirred about him, with such misdirected violence, however, that he not only failed to strike it even once, but at the same time lost his balance and fell forward from the chair whereon he perched—straight into it.

And then came the most curious thing of all, for as he dropped, the figure also dropped, stooped low down, crouched, dwindled amazingly in size, and rushed past him close to the ground like an animal on all fours. John Gilmer screamed, for he could no longer contain himself. Stumbling over the chair as he turned to follow, cutting and slashing wildly with his sword, he saw half-way down the darkened corridor beyond the scuttling outline of, apparently, an enormous—cat!

The door into the outer landing was somehow ajar, and the next second the beast was out, but not before the steel had fallen with a crashing blow upon the front disappearing leg, almost severing it from the body.

It was dreadful. Turning up the lights as he went, he ran after it to the outer landing. But the thing he followed was already well away, and he heard, on the floor below him, the same oddly gliding, slithering, stealthy sound, yet hurrying, that he heard weeks before when something had passed him in the lift, and Morgan, in his terror, had likewise cried aloud.

For a time he stood there on that dark landing, listening, thinking, trembling; then turned into the flat and shut the door. In the sitting-room he carefully replaced the glass case over the treasured violin, puzzled to the point of foolishness, and strangely routed in his mind. For the violin itself, he saw, had been dragged several inches from its cushioned bed of plush.

Next morning, however, he made no allusion to the occurrence of the night. His brother apparently had not been disturbed.

V

The only thing that called for explanation—an explanation not fully forthcoming—was the curious aspect of Mr. Morgan's countenance. The fact that this individual gave notice to the owners of the building, and at the end of the month left for a new post, was, of course, known to both brothers; whereas the story he told in explanation of his face was known only to the one who questioned him about it—John. And John, for reasons best known to himself, did not pass it on to the other. Also, for reasons best known to himself, he did not cross-question the liftman about those singular marks, or report the matter to the police.

Mr. Morgan's pasty visage was badly scratched, and there were red lines running from the cheek into the neck that had the appearance of having been produced by sharp points viciously applied—claws. He had been disturbed by a noise in the hall, he said, about three in the morning. A scuffle had ensued in the darkness, but the intruder had got clear away. ...

'A cat, or something of the kind, no doubt,' suggested John Gilmer at the end of the brief recital. And Morgan replied in his usual way: 'A cat, or something of the kind, Mr. John, no doubt.'

All the same, he had not cared to risk a second encounter, but had departed to wear his billycock and uniform in a building less haunted.

THE EMPTY SLEEVE

Hyman, meanwhile, made no attempt to call and talk over his dismissal. The reason for this was only apparent, however, several months later when, quite by chance, coming along Piccadilly in an omnibus, the brothers found themselves seated opposite to a man with a thick black beard and blue glasses. William Gilmer hastily rang the bell and got out, saying something half intelligible about feeling faint. John followed him.

'Did you see who it was?' he whispered to his brother the moment they were safely on the pavement.

John nodded.

'Hyman, in spectacles. He's grown a beard, too.'

'Yes, but didn't you also notice——'

'What?'

'He had an empty sleeve.'

'An empty sleeve?'

'Yes,' said William; 'he's lost an arm.'

There was a long pause before John spoke. At the door of their club the elder brother added:

'Poor devil! He'll never again play on'—then, suddenly changing the preposition—'*with* a pedigree violin!'

And that night in the flat, after William had gone to bed, he looked up a curious old volume he had once picked up on a secondhand bookstall, and read therein quaint descriptions of how the 'desire-body of a violent man' may assume animal shape, operate on concrete matter even at a distance; and, further, how a wound inflicted thereon can reproduce itself upon its physical counterpart by means of the mysterious so-called phenomenon of 're-percussion.'

VIOLENCE

'But what seems so odd to me, so horribly pathetic, is that such people don't resist,' said Leidall, suddenly entering the conversation. The intensity of his tone startled everybody; it was so passionate, yet with a beseeching touch that made the women feel uncomfortable a little. 'As a rule, I'm told, they submit willingly, almost as though——'

He hesitated, grew confused, and dropped his glance to the floor; and a smartly dressed woman, eager to be heard, seized the opening. 'Oh, come now,' she laughed; 'one always hears of a man being *put* into a strait waistcoat. I'm sure he doesn't slip it on as if he were going to a dance!' And she looked flippantly at Leidall, whose casual manners she resented. 'People are *put* under restraint. It's not in human nature to accept it— healthy human nature, that is?' But for some reason no one took her question up. 'That is so, I believe, yes,' a polite voice murmured, while the group at tea in the Dover Street Club turned with one accord to Leidall as to one whose interesting sentence still remained unfinished. He had hardly spoken before, and a silent man is ever credited with wisdom.

'As though—you were just saying, Mr. Leidall?' a quiet little man in a dark corner helped him.

'As though, I meant, a man in that condition of mind is not insane—all though,' Leidall continued stammeringly; 'but that some wise portion of him watches the proceeding with gratitude, and welcomes the protection against himself. It seems awfully pathetic. Still,' again hesitating and fumbling in his speech— 'er—it seems queer to me that he should yield quietly to enforced restraint—the waistcoat, handcuffs, and the rest.' He looked round hurriedly, half suspiciously, at the faces in the circle, then dropped his eyes again to the floor. He sighed, leaning back in his chair. 'I cannot understand it,' he added, as no one spoke, but in a very low voice, and almost to himself. 'One would expect them to struggle furiously.'

Someone had mentioned that remarkable book, *The Mind that Found Itself,* and the conversation had slipped into this serious vein. The women did not like it. What kept it alive was the fact that the silent Leidall, with his handsome, melancholy face, had suddenly wakened into speech, and that the little man opposite to him, half invisible in his dark corner, was assistant to one of London's great hypnotic doctors, who could, an' he would, tell interesting and terrible things. No one cared to ask the direct question, but all hoped for revelations, possibly about people they actually knew. It was a very ordinary tea-party indeed. And this little man now spoke, though hardly in the desired vein. He addressed his remarks to Leidall across the disappointed lady.

'I think, probably, your explanation *is* the true one,' he said gently, 'for madness in its commoner forms is merely want of proportion; the mind gets out of right and proper relations with its environment. The majority of madmen are mad on one thing only, while the rest of them is as sane as myself—or you.'

The words fell into the silence. Leidall bowed his agreement, saying no actual word. The ladies fidgeted. Someone made a jocular remark to the effect that most of the world was mad anyhow, and the conversation shifted with relief into a lighter vein—the scandal in the family of a politician. Everybody talked at once. Cigarettes were lit. The corner soon became excited and even uproarious. The tea-party was a great success, and the offended lady, no longer ignored, led all the skirmishes—towards herself. She was in her element. Only Leidall and the little invisible man in the corner took small part in it; and presently, seizing the opportunity when some new arrivals joined the group, Leidall rose to say his adieux, and slipped away, his departure scarcely noticed. Dr. Hancock followed him a minute later. The two men met in the hall; Leidall already had his hat and coat on.

'I'm going West, Mr. Leidall. If that's your way too, and you feel inclined for the walk we might go together.' Leidall turned with a start. His glance took in the other with avidity—a keenly-searching, hungry glance. He hesitated for an imperceptible moment, then made a movement towards him, half inviting, while a curious shadow dropped across his face and vanished. It was both pathetic and terrible. The lips trembled. He seemed to say, 'God bless you; *do* come with me!' But no words were audible.

'It's a pleasant evening for a walk,' added Dr. Hancock gently; 'clean and dry under foot for a change. I'll get my hat and join you in a second.' And there was a hint, the merest flavour of authority in his voice.

That touch of authority was his mistake. Instantly Leidall's hesitation passed. 'I'm sorry,' he said abruptly, 'but I'm afraid I must take a taxi. I have an appointment at the Club and I'm late already.' 'Oh, I see,' the other replied, with a kindly smile; 'then I mustn't keep you. But if you ever have a free evening, won't you look me up, or come and dine? You'll find my telephone number in the book. I should like to talk with you about—those things we mentioned at tea.' Leidall thanked him politely and went out. The memory of the little man's kindly sympathy and understanding eyes went with him.

'Who was that man?' someone asked, the moment Leidall had left the tea-table. 'Surely he's not the Leidall who wrote that awful book some years ago?'

'Yes—the *Gulf of Darkness*. Did you read it?'

They discussed it and its author for five minutes, deciding by a large majority that it was the book of a madman. Silent, rude men like that always had a screw loose somewhere, they agreed. Silence was invariably morbid.

'And did you notice Dr. Hancock? He never took his eyes off him. That's why he followed him out like that. I wonder if *he* thought anything!'

'I know Hancock well,' said the lady of the wounded vanity. 'I'll ask him and find out.' They chattered on, somebody mentioned a *risqué* play, and talk switched into other fields, and in due course the tea-party came to an end.

And Leidall, meanwhile, made his way towards the Park on foot, for he had not taken a taxi after all. The suggestion of the other man, perhaps, had worked upon him. He was very open to suggestion. With hands deep in his overcoat pockets, and head sunk forward between his shoulders, he walked briskly, entering the Park at one of the smaller gates. He made his way across the wet turf, avoiding the paths and people. The February sky was shining in the west; beautiful clouds floated over the houses; they looked like the shore-line of some radiant strand his childhood once had known. He sighed; thought dived and searched within; self-analysis, that old, implacable demon, lifted its voice; introspection took the reins again as usual. There seemed a strain upon the mind he could not dispel. Thought circled poignantly. He knew it was unhealthy, morbid, a sign of these many years of difficulty and stress that had marked him so deeply, but for the life of him he could not escape from the hideous spell that held him. The same old thoughts bored their way into his mind like burning wires, tracing the same unanswerable questions. From this torture, waking or sleeping, there was no escape. Had a companion been with him it might have been different. If, for instance, Dr. Hancock——

He was angry with himself for having refused—furious; it was that vile, false pride his long loneliness had fostered. The man was sympathetic to him, friendly, marvellously understanding; he could have talked freely with him, and found relief. His intuition had picked out the little doctor as a man in ten thousand. Why had he so curtly declined his gentle invitation? Dr. Hancock *knew*; he guessed his awful secret. But how? In what had he betrayed himself?

The weary self-questioning began again, till he sighed and groaned from sheer exhaustion. He *must* find people, companionship, someone to talk to. The Club—it crossed his tortured mind for a second—was impossible; there was a conspiracy among the members against him. He had left his usual haunts everywhere for the same reason—his restaurants, where he had his lonely meals; his music hall, where he tried sometimes to forget himself; his favourite walks, where the very policemen knew and eyed him. And, coming to the bridge across the Serpentine just then, he paused and leaned over the edge, watching a bubble rise to the surface. 'I suppose there *are* fish in the Serpentine?' he said to a man a few feet away.

They talked a moment—the other was evidently a clerk on his way home—and then the stranger edged off and continued his walk, looking back once or twice at the sad-faced man who had addressed him. 'It's ridiculous, that with all our science we can't live under water as the fish do,' reflected Leidall, and moved on round the other bank of the water, where he watched a flight of duck whirl down from the darkening air and settle with a long, mournful splash beside the bushy island. 'Or that, for all our pride of mechanism in a mechanical age, we cannot really fly.' But these attempts to escape from self were never very successful. Another part of him looked on and mocked. He returned ever to the endless introspection and self-analysis, and in the deepest moment of it—ran into a big, motionless figure that blocked his way. It was the Park policeman, the one who always eyed him. He sheered off suddenly towards the trees, while the man, recognising him, touched his cap respectfully. 'It's a pleasant evening, sir; turned quite mild again.' Leidall mumbled some reply or other, and hurried on to hide himself among the shadows of the trees. The policeman stood and watched him, till the darkness swallowed him. 'He knows too!' groaned the wretched man. And every bench was occupied; every face turned to watch him; there were even figures behind the trees. He dared not go into the street, for the very taxi-drivers were against him. If he gave an address, he would not be driven to it; the man would *know,* and take him elsewhere. And something in his heart, sick with anguish, weary with the endless battle, suddenly yielded.

'There *are* fish in the Serpentine,' he remembered the stranger had said. 'And,' he added to himself, with a wave of delicious comfort, 'they lead secret, hidden lives that no one can disturb.' His mind cleared surprisingly. In the water he could find peace and rest and healing. Good Lord! How easy it all was! Yet he had never thought of it before. He turned sharply to retrace his steps, but in that very second the clouds descended upon his thought again, his mind darkened, he hesitated. Could he get out again when he had had enough? Would he rise to the surface? A battle bega over these questions. He ran quickly, then stood still again to think the matter out. Darkness shrouded him. He heard the wind rush laughing through the trees. The picture of the whirring duck flashed back a moment, and he decided that the best way was by air, and not by water. He would *fly* into the place of rest, not sink or merely float; and he remembered the view from his bedroom window, high over old smoky London town, with a drop of eighty feet on to the pavements. Yes, that was the best way. He waited a moment, trying to think it all out clearly, but one moment the fish had it, and the next the birds. It was really impossible to decide. Was there no one who could help him, no one in all this enormous town who was sufficiently on his side to advise him on the point? Some clear-headed, experienced, kindly man?

And the face of Dr. Hancock flashed before his vision. He saw the gentle eyes and sympathetic smile, remembered the soothing voice and the offer of companionship he had refused. Of course, there was one serious drawback: Hancock *knew*. But he was far too tactful, too sweet and good a man to let that influence his judgment, or to betray in any way at all that he did know.

Leidall found it in him to decide. Facing the entire hostile world, he hailed a taxi from the nearest gate upon the street, looked up the address in a chemist's telephone-book, and reached the door in a condition of delight and relief. Yes, Dr. Hancock was at home. Leidall sent his name in. A few minutes later the two men were chatting pleasantly together, almost like old friends, so keen was the little man's intuitive sympathy and tact. Only Hancock, patient listener though he proved himself to be, was uncommonly full of words. Leidall explained the matter very clearly. 'Now, what is your decision, Dr. Hancock? Is it to be the way of the fish or the way of the duck?' And, while Hancock began his answer with slow, well-chosen words, a new idea, better than either, leaped with a flash into his listener's mind. It was an inspiration. For where could he find a better hiding-place from all his troubles than—inside Hancock himself? The man was kindly; he surely would not object. Leidall this time did not hesitate a second. He was tall and broad; Hancock was small; yet he was sure there would be room. He sprang upon him like a wild animal. He felt the warm, thin throat yeld and bend between his great hands... then darkness, peace and rest, a nothingness that surely was the oblivion he had so long prayed for. He had accomplished his desire. He had secreted himself for ever from persecution—inside the kindliest little man he had ever met—inside Hancock. ...

He opened his eyes and looked about him into a room he did not know. The walls were soft and dimly coloured. It was very silent. Cushions were everywhere. Peaceful it was, and out of the world. Overhead was a skylight, and one window, opposite the door, was heavily barred. Delicious! No one could get in. He was sitting in a deep comfortable chair. He felt rested and happy. There was a click, and he saw a tiny window in the door drop down, as though worked by a sliding panel. Then the door opened noiselessly, and in came a little man with smiling face and soft brown yes—Dr. Hancock.

Leidall's first feeling was amazement. 'Then I didn't get into him properly after all! Or I've slipped out again, perhaps! The dear, good fellow!' And he rose to greet him. He put his hand out, and found that the other came with it in some inexplicable fashion. Movement was cramped. 'Ah, then I've had a stroke,' he thought, as Hancock pressed him, ever so gently, back into the big chair. 'Do not get up,' he said soothingly but with authority; 'sit where you are and rest. You must take it very easy for a bit; like all clever men who have overworked——'

'I'll get in the moment he turns,' thought Leidall. 'I did it

VIOLENCE

badly before. It must be through the back of his head, of course, where the spine runs up into the brain,' and he waited till Hancock should turn. But Hancock never turned. He kept his face towards him all the time, while he chatted, moving gradually nearer to the door. On Leidall's face was the smile of an innocent child, but there lay a hideous cunning behind that smile, and the eyes were terrible.

'Are those bars firm and strong,' asked Leidall, 'so that no one can get in?' He pointed craftily, and the doctor, caught for a second unawares, turned his head. That instant Leidall was upon him with a roar, then sank back powerless into the chair, unable to move his arms more than a few inches in any direction. Hancock stepped up quietly and made him comfortable again with cushions.

And something in Leidall's soul turned round and looked another way. His mind became clear as daylight for a moment. The effort perhaps had caused the sudden change from darkness to great light. A memory rushed over him. 'Good God!' he cried. 'I am violent. I was going do you an injury—you, who are so sweet and good to me!' He trembled dreadfully, and burst into tears. 'For the sake of Heaven,' he implored, looking up, ashamed and keenly penitent, 'put me under restraint. Fasten my hands before I try it again.' He held both hands out willingly, beseechingly, then looked down, following the direction of the other's kind brown eyes. His wrists, he saw, already wore steel handcuffs, and a strait waistcoat was across his chest and arms and shoulders.

THE LOST VALLEY

I

Mark and Stephen, twins, were remarkable even of their kind: they were not so much one soul split in twain, as two souls fashioned in precisely the same mould. Their characters were almost identical—tastes, hopes, fears, desires, everything. They even liked the same food, wore the same kind of hats, ties, suits; and, strongest link of all, of course disliked the same things too. At the age of thirty-five neither had married, for they invariably liked the same woman; and when a certain type of girl appeared upon their horizon they talked it over frankly, agreed it was impossible to separate, and together turned their backs upon her for a change of scene before she could endanger their peace.

For their love for one another was unbounded—irresistible as a force of nature, tender beyond words—and their one keen terror was that they might one day be separated.

To look at, even for twins, they were uncommonly alike. Even their eyes were similar: that grey-green of the sea that sometimes changes to blue, and at night becomes charged with shadows. And both faces were of the same strong type with aquiline noses, stern-lipped mouths, and jaws well marked. They possessed imagination, real imagination of the winged kind, and at the same time the fine controlling will without which such a gift is apt to prove a source of weakness. Their emotions, too, were real and living: not the sort that merely tickle the surface of the heart, but the sort that plough.

Both had private means, yet both had studied medicine because it interested them, Mark specialising in diseases of eye and ear, Stephen in mental and nervous cases; and they carried on a select, even a distinguished, practice in the same house in Wimpole Street with their names on the brass plate thus: Dr. Mark Winters, Dr. Stephen Winters.

THE LOST VALLEY

In the summer of 1900 they went abroad together as usual for the months of July and August. It was their custom to explore successive ranges of mountains, collecting the folklore, and natural history of the region into small volumes, neatly illustrated with Stephen's photographs. And this particular year they chose the Jura, that portion of it, rather, that lies between the Lac de Joux, Baulmes and Fleurier. For, obviously, they could not exhaust a whole range in a single brief holiday. They explored it in sections, year by year. And they invariably chose for their head-quarters quiet, unfashionable places where there was less danger of meeting attractive people who might break in upon the happiness of their profound brotherly devotion—the incalculable, mystical devotion of twins.

'For abroad, you know,' Mark would say, 'people have an insinuating way with them that is often hard to withstand. The chilly English reserve disappears. Acquaintanceship becomes intimacy before one has time to weigh it.'

'Exactly,' Stephen added. 'The conventions that protect one at home suddenly wear thin, don't they? And one becomes soft and open to attack—unexpected attack.'

They looked up and laughed, reading each other's thoughts like trained telepathists. What each meant was the dread that one should, after all, be taken and the other left—by a woman.

'Though at our age, you know, one is almost immune,' Mark observed; while Stephen smiling agreed philosophically——

'Or *ought* to be.'

'*Is*,' quoth Mark decisively. For by common consent Mark played the *rôle* of the elder brother. His character, if anything, was a shade more practical. He was slightly more critical of life, perhaps, Stephen being ever more apt to accept without analysis, even without reflection. But Stephen had that richer heritage of dreams which comes from an imagination loved for its own sake.

II

In the peasant's chalet, where they had a sitting-room and two bedrooms, they were very comfortable. It stood on the edge of the forests that run along the slopes of Chasseront, on the side of Les Rasses farthest from Ste Croix. Marie Petavel provided them with the simple cooking they liked; and they spent their days walking, climbing, exploring, Mark collecting legend and folklore, Stephen making his natural history studies, with the little maps and surveys he drew so cleverly. Even this was only a division of labour, for each was equally interested in the occupation of the other; and they shared results in the long evenings, when expeditions brought them back in time, smoking on the rickety wooden balcony, comparing notes, shaping chapters, happy as two children. They brought the enthusiasm of boys to all they did, and they enjoyed the days apart almost as much as those they spent together. After separate expeditions each invariably returned with surprises which awakened the other's interest—even amazement.

Thus, the life of the foreign element in the hotels—unpicturesque in the daytime, noisy and overdressed at night—passed them by. The glimpses they caught as they passed these caravanserais, when gaieties were the order of the evening, made them value their peaceful retreat among the skirts of the forest. They brought no evening dress with them, not even 'le smoking'.

'The atmosphere of these huge hotels simply poisons the mountains,' quoth Stephen. 'All that "haunted" feeling goes.'

'Those people,' agreed Mark, with scorn in his eyes, 'would be far happier at Trouville or Dieppe, gambling, flirting, and the rest.'

Feeling, thus, secure from that jealousy which lies so terribly close to the surface of all giant devotions where the entire life depends upon exclusive possession, the brothers regarded with indifference the signs of this gayer world about them. In that throng there was no one who could introduce an element of danger into their lives—no woman, at least, either of them could like would be found *there*!

For this thought must be emphasised, though not exaggerated. Certain incidents in the past, from which only their strength of will had made escape possible, proved the danger to be a real one. (Usually, too, it was some un-English woman: to wit, the Budapest adventure, or the incident in London with the Greek girl who was first Mark's patient and then Stephen's.) Neither of them made definite reference to the danger, though undoubtedly it was present in their minds more or less vividly whenever they came to a new place: this singular dream that one day a woman would carry off one, and leave the other lonely. It was instinctive, probably, just as the dread of the wolf is instinctive in the deer. The curious fact, though natural enough, was that each brother feared for the other and not for himself. Had any one told Mark that some day he would marry, Mark would have shrugged his shoulders with a smile, and replied, 'No; but I'm awfully afraid Stephen may!' And *vice versa*.

III

Then out of a clear sky the bolt fell—upon Stephen. Catching him utterly unawares it sent him fairly reeling. For Stephen, even more than his brother, posssessed that glorious yet fatal gift, common to poets and children, by which out of a few insignificant details the soul builds for itself a whole sweet heaven to dwell in.

It was at the end of their first month, a month of unclouded happiness together. Since their exploration of the Abruzzi, two years before, they had never enjoyed anything so much. And not a soul had come to disturb their privacy. Plans were being mooted for moving their head-quarters some miles farther towards the Val de Travers and the Creux du Van; only the day of departure, indeed, remained to be fixed, when Stephen, coming home from an afternoon of photography alone, saw, with bewildering and arresting suddenness—a Face. And with the effect of a blow full upon the heart it literally struck him.

How such a thing can come upon a strong man, a man of balanced mind, healthy in nerves and spirit, and in a single moment change serenity into a state of feverish and passionate desire for possession, is a mystery that lies too deep for philosophy or science to explain. It turned him dizzy with a sudden and tempestuous delight—a veritable sickness of the soul, wonderous sweet as it was deadly. Rare enough, of course, such instances may be, but that they happen is undeniable.

He was making his way home in the dusk somewhat wearily. The sun had already dipped below the horizon of France behind him. Across the open country that stretched away to the distant mountains of the Rhone Valley, the moonlight climbed with wings of ghostly radiance that fanned their way into the clefts and pinewoods of the Jura all about him. Cool airs of night stirred and whispered; lights twinkled through the openings among the trees, and all was scented like a garden.

He must have strayed considerably from the right trail—path there was none—for instead of striking the mountain road that led straight to his chalet, he suddenly emerged into a pool of electric light that shone round one of the smaller wooden hotels by the borders of the forest. He recognised it at once, because he and his brother always avoided it deliberately. Not so gay or crowded as the larger caravanserais, it was nevertheless full of people of the kind they did not care about. Stephen was a good half-mile out of his way.

When the mind is empty and the body tired it would seem that the system is sensitive to impressions with an acuteness impossible when these are vigorously employed. The face of this girl, framed against the glass of the hotel verandah, rushed out towards him with a sudden invading glory, and took the most complete imaginable possession of this temporary unemployment of his spirit. Before he could think or act, accept or reject, it had lodged itself eternally at the very centre of his being. He stopped, as before an unexpected flash of lightning, caught his breath—and stared.

A little apart from the throng of 'dressy' folk who sat there in the glitter of the electric light, this face of melancholy dark splendour rose close before his eyes, all soft and wondrous as though the beauty of the night—of forest, stars and moon-rise—had dropped down and focussed itself within the compass of a single human countenance. Framed within a corner pane of the big windows, peering sideways into the darkness, the vision of this girl, not twenty feet rom where he stood, produced upon him a shock of the most convincing delight he had ever known. It was almost as though he saw some one who had dropped down among all these hotel people from another world. And from another world, in a sense, she undoubtedly, was; for her face held in it nothing that belonged to the European countries he knew. She was of the East. The magic of other suns swept into his soul with the vision; the pageantry of other skies flashed brilliantly and was gone. Torches flamed in recesses of his being hitherto dark.

The incongruous surroundings unquestionably deepened the contrast to her advantage, but what made this first sight of her so extraordinarily arresting was the curious chance that where she sat the glare of the electric light did not touch her. She was in shadow from the shoulders downwards. Only, as she leaned backwards against the window, the face and neck turned slightly, there fell upon her exquisite Eastern features the soft glory of the rising moon. And comely she was in Stephen's eyes as nothing in his life had hitherto seemed comely. Apart from the vulgar throng as an exotic is apart from the weeds that choke its growth, this face seemed to swim towards him along the pathway of the slanting moonbeams. And, with it, came literally herself. Some released projection of his consciousness flew forth to meet her. The sense of nearness took his breath away with the faintness of too great happiness. She was in his arms, and his lips were buried in her scented hair. The sensation was vivid with pain and joy, as an ecstasy. And of the nature of true ecstasy, perhaps, it was: for he stood, it seemed, *outside himself.*

He remained there rivetted in the patch of moonlight at the forest edge, for perhaps a whole minute, perhaps two, before he realized what had happened. Then came a second shock, that was even more conquering than the first, for the girl, he saw, was not only gazing into his very face, she was also rising, as with an incipient gesture of recognition. As though she knew him, the little head bent itself forward gently, gracefully, and the dear eyes positively smiled.

The impetuous yearning that leaped full-fledged into his blood taught him in that instant the spiritual secret that pain and pleasure are fundamentally the same force. His attempt at self-control, made instinctively, was utterly overwhelmed. Something flashed to him from her eyes that melted the very roots of resolve; he staggered backwards, catching at the nearest tree for support, and in so doing left the patch of moonlight and stood concealed from view within the deep shadows behind.

Incredible as it must seem in these days of starved romance, this man of strength and firm character, who had hitherto known of such attacks only vicariously from the description of others, now reeled back against the trunk of a pine-tree, knowing all the sweet faintness of an overpowering love at first sight.

'For that, by God, I'd let myself waste utterly to death! To bring her an instant's happiness I'd suffer torture for a century——!'

For the words, with their clumsy, concentrated passion, were out before he realised what he was saying, what he was doing; but, at once out, he knew how pitifully inadequate they were to express a tithe of what was in him a rising sterm. All words dropped away from him; the breath that came and went so quickly clothed no further speech.

With his retreat into the shadows the girl had sat down again, but she still gazed steadily at the place where he had stood. Stephen, who had lost the power of further movement, also stood and stared. The picture, meanwhile, was being traced with hot iron upon plastic deeps in his soul of which he had never before divined the existence. And, again, with the magic of this master-yearning, it seemed that he drew her out from that horde of hotel guests till she stood close before his eyes, warm, perfumed, caressing. The delicate, sharp splendour of her face, already dear beyond all else in life, flamed there within actual touch of his lips. He turned giddy with the joy, wonder and mystery of it all. The frontiers of his being melted—then extended to include her.

From the words a lover fights among to describe the face he worships one divines only a little of the picture; these dimly-coloured symbols conceal more beauty than they reveal. And of this dark, young oval face, first seen sideways in the moonlight, with drooping lids over the almond-shaped eyes, soft cloudy hair, all enwrapped with the haunting and penetrating mystery of love, Stephen never attempted to analyse the ineffable secret. He just accepted it with a plunge of utter self-abandonment. He only realised vaguely by way of detail that the little nose, without being Jewish, curved singularly down towards a chin daintily chiselled in firmness; that the mouth held in its lips the invitation of all womankind as expressed in another race, a race alien to his own—an Eastern race; and that something untamed, almost savage, in the face was corrected by the exquisite tenderness of the large dreamy, brown eyes. The mighty revolution of love spread its soft tide into every corner of his being.

Moreover, that gesture of welcome, so utterly unexpected yet so spontaneous (so natural, it seemed to him now!), the smile of recognition that had so deliciously perplexed him, he accepted in the same way. The girl had felt what he had felt, and had betrayed herself even as he had done by a sudden, uncontrollable movement of revelation and delight; and to explain it otherwise by any vulgar standard of worldly wisdom, would be to rob it of all its dear modesty, truth and wonder. She yearned to know him, even as he yearned to know her.

And all this in the little space, as men count time, of two minutes, even less.

How he was able at the moment to restrain all precipitate and impulsive action, Stephen has never properly understood. There was a fight, and it was short, painful and confused. But it ended on a note of triumphant joy—the rapture of happiness to come...

With a great effort he remembers that he found the use of his feet and continued his journey homewards, passing out once more into the moonlight. The girl in the verandah followed his disappearing figure with her turning head; she craned her neck to watch till he disappeared beyond the angle of vision; she even waved her little dark hand.

'I shall be late,' ran the thought sharply through Stephen's mind. It was cold; vivid with keen pain. 'Mark will wonder what in the world has become of me——!'

For, with swift and terrible reaction, the meaning of it all—the possible consequences of The Face—swept over his heart and drowned it in a flood of icy water. In estimating his brotherly love, even the love of the twin, he had never conceived such a thing as this—had never reckoned with the possibility of a force that could make all else in the world seem so trivial. ...

Mark, had he been there, with his more critical attitude to life, might have analysed something of it away. But Mark was not there. And Stephen had—*seen*.

Those mighty strings of life upon which, as upon an instrument, the heart of man lies stretched, had been set powerfully a-quiver. The new vibrations poured and beat through him. Something within him swiftly disintegrated; in its place something else grew marvellously. The Face had established dominion over the secret places of his soul; thenceforward the process was automatic and inevitable.

IV

Then, spectre-like and cold, the image of his brother rose before his inner vision. The profound brotherly love of the twin confronted him in the path.

He stumbled among the roots and stones, searching for the

means of self-control, but finding them with difficulty. Windows had opened everywhere in his soul; he looked out through them upon a new world, immense and gloriously coloured. Behind him in the shadows, as his vision searched and his heart sang, reared the single thought that hitherto had dominated his life: his love for Mark. It had already grown indisputably dim.

For both passions were genuine and commanding, the one built up through thirty-five years of devotion cemented by ten thousand associations and sacrifices, the other dropping out of heaven upon him with a suddenness simply appalling. And from the very first instant he understood that both could not live. One must die to feed the other...

On the staircase was the perfume of a strange tobacco, and, to his surprise and intense relief, when he entered the chalet he found that his brother for the first time was not alone. A small, dark man stood talking earnestly with him by the open window—the window where Mark had obviously been watching with anxiety for his arrival. Before introducing him to the stranger, Mark at once gave expression to his relief.

'I was beginning to be afraid something had happened to you,' he said quietly enough, but in a way that the other understood. And after a moment's pause, in which he searched Stephen's face keenly, he added, 'but we didn't wait supper as you see, and old Petavel has kept yours all hot and ready for you in the kitchen.'

'I—er—lost my way,' Stephen said quickly, glancing from Mark to the stranger, wondering vaguely who he was. 'I got confused somehow in the dusk——'

Mark, remembering his manners now that his anxiety was set at rest, hastened to introduce him—a Professor in a Russian University, interested in folklore and legend, who had read the book on the Abruzzi and discovered quite by chance that they were neighbours here in the forest. He was staying in a little hotel at Les Rasses, and had ventured to come up and introduce himself. Stephen was far too occupied trying to conceal his new battling emotions to notice that Mark and the stranger seemed on quite familiar terms. He was so fearful lest the perturbations of his own heart should betray him that he had no power to detect anything subtle or unusual in anybody else.

'Professor Samarianz comes originally from Tiflis,' Mark was explaining, 'and had been telling me the most fascinating things about the legends and folklore of the Caucasus. We really muts go there another year, Stephen... Mr. Samarianz most kindly has promised me letters to helpful people... He tells me, too, of a charming and exquisite legend of a "Lost Valley" that exists hereabouts, where the spirits of all who die by their own hands, or otherwise suffer violent deaths, find perpetual peace—the peace denied them by all the religions, that is...'

Mark went on talking for some minutes while Stephen took off his knapsack and exchanged a few words with their visitor, who spoke excellent English. He was not quite sure what he said, but hoped he talked quietly and sensibly enough, in spite of the passions that waged war so terrifically in his breast. He noticed, however, that the man's face held an unusual charm, though he could not detect wherein its secret specifically lay. Presently, with excuses of hunger, he went into the kitchen for his supper, hugely relieved to find the opportunity to collect his thoughts a little; and when he returned twenty minutes later he found that his brother was alone. Professor Samarianz had taken his leave. In the room still lingered the perfume of his peculiarly flavoured cigarettes.

Mark, after listening with half an ear to his brother's description of the day, began pouring out his new interest; he was full of the Caucasus, and its folklore, and of the fortunate chance that had broght the stranger their way. The legend of the 'Lost Valley' in the Jura, too, particularly interested him, and he spoke of his astonishment that he had hitherto come across no trace anywhere of the story.

'And fancy,' he exclaimed, after a recital that lasted half-an-hour, 'the man came up from one of those little hotels on the edge of the forest—that noisy one we have always been so careful to avoid. You never know where your luck hides, do you?' he added, with a laugh.

'You never do, indeed,' replied Stephen quietly, now wholly master of himself, or, at least, of his voice and eyes.

And, to his secret satisfaction and delight, it was Mark who provided the excuses for staying on in the chalet, instead of moving further down the valley as they had intended. Besides, it would have been unnatural and absurd to leave without investigating so picturesque a legend as the 'Lost Valley'.

'We're uncommonly happy here,' Mark added quietly; 'why not stay on a bit?'

'Why, not, indeed?' answered Stephen, trusting that the fearful inner storm instantly roused again by the prospect did not betray itself.

'You're not very keen, perhaps, old fellow?' suggested Mark gently.

'On the contrary—I am, *very*,' was the reply.

'Good. Then we'll stay.'

The words were spoken after a pause of some seconds. Stephen, who was down at the end of the room sorting his specimens by the lamp, looked up sharply. Mark's face, where he sat on the window-ledge in the dusk, was hardly visible. It must have been something in his voice that had shot into Stephen's heart with a flash of sudden warning.

A sensation of cold passed swiftly over him and was gone. Had he already betrayed himself? Was the subtle, almost telepathic sympathy between the twins developed to such a point that emotions could be thus transferred with the minumum of word or gesture, within the very shades of their silence even? And another thought: Was there something different in Mark too—something in him also that had changed? Or was it merely his own raging, heaving passion, though so sternly repressed, that distorted his judgment and made him imaginative?

What stood so darkly in the room—between them?

A sudden and fearful pain seared him inwardly as he realised, practically, and with cruelly acute comprehension, that one of these two loves in his heart must inevitably die to feed the other; and that it might have to be—Mark. The complete meaning of it came home to him. And at the thought all his deep love of thirty years rose in a tide within him, flooding through the gates of life, seeking to overwhelm and merge in itself all obstacles that threatened to turn it aside. Unshed tears burned behind his eyes. He ached with a degree of actual, physical pain.

After a moment of savage self-control he turned and crossed the room: but before he had covered half the distance that separated him from the window where his brother sat smoking, the rush of burning words—were they to have been of confession, of self reproach, or of renewed devotion?—swept away from him, so that he wholly forgot them. In their place came the ordinary dead phrases of convention. He hardly heard them himself, though his lips uttered them.

'Come along, Mark, old chap,' he said, conscious that his voice trembled, and that another face slipped imperiously in front of the one his eyes looked upon; 'it's time to go to bed. I'm dead tired like yourself.'

'You are right,' Mark replied, looking at him steadily as he turned towards the lamplight. 'Besides, the night air's getting chilly—and we've been sitting in a draught, you know, all along.'

For the first time in their lives the eyes of the two brothers could not quite find each other. Neither gaze hit precisely the middle of the other. It was as though a veil hung down between them and a deliberate act of focus was necessary. They looked one another straight in the face as usual, but with an effort—with momentary difficulty. The room, too, as Mark had said, was cold, and the lamp, exhausted of its oil, was beginning to smell. Both light and heat were going. It was certainly time for bed.

The brothers went out together, arm in arm, and the long shadows of the pines, thrown by the rising moon through the window, fell across the floor like arms that waved. And from the black branches outside, the wind caught up a shower of sighs and dropped them about the roofs and walls as they made their way to their bedrooms on opposite sides of the little corridor.

V

Four hours later, when the moon was high overhead and the room held but a single big shadow, the door opened softly and in came—Stephen. He was dressed. He crossed the floor stealthily, unfastened the windows, and let himself out upon the balcony. A minute afterwards he had disappeared into the forest beyond the strip of vegetable garden at the back of the chalet.

It was two o'clock in the morning, and no sleep had touched his eyes. For his heart burned, ached, and fought within him, and he felt the need of open spaces and the great forces of the night and mountains. No such battle had he ever known before. He remembered his brother saying years ago, with a laugh half serious, half playful, '...for if ever one of us comes a cropper in love, old fellow, it will be time for the other to—go!' And by 'go' they both understood the ultimate meaning of the word.

Through the glades of forest, sweet-scented by the night, he made his way till he reached the spot where that Face of soft splendour had first blessed his soul with its mysterious glory. There he sat down and, with his back against the very tree that had supported him a few hours ago, he drove his thoughts forward into battle with the whole strength of his will and character behind him. Very quietly, and with all the care, precision and steadiness of mind that he would have brought to bear upon a difficult 'case' at Wimpole Street, he faced the situation and wrestled with it. The emotions during four hours, tossing upon a sleepless bed, had worn themselves out a little. He was, in one sense of the word, calm, master of himself. The facts, with the huge issue that lay in their hands, he saw naked. And, as he thus saw them, he discerned how very, very far he had already travelled down the sweet path that led him towards the girl—and away from his brother.

Details about her, of course, he knew none; whether she was free even; for he only knew that he loved, and that his entire life was already breaking with the yearning to sacrifice itself for that love. That was the naked fact. The problem bludgeoned him. Could he do anything to hold back the flood still rising, to arrest its terrific flow? Could he divert its torrent, and take it, girl and all, to offer upon the altar of that other love—the devotion of the twin for its twin, the mysterious affinity that hitherto had ruled and directed all the currents of his soul?

There was no question of undoing what had already been done. Even if he never saw that face again, or heard the accents of those beloved lips; if he never was to know the magic of touch, the perfume of close thought, or the strange blessedness of telling her his burning message and hearing the murmur of her own—the fact of love was already accomplished between them. That was ineradicable. He had seen. The sensitive plate had received its undying picture.

For this was no foolish passion arising from the mere propinquity that causes so many of the world's misfit marriages. It was a profound and mystical union already accomplished, psychical in the utter sense, inevitable as the marriage of wind and fire. He almost heard his soul laugh as he thought of the revolution effected in an instant of time by the message of a single glance. What had science, or his own special department of science, to say to this tempest of force that invaded him, and swept with its beautiful terrors of wind and lightning the furthest recesses of his being? This whirlwind that so shook him, that so deliciously wounded him, that already made the thought of sacrificing his brother seem sweet—what was there to say to it, or do with it, or think of it?

Nothing, nothing, nothing!... He could only lie in its arms and rest, with that peace, deeper than all else in life, which the mystic knows when he is conscious that the everlasting arms are about him and that his union with the greatest force of the world is accomplished.

Yet Stephen struggled like a lion. His will rose up and opposed itself to the whole invasion... and in the end his will of steel, trained as all men of character train their wills against the difficulties of life, did actually produce a certain, definite result. This result was almost a *tour de force,* perhaps, yet it seemed valid. By its aid Stephen forced himself into a position he felt intuitively was an impossible one, but in which nevertheless he determined, by a deliberate act of almost incredible volition, that he would remain fixed. He decided to conquer his obsession, and to remain true to Mark. ...

The distant ridges of the dim blue Jura were tipped with the splendours of the coming dawn when at length he rose, chilly and exhausted, to retrace his steps to the chalet.

He realised fully the meaning of the resolve he had come to. And the knowledge of it froze something within him into a stiffness that was like the stiffness of death. The pain in his heart battling against the resolution was atrocious. He had estimated, or thought so, at least, the meaning of his sacrifice. As a matter of fact his decision was entirely artificial, of course, and his resolve dictated by a moral code rather than by the living forces that direct life and can alone make its changes permanent. Stephen had in him the stuff of the hero, and, having said that, one has said all that language can say.

On the way home in the cool white dawn, as he crossed the open spaces of meadow where the mist rose and the dew lay like rain, he suddenly thought of her lying dead—dead, that is, as he had thus decided she was to be dead—for him. And instantly, as by a word of command, the entire light went out of the landscape and out of the world. His soul turned wintry, and all the sweetness of his life went bleak. For it was the ancient soul in him that loved, and to deny it was to deny life itself. He had pronounced upon himself a sentence of death by starvation—a lingering and prolonged death accompanied by tortures of the most exquisite description. And along this path he really believed at the moment his little human will could hold him firm.

He made his way through the dew-drenched grass with the elation caused by so vast a sacrifice singing curiously in his blood. The splendour of the mountain sunrise and all the vital freshness of the dawn was in his heart. He was upon the chalet almost before he knew it, and there on the balcony, waiting to receive him, his grey dressing-gown wrapped about his ears in the sharp air, stood—Mark!

And, somehow or other, at the sight, all this false elation passed and dropped. Stephen looked up at him, standing suddenly still there in his tracks, as he might have looked up at his executioner. The picture had restored him most abruptly, with sharpest pain, to reality again.

'Like me, you couldn't sleep, eh?' Mark called softly, so as not to waken the peasants who slept on the ground floor.

‚Have *you* been lying awake, too?' Stephen replied.

'All night. I haven't closed an eye.' Then Mark added, as his brother came up the wooden steps towards him, 'I knew you were awake. I felt it. I knew, too—you had gone out.'

A silence passed between them. Both had spoken quietly, naturally, neither expressing surprise.

'Yes,' Stephen said slowly at length; 'we always reflect each other's pain—each other's moods——' He stopped abruptly, leaving the sentence unfinished.

Their eyes met as of old. Stephen knew an instant of quite freezing terror in which he felt that his brother had divined the truth. Then Mark took his arm and led the way indoors on tiptoe.

'Look here, Stevie, old fellow,' he said, with extraordinary tenderness, 'there's no good saying anything, but I know perfectly well that you're unhappy about something; and so, of course, I am unhappy too.' He paused, as though searching for words. Under ordinary circumstances Stephen would have caught his precise thought, but now the tumult of suppressed emotion in him clouded his divining power. He felt his arm clutched in a sudden vice. They drew closer to one another. Neither spoke. Then Mark, low and hurriedly, said—he almost mumbled it—'It's all my fault *really,* all my fault—dear old boy!'

Stephen turned in amazement and stared. What in the world did his brother mean? What was he talking about? Before he could find speech, however, Mark continued, speaking distinctly now, and with evidences of strong emotion in his voice—

'I'll tell you what we'll do,' he exclaimed, with sudden decision; 'we'll go away; we'll leave! We've stayed here a bit too long, perhaps. Eh? What d'you say to that?'

Stephen did not notice how sharply Mark searched his face. At the thought of separation all his mighty resolution dropped like a house of cards. His entire life seemed to melt away and run in a stream of impetuous yearning towards the Face.

But he answered quietly, sustaining his purpose artificially by a force of will that seemed to break and twist his life at the source with extraordinary pain. He could not have endured the strain for more than a few seconds. His voice sounded strange and distant.

'All right; at the end of the week,' he said—the faintness in him was dreadful, filling him with cold—'and that'll give us just three days to make our plans, won't it?'

Mark nodded his head. Both faces were lined and drawn like the faces of old men; only there was no one there to remark upon it—nor upon the fixed sternness that had dropped so suddenly upon their eyes and lips.

Arm in arm they entered the chalet and went to their bedrooms without another word. The sun, as they went, rose close over the tree-tops and dropped its first rays upon the spot where they had just stood.

VI

They came down in dressing-gowns to a very late breakfast. They were quiet, grave and slightly preoccupied. Neither made the least reference to their meeting at sunrise. New lines had graved themselves upon their faces, identical lines it seemed, drawing the mouth down at the corners with a touch of grimness where hitherto had been merely firmness.

And the eyes of both saw new things, new distances, new terrors. Something, feared till now only as a possibility, had come close, and stood at their elbows for the first time as an actuality. Sleep, in which changes offered to the soul during the day are confirmed and ratified, had established this new element in their personal equation. They had changed—if not towards one another, then towards something else.

But Stephen saw the matter only from his own point of view. For the first time in his memory he seemed to have lost the intuitive sympathy which enabled him to see things from his brother's point of view as well. The change, he felt positive, was in himself, not in Mark.

'He knows—he feels—something in me has altered dreadfully, but he doesn't yet understand what,' his thoughts ran. 'Pray to God he need never know—at least until I have utterly conquered it!'

For he still held with all the native tenacity of his strong will to the course he had so heroically chosen. The degree of self-deception his imagination brought into the contest seemed incredible when his mind looked back upon it all from the calmness of the end. But at the time he genuinely hoped, wished, intended to conquer, even *believed* that he would conquer.

Mark, he noticed, reacted in little ways that curiously betrayed his mental perturbation, and at any other time might have roused his brother's suspicions. He put sugar in Stephen's coffee, for instance; he forgot to bring him a cigarette when he went to the cupboard to get one for himself; he said and did numerous little things that were contrary to his habits, or to the habits of his twin.

In all of which, however, Stephen saw only the brotherly reaction to the change he was conscious of in himself. Nothing happened to convince him that anything in Mark had suffered revolution. With the mystical devotion peculiar to the twin he was too keenly aware of his own falling away to imagine the falling away of the other. He, Stephen, was the guilty one, and he suffered atrociously. Moreover, the pain of his renunciation was heightened by the sense that his ideal love for Mark had undergone a change—that he was making this fatal sacrifice, therefore, for something that perhaps no longer existed. This, however, he did not realise yet as an accomplished fact. Even if it were true, the resolution he had come to, acted by way of hypnotic suggestion to conceal it. At the same time it added enormously to the confusion and perplexity of his mind.

That day for the brothers was practically a *dies non*. They spent what was left of the morning over many aimless and unnecessary little duties, somewhat after the way of women. Although neither referred to the decision to leave at the end of the week, both acted upon it in desultory fashion, almost as though they wished to make a point of proving to one another that it was *not* forgotten—not wholly forgotten, at any rate. They made a brave pretence of collecting various things with a view to ultimate packing. No word was spoken, however, that bore more closely upon it than occasional phrases such as, 'When the time comes to go'—'when we leave'—'better put *that* out, or it will be forgotten, you know.'

The sentences dropped from their mouths alternately at long intervals, the only one deceived being the utterer. It was not unlike the pretence of schoolboys, only more elaborate and infinitely more clumsy and ill-done. Stephen, at any other time, would probably have laughed aloud. Yet the curious thing was that he noticed the pretence only in his own case. Mark, he thought, was genuine, though perhaps not too eager. 'He's agreed to leave, the dear old chap, because he thinks I want it, and not for himself,' he said. And the idea of the small brotherly sacrifice pleased, yet pained him horribly at the same time. For it tended to rehabilitate the old love which stood in the way of the new one.

He began, however, to take less trouble to sort and find his things for packing; he wrote letters, put out photographs to print in the sun, even studied his maps for expeditions, making occasional remarks thereon aloud which Mark did not negative. Presently, he forgot altogether about packing. Mark said nothing. Mark followed his example, however.

During the afternoon both lay down and slept, meeting again for tea at five. It was rare that they found themselves in for tea. Mark to-day made a special little ritual of it; he made it over their own spirit-lamp—almost tenderly, looking after his brother's wants like a woman. And the little meal was hardly over when a boy in hotel livery arrived with a note—an invitation from Professor Samarianz.

'He has looked up a lot of his papers,' observed Mark carelessly as he tossed the note down, 'and suggests my coming in for dinner, so that he can show me everything afterwards without hurry.'

'I should accept,' said Stephen. 'It might be valuable for us if we go to the Caucasus later.'

Mark hesitated a minute or two, telling the boy to wait in the kitchen. 'I think I'll go in *after* dinner instead,' he decided presently. There was a trace of eagerness in his manner which Stephen, however, did not notice.

'Take your note-book and pump the old boy dry,' Stephen added, with a slight laugh. 'I shall go to bed early myself probably.' And Mark, stuffing the note into his pocket, laughed back and consented, to the other's great relief.

It was very late when Mark returned form the visit, but his brother did not hear him come, having taken a draught to ensure sleeping. And next morning Mark was so full of the interesting information he had collected, and would continue to collect, that the question of leaving at the end of the week dropped of its own accord without further ado. Neither of the brothers made the least pretence of packing. Both wished and intended to stay on where they were.

'I shall look up Samarianz again this afternoon,' Mark said casually during the morning, 'and—if you've no objection—I might bring him back to supper. He's the most obliging fellow I've ever met, and crammed with information.'

Stephen, signifying his agreement, took his camera, his specimen-tin and his geological hammer and went out with bread and chocolate in his knapsack for the rest of the afternoon by himself.

VII

Moreover, he not only set out bravely, but for many hours held true, keeping so rigid a control over his feelings that it seemed literally to cost him blood. All the time, however, a passionate yearning most craftily attacked him, and the very memory he strove to smother rose with a persistence that ridiculed repression. Like snowflakes, whose individual weight is inappreciable but their cumulative burden irresistible, the thoughts of *her* gathered behind his spirit, ready at a given moment to overwhelm; and it was on the way home again in the evening that the temptation came upon him like a tidal wave that made the mere idea of resistance seem utterly absurd.

He remembered wondering with a kind of wild delight whether it could be possible for any human will to withstand such a tempest of pressure as that which took him by the shoulders and literally pushed him out of his course towards the little hotel on the edge of the forest.

It was utterly inconsistent, of course, and he made no pretence of argument or excuse. He hardly knew, indeed, what he expected to see or do; his mind, at least, framed no definite idea. But far within him that deep heart which refused to be stifled cried out for a drop of the living water that was now its very life. And, chiefly, he wanted to *see*. If only he could see her once again—even from a distance—the merest glimpse——! With one more sight of her that should charge his memory to the brim for life he might face the future with more courage perhaps. Ah! that *perhaps*!... For she was drawing him with those million invisible cords of love that persuade a man he is acting of his own volition when actually he is but obeying the inevitable forces that bind the planets and the suns.

And this time there was no hurry; there was a good hour before Mark would expect him home for supper; he could sit among the shadows of the wood, and wait.

In his pocket were the field-glasses, and he realized with a sudden secret shame that it was not by accident that they were there. He stumbled, even before he got within a quarter of a mile of the place, for the idea that perhaps he would see her again made him ridiculously happy, and like a schoolboy he positively trembled, tripping over roots and misjudging the distance of his steps. It was all part of a great whirling dream in which his soul sang and shouted the first delirious nonsense that came into his head. The possibility of his eyes again meeting hers produced a sensation of triumph and exultation that only one word describes—intoxication.

As he approached the opening in the trees whence the hotel was so easily visible, he went more slowly, moving even on tiptoe. It was instinctive; for he was nearing a place made holy by his love. Picking his way almost stealthily, he found the very tree; then leaned against it while his eyes searched eagerly for a sign of her in the glass verandah. The swiftness and accuracy of sight at such a time may be cause for wonder, but it is beyond question that in less than a single second he knew that the throng of moving figures did not contain the one he sought. She was not among them.

And he was just preparing to make himself comfortable for an extended watch when a sound or movement, perhaps both, somewhere among the trees on his right attracted his attention. There was a faint rustling; a twig snapped.

Stephen turned sharply. Under a big spruce, not half-a-dozen yards away, something moved—then rose up. At first, owing to the gloom, he took it for an animal of some kind, but the same second saw that it was a human figure. It was *two* human figures, standing close together. Then one moved apart from the other; he saw the outline of a man against a space of sky between the trees. And a voice spoke—a voice charged with great tenderness, yet driven by high passion——

'But it's nothing, nothing! I shall not be gone two minutes. And to save you an instant's discomfort you know that I would run the whole circle of the earth! Wait here for me——!'

That was all; but the voice and figure caused Stephen's heart to stop beating as though it had been suddenly plunged into ice, for they were the voice and the figure of his brother Mark.

Quickly running down the slope towards the hotel, Mark disappeared.

The other figure, leaning against the tree, was the figure of a girl; and Stephen, even in that first instant of fearful bewilderment, understood why it was that the face of the man Samarianz had so charmed him. For this, of course, was his daughter. And then the whole thing flashed mercilessly clear upon his inner vision, and he knew that Mark, too, had been swept from his feet, and was undergoing the same fierce tortures, and fighting the same dread battle, as himself. ....

There seemed to be no conscious act of recognition. The fire that flamed through him and set his frozen heart so fearfully beating again, hammering against his ribs, left him apparently without volition or any power of cerebral action at all. *She* stood there, not half-a-dozen yards away from where he sat all huddled upon the ground, stood there in all her beauty, her mystery, her wonder, near enough for him to have taken her almost with a single leap into his arms;—stood there, veiled a little by the shadows of the dusk—waiting for the return of—Mark!

He remembers what happened with the blurred indistinctness common to moments of overwhelming passion. For in the next few seconds, that mocked all scale of time, he lived through a series of concentrated emotions that burned his brain too vividly for precise recollection. He rose to his feet unsteadily, his hand upon the rough bark of the tree. Absurd details only seem to remain of these few moments: that a foot was 'asleep' with pins and needles up to the knee, and that his slouch hat fell from his head, filling him with fury because it hid her from him for the fraction of a second. These odd details he remembers.

And then, as though the driving-power of the universe had deliberately pushed him from behind, he was advancing slowly, with short, broken steps, towards the tree where the girl stood with her back half turned against him.

He did not know her name, had never heard her voice, had

never even stood close enough to 'feel' her atmosphere; yet, so deeply had his love and imagination already prepared the little paths of intimacy within him, that he felt he was moving towards some one whom he had known ever since he could remember, and who belonged to him as utterly as if from the beginning of time his possession of her had been absolute. Had they shared together a whole series of previous lives, the sensation could not have been more convincing and complete.

And out of all this whirlwind and tumult two small actions, he remembers, were delivered: a confused cry that was no definite word came from his lips, and—he opened his arms to take her to his heart. Whereupon, of course, she turned with a quick start, and became for the first time aware of his near presence.

'Oh, oh! But how so softly quick you return!' she cried falteringly, looking into his eyes with a smile both of welcome and alarm. 'You a little frightened me, I tell you.'

It was just the voice he had known would come, with the curiously slow, dragging tone of its broken English, the words lingering against the lips as if loath to leave, the soft warmth of their sound in the throat like a caress. The next instant he held her smothered in his arms, his face buried in the scented hair about her neck.

There was an unbelievable time of forgetfulness in which touch, perfume, and a healing power that emanated from her blessed the depths of his soul with a peace that calmed all pain, stilled all tumult—a moment in which Time itself for once stopped its remorseless journey, and the very processes of life stood still to watch. Then there was a frightened cry, and she had pushed him from her. She stood there, her soft eyes puzzled and surprised, looking hard at him; panting a little, her breast heaving.

And Stephen understood then, if he had not already understood before. The gesture of recognition in the hotel verandah two days ago, and this glorious realization it of that now seemed to have happened a century ago, shared a common origin. They were intended for another, and on both occasions the girl had taken him for his brother Mark.

And, turning sharply, almost falling with the abruptness of it all, as the girl's lips uttered that sudden cry, he saw close beside them the very person for whom they were intended. Mark had come up the slope behind them unobserved, carrying upon his arm the little red cloak he had been to fetch.

It was as though a wind of ice had struck him in the face. The revulsion of feeling with which Stephen saw the return of his brother passed rapidly into a state of numbness where all emotion whatsoever ebbed like the tides of death. He lost momentarily the power of realisation. He forgot who he was, what he was doing there. He was dazed by the fact that Mark had so completely forestalled him. His life shook and tottered upon its foundations...

Then the face and figure of his brother swayed before his eyes tike the branch of a tree, as an attack of passing dizziness seized him. It may have been a mere hazard that led his fingers to close, moist and clammy, upon the geological hammer at his belt. Certainly, he let it go again almost at once. ... And, when the tide of emotion returned upon him with the dreadful momentum it had gathered during the interval, the possibility of his yielding to wild impulse and doing something mad or criminal, was obviated by the swift enactment of an exceedingly poignant little drama that made both brothers forget themselves in their desire to save the girl.

In sweetest bewilderment, like a frightened little child or animal, the girl looked from one brother to the other. Her eyes shone in the dusk. Strangely appealing her loveliness was in that moment of seeking some explanation of the double vision. She made a movement first towards Mark—turned halfway in her steps, and ran, startled, upon Stephen—then, with a sharp scream of fear, dropped in a heap to the ground midway between the two.

Her indecision of half-a-second, however, seemed to Stephen to have lasted many minutes. Had she fallen finally into the arms of his brother, he felt nothing on earth could have prevented his leaping upon him with the hands of a murderer. As it was—mercifully—the singular beauty of her little Eastern face, touched as it was by the white terror of her soul, momentarily arrested all other feeling in him. A shudder of fearful admiration passed through him as he saw her sway and fall. Thus might have dropped some soft angel from the skies. ...

It was Mark, however, with his usual decision, who brought some possibility of focus back to his mind; and he did it with an action and a sentence so utterly unexpected, so incongruous amid this whirlwind of passion, that had he seen it on the stage or read it in a novel, he must surely have burst out laughing. For, in that very second after the dear form swayed and fell, while the eyes of the brothers met across her in one swift look that held the possibilities of the direst results, Mark, his face abruptly clearing to calmness, stooped down beside the prostrate girl, and, looking up at Stephen steadily, said in a gentle voice, but with his most deliberate professional manner—

'Stephen, old fellow, this is—*my* patient. One of us, perhaps, had better—go.'

He bent down to loosen the dress at the throat and chafe the cold hands, and Stephen, uncertain exactly what he did, and trembling like a child, turned and disappeared among the thick trees in the direction of their little house. For he understood only one thing clearly in that awful moment: that he must either kill—or not see. And his will, well-nigh breaking beneath the pressure, was just able to take the latter course.

'*Go!*' it said peremptorily.

And the little word sounded through the depths of his soul like the tolling of a last bell.

VIII

'*This is my patient!*' The dreadful comedy of the phrase, the grim mockery of the professional manner, the contrast between the words that some one *ought* to have uttered and the words Mark actually *had* uttered—all this had the effect of restoring Stephen to some measure of sanity. No one but his brother, he felt, could have said the thing so exactly calculated to relieve the choking passion of the situation. It was an inspiration—yet horrible in ist bizarre mingling of true and false.

'But it's all like a thing in a dream,' he heard an inner voice murmur as he stumbled homewards without once looking back; 'the kind of thing people say and do in the rooms of strange sleep-houses. We are all surely in a dream, and presently I shall wake up——!'

The voice continued talking, but he did not listen. A web of confusion began to spin itself about his thoughts, and there stole over him an odd sensation of remoteness from the actual things of life. It was surely one of those vivid, haunting dreams he sometimes had when his spirit seemed to take part in real scenes, with real people only far, far away, and on quite another scale of time and values.

'I shall find myself in my bed at Wimpole Street!' he exclaimed. He even tried to escape from the pain closing about him like a vice—tried to escape by waking up, only to find, of course, that the effort drove him more closely to the reality of his position.

Yet the texture of a dream certainly ran through the whole thing; the outlandish proportions of dream-events showed themselves everywhere; the tiny causes and prodigious effects: the terrific power of the Face upon his soul; the uncanny semi-quenching of his love for Mark; the ridiculous way he had come upon these two in the forest, with the nightmare discovery that they had known one another for days; and then the sight of that dear, magical face dropping through the dusky forest air between the two of them. Moreover—just when the dream ought to have ended with his sudden awakening, it had taken this abrupt and inconsequent turn, and Mark had uttered the language of—well, the impossible and rather horrible language of the nightmare world——

'*This is my patient. ...*'

Moreover, his face of ice as he said it; yet, at the same time, the wisdom, the gentleness of the decision that lay behind the words: the desire to relieve an impossibly painful situation. And then—the other words, meant kindly, even meant nobly, but charged for all that with the naked cruelty of life—

'One of us, perhaps, had better—go.'

And he had gone—fortunately, he had gone. .....

Yet an hour later, after lying motionless upon his bed seeking with all his power for a course of action his will could follow and his mind approve, it was no dream-voice that called softly to him through the keyhole—

'Stevie, old fellow ... she is well ... she is all right now. She leaves in the morning with her father... the first thing... very early. ...'

And then, after a pause in which Stephen said nothing lest he should at the same time say all—

'...and it is best, perhaps...we should not see one another ...you and I...for a bit. Let us go our ways...till to-morrow night. Then we shall be...alone together again... you and I...as of old. ...'

The voice of Mark did not tremble; but it sounded far away and unreal, almost like wind in the keyhole, thin, reedy, sighing; oddly broken and interrupted.

'...I'm yours Stevie, old fellow, always yours,' it added far down the corridor, more like the voice of dream again than ever.

But, though he made no reply at the moment, Stephen welcomed and approved both the proposal and the spirit in which it was made; and next day, soon after sunrise, he left the chalet very quietly and went off alone into the mountains with his thoughts, and with the pain that all night long had simply been eating him alive.

IX

It is impossible to know precisely what he felt all that morning in the mountains. His emotions charged like wild bulls to and fro. He seemed conscious only of two master-feelings: first that his life now belonged beyond possibility of change or control—to another; yet, secondly, that his will, tried and tempered weapon of steel that it was, held firm.

Thus his powerful feelings flung him from one wall of his dreadful prison to another without possible means of escape. For his position involved a fundamental contradiction: the new love owned him, yet his will cried, 'I love Mark; I hold true to that; in the end I shall conquer!' He refused, that is, to capitulate, or rather to acknowledge that he had capitulated. And meanwhile, even while he cried, his inmost soul listened, watched, and laughed, well content to abide the issue.

But if his feelings were in too great commotion for clear analysis, his thoughts, on the other hand, were painfully definite—some of them, at least; and, as the physical exercise lessens the assaults of emotion, these stood forth in sharp relief against the confusion of his inner world. It was now clear as the day, for instance, that Mark had been through a battle similar to his own. The chance meeting with the Professor had led to the acquaintance with his daughter. Then, swiftly and inevitably, just as it would have happened to Stephen in his place, love had accomplished its full magic. And Mark had been afraid to tell him. The twins had travelled the same path, only personal, feeling having clouded their usual intuition, neither had divined the truth.

Stephen saw it now with pitiless clarity: his brother's frequent visits to the hotel, omitting to mention that the notes of invitation probably also included himself; the desire, nay, the intention to stay on; the delay in packing—and a dozen other details stood out clearly. He remembered, too, with a pang how Mark had not slept that memorable night; he recalled their enigmatical conversation on the balcony as the sun rose... and all the rest of the miserable puzzle.

And, as he realised from his own torments what Mark must also have suffered—be suffering now—he was conscious of a strenghtening of his will to conquer. The thought linked him fiercely again to his twin; for nothing in their lives had yet been separate, and the chain of their spiritual intimacy was of incalculably vast strength. They would win—win back to one another's side again. Mark would conquer her. He, Stephen, would also in the end conquer... her...!.

But with the thought of her lying thus dead to him, and his life cold and empty without her, came the inevitable revulsion of feeling. It was the anarchy of love. The Face, the perfume, the rushing power of her melancholy dear eyes, with their singular touch of proud languor—in a word, all the amazing magic that had swept himself and Mark from their feet, tore back upon him with such an invasion of entreaty and command, that he sat down upon the very rock where he was and buried his face in his hands, literally groaning with the pain of it. For the thought lacerated within. To give her up was a sheer impossibility;... to give up his brother was equally inconceivable. The weight of thirty-five years' love and associations thus gave battle against the telling blow of a single moment. Behind the first lay all that life had built into the woof of his personality hitherto, but *beyond* the second lay the potent magic, the huge seductive invitation of what he might become in the future—with her.

The contest, in the nature of the forces engaged, was an unequal one. Yet all that morning as he wandered aimlessly over ridge and summit, and across the high Jura pastures above the forests, meeting no single human being, he fought with himself as only men with innate energy of soul know how to fight—bitterly, savagely, blindly. He did not stop to realise that he was somewhat in the position of a fly that strives to push from its appointed course the planet on which it rides through space. For the tides of life itself bore him upon their crest, and at thirty-five these tides are at the full.

Thus, gradually it was, then, as the hopelessness of the struggle became more and more apparent, that the door of the only alternative opened slightly and let him peer through. Once ajar, however, it seemed the same second wide open: he was through; and it was closed—behind him.

THE LOST VALLEY

For a different nature the alternative might have taken a different form. As has been seen, he was too strong a man to drift merely; a definite way out that could commend itself to a man of action had to be found; and, though the raw material of heroism may have been in him, he made no claim to a martyrdom that should last as long as life itself. And this alternative dawned upon him now as the grey light of a last morning must dawn upon the condemned prisoner: given Stephen, and given this particular problem, it was the only way out.

He envisaged it thus suddenly with a kind of ultimate calmness and determination that was characteristic of the man. And in every way it *was* characteristic of the man, for it involved the precise combination of courage and cowardice, weakness and strength, selfishness and sacrifice, that expressed the true resultant of all the forces at work in his soul. To him, at the moment of his rapid decision, however, it seemed that the dominant motive was the sacrifice to be offered upon the altar of his love for Mark. The twisted notion possessed him that in this way he might atone in some measure for the waning of his brotherly devotion. His love for the girl, her possible love for him—both were to be sacrificed to obtain the happiness—the eventual happiness—of these other two. Long ago Mark had himself said that under such circumstances one or other of them would have to—*go*. And the decision Stephen had come to was that the one to 'go' was—himself.

This day among the woods and mountains should be his last on earth. By the evening of the following day Mark should be free.

'I'll give my life for him.'

His face was grey set as he said it. He stood on the high ridge, bathed by sun and wind. He looked over the fair world of wooded vales and mountains at his feet, but his eyes, turned inwards, saw only his brother—and that sweet Eastern face—then darkness.

'He will understand—and perforce accept it—and with time, yes, with time, the new happiness shall fill his soul utterly—and hers. It is for her, too, that I give it. It *must*—under these unparalled circumstances be right ... !'

And although there was no single cloud in the sky, the landscape at his feet suddenly went dark and sunless from one horizon to the other.

X

Then, having come into the gloom of this terrible decision, his imaginative nature at once bounded to the opposite extreme, and a kind of exaltation possessed him. The stereotyped verdict of a coroner's jury might in this instance have been true. The prolonged stress of emotion under which he had so long been labouring had at last produced a condition of mind that could only be considered—unsound.

A cool wind swept his face as he let his tired eyes wander over the leagues of silent forest below. The blue Jura with its myriad folded valleys lay about him like waves of a giant sea ready to swallow up the little atom of his life within its deep heart of forgetfulness. Clear away into France he saw on the one side where, beyond the fortress of Pontarlier, white clouds sailed the horizon before a westerly wind; and, on the other, towards the white-robed Alps rising mistily through the haze of the autumn sunshine. Between these extreme distances lay all that world of a hundred intricate valleys, curiously winding, deeply wooded, little inhabited, a region of soft, confusing loveliness where a traveller might well lose himself for days together before he discovered a way out of so vast a maze.

And, as he gazed, there passed across his mind, like the dim memory of something heard in childhood, that legend of the 'Lost Valley' in which the souls of the unhappy dead find the deep peace that is denied to them by all the religions—and to which hundreds, who have not yet the sad right of entry, seek to find the mournful forest gates. The memory was vivid, but swiftly engulfed by others and forgotten. They chased each other in rapid succession across his mind, as clouds at sunset pass before a high wind, merging on the horizon in a common mass.

Then, slowly, at length, he turned and made his way down the mountain-side in the direction of the French frontier for a last journey upon the sweet surface of the world he loved. In his soul was the one dominant feeling: this singular exaltation arising from the knowledge that in the long run his great sacrifice must ensure the happiness of the two beings he loved more than all else in life.

At the solitary farm where an hour later he had his lunch of bread and cheese and milk, he learned that he had wandered many miles out of the routes with which he was more or less familiar. He had been walking faster than he knew all these hours of battle. A physical weariness came upon him that made him conscious of every muscle in his body as he realised what a long road over mountain and valley he had to retrace. But, with the heaviness of fatigue, ran still the sense of interior spiritual exaltation. Something in him walked on air with springs of steel—something that was independent of the dragging limbs and the aching back. For the rest, his sensation seemed numb. His great Decision stood black before him, blocking the way. Thoughts and feelings forsook him as rats leave a sinking ship. The time for these was past. Two overmatering desires, however, clung fast: one, to see Mark again, and be with him; the other, to be once more—with her. These two desires left no room for others. With the former, indeed, it was almost as though Mark had called aloud to him by name.

He stood a moment where the depth of the valley he had to thread lay like a twisting shadow at his feet; it ran, soft and dim, through the slanting sunshine. From the whole surface of the woods rose a single murmur; like the whirring of voices heard in a dream, he thought. The individual purring of separate trees was merged. Peace, most ancient and profound, lay in it, and its hushed whisper soothed his spirit.

He hurried his pace a little. The cool wind that had swept his face on the heights earlier in the afternoon followed him down, urging him forwards with deliberate pressure, as though a thousand soft hands were laid upon his back. And there were spirits in the wind that day. He heard their voices; and far below he traced by the motion of the tree-tops, where they coiled upwards to him through miles of forest. His way, meanwhile, dived down through dense growths of spruce and pine into a region unfamiliar. There was an aspect of the scenery that almost suggested it was unknown—an undiscovered corner of the world. The countless signs that mark the passage of humanity were absent, or at least did not obtrude themselves upon him. Something remote from life, alien, at any rate, to the normal life he had hitherto known, began to steal gently over his burdened soul. ...

In this way, perhaps, the effect of his dreadful Decision already showed its influence upon his mind and senses. So very soon now he would be—*going*!

The sadness of autumn lay all about him, and the loneliness of this secluded vale spoke to him of the melancholy of things that die—of vanished springs, of summers unfulfilled, of things for ever incomplete and unsatisfying. Human effort, he felt, this valley had never known. No hoofs had ever pressed the mossy turf of these forest clearings; no traffic of peasants or woodsmen won echoes from these limestone cliffs. All was hushed, lonely, deserted.

And yet——? The depths to which it apparently plunged astonished him more and more. Nowhere more than a half-mile across, each turn of the shadowy trail revealed new distances below. With spots of a haunting, fairy loveliness too: for here and there, on isolated patches of lawn-like grass, stood wild lilac bushes, rounded by the wind; willows from the swampy banks of the stream waved pale hands; firs, dark and erect, guarded their eternal secrets on the heights. In one little opening, standing all by itself, he found a lime-tree; while beyond it, shining among the pines, was a group of shimmering beeches. And, although there was no wild life, there were flowers; he saw clumps of them—tall, graceful, blue flowers whose name he did not know, nodding in dream across the foaming water of the little torrent.

And his thoughts ran incessantly to Mark. Never before had he been conscious of so imperious a desire to see him, to hear his voice, to stand at his side. At moments it almost obliterated that other great desire. ... Again he increased his pace. And the path plunged more and more deeply into the heart of the mountains, sinking ever into deeper silence, ever into an atmosphere of deeper peace. For no sound could reach him here without first passing along great distances that were cushioned with soft wind, and padded, as it were, with a million feathery pine-tops. A sense of peace that was beyond reach of all possible disturbance began to cover his breaking life with a garment as of softest shadows. Never before had he experienced anything approaching the wonder and completeness of it. It was a peace, still as the depths of the sea which are motionless because they *cannot* move—cannot even tremble. It was a peace unchangeable —what some have called, perhaps, the Peace of God. ...

'Soon the turn *must* come,' he thought, yet without a trace of impatience or alarm, 'and the road wind upwards again to cross the last ridge!' But he cared little enough; for this enveloping peace drowned him, hiding even the fear of death.

And still the road sank downwards into the sleep-laden atmosphere of the crowding trees, and with it his thoughts, oddly enough, sank deeper and deeper into dim recesses of his own being. As though a secret sympathy lay between the path that dived and the thoughts that plunged. Only, from time to time, the thought of his brother Mark brought him back to the surface with a violent rush. Dreadfully, in those moments, he wanted him—to feel his warm, strong hand within his own— to ask his forgiveness—perhaps, too, to grant his own... he hardly knew.

'But is there no end to this delicious valley?' he wondered, with something between vagueness and confusion in his mind. 'Does it never stop, and the path climb again to the mountains beyond?' Drowsily, divorced from any positive interest, the question passed through his thoughts. Underfoot the grass already grew thickly enough to muffle the sound of his footsteps. The trail even had vanished, swallowed by moss. His feet sank in.

'I wish Mark were with me now—to see and feel all this——'

He stopped short and looked keenly about him for a moment, leaving the thought incomplete. A deep sighing, instantly caught by the wind and merged in the soughing of the trees, had sounded close beside him. Was it perhaps himself that sighed—unconsciously? His heart was surely charged enough!...

A faint smile played over his lips—instantly frozen, however, as another sigh, more distinct than the first, and quite obviously external to himself, passed him closely in the darkening air. More like deep breathing, though, it was, than sighing. ... It was nothing but the wind, of course. Stephen hurried on again, not surprised that he had been so easily deceived, for this valley was full of sighings and breathings—of trees and wind. It ventured upon no louder noise. Noise of any kind, indeed, seemed impossible and forbidden in this muted vale. And so deeply had he descended now, that the sunshine, silver rather than golden, already streamed past far over his head along the ridges, and no gleam found its way to where he was. The shadows, too, no longer blue and purple, had changed to black, as though woven of some delicate substance that had definite thickness, like a veil. Across the opposite slope, one of the mountain summits in the western sky already dropped its monstrous shadow fringed with pines. The day was rapidly drawing in.

XI

And here, very gradually, there began to dawn upon his overwrought mind certain curious things. They pierced clean though the mingled gloom and exaltation that characterised his mood. And they made the skin upon his back a little to—stir and crawl.

For he now became distinctly aware that the emptiness of this lonely valley was only apparent. It is impossible to say through what sense, or combination of senses, this singular certainty was brought to him that the valley was not really as forsaken and deserted as it seemed—that, on the contrary, is was the very reverse. It came to him suddenly—as a certainty. The valley as a matter of fact was—full. Packed, thronged and crowded it was to the very brim of its mighty wooded walls—with life. It was now borne in upon him, with an inner conviction that left no room for doubt, that on all sides living things—persons—were jostling him, rubbing elbows, watching all his movements, and only waiting till the darkness came to reveal themselves.

Moreover, with this eerie discovery came also the further knowledge that a vast multitude of others, again, with pallid faces and yearning eyes, with arms outstretched and groping feet, were searching everywhere for the way of entrance that he himself had found so easily. All about him, he felt, were people by the hundred, by the thousand, seeking with a kind of restless fever for the narrow trail that led down into the valley, longing with an intensity that beat upon his soul in a million waves, for the rest, the calm silence of the place—but most of all for its strange, deep, and unalterable peace.

He, alone of all these, had found the Entrance; he, *and one other*.

For out of his singular conviction grew another even more singular: his brother Mark was also somewhere in this valley with him. Mark, too, was wandering like himself in and out among its intricate dim turns. He had said but a short time ago, 'I wish Mark were here!' Mark *was* here. And it was precisely then—while he stood still a moment, trying to face these overwhelming obsessions and deal with them—that the figure of a man, moving swiftly through the trees, passed him with a great gliding stride, and with averted face. Stephen started horribly, catching his breath. In an instant the man was gone again, swallowed up by the crowding pines.

With a quick movement of pursuit and a cry that should make the man turn, he sprang forward—but stopped again almost the same moment, realising that the extraordinary speed at which the man had shot past him rendered pursuit out of the question. He had been going downhill into the valley; by this time he was already far, far ahead. But in that momentary glimpse of him he had seen enough to know. The face was turned away, and the shadows under the trees were heavy, but the figure was beyond question the figure of—his brother Mark.

It was his brother, yet not his brother. It was Mark—but Mark altered. And the alteration was in some way—awful; just as the silent speed at which he had moved—the impossible speed in so dense a forest—was likewise awful. Then, still shaking inwardly with the suddenness of it all, Stephen realised that when he called aloud he had uttered certain definite words. And these words now came back to him—

'Mark. Mark! Don't go yet! Don't go—without me!'

Before, however, he could act, a most curious and unaccountable sensation of deadly faintness and pain came upon him, without cause, without explanation, so that he dropped backwards in momentary collapse, and but for the closeness of the tree stems would have fallen full length to the ground. From the centre of the heart it came, spreading thence throughout his whole being like a swift and dreadful fever. All the muscles of his body relaxed; icy perspiration burst forth upon his skin; the pulses of life seemed suddenly reduced to the threshold beyond which they stop. There was a thick, rushing sound in his ears and his mind went utterly blank.

There were the sensations of death by suffocation. He knew this as certainly as though another doctor stood by his side and labelled each spasm, explained each successive sinking of the vital flame. He was passing through the last throes of a dying man. And then into his mind, thus deliberately left blank, rushed at lightning speed a whole series of the pictures of his past life. Even while his breath failed, he saw his thirty-five years pictorially, successively, yet in some queer fashion *at once*, pass through the lighted chambers of his brain. In this way, it is said, they pass through the brain of a drowning man during the last second before death.

Childhood rose about him with its scenes, figures, voices; the

THE LOST VALLEY

Kentish lawns where he had played with Mark in stained overalls, the summer-house where they had tea, the hay-fields where they romped. The scent of lime and walnut, of garden pinks and roses by the tumbled rockery came back to his nostrils... He heard the voices of grown-ups in the distance... faint barking of dogs... the carriage wheels upon the gravel drive... and then the sharp summons from the opened window—'Time to come in now! Time to come in!' ...

Time to come in now. It all drove before him as of yesterday on the scented winds of childhood's summer days... He heard his brother's voice—dreadfully faint and far away—calling him by name in the shrill accents of the boy: 'Stevie—I say, you *might* shut up... and play properly...'

And then followed the panorama of the thirty years, all the chief events drawn in steel-like lines of white and black, vivid in sunshine, alive—right down to the present moment with the portentous dark shadow of his terrible Decision closing the series like a cloud.

Yes, like a smothering black cloud that blocked the way. There was nothing visible beyond it. There, for him, life ceased——

Only, as he gazed with inward-turned eyes that could not close even if they would, he saw to his amazement that the black cloud suddenly opened, and into a space of clear light there swam the vision, radiant as morning, of that dark young Eastern face—the face that held for him all the beauty in the world. The eyes instantly found his own, and smiled. Behind her, moreover, and beyond, before the moving vapours closed upon it, he saw a long vista of brilliance, crowded with pictures he could but half discern—as though, in spite of himself and his Decision, life continued—as though, too, it *continued with her.*

And instantly, with the sight and thought of her, the consuming faintness passed; strength returned to his body with the glow of life; the pain went; the pictures vanished; the cloud was no more. In his blood the pulses of life once again beat strong, and the blackness left his soul. The smile of those beloved eyes had been charged with the invitation to live. Although his determination remained unshaken, there shone behind it the joy of this potent magic: life with her...

With a strong effort, at length he recovered himself and continued on his way. More or less familiar, of course, with the psychology of vision, he dimly understood that his experiences had been in some measure subjective—within himself. To find the line of demarcation, however, was beyond him. That Mark had wandered out to fight his own battle upon the mountains, and so come into this same valley, was well within the bounds of coincidence. But the nameless and dreadful alteration discerned in that swift moment of his passing—that remained inexplicable. Only he no longer thought about it. The glory of that sweet vision had bewildered him beyond any possibility of reason or analysis.

His watch told him that the hour was past five o'clock—ten minutes past, to be exact. He still had several hours before reaching the country he was familiar with nearer home. Following the trail at an increased pace, he presently saw patches of meadow glimmering between the thinning trees, and knew that the bottom of the valley was at last in sight.

'And Mark, God bless him, is down there too—somewhere!' he exclaimed aloud. 'I shall surely find him.' For, strange to say, nothing could have persuaded him that his twin was not wandering among the shadows of this peaceful and haunted valley with himself, and—that he would shortly find him.

XII

And a few minutes later he passed from the forest as through an open door and found himself before a farmhouse standing in a patch of bright green meadow against the mountain-side. He was in need both of food and information.

The chalet, less lumbering and picturesque than those found in the Alps, had, nevertheless, the appearance of being exceedingly ancient. It was not toy-like—as the Jura chalets sometimes are.

Solidly built, its balcony and overhanging roof supported by immense beams of deeply stained wood, it stood so that the back walls merged into the mountain slope behind, and the arms of pine, spruce and fir seemed stretched out to include it among their shadows. A last ray of sunshine, dipping between two far summits overhead, touched it with pale gold, bringing out the rich beauty of the heavily-dyed beams. Though no one was visible at the moment, and no smoke rose from the shingled chimney, it had the appearance of being occupied, and Stephen approached it with the caution due to the first evidence of humanity he had come across since he entered the valley.

Under the shadow of the broad balcony roof he noticed that the door, like that of a stable, was in two parts, and, wondering rather to find it closed, he knocked firmly upon the upper half. Under the pressure of a second knock this upper half yielded slightly, though without opening. The lower half, however, evidently barred and bolted, remained unmoved.

The third time he knocked with more force than he intended, and the knock sounded loud and clamorous as a summons. From within, as though great spaces stretched beyond, came a murmur of voices, faint and muffled, and then almost immediately—the footsteps of some one coming softly up to open.

But, instead of the heavy brown door opening, there came a voice. He heard it, petrified with amazement. For it was a voice he knew—hushed, soft, lingering. His heart, hammering atrociously, seemed to leave its place, and cut his breath away.

'Stephen!' it murmured, calling him by name, 'what are *you* doing here so soon? And what is it that you want?'

The knowledge that only this dark door separated him from her, at first bereft him of all power of speech or movement; and the possible significance of her words escaped him. Through the sweet confusion that turned his spirit faint he only remembered, flash-like, that she and her father were indeed to have left the hotel that very morning. After that his thought stopped dead.

Then, also flash-like, swept back upon him the memory of the figure that had passed him with averted face—and, with it, the clear conviction that at this moment Mark, too, was somewhere in this very valley, even close beside him. More: Mark was in this chalet—with her.

The torrent of speech that instantly crowded to his lips was almost too thick for utterance.

'Open, open, open!' was all he heard intelligibly from the throng of words that poured out. He raised his hands to push and force; but her reply again stopped him.

'Even if I open—you may not enter yet,' came the whisper through the door. And this time he could almost have sworn that it sounded within himself rather than without.

'I must enter,' he cried. 'Open to me, I say!'

'But you are trembling——'

'Open to me, O my life! Open to me!'

'But your heart—it is shaking.'

'Because you—you are so near,' came in passionate, stammering tones. 'Because you stand there beside me!' And then, before she could answer, or his will control the words, he had added: 'And because Mark—my brother—is in there—with you——'

'Hush, hush!' came the soft, astonishing reply. 'He is in here, true; but he is not with me. And it is for my sake that he has come—for my sake and for yours. My soul, alas! has led him to the gates...'

But Stephen's emotions had reached the breaking-point, and the necessity for action was upon him like a storm. He drew back a pace so as to fling himself better against the closed door, when to his utter surprise, it moved. The upper half swung slowly outwards, and he—saw.

He was aware of a vast room, with closely shuttered windows, that seemed to stretch beyond the walls into the wooded mountainside, thronged with moving figures, like forms of life gently gliding to and fro in some huge darkened tank; and there, framed against this opening—the girl herself. She stood, visible to the waist, radiant in the solitary beam of sunshine that reached the chalet, smiling down wondrously into his face with the same exquisite beauty in her eyes that he had seen before in the vision of the cloud: with, too, that supreme invitation in them—the invitation to live.

The loveliness blinded him. He could see the down upon her little dark cheeks where the sunlight kissed them; there was the cloud of hair upon her neck where his lips had lain; there, too, the dear, slight breast that not twenty-four hours ago had known the pressure of his arms. And, once again, driven forward by the love that triumphed over all obstacles, real or artificial, he advanced headlong with outstretched arms to take her.

'Katýa!' he cried, never thinking how passing strange it was that he knew her name at all, much more the endearing and shortened form of it. 'Katýa!'

But the young girl held up her little brown hand against him with a gesture that was more strong to restrain than any number of bolted doors.

'Not here,' she murmured, with her grave smile, while behind the words he caught in that darkened room the alternate hush and sighing as of a thousand sleepers. 'Not here! You cannot see him now; for these are the Reception Halls of Death and here I stand in the Vestibule of the Beyond. Our way... your way and mine... lies farther yet... traced there since the beginning of the world... together...'

In quaintly broken English it was spoken, but his mind remembers the singular words in their more perfect form. Even this, however, came later. At the moment he only felt the twofold wave of love surge through him with a tide of power that threatened to break him asunder: he *must* hold her to his heart; he *must* come instantly to his brother's side, meet his eyes, have speech with him. The desire to enter that great darkened room and force a path through the dimly gliding forms to his brother became irresistible, while tearing upon its heels came like a fever of joy the meaning of the words she had just uttered, and especially of that last word: '*Together!*'

Then, for an instant, all the forces in his being turned negative so that his will refused to act. The excess of feeling numbed him.

A flying interval of knowledge, calm and certain, came to him. The exaltation of spirit which produced the picture of all this spiritual clairvoyance moved a stage higher, and he realised that he witnessed an order of things pertaining to the world of eternal causes rather than of temporary effects. Some one had lifted the Veil.

With a feeling that he could only wait and let things take their extraordinary course, he stood still. For an instant, even less, he must have hidden his eyes in his hand, for when, a moment later, he again looked up, he saw that the half of the swinging door which had been open, was now closed. He stood alone upon the balcony. And the sunshine had faded entirely from the scene.

It was here, it seems, that the last vestige of self-control disappeared. He flung himself against the door; and the door met his assault like a wall of solid rock. Crying aloud alternately the names of his two loved ones, he turned, scarcely knowing what he did, and ran into the meadow. Dusk was about the chalet, drawing the encircling forests closer. Soon the true darkness would stalk down the slopes. The walls of the valley reached, it seemed, up to heaven.

Still calling, he ran about the walls, searching wildly for a way of entrance, his mind charged with bewildering fragments of what he had heard: 'The Reception Halls of Death'—'The Vestibule of the Beyond'—'You cannot see him now'—'Our way lies farther—*and together*!'

And, on the far side of the chalet, by the corner that touched the trees, he suddenly stopped, feeling his gaze drawn upwards, and there, pressed close against the window-pane of an upper room, saw that some one was peering down upon him.

With a sensation of freezing terror he realised that he was staring straight into the eyes of his brother Mark. Bent a little forward with the effort to look down, the face, pale and motionless, gazed into his own, but without the least sign of recognition. Not a feature moved: and although but a few feet separated the brothers, the face wore the dim, misty appearance of great distance. It was like the face of a man called suddenly from deep sleep—dazed, perplexed; nay, more—frightened and horribly distraught.

What Stephen read upon it, however, in that first moment of sight, was the signature of the great, eternal question men have asked since the beginning of time, yet never heard the answer. And into the heart of the twin the pain of it plunged like a sword.

'Mark!' he stammered, in that low voice the valley seemed to exact; 'Mark! Is that really *you*?' Tears swam already in his eyes, and yearning in a flood choked his utterance.

And Mark, with a dreadful, steady stare that still held no touch of recognition, gazed down upon him from the closed window of that upper chamber, motionless, unblinking as an image of stone. It was almost like an imitation figure of himself—only with the effect of some added alteration. For alteration certainly there was —awful and unknown alteration—though Stephen was utterly unable to detect wherein it lay. And he remembered how the figure had passed him in the woods with averted face.

He made then, it seems, some violent sign or other, in response to which his brother at last moved—slowly opening the window. He leaned forward, stooping with lowered head and shoulders over the sill, while Stephen ran up against the wall beneath and craned up towards him. The two faces drew close; their eyes met clean and straight. Then the lips of Mark moved, and the distraught look half vanished within the borders of a little smile of puzzled and affectionate wonder.

'Stevie, old fellow,' issued a tiny, far-away voice; 'but where are you? I see you—so dimly?'

It was like a voice crying faintly down half-a-mile of distance. He shuddered to hear it.

'I'm here, Mark—close to you,' he whispered.

'I hear your voice, I feel your presence,' came the reply like a man talking in his sleep, 'but I see you—as through a glass darkly. And I want to see you all clear, and close——'

'But *you*! Where are *you*?' interrupted Stephen, with anguish.

'Alone; quite alone—over here. And it's cold, oh, so cold!' The words came gently, half veiling a complaint. The wind caught them and ran round the walls towards the forest, wailing as it went.

'But how did you come, how did you come?' Stephen raised himself on tiptoe to catch the answer. But there was no answer. The face receded a little, and as it did so the wind, passing up the walls again, stirred the hair on the forehead. Stephen saw it move. He thought, too, the head moved with it, shaking slightly to and fro.

'Oh, but tell me, my dear, dear brother! Tell me——!' he cried, sweating horribly, his limbs shaking.

Mark made a curious gesture, withdrawing at the same time a little farther into the room behind, so that he now stood upright, half shadow by the window. The alteration in him proclaimed itself more plainly, though still without betraying its exact nature. There was something about him that was terrible. And the air that came from the open window upon Stephen was so freezing that it seemed to turn the perspiration on his face into ice.

'I do not know; I do not remember,' he heard the tiny voice inside the room, ever withdrawing. 'Besides—I may not speak with you—yet; it is so difficult—and it hurts.'

Stephen stretched out his body, the arms scraping the wooden walls above his head, trying to climb the smooth and slippery surface.

'For the love of God!' he cried with passion, 'tell me what it all means and what you are doing here—you and—and—oh, and *all three of us*?' The words rang out through the silent valley.

But the other stood there motionless again by the window, his face distraught and dazed as though the effort of speech had already been too much for him. His image had begun to fade a little. He seemed, without moving, yet to be retreating into some sort of interior distance. Presently, it seemed, he would disappear altogether.

'I don't know,' came the voice at length, fainter than before, half muffled. 'I have been asleep, I think. I have just waked up, and come across from somewhere else—where we were all together, you and I and—and——'

Like his brother, he was unable to speak the name. He ended the sentence a moment later in a whisper that was only just audible. 'But I cannot tell you *how* I came,' he said, 'for I do not know the words.'

Stephen, then, with a violent leap tried to reach the window-sill and pull himself up. The distance was too great, however, and he fell back upon the grass, only just keeping his feet.

'I'm coming in to you,' he cried out very loud. 'Wait there for me! For the love of heaven, wait till I come to you. I'll break the doors in——!'

Once again Mark made that singular gesture; again he seemed to recede a little farther into a kind of veiled perspective that caused his appearance to fade still more; and, from an incredible distance—a distance that somehow conveyed an idea of appalling height—his thin, tiny voice floated down upon his brother from the fading lips of shadow.

'Old fellow, don't you come! You are not ready—and it is too cold here. I shall wait, Stevie, I shall wait for you. Later —I mean farther from here—we shall one day all three be together. ... Only you cannot understand now. I am here for your sake, old fellow, and for hers. She loves us both, but... it is... you ... she loves... the best...'

The whispering voice rose suddenly on these last words into a long high cry that the wind instantly caught away and buried far in the smothering silences of the woods. For, at the same moment, Mark had come with a swift rush back to the window, had leaned out and stretched both hands towards his brother underneath. And his face had cleared and smiled. Caught within that smile, the awful change in him had vanished.

Stephen turned and made a mad rush round the chalet to find the door he would batter in with his hands and feet and body. He searched in vain, however, for in the shadows the supporting beams of the building were indistinguishable from the stems of the trees behind; the roof sank away, blotted out by the gloom of the branches, and the darkness now wove forest, sky and mountain into a uniform black sheet against which no item was separately visible.

There was no chalet any longer. He was simply battering with bruised hands and feet upon the solid trunks of pines and spruces in his path; which he continued to do, calling ever aloud for Mark, until finally he grew dizzy with exhaustion and fell to the ground in a state of semi-consciousness.

And for the best part of half-an-hour he lay there motionless upon the moss, while the vast hands of Night drew the cloak of her softest darkness over valley and mountain, covering his small body with as much care as she covered the sky, the hemisphere, and all those leagues of velvet forest.

XIII

It was long before he came to himself again—shivering with cold, for the perspiration had dried upon him where he lay. He got up and ran. The night was now fairly down, and the keen air stung his cheeks. But, with a sure instinct not to be denied, he took the direction of home.

He travelled at an extraordinary pace, considering the thickness of the trees and the darkness. How he got out of the valley he does not remember; nor how he found his way over the intervening ridges that lay between him and the country he knew. At the back of his mind crashed and tumbled the loose fragments of all he had seen and heard, forming as yet no coherent pattern. For himself, indeed, the details were of small interest. He was a man under sentence of death. His determination, in spite of everything, remained unshaken. In a few short hours he would be gone.

Yet, with the habit of the professional mind, he tried a little to sort out things. During that state of singular exaltation, for instance, he understood vaguely that his deep longings had somehow translated themselves into act and scene. For these longings were life; his decision negatived them; hence, they dramatized themselves pictorially with what vividness his imagination allowed.

They were dramatised inventions, singularly elaborate, of the emotions that burned so fiercely within. All were projections of his consciousness, maimed and incomplete, masquerading as persons before his inner vision. It began with the singular sensations of death by drowning he had experienced. From that moment the other forces at work in the problem had taken their cue and played their part more or less convincingly, according to their strength...

He thought and argued a great deal as he hurried homewards through the night. But all the time he knew that it was untrue. He had no real explanation at all!

From the high ridges, cold and bleak under the stars, swept by the free wind of night, he ran almost the entire way. It was downhill. And during that violet descent of nearly an hour the details of his 'going' shaped themselves. Until then he had formed no definite plans. Now he settled everything. He chose the very pool where the water coiled and bubbled as in a cauldron just where the little torrent made a turn above their house; he decided upon the very terms of the letter he would leave behind. He would put it on the kitchen table so that they should know where to find him.

He urged his pace tremendously, for the idea that his brother would have left—that he would find him gone—haunted him. It grew, doubtless, out of that singular, detailed vision that had come upon him in his great weakness in the valley. He was terrified that he would not see his brother again—that he had already gone deliberately—after her...

'I *must* see Mark once more. I *must* get home before he leaves!' flashed the strong thought continually in his mind, making him run like a deer down the winding trail.

It was after ten o'clock when he reached the little clearing behind the chalet, panting with exhaustion, blinded with perspiration. There was no light visible; all the windows were dark; but presently he made out a figure moving to and fro below the balcony. It was *not* Mark—he saw that in a flash. It moved oddly. A sound of moaning reached him at the same time. And then he saw that it was the figure of the peasant woman who cooked for them, Marie Petavel.

And the instant he saw who it was, and heard her moaning, he knew what had happened. Mark had left a letter to explain— and gone: gone after the girl. His heart sank into death.

The woman came forward heavily through the darkness, the dew-drenched grass swishing audibly against her skirts. And the words he heard were precisely what he had expected to hear, though patois and excitement rendered them difficult—

'Your brother—oh, your poor brother, Monsieur le Docteur— he—has gone!'

And then he saw the piece of white paper glimmering in her hands as she stood quite close. He took it mechanically from her. It was the letter Mark had left behind to explain.

But before Stephen had time to read it, a man with a lantern came out of the barn that stood behind the house. It was her husband. He came slowly towards them.

'We searched for you, oh, we searched,' he said in a thick voice, 'my son went as far as Buttes even, and hasn't come back yet. You've been long, too long away——'

He stopped short and glanced down at his wife, telling her roughly to cease her stupid weeping. Stephen, shaking inwardly, with an icy terror in his blood, began to feel that things were not precisely as he had anticipated. Something else was the matter. The expression in the face of the peasant as the lantern's glare fell upon it came to him suddenly with the shock of a revelation.

'You have told monsieur—all?' the man whispered, stooping to his wife. She shook her head; and her husband led the way without another word. The interval of a few seconds seemed endless to Stephen; he was trembling all over like a man with the ague. Behind them the old woman floundered through the wet grass, moaning to herself.

'No one would have believed it could have happened—anything of *that* sort,' the man mumbled. The lantern was unsteady in his hand. The next minute the barn, like some monstrous animal, rose against the stars, and the huge wooden doors gaped wide before them.

The peasant, uncovering his head, went first, and Stephen, following with stumbling footsteps, saw the shadows of the beams and posts shift across the boarded floor. Against the wall, whither the man led, was a small littered heap of hay, and upon this, covered by a white sheet, was stretched a human body. The peasant drew back the sheet gently with his heavy brown hand, stooping close over it so that the lantern threw its light full upon the act.

And Stephen, stumbling forward, scarcely knowing what he did, without further warning or preparation, looked down upon the face of his brother Mark. The eyes stared fixedly into nothing; the features wore the distraught expression he had seen upon them a few hours before through the window-pane of that upper chamber.

'We found him in that deep pool just where the stream makes the quick turn above the house,' the peasant whispered. 'He left a bit of paper on the kitchen table to say where he would be. It was after dark when we got there. His watch had stopped, though, long before——' He muttered on unintelligibly.

Stephen looked up at the man, unable to utter a word, and the man replied to the unspoken question—

'At ten minutes past five the watch had stopped,' he said. 'That was when the water reached it.'

By the flicker of the lantern, then, sitting beside that still figure covered with the sheet, Stephen read the letter Mark had left for him—

'Stevie, old fellow, one of us, you know, has got to—go; and it is better, I think, that it should not be you. I know all you have been through, for I have fought and suffered every step with you. I have been along the same path, loving her too much for you, and you too much for her. And I leave her to you, boy, because I am convinced she now loves you even as she first believed she loved me. But all that evening she cried incessantly for you. More I cannot explain to you now; she will do that. And she need never know more than that I have withdrawn in your favour: she need never know *how*. Perhaps, one day, when there is no marriage or giving in marriage, we may all three be together, and happy. I have often wondered, as you know...'

The remainder of the sentence was scratched out and illegible.

'...And, if it be possible, old fellow, of course *I shall wait*.'

Then came more words blackened out.

'...I am now going, within a few minutes of writing this last word to you of blessing and forgiveness (for I know you will want that, although there is nothing, *nothing* to forgive!)—going down into that Lost Valley her father told us about—the Valley hidden among these mountains we love—the Lost Valley where even the unhappy dead find peace. There I shall wait for you both.—Mark.'

* * * *

Several weeks later, before he took the train eastwards, Stephen retraced his steps to the farmhouse where he had bought milk and asked for directions. Thence for some distance he followed the path he well remembered. At a point, however, the confusion of the woods grew strangely upon him. The mountains, true to the map, were not true to his recollections. The trail stopped; high, unknown ridges intervened; and no such deep and winding valley as he had travelled that afternoon for so many hours was anywhere to be found. The map, the peasants, the very configuration of the landscape even, denied its existence.

Part Two
Tales of the Mysterious and Macabre

CONTENTS					PAGE

Chinese Magic				429
First Hate					452
The Olive					463
The Sacrifice				475
The Damned				501
Wayfarers					587
The Sea Fit					609
The Attic					624
The Heath Fire				631
The Return					640
The Transfer				646
Clairvoyance				658
The Golden Fly				664
Special Delivery				670
The Destruction of Smith		681
The Tryst					689
The Wings of Horus			702
Initiation					725
A Desert Episode				751
Transition					767
The Other Wing				774

CHINESE MAGIC

Dr. Owen Francis felt a sudden wave of pleasure and admiration sweep over him as he saw her enter the room. He was in the act of going out; in fact, he had already said good-bye to his hostess, glad to make his escape from the chattering throng, when the tall and graceful young woman glided past him. Her carriage was superb; she had black eyes with a twinkling happiness in them; her mouth was exquisite. Round her neck, in spite of the warm afternoon, she wore a soft thing of fur or feathers; and as she brushed by to shake the hand he had just shaken himself, the tail of this touched his very cheek. Their eyes met fair and square. He felt as though her eyes also touched him.

Changing his mind, he lingered another ten minutes, chatting with various ladies he did not in the least remember, but who remembered him. He did not, of course, desire to exchange banalities with these other ladies, yet did so gallantly enough. If they found him absent-minded, they excused him since he was the famous mental specialist whom everybody was proud to know. And all the time his eyes never left the tall graceful figure that allured him almost to the point of casting a spell upon him.

His first impression deepened as he watched. He was aware of excitement, curiosity, longing; there was a touch even of exaltation in him; yet he took no steps to seek the introduction which was easily enough procurable. He checked himself, if with an effort. Several times their eyes met across the crowded room; he dared to believe—he felt instinctively—that his interest was returned. Indeed, it was more than instinct, for she was certainly aware of his presence, and he even caught her indicating him to a woman she spoke with, and evidently asking who he was. Once he half bowed, and once, in spite of himself, he went so far as to smile, and there came, he was sure, a faint, delicious brightening of the eyes in answer.

There was he fancied, a look of yearning in the face. The young woman charmed him inexpressibly; the very way she moved delighted him. Yet at last he slipped out the room without a word, without an introduction, without even knowing her name. He chose his moment when her back was turned. It was characteristic of him.

For Owen Francis had ever regarded marriage, for himself at least, as a disaster that could be avoided. He was in love with his work, and his work was necessary to humanity. Others might perpetuate the race, but he must heal it. He had come to regard love as the bait wherewith Nature lays her trap to fulfil her own ends. A man in love was a man enjoying a delusion, a deluded man. In his case, and he was nearing forty-five, the theory had worked admirably, and the dangerous exception that proved it had as yet not troubled him.

'It's come at last—I do believe,' he thought to himself, as he walked home, a new tumultuous emotion in his blood; 'the exception, quite possibly, has come at last. I wonder....'

And it seemed he said it to the tall graceful figure by his side, who turned up dark eyes smilingly to meet his own, and whose lips repeated softly his last two words 'I wonder....'

The experience, being new to him, was baffling. A part of his nature, long dormant, received the authentic thrill that pertains actually to youth. He was a man of chaste, abstemious custom. The reaction was vehement. That dormant part of him became obstreperous. He thought of his age, his appearance, his prospects; he looked thirty-eight, he was not unhandsome, his position was secure, even remarkable. That gorgeous young woman—he called her gorgeous—haunted him. Never could he forget that face, those eyes. It was extraordinary—he had left her there unspoken to, unknown, when an introduction would have been the simplest thing in the world.

'But it still is,' he reflected. And the reflection filled his being with a flood of joy.

He checked himself again. Not so easily is established habit routed. He felt instinctively that, at last, he had met his mate; if he followed it up, he was a man in love, a lost man enjoying a delusion, a deluded man. But the way she had looked at him! That air of intuitive invitation which not even the sweetest modesty could conceal! He felt an immense confidence in himself; also he felt oddly sure of her.

The presence of that following figure, already precious, came with him into his house, even into his study at the back where he sat over a number of letters by the open window. The pathetic little London garden showed its pitiful patch. The lilac had faded, but a smell of roses entered. The sun was just behind the buildings opposite, and the garden lay soft and warm in summer shadows.

He read and tossed aside the letters; one only interested him, from Edward Farque, whose journey to China had interrupted a friendship of long standing. Edward Farque's work on Eastern art and philosophy, on Chinese painting and Chinese thought in particular, had made its mark. He was an authority. He was to be back about this time, and his friend smiled with pleasure. ' "Dear old unpractical dreamer," as I used to call him,' he mused. 'He's a success, anyhow!' And as he mused the presence that sat beside him came a little closer, yet at the same time faded. Not that he forgot her—that was impossible—but that just before opening the letter from his friend he had come to a decision. He had definitely made up his mind to seek acquaintance. The reality replaced the remembered substitute.

'As the newspapers may have warned you' [ran the familiar and kinky writing], 'I am back in England after what the scribes term my ten years of exile in Cathay. I have taken a little house in Hampstead for six months, and am just settling in. Come to us to-morrow night and let me prove it to you. Come to dinner. We shall have much to say; we both are ten years wiser. You know how glad I shall be to see my old-time critic and disparager, but let me add frankly that I want to ask you a few professional, or, rather, technical, questions. So prepare yourself to come as doctor and as friend. I am writing, as the papers said truthfully, a treatise on Chinese thought. But—don't shy!—it is about Chinese Magic that I want your technical advice' [the last two words were substituted for "professional wisdom", which had been crossed out] 'and the benefit of your vast experience. So come, old friend, come quickly, and come hungry! I'll feed your body as you shall feed my mind.

Yours,
Edward Farque

'P.S.—The coming of a friend from a far-off land—is not this true joy?'

Dr. Francis laid down the letter with a pleased anticipatory chuckle, and it was the touch in the final sentence that amused him. In spite of being an authority, Farque was clearly the same fanciful, poetic dreamer as of old. He quoted Confucius as in other days. The firm but kinky writing had not altered either. The only sign of novelty he noticed was the use of scented paper, for a faint and pungent aroma clung to the big quarto sheet.

'A Chinese habit, doubtless,' he decided, sniffing it with a puzzled air of disapproval. Yet it had nothing in common with the scented sachets some ladies use too lavishly, so that even the air of the street is polluted by their passing for a dozen yards. He was familiar with every kind of perfumed note-paper used in London, Paris, and Constantinople. This one was different. It was delicate and penetrating for all its faintness, pleasurable too. He rather liked it, and while annoyed that he could not name it, he sniffed at the letter several times, as though it were a flower.

'I'll go,' he decided at once, and wrote an acceptance then and there. He went out and posted it. He meant to prolong his walk into the Park, taking his chief preoccupation, the face, the eyes, the figure, with him. Already he was composing the note of inquiry to Mrs. Malleson, his hostess of the tea-party, the note whose willing answer should give him the name, the address, the means of introduction he had now deteremined to secure. He visualized that note of inquiry, seeing it in his mind's eye; only, for some odd reason, he saw the kinky writing of Farque instead of his own more elegant script. Association of ideas and emotions readily explained this. Two new and unexpected interests had entered his life on the same day, and within half an hour of each other. What he could not so readily explain, however, was that two words in his friend's ridiculous letter, and in that kinky writing, stood out sharply from the rest. As he slipped his envelope into the mouth of the red pillar-box they shone vividly in his mind. These two words were 'Chinese Magic.'

II

It was the warmth of his friend's invitation as much as his own state of inward excitement that decided him suddenly to anticipate his visit by twenty-four hours. It would clear his judgment and help his mind if he spent the evening at Hampstead rather than alone with his own thoughts. 'A dose of China,' he thought, with a smile, 'will do me good. Edward won't mind. I'll telephone.'

He left the Park soon after six o'clock and acted upon his impulse. The connexion was bad, the wire buzzed and popped and crackled; talk was difficult; he did not hear properly. The Professor had not yet come in, apparently. Francis said he would come up anyhow on the chance.

'Velly pleased,' said the voice in his ear, as he rang off.

Going into his study, he drafted the note that should result in the introduction that was now, it appeared, the chief object of his life. The way this woman with the black, twinkling eyes obsessed him was—he admitted it with joy—extraordinary. The draft he put in his pocket, intending to rewrite it next morning, and all the way up to Hampstead Heath the gracious figure glided silently beside him, the eyes were ever present, his cheek still glowed where the feather boa had touched his skin. Edward Farque remained in the background. In fact, it was on the very door-step, having rung the bell, that Francis realised he must pull himself together. 'I've come to see old Farque,' he reminded himself, with a smile. 'I've got to be interested in him and his, and, probably, for an hour or two, to talk Chinese——' when the door opened noiselessly, and he saw facing him, with a grin of celestial welcome on his yellow face, a Chinaman.

'Oh!' he said, with a start. He had not expected a Chinese servant.

'Velly pleased,' the man bowed him in.

Dr Francis stared round him with astonishment he could not conceal. A great golden idol faced him in the hall, its gleaming visage blazing out of a sort of miniature golden palanquin, with a grin, half dignified, half cruel. Fully double human size, it blocked the way, looking so life-like that it might have moved to meet him without too great a shock to what seemed possible. It rested on a throne with four massive legs, carved, the doctor saw, with serpents, dragons, and mythical monsters generally. Round it on every side were other things in keeping. Name them he could not, describe them he did not try. He summed them up in one word—China: pictures, weapons, cloths and tapestries, bells, gongs, and figures of every sort and kind imaginable.

Being ignorant of Chinese matters, Dr. Francis stood and looked about him in a mental state of some confusion. He had the feeling that he had entered a Chinese temple, for there was a faint smell of incense hanging about the house that was, to say the least, un-English. Nothing English, in fact, was visible at all. The matting on the floor, the swinging curtains of bamboo beads that replaced the customary doors, the silk draperies and pictured cushions, the bronze and ivory, the screens hung with fantastic embroideries, everything was Chinese. Hampstead vanished from his thoughts. The very lamps were in keeping, the ancient lacquered furniture as well. The value of what he saw, an expert could have told him, was considerable.

'You likee?' queried the voice at his side.

He had forgotten the servant. He turned sharply.

'Very much; it's wonderfully done,' he said. 'Makes you feel at home, John, eh?' he added tactfully, with a smile, and was going to ask how long all this preparation had taken, when a voice sounded on the stairs beyond. It was a voice he knew, a note of hearty welcome in its deep tones.

'The coming of a friend from a far-off land, even from Harley Street—is not this true joy?' he heard, and the next minute was shaking the hand of his old and valued friend. The intimacy between them had always been of the truest.

'I almost expected a pigtail,' observed Francis, looking him affectionately up and down, 'but, really—why, you've hardly changed at all!'

'Outwardly, not as much, perhaps, as Time expects,' was the happy reply, 'but inwardly——!' He scanned appreciatively the burly figure of the doctor in his turn. 'And I can say the same of you,' he declared, still holding his hand tight. 'This is a real pleasure, Owen,' he went on in his deep voice; 'to see you again is a joy to me. Old friends meeting again—there's nothing like it in life, I believe, nothing.' He gave the hand another squeeze before he let it go. 'And we,' he added, leading the way into a room across the hall, 'neither of us is a fugitive from life. We take what we can, I mean.'

The doctor smiled as he noted the un-English turn of language, and together they entered a sitting-room that was, again, more like some inner chamber of a Chinese temple than a back room in a rented Hampstead house.

'I only knew ten minutes ago that you were coming, my dear fellow,' the scholar was saying, as his friend gazed round him with increased astonishment, 'or I would have prepared more suitably for your reception. I was out till late. All this' —he waved his hand— 'surprises you, of course, but the fact is I have been home some days already, and most of what you see was arranged for me in advance of my arrival. Hence its apparent completion. I say "apparent," because, actually, it is far from faithfully carried out. Yet to exceed,' he added, 'is as bad as to fall short.'

The doctor watched him while he listened to a somewhat

lengthy explanation of the various articles surrounding them. The speaker—he confirmed his first impression—had changed little during the long interval; the same enthusiasm was in him as before, the same fire and dreaminess alternately in the fine grey eyes, the same humour and passion about the mouth, the same free gestures, and the same big voice. Only the lines had deepened on the forehead, and on the fine face the air of thoughtfulness was also deeper. It was Edward Farque as of old, scholar, poet, dreamer and enthusiast, despiser of Western civilisation, contemptuous of money, generous and upright, a type of value, an individual.

'You've done well, done splendidly, Edward, old man,' said his friend presently, after hearing of Chinese wonders that took him somewhat beyond his depth perhaps. 'No one is more pleased than I. I've watched your books. You haven't regretted England, I'll be bound?' he asked.

'The philosopher has no country, in any case,' was the reply, steadily given. 'But out there I confess I've found my home.' He leaned forward, a deeper earnestness in his tone and expression. And into his face, as he spoke, came a glow of happiness. 'My heart,' he said softly, 'is in China.'

'I see it is, I see it is,' put in the other, conscious that he could not honestly share his friend's enthusiasm. 'And you're fortunate to be free to live where your treasure is,' he added after a moment's pause. 'You must be a happy man. Your passion amounts to nostalgia, I suspect. Already yearning to get back there, probably?'

Farque gazed at him for some seconds with shining eyes. 'You remember the Persian saying, I'm sure,' he said. ' "You see a man drink, but you do not see his thirst." Well,' he added, laughing happily, 'you may see me off in six months' time, but you will not see my happiness.'

While he went on talking the doctor glanced round the room, marvelling still at the exquisite taste of everything, the neat arrangement, the perfect matching of form and colour. A woman might have done this thing, occurred to him, as the haunting figure shifted deliciously into the foreground of his mind again. The thought of her had been momentarily replaced by all he heard and saw. She now returned, filling him with joy, anticipation, and enthusiasm. Presently, when it was his turn to talk, he would tell his friend about this new, unimagined happiness that had burst upon him like a sunrise. Presently, but not just yet. He remembered, too, with a passing twinge of possible boredom to come, that there must be some delay before his own heart could unburden itself in its turn. Farque wanted to ask some professional questions, of course. He had for the moment forgotten that part of the letter in his general interest and astonishment.

'Happiness, yes...' he murmured, aware that his thoughts had wandered and catching at the last word he remembered hearing. 'As you said just now in your own queer way—you haven't changed a bit, let me tell you, in your picturesqueness of quotation, Edward!—one must not be fugitive from life; one must seize happiness when and where it offers'.

He said it lightly enough, hugging internally his own sweet secret; but he was a little surprised at the earnestness of his friend's rejoinder: 'Both of us, I see,' came the deep voice, backed by the flash of the far-seeing grey eyes, 'have made some progress in the doctrine of life and death.' He paused, gazing at the other with sight that was obviously turned inwards upon his own thoughts. 'Beauty,' he went on presently, his tone even more serious, 'has been my lure; yours, Reality....'

'You don't flatter either of us, Edward. That's too exclusive a statement,' put in the doctor. He was becoming every minute more and more interested in the workings of his friend's mind. Something about the signs offered eluded his understanding. 'Explain yourself, old scholar-poet. I'm a dull, practical mind, remember, and can't keep pace with Chinese subtleties.'

'*You've* left out Beauty,' was the quiet rejoinder, 'while *I* left out Reality. That's neither Chinese nor subtle. It's simply true.'

'A bit wholesale, isn't it?' laughed Francis. 'A big generalisation, rather.'

A bright light seemed to illuminate the scholar's face. It was as though an inner lamp was suddenly lit. At the same moment the sound of a soft gong floated in from the hall outside, so soft that the actual strokes were not distinguishable in the wave of musical vibration that reached the ear.

Farque rose to lead the way in to dinner.

'What if I—' he whispered, 'have combined the two?' And upon his face was a look of joy that reached down into the other's own full heart with its unexpectedness and wonder. It was the last remark in the world he had looked for. He wondered for a moment whether he interpreted it correctly.

'By Jove...!' he exclaimed. 'Edward, what d'you mean?'

'You shall hear—after dinner,' said Farque, his voice mysterious, his eyes still shining with his inner joy. 'I told you I have some questions to ask you—professionally.' And they took their seats round an ancient, marvellous table, lit by two swinging lamps of soft green jade, while the Chinese servant waited on them with the silent movements and deft neatness of his imperturbable celestial race.

III

To say that he was bored during the meal were an over-statement of Dr. Francis's mental condition, but to say that he was half-bored seemed the literal truth; for one half of him, while he ate his steak and savoury and watched Farque manipulating *chou chop suey* and *chou om dong* most cleverly with chop-sticks, was too preoccupied with his own new romance to allow the other half to give its full attention to the conversation.

He had entered the room, however, with a distinct quickening of what may be termed his instinctive and infallible sense of diagnosis. That last remark of his friend's had stimulated him. He was aware of surprise, curiosity, and impatience. Willy-nilly, he began automatically to study him with a profounder interest. Something, he gathered, was not quite as it should be in

Edward Farque's mental composition. There was what might be called an elusive emotional disturbance. He began to wonder and to watch.

They talked, naturally, of China and of things Chinese, for the scholar responded to little else, and Francis listened with what sympathy and patience he could muster. Of art and beauty he had hitherto known little, his mind was practical and utilitarian. He now learned that all art was derived from China, where a high, fine, subtle culture had reigned since time immemorial. Older than Egypt was their wisdom. When the Western races were eating one another, before Greece was even heard of, the Chinese had reached a level of knowledge and achievement that few realised. Never had they, even in earliest times, been deluded by anthropomorphic conceptions of the Deity, but perceived in everything the expressions of a single whole whose vast activities they reverently worshipped. Their contempt for the Western scurry after knowledge, wealth, machinery, was justified, if Farque was worthy of belief. He seemed saturated with Chinese thought, art, philosophy, and his natural bias toward the celestial race had hardened into an attitude to life that had now become ineradicable.

'They deal, as it were, in essences,' he declared, 'they discern the essence of everything, leaving out the superfluous, the unessential, the trivial. Their pictures alone prove it. Come with me,' he concluded, 'and see the *Earthly Paradise*, now in the British Museum. It is like Botticelli, but better than anything Botticelli ever did. It was painted'—he paused for emphasis—'600 years B.C.'

The wonder of this quiet, ancient civilization, a sense of its depth, its wisdom, grew upon his listener as the enthusiastic poet described its charm and influence upon himself. He willingly allowed the enchantment of the other's Paradise to steal upon his own awakened heart. There was a good deal Francis might have offered by way of criticism and objection, but he preferred on the whole to keep his own views to himself, and to let his friend wander unhindered through the mazes of his passionate evocation. All men, he well knew, needed a dream to carry them through life's disappointments, a dream that they could enter at will and find peace, contentment, happiness. Farque's dream was China. Why not? It was as good as another, and a man like Farque was entitled to what dream he pleased.

'And their women?' he inquired at last, letting both halves of his mind speak together for the first time.

But he was not prepared for the expression that leaped upon his friend's face at the simple question. Nor for his method of reply. It was no reply, in point of fact. It was simply an attack upon all other types of woman, and upon the white, the English, in particular—their emptiness, their triviality, their want of intuitive imagination, of spiritual grace, of everything, in a word, that should constitute woman a meet companion for man, and a little higher than the angels into the bargain. The doctor listened spellbound. Too humorous to be shocked, he was, at any rate, disturbed by what he heard, displeased a little, too. It threatened too directly his own new tender dream.

Only with the utmost self-restraint did he keep his temper under, and prevent hot words he would have regretted later from tearing his friend's absurd claim into ragged shreds. He was wounded personally as well. Never now could he bring himself to tell his own secret to him. The outburst chilled and disappointed him. But it had another effect—it cooled his judgment. His sense of diagnosis quickened. He divined an *idée fixe,* a mania possibly. His interest deepened abruptly. He watched. He began to look about him with more wary eyes, and a sense of uneasiness, once the anger passed, stirred in his friendly and affectionate heart.

They had been sitting alone over their port for some considerable time, the servant having long since left the room. The doctor had sought to change the subject many times without much success, when suddenly Farque changed it for him.

'Now,' he announced, 'I'll tell you something,' and Francis guessed that the professional questions were on the way at last.

'We must pity the living, remember, and part with the dead. Have you forgotten old Shan-Yu?'

The forgotten name came back to him, the picturesque East End dealer of many years ago. 'The old merchant who taught you your first Chinese? I do recall him dimly, now you mention it. You made quite a friend of him, didn't you? He thought very highly of you—ah, it comes back to me now—he offered something or other very wonderful in his gratitude, unless my memory fails me.'

'His most valuable possession,' Farque went on, a strange look deepening on his face, an expression of mysterious rapture, as it were, and one that Francis recognised and swiftly pigeonholed in his now attentive mind.

'Which was?' he asked sympathetically. 'You told me once, but so long ago that really it's slipped my mind. Something magical, wasn't it?' He watched closely for his friend's reply.

Farque lowered his voice to a whisper almost devotional:

'The Perfume of the Garden of Happiness,' he murmured, with an expression in his eyes as though the mere recollection gave him joy. ' "Burn it," he told me, "in a brazier; then inhale. You will enter the Valley of a Thousand Temples wherein lies the Garden of Happiness, and there you will meet your Love. You will have seven years of happiness with your Love before the Waters of Separation flow between you. I give this to you who alone of men here have appreciated the wisdom of my land. Follow my body toward the Sunrise. You, an Eastern soul in a barbarian body, will meet your Destiny." '

The doctor's attention, such is the power of self-interest, quickened amazingly as he heard. His own romance flamed up with power. His friend—it dawned upon him suddenly—loved a woman.

'Come,' said Farque, rising quietly, 'we will go into the other room, and I will show you what I have shown to but one other in the world before. You are a doctor,' he continued, as he led the way to the silk-covered divan where golden dragons swallowed crimson suns, and wonderful jade horses hovered near. 'You understand the mind and nerves. States of consciousness you also can explain, and the effect of drugs is, doubtless, known to you.' He swung to the heavy curtains that took the place of a door, handed a lacquered box of cigarettes to his friend, and lit one himself. 'Perfumes, too,' he added, 'you probably have studied, with their extraordinary evocative power.' He stood in the middle of the room, the green light falling on his interesting and thoughtful face, and for a passing second Francis, watching keenly, observed a change flit over it and vanish. The eyes grew narrow and slid tilted upward, the skin wore a shade of yellow underneath the green from the lamp of jade, the nose slipped back a little, the cheek-bones forward.

'Perfumes,' said the doctor, 'no. Of perfumes I know nothing, beyond their interesting effect upon the memory. I cannot help you there. But you, I suspect,' and he looked up with an inviting sympathy that concealed the close observation underneath, 'you yourself, I feel sure, can tell me something of value about them?'

'Perhaps,' was the calm reply, 'perhaps, for I have smelt the Perfume of the Garden of Happiness, and I have been in the Valley of a Thousand Temples.' He spoke with a glow of joy and reverence almost devotional.

The doctor waited in some suspense, while his friend moved toward an inlaid cabinet across the room. More than broad-minded, he was that much rarer thing, an open-minded man, ready at a moment's notice to discard all preconceived ideas, provided new knowledge that necessitated the holocaust were shown to him. At present, none the less, he held very definite views of his own. 'Please ask me any questions you like,' he added. 'All I know is entirely yours, as always.' He was aware of suppressed excitement in his friend that betrayed itself in every word and look and gesture, an excitement intense, and not as yet explained by anything he had seen or heard.

The scholar, meanwhile, had opened a drawer in the cabinet and taken from it a neat little packet tied up with purple silk.

He held it with tender, almost loving care, as he came and sat down on the divan beside his friend.

'This,' he said, in a tone, again, of something between reverence and worship, 'contains what I have to show you first.' He slowly unrolled it, disclosing a yet smaller silken bag within, coloured a deep rich orange. There were two vertical columns of writing on it, painted in Chinese characters. The doctor leaned forward to examine them. His friend translated:

'The Perfume of the Garden of Happiness,' he read aloud, tracing the letters of the first column with his finger. 'The Destroyer of Honourable Homes,' he finished, passing to the second, and then proceeded to unwrap the little silken bag. Befory it was actually open, however, and the pale shredded material resembling coloured chaff visible to the eyes, the doctor's nostrils had recognised the strange aroma he had first noticed about his friend's letter received earlier in the day. The same soft, penetrating odour, sharply piercing, sweet and delicate, rose to his brain. It stirred at once a deep emotional pleasure in him. Having come to him first when he was aglow with his own unexpected romance, his mind and heart full of the woman he had just left, that delicious, torturing state revived in him quite naturally. The evocative power of perfume with regard to memory is compelling. A livelier sympathy toward his friend, and toward what he was about to hear, awoke in him spontaneously.

He did not mention the letter, however. He merely leaned over to smell the fragrant perfume more easily.

Farque drew back the open packet instantly, at the same time holding out a warning hand. 'Careful,' he said gravely, 'be careful, my old friend—unless you desire to share the rapture and the risk that have been mine. To enjoy its full effect, true, this dust must be burned in a brazier and its smoke inhaled; but even sniffed, as you now would sniff it, and you are in danger——'

'Of what?' asked Francis, impressed by the other's extraordinary intensity of voice and manner.

'Of Heaven; but, possibly, of Heaven before your time.'

IV

The tale that Farque unfolded then had certainly a strange celestial flavour, a glory not of this dull world; and as his friend listened, his interest deepened with every minute, while his bewilderment increased. He watched closely, expert that he was, for clues that might guide his deductions aright, but for all his keen observation and experience he could detect no inconsistency, no weakness, nothing that betrayed the smallest mental aberration. The origin and nature of what he already decided was an *idée fixe,* a mania, evaded him entirely. This evasion piqued and vexed him; he had heard a thousand tales of similar type before; that this one in particular should baffle his unusual skill touched his pride. Yet he faced the position honestly; he confessed himself baffled until the end of the evening. When he went away, however, he went away satisfied, even forgetful—because a new problem of yet more poignant interest had replaced the first.

'It was after three years out there,' said Farque, 'that a sense of my loneliness first came upon me. It came upon me bitterly. My work had not then been recognised; obstacles and difficulties had increased; I felt a failure; I had accomplished nothing. And it seemed to me I had misjudged my capacities, taken a wrong direction, and wasted my life accordingly. For my move to China, remember, was a radical move, and my boats were burnt behind me. This sense of loneliness was really devastating.'

Francis, already fidgeting, put up his hand.

'One question, if I may,' he said, 'and I'll not interrupt again.'

'By all means,' said the other patiently. 'What is it?'

'Were you—we are such old friend's—he apologised—'were you still celibate as ever?'

Farque looked surprised, then smiled. 'My habits had not changed,' he replied. 'I was, as always, celibate.'

'Ah!' murmured the doctor, and settled down to listen.

'And I think now,' his friend went on, 'that it was the lack of companionship that first turned my thoughts toward conscious disappointment. However that may be, it was one evening, as I walked homeward to my little house, that I caught my imagination lingering upon English memories, though chiefly, I admit, upon my old Chinese tutor, the dead Shan-Yu.

'It was dusk, the stars were coming out in the pale evening air, and the orchards, as I passed them, stood like wavering ghosts of unbelievable beauty. The effect of thousands upon thousands of these trees, flooding the twilight of a spring evening with their sea of blossom, is almost unearthly. They seem transparencies, their colour hangs sheets upon the very sky. I crossed a small wooden bridge that joined two of these orchards above a stream, and in the dark water I watched a moment the mingled reflection of stars and flowering branches on the quiet surface. It seemed too exquisite to belong to earth, this fairy garden of stars and blossoms, shining faintly in the crystal depths, and my thought, as I gazed, dived suddenly down the little avenue that memory opened into former days. I remembered Shan-Yu's present, given to me when he died. His very words came back to me: The Garden of Happiness in the Valley of the Thousand Temples, with its promise of love, of seven years of happiness, and the prophecy that I should follow his body toward the Sunrise and meet my destiny.

'This memory I took home with me into my lonely little one-story house upon the hill. My servants did not sleep there. There was no one near. I sat by the open window with my thoughts, and you may easily guess that before very long I had unearthed the long-forgotten packet from among my things, spread a portion of its contents on a metal tray above a lighted brazier, and was comfortably seated before it, inhaling the light blue smoke with its exquisite and fragrant perfume.

'A light air entered through the window, the distant orchards below me trembled, rose, and floated through the dusk, and I found myself, almost at once, in a pavilion of flowers; a blue river lay shining in the sun before me, as it wandered through a lovely valley where I saw groves of flowering trees among a thousand scattered temples. Drenched in light and colour, the Valley lay dreaming amid a peaceful loveliness that woke what seemed impossible, unrealisable, longings in my heart. I yearned toward its groves and temples; I would bathe my soul in that flood of tender light and my body in the blue coolness of that winding river. In a thousand temples must I worship. Yet these impossible yearnings instantly were satisfied. I found myself there at once... and the time that passed over my head you may reckon in centuries, if not in ages. I was in the Garden of Happiness, and its marvellous perfume banished time and sorrow; there was no end to chill the soul, nor any beginning, which is its foolish counterpart.

'Nor was there loneliness.' The speaker clasped his thin hands, and closed his eyes a moment in what was evidently an ecstasy of the sweetest memory man may ever know. A slight trembling ran through his frame, communicating itself to his friend upon the divan beside him—this understanding, listening, sympathetic friend, whose eyes had never once yet withdrawn their attentive gaze from the narator's face.

'I was not alone,' the scholar resumed, opening his eyes again, and smiling out of some deep inner joy. 'Shan-Yu came down the steps of the first temple and took my hand, while the great golden figures in the dim interior turned their splendid shining heads to watch. Then, breathing the soul of his ancient wisdom in my ear, he led me through all the perfumed ways of that enchanted Garden, worshipping with me at a hundred deathless shrines; led me, I tell you, to the sound of soft gongs and gentle bells, by fragrant groves and sparkling streams, mid a million gorgeous flowers, until beneath that unsetting sun, we reached the heart of the Valley, where the source of the river gushed forth beneath the lighted mountains. He stopped and pointed across the narrow waters. I saw the woman—'

'*The* woman,' his listener murmured beneath his breath, though Farque seemed unaware of interruption.

'She smiled at me and held her hands out, and while she did so, even before I could express my joy and wonder in response, Shan-Yu, I saw, had crossed the narrow stream and stood beside her. I made to follow them, my heart burning with inexpressible delight. But Shan-Yu held up his hand, as they began to move down the flowered bank together, making a sign that I should keep pace with them, though on my own side.

'Thus, side by side, yet with the blue, sparkling stream between us, we followed back along its winding course, through the heart of that enchanted Valley, my hands stretched out toward the radiant figure of my Love, and hers stretched out toward me. They did not touch, but our eyes, our smiles, our thoughts, these met and mingled in a sweet union of unimagined bliss, so that the absence of physical contact was unnoticed and laid no injury on our marvellous joy. It was a spirit union, and our kiss a spirit kiss. Therein lay the subtlety and glory of the Chinese wonder, for it was our *essences* that met, and for such union there is no satiety and, equally, no possible end. The Perfume of the Garden of Happiness is an essence. We were in Eternity.

'The stream, meanwhile, widened between us, and as it widened, my Love grew farther from me in space, smaller, less visibly defined, yet ever essentially more perfect, and never once with a sense of distance that made our union less divinely close. Across the widening reaches of blue, sunlit water I still knew her smile, her eyes, the gestures of her radiant being; I saw her exquisite reflection in the stream; and, mid the music of those soft gongs and gentle bells, the voice of Shan-Yu came like a melody to my ears:

' "You have followed me into the Sunrise, and have found your Destiny. Behold now your Love. In this Valley of a Thousand Temples you have known the Garden of Happiness, and its Perfume your soul now inhales."

' "I am bathed," I answered, "in a happiness divine. It is for ever."

' "The Waters of Separation," his answer floated like a bell, "lie widening between you."

'I moved nearer to the bank, impelled by the pain in his words to take my Love and hold her to my breast.

'"But I would cross to her," I cried, and saw that, as I moved, Shan-Yu and my Love came likewise closer to the water's edge across the widening river. They both obeyed, I was aware, my slightest wish.

'"Seven years of happiness you may know," sang his gentle tones across the brimming flood, "if you would cross to her. Yet the Destroyer of Honourable Homes lies in the shadows that you must cast outside."

'I heard his words, I noticed for the first time that in the blaze of this radiant sunshine we cast no shadows on the sea of flowers at our feet, and—I stretched out my arms toward my Love across the river.

'"I accept my destiny," I cried, "I will have my seven years of bliss," and stepped forward into the running flood. As the cool water took my feet, my Love's hands stretched out both to hold me and to bid me stay. There was acceptance in her gesture, but there was warning too.

'I did not falter. I advanced until the water bathed my knees, and my Love, too, came to meet me, the stream already to her waist, while our arms stretched forth above the running flood toward each other.

'The change came suddenly. Shan-Yu first faded behind her advancing figure into air; there stole a chill upon the sunlight; a cool mist rose from the water, hiding the Garden and the hills beyond; our fingers touched, I gazed into her eyes, our lips lay level with the water—and the room was dark and cold about me. The brazier stood extinguished at my side. The dust had burnt out, and no smoke rose. I slowly left my chair and closed the window, for the air was chill.'

V

It was difficult at first to return to Hampstead and the details of ordinary life about him. Francis looked round him slowly, freeing himself gradually from the spell his friend's words had laid even upon his analytical temperament. The transition was helped, however, by the details that everywhere met his eye. The Chinese atmosphere remained. More, its effect had gained, if anything. The embroideries of yellow gold, the pictures, the lacquered stools and inlaid cabinets—above all, the exquisite figures in green jade upon the shelf beside him—all this, in the shimmering pale olive light the lamps shed everywhere, helped his puzzled mind to bridge the gulf from the Garden of Happiness into the decorated villa upon Hampstead Heath.

There was silence between the two men for several minutes. Far was it from the doctor's desire to injure his old friend's delightful fantasy. For he called it fantasy, although something in him doubted. He remained, therefore, silent. Truth to tell, perhaps, he knew not exactly what to say.

Farque broke the silence himself. He had not moved since the story ended; he sat motionless, his hands tightly clasped, his eyes alight with the memory of his strange imagined joy, his face rapt and almost luminous, as though he still wandered through the groves of the enchanted Garden and inhaled the perfume of its perfect happiness in the Valley of the Thousand Temples.

'It was two days later,' he went on suddenly in his quiet voice, 'only two days afterwards, that I met her.'

'You met her? You met the woman of your dream?' Francis's eyes opened very wide.

'In that little harbour town,' repeated Farque calmly, 'I met her in the flesh. She had just landed in a steamer from up the coast. The details are of no particular interest. She knew me, of course, at once. And, naturally, I knew her.'

The doctor's tongue refused to act as he heard. It dawned upon him suddenly that his friend was married. He remembered the woman's touch about the house; he recalled, too, for the first time that the letter of invitation to dinner had said 'come to *us*'. He was full of a bewildered astonishment.

The reaction upon himself was odd, perhaps, yet wholly natural. His heart warmed toward his imaginative friend. He could now tell him his own new strange romance. The woman who haunted him crept back into the room and sat between them. He found his tongue.

'You married her, Edward?' he exclaimed.

'She is my wife,' was the reply, in a gentle, happy voice.

'A Ch——' he could not bring himself to say the word. 'A foreigner?'

'My wife is a Chinese woman,' Farque helped him easily, with a delighted smile.

So great was the other's absorption in the actual moment that he had not heard the step in the passage that his host had heard. The latter stood up suddenly.

'I hear her now,' he said. 'I'm glad she's come back before you left.' He stepped toward the door.

But before he reached it, the door was opened and in came the woman herself. Francis tried to rise, but something had happened to him. His heart missed a beat. Something, it seemed, broke in him. He faced a tall, graceful young Englishwoman with black eyes of sparkling happiness, the woman of his own romance. She still wore the feather boa round her neck. She was no more Chinese than he was.

'My wife,' he heard Farque introducing them, as he struggled to his feet, searching feverishly for words of congratulation, normal, everyday words he ought to use. 'I'm so pleased, oh, so pleased,' Farque was saying—he heard the sound from a distance, his sight was blurred as well—'my two best friends in the world, my English comrade and my Chinese wife.' His voice was absolutely sincere with conviction and belief.

'But we have already met,' came the woman's delightful voice, her eyes full upon his face with smiling pleasure. 'I saw yout at Mrs. Malleson's tea only this afternoon.'

And Francis remembered suddenly that the Mallesons were old acquaintances of Farque's as well as of himself. 'And I even dared to ask who you were,' the voice went on, floating from some other space, it seemed, to his ears. 'I had you pointed out to me. I had heard of you from Edward, of course. But you vanished before I could be introduced.'

The doctor mumbled something or other polite and, he hoped, adequate. But the truth had flashed upon him with remorseless suddenness. She had 'heard of' him—the famous mental specialist. Her interest in him was cruelly explained, cruelly both for himself and for his friend. Farque's delusion lay clear before his eyes. An awakening to reality might involve dislocation of the mind. *She*, too moreover, knew the truth. She was involved as well. And her interest in himself was—consultation.

'Seven years we've been married, just seven years to-day,' Farque was saying thoughtfully, as he looked at them. 'Curius, rather, isn't it?'

'Very,' said Francis, turning his regard from the black eyes to the grey.

Thus it was that Owen Francis left the house a little later with a mind in a measure satisfied, yet in a measure forgetful too—forgetful of his own deep problem, because another of even greater interest had replaced it.

'Why undeceive him?' ran his thought. 'He need never know. It's harmless, anyhow—I can tell her that.'

But side by side with this reflection ran another that was oddly haunting, considering his type of mind: 'Destroyer of Honourable Homes,' was the form of words it took. And with a sigh he added, 'Chinese Magic.'

FIRST HATE

They had been shooting all day; the weather had been perfect and the powder straight, so that when they assembled in the smoking-room after dinner they were well-pleased with themselves. From discussing the day's sport and the weather outlook, the conversation drifted to other, though still cognate, fields. Lawson, the crack shot of the party, mentioned the instinctive recognition all animals feel for their natural enemies, and gave several instances in which he had tested it—tame rats with a ferret, birds with a snake, and so forth.

'Even after being domesticated for generations,' he said, 'they recognise their natural enemy at once by instinct, an enemy they can never even have seen before. It's infallible. They know instantly.'

'Undoubtedly,' said a voice from the corner chair; 'and so do we.'

The speaker was Ericssen, their host, a great hunter before the Lord, generally uncommunicative but a good listener, leaving the talk to others. For this latter reason, as well as for a certain note of challenge in his voice, his abrupt statement gained attention.

'What do you mean exactly by "so do we"?' asked three men together, after waiting some seconds to see whether he meant to elaborate, which he evidently did not.

'We belong to the animal kingdom, of course,' put in a fourth, for behind the challenge there obviously lay a story, though a story that might be difficult to drag out of him. It was.

Ericssen, who had leaned forward a moment so that his strong, humorous face was in clear light, now sank back again into his chair, his expression concealed by the red lampshade at his side. The light played tricks, obliterating the humorous, almost tender, lines, while emphasising the stength of the jaw and nose. The red glare lent to the whole a rather grim expression.

FIRST HATE

Lawson, man of authority among them, broke the little pause.

'You're dead right,' he observed; 'but how do you know it?'—for John Ericssen never made a positive statement without a good reason for it. That good reason, he felt sure, involved a personal proof, but a story Ericssen would never tell before a general audience. He would tell it later, however when the others had left. 'There's such a thing as instinctive antipathy, of course,' he added, with a laugh, looking round him. 'That's what you mean, probably.'

'I meant exactly what I said,' replied the host bluntly. 'There's first love. There's first hate, too.'

'Hate's a strong word,' remarked Lawson.

'So is love,' put in another.

'Hate's strongest,' said Ericssen grimly. 'In the animal kingdom, at least,' he added suggestively, and then kept his lips closed, except to sip his liquor, for the rest of the evening—until the party at length broke up, leaving Lawson and one other man, both old trusted friends of many years' standing.

'It's not a tale I'd tell to everybody,' he began, when they were alone. 'It's true, for one thing; for another, you see, some of those good fellows'—he indicated the empty chairs with an expressive nod of his great head—'some of 'em knew him. You both knew him too, probably.'

'The man you hated,' said the understanding Lawson.

'And who hated me,' came the quiet confirmation. 'My other reason,' he went on, 'for keeping quiet was that the tale involves my wife.'

The two listeners said nothing, but each remembered the curiously long courtship that had been the prelude to his marriage. No engagement had been announced, the pair were devoted to one another, there was no known rival on either side, yet the courtship continued without coming to its expected conclusion. Many stories were afloat in consequence. It was a social mystery that intrigued the gossips.

'I may tell you two,' Ericssen continued, 'the reason my wife refused for so long to marry me. It is hard to believe, perhaps, but it is true. Another man wished to make her his wife, and she would not consent to marry me until that other man was dead. Quixotic, absurd, unreasonable? If you like. I'll tell you what she said.' He looked up with a significant expression in his face which proved that he, at least, did not now judge her reason foolish. ' "Because it would be murder," she told me. "Another man who wants to marry me would kill you." '

'She had some proof for the assertion, no doubt?' suggested Lawson.

'None whatever,' was the reply. 'Merely her woman's instinct. Moreover, *I* did not know who the other man was, nor would she ever tell me.'

'Otherwise you might have murdered him instead?' said Baynes, the second listener.

'I did', said Ericssen grimly. 'But without knowing he was the man.' He sipped his whisky and relit his pipe. The others waited.

'Our marriage took place two months later—just after Hazel's disappearance.'

'Hazel?' exclaimed Lawson and Baynes in a single breath. 'Hazel! Member of the Hunters!' His mysterious disappearance had been a nine days' wonder some ten years ago. It had never been explained. They had all been members of the Hunters' Club together.

'That's the chap,' Ericssen said. 'Now I'll tell you the tale, if you care to hear it.' They settled back in their chairs to listen. and Ericssen, who had evidently never told the affair to another living soul except his own wife, doubtless, seemed glad this time to tell it to two men.

'It began some dozen years ago when my brother Jack and I came home from a shooting trip in China. I've often told you about our adventures there, and you see the heads hanging up here in the smoking-room—some of 'em'. He glanced round proudly at the walls. 'We were glad to be in town again after two years' roughing it, and we looked forward to our first good dinner at the Club, to make up for the rotten cooking we had endured so long. We had ordered that dinner in anticipatory detail many a time together. Well, we had it and enjoyed it up to a point—the point of the *entrée,* to be exact.

'Up to that point it was delicious, and we let ourselves go, I can tell you. We had ordered the very wine we had planned months before when we were snow-bound and half starving in the mountains.' He smacked his lips as he mentioned it. 'I was just starting on a beautifully cooked grouse,' he went on, 'when a figure went by our table, and Jack looked up and nodded. The two exchanged a brief word of greeting and explanation, and the other man passed on. Evidently they knew each other just enough to make a word or two necessary, but enough.

' "Who's that?" I asked.

' "A new member, named Hazel," Jack told me. "A great shot." He knew him slightly, he explained; he had once been a client of his—Jack was a barrister, you remember—and had defended him in some financial case or other. Rather an unpleasant case, he added. Jack did not 'care about' the fellow, he told me, as he went on with his tender wing of grouse.'

Ericssen paused to relight his pipe a moment.

'Not care about him!' he continued. 'It didn't surprise me, for my own feeling, the instant I set eyes on the fellow, was one of violent, instinctive dislike that amounted to loathing. Loathing! No. I'll give it the right word—hatred. I simpy couldn't help myself; I hated the man from the very first go off. A wave of repulsion swept over me as I followed him down the room a moment with my eyes, till he took his seat at a distant table and was out of sight. Ugh! He was a big, fat-faced man, with an eyeglass glued into one of his pale-blue cod-like eyes—out of condition, ugly as a toad, with a smug expression of intense self-satisfaction on his jowl that made me long to———

'I leave it to you to guess what I would have liked to do to him. But the instinctive loathing he inspired in me had another aspect, too. Jack had not introduced us during the momentary pause beside our table, but as I looked up I caught the fellow's eye on mine—he was glaring at me instead of at Jack, to whom he was talking—with an expression of malignant dislike, as keen evidently as my own. That's the other aspect I meant. He hated me as violently as I hated him. We were instinctive enemies, just as the rat and ferret are instinctive enemies. Each recognised a mortal foe. It was a case—I swear it—of whoever got first chance.'

'Bad as that!' exclaimed Baynes. 'I knew him by sight. He wasn't pretty, I'll admit.'

'I knew him to nod to,' Lawson mentioned. 'I never heard anything particular against him.' He shrugged his shoulders.

Ericssen went on. 'It was not his character or qualities I hated,' he said. 'I didn't even know them. That's the whole point. There's no reason you fellows should have disliked him. *My* hatred—our mutual hatred—was instinctive, as instinctive as first love. A man knows his natural mate; also he knows his natural enemy. I did, at any rate, both with him and with my wife. Given the chance, Hazel would have done me in; just as surely, given the chance, I would have done him in. No blame to either of us, what's more, in my opinion.'

'I've felt dislike, but never hatred like that,' Baynes mentioned. 'I came across it in a book once, though. The writer did not mention the instinctive fear of the human animal for its natural enemy, or anything of that sort. He thought it was a continuance of a bitter feud begun in an earlier existence. He called it memory.'

'Possibly,' said Ericssen briefly. 'My mind is not speculative. But I'm glad you spoke of fear. I left that out. The truth is, I feared the fellow, too, in a way; and had we ever met face to face in some wild country without witnesses I should have felt justified in drawing on him at sight, and he would have felt the same. Murder? If you like. I should call it self-defence. Anyhow, the fellow polluted the room for me. He spoilt the enjoyment of that dinner we had ordered months before in China.'

'But you saw him again, of course, later?'

'Lots of times. Not that night, because we went on to a theatre. But in the Club we were always running across one another—in the houses of friends at lunch or dinner; at race-meetings; all over the place; in fact, I even had some trouble to avoid being introduced to him. And every time we met, our eyes betrayed us. He felt in his heart what I felt in mine. Ugh! He was as loathsome to me as leprosy, and as dangerous. Odd, isn't it? The most intense feeling, except love, I've ever known. I remember'—he laughed gruffly—'I used to feel quite sorry for him. If he felt what I felt, and I'm convinced he did, he must have suffered. His one object—to get me out of the way for good—was so impossible. Then Fate played a hand in the game. I'll tell you how.

'My brother died a year or two later, and I went abroad to try and forget it. I went salmon fishing in Canada. But, though the sport was good, it was not like the old times with Jack. The camp never felt the same without him. I missed him badly. But I forgot Hazel for the time; hating did not seem worth while, somehow.

'When the best of the fishing was over on the Atlantic side I took a run back to Vancouver and fished there for a bit. I went up the Campbell River, which was not so crowded then as it is now, and had some rattling sport. Then I grew tired of the rod and decided to go after wapiti for a change. I came back to Victoria and learned what I could about the best places, and decided finally to go up the west coast of the island. By luck I happened to pick up a good guide, who was in the town at the moment on business, and we started off together in one of the little Canadian Pacific Railway boats that ply along that coast.

'Outfitting two days later at a small place the steamer stopped at, the guide said we needed another man to help pack our kit over portages, and so forth, but the only fellow available was a Siwash of whom he disapproved. My guide would not have him at any price; he was lazy, a drunkard, a liar, and even worse, for on one occasion he came back without the sportsman he had taken up country on a shooting trip, and his story was not convincing, to say the least. These disappearances are always awkward, of course, as you both know. We preferred, anyhow, to go without the Siwash, and off we started.

'At first our luck was bad. I saw many wapiti, but no good heads; only after a fortnight's hunting did I manage to get a decent head, though even that was not so good as I should have liked.

'We were then near the head waters of a little river that ran down into the Inlet; heavy rains had made the river rise; running downstream was a risky job, what with old log-jams shifting and new ones forming; and, after many narrow escapes, we upset one afternoon and had the misfortune to lose a lot of our kit, amongst it most of our cartridges. We could only muster a few between us. The guide had a dozen; I had two—just enough, we considered, to take us out all right. Still, it was an infernal nuisance. We camped at once to dry out our soaked things in front of a big fire, and while this laundry work was going on the guide suggested my filling in the time by taking a look at the next little valley, which ran parallel to ours. He had seen some good heads over there a few weeks ago. Possibly I might come upon the herd. I started at once, taking my two cartridges with me.

'It was the devil of a job getting over the divide, for it was a badly bushed-up place, and where there were no bushes there were boulders and fallen trees, and the going was slow and tiring. But I got across at last and came out upon another stream at the bottom of the new valley. Signs of wapiti were plentiful, though I never came up with a single beast all the afternoon. Blacktail deer were everywhere, but the wapiti remained invisible. Providence, or whatever you like to call that fate which there is no escaping in our lives, made me save my two cartridges.'

Ericssen stopped a minute then, It was not to light his pipe or sip his whisky. Nor was it because the remainder of his story failed in the recollection of any vivid detail. He paused a moment to think.

'Tell us the lot,' pleaded Lawson. 'Don't leave out anything.'

Ericssen looked up. His friend's remark had helped him to

make up his mind apparently. He *had* hesitated about something or other, but the hesitation passed. He glanced at both his listeners.

'Right,' he said. 'I'll tell you everything. I'm not imaginative, as you know, and my amount of superstition, I should judge, is microscopic.' He took a longer breath, then lowered his voice a trifle. 'Anyhow,' he went on, 'it's true, so I don't see why I should feel shy about admitting it—but as I stood there, in that lonely valley, where only the noises of wind and water were audible, and no human being, except my guide, some miles away, was within reach, a curious feeling came over me I find difficult to describe. I felt'—obviously he made an effort to get the word out—'I felt creepy.'

'You,' murmured Lawson, with an incredulous smile—'you creepy?' he repeated under his breath.

'I felt creepy and afraid,' continued the other, with conviction. 'I had the sensation of being seen by someone—as if someone, I mean, was watching me. It was so unlikely that anyone was near me in that God-forsaken bit of wilderness that I simply couldn't believe it at first. But the feeling persisted. I felt absolutely positive somebody was not far away among the red maples, behind a boulder, across the little stream, perhaps —somewhere, at any rate, so near that I was plainly visible to him. It was not an animal. It was human. Also, it was hostile.

'I was in danger.

'You may laugh, both of you, but I assure you the feeling was so positive that I crouched down instinctively to hide myself behind a rock. My first thought, that the guide had followed me for some reason or other, I at once discarded. It was not the guide. It was an enemy.

'No, no, I thought of no one in particular. No name, no face occurred to me. Merely that an enemy was on my trail, that he saw me, and I did not see him, and that he was near enough to me to—well, to take instant action. This deep instinctive feeling of danger, of fear, of anything you like to call it, was simply overwhelming.

'Another curious detail I must also mention. About half an hour before, having given up all hope of seeing wapiti, I had decided to kill a blacktail deer for meat. A good shot offered itself, not thirty yards away. I aimed. But just as I was going to pull the trigger a queer emotion touched me, and I lowered the rifle. It was exactly as though a voice said, "Don't!" I heard no voice, mind you; it was an emotion only, a feeling, a sudden inexplicable change of mind—a warning, if you like. I didn't fire, anyhow.

'But now, as I crouched behind that rock, I remembered this curious little incident, and was glad I had not used up my last two cartridges. More than that I cannot tell you. Things of that kind are new to me. They're difficult enough to tell let alone to explain. But they were *real*.

'I crouched there, wondering what on earth was happening to me, and feeling a bit of a fool, if you want to know, when suddenly, over the top of the boulder, I saw something moving. It was a man's hat. I peered cautiously. Some sixty yards away the bushes parted, and two men came out on to the river's bank, and I knew them both. One was the Siwash I had seen at the store. The other was Hazel. Before I had time to think I cocked my rifle.'

'Hazel. Good Lord!' exclaimed the listeners.

'For a moment I was too surprised to do anything but cock that rifle. I waited, for what puzzled me was that, after all, Hazel had *not* seen me. It was only the feeling of his beastly proximity that had made me feel I was seen and watched by him. There was something else, too, that made me pause before—er—doing anything. Two other things, in fact. One was that I was so intensely interested in watching the fellow's actions. Obviously he had the same uneasy sensation that I had. He shared with me the nasty feeling that danger was about. His rifle, I saw, was cocked and ready; he kept looking behind him, over his shoulder, peering this way and that, and sometimes addressing a remark to the Siwash at his side. I caught the laughter of the latter. The Siwash evidently did not think there was danger anywhere. It was, of course, unlikely enough——'

'And the other thing that stopped you?' urged Lawson, impatiently interrupting.

Ericssen turned with a look of grim humour on his face.

'Some confounded or perverted sense of chivalry in me, I suppose,' he said, 'that made it impossible to shoot him down in cold blood, or, rather, without letting him have a chance. Fo my blood, as a matter of fact, was far from cold at the moment. Perhaps, too, I wanted the added satisfaction of letting him know who fired the shot that was to end his vile existence.'

He laughed again. 'It was rat and ferret in the human kingdom,' he went on, 'but I wanted my rat to have a chance, I suppose. Anyhow, though I had a perfect shot in front of me at easy distance, I did not fire. Instead I got up, holding my cocked rifle ready, finger on trigger, and came out of my hiding-place. I called to him. "Hazel, you beast! So there you are—at last!"

'He turned, but turned away from me, offering his horrid back. The direction of the voice he misjudged. He pointed down-stream, and the Siwash turned to look. Neither of them had seen me yet. There was a big log-jam below them. The roar of the water in their ears concealed my footsteps. I was, perhaps, twenty paces from them when Hazel, with a jerk of his whole body, abruptly turned clean round and faced me. We stared into each other's eyes.

'The amazement on his face changed instantly to hatred and resolve. He acted with incredible rapidity. I think the unexpected suddenness of his turn made me lose a precious second or two. Anyhow he was ahead of me. He flung his rifle to his shoulder. 'You devil!' I heard his voice. 'I've got you at last!' His rifle cracked, for he let drive the same instant. The hair stirred just above my ear.

'He had missed!

'Before he could draw back his bolt for another shot I had acted.

' "You're not fit to live!" I shouted, as my bullet crashed

into his temple. I had the satisfaction, too, of knowing that he heard my words. I saw the swift expression of frustrated loathing in his eyes.

'He fell like an ox, his face splashing in the stream. I shoved the body out. I saw it sucked beneath the log-jam instantly. It disappeared. There could be no inquest on him, I reflected comfortably. Hazel was gone—gone from this earth, from my life, our mutual hatred over at last.'

The speaker paused a moment. 'Odd,' he continued presently—'very odd indeed.' He turned to the others. 'I felt quite sorry for him suddenly. I suppose,' he added,' the philosophers are right when they gas about hate being very close to love.'

His friends contributed no remark.

'Then I came away,' he resumed shortly. 'My wife—well, you know the rest, don't you? I told her the whole thing. She—she said nothing. But she married me, you see.'

There was a moment's silence. Baynes was the first to break it. 'But—the Siwash?' he asked. 'The witness?'

Lawson turned upon him with something of contemptuous impatience.

'He told you he had *two* cartridges.'

Ericssen, smiling grimly, said nothing at all.

THE OLIVE

HE laughed involuntarily as the olive rolled toward his chair across the shiny parquet floor of the hotel dining-room.

His table in the cavernous *salle à manger* was apart: he sat alone, a solitary guest; the table from which the olive fell and rolled toward him was some distance away. The angle, however, made him an unlikely objective. Yet the lob-sided, juicy thing, after hesitating once or twice *en route* as it plopped along, came to rest finally against his feet.

It settled with an inviting, almost an aggressive, air. And he stooped and picked it up, putting it rather self-consciously, because of the girl from whose table it had come, on the white tablecloth beside his plate.

Then, looking up, he caught her eye, and saw that she, too, was laughing, though not a bit self-consciously. As she helped herself to the *hors-d'oeuvre* a false move had sent it flying. She watched him pick the olive up and set it beside his plate. Her eyes then suddenly looked away again—at her mother—questioningly.

The incident was closed. But the little oblong, succulent olive lay beside his plate, so that his fingers played with it. He fingered it automatically from time to time until his lonely meal was finished.

When no one was looking he slipped it into his pocket, as though, having taken the trouble to pick it up, this was the very least he could do with it. Heaven alone knows why, but he then took it upstairs with him, setting it on the marble mantelpiece among his field-glasses, tobacco tins, ink-bottles, pipes, and candlestick. At any rate, he kept it—the moist, shiny, lob-sided, juicy little oblong olive. The hotel lounge wearied him; he came to his room after dinner to smoke at his ease, his coat off and his feet on a chair; to read another chapter of Freud, to write a letter or two he didn't in the least want to write, and then to go to bed at ten o'clock. But this evening the olive kept rolling between him and the thing he read; it rolled between the paragraphs, between the lines; the olive was more vital than the interest of these eternal 'complexes' and 'suppressed desires.'

The truth was that he kept seeing the eyes of the laughing girl beyond the bouncing olive. She had smiled at him in such a natural, spontaneous, friendly way before her mother's glance had checked her—a smile, he felt, that might lead to acquaintance on the morrow.

He wondered! A thrill of possible adventure ran through him.

She was a merry-looking sort of girl, with a happy, half-roguish face that seemed on the look-out for somebody to play with. Her mother, like most of the people in the big hotel, was an invalid; the girl, a dutiful and patient daughter. They had arrived that very day, apparently.

A laugh is a revealing thing, he thought as he fell asleep to dream of a lob-sided olive rolling consciously toward him, and of a girl's eyes that watched its awkward movements, then looked up into his own and laughed. In his dream the olive had been deliberately and cleverly dispatched upon its uncertain journey. It was a message.

He did not know, of course, that the mother, chiding her daughter's awkwardness, had muttered:

'There you are again, child! True to your name, you never see an olive without doing something queer and odd with it!'

A youngish man, whose knowledge of chemistry, including invisible inks and suchlike mysteries, had proved so valuable to the Censor's Department that for five years he had overworked without a holiday, the Italian Riviera had attracted him, and he had come out for a two months' rest. It was his first visit. Sun, mimosa, blue seas and brilliant skies had tempted him; exchange made a pound worth forty, fifty, sixty, and seventy shillings. He found the place lovely, but somewhat untenanted.

He stayed on, however, caught by the sunshine and the good exchange, also without the physical energy to discover a better,

THE OLIVE

livelier place. He went for walks among the olive-groves; he sat beside the sea and palms; he visited shops and bought things he did not want because the exchange made them seem cheap; he paid immense 'extras' in his weekly bill, then chuckled as he reduced them to shillings and found that a few pence covered them; he lay with a book for hours among the olive-groves.

The olive-groves! His daily life could not escape the olive-groves; to olive-groves, sooner or later, his walks, his expeditions, his meanderings by the sea, his shopping—all led him to these ubiquitous olive-groves.

If he bought a picture postcard to send home, there was sure to be an olive-grove in one corner of it. The whole place was smothered with olive groves, the people owed their incomes and existence to these irrepressible trees. The villages among the hills swam roof-deep in them. They swarmed even in the hotel gardens.

The guide-books praised them as persistently as the residents brought them, sooner or later, into every conversation. They grew lyrical over them:

'And how do you like our olive-trees? Ah, you think them pretty. At first, most people are disappointed. They grow on one.'

'They do,' he agreed.

'I'm glad you appreciate them. I find them the embodiment of grace. And when the wind lifts the underleaves across a whole mountain slope—why, it's wonderful, isn't it? One realises the meaning of "olive-green." '

'One does.' He sighed. 'But, all the same, I should like to get one to eat—an olive, I mean.'

'Ah, to eat, yes. That's not so easy. You see, the crop is...'

'Exactly,' he interrupted impatiently, weary of the habitual and evasive explanations. 'But I should like to taste the *fruit*. I should like to enjoy one.'

For, after a stay of six weeks, he had never once seen an olive on the table, in the shops, nor even on the street barrows at the market-place. He had never tasted one. No one sold olives, though olive-trees were a drug in the place; no one bought them, no one asked for them; it seemed that no one wanted them. The trees, when he looked closely, were thick with a dark little berry that seemed more like a sour sloe than the succulent, delicious, spicy fruit associated with its name.

Men climbed the trunks, everywhere shaking the laden branches and hitting them with long bamboo poles to knock the fruit off, while women and children, squatting on their haunches, spent laborious hours filling baskets underneath, then loading mules and donkeys with their daily 'catch.' But an olive to eat was unobtainable. He had never cared for olives, but now he craved with all his soul to feel his teeth in one.

'Ach! But it is the Spanish olive that you *eat*,' explained the head waiter, a German 'from Basel'. 'These are for oil only.' After which he disliked the olive more than ever—until that night when he saw the first eatable specimen rolling across the shiny parquet floor, propelled toward him by the careless hand of a pretty girl, who then looked up into his eyes and smiled.

He was convinced that Eve, similarly, had rolled the apple toward Adam across the emerald sward of the first garden in the world. The dull, accumulated resentment he had come to feel, subconsciously perhaps, against an elusive fruit was changed in the twinkling of an eye into a source of joy, a symbol of romance.

.   .   .   .   .

He slept usually like the dead. It must have been something very real that made him open his eyes and sit up in bed alertly. There was a noise against his door. He listened. The room was still quite dark. It was early morning. The noise was not repeated.

'Who's there?' he asked in a sleepy whisper. 'What is it?'

The noise came again. Someone was scratching on the door. No, it was somebody tapping.

THE OLIVE

'What d'you want?' he demanded in a louder voice. 'Come in,' he added, wondering sleepily whether he was presentable. Either the hotel was on fire or the porter was waking the wrong person for some sunrise expedition.

Nothing happened. Wide awake now, he turned the switch on, but no light flooded the room. The electricians, he remembered with a curse, were out on strike. He fumbled for the matches, and as he did so a voice in the corridor became distincly audible. It was just outside his door.

'Aren't you ready?' he heard. 'You sleep for ever.'

And the voice, although, never having heard it before, he could not have recognised, belonged, he knew suddenly, to the girl who had let the olive fall. In an instant he was out of bed. He lit a candle.

'I'm coming,' he called softly, as he slipped rapidly into some clothes. 'I'm sorry I've kept you. I shan't be a minute.'

'Be quick then!' he heard, while the candle-flame slowly grew, and he found his garments. Less than three minutes later he openecd the door and, candle in hand, peered into the dark passage.

'Blow it out!' came a peremptory whisper. He obeyed, but not quick enough. A pair of red lips emerged from the shadows. There was a puff, and the candle was extinguished. 'I've got my reputation to consider. We mustn't be seen, of course!'

The face vanished in the darkness, but he had recognised it—the shining skin, the bright, glancing eyes. The sweet breath touched his cheek. The candlestick was taken from him by a swift, deft movement. He heard it knock the wainscoting as it was set down. He went out into a pitch-black corridor, where a soft hand seized his own and led him—by a back-door, it seemed—out into the open air of the hillside immediately behind the hotel.

He saw the stars. The morning was cool and fragrant, the sharp air waked him, and the last vestiges of sleep went flying. He had been drowsy and confused, had obeyed the summons without thinking. He now realised suddenly that he was engaged in an act of madness.

The girl, dressed in some flimsy material thrown loosely about her head and body, stood a few feet away, looking, he thought, like some figure called out of dreams and slumber of a forgotten world, out of legend almost. He saw her evening shoes peep out; he divined an evening dress beneath the gauzy covering. The light wind blew it close against her figure. He thought of a nymph.

'I say—but haven't you been to bed?' he asked stupidly.

He had meant to expostulate, to apologize for his foolish rashness, to scold and say they must go back at once. Instead, this sentence came. He guessed she had been sitting up all night. He stood still a second, staring in mute admiration, his eyes full of bewildered question.

'Watching the stars,' she met his thought with a happy laugh. 'Orion has touched the horizon. I came for you at once. We've got just four hours!' The voice, the smile, the eyes, the reference to Orion, swept him off his feet. Something in him broke loose and flew wildly, recklessly to the stars.

'Let us be off!' he cried, 'before the Bear tilts down. Already Alcyone begins to fade. I'm ready. Come!'

She laughed. The wind blew the gauze aside to show two ivory-white limbs. She caught his hand again, and they scampered together up the steep hillside toward the woods. Soon the big hotel, the villas, the white houses of the little town where natives and visitors still lay soundly sleeping, were out of sight. The farther sky came down to meet them. The stars were paling, but no sign of actual dawn was yet visible. The freshness stung their cheeks. Slowly, the heavens grew lighter, the east turned rose, the outline of the trees defined themselves, there was a stirring of the silvery-green leaves. They were among olive-groves—but the spirits of the trees were dancing. Far below them, a pool of deep colour, they saw the ancient sea. They saw the tiny specks of distant fishing-boats. The sailors were singing to the dawn, and birds among the mimosa of the hanging gardens answered them.

Pausing a moment at length beneath a gaunt old tree, whose struggle to leave the clinging earth had tortured its great writhing arms and trunk, they took their breath, gazing at one another with eyes full of happy dreams.

'You understood so quickly,' said the girl, 'my little message. I knew by your eyes and ears you would.' And she first tweaked his ears with two slender fingers mischievously, then laid her soft palm with a momentary light pressure on both eyes.

'You're half-and-half, at any rate,' she went on looking him up and down for a swift instant of appraisement, 'if you're not altogether.' The laughter showed her white, even little teeth.

'You know how to play, and that's something,' she added. Then, as if to herself, 'You'll be altogether before I've done with you.'

'Shall I?' he stammered, afraid to look at her.

Puzzled, some spirit of compromise still lingering in him, he knew not what she meant; he knew only that the current of life flowed increasingly through his veins, but that her eyes confused him.

'I'm longing for it,' he added. 'How wonderfully you did it! They roll so awkwardly——'

'Oh, that!' She peered at him through a wisp of hair. 'You've kept it, I hope.'

'Rather. It's on my mantelpiece——'

'You're sure you haven't eaten it?' and she made a delicious mimicry with her red lips, so that he saw the tip of a small, pointed tongue.

'I shall keep it,' he swore, 'as long as these arms have life in them,' and he seized her just as she was crouching to escape, and covered her with kisses.

'I knew you longed to play,' she panted, when he released her. 'Still, it was sweet of you to pick it up before another got it.'

'Another!' he exclaimed.

'The gods decide. It's a lob-sided thing, remember. It can't roll straight.' She looked oddly mischievous, elusive.

He stared at her.

'If it had rolled elsewhere—and another had picked it up——?'

he began.

'I should be with that other now!' And this time she was off and away before he could prevent her, and the sound of her silvery laughter mocked him among the olive-trees beyond. He was up and after her in a second, following her slim whiteness in and out of the old-world grove, as she flitted lightly, her hair flying in the wind, her figure flashing like a ray of sunlight or the race of foaming water—till at last he caught her and drew her down upon his knees, and kissed her wildly, forgetting who and where and what he was.

'Hark!' she whispered breathlessly, one arm close about his neck. 'I hear their footsteps. Listen! It is the pipe!'

'The pipe——!' he repeated, conscious of a tiny but delicious shudder.

For a sudden chill ran through him as she said it. He gazed at her. Her hair fell loose about her cheeks, flushed and rosy with his hot kisses. Her eyes were bright and wild for all their softness. Her face, turned sideways to him as she listened, wore an extraordinary look that for an instant made his blood run cold. He saw the parted lips, the small white teeth, the slim neck of ivory, the young bosom panting from his tempestuous embrace. Of an unearthly loveliness and brightness she seemed to him, yet with this strange, remote expression that touched his soul with sudden terror.

Her face turned slowly.

'Who *are* you?' he whispered. He sprang to his feet without waiting for her answer.

He was young and agile; strong, too, with that quick response of muscle they have who keep their bodies well; but he was no match for her. Her speed and agility outclassed his own with ease. She leaped. Before he had moved one leg forward toward escape, she was clinging with soft, supple arms and limbs about him, so that he could not free himself, and as her weight bore him downward to the ground her lips found his own and kissed them into silence. She lay buried again in his embrace, her hair across his eyes, her heart against his heart, and he forgot his question, forgot his little fear, forgot the very world he knew....

'They come, they come,' she cried gaily. 'The Dawn is here. Are you ready?'

'I've been ready for five thousand years,' he answered, leaping to his feet beside her.

'Altogether!' came upon a sparkling laugh that was like wind among the olive-leaves.

Shaking her last gauzy covering from her, she snatched his hand, and they ran forward together to join the dancing throng now crowding up the slope beneath the tress. Their happy singing filled the sky, Decked with vine and ivy, and trailing silvery-green branches, they poured in a flood of radiant life along the mountain-side. Slowly they melted away into the blue distance of the breaking dawn, and, as the last figure disappeared, the sun came up slowly out of a purple sea....

They came to the place he knew—the deserted earthquake village—and a faint memory stirred in him. He did not actually recall that he had visited it already, had eaten his sandwiches with 'hotel friends' beneath its crumbling walls; but there was a dim troubling sense of familiarity—nothing more. The houses still stood, but pigeons lived in them, and weasels, stoats, and snakes had their uncertain homes in ancient bedrooms. Not twenty years ago the peasants thronged its narrow streets, through which the dawn now peered and cool wind breathed among dew-laden brambles.

'I know the house,' she cried, 'the house where we would live!' and raced, a flying form of air and sunlight, into a tumbled cottage that had no roof, no floor or windows. Wild bees had hung a nest against the broken wall.

He followed her. There was sunlight in the room, and there were flowers. Upon a rude, simple table lay a bowl of cream, with eggs, and honey and butter close against a homemade loaf. They sank into each orher's arms upon a couch of fragrant grass and boughs against the window where wild roses bloomed ... and the bees flew in and out.

It was Bussana, the so-called earthquake village, because a sudden earthquake had fallen on it one summer morning when all the inhabitants were at church. The crashing roof killed sixty, the tumbling walls another hundred, and the rest had left it where it stood.

'The church,' he said, vaguely remembering the story. 'They were at prayer——'

The girl laughed carelessly in his ear, setting his blood in a rush and quiver of delicious joy. He felt himself untamed, wild as the wind and animals. 'The true God claimed His own,' she whispered. 'He came back. Ah, they were not ready——the old priests had seen to that. But He came. They heard His music. Then His tread shook the olive-groves, the old ground danced, the hills leapt for joy——'

'They called it earthquake! And the houses crumbled,' he laughed as he pressed her closer to his heart.

'And now we've come back!' she cried merrily. 'We've come back to worship and be glad!' She nestled into him, while the sun rose higher. 'I hear them—hark!' she cried, and again leapt, dancing, from his side. Again he followed her like wind. Through the broken window they saw the naked fauns and nymphs and satyrs rolling, dancing, shaking their soft hoofs amid the ferns and brambles. Toward the ruptured church they sped with feet of light and air. A roar of happy song and laughter rose.

'Come!' he cried. 'We must go too.'

Hand in hand they raced to join the tumbling, dancing throng. She was in his arms and on his back and flung across his shoulders as he ran. They reached the broken building, its whole roof gone sliding years ago, its walls atremble still, its shattered shrines alive with nestling birds.

'Hush!' she whispered, in a tone of awe, yet pleasure. '*He* is there!' She pointed, her bare arm outstretched, above the bending heads.

There, in the empty space, where once stood sacred Host and cup, He sat, filling the niche sublimely and with awful power. His shaggy form, benign yet terrible, rose through the broken stone. The great eyes shone and smiled. The feet were lost in brambles....

'God!' cried a wild, frightened voice, yet with deep worship in it—and the old familiar panic came with portentous swiftness. The great Figure rose.

The birds flew screaming, the animals sought holes, the worshippers, laughing and glad a moment ago, rushed tumbling over one another for the doors.

'He goes again! Who called? Who called like that? His feet shake the ground!'

'It is the earthquake!' screamed a woman's shrill accents in ghastly terror.

'Kiss me—one kiss before we forget again!...' sighed a laughing, passionate voice against his ear. 'Once more your arms, your heart beating on my lips...! You recognised His power. You are now *altogether!* We shall remember!'

But he woke, with the heavy bedclothes stuffed against his mouth and the wind of early morning sighing mournfully about the hotel walls.

.　　.　　.　　.　　.

'Have they left again—those ladies?' he inquired casually of the head waiter, pointing to the table. 'They were here last night at dinner.'

'Who do you mean?' replied the man stupidly, gazing at the spot indicated with a face quite blank. 'Last night—at dinner?' He tried to think.

'An English lady, elderly, with—her daughter——' at which moment precisely the girl came in alone. Lunch was over, the room empty.

There was a second's difficult pause. It seemed ridiculous not to speak. Their eyes met. The girl blushed furiously.

He was very quick for an Englishman. 'I was allowing, myself to ask after your mother,' he began. 'I was afraid' —he glanced at the table laid for one— 'she was not well, perhaps?'

'Oh, but that's very kind of you, I'm sure.' She smiled. He saw the small white even teeth....

And before three days had passed he was so deeply in love that he simply couldn't help himself.

'I believe,' he said lamely, 'this is yours. You dropped it, you know. Er—may I keep it? It's only an olive.'

They were, of course, in an olive-grove when he asked it, and the sun was setting.

She looked at him, looked him up and down, looked at his ears, his eyes. He felt that in another second her little fingers would slip up and tweak the first or close the second with a soft pressure——

'Tell me,' he begged: 'did you dream anything—that first night I saw you?'

She took a quick step backward. 'No,' she said, as he followed her more quickly still, 'I don't think I did. But,' she went on breathlessly as he caught her up, 'I knew—from the way you picked it up——'

'Knew what?' he demanded, holding her tightly so that she could not ge away again.

'That you were already half and half, but would soon be altogether.'

And, as he kissed her, he felt her soft fingers tweak his ears.

THE SACRIFICE

I

LIMASSON was a religious man, though of what depth and quality were unknown, since no trial of ultimate severity had yet tested him. An adherent of no particular creed, he yet had his gods; and his self-discipline was probably more rigorous than his friends conjectured. He was so reserved. Few guessed, perhaps, the desires conquered, the passions regulated, the inner tendencies trained and schooled—not by denying their expression, but by transmuting them alchemically into nobler channels. He had in him the makings of an enthusiastic devotee, and might have become such but for two limitations that prevented. He loved his wealth, labouring to increase it to the neglect of other interests; and, secondly, instead of following up one steady line of search, he scattered himself upon many picturesque theories, like an actor who wants to play all parts rather than concentrate on one. And the more picturesque the part, the more he was attracted. Thus, though he did his duty unshrinkingly and with a touch of love, he accused himself sometimes of merely gratifying a sensuous taste in spiritual sensations. There was this unbalance in him that argued want of depth.

As for his gods—in the end he discovered their reality by first doubting, then denying their existence.

It was this denial and doubt that restored them to their thrones, converting his dilettante skirmishes into genuine, deep belief; and the proof came to him one summer in early June when he was making ready to leave town for his annual month among the mountains.

With Limasson mountains, in some inexplicable sense, were a passion almost, and climbing so deep a pleasure that the ordinary scrambler hardly understood it. Grave as a kind of worship it was to him; the preparations for an ascent, the ascent itself in particular, involved a concentration that seemed symbolical as of a ritual. He not only loved the heights, the massive grandeur, the splendour of vast proportions blocked in space, but loved them with a respect that held a touch of awe. The emotion mountains stirred in him, one might say, was of that profound, incalculable kind that held kinship with his religious feelings, half realised though these were. His gods had their invisible thrones somewhere among the grim, forbidding heights. He prepared himself for this annual mountaineering with the same earnestness that a holy man might approach a solemn festival of his church.

And the impetus of his mind was running with big momentum in this direction, when there fell upon him, almost on the eve of starting, a swift series of disasters that shook his being to its last foundations, and left him stunned among the ruins. To describe these is unnecessary. People said, 'One thing after another like that! What appalling luck! Poor wretch!' then wondered, with the curiosity of children, how in the world he would take it. Due to no apparent fault of his own, these disasters were so sudden that life seemed in a moment shattered, and his interest in existence almost ceased. People shook their heads and thought of the emergency exit. But Limasson was too vital a man to dream of annihilation. Upon him it had a different effect—he turned and questioned what he called his gods. They did not answer or explain. For the first time in his life he doubted. A hair's breadth beyond lay definite denial.

The ruin in which he sat, however, was not material; no man of his age, possessed of courage and a working scheme of life, would permit disaster of a material order to overwhelm him. It was collapse of a mental, spiritual kind, an assault upon the roots of character and temperament. Moral duties laid suddenly upon him threatened to crush. His *personal* existence was assailed, and apparently must end. He must spend the remainder of his life caring for others who were nothing to him. No outlet showed, no way of escape, so diabolically complete was the combination of events that

THE SACRIFICE

rushed his inner trenches. His faith was shaken. A man can but endure so much, and remain human. For him the saturation point seemed reached. He experienced the spiritual equivalent of that physical numbness which supervenes when pain has touched the limit of endurance. He laughed, grew callous, then mocked his silent gods.

It is said that upon this state of blank negation there follows sometimes a condition of lucidity which mirrors with crystal clearness the forces driving behind life at a given moment, a kind of clairvoyance that brings explanation and therefore peace. Limasson looked for this in vain. There was the doubt that questioned, there was the sneer that mocked the silence into which his questions fell; but there was neither answer nor explanation, and certainly not peace. There was no relief. In this tumult of revolt he did none of the things his friends suggested or expected; he merely followed the line of least resistance. He yielded to the impetus that was upon him when the catastrophe came. To their indignant amazement he went out to his mountains.

All marvelled that at such a time he could adopt so trivial a line of action, neglecting duties that seemed paramount; they disapproved. Yet in reality he was taking no definite action at all, but merely drifting, with the momentum that had been acquired just before. He was bewildered with so much pain, confused with suffering, stunned with the crash that flung him helpless amid undeserved calamity. He turned to the mountains as a child to its mother, instinctively. Mountains had never failed to bring him consolation, comfort, peace. Their grandeur restored proportion whenever disorder threatened life. No calculation, properly speaking, was in his move at all; but a blind desire for a violent physical reaction such as climbing brings. And the instinct was more wholesome than he knew.

In the high upland valley among lonely peaks whither Limasson then went, he found in some measure the proportion he had lost. He studiously avoided thinking; he lived in his muscles recklessly. The region with its little Inn was familiar to him; peak after peak he attacked, sometimes with, but more often without a guide, until his reputation as a sane climber, a laurelled member of all the foreign Alpine Clubs, was seriously in danger. That he overdid it physically is beyond question, but that the mountains breathed into him some portion of their enormous calm and deep endurance is also true. His gods, meanwhile, he neglected utterly for the first time in his life. If he thought of them at all, it was as tinsel figures imagination had created, figures upon a stage that merely decorated life for those whom pretty pictures pleased. Only—he had left the theatre and their make-believe no longer hypnotised his mind. He realised their impotence and disowned them. This attitude, however, was subconscious; he lent to it no substance, either of thought or speech. He ignored rather than challenged their existence.

And it was somewhat in this frame of mind—thinking little, feeling even less—that he came out into the hotel vestibule after dinner one evening, and took mechanically the bundle of letters the porter handed to him. They had no possible interest for him; in a corner where the big steam-heater mitigated the chilliness of the hall, he idly sorted them. The score or so of other guests, chiefly expert climbing men, were trailing out in twos and threes from the dining-room; but he felt as little interest in them as in his letters: no conversation could alter facts, no written phrases change his circumstances. At random, then, he opened a business letter with a typewritten address—it would probably be impersonal, less of a mockery, therefore, than the others with their tiresome sham condolences. And, in a sense, it was impersonal; sympathy from a solicitor's office is mere formula, a few extra ticks upon the universal keyboard of a Remington. But as he read it, Limasson made a discovery that startled him into acute and bitter sensation. He had imagined the limit of bearable suffering and disaster already reached. Now, in a few dozen words, his error was proved convincingly. The fresh blow was dislocating.

This culminating news of additional catastrophe disclosed within him entirely new reaches of pain, of biting, resentful fury. Limasson experienced a momentary stopping of the heart as he took it in, a dizziness, a violent sensation of revolt whose impotence induced almost physical nausea. He felt like—death.

'Must I suffer all things?' flashed through his arrested intelligence in letters of fire.

There was a sullen rage in him, a dazed bewilderment, but no positive suffering as yet. His emotion was too sickening to include the smaller pains of disappointment; it was primitive, blind anger that he knew. He read the letter calmly, even to the neat paragraph of machine-made sympathy at the last, then placed it in his inner pocket. No outward sign of disturbance was upon him; his breath came slowly; he reached over to the table for a match, holding it at arm's length lest the sulphur fumes should sting his nostrils.

And in that moment he made his second discovery. The fact that further suffering was still possible included also the fact that some touch of resignation had been left in him, and therefore some vestige of belief as well. Now, as he felt the crackling sheet of stiff paper in his pocket, watched the sulphur die, and saw the wood ignite, this remnant faded utterly away. Like the blackened end of the match, it shrivelled and dropped off. It vanished. Savagely, yet with an external calmness that enabled him to light his pipe with untrembling hand, he addressed his futile deities. And once more in fiery letters there flashed across the darkness of his passionate thought:

'Even this you demand of me—this cruel, ultimate sacrifice?'

And he rejected them, bag and baggage; for they were a mockery and a lie. With contempt he repudiated them for ever. The stage of doubt had passed. He denied his gods. Yet, with a smile upon his lips; for what were they after all but the puppets his religious fancy had imagined? They never had existed. Was it, then merely the picturesque, sensational aspect of his devotional temperament that had created them? That side of his nature, in any case, was dead now, killed by a single devastating blow. The gods went with it.

Surveying what remained of his life, it seemed to him like a city that an earthquake has reduced to ruins. The inhabitants think no worse thing could happen. Then comes the fire.

Two lines of thought, it seems, then developed parallel in him and simultaneously, for while underneath he stormed against this culminating blow, his upper mind dealt calmly with the project of a great expedition he would make at dawn. He had engaged no guide. As an experienced mountaineer, he knew the district well; his name was tolerably familiar, and in half an hour he could have settled all details, and retired to bed with instructions to be called at two. But, instead, he sat there waiting, unable to stir, a human volcano that any moment might break forth into violence. He smoked his pipe as quietly as though nothing had happened, while through the blazing depths of him ran ever this one self-repeating statement: 'Even this you demand of me, this cruel, ultimate sacrifice!...' His self-control, dynamically estimated, just then must have been very great and, thus repressed, the store of potential energy accumulated enormously.

With thought concentrated largely upon this final blow, Limasson had not noticed the people who streamed out of the *salle à manger* and scattered themselves in groups about the hall. Some individual, now and again, approached his chair with the idea of conversation, then, seeing his absorption, turned away. Even when a climber whom he slightly knew reached across him with a word of apology for the matches, Limasson made no response, for he did not see him. He noticed nothing. In particular he did not notice two men, who, from an opposite corner, had for some time been observing him. He now looked up—by chance?—and was vaguely aware that they were discussing him. He met their eyes across the hall, and started.

For at first he thought he knew them. Possibly he had seen them about in the hotel—they seemed familiar—yet he certainly had never spoken with them. Aware of his mistake, he turned his glance elsewhere, though still vividly conscious of their attention. One was a clergyman or a priest; his face wore an air of gravity touched by sadness, a sternness about the lips counteracted by a kindling beauty in the eyes that betrayed enthusiasm nobly regulated. There was a suggestion of stateliness in the man that made the impression very sharp. His clothing emphasised it. He wore a dark tweed suit that was strict in its simplicity. There was austerity in him somewhere.

His companion, perhaps by contrast, seemed inconsiderable in his conventional evening dress. A good deal younger than his friend, his hair, always a tell-tale detail, was a trifle long; the thin fingers that flourished a cigarette wore rings; the face, though picturesque, was flippant, and his entire attitude conveyed a certain insignificance. Gesture, that faultless language which challenges counterfeit, betrayed unbalance somewhere. The impression he produced, however, was shadowy compared to the sharpness of the other. 'Theatrical' was the word in Limasson's mind, as he turned his glance elsewhere. But as he looked away he fidgeted. The interior darkness caused by the dreadful letter rose about him. It engulfed him. Dizziness came with it....

Far away the blackness was fringed with light, and through this light, stepping with speed and carelessness as from gigantic distance, the two men, suddenly grown large, came at him. Limasson, in self-protection, turned to meet them. Conversation he did not desire. Somehow he had expected this attack.

Yet the instant they began to speak—it was the priest who opened fire—it was all so natural and easy that he almost welcomed the diversion. A phrase by way of introduction—and he was speaking of the summits. Something in Limasson's mind turned over. The man was a serious climber, one of his own species. The sufferer felt a certain relief as he heard the invitation, and realised, though dully, the compliment involved.

'If you felt inclined to join us—if you would honour us with your company,' the man was saying quietly, adding something then about 'your great experience' and 'invaluable advice and judgment.'

Limasson looked up, trying hard to concentrate and understand.

'The Tour du Néant?' he repeated, mentioning the peak proposed. Rarely attempted, never conquered, and with an ominous record of disaster, it happened to be the very summit he had meant to attack himself next day.

'You have engaged guides?' He knew the question foolish.

'No guide will try it,' the priest answered, smiling, while his companion added with a flourish, 'but we—we need no guide—if *you* will come.'

'You are unattached, I believe? You are alone?' the priest enquired, moving a little in front of his friend, as though to keep him in the background.

'Yes,' replied Limasson. 'I am quite alone.'

He was listening attentively, but with only part of his mind. He realised the flattery of the invitation. Yet it was like flattery addressed to some one else. He felt himself so indifferent, so—dead. These men wanted his skilful body, his experienced mind; and it was his body and mind that talked with them, and finally agreed to go. Many a time expeditions had been planned in just this way, but to-night he felt there was a difference. Mind and body signed the agreement, but his soul, listening elsewhere and looking on, was silent. With his rejected gods it had left him, though hovering close still. It did not interfere; it did not warn; it even approved; it sang to him from great distance that this expedition cloaked another. He was bewildered by the clashing of his higher and his lower mind.

'At one in the morning then, if that will suit you...' the older man concluded.

'I'll see to the provisions,' exclaimed the younger enthusiastically, 'and I shall take my telephoto for the summit. The porters can come as far as the Great Tower. We're over six thousand feet here already, you see, so...' and his voice died away in the distance as his companion led him off.

Limasson saw him go with relief. But for the other man he would have declined the invitation. At heart he was indifferent enough. What decided him really was the coincidence that the Tour du Néant was the very peak he had intended to attack himself *alone,* and the curious feeling that this expedition cloaked another somehow—almost that these men had a hidden motive. But he dismissed the idea—it was not worth thinking about. A moment later he followed them to bed. So careless was he of the affairs of the world, so dead to mundane interests, that he tore up his other letters and tossed them into a corner of the room—unread.

II

Once in his chilly bedroom he realised that his upper mind had permitted him to do a foolish thing; he had drifted like a schoolboy into an unwise situation. He had pledged himself to an expedition with two strangers, an expedition for which normally he would have chosen his companions with the utmost caution. Moreover, he was guide; they looked to him for safety, while yet it was they had arranged and planned it. But who were these men with whom he proposed to run grave bodily risks? He knew them as little as they knew him. Whence came, he wondered, the curious idea that this climb was really planned by another who was no one of them?

The thought slipped idly across his mind; going out by one door, it came back, however, quickly by another. He did not think about it more than to note its passage through the disorder that passed with him just then for thinking. Indeed, there was nothing in the whole world for which he cared a single brass farthing. As he undressed for bed, he said to himself: 'I shall be called at one... but why am I going with these two on this wild plan?... And who made the plan?'...

It seemed to have settled itself. It came about so naturally and easily, so quickly. He probed no deeper. He didn't care. And for the first time he omitted the little ritual, half prayer, half adoration, it had always been his custom to offer to his deities upon retiring to rest. He no longer recognised them.

How utterly broken his life was! How blank and terrible and lonely! He felt cold, and piled his overcoats upon the bed, as though his mental isolation involved a physical effect as well. Switching off the light by the door, he was in the act of crossing the floor in the darkness when a sound beneath the window caught his ear. Outside there were voices talking. The roar of falling water made them indistinct, yet he was sure they were voices, and that one of them he knew. He stopped still to listen. He heard his own name uttered—'John Limasson.' They ceased. He stood a moment shivering on the boards, then crawled into bed beneath the heavy clothing. But in the act of settling down, they began again. He raised himself again hurriedly to listen. What little wind there was passed in that moment down the valley, carrying off the roar of falling water; and into the moment's space of silence dropped fragments of definite sentences:

'They are close, you say—close down upon the world?' It was the voice of the priest surely.

'For days they have been passing,' was the answer—a rough, deep tone that might have been a peasant's, and a kind of fear in it, 'for all my flocks are scattered.'

'The signs are sure? You know them?'

'Tumult,' was the answer in much lower tones. 'There has been tumult in the mountains...'

There was a break then as though the voices sank too low to be heard. Two broken fragments came next, end of a question—beginning of an answer.

'...the opportunity of a lifetime?'

'...if he goes of his own free will, success is sure. For acceptance is...'

And the wind, returning, bore back the sound of the falling water, so that Limasson heard no more...

An indefinable emotion stirred in him as he turned over to sleep. He stuffed his ears lest he should hear more. He was aware of a sinking of the heart that was inexplicable. What in the world were they talking about, these two? What was the meaning of these disjointed phrases? There lay behind them a grave significance almost solemn. That 'tumult in the mountains' was somehow ominous, its suggestion terrible and mighty. He felt disturbed, uncomfortable, the first emotion that had stirred in him for days. The numbness melted before its faint awakening. Conscience was in it—he felt vague prickings —but it was deeper far than conscience. Somewhere out of sight, in a region life had as yet not plumbed, the words sank down and vibrated like pedal notes. They rumbled away into the night of undecipherable things. And, though explanation failed him, he felt they had reference somehow to the morrow's expedition: how, what, wherefore, he knew not; his name had been spoken—then these curious sentences; that was all. Yet to-morrow's expedition, what was it but an expedition of impersonal kind, not even planned by himself? Merely his own plan taken and altered by others—made over? His personal business, his personal life, were not really in it at all.

The thought startled him a moment. He had no personal life...!

Struggling with sleep, his brain played the endless game of disentanglement without winning a single point, while the under-mind in him looked on and smiled—because it *knew*. Then, suddenly, a great peace fell over him. Exhaustion brought it perhaps. He fell asleep; and next moment, it seemed, he was aware of a thundering at the door and an unwelcome growling voice, " *'s ist bald ein Uhr, Herr! Aufstehen!*'

Rising at such an hour, unless the heart be in it, is a sordid and depressing business; Limasson dressed without enthusiasm, conscious that thought and feeling were exactly where he had left them on going to sleep. The same confusion and bewilderment were in him; also the same deep solemn emotion stirred by the whispering voices. Only long habit enabled him to attend to detail, and ensured that nothing was forgotten. He felt heavy and oppressed, a kind of anxiety about him; the routine of preparation he followed gravely, utterly untouched by the customary joy; it was mechanical. Yet through it ran the old familiar sense of ritual, due to the practice of so many years, that cleansing of mind and body for a big Ascent—like initiatory rites that once had been as important to him as those of some priest who approached the worship of his deity in the temples of ancient time. He performed the ceremony with the same care as though no ghost of vanished faith still watched him, beckoning from the air as formerly.... His knapsack carefully packed, he took his ice-axe from beside the bed, turned out the light, and went down the creaking wooden stairs in stockinged feed, lest his heavy boots should waken the other sleepers. And in his head still rang the phrase he had fallen asleep on—as though just uttered:

'The signs are sure; for days they have been passing—close down upon the world. The flocks are scattered. There has been tumult—tumult in the mountains.' The other fragments he had forgotten. But who were 'they'? And why did the word bring a chill of awe into his blood?

And as the words rolled through him Limasson felt tumult in his thoughts and feelings too. There had been tumult in his life, and all his joys were scattered—joys that hitherto had fed his days. The signs were sure. Something was close down upon his little world—passing—sweeping. He felt a touch of terror.

Outside in the fresh darkness of very early morning the strangers stood waiting for him. Rather, they seemed to arrive in the same instant as himself, equally punctual. The clock in the church tower sounded one. They exchanged low greetings, remarked that the weather promised to hold good, and started off in single file over soaking meadows towards the first belt of forest. The porter—mere peasant, unfamiliar of face and not connected with the hotel led the way with a hurricane lantern. The air was marvellously sweet and fragrant. In the sky overhead the stars shone in their thousands. Only the noise of falling water from the heights, and the regular thud of their heavy boots broke the stillness. And, black against the sky, towered the enormous pyramid of the Tour du Néant they meant to conquer.

Perhaps the most delightful portion of a big ascent is the beginning in the scented darkness while the thrill of possible conquest lies still far off. The hours stretch themselves queerly;

last night's sunset might be days ago; sunrise and the brilliance coming seem in another week, part of dim futurity like children's holidays. It is difficult to realise that this biting cold before the dawn, and the blazing heat to come, both belong to the same to-day.

There were no sounds as they toiled slowly up the zigzag path through the first fifteen hundred feet of pine-woods; no one spoke; the clink of nails and ice-axe points against the stones was all they heard. For the roar of water was felt rather than heard; it beat against the ears and the skin of the whole body at once. The deeper notes were below them now in the sleeping valley; the shriller ones sounded far above, where streams just born out of ponderous snow-beds tinkled sharply....

The change came delicately. The stars turned a shade less brilliant, a softness in them as of human eyes that say farewell. Between the highest branches the sky grew visible. A sighing air smoothed all their crests one way; moss, earth, and open spaces brought keen perfumes; and the little human procession, leaving the forest, stepped out into the vastness of the world above the tree-line. They paused while the porter stooped to put his lantern out. In the eastern sky was colour. The peaks and crags rushed closer.

Was it the Dawn? Limasson turned his eyes from the height of sky where the summits pierced a path for the coming day, to the faces of his companions, pale and wan in the early twilight. How small, how insignificant they seemed amid this hungry emptiness of desolation. The stupendous cliffs fled past them, led by headstrong peaks crowned with eternal snows. Thin lines of cloud, trailing half way up precipice and ridge, seemed like the swish of movement—as though he caught the earth turning as she raced through space. The four of them, timid riders on the gigantic saddle, clung for their lives against her titan ribs, while currents of some majestic life swept up at them from every side. He drew deep draughts of the rarefied air into his lungs. It was very cold. Avoiding the pallid, insignificant faces of his companions, he pretended interest in the porter's operations; he stared fixedly on the ground. It seemed twenty minutes before the flame was extinguished, and the lantern fastened to the pack behind. This Dawn was unlike any he had seen before.

For, in reality, all the while Limasson was trying to bring order out of the extraordinary thoughts and feelings that had possessed him during the slow forest ascent, and the task was not crowned with much success. The Plan, made by others, had taken charge of him, he felt; and he had thrown the reins of personal will and interest loosely upon its steady gait. He had abandoned himself carelessly to what might come. Knowing that he was leader of the expedition, he yet had suffered the porter to go first, taking his own place as it was appointed to him, behind the younger man, but before the priest. In this order, they had plodded, as only experienced climbers plod, for hours without a rest, until half way up a change had taken place. He had wished it, and instantly it was effected. The priest moved past him, while his companion dropped to the rear—the companion who forever stumbled in his speed, whereas the older man climbed surely, confidently. And thereafter Limasson walked more easily—as though the relative positions of the three were of importance somehow. The steep ascent of smothering darkness through the woods became less arduous. He was glad to have the younger man behind him.

For the impression had strengthened as they climbed in silence that this ascent pertained to some significant Ceremony, and the idea had grown insistently, almost stealthily, upon him. The movements of himself and his companions, especially the positions each occupied relatively to the other, established some kind of intimacy that resembled speech, suggesting even question and answer. And the entire performance, while occupying hours by his watch, it seemed to him more than once, had been in reality briefer than the flash of a passing thought, so that he saw it within himself—pictorially. He thought of a picture worked in colours upon a strip of elastic. Some one pulled the strip, and the picture stretched. Or some one released it again, and the picture flew back, reduced to a mere stationary speck. All happened in a single speck of time.

And the little change of position, apparently so trivial, gave point to this singular notion working in his under-mind—that this ascent was a ritual and a ceremony as in older days, its significance approaching revelation, however, for the first time—now. Without language, this stole over him; no words could quite describe it. For it came to him that these three formed a unit, himself being in some fashion yet the acknowledged principal, the leader. The labouring porter had no place in it, for this first toiling through the darkness was a preparation, and when the actual climb began, he would disappear, while Limasson himself went first. This idea that they took part together in a Ceremony established itself firmly in him, with the added wonder that, though so often done, he performed it now for the first time with full comprehension, knowledge, truth. Empty of personal desire, indifferent to an ascent that formerly would have thrilled his heart with ambition and delight, he understood that climbing had ever been a ritual for his soul and of his soul, and that power must result from its sincere accomplishment. It was a symbolical ascent.

In words this did not come to him. He felt it, never criticising. That is, he neither rejected nor accepted. It stole most sweetly, grandly, over him. It floated into him while he climbed, yet so convincingly that he had felt his relative position must be changed. The younger man held too prominent a post, or at least a wrong one—in advance. Then, after the change, effected mysteriously as though all recognised it, this line of certainty increased, and there came upon him the big, strange knowledge that all of life is a Ceremony on a giant scale, and that by performing the movements accurately, with sincere fidelity, there may come—knowledge. There was gravity in him from that moment.

This ran in his mind with certainty. Though his thought assumed no form of little phrases, his brain yet furnished detailed statements that clinched the marvellous thing with simile and incident which daily life might apprehend: that knowledge arises from action; that to do the thing invites the teaching and explains it. Action, moreover, is symbolical; a group of men, a family, an entire nation, engaged in those daily movements which are the working out of their destiny, perform a Ceremony which is in direct relation somewhere to the pattern of greater happenings which are the teachings of the Gods. Let the body imitate, reproduce—in a bedroom, in a wood—anywhere—the movements of the stars, and the meaning of those stars shall sink down into the heart. The movements constitute a script, a language. To mimic the gestures of a stranger is to understand his mood, his point of view—to establish a grave and solemn intimacy. Temples are everywhere, for the entire earth is a temple, and the body, House of Royalty, is the biggest temple of them all. To ascertain the pattern its movements trace in daily life, *could* be to determine the relation of that particular ceremony to the Cosmos, and so learn power. The entire system of Pythagoras, he realised, could be taught without a single word—by movements; and in everyday life even the commonest act and vulgarest movement are part of some big Ceremony—a message from the Gods. Ceremony, in a word, is three-dimensional language, and action, therefore, is the language of the Gods. The Gods he had denied were speaking to him... passing with tumult close across his broken life.... Their passage it was, indeed, that had caused the breaking!

In this cryptic, condensed fashion the great fact came over him—that he and these other two, here and now, took part in some great Ceremony of whose ultimate object as yet he was in ignorance. The impact with which it dropped upon his mind was tremendous. He realised it most fully when he stepped from the darkness of the forest and entered the expanse of glimmering, early light; up till this moment his mind was being prepared only, whereas now he knew. The innate desire to worship which all along had been his, the momentum his religious temperament had acquired during forty years, the yearning to have proof, in a word, that the Gods he once acknowledged were really true, swept back upon him wih that violent reaction which denial had aroused.

He wavered where he stood....

Looking about him, then, while the others rearranged burdens the returning porter now discarded, he perceived the astonishing beauty of the time and place, feeling it soak into him as by the very pores of his skin. From all sides this beauty rushed upon him. Some radiant, winged sense of wonder sped past him through the silent air. A thrill of ecstasy ran down every nerve. The hair of his head stood up. It was far from unfamiliar to him, this sight of the upper mountain world awakening from its sleep of the summer night, but never before had he stood shuddering thus at its exquisite cold glory, nor felt its significance as now, so mysteriously *within himself*. Some transcendent power that held sublimity was passing across this huge desolate plateau, far more majestic than the mere sunrise among mountains he had so often witnessed. There was Movement. He understood why he had seen his companions insignificant. Again he shivered and looked about him, touched by a solemnity that held deep awe.

Personal life, indeed, was wrecked, destroyed, but something greater was on the way. His fragile alliance with a spiritual world was strengthened. He realised his own past insolence. He became afraid.

III

The treeless plateau, littered with enormous boulders, stretched for miles to right and left, grey in the dusk of very early morning. Behind him dropped thick guardian pine-woods into the sleeping valley that still detained the darkness of the night. Here and there lay patches of deep snow, gleaming faintly through thin rising mist; singing streams of icy water spread everywhere among the stones, soaking the coarse rough grass that was the only sign of vegetation. No life was visible; nothing stirred; nor anywhere was movement, but of the quiet trailing mist and of his own breath that drifted past his face like smoke. Yet through the splendid stillness there *was* movement; that sense of absolute movement which results in stillness—it was owing to the stillness that he became aware of it—so vast, indeed, that only immobility could express it. Thus, on the calmest day in summer, may the headlong rushing of the earth through space seem more real than when the tempest shakes the trees and water on its surface; or great machinery turn with such vertiginous velocity that it appears steady to the deceived function of the eye. For it was not through the eye that this solemn Movement made itself known, but rather through a massive sensation that owned his entire body as its organ. Within the league-long amphitheatre of enormous peaks and precipices that enclosed the plateau, piling themselves upon the horizon, Limasson felt the outline of a Ceremony extended. The pulses of its grandeur poured into him where he stood. Its vast design was knowable because they themselves had traced—were even then tracing—its earthly counterpart in little. And the awe in him increased.

'This light is false. We have an hour yet before the true dawn,' he heard the younger man say lightly. 'The summits still are ghostly. Let us enjoy the sensation, and see what we can make of it.'

And Limasson, looking up startled from his reverie, saw that the far-away heights and towers indeed were heavy with shadow, faint still with the light of stars. It seemed to him they bowed their awful heads and that their stupendous shoulders lowered. They drew together, shutting out the world.

'True,' said his companion, 'and the upper snows still wear the spectral shine of night. But let us now move faster, for we travel very light. The sensations you propose will but delay and weaken us.'

He handed a share of the burdens to his companion and to Limasson. Slowly they all moved forward, and the mountains shut them in.

And two things Limasson noted then, as he shouldered his heavier pack and led the way: first, that he suddenly knew their destination though its purpose still lay hidden; and, secondly, that the porter's leaving before the ascent proper began signified finally that ordinary climbing was not their real objective. Also—the dawn was a lifting of inner veils from off his mind, rather than a brightening of the visible earth due to the nearing sun. Thick darkness, indeed, draped this enormous, lonely amphitheatre where they moved.

'You lead us well,' said the priest a few feet behind him, as he picked his way unfalteringly among the boulders and the streams.

'Strange that I do so,' replied Limasson in a low tone, 'for the way is new to me, and the darkness grows instead of lessening.' The language seemed hardly of his choosing. He spoke and walked as in a dream.

Far in the rear the voice of the younger man called plaintively after them:

'You go so fast, I can't keep up with you,' and again he stumbled and dropped his ice-axe among the rocks. He seemed for ever stooping to drink the icy water, or clambering off the trail to test the patches of snow as to quality and depth. 'You're missing all the excitement,' he cried repeatedly. 'There are a hundred pleasures and sensations by the way.'

They paused a moment for him to overtake them; he came up panting and exhausted, making remarks about the fading stars, the wind upon the heights, new routes he longed to try up dangerous couloirs, about everything, it seemed, except the work in hand. There was eagerness in him, the kind of excitement that saps energy and wastes the nervous force, threatening a probable collapse before the arduous object is attained.

'Keep to the thing in hand,' replied the priest sternly. 'We are not really going fast; it is you who are scattering yourself to no purpose. It wears us all. We must husband out resources,' and he pointed significantly to the pyramid of the Tour du Néant that gleamed above them at an incredible altitude.

'We are here to amuse ourselves; life is a pleasure, a sensation, or it is nothing,' grumbled his companion; but there was a gravity in the tone of the older man that discouraged argument and made resistance difficult. The other arranged his pack for the tenth time, twisting his axe through an ingenious scheme of straps and string, and fell silently into line behind his leaders. Limasson moved on again... and the darkness at length began to lift. Far overhead, at first, the snowy summits shone with a hue less spectral; a delicate pink spread softly from the east; there was a freshening of the chilly wind; then suddenly the highest peak that topped the others by a thousand feet of soaring rock, stepped sharply into sight, half golden and half rose. At the same instant, the vast Movement of the entire scene slowed down; there came one or two terrific gusts of wind in quick succession; a roar like an avalanche of falling stones boomed distantly—and Limasson stopped dead and held his breath.

For something blocked the way before him, something he knew he could not pass. Gigantic and unformed, it seemed part of the architecture of the desolate waste about him, while yet it bulked there, enormous in the trembling dawn, as belonging neither to plain nor mountain. Suddenly it was there, where a moment before had been mere emptiness of air. Its massive outline shifted into visibility as though it had risen from the ground. He stood stock still. A cold that was not of this world turned him rigid in his tracks. A few yards behind him the priest had halted too. Farther in the rear they heard the stumbling tread of the younger man, and the faint calling of his voice—a feeble broken sound as of a man whom sudden fear distressed to helplessness.

'We're off the track, and I've lost my way,' the words came on the still air. 'My axe is gone... let us put on the rope!... Hark! Do you hear that roar?' And then a sound as though he came slowly groping on his hands and kness.

'You have exhausted yourself too soon,' the priest answered sternly. 'Stay where you are and rest, for we go no farther. This is the place we sought.'

There was in his tone a kind of ultimate solemnity that for a moment turned Limasson's attention from the great obstacle that blocked his farther way. The darkness lifted veil by veil, not gradually, but by a series of leaps as when some one inexpertly turns a wick. He perceived then that not a single Grandeur loomed in front, but that others of similar kind, some huger than the first, stood all about him, forming an enclosing circle that hemmed him in.

Then, with a start, he recovered himself. Equilibrium and common sense returned. The trick that sight had played upon him, assisted by the rarefied atmosphere of the heights and by the witchery of dawn, was no uncommon one, after all. The long straining of the eyes to pick the way in a uncertain light so easily deceives perspective. Delusion ever follows abrupt change of focus. These shadowy encircling forms were but the rampart of still distant precipices whose giant walls framed the tremendous amphitheatre to the sky.

Their closeness was a mere gesture of the dusk and distance. The shock of the discovery produced an instant's unsteadiness in him that brought bewilderment. He straightened up, raised his head, and looked about him. The cliffs, it seemed, to him, shifted back instantly to their accustomed places; as though after all they *had* been close; there was a reeling among the topmost crags; they balanced fearfully, then stood still against a sky already faintly crimson. The roar he heard, that might well have seemed the tumult of their hurrying speed, was in reality but the wind of dawn that rushed against their ribs, beating the echoes out with angry wings. And the lines of trailing mist, streaking the air like proofs of rapid motion, merely coiled and floated in the empty spaces.

He turned to the priest, who had moved up beside him.

'How strange,' he said, 'is this beginning of new light. My sight went all astray for a passing moment. I thought the mountains stood right across my path. And when I looked up just now it seemed they all ran back.' His voice was small and lost in the great listening air.

The man looked fixedly at him. He had removed his slouch hat, hot with the long ascent, and as he answered, a long thin shadow flitted across his features. A breadth of darkness dropped about them. It was as though a mask were forming. The face that now was covered had been—naked. He was so long in answering that Limasson heard his mind sharpening the sentence like a pencil.

He spoke very slowly. '*They* move perhaps even as Their powers move, and Their minutes are our years. Their passage ever is in tumult. There is disorder then among the affairs of men; there is confusion in their minds. There may be ruin and disaster, but out of the wreckage shall issue strong, fresh growth. For like a sea, They pass.'

There was in his mien a grandeur that seemed borrowed marvellously from the mountains. His voice was grave and deep; he made no sign or gesture; and in his manner was a curious steadiness that breathed through the language a kind of sacred prophecy.

Long, thundering gusts of wind passed distantly across the precipices as he spoke. The same moment, expecting apparently no rejoinder to his strange utterance, he stooped and began to unpack his knapsack. The change from the sacerdotal language to this commonplace and practical detail was singularly bewildering.

'It is the time to rest,' he added, 'and the time to eat. Let us prepare.' And he drew out several small packets and laid them in a row upon the ground. Awe deepened over Limasson as he watched, and with it a great wonder too. For the words seemed ominous, as though this man, upon the floor of some vast Temple, said: 'Let us prepare a sacrifice...!' There flashed into him, out of depths that had hitherto concealed it, a lightning clue that hinted at explanation of the entire strange proceeding—of the abrupt meeting with the strangers, the impulsive acceptance of their project for the great ascent, their grave behaviour as though it were a Ceremonial of immense design, his change of position, the bewildering tricks of sight, and the solemn language, finally, of the older man that corroborated what he himself had deemed at first illusion. In a flying second of time this all swept through him—and with it the sharp desire to turn aside, retreat, to run away.

THE SACRIFICE

Noting the movement, or perhaps divining the emotion prompting it the priest looked up quickly. In his tone was a coldness that seemed as though this scene of wintry desolation uttered words:

'You have come too far to think of turning back. It is not possible. You stand now at the gates of birth—and death. All that might hinder, you have so bravely cast aside. Be brave now to the end.'

And, as Limasson heard the words, there dropped suddenly into him a new and awful insight into humanity, a power that unerringly discovered the spiritual necessities of others, and therefore of himself. With a shock he realised that the younger man who had accompanied them with increasing difficulty as they climbed higher and higher—was but a shadow of reality. Like the porter, he was but an encumbrance who impeded progress. And he turned his eyes to search the desolate landscape.

'You will not find him,' said his companion, 'for he is gone, Never, unless you weakly call, shall you see him again, nor desire to hear his voice.' And Limasson realised that in his heart he had all the while disapproved of the man, disliked him for his theatrical fondness of sensation and effect, more, that he had even hated and despised him. Starvation might crawl upon him where he had fallen and eat his life away before he would stir a finger to save him. It was with the older man he now had dreadful business in hand.

'I am glad,' he answered, 'for in the end he must have proved my death—our death!'

And they drew closer round the little circle of food the priest had laid upon the rocky ground, an intimate understanding linking them together in a sympathy that completed Limasson's bewilderment. There was bread, he saw, and there was salt; there was also a little flask of deep red wine. In the centre of the circle was a miniature fire of sticks the priest had collected from the bushes of wild rhododendron. The smoke rose upwards in a thin blue line. It did not even quiver, so profound was the surrounding stillness of the mountain air, but far away among the precipices ran the boom of falling water, and behind it again, the muffled roar as of peaks and snow-fields that swept with a rolling thunder through the heavens.

'They are passing,' the priest said in a low voice, 'and They know that you are here. You have now the opportunity of a lifetime; for, if you yield acceptance of your own free will, success is sure. You stand before the gates of birth and death. They offer you life.'

'Yet... I denied Them!' He murmured it below his breath.

'Denial is evocation. You called to them, and They have come. The sacrifice of your little personal life is all They ask. Be brave—and yield it.'

He took the bread as he spoke, and, breaking it in three pieces, he placed one before Limasson, one before himself, and the third he laid upon the flame which first blackened and then consumed it.

'Eat it and understand,' he said, 'for it is the nourishment that shall revive your fading life.'

Next, with the salt, he did the same. Then, raising the flask of wine, he put it to his lips, offering it afterwards to his companion. When both had drunk there still remained the greater part of the contents. He lifted the vessel with both hands reverently towards the sky. He stood upright.

'The blood of your personal life I offer to Them in your name. By the renunciation which seems to you as death shall you pass through the gates of birth to the life of freedom beyond. For the ultimate sacrifice that They ask of you is—this.'

And bending low before the distant heights, he poured the wine upon the rocky ground.

For a period of time Limasson found no means of measuring, so terrible were the emotions in his heart, the priest remained in this attitude of worship and obeisance. The tumult in the mountains ceased. An absolute hush dropped down upon the world. There seemed a pause in the inner history of the universe itself. All waited—till he rose again. And, when he did so, the mask that had for hours now been spreading across his features, was accomplished. The eyes gazed sternly down into his own. Limasson looked—and recognised. He stood face to face with the man whom he knew best of all others in the world... himself.

There had been death. There had also been that recovery of splendour which is birth and resurrection.

And the sun that moment, with the sudden surprise that mountains only know, rushed clear above the heights, bathing the landscape and the standing figure with a stainless glory. Into the vast Temple where he knelt, as into that greater inner Temple which is mankind's true House of Royalty, there poured the completing Presence which is—Light.

'For in this way, and in this way only, shall you pass from death to life,' sang a chanting voice he recognised also now for the first time as indubitably his own.

It was marvellous. But the birth of light is ever marvellous. It was anguish; but the pangs of resurrection since time began have been accomplished by the sweetness of fierce pain. For the majority still lie in the pre-natal stage, unborn, unconscious of a definite spiritual existence. In the womb they grope and stifle, depending ever upon another. Denial is ever the call to life, a protest against continued darkness for deliverance. Yet birth is the ruin of all that has hitherto been depended on. There comes then that standing alone which at first seems desolate isolation. The tumult of destruction precedes release.

Limasson rose to his feet, stood with difficulty upright, looked about him from the figure so close now at his side to the snowy summit of that Tour du Néant he would never climb. The roar and thunder of *Their* passage was resumed. It seemed the mountains reeled.

'They are passing,' sang the voice that was beside him and within him too, 'but They have known you, and your offering is accepted. When They come close upon the world there is ever wreckage and disaster in the affairs of men. They bring disorder and confusion into the mind, a confusion that seems final, a disorder that seems to threaten death. For there is tumult in Their Presence, and apparent chaos that seems the abandonment of order. Out of this vast ruin, then, there issues life in new design. The dislocation is its entrance, the dishevelment its strength. There has been birth....'

The sunlight dazzled his eyes. That distant roar, like a wind, came close and swept his face. An icy air, as from a passing star, breathed over him.

'Are you prepared?' he heard.

He knelt again. Without a sign of hesitation or reluctance, he bared his chest to the sun and wind. The flash came swiftly, instantly, descending into his heart with unerring aim. He saw the gleam in the air, he felt the fiery impact of the blow, he even saw the stream gush forth and sink into the rocky ground, far redder than the wine....

He gasped for breath a moment, staggered, reeled, collapsed... and within the moment, so quickly did all happen, he was aware of hands that supported him and helped him to his feet. But he was too weak to stand. They carried him up to bed. The porter, and the man who had reached across him for the matches five minutes before, intending conversation, stood, one at his feet and the other at his head. As he passed through the vestibule of the hotel, he saw the people staring, and in his hand he crumpled up the unopened letters he had received so short a time ago.

'I really think—I can manage alone,' he thanked them. 'If you will set me down I can walk. I felt dizzy for a moment.'

'The heat in the hall——' the gentleman began in a quiet, sympathetic voice.

They left him standing on the stairs, watching a moment to see that he had quite recovered. Limasson walked up the two flights to his room without faltering. The momentary dizziness had passed. He felt quite himself again, strong, confident, able to stand alone, able to move forward, able to *climb*.

THE DAMNED

I

'I'M over forty, Frances, and rather set in my ways,' I said good-naturedly, ready to yield if she insisted that our going together on the visit involved her happiness. 'My work is rather heavy just now too, as you know. The question is, *could* I work there—with a lot of unassorted people in the house?'

'Mabel doesn't mention any other people, Bill,' was my sister's rejoinder. 'I gather she's alone—as well as lonely.'

By the way she looked sideways out of the window at nothing, it was obvious she was disappointed, but to my surprise she did not urge the point; and as I glanced at Mrs. Franklyn's invitation lying upon her sloping lap, the neat, childish hand-writing conjured up a mental picture of the banker's widow, with her timid, insignificant personality, her pale grey eyes and her expression as of a backward child. I thought, too, of the roomy country mansion her late husband had altered to suit his particular needs, and of my visit to it a few years ago when its barren spaciousness suggested a wing of Kensington Museum fitted up temporarily as a place to eat and sleep in. Comparing it mentally with the poky Chelsea flat where I and my sister kept impecunious house, I realised other points as well. Unworthy details flashed across me to entice: the fine library, the organ, the quiet work-room I should have, perfect service, the delicious cup of early tea, and hot baths at any moment of the day—without a geyser!

'It's a longish visit, a month—isn't it?' I hedged, smiling at the details that seduced me, and ashamed of my man's selfishness, yet knowing that Frances expected it of me. 'There *are* points about it, I admit. If you're set on my going with you, I could manage it all right.'

I spoke at length in this way because my sister made no

answer. I saw her tired eyes gazing into the dreariness of Oakley Street and felt a pang strike through me. After a pause, in which again she said no word, I added: 'So, when you write the letter, you might hint, perhaps, that I usually work all the morning, and—er—am not a very lively visitor! Then she'll understand, you see.' And I half-rose to return to my diminutive study, where I was slaving, just then, at an absorbing article on Comparative Aesthetic Values in the Blind and Deaf.

But Frances did not move. She kept her grey eyes upon Oakley Street where the evening mist from the river drew mournful perspectives into view. It was late October. We heard the omnibuses thundering across the bridge. The monotony of that broad, characterless street seemed more than usually depressing. Even in June sunshine it was dead, but with autumn its melancholy soaked into every house between King's Road and the Embankment. It washed thought into the past, instead of inviting it hopefully towards the future. For me, its easy width was an avenue through which nameless slums across the river sent creeping messages of depression, and I always regarded it as Winter's main entrance into London —fog, slush, gloom trooped down it every November, waving their forbidding banners till March came to rout them. Its one claim upon my love was that the south wind swept sometimes unobstructed up it, soft with suggestions of the sea. These lugubrious thoughts I naturally kept to myself, though I never ceased to regret the little flat whose cheapness had seduced us. Now, as I watched my sister's impassive face, I realised that perhaps she, too, felt as I felt, yet, brave woman, without betraying it.

'And, look here, Fanny,' I said, putting a hand upon her shoulder as I crossed the room, 'it would be the very thing for you. You're worn out with catering and housekeeping. Mabel is your oldest friend, besides, and you've hardly seen her since *he* died———'

'She's been abroad for a year, Bill, and only just came back,' my sister interposed. 'She came back rather unexpectedly, though I never thought she would go *there* to live——' She stopped abruptly. Clearly, she was only speaking half her mind. 'Probably,' she went on, 'Mabel wants to pick up old links again.'

'Naturally,' I put in, 'yourself chief among them.' The veiled reference to the house I let pass. It involved discussing the dead man for one thing.

'I feel *I* ought to go anyhow,' she resumed, 'and of course it would be jollier if you came too. You'd get in such a muddle here by yourself, and eat wrong things, and forget to air the rooms, and—oh, everything!' She looked up laughing. 'Only,' she added, 'there's the British Museum——?'

'But there's a big library there', I answered, 'and all the books of reference I could possibly want. It was of you I was thinking. You could take up your painting again; you always sell half of what you paint. It would be a splendid rest too, and Sussex is a jolly country to walk in. By all means, Fanny, I advise——'

Our eyes met, as I stammered in my attempts to avoid expressing the thought that hid in both our minds. My sister had a weakness for dabbling in the various 'new' theories of the day, and Mabel, who before her marriage had belonged to foolish societes for investigating the future life to the neglect of the present one, had fostered this undersirable tendency. Her amiable, impressionable temperament was open to every psychic wind that blew. I deplored, detested the whole business. But even more than this I abhorred the later influence that Mr. Franklyn had steeped his wife in, capturing her body and soul in his sombre doctrines. I had dreaded lest my sister also might be caught.

'Now that she is alone again——'

I stopped short. Our eyes now made pretence impossible, for the truth had slipped out inevitably, stupidly, although unexpressed in definite language. We laughed, turning our faces a moment to look at other things in the room. Frances picked up a book and examined its cover as though she had made an important discovery, while I took my case out and lit a cigarette I did not want to smoke. We left the matter there. I went out of the room before further explanation could cause tension. Disagreements grow into discord from such tiny things—wrong adjectives, or a chance inflection of the voice. Frances had a right to her views of life as much as I had. At least, I reflected comfortably, we had separated upon an agreement this time, recognised mutually, though not actually stated.

And this point of meeting was, oddly enough, our way of regarding some one who was dead. For we had both disliked the husband with a great dislike, and during his three years' married life had only been to the house once—for a week-end visit; arriving late on Saturday, we had left after an early breakfast on Monday morning. Ascribing my sister's dislike to a natural jealousy at losing her old friend, I said merely that he displeased me. Yet we both knew that the real emotion lay much deeper. Frances, loyal, honourable creature, had kept silence; and beyond saying that house and grounds—he altered one and laid out the other—distressed her as an expression of his personality somehow ("distressed" was the word she used), no further explanation had passed her lips.

Our dislike of his personality was easily accounted for—up to a point, since both of us shared the artist's point of view that a creed, cut to measure and carefully dried, was an ugly thing, and that a dogma to which believers must subscribe or perish everlastingly was a barbarism resting upon cruelty. But while my own dislike was purely due to an abstract worship of Beauty, my sister's had another twist in it, for with her 'new' tendencies, she believed that all religions were an aspect of truth and that no one, even the lowest wretch, could escape 'heaven' in the long run.

Samuel Franklyn, the rich banker, was a man universally respected and admired, and the marriage, though Mabel was fifteen years his junior, won general applause; his bride was an heiress in her own right—breweries—and the story of her conversion at a revivalist meeting where Samuel Franklyn had spoken fervidly of heaven, and terrifyingly of sin, hell and damnation, even contained a touch of genuine romance. She was a brand snatched from the burning; his detailed eloquence had frightened her into heaven; salvation came in the nick of time; his words had plucked her from the edge of that lake of fire and brimstone where their worm dieth not and the fire is not quenched. She regarded him as a hero, sighed her relief upon his saintly shoulder, and accepted the peace he offered her with a grateful resignation.

For her husband was a 'religious man' who successfully combined great riches with the glamour of winning souls. He was a portly figure, though tall, with masterful, big hands, the fingers rather thick and red; and his dignity, that just escaped being pompous, held in it something that was implacable. A convinced assurance, almost remorseless, gleamed in his eyes when he preached especially, and his threats of hell fire must have scared souls stronger than the timid, receptive Mabel whom he married. He clad himself in long frock-coats that buttoned unevenly, big square boots, and trousers that invariably bagged at the knee and were a little short; he wore low collars, spats occasionally, and a tall black hat that was not of silk. His voice was alternately hard and unctuous; and he regarded theatres, ball-rooms and race-courses as the vestibule of that brimstone lake of whose geography he was as positive as of his great banking offices in the City. A philanthropist up to the hilt, however, no one ever doubted his complete sincerity; his convictions were ingrained, his faith borne out by his life—as witness his name upon so many admirable Societes, as treasurer, patron, or heading the donation list. He bulked large in the world of doing good, a broad and stately stone in the rampart against evil. And his heart was genuinely king and soft for others—who believed as he did.

Yet, in spite of this true sympathy with suffering and his desire to help, he was narrow as a telegraph wire and unbending as a church pillar; he was intensely selfish; intolerant as an officer of the Inquisition, his bourgeois soul constructed a revolting scheme of heaven that was reproduced in miniature in all he did and planned. Faith was the *sine qua non* of salvation, and by 'faith' he meant belief in his own particular view of things—'which faith, except every one do keep whole and undefiled, without doubt he shall perish everlastingly.' All the world but his own small, exclusive sect must be damned eternally—a pity, but alas, inevitable. *He* was right.

Yet he prayed without ceasing, and gave heavily to the poor—the only thing he could not give being big ideas to his provincial and suburban deity. Pettier than an insect, and more obstinate than a mule, he had also the superior, sleek humility of a 'chosen one'. He was churchwarden too. He read the Lesson in a 'place of worship', either chilly or over-heated, where neither organ, vestments, nor lighted candles were permitted, but where the odour of hair-wash on the boys' heads in the back rows pervaded the entire building.

This portrait of the banker, who accumulated riches both on earth and in heaven, may possibly be overdrawn, however, because Frances and I were 'artistic temperaments' that viewed the type with a dislike and distrust amounting to contempt. The majority considered Samuel Franklyn a worthy man and a good citizen. The majority, doubtless, held the saner view. A few years more, and he certainly would have been made a baronet. He relieved much suffering in the world, as assuredly as he caused many souls the agonies of torturing fear by his emphasis upon damnation. Had there been one point of beauty in him, we might have been more lenient; only we found it not, and, I admit, took little pains to search. I shall never forget the look of dour forgiveness with which he heard our excuses for missing Morning Prayers that Sunday morning of our single visit to The Towers. My sister learned that a change was made soon afterwards, prayers being 'conducted' after breakfast instead of before.

The Towers stood solemnly upon a Sussex hill amid park-like modern grounds, but the house cannot better be described—it would be so wearisome for one thing—than by saying that it was a cross between an overgrown, pretentious Norwood villa and one of those saturnine Institutes for cripples the train passes as it slinks ashamed through South London into

Surrey. It was 'wealthily' furnished and at first sight imposing, but on closer acquaintance revealed a meagre personality, barren and austere. One looked for Rules and Regulations on the walls, all signed By Order. The place was a prison that shut out 'the world.' There was, of course, no billiard-room, no smoking-room, no room for play of any kind, and the great hall at the back, once a chapel, which might have been used for dancing, theatricals, or other innocent amusements, was consecrated in his day to meetings of various kinds, chiefly brigades, temperance or missionary societies. There was a harmonium at one end—on the level floor—a raised dais or platform at the other, and a gallery above for the servants, gardeners and coachmen. It was heated with hot-water pipes, and hung with Doré's pictures, though these latter were soon removed and stored out of sight in the attics as being too unspiritual. In polished, shiny wood, it was a representation in miniature of that poky exclusive Heaven he took about with him, externalising it in all he did and planned, even in the grounds about the house.

Changes in The Towers, Frances told me, had been made during Mabel's year of widowhood abroad—an organ put into the big hall, the library made liveable and recatalogued—when it was permissible to suppose she had found her soul again and returned to her normal, healthy views of life, which included enjoyment and play, literature, music and the arts, without, however, a touch of that trivial thoughtlessness usually termed worldliness. Mrs. Franklyn, as I remembered her, was a quiet little woman, shallow, perhaps, and easily influenced, but sincere as a dog and thorough in her faithful friendship. Her tastes at heart were catholic, and that heart was simple and unimaginative. That she took up with the various movements of the day was sign merely that she was searching in her limited way for a belief that should bring her peace. She was, in fact, a very ordinary woman, her calibre a little less than that of Frances. I knew they used to discuss all kinds of theories together, but as these discussions never resulted in action, I had come to regard her as harmless. Still,

I was not sorry when she married, and I did not welcome now a renewal of the former intimacy. The philanthropist she had given no children, or she would have made a good and sensible mother. No doubt she would marry again.

'Mabel mentions that she's been alone at The Towers since the end of August,' Frances told me at tea-time; 'and I'm sure she feels out of it and lonely. It would be a kindness to go. Besides, I always liked her.'

I agreed. I had recovered from my attack of selfishness. I expressed my pleasure.

'You've written to accept,' I said, half statement and half question.

Frances nodded. 'I thanked for you,' she added quietly, 'explaining that you were not free at the moment, but that later, if not inconvenient, you might come down for a bit and join me.'

I stared. Frances sometimes had this independent way of deciding things. I was convicted, and punished into the bargain.

Of course there followed argument and explanation, as between brother and sister who were affectionate, but the recording of our talk could be of little interest. It was arranged thus, Frances and I both satisfied. Two days later she departed for The Towers, leaving me alone in the flat with everything planned for my comfort and good behaviour—she was rather a tyrant in her quiet way—and her last words as I saw her off from Charing Cross rang in my head for a long time after she was gone:

'I'll write and let you know, Bill. Eat properly, mind, and let me know if anything goes wrong.'

She waved her small gloved hand, nodded her head till the feather brushed the window, and was gone.

II

After the note announcing her safe arrival a week of silence passed, and then a letter came; there were various suggestions for my welfare, and the rest was the usual rambling information and description Frances loved, generously italicised.

'... and we are quite alone,' she went on in her enormous handwriting that seemed such a waste of space and labour, 'though some others are coming presently, I believe. You could work here to your heart's content. Mabel *quite* understands, and says she would love to have you when you feel free to come. She has changed a bit—back to her old natural self: she never mentions *him*. The place has changed too in certain ways: it has more cheerfulness, I think. *She* has put it in, this cheerfulness, spaded it in, if you know what I mean; but it lies about uneasily and is not natural—quite. The organ is a beauty. She must be very rich now, but she's as gentle and sweet as ever. Do you know, Bill, I think he must have *frightened* her into marrying him. I get the impression she was afraid of him.' This last sentence was inked out, but I read it through the scratching; the letters being too big to hide. 'He had an inflexible will beneath all that oily kindness which passed for spiritual. He was a real personality, I mean. I'm sure he'd have sent you and me cheerfully to the stake in another century—*for our own good*. Isn't it odd she never speaks of him, even to me?' This, again, was stroked through, though without the intention to obliterate—merely because it was repetition, probably. 'The only reminder of him in the house now is a big copy of the presentation portrait that stands on the stairs of the Multitechnic Institute at Peckham—you know—that life-size one with his fat hand sprinkled with rings resting on a thick Bible and the other slipped between the buttons of a tight frock-coat. It hangs in the dining-room and rather dominates our meals. I wish Mabel would take it down. I think she'd like to, if she *dared*. There's not a single photograph of him anywhere, even in her own room. Mrs. Marsh is here—you remember her, *his* housekeeper, the wife of the man who got penal servitude for killing a baby or something—*you* said she robbed him and justified her stealing because the story of the unjust steward was in the Bible! How we laughed over that! *She's* just the same too, gliding about all over the house and turning up when least expected.'

Other reminiscences filled the next two sides of the letter, and ran, without a trace of punctuation, into instructions about a Salamander stove for heating my work-room in the flat; these were followed by things I was to tell the cook, and by requests for several articles she had forgotten and would like sent after her, two of them blouses, with descriptions so lengthy and contradictory that I sighed as I read them—'unless you come down soon, in which case perhaps you wouldn't mind bringing them; *not* the mauve one I wear in the evening sometimes, but the pale blue one with lace round the collar and the crinkly front. They're in the cupboard—or the drawer, I'm not sure which—of my bedroom. *Ask Annie* if you're in doubt. Thanks most *awfully*. Send a telegram, remember, and we'll meet you in the motor *any time*. I don't quite know if I shall stay the whole month—*alone*. It all depends....' And she closed the letter, the italicised words increasing recklessly towards the end, with a repetition that Mabel would love to have me 'for myself,' as also to have a 'man in the house', and that I only had to telegraph the day and the train.... This letter, coming by the second post, interrupted me in a moment of absorbing work, and, having read it through to make sure there was nothing requiring instant attention, I threw it aside and went on with my notes and reading. Within five minutes, however, it was back at me again. That restless thing called 'between the lines' fluttered about my mind. My interest in the Balkan States—political article that had been 'ordered'—faded. Somewhere, somehow I felt disquieted, disturbed. At first I persisted in my work, forcing myself to concentrate, but soon found that a layer of new impressions floated between the article and my attention. It was like a shadow, though a shadow that dissolved upon inspection. Once or twice I glanced up, expecting to find some one in the room, that the door had opened unobserved and Annie was waiting for instructions. I heard the 'buses thundering across the bridge. I was aware of Oakley Street. Montenegro and the blue Adriatic melted into the October haze along that depressing Embankment that aped a river bank, and sentences from the letter flashed before my eyes and stung me. Picking it up and reading it through more carefully, I rang the bell and told Annie to find the blouses and pack them for the post, showing her finally the written description, and resenting the superior smile with which she at once interrupted. '*I* know them, sir,' and disappeared.

But it was not the blouses: it was that exasperating thing 'between the lines' that put an end to my work with its elusive teasing nuisance. The first sharp impression is alone of value in such a case, for once analysis begins the imagination constructs all kinds of false interpretation. The more I thought, the more I grew fuddled. The letter, it seemed to me, wanted to say another thing; instead the eight sheets *conveyed* it merely. It came to the edge of disclosure, then halted. There was something on the writer's mind, and I felt uneasy. Studying the sentences brought, however, no revelation, but increased confusion only; for while the uneasiness reamined, the first clear hint had vanished. In the end I closed my books and went out to look up another matter at the British Museum Library. Perhaps I should discover it that way—by turning the mind in a totally new direction. I lunched at the Express Dairy in Oxford Street close by, and telephoned to Annie that I would be home to tea at five.

And at tea, tired physically and mentally after breathing the exhausted air of the Rotunda for five hours, my mind suddenly delivered up its original impression, vivid and clear-cut; no proof accompanied the revelation; it was mere presentiment, but convincing. Frances was disturbed in her mind, her orderly, sensible, housekeeping mind; she was uneasy, even perhaps afraid; something in the house distressed her, and she had need of me. Unless I went down, her time of rest and change, her quite necessary holiday, in fact, would be spoilt. She was too unselfish to say this, but it ran everywhere between the lines. I saw it clearly now. Mrs. Franklyn, moreover—and that meant Frances too—would like a 'man in the house.' It was a disagreeable phrase, a suggestive way of hinting something she dared not state definitely. The two women in that great, lonely barrack of a house were afraid.

My sense of duty, affection, unselfishness, whatever the composite emotion may be termed, was stirred; also my vanity. I acted quickly, lest reflection should warp clear, decent judgment. 'Annie,' I said, when she answered the bell, 'you need not send those blouses by the post. I'll take them down tomorrow when I go. I shall be away a week or two, possibly longer.' And, having looked up a train, I hastened out to telegraph before I could change my fickle mind.

But no desire came that night to change my mind. I was doing the right, the necessary thing. I was even in something of a hurry to get down to The Towers as soon as possible. I chose an early afternoon train.

III

A telegram had told me to come to a town ten miles from the house, so I was saved the crawling train to the local station, and travelled down by an express. As soon as we left London the fog cleared off, and an autumn sun, though without heat in it, painted the landscape with golden browns and yellows. My spirits rose as I lay back in the luxurious motor and sped between the woods and hedges. Oddly enough, my anxiety of overnight had disappeared. It was due, no doubt, to that exaggeration of detail which reflection in loneliness brings. Frances and I had not been separated for over a year, and her letters from The Towers told so little. It had seemed unnatural to be deprived of those intimate particulars of mood and feeling I was accustomed to. We had such confidence in one another, and our affection was so deep. Though she was but five years younger than myself, I regarded her as a child. My attitude was fatherly. In return, she certainly mothered me with a solicitude that never cloyed. I felt no desire to marry while she was still alive. She painted in water-colours with a reasonable success, and kept house for me; I wrote, reviewed books and lectured on aesthetics; we were a humdrum couple of quasi-artists, well satisfied with life, and all I feared for her was that she might become a suffragette or be taken captive by one of these wild theories that caught her imagination sometimes, and that Mabel, for one, had fostered. As for myself, no doubt she deemed me a trifle solid or stolid—I forget which word she preferred—but on the whole there was just sufficient difference of opinion to make intercourse suggestive without monotony, and certainly without quarrelling. Drawing in deep draughts of the stinging autumu air, I felt happy and exhilarated. It was like going for a holiday, with comfort at the end of the journey instead of bargaining for centimes.

But my heart sank noticeably the moment the house came into view. The long drive, lined with hostile monkey trees and formal wellingtonias that were solemn and sedate, was mere extension of the miniature approach to a thousand semi-detached suburban 'residences'; and the appearance of The Towers, as we turned the corner with a rush, suggested a commonplace climax to a story that had begun interestingly, almost thrillingly. A villa had escaped from the shadow of the Crystal Palace, thumped its way down by night, grown suddenly monstrous in a shower of rich rain, and settled itself insolently to stay. Ivy climbed about the opulent red-brick walls, but climbed neatly and with disfiguring effect, sham as on a prison or—the simile made me smile—an orphan asylum. There was no hint of the comely roughness of untidy ivy on a ruin. Clipped, trained and precise it was, as on a brand-new protestant church. I swear there was not a bird's nest nor a single earwig in it anywhere. About the porch it was particularly thick, smothering a seventeenth-century lamp with a contrast that was quite horrible. Extensive glass-houses spread away on the farther side of the house; the numerous towers to which the building owed its name seemed made to hold school bells; and the window-sills, thick with potted flowers, made me think of the desolate suburbs of Brighton or Bexhill. In a commanding position upon the crest of a hill, it overlooked miles of undulating, wooded country southwards to the Downs, but behind it, to the north, thick banks of ilex, holly and privet protected it from the cleaner and more stimulating winds. Hence, though highly placed, it was shut in. Three years had passed since I last set eyes upon, it, but the unsightly memory I had retained was justified by the reality. The place was deplorable.

It is my habit to express my opinions audibly sometimes, when impressions are strong enough to warrant it; but now I only sighed 'Oh, dear,' as I extricated my legs from many rugs and went into the house. A tall parlour-maid, with the bearing of a grenadier, received me, and standing behind her was Mrs. Marsh, the housekeeper, whom I remembered because her untidy back hair had suggested to me that it had been burnt. I went at once to my room, my hostess already dressing for dinner, but Frances came in to see me just as I was struggling with my black tie that had got tangled like a bootlace. She fastened it for me in a neat, effective bow, and while I held my chin up for the operation, staring blankly at the ceiling, the impression came—I wondered, was it her touch that caused it?—that something in her trembled. Shrinking perhaps is the truer word. Nothing in her face or manner betrayed it, nor in her pleasant, easy talk while she tidied my things and scolded my slovenly packing, as her habit was, questioning me about the servants at the flat. The blouses, though right, were crumpled, and my scolding was deserved. There was no impatience even. Yet somehow or other the suggestion of a shrinking reserve and holding back reached my mind. She had been lonely, of course, but it was more than that; she was glad that I had come, yet for some reason unstated she could have wished that I had stayed away. We discussed the news that had accumulated during our brief separation, and in doing so the impression, at best exceedingly slight, was forgotten. My chamber was large and beautifully furnished; the hall and dining-room of our flat would have gone into it with a good remainder; yet it was not a place I could settle down in for work. It conveyed the idea of impermanence, making me feel transient as in a hotel bedroom. This, of course, was the fact. But some rooms convey a settled, lasting hospitality even in a hotel; this one did not; and as I was accustomed to work in the room I slept in, at least when visiting, a slight frown must have crept between my eyes.

'Mabel has fitted a work-room for you just out of the library,' said the clairvoyant Frances. 'No one will disturb you there, and you'll have fifteen thousand books all catalogued within easy reach. There's a private staircase too. You can breakfast in your room and slip down in your dressing-gown if you want to.' She laughed. My spirits took a turn upwards as adsurdly as they had gone down.

'And how are *you*?' I asked, giving her a belated kiss. 'It's jolly to be together again. I did feel rather lost without you, I'll admit.'

'That's natural,' she laughed. 'I'm so glad.'

She looked well and had country colour in her cheeks. She informed me that she was eating and sleeping well, going out for little walks with Mabel, painting bits of scenery again, and enjoying a complete change and rest; and yet, for all her brave description, the word somehow did not quite ring true. Those last words in particular did not ring true. There lay in her manner, just out of sight, I felt, this suggestion of the exact reverse—of unrest, shrinking, almost of anxiety. Certain small strings in her seemed over-tight. 'Keyed-up' was the slang expression that crossed my mind. I looked rather searchingly into her face as she was telling me this.

'Only—the evenings,' she added, noticing my query, yet rather avoiding my eyes, 'the evenings are—well, rather heavy sometimes, and I find it difficult to keep awake.'

'The strong air after London makes you drowsy,' I suggested, 'and you like to get early to bed.'

Frances turned and looked at me for a moment steadily. 'On the contrary, Bill, I dislike going to bed—here. And Mabel goes so early.' She said it lightly enough, fingering the disorder upon my dressing-table in such a stupid way that I saw her mind was working in another direction altogether. She looked up suddenly with a kind of nervousness from the brush and scissors. 'Billy,' she said abruptly, lowering her voice, 'isn't it odd, but I *hate* sleeping alone here? I can't make it out quite; I've never felt such a thing before in my life. Do you—think it's all nonsense?' And she laughed, with her lips but not with her eyes; there was a note of defiance in her I failed to understand.

'Nothing a nature like yours feels strongly is nonsense, Frances,' I replied soothingly.

But I, too, answered with my lips only, for another part of my mind was working elsewhere, and among uncomfortable things. A touch of bewilderment passed over me. I was not certain how best to continue. If I laughed she would tell me no more, yet if I took her too seriously the strings would tighten further. Instinctively, then, this flashed rapidly across me: that something of what she felt, I had also felt, though interpreting it differently. Vague it was, as the coming of rain or storm that announce themselves hours in advance with their hint of faint, unsettling excitement in the air. I had been but a short hour in the house—big, comfortable, luxurious house—but had experienced this sense of being unsettled, unfixed, fluctuating—a kind of impermanence that transient lodgers in hotels must feel, but that a guest in a friend's home ought not to feel, be the visit short or long. To Frances, an impressionable woman, the feeling had come in the terms of alarm. She disliked sleeping alone, while yet she longed to sleep. The precise idea in my mind evaded capture, merely brushing through me, three-quarters out of sight; I realised only that we both felt the same thing, and that neither of us could get at it clearly. Degrees of unrest we felt, but the actual thing did not disclose itself. It did not happen.

I felt strangely at sea for a moment. Frances would interpret hesitation as endorsement, and encouragement might be the last thing that could help her.

'Sleeping in a strange house,' I answered at length, 'is often difficult at first, and one feels lonely. After fifteen months in our tiny flat one feels lost and uncared-for in a big house. It's an uncomfortable feeling—I know it well. And this *is* a barrack, isn't it? The masses of furniture only make it worse. One feels in storage somewhere underground—the furniture doesn't furnish. One must never yield to fancies, though——'

Frances looked away towards the windows; she seemed disappointed a little.

'After our thickly-populated Chelsea,' I went on quickly, 'it seems isolated here.'

But she did not turn back, and clearly I was saying the wrong thing. A wave of pity rushed suddenly over me. Was she really frightened, perhaps? She was imaginative, I knew, but never moody; common sense was strong in her, though she had her times of hypersensitiveness. I caught the echo of some unreasoning, big alarm in her. She stood there, gazing across my balcony towards the sea of wooded country that spread dim and vague in the obscurity of the dusk. The deepening shadows entered the room, I fancied, from the grounds below. Following her abstracted gaze a moment, I experienced a curious sharp desire to leave, to escape. Out yonder was wind and space and freedom. This enormous building was oppressive, silent, still. Great catacombs occured to me, things beneath the ground, imprisonment and capture. I believe I even shuddered a little.

I touched her shoulder. She turned round slowly, and we looked with a certain deliberation into each other's eyes.

'Fanny,' I asked, more gravely than I intended, 'you are not frightened, are you? Nothing has happened, has it?'

She replied with emphasis, 'Of course not! How could it—I mean, why should I?' She stammered, as though the wrong sentence flustered her a second. 'I'ts simply—that I have this ter—this dislike of sleeping alone.'

Naturally, my first thought was how easy it would be to cut our visit short. But I did not say this. Had it been a true solution, Frances would have said it for me long ago.

'Wouldn't Mabel double-up with you?' I said instead, 'or give you an adjoining room, so that you could leave the door between you open? There's space enough, heaven knows.'

And then, as the gong sounded in the hall below for dinner, she said, as with an effort, this thing:

'Mabel did ask me—on the third night—after I had told her. But I declined.'

'You'd rather be alone than with her?' I asked, with a certain relief.

Her reply was so gravely given, a child would have known there was more behind it: 'Not that; but that she did not really want it.'

I had a moment's intuition and acted on it impulsively. 'She feels it too, perhaps, but wishes to face it by herself—and get over it?'

My sister bowed her head, and the gesture made me realise of a sudden how grave and solemn our talk had grown, as though some portentous thing were under discussion. It had come of itself—indefinite as a gradual change of temperature. Yet neither of us knew its nature, for apparently neither of us could state it plainly. Nothing happened, even in our words.

'That *was* my impression,' she said, '—that if she yields to it she encourages it. And a habit forms so easily. Just think,' she added with a faint smile that was the first sign of lightness she had yet betrayed, 'what a nuisance it would be—everywhere —if everybody was afraid of being alone—like that.'

I snatched readily at the chance. We laughed a little, though it was a quiet kind of laughter that seemed wrong. I took her arm and led her towards the door.

'Disastrous, in fact,' I agreed.

She raised her voice to its normal pitch again, as I had done. 'No doubt it will pass,' she said, 'now that you have come. Of course, it's chiefly my imagination.' Her tone was lighter, though nothing could convince me that the matter itself was light—just then. 'And in any case,' tightening her grip on my arm as we passed into the bright enormous corridor and caught sight of Mrs. Franklyn waiting in the cheerless hall below, 'I'm *very* glad you're here, Bill, and Mabel, I know, is too.'

'If it doesn't pass,' I just had time to whisper with a feeble attempt at jollity, 'I'll come at night and snore outside your door. After that you'll be so glad to get rid of me that you won't mind being alone.'

'That's a bargain,' said Frances.

I shook my hostess by the hand, made a banal remark about the long interval since last we met, and walked behind them into the great dining-room, dimly lit by candles, wondering in my heart how long my sister and I should stay, and why in the world we had ever left our cosy little flat to enter this desolation of riches and false luxury at all. The unsightly picture of the late Samuel Franklyn, Esq., stared down upon me from the farther end of the room above the mighty mantelpiece. He looked, I thought, like some pompous Heavenly Butler who denied to all the world, and to us in particular, the right of entry without presentation cards signed by his hand as proof that we belonged to his own exclusive set. The majority, to his deep grief, and in spite of all his prayers on their behalf, must burn and 'perish everlastingly.'

IV

With the instinct of the healthy bachelor I always try to make myself a nest in the place I live in, be it for long or short. Whether visiting, in lodging-house, or in hotel, the first essential is this nest—one's own things built into the walls as a bird builds in its feathers. It may look desolate and uncomfortable enough to others, because the central detail is neither bed nor wardrobe, sofa nor arm-chair, but a good solid writing-table that does not wriggle, and that has wide elbow-room. And The Towers is vividly described for me by the single fact that I could not 'nest' there. I took several days to discover this, but the first impression of impermanence was truer than I knew. The feathers of the mind refused here to lie one way. They ruffled, pointed and grew wild.

Luxurious furniture does not mean comfort; I might as well have tried to settle down in the sofa and arm-chair department of a big shop. My bedroom was easily managed; it was the private workroom, prepared especially for my reception, that made me feel alien and outcast. Externally, it was all one could desire: an ante-chamber to the great library, with not one, but two generous oak tables, to say nothing of smaller ones against the walls with capacious drawers. There were reading-desks, mechanical devices for holding books, perfect light, quiet as in a church, and no approach but across the huge adjoining room. Yet it did not invite.

'I hope you'll be able to work here,' said my little hostess the next morning, as she took me in—her only visit to it while I stayed in the house—and showed me the ten-volume Catalogue. 'It's absolutely quiet and no one will disturb you.'

'If you can't, Bill, you're not much good,' laughed Frances, who was on her arm. 'Even I could write in a study like this!'

I glanced with pleasure at the ample tables, the sheets of thick blotting-paper, the rulers, sealing-wax, paper-knives, and all the other immaculate paraphernalia. 'It's perfect,' I answered with a secret thrill, yet feeling a little foolish. This was for Gibbon or Carlyle, rather than for my pot-boiling insignificancies. 'If I can't write masterpieces here, it's certainly not *your* fault,' and I turned with gratitude to Mrs. Franklyn. She was looking straight at me, and there was a question in her small pale eyes I did not understand. Was she noting the effect upon me, I wondered?

'You'll write here—perhaps a story about the house,' she said, 'Thompson will bring you anything you want; you only have to ring.' She pointed to the electric bell on the central table, the wire running neatly down the leg. 'No one has ever worked here before, and the library has been hardly used since it was put in. So there's no previous atmosphere to affect your imagination—er—adversely.'

We laughed. 'Bill isn't that sort,' said my sister; while I wished they would go out and leave me to arrange my little nest and set to work.

I thought, of course, it was the huge listening library that made me feel so inconsiderable—the fifteen thousand silent, staring books, the solemn aisles, the deep, eloquent shelves. But when the women had gone and I was alone, the beginning of the truth crept over me, and I felt that first hint of disconsolateness which later became an imperative No. The mind shut down, images ceased to rise and flow. I read, made copious notes, but I wrote no single line at The Towers. Nothing completed itself there. Nothing happened.

The morning sunshine poured into the library through ten long narrow windows; birds were singing; the autumn air, rich with a faint aroma of November melancholy that stung the imagination pleasantly, filled my ante-chamber. I looked out upon the undulating wooded landscape, hemmed in by the sweep of distant Downs, and I tasted a whiff of the sea. Rooks cawed as they floated above the elms, and there were lazy cows in the nearer meadows. A dozen times I tried to make my nest and settle down to work, and a dozen times, like a turning fastidious dog upon a hearth-rug, I rearranged my chair and books and papers. The temptation of the Catalogue and shelves, of course, was accountable for much, yet not, I felt, for all. That was a manageable seduction. My work, moreover, was not of the creative kind that requires absolute absorption; it was the mere readable presentation of data I had accumulated. My note-books were charged with facts ready to tabulate—facts, too, that interested me keenly. A mere effort of the will was necessary, and concentration of no difficult kind. Yet, somehow, it seemed beyond me: something for ever pushed the facts into disorder... and in the end I sat in the sunshine, dipping into a dozen books selected from the shelves outside, vexed with myself and only half-enjoying it. I felt restless. I wanted to be elsewhere.

And even while I read, attention wandered. Frances, Mabel, her late husband, the house and grounds, each in turn and sometimes all together, rose uninvited into the stream of thought, hindering any consecutive flow of work. In disconnected fashion came these pictures that interrupted concentration, yet presenting themselves as broken fragments of a bigger thing my mind already groped for unconsciously. They fluttered round this hidden thing of which they were aspects, fugitive interpretations, no one of them bringing complete revelation. There was no adjective, such as pleasant or unpleasant, that I could attach to what I felt, beyond that the result was unsettling. Vague as the atmosphere of a dream, it yet persisted, and I could not dissipate it. Isolated words or phrases in the lines I read sent questions scouring across my mind, sure sign that the deeper part of me was restless and ill at ease.

Rather trivial questions too—half-foolish interrogations, as of a puzzled or curious child: Why was my sister afraid to sleep alone, and why did her friend feel a similar repugnance, yet seek to conquer it? Why was the solid luxury of the house without comfort, its shelter without the sense of permanence? Why had Mrs. Franklin asked *us* to come, artists, unbelieving vagabonds, types at the farthest possible remove from the saved sheep of her husband's household? Had a reaction set in against the hysteria of her conversion? I had seen no signs of religious fervour in her; her atmosphere was that of an ordinary, high-minded woman, yet a woman of the world. Lifeless, though, a little, perhaps, now that I came to think about it: she had made no definite impression upon me of any kind. And my thoughts ran vaguely after this fragile clue.

Closing my book, I let them run. For, with this chance reflection came the discovery that I could not *see* her clearly —could not feel her soul, her personality. Her face, her small pale eyes, her dress and body and walk, all these stood before me like a photograph; but her Self evaded me. She seemed not there, lifeless, empty, a shadow—nothing. The picture was disagreeable, and I put it by. Instantly she melted out, as though light thought had conjured up a phantom that had no real existence. And at that very moment, singularly enough, my eye caught sight of her moving past the window, going silently along the gravel path. I watched her, a sudden new sensation gripping me. 'There goes a prisoner,' my thought instantly ran, 'one who wishes to escape, but cannot.'

What brought the outlandish notion, heaven only knows. The house was of her own choice, she was twice an heiress, and the world lay open at her feet. Yet she stayed—unhappy, frightened, caught. All this flashed over me, and made a sharp impression even before I had time to dismiss it as absurd. But a moment later explanation offered itself, though it seemed as far-fetched as the original impression. My mind, being logical, was obliged to provide something, apparently. For Mrs. Franklyn, while dressed to go out, with thick walking-boots, a pointed stick, and a motor-cap tied on with a veil as for the windy lanes, was obviously content to go no farther than the little garden paths. The costume was a sham and a pretence. It was this, and her lithe, quick movements that suggested a caged creature—a creature tamed by fear and cruelty that cloaked themselves in kindness—pacing up and down, unable to realise why it got no farther, but always met the same bars in exactly the same place. The mind in her was barred.

I watched her go along the paths and down the steps from one terrace to another, until the laurels hid her altogether; and into this mere imagining of a moment came a hint of something slightly disagreeable, for which my mind, search as it would, found no explanation at all. I remembered then certain other little things. They dropped into the picture of their own accord. In a mind not deliberately hunting for clues, pieces of a puzzle sometimes come together in this way, bringing revelation, so that for a second there flashed across me, vanishing instantly again before I could consider it, a large, distressing thought. I can only describe vaguely as a Shadow. Dark and ugly, oppressive certainly it might be described, with something torn and dreadful about the edges that suggested pain and strife and terror. The interior of a prison with two rows of occupied condemned cells, seen years ago in New York, sprang to memory after it—the connection between the two impossible to surmise even. But the 'certain other little things' mentioned above were these: that Mrs. Franklyn, in last night's dinner talk, had always referred to 'this house', but never called it 'home'; and had emphasised unnecessarily, for a well-bred woman, our 'great kindness' in coming down to stay so long with her. Another time, in answer to my futile compliment about the 'stately rooms', she said quietly, 'It is an enormous house for so small a party; but I stay here very little, and only till I get it straight again.' The three of us were going up the great staircase to bed as this was said, and, not knowing quite her meaning, I dropped the subject. It edged delicate ground, I felt. Frances added no word of her own. It now occurred to me abruptly that 'stay' was the word made use of, when 'live' would have been more natural. How insignificant to recall! Yet why did they suggest themselves just at this moment?... And, on going to Frances's room to make sure she was not nervous or lonely, I realised abruptly, that Mrs. Franklyn, of course, had talked with *her* in a confidential sense that I, as a mere visiting brother, could not share. Frances had told me nothing. I might easily have wormed it out of her, had I not felt that for us to discuss further our hostess and her house merely because we were under the roof together, was not quite nice or loyal.

'I'll call you, Bill, if I'm scared,' she had laughed as we parted, my room being just across the big corridor from her own. I had fallen asleep, thinking what in the world was meant by 'getting it straight again'.

And now in my ante-chamber to the library, on the second morning, sitting among piles of foolscap and sheets of spotless blotting-paper, all useless to me, these slight hints came back and helped to frame the big, vague Shadow I have mentioned. Up to the neck in this Shadow, almost drowned, yet just treading water, stood the figure of my hostess in her walking costume. Frances and I seemed swimming to her aid. The Shadow was large enough to include both house and grounds, but farther than that I could not see.... Dismissing it, I fell to reading my purloined book again. Before I turned another page, however, another startling detail leaped out at me: the figure of Mrs. Franklyn in the Shadow was not living. It floated helplessly, like a doll or puppet that has no life in it. It was both pathetic and dreadful.

Any one who sits in reverie thus, of course, may see similar ridiculous pictures when the will no longer guides construction. The incongruities of dreams are thus explained. I merely record the picture as it came. That it remained by me for several days, just as vivid dreams do, is neither here nor there. I did not allow myself to dwell upon it. The curious thing, perhaps, is that from this moment I date my inclination, though not yet my desire, to leave. I purposely say 'to leave.' I cannot quite remember when the word changed to that aggressive, frantic thing which is escape.

V

We were left delightfully to ourselves in this pretentious country mansion with the soul of a villa. Frances took up her painting again, and, the weather being propitious, spent hours out of doors, sketching flowers, trees and nooks of woodland, garden, even the house itself where bits of it peered suggestively across the orchards. Mrs. Franklyn seemed always busy about something or other, and never interfered with us except to propose motoring, tea in another part of the lawn, and so forth. She flitted everywhere, preoccupied, yet apparently doing nothing. The house engulfed her rather. No visitor called. For one thing, she was not supposed to be back from abroad yet; and for another, I think, the neighbourhood—her husband's neighbourhood—was puzzled by her sudden cessation from good works. Brigades and temperance societies did not ask to hold their meetings in the big hall, and the vicar arranged the school-treats in another's field without explanation. The full-length portrait in the dining-room, and the presence of the housekeeper with the 'burnt' backhair, indeed, were the only reminders of the man who once had lived here. Mrs. Marsh retained her place in silence, well-paid sinecure as it doubtless was, yet with no hint of that suppressed disapproval one might have expected from her. Indeed there was nothing positive to disapprove, since nothing 'worldly' entered grounds or building. In her master's lifetime she had been another 'brand snatched from the burning', and it had then been her custom to give vociferous 'testimony' at the revival meetings where he adorned the platform and led in streams of prayer. I saw her sometimes on the stairs, hovering, wandering, half-watching and half-listening, and the idea came to me once that this woman somehow formed a link with the departed influence of her bigoted employer. She, alone among us, *belonged* to the house, and looked at home there. When I saw her talking—oh, with such correct and respectful mien—to Mrs. Franklyn, I had the feeling that for all her unaggressive attitude, she yet exerted some influence that sought to make her mistress stay in the building for ever —live there. She would prevent her escape, prevent 'getting it straight again,' thwart somehow her will to freedom, if she could. The idea in me was of the most fleeting kind. But another time, when I came down late at night to get a book from the library ante-chamber, and found her sitting in the hall—alone—the impression left upon me was the reverse of fleeting. I can never forget the vivid, disagreeable effect it produced upon me. What was she doing there at half-past eleven at night, all alone in the darkness? She was sitting upright, stiff, in a big chair below the clock. It gave me a turn. It was so incongruous and odd. She rose quietly as I turned the corner of the stairs, and asked me respectfully, her eyes cast down as usual, whether I had finished with the library, so that she might lock up. There was no more to it than that; but the picture stayed with me—unpleasantly.

These various impressions came to me at odd moments, of course, and not in a single sequence as I now relate them. I was hard at work before three days were past, not writing, as explained, but reading, making notes, and gathering material from the library for future use. It was in chance moments that these curious flashes came, catching me unawares with a touch of surprise that sometimes made me start. For they proved that my under-mind was still conscious of the Shadow, and that far away out of sight lay the cause of it that left me with a vague unrest, unsettled, seeking to 'nest' in a place that did not want me. Only when this deeper part knows harmony, perhaps, can good brain work result, and my inability to write was thus explained. Certainly, I was always seeking for something here I could not find—an explanation that continually evaded me. Nothing but these trivial hints offered themselves. Lumped together, however, they had the effect of defining the Shadow a little. I became more and more aware of its very real existence. And, if I have made little mention of Frances and my hostess in this connection, it is because they contributed at first little or nothing towards the discovery of what this story tries to tell. Our life was wholly external, normal, quiet, and uneventful; conversation banal—Mrs. Franklyn's conversation in particular. They said nothing that suggested revelation. Both were in this Shadow, and both knew that they were in it, but neither betrayed by word or act a hint of interpretation. They talked privately, no doubt, but of that I can report no details.

And so it was that, after ten days of a very commonplace visit, I found myself looking straight into the face of a Strangeness that defied capture at close quarters. 'There's something here that never happens,' were the words that rose in my mind, 'and that's why none of us can speak of it.' And as I looked out of the window and watched the vulgar blackbirds, with toes turned in, boring out their worms, I realised sharply that even they, as indeed everything large and small in the house and grounds, shared this strangeness, and were twisted out of normal appearance because of it. Life, as expressed in the entire place, was crumpled, dwarfed, emasculated. God's meanings here were crippled, His love of joy was stunted. Nothing in the garden danced or sang. There was hate in it. 'The Shadow,' my thought hurried on to completion, 'is a manifestation of hate; and hate is the Devil.' And then I sat back frightened in my chair, for I knew that I had partly found the truth.

Leaving my books I went out into the open. The sky was overcast, yet the day by no means gloomy, for a soft, diffused light oozed through the clouds and turned all things warm and almost summery. But I saw the grounds now in their nakedness because I understood. Hate means strife, and the two together weave the robe that terror wears. Having no so-called religious beliefs myslf, nor belonging to any set of dogmas called a creed, I could stand outside these feelings and observe. Yet they soaked into me sufficiently for me to grasp sympathetically what others, with more cabined souls (I flattered myself), might feel. That picture in the dining-room stalked everywhere, hid behind every tree, peered down upon me from the peaked ugliness of the bourgeois towers, and left the impress of its powerful hand upon every bed of flowers. 'You must not do this, you must not do that,' went past me through the air. 'You must not leave these narrow paths,' said the rigid iron railings of black. 'You shall not walk here,' was written on the lawns. 'Keep to the steps,' 'Don't pick the flowers; make no noise of laughter, singing, dancing,' was placarded all over the rose-garden, and 'Trespassers will be—not prosecuted but—*destroyed*' hung from the crest of monkey-tree and holly. Guarding the ends of each artificial terrace stood gaunt, implacable policemen, warders, gaolers. 'Come with us,' they chanted, 'or be damned eternally.'

I remember feeling quite pleased with myself that I had discovered this obvious explanation of the prison-feeling the place breathed out. That the posthumous influence of heavy old Samuel Franklyn might be an inadequate solution did not occur to me. By 'getting the place straight again,' his widow, of course, meant forgetting the glamour of fear and foreboding his depressing creed had temporarily forced upon her; and Frances, delicately-minded being, did not speak of it because it was the influence of the man her friend had loved. I felt lighter; a load was lifted from me. 'To trace the unfamiliar to the familiar,' came back a sentence I had read somewhere, 'is to understand.' It was a real relief. I could talk with Frances now, even with my hostess, no danger of treading clumsily. For the key was in my hands. I might even help to dissipate the Shadow, 'to get it straight again.' It seemed, perhaps, our long invitation was explained!

I went into the house laughing—at myself a little. 'Perhaps after all the artist's outlook, with no hard and fast dogmas, is as narrow as the others! How small humanity is! And why is there no possible and true combination of *all* outlooks?'

The feeling of 'unsettling' was very strong in me just then, in spite of my big discovery which was to clear everything up. And at the moment I ran into Frances on the stairs, with a portfolio of sketches under her arm.

It came across me then abruptly that, although she had worked a great deal since we came, she had shown me nothing. It struck me suddenly as odd, unnatural. The way she tried to pass me now confirmed my new-born suspicion that—well, that her results were hardly what they ought to be.

'Stand and deliver!' I laughed, stepping in front of her. 'I've seen nothing you've done since you've been here, and as a rule you show me all your things. I believe they are atrocious and degrading!' Then my laughter froze.

She made a sly gesture to slip past me, and I almost decided to let her go, for the expression that flashed across her face shocked me. She looked uncomfortable and ashamed; the colour came and went a moment in he cheeks, making me think of a child detected in some secret naughtiness. It was almost fear.

'It's because they're not finished then?' I said, dropping the tone of banter, 'or because they're too good for me to understand?' For my criticism of painting, she told me, was crude and ignorant sometimes. 'But you'll let me see them later, won't you?'

Frances, however, did not take the way of escape I offered. She changed her mind. She drew the portfolio from beneath her arm instead. 'You can see them if you *really* want to, Bill,' she said quietly, and her tone reminded me of a nurse who says to a boy just grown out of childhood, 'you are old enough now to look upon horror and ugliness—only I don't advise it.'

'I do want to,' I said, and made to go downstairs with her. But, instead, she said in the same low voice as before, 'Come up to my room, we shall be undisturbed there.' So I guessed that she had been on her way to show the paintings to our hostess, but did not care for us all three to see them together.

My mind worked furiously.

'Mabel asked me to do them,' she explained in a tone of submissive horror, once the door was shut, 'in fact, she begged it of me. You know how persistent she is in her quiet way. I—er—had to.'

She flushed and opened the portfolio on the little table by the window, standing behind me as I turned the sketches over—sketches of the grounds and trees and garden. In the first moment of inspection, however, I did not take in clearly why my sister's sense of modesty had been offended. For my attention flashed a second elsewhere. Another bit of the puzzle had dropped into place, defining still further the nature of what I called 'the Shadow'. Mrs. Franklyn, I now remembered, has suggested to me in the library that I might perhaps write something about the place, and I had taken it for one of her banal sentences and paid no further attention. I realised now that it was said in earnest. She wanted our interpretations, as expressed in our respective 'talents', painting and writing. Her invitation *was* explained. She left us to ourselves on purpose.

'I should like to tear them up,' Frances was whispering behind me with a shudder, 'only I promised——' She hesitated a moment.

'Promised not to?' I asked with a queer feeling of distress, my eyes glued to the papers.

'Promised always to show them to her first,' she finished so low I barely caught it.

I have no intuitive, immediate grasp of the value of paintings; results come to me slowly, and though every one believes his own judgment to be good, I dare not claim that mine is worth more than that of any other layman, Frances had too often convicted me of gross ignorance and error. I can only say that I examined these sketches with a feeling of amazement that contained revulsion, if not actually horror and disgust. They were outrageous. I felt hot for my sister, and it was a relief to know she had moved across the room on some pretence or other, and did not examine them with me. Her talent, of course, is mediocre, yet she has her moments of inspiration — moments, that is to say, when a view of Beauty not normally her own flames divinely through her. And these interpretations struck me forcibly as being thus 'inspired'—not her own. They were uncommonly well done; they were also atrocious. The meaning in them, however, was never more than hinted. There the unholy skill and power came in: they suggested so abominably, leaving most to the imagination. To find such significance in a bourgeois villa garden, and to interpret it with such delicate yet legible certainty, was a kind of symbolism that was sinister, even diabolical. The delicacy was her own, but the point of view was another's. And the word that rose in my mind was not the gross description of 'impure', but the more fundamental qualification—'un-pure'.

In silence I turned the sketches over one by one, as a boy hurries through the pages of an evil book lest he be caught.

'What does Mabel do with them?' I asked presently in a low tone, as I neared the end. 'Does she keep them?'

'She makes notes about them in a book and then destroys them,' was the reply from the end of the room. I heard a sigh of relief. 'I'm glad you've seen them, Bill. I wanted you to— but was afraid to show them. You understand?'

'I understand,' was my reply, though it was not a question intended to be answered. All I understood really was that Mabel's mind was as sweet and pure as my sister's, and that she had some good reason for what she did. She destroyed the sketches, but first made notes! It was an interpretation of the place she sought. Brother-like, I felt resentment, though, that Frances should waste her time and talent, when she might be doing work that she could sell. Naturally, I felt other things as well....

'Mabel pays me five guineas for each one,' I heard. 'Absolutely insists.'

I stared at her stupidly a moment, bereft of speech or wit.

'I must either accept, or go away,' she went on calmly, but a little white. 'I've tried everything. There was a scene the third day I was here—when I showed her my first result. I wanted to write to you, but hesitated——'

'It's unintentional, then, on your part—forgive my asking it, Frances, dear?' I blundered, hardly knowing what to think or say. 'Between the lines' of her letter came back to me. 'I mean, you make the sketches in your ordinary way and—the result comes out of itself, so to speak?'

She nodded, throwing her hands out like a Frenchman. 'We needn't keep the money for ourselves, Bill. We can give it away, but—I must either accept or leave,' and she repeated the shrugging gesture. She sat down on the chair facing me, staring helplessly at the carpet.

'You say there was a scene?' I went on presently, 'She insisted?'

'She begged me to continue,' my sister replied very quietly. 'She thinks—that is, she has an idea or theory that there's something about the place—something she can't get at quite.' Frances stammered badly. She knew I did not encourage her wild theories.

'Something she feels—yes,' I helped her, more than curious.

'Oh, you know what I mean, Bill,' she said desperately. 'That the place is saturated with some influence that she is herself too positive or too stupid to interpret. She's trying to make herself negative and receptive, as she calls it, but can't, of course, succeed. Haven't you noticed how dull and impersonal and insipid she seems, as though she had no personality? She thinks impressions will come to her that way. But they don't——'

'Naturally.'

'So she's trying me—us—what she calls the sensitive and impressionable artistic temperament. She says that until she is sure exactly what this influence is, she can't fight it, turn it out, "get the house straight", as she phrases it.'

Remembering my own singular impressions, I felt more lenient than I might otherwise have done. I tried te keep impatience out of my voice.

'And this influence, what—whose is it?'

We used the pronoun that followed in the same breath, for I answered my own question at the same moment as she did:

'*His*.' Our heads nodded involuntarily towards the floor, the dining-room being directly underneath.

And my heart sank, my curiosity died away on the instant; I felt bored. A commonplace haunted house was the last thing in the world to amuse or interest me. The mere thought exasperated, with its suggestions of imagination, overwrought nerves, hysteria, and the rest. Mingled with my other feelings was certainly disappointment. To see a figure or feel a 'presence', and report from day to day strange incidents to each other would be a form of weariness I could never tolerate.

'But really, Frances,' I said firmly, after a moment's pause, 'it's too far-fetched, this explanation. A curse, you know, belongs to the ghost stories of early Victorian days.' And only my positive conviction that there *was* something after all worth discovering, and that it most certainly was *not* this, prevented my suggesting that we terminate our visit forthwith, or as soon as we decently could. 'This is not a haunted house, whatever it is,' I concluded somewhat vehemently, bringing my hand down upon her odious portfolio.

My sister's reply revived my curiosity sharply.

'I was waiting for you to say that. Mabel says exactly the same. *He* is in it—but it's something more than that alone, something far bigger and more complicated.' Her sentence seemed to indicate the sketches, and though I caught the inference I did not take it up, having no desire to discuss them with her just them indeed, if ever.

I merely stared at her and listened. Questions, I felt sure, would be of little use. It was better she should say her thought in her own way.

'He is one influence, the most recent,' she went on slowly, and always very calmly, 'but there are others—deeper layers, as it were—underneath. If his were the only one, something would happen. But nothing ever does happen. The others hinder and prevent—as though each were struggling to predominate.'

I had felt it already myself. The idea was rather horrible. I shivered.

'That's what is so ugly about it—that nothing ever happens,' she said. 'There is this endless anticipation—always on the dry edge of a result that never materialises. It is torture. Mabel is at her wits' end, you see. And when she begged me—what I felt about my sketches—I mean——' She stammered badly as before.

I stopped her. I had judged too hastily. That queer symbolism in her paintings, pagan and yet not innocent, was, I understood, the result of mixture. I did not pretend to understand, but at least I could be patient. I consequently held my peace. We did talk on a little longer, but it was more general talk that avoided successfully our hostess, the paintings, wild theories, and *him*—until at length the emotion Frances had hitherto so successfully kept under burst vehemently forth again. It had hidden between her calm sentences, as it had hidden between the lines of her letter. It swept her now from head to foot, packed tight in the thing she then said.

'Then, Bill, if it is not an ordinary haunted house,' she asked, *'what is it?'*

The words were commonplace enough. The emotion was in the tone of her voice that trembled; in the gesture she made, leaning forward and clasping both hands upon her knees, and in the slight blanching of her cheeks as her brave eyes asked the question and searched my own with anxiety that bordered upon panic. In that moment she put herself under my protection. I winced.

'And why,' she added, lowering her voice to a still and furtive whisper, 'does nothing ever happen? If only,'—this with great emphasis—'something *would* happen—break this awful tension —bring relief. It's the waiting I cannot stand.' And she shivered all over as she said it, a touch of wildness in her eyes.

I would have given much to have made a true and satisfactory answer. My mind searched frantically for a moment, but in vain. There lay no sufficient answer in me. I felt what she felt, though with differences. No conclusive explanation lay within reach. Nothing happened. Eager as I was to shoot the entire business into the rubbish heap where ignorance and superstition discharge their poisonous weeds, I could not honestly accomplish this. To treat Frances as a child, and merely 'explain away' would be to strain her confidence in my protection, so affectionately claimed. It would further be dishonest to myself—weak, besides—to deny that I had also felt the strain and tension even as she did. While my mind continued searching, I returned her stare in silence; and Frances then, with more honesty and insight than my own, gave suddenly the answer herself—an answer whose truth and adequacy, so far as they went, I could not readily gainsay:

'I think, Bill, because it is too big to happen here—to happen anywhere, indeed, all at once—and too awful!'

To have tossed the sentence aside as nonsense, argued it away, proved that it was really meaningless, would have been easy—at any other time or in any other place; and, had the past week brought me none of the vivid impressions it had brought me, this is doubtless what I should have done. My narrowness again was proved. We understand in others only what we have in ourselves. But her explanation, in a measure, I knew was true. It hinted at the strife and struggle that my notion of a Shadow had seemed to cover thinly.

'Perhaps,' I murmured lamely, waiting in vain for her to say more. 'But you said just now that you felt the thing was "in layers", as it were. Do you mean each one—each influence—fighting for the upper hand?'

I used her phraseology to conceal my own poverty. Terminology, after all, was nothing, provided we could reach the idea itself.

Her eyes said yes. She had her clear conception, arrived at independently, as was her way. And, unlike her sex, she kept it clear, unsmothered by too many words.

'One set of influences gets at me, another gets at you. It's according to our temperaments, I think.' She glanced significantly at the vile portfolio. 'Sometimes they are mixed—and therefore false. There has always been in me, more than in you, the pagan thing, perhaps, though never, thank God, like *that*.'

The frank confession of course invited my own, as it was meant to do. Yet it was difficult to find the words.

'What I have felt in this place, Frances, I honestly can hardly tell you, because—er—my impressions have not arranged themselves in any definite form I can describe. The strife, the agony of vainly-sought escape, and the unrest—a sort of prison atmosphere—this I have felt at different times and with varying degrees of strength. But I find, as yet, no final label to attach. I couldn't say pagan, Christian, or anything like that, I mean, as you do. As with the blind and deaf, you may have an intensification of certain senses denied to me, or even another sense altogether in embryo——'

'Perhaps,' she stopped me, anxious to keep to the point, 'you feel it as Mabel does. She feels the whole thing *complete*.'

'That also is possible,' I said very slowly. I was thinking behind my words. Her odd remark that it was 'big and awful' came back upon me as true. A vast sensation of distress and discomfort swept me suddenly. Pity was in it, and a fierce contempt, a savage, bitter anger as well. Fury against some sham authority was part of it.

'Frances,' I said, caught unawares, and dropping all pretence, 'what in the world can it be?' I looked hard at her. For some minutes neither of us spoke.

'Have *you* felt no desire to interpret it?' she asked presently,

'Mabel did suggest my writing something about the house,' was my reply, 'but I've felt nothing imperative. That sort of writing is not my line, you know. My only feeling,' I added, noticing that she waited for more, 'is the impulse to explain, discover, get it out of me somehow, and so get rid of it. Not by writing, though—as yet.' And again I repeated my former question: 'What in the world do you think it is?' My voice had become involuntarily hushed. There was awe in it.

Her answer, given with slow emphasis, brought back all my reserve: the phraseology provoked me rather:—

'Whatever it is, Bill, it is not of God.'

I got up to go downstairs. I believe I shrugged my shoulders. 'Would you like to leave, Frances? Shall we go back to town?' I suggested this at the door, and hearing no immediate reply, I turned back to look. Frances was sitting with her head bowed over and buried in her hands. The attitude horribly suggested tears. No woman, I realised, can keep back the pressure of strong emotion as long as Frances had done, without ending in a fluid collapse. I waited a moment uneasily, longing to comfort, yet afraid to act—and in this way discovered the existence of the appalling emotion in myself, hitherto but half guessed. At all costs a scene must be prevented: it would involve such exaggeration and over-statement. Brutally, such is the weakness of the ordinary man, I turned the handle to go out, but my sister then raised her head. The sunlight caught her face, framed untidily in its auburn hair, and I saw her wonderful expression with a start. Pity, tenderness and sympathy shone in it like a flame. It was undeniable. There shone through all her features the imperishable love and yearning to sacrifice self for others which I have seen in only one type of human being. It was the great mother look.

'We must stay by Mabel and help her get it straight,' she whispered, making the decision for us both.

I murmured agreement. Abashed and half ashamed, I stole softly from the room and went out into the grounds. And the first thing clearly realised when alone was this: that the long scene between us was without definite result. The exchange of confidence was really nothing but hints and vague suggestion. We had decided to stay, but it was a negative decision not to leave rather than a positive action. All our words and questions, our guesses, inferences, explanations, our most subtle allusions and insinuations, even the odious paintings themselves, were without definite result. Nothing had happened.

VI

And instinctively, once alone, I made for the places where she had painted her extraordinary pictures; I tried to see what she had seen. Perhaps, now that she had opened my mind to another view, I should be sensitive to some similar interpretation—and possibly by way of literary expression. If I were to write about the place, I asked myself, how should I treat it? I deliberately invited an interpretation in the way that came easiest to me—writing.

But in this case there came no such revelation. Looking closely at the trees and flowers, the bits of lawn and terrace, the rose-garden and corner of the house where the flaming creeper hung so thickly, I discovered nothing of the odious, unpure thing her colour and grouping had unconsciously revealed. At first, that is, I discovered nothing. The reality stood there, commonplace and ugly, side by side with her distorted version of it that lay in my mind. It seemed incredible. I tried to force it, but in vain. My imagination, ploughed less deeply than hers, or to another pattern, grew different seed. Where I saw the gross soul of an overgrown suburban garden, inspired by the spirit of a vulgar, rich revivalist who loved to preach damnation, she saw this rush of pagan liberty and joy, this strange licence of primitive flesh which, tainted by the other, produced the adulterated, vile result.

Certain things, however, gradually then became apparent, forcing themselves upon me, willy nilly. They came slowly, but overwhelmingly. Not that facts had changed, or natural details altered in the grounds—this was impossible—but that I noticed for the first time various aspects I had not noticed before—trivial enough, yet for me, just then, significant. Some I remembered from previous days; others I saw now as I wandered to and fro, uneasy, uncomfortable,—almost, it seemed, watched by some one who took note of my impressions. The details were so foolish, the total result so formidable. I was half aware that others tried hard to make me see. It was deliberate. My sister's phrase, 'one layer got at me, another gets at you', flashed, undesired, upon me.

For I saw, as with the eyes of a child, what I can only call a goblin garden—house, grounds, trees, and flowers belonged to a goblin world that children enter through the pages of their fairy tales. And what made me first aware of it was the whisper of the wind behind me, so that I turned with a sudden start, feeling that something had moved closer. An old ash tree, ugly and ungainly, had been artificially trained to form an arbour at one end of the terrace that was a tennis lawn, and the leaves of it now went rustling together, swishing as they rose and fell. I looked at the ash tree, and felt as though I had passed that moment between doors into this goblin garden that crouched behind the real one. Below, at a deeper layer perhaps, lay hidden the one my sister had entered.

To deal with my own, however, I call it goblin, because an odd aspect of the quaint in it yet never quite achieved the picturesque. Grotesque, probably, is the truer word, for everywhere I noticed, and for the first time, this slight alteration of the natural due either to the exaggeration of some detail, or to its suppression, generally, I think, to the latter. Life everywhere appeared to me as blocked from the full delivery of its sweet and lovely message. Some counter influence stopped it—suppression; or sent it awry—exaggeration. The house itself, mere expression, of course, of a narrow, limited mind, was sheer ugliness; it required no further explanation. With the grounds and garden, so far as shape and general plan were concerned, this was also true; but that trees and flowers and other natural details should share the same deficiency perplexed my logical soul, and even dismayed it. I stood and stared, then moved about, and stood and stared again. Everywhere was this mockery of a sinister, unfinished aspect. I sought in vain to recover my normal point of view. My mind had found this goblin garden and wandered to and fro in it, unable to escape.

The change was in myself, of course, and so trivial were the details which illustrated it, that they sound absurd, thus mentioned one by one. For me, they proved it, is all I can affirm. The goblin touch lay plainly everywhere: in the forms of the trees, planted at neat intervals along the lawns; in this twisted ash that rustled just behind me; in the shadow of the gloomy wellingtonias, whose sweeping skirts obscured the grass; but especially, I noticed, in the tops and crests of them. For here, the delicate, graceful curves of last year's growth seemed to shrink back into themselves. None of them pointed upwards. Their life had failed and turned aside just when it should have become triumphant. The character of a tree reveals itself chiefly at the extremities, and it was precisely here that they all drooped and achieved this hint of goblin distortion—in the growth, that is, of the last few years. What ought to have been fairy, joyful, natural, was instead uncomely to the verge of the grotesque. Spontaneous expression was arrested. My mind perceived a goblin garden, and was caught in it. The place grimaced at me.

With the flowers it was similar, though far more difficult to detect in detail for description. I saw the smaller vegetable growth as impish, half-malicious. Even the terraces sloped ill, as though their ends had sagged since they had been so lavishly constructed; their varying angles gave a queerly bewildering aspect to their sequence that was unpleasant to the eye. One might wander among their deceptive lengths and get lost—lost among open terraces!—with the house quite close at hand. Unhomely seemed the entire garden, unable to give repose, restlessness in it everywhere, almost strife, and discord certainly.

Moreover, the garden grew into the house, the house into the garden, and in both was this idea of resistance to the natural—the spirit that says No to joy. All over it I was aware of the effort to achieve another end, the struggle to burst forth and escape into free, spontaneous expression that should be happy and natural, yet the effort for ever frustrated by the weight of this dark shadow that rendered it abortive. Life crawled aside into a channel that was a cul-de-sac, then turned horribly upon itself. Instead of blossom and fruit, there were weeds. This approach of life I was conscious of—then dismal failure. There was no fulfilment. Nothing happened.

And so, through this singular mood, I came a little nearer to understand the unpure thing that had stammered out into expression through my sister's talent. For the unpure is merely negative; it has no existence; it is but the cramped expression of what is true, stammering its way brokenly over false boundaries that seek to limit and confine. Great, full expression of anything is pure, whereas here was only the incomplete, unfinished, and therefore ugly. There was a strife and pain and desire to escape. I found myself shrinking from house and grounds as one shrinks from the touch of the mentally arrested, those in whom life has turned awry. There was almost mutilation in it.

Past items, too, now flocked to confirm this feeling that I walked, liberty captured and half-maimed, in a monstrous garden. I remembered days of rain that refreshed the countryside, but left these grounds, cracked with the summer heat, unsatisfied and thirsty; and how the big winds, that cleaned the woods and fields elsewhere, crawled here with difficulty through the dense foliage that protected The Towers from the North and West and East. They were ineffective, sluggish currents. There was no real wind. Nothing happened. I began to realise—far more clearly than in my sister's fanciful explanation about 'layers'—that here were many contrary influences at work, mutually destructive of one another. House and grounds were not haunted merely; they were the arena of past thinking and feeling, perhaps of terrible, impure beliefs, each striving to suppress the others, yet no one of them achieving supremacy because no one of them was strong enough, no one of them was true. Each, moreover, tried to win me over, though only one was able to reach my mind at all. For some obscure reason—possibly because my temperament had a natural bias towards the grotesque—it was the goblin layer. With me, it was the line of least resistance....

In my own thoughts this 'goblin garden' revealed, of course, merely my personal interpretation. I felt now objectively what long ago my mind had felt subjectively. My work, essential sign of spontaneous life with me, had stopped dead; production had become impossible. I stood now considerably closer to the cause of this sterility. The Cause, rather, turned bolder, had stepped insolently nearer. Nothing happened anywhere; house, garden, mind alike were barren, abortive, torn by the strife of frustrate impulse, ugly, hateful, sinful. Yet behind it all was still the desire of life—desire to escape—accomplish. Hope—an intolerable hope—I became startlingly aware— crowned torture.

And, realising this, though in some part of me where Reason lost her hold, there rose upon me then another and a darker thing that caught me by the throat and made me shrink with a sense of revulsion that touched actual loathing. I knew instantly whence it came, this wave of abhorrence and disgust, for even while I saw red and felt revolt rise in me, it seemed that I grew partially aware of the layer next below the goblin. I perceived the existence of this deeper stratum. One opened the way for the other, as it were. There were so many, yet all inter-related; to admit one was to clear the way for all. If I lingered I should be caught—horribly. They struggled with such violence for supremacy among themselves, however, that this latest uprising was instantly smothered and crushed back, though not before a glimpse had been revealed to me, and the redness in my thoughts transferred itself to colour my surroundings thickly and appallingly—with blood. This lurid aspect drenched the garden, smeared the terraces, lent to the very soil a tinge as of sacrificial rites, that choked the breath in me, while it seemed to fix me to the earth my feet so longed to leave. It was so revolting that at the same time I felt a dreadful curiosity as of fascination—I wished to stay. Between these contrary impulses I think I actually reeled a moment, transfixed by a fascination of the Awful. Through the lighter goblin veil I felt myself sinking down, down, down into this turgid layer that was so much more violent and so much more ancient. The upper layer, indeed, seemed fairy by comparison with this terror born of the lust for blood, thick with the anguish of human sacrificial victims.

THE DAMNED

Upper! Then I was already sinking; my feet were caught; I was actually in it! What atavistic strain, hidden deep within me, had been touched into vile response, giving this flash of intuitive comprehension, I cannot say. The coatings laid on by civilisation are probably thin enough in all of us. I made a supreme effort. The sun and wind came back. I could almost swear I opened my eyes. Something very atrocious surged back into the depths, carrying with it a thought of tangled woods, of big stones standing in a circle, motionless, white figures, the one form bound with ropes, and the ghastly gleam of the knife. Like smoke upon a battlefield, it rolled away....

I was standing on the gravel path below the second terrace when the familiar goblin garden danced back again, doubly grotesque now, doubly mocking, yet, by way of contrast, almost welcome. My glimpse into the depths was momentary, it seems, and had passed utterly away. The common world rushed back with a sense of glad relief, yet ominous now for ever, I felt, for the knowledge of what its past had built upon. In street, in theatre, in the festivities of friends, in music-room or playing-field, even indeed in church—how could the memory of what I had seen and felt leave its hideous trace? The very structure of my Thought, it seemed to me, was stained. What has been thought by others can never be obliterated until....

With a start my reverie broke and fled, scattered by a violent sound that I recognised for the first time in my life as wholly desirable. The returning motor meant that my hostess was back. Yet, so urgent had been my temporary obsession, that my first presentation of her was—well, not as I knew her now. Floating along with a face of anguished torture I saw Mabel, a mere effigy captured by others' thinking, pass down into those depths of fire and blood that only just had closed beneath my feet. She dipped away. She vanished, her fading eyes turned to the last towards some saviour who had failed her. And that strange intolerable hope was in her face.

The mystery of the place was pretty thick about me just then. It was the fall of dusk, and the ghost of slanting sunshine was as unreal as though badly painted. The garden stood at attention all about me. I cannot explain it, but I can tell it, I think, exactly as it happened, for it remains vivid in me for ever—that, for the first time, something *almost happened,* myself apparently the combining link through which it pressed towards delivery:

I had already turned towards the house. In my mind were pictures—not actual thoughts—of the motor, tea on the verandah, my sister, Mabel—when there came behind me this tumultuous, awful rush—as I left the garden. The ugliness, the pain, the striving to escape, the whole negative and suppressed agony that *was* the Place, focused that second into a concentrated effort to produce a result. It was a blinding tempest of long-frustrate desire that heaved at me, surging appallingly behind me like an anguished mob. I was in the act of crossing the frontier into my normal self again, when it came, catching fearfully at my skirts. I might use an entire dictionary of descriptive adjectives yet come no nearer to it than this—the conception of a huge assemblage determined to escape with me, or to snatch me back among themselves. My legs trembled for an instant, and I caught my breath—then turned and ran as fast as possible up the ugly terraces.

At the same instant, as though the clanging of an iron gate cut short the unfinished phrase, I *thought* the beginning of an awful thing:

'The Damned...'

Like this it rushed after me from that goblin garden that had sought to keep me:

'The Damned!'

For there was sound in it. I know full well it was subjective, not actually heard at all; yet somehow sound was in it—a great volume, roaring and booming thunderously, far away, and below me. The sentence dipped back into the depths that gave it birth, unfinished. Its completion was prevented. As usual, nothing happened. But it drove behind me like a hurricane as I ran towards the house, and the sound of it I can only liken to those terrible undertones you may hear standing beside Niagara. They lie behind the mere crash of the falling flood, within it somehow, not audible to all—felt rather than definitely heard.

It seemed to echo back from the surface of those sagging terraces as I flew across their sloping ends, for it was somehow underneath them. It was in the rustle of the wind that stirred the skirts of the drooping wellingtonias. The beds of formal flowers passed it on to the creepers, red as blood, that crept over the unsightly building. Into the structure of the vulgar and forbidding house it sank away; The Towers took it home. The uncomely doors and windows seemed almost like mouths that had uttered the words themselves, and on the upper floors at that very moment I saw two maids in the act of closing them again.

And on the verandah, as I arrived breathless, and shaken in my soul, Frances and Mabel, standing by the tea-table, looked up to greet me. In the faces of both were clearly legible the signs of shock. They watched me coming, yet so full of their own distress that they hardly noticed the state in which I came. In the face of my hostess, however, I read another and a bigger thing than in the face of Frances. Mabel *knew*. She had experienced what I had experienced. She had heard that awful sentence I had heard but heard it not for the first time; heard it, moreover, I verily believe, complete and to its dreadful end.

'Bill, did you hear that curious noise just now?' Frances asked it sharply before I could say a word. Her manner was confused; she looked straight at me; and there was a tremor in her voice she could not hide.

'There's wind about,' I said, 'wind in the trees and sweeping round the walls. It's risen rather suddenly.' My voice faltered rather.

'No. It wasn't wind,' she insisted, with a significance meant for me alone, but badly hidden. 'It was more like distant thunder, we thought. How you ran too!' she added. 'What a pace you came across the terraces!'

I knew instantly from the way she said it that they both

had already heard the sound before and were anxious to know if I had heard it, and how. My interpretation was what they sought.

'It was a curiously deep sound, I admit. It may have been big guns at sea,' I suggested, 'forts or cruisers practising. The coast isn't so very far, and with the wind in the right direction——'

The expression on Mabel's face stopped me dead.

'Like huge doors closing,' she said softly in her colourless voice, 'enormous metal doors shutting against a mass of people clamouring to get out.' The gravity, the note of hopelessness in her tones, was shocking.

Frances had gone into the house the instant Mabel began to speak. 'I'm cold,' she had said; 'I think I'll get a shawl.' Mabel and I were alone. I believe it was the first time we had been really alone since I arrived. She looked up from the teacups, fixing her pallid eyes on mine. She had made a question of the sentence.

'You hear it like that?' I asked innocently. I purposely used the present tense.

She changed her stare from one eye to the other; it was absolutely expressionless. My sister's step sounded on the floor of the room behind us.

'If only——' Mabel began, then stopped, and my own feelings leaping out instinctively completed the sentence I felt was in her mind:

'——something would happen.'

She instantly corrected me. I had caught her thought, yet somehow phrased it wrongly.

'We could escape!' She lowered her tone a little, saying it hurriedly. The 'we' amazed and horrified me; but something in her voice and manner struck me utterly dumb. There was ice and teror in it. It was a dying woman speaking— a lost and hopeless soul.

In that atrocious moment I hardly noticed what was said exactly, but I remember that my sister returned with a grey shawl about her shoulders, and that Mabel said, in her ordinary voice again, 'It *is* chilly, yes; let's have tea inside,' and that two maids, one of them the grenadier, speedily carried the loaded trays into the morning-room and put a match to the logs in the great open fireplace. It was, after all, foolish to risk the sharp evening air, for dusk was falling steadily, and even the sunshine of the day just fading could not turn autumn into summer. I was the last to come in. Just as I left the verandah a large black bird swooped down in front of me past the pillars; it dropped from overhead, swerved abruptly to one side as it caught sight of me, and flapped heavily towards the shrubberies on the left of the terraces, where it disappeared into the gloom. It flew very low, very close. And it startled me, I think because in some way it seemed like my Shadow materialised—as though the dark horror that was rising everywhere from house and garden, then settling back so thickly yet so imperceptibly upon us all, were incarnated in that whirring creature that passed between the daylight and the coming night.

I stood a moment, wondering if it would appear again, before I followed the others indoors, and as I was in the act of closing the windows after me, I caught a glimpse of a figure on the lawn. It was some distance away, on the other side of the shrubberies, in fact where the bird had vanished. But in spite of the twilight that half magnified, half obscured it, the identity was unmistakable. I knew the housekeeper's stiff walk too well to be deceived. 'Mrs. Marsh taking the air,' I said to myself. I felt the necessity of saying it, and I wondered why she was doing so at this particular hour. If I had other thoughts they were so vague, and so quickly and utterly suppressed, that I cannot recall them sufficiently to relate them here.

And, once indoors, it was to be expected that there would come explanation, discussion, conversation, at any rate, regarding the singular noise and its cause, some uttered evidence of the mood that had been strong enough to drive us all inside. Yet there was none. Each of us purposely, and with various skill, ignored it. We talked little, and when we did it was of anything in the world but that. Personally, I experienced a touch of that same bewilderment which had come over me during my first talk with Frances on the evening of my arrival, for I recall now the acute tension, and the hope, yet dread, that one or other of us must sooner or later introduce the subject. It did not happen, however; no reference was made to it even remotely. It was the presence of Mabel, I felt positive, that prohibited. As soon might we have discussed Death in the bedroom of a dying woman.

The only scrap of conversation I remember, where all was ordinary and commonplace, was when Mabel spoke casually to the grenadier asking why Mrs. Marsh had omitted to do something or other—what it was I forget—and that the maid replied respectfully that 'Mrs. Marsh was very sorry, but her 'and still pained her.' I enquired, though so casually that I scarcely know what prompted the words, whether she had injured herself severely, and the reply, 'She upset a lamp and burnt herself,' was said in a tone that made me feel my curiosity was indiscreet, 'but she always has an excuse for not doing things she ought to do.' The little bit of conversation remained with me, and I remember particularly the quick way Frances interrupted and turned the talk upon the delinquencies of servants in general, telling incidents of her own at our flat with a volubility that perhaps seemed forced, and that certainly did not encourage general talk as it may have been intended to do. We lapsed into silence immediately she finished.

But for all our care and all our calculated silence, each knew that something had, in these last moments, come very close; it had brushed us in passing; it had retired; and I am inclined to think now that the large dark thing I saw, riding the dusk, probably bird of prey, was in some sense a symbol of it in my mind—that actually there had been no bird at all, I mean, but that my mood of apprehension and dismay had formed the vivid picture in my thoughts. It had swept past us, it had retreated, but it was now, at this moment, in hiding very close. And it was watching us.

Perhaps, too, it was mere coincidence that I encountered

Mrs. Marsh, *his* housekeeper, several times that evening in the short interval between tea and dinner, and that on each occasion the sight of this gaunt, half-saturnine woman fed my prejudice against her. Once, on my way to the telephone. I ran into her just where the passage is somewhat jammed by a square table carrying the Chinese gong, a grandfather's clock and a box of croquet mallets. We both gave way, then both advanced, then again gave way—simultaneously. It seemed, impossible to pass. We stepped with decision to the same side, finally colliding in the middle, while saying those futile little things, half apology, half excuse, that are inevitable at such times. In the end she stood upright against the wall for me to pass, taking her place against the very door I wished to open. It was ludicrous.

'Excuse me—I was just going in—to telephone,' I explained. And she sidled off, murmuring apologies, but opening the door for me while she did so. Our hands met a moment on the handle. There was a second's awkwardness—it was too stupid. I remembered her injury, and by way of something to say, I enquired after it. She thanked me; it was entirely healed now, but it might have been much worse; and there was something about the 'mercy of the Lord' that I didn't quite catch. While telephoning, however—a London call, and my attention focused on it—I realised sharply that this was the first time I had spoken with her; also, that I had—touched her.

It happened to be a Sunday, and the lines were clear. I got my connection quickly, and the incident was forgotten while my thoughts went up to London. On my way upstairs, then, the woman came back into my mind, so that I recalled other things about her—how she seemed all over the house, in unlikely places often; how I had caught her sitting in the hall alone that night; how she was for ever coming and going with her lugubrious visage and that untidy hair at the back that had made me laugh three years ago with the idea that it looked singed or burnt; and how the impression on my first arrival at The Towers was that this woman somehow kept alive, though its evidence was outwardly suppressed, the influence of her late employer and of his sombre teachings. Somewhere with her was associated the idea of punishment, vindictiveness, revenge. I remembered again suddenly my odd notion that she sought to keep her present mistress here, a prisoner in this bleak and comfortless house, and that really, in spite of her obsequious silence, she was intensely opposed to the change of thought that had reclaimed Mabel to a happier view of life.

All this in a passing second flashed in review before me, and I discovered, or at any rate reconstructed, the real Mrs. Marsh. She was decidedly in the Shadow. More, she stood in the forefront of it, stealthily leading an assault, as it were, against The Towers and its occupants, as though, consciously or unconsciously, she laboured incessantly to this hateful end.

I can only judge that some state of nervousness in me permitted the series of insignificant thoughts to assume this dramatic shape, and that what had gone before prepared the way and led her up at the head of so formidable a procession. I relate it exactly as it came to me. My nerves were doubtless somewhat on edge by now. Otherwise I should hardly have been a prey to the exaggeration at all. I seemed open to so many strange, impressions.

Nothing else, perhaps, can explain my ridiculous conversation with her, when, for the third time that evening, I came suddenly upon the woman half-way down the stairs, standing by an open window as if in the act of listening. She was dressed in black, a black shawl over her square shoulders and black gloves on her big, broad hands. Two black objects, prayerbooks apparently, she clasped, and on her head she wore a bonnet with shaking beads of jet. At first I did not know her, as I came running down upon her from the landing; it was only when she stood aside to let me pass that I saw her profile against the tapestry and recognised Mrs. Marsh. And to catch her on the front stairs, dressed like this, struck me as incongruous —impertiment. I paused in my dangerous descent. Through the opened window came the sound of bells—church bells—

a sound more depressing to me than superstition, and as nauseating. Though the action was ill-judged, I obeyed the sudden prompting—was it a secret desire to attack, perhaps?—and spoke to her.

'Been to church, I suppose, Mrs. Marsh?' I said. 'Or just going, perhaps?'

Her face, as she looked up a second to reply, was like an iron doll that moved its lips and turned its eyes, but made no other imitation of life at all.

'Some of us still goes, sir,' she said unctuously.

It was respectful enough, yet the implied judgment of the rest of the world made me almost angry. A deferential insolence lay behind the affected meekness.

'For those who believe no doubt it *is* helpful,' I smiled. 'True religion brings peace and happiness, I'm sure—joy, Mrs. Marsh, JOY!' I found keen satisfaction in the emphasis.

She looked at me like a knife. I cannot describe the implacable thing that shone in her fixed, stern eyes, nor the shadow of felt darkness that stole across her face. She glittered. I felt hate in her. I knew—she knew too—who was in the thoughts of us both at that moment.

She replied softly, never forgetting her place for an instant:

'There is joy, sir—in 'eaven—over one sinner that repenteth, and in church there goes up prayer to Gawd for those'oo—well, for the others, sir, 'oo——'

She cut short her sentence thus. The gloom about her as she said it was like the gloom about a hearse, a tomb, a darkness of great hopeless dungeons. My tongue ran on of itself with a kind of bitter satisfaction:

'We must believe there are *no* others, Mrs. Marsh. Salvation, you know, would be such a failure if there were. No merciful, all-foreseeing God could ever have devised such a fearful plan——'

Her voice, interrupting me, seemed to rise out of the bowels of the earth:

'They rejected the salvation when it was offered to them, sir, on earth.'

'But you wouldn't have them tortured for ever because of one mistake in ignorance,' I said, fixing her with my eye. 'Come now, would you, Mrs. Marsh? No God worth worshipping could permit such cruelty. Think a moment what it means.'

She stared at me, a curious expression in her stupid eyes. It seemed to me as though the 'woman' in her revolted, while yet she dared not suffer her grim belief to trip. That is, she would willingly have had it otherwise but for a terror that prevented.

'We may pray for them, sir, and we do—we *may* 'ope'. She dropped her eyes to the carpet.

'Good, good!' I put in cheerfully, sorry now that I had spoken at all. 'That's more hopeful, at any rate isn't it?'

She murmured something about Abraham's bosom, and the 'time of salvation not being for ever,' as I tried to pass her. Then a half gesture that she made stopped me. There was something more she wished to say—to ask. She looked up furtively. In her eyes I saw the 'woman' peering out through fear.

'Per'aps, sir.' she faltered, as though lightning must strike her dead, 'per'aps, would you think, a drop of cold water, given in His name, might moisten——?'

But I stopped her, for the foolish talk had lasted long enough.

'Of course,' I exclaimed, 'of course. For God is love, remember, and love means charity, tolerance, sympathy, and sparing others pain,' and I hurried past her, determined to end the outrageous conversation for which yet I knew myself entirely to blame. Behind me, she stood stock-still for several minutes, half bewildered, half alarmed, as I suspected. I caught the fragment of another sentence, one word of it, rather—'punishment'—but the rest escaped me. Her arrogance and condescending tolerance exasperated me, while I was at the same time secretly pleased that I might have touched some string of remorse or sympathy in her after all. Her belief was iron; she dared not let it go; yet somewhere underneath there lurked the germ of a wholesome revulsion. She would help 'them'—if she dared. Her question proved it.

THE DAMNED

Half ashamed of myself, I turned and crossed the hall quickly lest I should be tempted to say more, and in me was a disagreeable sensation as though I had just left the Incurable Ward of some great hospital. A reaction caught me as of nausea. Ugh! I wanted such people cleansed by fire. They seemed to me as centres of contamination whose vicious thoughts flowed out to stain God's glorious world. I saw myself, Frances, Mabel too especially, on the rack, while that odious figure of cruelty and darkness stood over us and ordered the awful handles turned in order that we might be 'saved'—forced, that is, to think and believe exactly as *she* thought and believed.

I found relief for my somewhat childish indignation by letting myself loose upon the organ then. The flood of Bach and Beethoven brought back the sense of proportion. It proved, however, at the same time that there *had* been this growth of distortion in me, and that it had been provided apparently by my closer contact—for the first time—with that funereal personality, the woman who, like her master, believed that all holding views of God that differed from her own, must be damned eternally. It gave me, moreover, some faint clue perhaps, though a clue I was unequal of following up, to the nature of the strife and terror and frustrate influence in the house. That housekeeper had to do with it. She kept it alive. Her thought was like a spell she waved above her mistress's head.

VII

That night I was wakened by a hurried tapping at my door, and before I could answer, Frances stood beside my bed. She had switched on the light as she came in. Her hair fell straggling over her dressing-gown. Her face was deathly pale, its expression so distraught it was almost haggard. The eyes were very wide. She looked almost like another woman.

She was whispering at a great pace: 'Bill, Bill, wake up, quick!'

'I *am* awake. What is it?' I whispered too. I was startled.

'Listen!' was all she said. Her eyes stared into vacancy. There was not a sound in the great house. The wind had dropped, and all was still. Only the tapping seemed to continue endlessly in my brain. The clock on the mantelpiece pointed to half-past two.

'I heard nothing, Frances. What is it?' I rubbed my eyes; I had been very deeply asleep.

'Listen!' she repeated very softly, holding up one finger and turning her eyes towards the door she had left ajar. Her usual calmness had deserted her. She was in the grip of some distressing terror.

For a full minute we held our breath and listened. Then her eyes rolled round again and met my own, and her skin went even whiter than before.

'It woke me,' she said beneath her breath, and moving a step nearer to my bed. 'It was the Noise.' Even her whisper trembled.

'The Noise!' The word repeated itself dully of its own accord. I would rather it had been anything in the world but that—earthquake, foreign cannon, collapse of the house above our heads! 'The Noise, Frances! Are you *sure?*' I was playing really for a little time.

'It was like thunder. At first I thought it *was* thunder. But a minute later it came again—from underground. It's appalling.' She muttered the words, her voice not properly under control.

There was a pause of perhaps a minute, and then we both spoke at once. We said foolish, obvious things that neither of us believed in for a second. The roof had fallen in, there were burglars downstairs, the safes had been blown open. It was to comfort each other as children do that we said these things; also it was to gain further time.

'There's some one in the house, of course,' I heard my voice say finally, as I sprang out of bed and hurried into dressing-gown and slippers. 'Don't be alarmed. I'll go down and see,' and from the drawer I took a pistol it was my habit to carry everywhere with me. I loaded it carefully while Frances stood stock-still beside the bed and watched. I moved towards the open door.

'You stay here, Frances,' I whispered, the beating of my heart making the words uneven, 'while I go down and make a search. Lock yourself in, girl. Nothing can happen to you. It was downstairs, you said?'

'Underneath,' she answered faintly, pointing through the floor.

She moved suddenly between me and the door.

'Listen! Hark!' she said, the eyes in her face quite fixed; 'it's coming again,' and she turned her head to catch the slightest sound. I stood there watching her, and while I watched her, shook. But nothing stirred. From the halls below rose only the whirr and quiet ticking of the numerous clocks. The blind by the open window behind us flapped out a little into the room as the draught caught it.

'I'll come with you, Bill—to the next floor,' she broke the silence. 'Then I'll stay with Mabel—till you come up again.' The blind sank down with a long sigh as she said it.

The question jumped to my lips before I could repress it:

'Mabel is awake. She heard it too?'

I hardly know why horror caught me at her answer. All was so vague and terrible as we stood there playing the great game of this sinister house where nothing ever happened.

'We met in the passage. She was on her way to me.'

What shook in me, shook inwardly. Frances, I mean, did not see it. I had the feeling just that the Noise was upon us, that any second it would boom and roar about our ears. But the deep silence held. I only heard my sister's little whisper coming across the room in answer to my question:

'Then what is Mabel doing now?'

And her reply proved that she was yielding at last beneath the dreadful tension, for she spoke at once, unable longer to keep up the pretence. With a kind of relief, as it were, she said it out, looking helplessly at me like a child:

'She is weeping and gna——'

My expression must have stopped her. I believe I clapped both hands upon her mouth, though when I realised things clearly again, I found they were covering my own ears instead. It was a moment of unutterable horror. The revulsion I felt was actually physical. It would have given me pleasure to fire off all the five chambers of my pistol into the air above my head; the sound—a definite, wholesome sound that explained itself—would have been a positive relief. Other feelings, though, were in me too, all over me, rushing to and fro. It was vain to seek their disentanglement; it was impossible. I confess that I experienced, among them, a touch of paralysing fear—though for a moment only; it passed as sharply as it came, leaving me with a violent flush of blood to the face such as bursts of anger bring, followed abruptly by an icy perspiration over the entire body. Yet I may honestly avow that it was not ordinary personal fear I felt, nor any common dread of physical injury. It was, rather, a vast, impersonal shrinking—a sympathetic shrinking—from the agony and terror that countless others, somewhere, somehow, felt for themselves. The first sensation of a prison overwhelmed me in that instant, of bitter strife and frenzied suffering, and the fiery torture of the yearning to escape that was yet hopelessly uttered.... It was of incredible power. It was real. The vain, intolerable hope swept over me.

I mastered myself, though hardly knowing how, and took my sister's hand. It was as cold as ice, as I led her firmly to the door and out into the passage. Apparently she noticed nothing of my so near collapse, for I caught her whisper as we went. 'You *are* brave, Bill; splendidly brave.'

The upper corridors of the great sleeping house were brightly lit; on her way to me she had turned on every electric switch her hand could reach; and as we passed the final flight of stairs to the floor below, I heard a door shut softly and knew that Mabel had been listening—waiting for us. I led my sister up to it. She knocked, and the door was opened cautiously an inch or so. The room was pitch black. I caught no glimpse of Mabel standing there. Frances turned to me with a hurried whisper, 'Billy, you *will* be careful, won't you?' and went in. I just had time to answer that I would not be long, and Frances to reply, 'You'll find us here——' when the door closed and cut her sentence short before its end.

But it was not alone the closing door that took the final words. Frances—by the way she disappeared I knew it—had made a swift and violent movement into the darkness that was as though she sprang. She leaped upon that other woman who stood back among the shadows, for, simultaneously with the clipping of the sentence, another sound was also stopped—stifled, smothered, choked back lest I should also hear it. Yet not in time. I heard it—a hard and horrible sound that explained both the leap and the abrupt cessation of the whispered words.

I stood irresolute a moment. It was as though all the bones had been withdrawn from my body, so that I must sink and fall. That sound plucked them out, and plucked out my self-possession with them. I am not sure that it was a sound I had ever heard before, though children, I half remembered, made it sometimes in blind rages when they knew not what they did. In a grown-up person certainly I had never known it. I associated it with animals rather—horribly. In the history of the world, no doubt, it has been common enough, alas, but fortunately to-day there can be but few who know it, or would recognise it even when heard. The bones shot back into my body the same instant, but red-hot and burning; the brief instant of irresolution passed; I was torn between the desire to break down the door and enter, and to run—run for my life from a thing I dared not face.

Out of the horrid tumult, then, I adopted neither course. Without reflection, certainly without analysis of what was best to do for my sister, myself or Mabel, I took up my action where it had been interrupted. I turned from the awful door and moved slowly towards the head of the stairs. But that dreadful little sound came with me. I believe my own teeth chattered. It seemed all over the house—in the empty halls that opened into the long passages towards the music-room, and even in the grounds outside the building. From the lawns and barren garden, from the ugly terraces themselves, it rose into the night, and behind it came a curious driving sound, incomplete, unfinished, as of wailing for deliverance, the wailing of desperate souls in anguish, the dull and dry beseeching of hopeless spirits in prison.

That I could have taken the little sound from the bedroom where I actually heard it, and spread it thus over the entire house and grounds, is evidence, perhaps, of the state my nerves were in. The wailing assuredly was in my mind alone. But the longer I hesitated, the more difficult became my task, and, gathering up my dressing-gown, lest I should trip in the darkness, I passed slowly down the staircase into the hall below. I carried neither candle nor matches; every switch in room and corridor was known to me. The covering of darkness was indeed rather comforting than otherwise, for if it prevented seeing, it also prevented being seen. The heavy pistol, knocking against my thigh as I moved, made me feel I was carrying a child's toy, foolishly. I experienced in every nerve that primitive vast dread which is the Thrill of darkness. Merely the child in me was comforted by that pistol.

The night was not entirely black; the iron bars across the glass front door were visible, and, equally, I discerned the big, stiff wooden chairs in the hall, the gaping fireplace, the upright pillars supporting the staircase, the round table in the centre with its books and flower-vases, and the basket that held visitors' cards. There, too, was the stick and umbrella stand and the shelf with railway guides, directory, and telegraph forms. Clocks ticked everywhere with sounds like quiet footfalls. Light fell here and there in patches from the floor above. I stood a moment in the hall, letting my eyes grow more accustomed to the gloom, while deciding on a plan of search. I made out the ivy trailing outside over one of the big windows... and then the tall clock by the front door made a grating noise deep down inside its body—it was the Presentation clock, large and hideous, given by the congregation of his church—and, dreading the booming strike it seemed to threaten, I made a quick decision. If others beside myself were about in the night, the sound of that striking might cover their approach.

So I tiptoed to the right, where the passage led towards the dining-room. In the other direction were the morning- and drawing-rooms, both little used, and various other rooms beyond that had been *his*, generally now kept locked. I thought of my sister, waiting upstairs with that frightened woman for my return. I went quickly, yet stealthily.

And, to my surprise, the door of the dining-room was open. It had been opened. I paused on the threshold, staring about me. I think I fully expected to see a figure blocked in the shadows against the heavy sideboard, or looming on the other side beneath his portrait. But the room was empty; I *felt* it empty. Through the wide bow-windows that gave on to the verandah came an uncertain glimmer that even shone reflected in the polished surface of the dinner-table, and again I perceived the stiff outline of chairs, waiting tenantless all round it, two larger ones with high carved backs at either end. The monkey-trees on the upper terrace, too, were visible outside against the sky, and the solemn crests of the wellingtonias on the terraces below. The enormous clock on the mantelpiece ticked very slowly, as though its machinery were running down, and I made out the pale round patch that was its face. Resisting my first inclination to turn the lights up—my hand had gone so far as to finger the friendly knob—I crossed the room so carefully that no single board creaked, nor a single chair, as I rested a hand upon its back, moved on the parquet flooring. I turned neither to the right nor left, nor did I once look back.

I went towards the long corridor filled with priceless *objets d'art,* that led through various antechambers into the spacious music-room, and only at the mouth of this corridor did I next halt a moment in uncertainty. For this long corridor, lit faintly by high windows on the left from the verandah, was very narrow, owing to the mass of shelves and fancy tables it contained. It was not that I feared to knock over precious things as I went, but, that, because of its ungenerous width, there would be no room to pass another person—if I met one. And the certainty had suddenly come upon me that somewhere in this corridor another person at this actual moment stood. Here, somehow, amid all this dead atmosphere of furniture and impersonal emptiness, lay the hint of a living human presence; and with such conviction did it come upon me, that my hand instinctively gripped the pistol in my pocket before I could even think. Either some one had passed along this corridor just before me, or some one lay waiting at its farther end—withdrawn or flattened into one of the little recesses, to let me pass. It was the person who had opened the door. And the blood ran from my heart as I realised it.

It was not courage that sent me on, but rather a strong impulsion from behind that made it impossible to retreat: the feeling that a throng pressed at my back, drawing nearer and nearer; that I was already half surrounded, swept, dragged, coaxed into a vast prison-house where there was wailing and gnashing of teeth, where their worm dieth not and their fire is not quenched. I can neither explain nor justify the storm of irrational emotion that swept me as I stood in that moment, staring down the length of the silent corridor towards the music-room at the far end, I can only repeat that no personal bravery sent me down it, but that the negative emotion of fear was swamped in this vast sea of pity and commiseration for others that surged upon me.

My senses, at least, were no whit confused; if anything, my brain registered impressions with keener accuracy than usual. I noticed, for instance, that the two swinging doors of baize that cut the corridor into definite lengths, making little rooms of the spaces between them, were both wide-open—in the dim light no mean achievement. Also that the fronds of a palm plant, some ten feet in front of me, still stirred gently from the air of some one who had recently gone past them. The long green leaves waved to and fro like hands. Then I went stealthily forward down the narrow space, proud even that I had this command of myself, and so carefully that my feet made no sound upon the Japanese matting on the floor.

THE DAMNED

It was a journey that seemed timeless. I have no idea how fast or slow I went, but I remember that I deliberately examined articles on each side of me, peering with particular closeness into the recesses of wall and window. I passed the first baize doors, and the passage beyond them widened out to hold shelves of books; there were sofas and small reading-tables against the wall. It narrowed again presently, as I entered the second stretch. The windows here were higher and smaller, and marble statuettes of classical subject lined the walls, watching me like figures of the dead. Their white and shining faces saw me, yet made no sign. I passed next between the second baize doors. They, too, had been fastened back with hooks against the wall. Thus all doors were open—had been recently opened.

And so, at length, I found myself in the final widening of the corridor which formed an antechamber to the music-room itself. It had been used formerly to hold the overflow of meetings. No door separated it from the great hall beyond, but heavy curtains hung usually to close it off, and these curtains were invariably drawn. They now stood wide. And here—I can merely state the impression that came upon me—I knew myself at last surrounded. The throng that pressed behind me, also surged in front: facing me in the big room, and waiting for my entry, stood a multitude; on either side of me, in the very air above my head, the vast assemblage paused upon my coming. The pause, however, was momentary, for instantly the deep tumultuous movement was resumed that yet was silent as a cavern underground. I felt the agony that was in it, the passionate striving, the awful struggle to escape. The semi-darkness held beseeching faces that fought to press themselves upon my vision, yearning yet hopeless eyes, lips scorched and dry, mouths that opened to implore but found no craved delivery in actual words, and a fury of misery and hate that made the life in me stop dead, frozen by the horror of vain pity. That intolerable, vain Hope was everywhere.

And the multitude, it came to me, was not a single multitude, but many; for, as soon as one huge division pressed too close upon the edge of escape, it was dragged back by another and prevented. The wild host was divided against itself. Here dwelt the Shadow I had 'imagined' weeks ago, and in it struggled armies of lost souls as in the depths of some bottomless pit whence there is no escape. The layers mingled, fighting against themselves in endless torture. It was in this great Shadow I had clairvoyantly seen Mabel, but about its fearful mouth, I now was certain, hovered another figure of darkness, a figure who sought to keep it in existence, since to her thought were due those lampless depths of woe without escape.... Towards me the multitudes now surged.

It was a sound and a movement that brought me back into myself. The great clock at the farther end of the room just then struck the hour of three. That was the sound. And the movement—? I was aware that a figure was passing across the distant centre of the floor. Instantly I dropped back into the arena of my little human terror. My hand again clutched stupidly at the pistol butt. I drew back into the folds of the heavy curtain. And the figure advanced.

I remember every detail. At first it seemed to me enormous—this advancing shadow—far beyond human scale; but as it came nearer, I measured it, though not consciously, by the organ pipes that gleamed in faint colours, just above its gradual soft approach. It passed them, already half-way across the great room. I saw then that its stature was that of ordinary men. The prolonged booming of the clock died away. I heard the footfall, shuffling upon the polished boards. I heard another sound—a voice, low and monotonous, droning as in prayer. The figure was speaking. It was a woman. And she carried in both hands before her a small object that faintly shimmered—a glass of water. And then I recognised her.

There was still an instant's time before she reached me, and I made use of it. I shrank back, flattening myself against the wall. Her voice ceased a moment, as she turned and carefully drew the curtains together behind her, closing them with one hand. Oblivious of my presence, though she actually touched my dressing-gown with the hand that pulled the cords, she resumed her dreadful, solemn march, disappearing at length down the long vista of the corridor like a shadow. But as she passed me, her voice began again, so that I heard each word distinctly as she uttered it, her head aloft, her figure upright, as though she moved at the head of a procession:

'A drop of cold water, given in His name, shall moisten their burning tongues.'

It was repeated monotonously over and over again, droning down into the distance as she went, until at length both voice and figure faded into the shadows at the farther end.

For a time, I have no means of measuring precisely, I stood in that dark corner, pressing my back against the wall, and would have drawn the curtains down to hide me had I dared to stretch an arm out. The dread that presently the woman would return passed gradually away. I realised that the air had emptied, the crowd her presence had stirred into activity had retreated; I was alone in the gloomy under-space of the odious building.... Then I remembered suddenly again the terrified women waiting for me on that upper landing; and realised that my skin was wet and freezing cold after a profuse perspiration. I prepared to retrace my steps. I remember the effort it cost me to leave the support of the wall and covering darkness of my corner, and step out into the grey light of the corridor. At first I sidled, then, finding this mode of walking impossible, turned my face boldly and walked quickly, regardless that my dressing-gown set the precious objects shaking as I passed. A wind that sighed mournfully against the high, small windows seemed to have got inside the corridor as well; it felt so cold; and every moment I dreaded to see the outline of the woman's figure as she waited in recess or angle against the wall for me to pass.

Was there another thing I dreaded even more? I cannot say. I only know that the first baize doors had swung to behind me, and the second ones were close at hand, when the great dim thunder caught me, pouring up with prodigious volume so that it seemed to roll out from another world. It shook the very bowels of the building. I was closer to it than that other time, when it had followed me from the goblin garden. There was strength and hardness in it, as of metal reverberation. Some touch of numbness, almost of paralysis, must surely have been upon me that I felt no actual terror, for I remember even turning and standing still to hear it better. 'That is the Noise,' my thought ran stupidly, and I think I whispered it aloud; *the Doors are closing.*

The wind outside against the windows was audible, so it cannot have been really loud, yet to me it was the biggest, deepest sound I have ever heard, but so far away, with such awful remoteness in it, that I had to doubt my own ears at the same time. It seemed underground—the rumbling of earthquake gates that shut remorselessly within the rocky Earth—stupendous ultimate thunder. *They* were shut off from help again. The doors had closed.

I felt a storm of pity, an agony of bitter, futile hate sweep through me. My memory of the figure changed then. The Woman with the glass of cooling water had stepped down from Heaven; but the Man—or was it Men?—who smeared this terrible layer of belief and Thought upon the world!...

I crossed the dining-room—it was fancy, of course, that held my eyes from glancing at the portrait for fear I should see it smiling approval—and so finally reached the hall, where the light from the floor above seemed now quite bright in comparison. All the doors I closed carefully behind me; but first I had to open them. The woman had closed every one. Up the stairs, then, I actually ran, two steps at a time. My sister was standing outside Mabel's door. By her face I knew that she had also heard. There was no need to ask. I quickly made my mind up.

'There's nothing,' I said, and detailed briefly my tour of search. 'All is quiet and undisturbed downstairs.' May God forgive me!

She beckoned to me, closing the door softly behind her. My heart beat violently a moment, then stood still.

'Mabel,' she said aloud.

It was like the sentence of a judge, that one short word.

I tried to push past her and go in, but she stopped me with her arm. She was wholly mistress of herself, I saw.

'Hush!' she said in a lower voice. 'I've got her round again with brandy. She's sleeping quietly now. We won't disturb her.'

She drew me farther out into the landing, and as she did so, the clock in the hall below struck half-past three. I had stood, then, thirty minutes in the corridor below. 'You've been such a long time.' she said simply. 'I feared for you,' and she took my hand in her own that was cold and clammy.

VIII

And then, while that dreadful house stood listening about us in the early hours of this chill morning upon the edge of winter, she told me, with laconic brevity, things about Mabel that I heard as from a distance. There was nothing so unusual or tremendous in the short recital, nothing indeed I might not have already guessed for myself. It was the time and scene, the inference, too, that made it so afflicting: the idea that Mabel believed herself so utterly and hopelessly lost—beyond recovery *damned*.

That she had loved him with so passionate a devotion that she had given her soul into his keeping, this certainly I had not divined—probably because I had never thought about it one way or the other. He had 'converted' her, I knew, but that she had subscribed whole-heartedly to that most cruel and ugly of his dogmas—this was new to me, and came with a certain shock as I heard it. In love, of course, the weaker nature is receptive to all manner of suggestion. This man had 'suggested' his pet brimstone lake so vividly that she had listened and believed. He had frightened her into heaven; and his heaven, a definite locality in the skies, had its foretaste here on earth in miniature—The Towers, house and garden. Into his dolorous scheme of a handful saved and millions damned, his enclosure, as it were, of sheep and goats, he had swept her before she was aware of it. Her mind no longer was her own. And it was Mrs. Marsh who kept the thought-stream open, though tempered, as she deemed, with that touch of craven, superstitious mercy.

But what I found it difficult to understand, and still more difficult to accept, was that, during her year abroad, she had been so haunted with a secret dread of that hideous after-death that she had finally revolted and tried to recover that clearer state of mind she had enjoyed before the religious bully had stunned her—yet had tried in vain. She had returned to The Towers to find her soul again, only to realise that it was lost eternally. The cleaner state of mind lay then beyond recovery. In the reaction that followed the removal of his terrible 'suggestion,' she felt the crumbling of all that he had taught her, but searched in vain for the peace and beauty his teachings had destroyed. Nothing came to replace these. She was empty, desolate, hopeless; craving her former joy and carelessness, she found only hate and diabolical calculation. This man, whom she had loved to the point of losing her soul for him, had bequeathed to her one black and fiery thing—the terror of the damned. His thinking wrapped her in this iron garment that held her fast.

All this Frances told me, far more briefly than I have here repeated it. In her eyes and gestures and laconic sentences lay the conviction of great beating issues and of menacing drama my own description fails to recapture. It was all so incongruous and remote from the world I lived in that more than once a smile, though a smile of pity, fluttered to my lips; but a glimpse of my face in the mirror showed rather the leer of a grimace. There was no real laughter anywhere that night. The entire adventure seemed so incredible, here, in this twentieth century —but yet delusion, that feeble word, did not occur once in the comments my mind suggested though did not utter. I remembered that forbidding Shadow too; my sister's watercolours; the vanished personality of our hostess; the inexplicable, thundering Noise, and the figure of Mrs. Marsh in her midnight ritual that was so childish yet so horrible. I shivered in spite of my own 'emancipated' cast of mind.

'Thete *is* no Mabel,' were the words with which my sister sent another shower of ice down my spine. 'He has killed her in his lake of fire and brimstone.'

I stared at her blankly, as in a nightmare where nothing true or possible ever happened.

'He killed her in his lake of fire and brimstone,' she repeated more faintly.

A desperate effort was in me to say the strong, sensible thing which should destroy the oppressive horror that grew so stiflingly about us both, but again the mirror drew the attempted smile into the merest grin, betraying the distortion that was everywhere in the place.

'You mean,' I stammered beneath my breath, 'that her faith has gone, but that the terror has remained?' I asked it, dully groping. I moved out of the line of the reflection in the glass.

She bowed her head as though beneath a weight; her skin was the pallor of grey ashes.

'You mean,' I said louder, 'that she has lost her—mind?'

'She is terror incarnate,' was the whispered answer. 'Mabel has lost her soul. Her soul is—there!' She pointed horribly below. 'She is seeking it...?'

The word 'soul' stung me into something of my normal self again.

'But her terror, poor thing, is not—cannot be—transferable to *us!*' I exclaimed more vehemently. 'It certainly is not convertible into feelings, sights and—even sounds!'

She interrupted me quickly, almost impatiently, speaking with that conviction by which she conquered me so easily that night.

'It is her terror that revived "the Others." It has brought her into touch with them. They are loose and driving after her. Her efforts at resistance have given them also hope—that escape, after all, *is* possible. Day and night they strive.'

'Escape! Others!' The anger fast rising in me dropped of its own accord at the moment of birth. It shrank into a shuddering beyond my control. In that moment, I think,

I would have believed in the possibility of anything and everything she might tell me. To argue or contradict seemed equally futile.

'His strong belief, as also the beliefs of others who have preceded him,' she replied, so sure of herself that I actually turned to look over my shoulder, 'have left their shadow like a thick deposit over the house and grounds. To them, poor souls imprisoned by thought, it was hopeless as granite walls—until her resistance, her effort to dissipate it—let in light. Now, in their thousands, they are flocking to this little light, seeking escape. Her own escape, don't you see, may release them all!'

It took my breath away. Had his predecessors, former occupants of this house, also preached damnation of all the world but their own exclusive sect? Was this the explanation of her obscure talk of 'layers,' each striving against the other for domination? And if men are spirits, and these spirits survive, could strong Thought thus determine their condition even afterwards?

So many questions flooded into me that I selected no one of them, but stared in uncomfortable silence, bewildered, out of my depth, and acutely, painfully distressed. There was so odd a mixture of possible truth and incredible, unacceptable explanation in it all; so much confirmed, yet so much left darker than before. What she said did, indeed, offer a quasi-interpretation of my own series of abominable sensations—strife, agony, pity, hate, escape—but so far-fetched that only the deep conviction in her voice and attitude made it tolerable for a second even. I found myself in a curious state of mind. I could neither think clearly nor say a word to refute her amazing statements, whispered there beside me in the shivering hours of the early morning with only a wall between ourselves and—Mabel. Close behind her words I remember this singular thing, however—that an atmosphere as of the Inquisition seemed to rise and stir about the room, beating awful wings of black above my head.

Abruptly, then, a moment's common-sense returned to me.

THE DAMNED

I faced her.

'And the Noise?' I said aloud, more firmly, 'the roar of the closing doors? We have *all* heard that! Is that subjective too?'

Frances looked sideways about her in a queer fashion that made my flesh creep again. I spoke brusquely, almost angrily. I repeated the question, and waited with anxiety for her reply.

'What noise?' she asked, with the frank expression of an innocent child. 'What closing doors?'

But her face turned from grey to white, and I saw that drops of perspiration glistened on her forehead. She caught at the back of a chair to steady herself, then glanced about her again with that sidelong look that made my blood run cold. I understood suddenly then. She did not take in what I said. I knew now. She was listening—for something else.

And the discovery revived in me a far stronger emotion than any mere desire for immediate explanation. Not only did I not insist upon an answer, but I was actually terrified lest she *would* answer. More, I felt in me a terror lest I should be moved to describe my own experiences below-stairs, thus increasing their reality and so the reality of all. She might even explain them too!

Still listening intently, she raised her head and looked me in the eyes. Her lips opened to speak. The words came to me from a great distance, it seemed, and her voice had a sound like a stone that drops into a deep well, its fate though hidden, known.

'We are in it with her, too, Bill. We are in it with her. Our interpretations vary—because we are—in parts of it only. Mabel is in it—*all*.'

The desire for violence came over me. If only she would say a definite thing in plain King's English! If only I could find it in me to give utterance to what shouted so loud within me! If only—the same old cry—something would happen! For all this elliptic talk that dazed my mind left obscurity everywhere. Her atrocious meaning, none the less, flashed through me, though vanishing before it wholly divulged itself.

It brought a certain reaction with it. I found my tongue.

Whether I actually believed what I said is more than I can swear to; that it seemed to me wise at the moment is all I remember. My mind was in a state of obscure perception less than that of normal consciousness.

'Yes, Frances, I believe that what you say is the truth, and that we are in it with her'—I meant to say I with loud, hostile emphasis, but instead I whispered it lest she should hear the trembling of my voice—'and for that reason, my dear sister, we leave to-morrow, you and I—to-day, rather, since it is long past midnight—we leave this house of the damned. We go back to London.'

Frances looked up, her face distraught almost beyond recognition. But it was not my words that caused the tumult in her heart. It was a sound—the sound she had been listening for—so faint I barely caught it myself, and had she not pointed I could never have known the direction whence it came. Small and terrible it rose again in the stillness of the night, the sound of gnashing teeth. And behind it came another—the tread of stealthy footsteps. Both were just outside the door.

The room swung round me for a second. My first instinct to prevent my sister going out—she had dashed past me frantically to the door—gave place to another when I saw the expression in her eyes. I followed her lead instead; it was surer than my own. The pistol in my pocket swung uselessly against my thigh. I was flustered beyond belief and ashamed that I was so.

'Keep close to me, Frances,' I said huskily, as the door swung wide and a shaft of light fell upon a figure moving rapidly. Mabel was going down the corridor. Beyond her, in the shadows on the staircase, a second figure stood beckoning, scarcely visible.

'Before they get her! Quick!' was screamed into my ears, and our arms were about her in the same moment. It was a horrible scene. Not that Mabel struggled in the least, but that she collapsed as we caught her and fell with her dead weight, as of a corpse, limp, against us. And her teeth began again. They continued, even beneath the hand that Frances clapped upon her lips....

We carried her back into her own bedroom, where she lay down peacefully enough. It was so soon over.... The rapidity of the whole thing robbed it of reality almost. It had the swiftness of something remembered rather than of something witnessed. She slept again so quickly that it was almost as if we had caught her sleep-walking. I cannot say. I asked no questions at the time; I have asked none since; and my help was needed as little as the protection of my pistol. Frances was strangely competent and collected.... I lingered for some time uselessly by the door, till at length, looking up with a sigh, she made a sign for me to go.

'I shall wait in your room next door,' I whispered, 'till you come.' But, though going out, I waited in the corridor instead, so as to hear the faintest call for help. In that dark corridor upstairs I waited, but not long. It may have been fifteen minutes when Frances reappeared, locking the door softly behind her. Leaning over the banisters, I saw her.

'I'll go in again about six o'clock,' she whispered, 'as soon as it gets light. She is sound asleep now. Please don't wait. If anything happens I'll call—you might leave your door ajar, perhaps.' And she came up, looking like a ghost.

But I saw her first safely into bed, and the rest of the night I spent in an armchair close to my opened door, listening for the slightest sound. Soon after five o'clock I heard Frances fumbling with the key, and, peering over the railing again, I waited till she reappeared and went back into her own room. She closed her door. Evidently she was satisfied that all was well.

Then, and then only, did I go to bed myself, but not to sleep. I could not get the scene out of my mind, especially that odious detail of it which I hoped and believed my sister had not seen—the still, dark figure of the housekeeper waiting on the stairs below—waiting, of course, for Mabel.

IX

It seems I became a mere spectator after that; my sister's lead was so assured for one thing, and, for another, the responsibility of leaving Mabel alone—Frances laid it bodily upon my shoulders—was a little more than I cared about. Moreover, when we all three met later in the day, things went on so exactly as before, so absolutely without friction or distress, that to present a sudden, obvious excuse for cutting our visit short seemed ill-judged. And on the lowest grounds it would have been desertion. At any rate, it was beyond my powers, and Frances was quite firm that *she* must stay. We therefore did stay. Things that happen in the night always seem exaggerated and distorted when the sun shines brightly next morning; no one can reconstruct the terror of a nightmare afterwards, nor comprehend why it seemed so overwhelming at the time.

I slept till ten o'clock, and when I rang for breakfast, a note from my sister lay upon the tray, its message of counsel couched in a calm and comforting strain. Mabel, she assured me, was herself again and remembered nothing of what had happened; there was no need of any violent measures; I was to treat her exactly as if I knew nothing. 'And, if you don't mind, Bill, let us leave the matter unmentioned between ourselves as well. Discussion exaggerates; such things are best not talked about. I'm sorry I disturbed you so unnecessarily; I was stupidly excited. Please forget all the things I said at the moment.' She had written 'nonsense' first instead of 'things', then scratched it out. She wished to convey that hysteria had been abroad in the night, and I readily gulped the explanation down, though it could not satisfy me in the smallest degree.

There was another week of our visit still, and we stayed it out to the end without disaster. My desire to leave at times became that frantic thing, desire to escape; but I controlled it, kept silent, watched and wondered. Nothing happened. As before, and everywhere, there was no sequence of development, no connection between cause and effect; and climax, none whatever. The thing swayed up and down, backwards and forwards like a great loose curtain in the wind, and I could only vaguely surmise what caused the draught or why there was a curtain at all. A novelist might mould the queer material into coherent sequence that would be interesting but could not be true. It remains, therefore, not a story but a history. Nothing happened.

Perhaps my intense dislike of the fall of darkness was due wholly to my stirred imagination, and perhaps my anger when I learned that Frances now occupied a bed in our hostess's room was unreasonable. Nerves were unquestionably on edge. I was for ever on the look-out for some event that should make escape imperative, but yet that never presented itself. I slept lightly, left my door ajar to catch the slightest sound, even made stealthy tours of the house below-stairs while everybody dreamed in their beds. But I discovered nothing; the doors were always locked; I neither saw the housekeeper again in unreasonable times and places, nor heard a footstep in the passages and halls. The Noise was never once repeated. That horrible, ultimate thunder, my intensest dread of all, lay withdrawn into the abyss whence it had twice arisen. And though in my thoughts it was sternly denied existence, the great black reason for the fact afflicted me unbelievably. Since Mabel's fruitless effort to escape, the Doors kept closed remorselessly. She had failed; *they* gave up hope. For this was the explanation that haunted the region of my mind where feelings stir and hint before they clothe themselves in actual language. Only I firmly kept it there; it never knew expression.

But, if my ears were open, my eyes were opened too, and it were idle to pretend that I did not notice a hundred details that were capable of sinister interpretation had I been weak enough to yield. Some protective barrier had fallen into ruins round me, so that Terror stalked behind the general collapse, feeling for me through all the gaping fissures. Much of this, I admit, must have been merely the elaboration of those sensations I had first vaguely felt, before subsequent events and my talks with Frances had dramatised them into living thoughts. I therefore leave them unmentioned in this history, just as my mind left them unmentioned in that interminable final week.

Our life went on precisely as before—Mabel unreal and outwardly so still; Frances, secretive, anxious, tactful to the point of slyness, and keen to save to the point of self-forgetfulness. There were the same stupid meals, the same wearisome long evenings, the stifling ugliness of house and grounds, the Shadow settling in so thickly that it seemed almost a visible, tangible thing. I came to feel the only friendly things in all this hostile, cruel place were the robins that hopped boldly over the monstrous terraces and even up to the windows of the unsightly house itself. The robins alone knew joy; they danced, believing no evil thing was possible in all God's radiant world. They believed in everybody; *their* god's plan of life had no room in it for hell, damnation and lakes of brimstone. I came to love the little birds. Had Samuel Franklyn known them, he might have preached a different sermon, bequeathing love in place of terror!...

Most of my time I spent writing; but it was a pretence at best, and rather a dangerous one besides. For it stirred the mind to production, with the result that other things came pouring in as well. With reading it was the same. In the end I found an aggressive, deliberate resistance to be the only way of feasible defence. To walk far afield was out of the question, for it meant leaving my sister too long alone, so that my exercise was confined to nearer home. My saunters in the grounds, however, never surprised the goblin garden again. It was close at hand, but I seemed unable to get wholly into it. Too many things assailed my mind for any one to hold exclusive possession, perhaps.

Indeed, all the interpretations, all the 'layers,' to use my sister's phrase, slipped in by turns and lodged there for a time. They came day and night, and though my reason denied them entrance they held their own as by a kind of squatter's right. They stirred moods already in me, that is, and did not introduce entirely new ones; for every mind conceals ancestral deposits that have been cultivated in turn along the whole line of its descent. Any day a chance shower may cause this one or that to blossom. Thus it came to me, at any rate. After darkness the Inquisition paced the empty corridors and set up ghastly apparatus in the dismal halls; and once, in the library, there swept over me that easy and delicious conviction that by confessing my wickedness I could resume it later, since Confession is expression, and expression brings relief and leaves one ready to accumulate again. And in such mood I felt bitter and unforgiving towards all others who thought differently. Another time it was a Pagan thing that assaulted me—so trivial yet oh, so significant at the time—when I dreamed that a herd of centaurs rolled up with a great stamping of hoofs round the house to destroy it, and then woke to hear the horses tramping across the field below the lawns; they neighed ominously and their noisy panting was audible as if it were just outside my windows.

But the tree episode, I think, was the most curious of all—except, perhaps, the incident with the children which I shall mention in a moment—for its closeness to reality was so unforgettable. Outside the east window of my room stood a giant wellingtonia on the lawn, its head rising level with the upper sash. It grew some twenty feet away, planted on the highest terrace, and I often saw it when closing my curtains for the night, noticing how it drew its heavy skirts about it, and how the light from other windows threw glimmering streaks and patches that turned it into the semblance of a towering, solemn image. It stood there then so strikingly, somehow like a great old-world idol, that it claimed attention. Its appearance was curiously formidable. Its branches rustled without visibly moving and it had a certain portentous, forbidding air, so grand and dark and monstrous in the night that I was always glad when my curtains shut it out. Yet, once in bed, I had never thought about it one way or the other, and by day had certainly never sought it out.

One night, then, as I went to bed and closed this window against a cutting easterly wind, I saw—that there were two of these trees. A brother wellingtonia rose mysteriously beside it, equally huge, equally towering, equally monstrous. The menacing pair of them faced me there upon the lawn. But in this new arrival lay a strange suggestion that frightened me before I could argue it away. Exact counterpart of its giant companion, it revealed also that gross, odious quality that all my sister's paintings held. I got the odd impression that the rest of these trees, stretching away dimly in a troop over the farther lawns, were similar, and that, led by this enormous pair, they had all moved boldly closer to my windows. At the same moment a blind was drawn down over an upper room; the second tree disappeared into the surrounding darkness. It was, of course, this chance light that had brought it into the field of vision, but when the black shutter dropped over it, hiding it from view, the manner of its vanishing produced the queer effect that it had slipped into its companion—almost that it had been an emanation of the one I so disliked, and not really a tree at all! In this way the garden turned vehicle for expressing what lay behind it all!...

The behaviour of the doors, the little, ordinary doors, seems scarcely worth mention at all, their queer way of opening and shutting of their own accord; for this was accountable in a hundred natural ways, and to tell the truth, I never caught one in the act of moving. Indeed, only after frequent repetitions did the detail force itself upon me, when, having noticed one, I noticed all. It produced, however, the unpleasant impression of a continual coming and going in the house, as though, screened cleverly and purposely from actual sight, some one in the building held constant invisible intercourse with—others.

Upon detailed descriptions of these uncertain incidents I do not venture, individually so trival, but taken all together so impressive and so insolent. But the episode of the children, mentioned above, was different. And I give it because it showed how vividly the intuitive child-mind received the impression—one impression, at any rate—of what was in the air. It may be told in a very few words. I believe they were the coachman's children, and that the man had been in Mr. Franklyn's service; but of neither point am I quite positive.

I heard screaming in the rose-garden that runs along the stable walls—it was one afternoon not far from the tea-hour—and on hurrying up I found a little girl of nine or ten fastened with ropes to a rustic seat, and two other children—boys, one about twelve and one much younger—gathering sticks beneath the climbing rose-trees. The girl was white and frightened, but the others were laughing and talking among themselves so busily while they picked that they did not notice my abrupt arrival. Some game, I understood, was in progress, but a game that had become too serious for the happiness of the prisoner, for there was a fear in the girl's eyes that was a very genuine fear indeed. I unfastened her at once; the ropes were so loosely and clumsily knotted that they had not hurt her skin; it was not that which made her pale. She collapsed a moment upon the bench, then picked up her tiny skirts and dived away at full speed into the safety of the stable-yard. There was no response to my brief comforting, but she ran as though for her life, and I divined that some horrid boys' cruelty had been afoot. It was probably mere thoughtlessness, as cruelty with children usually is, but something in me decided to discover exactly what it was.

And the boys, not one whit alarmed at my intervention, merely laughed shyly when I explained that their prisoner had escaped, and told me frankly what their 'gime' had been. There was no vestige of shame in them, nor any idea, of course, that they aped a monstrous reality. That it was mere pretence was neither here nor there. To them, though make-believe, it was a make-believe of something that was right and natural and in no sense cruel. Grown-ups did it too. It was necessary for her good.

'We was going to burn her up, sir,' the older one informed me, answering my 'Why?' with the explanation, 'Because she wouldn't believe what we wanted 'er to believe.'

And, game though it was, the feeling of reality about the little episode was so arresting, so terrific in some way, that only with difficulty did I confine my admonitions on this occasion to mere words. The boys slunk off, frightened in their turn, yet not, I felt, convinced that they had erred in principle. It was their inheritance. They had breathed it in with the atmosphere of their bringing-up. They would renew the salutary torture when they could—till she 'believed' as they did.

I went back into the house, afflicted with a passion of mingled pity and distress impossible to describe, yet on my short way across the garden was attacked by other moods in turn, each more real and bitter than its predecessor. I received the whole series, as it were, at once. I felt like a diver rising to the surface through layers of water at different temperatures, though here the natural order was reversed, and the cooler strata were uppermost, the heated ones below. Thus, I was caught by the goblin touch of the willows that fringed the field; by the sensuous curving of the twisted ash that formed a gateway to the little grove of sapling oaks where fauns and satyrs lurked to play in the moonlight before Pagan altars; and by the cloaking darkness, next, of the copse of stunted pines, close gathered each to each, where hooded figures stalked behind an awful cross. The episode with the children seemed to have opened me like a knife. The whole Place rushed at me.

I suspect this synthesis of many moods produced in me that climax of loathing and disgust which made me feel the limit of bearable emotion had been reached, so that I made straight to find Frances in order to convince her that at any rate *I* must leave. For, although this was our last day in the house, and we had arranged to go next day, the dread was in me that she would still find some persuasive reason for staying on. And an unexpected incident then made my dread unnecessary. The front door was open and a cab stood in the drive; a tall, elderly man was gravely talking in the hall with the parlourmaid we called the Grenadier. He held a piece of paper in his hand. 'I have called to see the house,' I heard him say, as I ran up the stairs to Frances, who was peering like an inquisitive child over the banisters....

'Yes,' she told me with a sigh, I know not whether of resignation or relief, 'the house *is* to be let or sold. Mabel has decided. Some Society or other, I believe——'

I was overjoyed: this made our leaving right and possible.
'You never told me, Frances!'

'Mabel only heard of it a few days ago. She told me herself this morning. It is a chance, she says. Alone she cannot get it "straight". '

'Defeat?' I asked, watching her closely.

'She thinks she has found a way out. It's not a family, you see, it's a Society, a sort of Community—they go in for thought——'

'A Community!' I gasped. 'You mean religious?'

She shook her head. 'Not exactly,' she said smiling, 'but some kind of association of men and women who want a headquarters in the country—a place where they can write and meditate—*think*—mature their plans and all the rest—I don't know exactly what.'

'Utopian dreamers?' I asked, yet feeling an immense relief come over me as I heard. But I asked in ignorance, not cynically. Frances would know. She knew all this kind of thing.

'No, not that exactly,' she smiled. 'Their teachings are grand and simple—old as the world too, really—the basis of every religion before men's minds perverted them with their manufactured creeds——'

Footsteps on the stairs, and the sound of voices, interrupted our odd impromptu conversation, as the Grenadier came up, followed by the tall, grave gentleman who was being shown over the house. My sister drew me along the corridor towards her room, where she went in and closed the door behind me, yet not before I had stolen a good look at the caller—long enough, at least, for his face and general appearance to have made a definite impression on me. For something strong and peaceful emanated from his presence; he moved with such quiet dignity; the glance of his eyes was so steady and reassuring, that my mind labelled him instantly as a type of man one would turn to in an emergency and not be disappointed. I had seen him but for a passing moment, but I had seen him twice, and the way he walked down the passage, looking competently about him, conveyed the same impression as when I saw him standing at the door—fearless, tolerant, wise. 'A sincere and kindly character,' I judged instantly, 'a man whom some big kind of love has trained in sweetness towards the world; no hate in him anywhere.' A great deal, no doubt, to read in so brief a glance! Yet his voice confirmed my intuition, a deep and very gentle voice, great firmness in it too.

'Have I become suddenly sensitive to people's atmospheres in this extraordinary fashion?' I asked myself, smiling, as I stood in the room and heard the door close behind me. 'Have I developed some clairvoyant faculty here?' At any other time I should have mocked.

And I sat down and faced my sister, feeling strangely comforted and at peace for the first time since I had stepped beneath The Towers' roof a month ago. Frances, I then saw, was smiling a little as she watched me.

'You know him?' I asked.

'You felt it too?' was her question in reply. 'No,' she added, 'I don't know him—beyond the fact that he is a leader in the Movement and has devoted years and money to its objects. Mabel felt the same thing in him that you have felt—and jumped at it.'

'But you've seen him before?' I urged, for the certainty was in me that he was no stranger to her.

She shook her head. 'He called one day early this week, when you were out. Mabel saw him. I believe——' she hesitated a moment, as though expecting me to stop her with my usual impatience of such subjects—'I believe he has explained everything to her—the beliefs he embodies, she declares, are her salvation—might be, rather, if she could adopt them.'

'Conversion again!' For I remembered her riches, and how gladly a Society would gobble them.

'The layers I told you about,' she continued calmly, shrugging her shoulders slightly—'the deposits that are left behind by strong thinking and *real* belief—but especially by ugly, hateful belief, because, you see—unfortunately there's more vital passion in that sort——'

'Frances, I don't understand a bit,' I said out loud, but said it a little humbly, for the impression the man had left was still strong upon me and I was grateful for the steady sense of peace and comfort he had somehow introduced. The horrors had been so dreadful. My nerves, doubtless, were more than a little overstrained. Absurd as it must sound, I classed him in my mind with the robins, the happy, confiding robins who believed in everybody and thought no evil! I laughed a moment at my ridiculous idea, and my sister, encouraged by this sign of patience in me, continued more fluently.

'Of course you don't understand, Bill? Why should you? You've never thought about such things. Needing no creed yourself, you think all creeds are rubbish.'

'I'm open to conviction—I'm tolerant,' I interrupted.

'You're as narrow as Sam Franklyn, and as crammed with prejudice,' she answered, knowing that she had me at her mercy.

'Then, pray, what may be his, or his Society's beliefs?' I asked, feeling no desire to argue, 'and how are they going to prove your Mabel's salvation? Can they bring beauty into all this aggressive hate and ugliness?'

'Certain hope and peace,' she said, 'that peace which is understanding, and that understanding which explains *all* creeds and therefore tolerates them.'

'Toleration! The one word a religous man loathes above all others! His pet word is damnation——'

'Tolerates them,' she repeated patiently, unperturbed by my explosion, 'because it includes them all.'

'Fine, if true' I admitted, 'very fine. But how, pray, does it include them all?'

'Because the key-word, the motto, of their Society is, "There is no religion higher than Truth," and it has no single dogma of any kind. Above all,' she went on, 'because it claims that no individual can be "lost." It teaches universal salvation. To damn outsiders is uncivilised, childish, impure. Some take longer than others—it's according to the way they think and live—but all find peace, through development, in the end. What the creeds call a hopeless soul, it regards as a soul having further to go. There is no damnation——'

'Well, well,' I exclaimed, feeling that she rode her hobby horse too wildly, too roughly over me, 'but what is the bearing of all this upon this dreadful place, and upon Mabel? I'll admit that there is this atmosphere—this—er—inexplicable horror in the house and grounds, and that if not of damnation exactly, it is certainly damnable. I'm not too prejudiced to deny *that*, for I've felt it myself.'

To my relief she was brief. She made her statement, leaving me to take it or reject it as I would.

'The thought and belief its former occupants—have left behind. For there has been coincidence here, a coincidence that must be rare. The site on which this modern house now stands was Roman, before that Early Britain, with burial mounds, before that again, Druid—the Druid stones still lie in that copse below the field, the Tumuli among the ilexes behind the drive. The older building Sam Franklyn altered and practically pulled down was a monastery; he changed the chapel into a meeting hall, which is now the music room; but, before he came here, the house was occupied by Manetti, a violent Catholic without tolerance or vision; and in the interval between these two, Julius Weinbaum had it, Hebrew of most rigid orthodox type imaginable—so they all have left their——'

'Even so,' I repeated, yet interested to hear the rest, 'what of it?'

'Simply this,' said Frances with conviction, 'that each in turn has left his layer of concentrated thinking and belief behind him; because each believed intensely, absolutely, beyond the least weakening of any doubt—the kind of strong belief and thinking that is rare anywhere to-day, the kind that wills, impregnates objects, saturates the atmosphere, haunts, in a word. And each, believing he was utterly and finally right, damned with equally positive conviction the rest of the world. One and all preached that implicitly if not explicitly. It's the root of every creed. Last of the bigoted, grim series came Samuel Franklyn.'

THE DAMNED

I listened in amazement that increased as she went on. Up to this point her explanation was so admirable. It was, indeed, a pretty study in psychology if it were true.

'Then why does nothing ever happen?' I enquired mildly. 'A place so thickly haunted ought to produce a crop of no ordinary results!'

'There lies the proof,' she went on in a lowered voice, 'the proof of the horror and the ugly reality. The thought and belief of each occupant in turn kept all the others under. They gave no sign of life at the time. But the results of thinking never die. They crop out again the moment there's an opening. And, with the return of Mabel in her negative state, believing nothing positive heself, the place for the first time found itself free to reproduce its buried stores. Damnation, hell-fire, and the rest—the most permanent and vital thought of all those creeds, since it was applied to the majority of the world—broke loose again, for there was no restraint to hold it back. Each sought to obtain its former supremacy. None conquered. There results a pandemonium of hate and fear, of striving to escape, of agonised, bitter warring to find safety, peace—salvation. The place is saturated by that appalling stream of thinking—the terror of the damned. It concentrated upon Mabel, whose negative attitude furnished the channel of deliverance. You and I, according to our sympathy with her, were similarly involved. Nothing happened, because no one layer could ever gain the supremacy.'

I was so interested—I dare not say amused—that I stared in silence while she paused a moment, afraid that she would draw rein and end the fairy tale too soon.

'The beliefs of this man, of his Society rather, vigorously thought and therefore vigorously given out here, will put the whole place straight. It will act as a solvent. These vitriolic layers actively denied, will fuse and disappear in the stream of gentle, tolerant sympathy which is love. For each member, worthy of the name, loves the world, and all creeds go into the melting-pot; Mabel, too, if she joins them out of real conviction, will find salvation——'

'Thinking, I know, is of the first importance,' I objected, 'but don't you, perhaps, exaggerate the power of feeling and emotion which in religion are *au fond* always hysterical?'

'What *is* the world,' she told me, 'but thinking and feeling? An individual's world is entirely what that individual thinks and believes—interpretation. There is no other. And unless he really thinks and really believes, he has no permanent world at all. I grant that few people think, and still fewer believe, and that most take ready-made suits and make them do. Only the strong make their own things; the lesser fry, Mabel among them, are merely swept up into what has been manufactured for them. They get along somehow. You and I have made for ourselves, Mabel has not. She is a nonentity, and when her belief is taken from her, she goes with it.'

It was not in me just then to criticise the evasion, or pick out the sophistry from the truth. I merely waited for her to continue.

'None of us have Truth, my dear Frances,' I ventured presently, seeing that she kept silent.

'Precisely,' she answered, 'but most of us have beliefs. And what one believes and thinks affects the world at large. Consider the legacy of hatred and cruelty involved in the doctrines men have built into their creeds where the *sine qua non* of salvation is absolute acceptance of one particular set of views or else perishing everlastingly—for only by repudiating history can they disavow it——'

'You're not quite accurate,' I put in. 'Not all the creeds teach damnation, do they? Franklyn did, of course, but the others are a bit modernised now surely?'

'Trying to get out of it,' she admitted, 'perhaps they are, but damnation of unbelievers—of most of the world, that is—is their rather favourite idea if you talk with them.'

'I never have.'

She smiled. 'But I have,' she said significantly, 'so, if you consider what the various occupants of this house have so strongly held and thought and believed, you need not be surprised that the influence they have left behind them should be a dark and dreadful legacy. For thought, you know, does leave——'

The opening of the door, to my great relief, interrupted her, as the Grenadier led in the visitor to see the room. He bowed to both of us with a brief word of apology, looked round him, and withdrew, and with his departure the conversation between us came naturally to an end. I followed him out. Neither of us in any case, I think, cared to argue further.

And, so far as I am aware, the curious history of The Towers ends here too. There was no climax in the story sense. Nothing ever really happened. We left next morning for London. I only know that the Society in question took the house and have since occupied it to their entire satisfaction, and that Mabel, who became a member shortly afterwards, now stays there frequently when in need of repose from the arduous and unselfish labours she took upon herself under its aegis. She dined with us only the other night, here in our tiny Chelsea flat, and a jollier, saner, more interesting and happy guest I could hardly wish for. She was vital—in the best sense; the lay-figure had come to life. I found it difficult to believe she was the same woman whose fearful effigy had floated down those dreary corridors and almost disappeared in the depths of that atrocious Shadow.

What her beliefs were now I was wise enough to leave unquestioned, and Frances, to my great relief, kept the conversation well away from such inappropriate topics. It was clear, however, that the woman had in herself some secret source of joy, that she was now an aggressive, positive force, sure of herself, and apparently afraid of nothing in heaven or hell. She radiated something very like hope and courage about her, and talked as though the world were a glorious place and everybody in it kind and beautiful. Her optimism was certainly infectious.

The Towers were mentioned only in passing. The name of Marsh came up—not *the* Marsh, it so happened, but a name in some book that was being discussed—and I was unable to restrain myself. Curiosity was too strong. I threw out a casual enquiry Mabel could leave unanswered if she wished. But there was no desire to avoid it. Her reply was frank and smiling.

'Would you believe it? She married,' Mabel told me, though obviously surprised that I remembered the housekeeper at all; 'and is happy as the day is long. She's found her right niche in life. A sergeant——'

'The army!' I ejaculated.

'Salvation Army,' she explained merrily.

Frances exchanged a glance with me. I laughed too, for the information took me by surprise. I cannot say why exactly, but I expected at least to hear that the woman had met some dreadful end, not impossibly by burning.

'And The Towers, now called the Rest House,' Mabel chattered on, 'seems to me the most peaceful and delightful spot in England——'

'Really,' I said politely.

'When I lived there in the old days—while you were there, perhaps, though I won't be sure,' Mabel went on, 'the story got abroad that it was haunted. Wasn't it odd? A less likely place for a ghost I've never seen. Why, it had no atmosphere at all.' She said this to Frances, glancing up at me with a smile that apparently had no hidden meaning. 'Did *you* notice anything queer about it when you were there?'

This was plainly addressed to me.

'I found it—er—difficult to settle down to anything,' I said, after an instant's hesitation. 'I couldn't work there——'

'But I thought you wrote that wonderful book on the Deaf and Blind while you stayed with me,' she asked innocently.

I stammered a little. 'Oh no, not then. I only made a few notes—er—at The Towers. My mind, oddly enough, refused to produce at all down there. But—why do you ask? Did anything—was anything *supposed* to happen there?'

She looked searchingly into my eyes a moment before she answered:

'Not that I know of,' she said simply.

WAYFARERS

I MISSED the train at Evian, and, after infinite trouble, discovered a motor that would take me, ice-axe and all, to Geneva. By hurrying, the connection might be just possible. I telegraphed to Haddon to meet me at the station, and lay back comfortably, dreaming of the precipices of Haute Savoie. We made good time; the roads were excellent, traffic of the slightest, when—crash! There was an instant's excruciating pain, the sun went out like a snuffed candle, and I fell into something as soft as a bed of flowers and as yielding to my weight as warm water....

It was *very* warm. There was a perfume of flowers. My eyes opened, focused vividly upon a detailed picture for a moment, then closed again. There was no context—at least, none that I could recall—for the scene, though familiar as home, brought nothing that I definitely remembered. Broken away from any sequence, unattached to any past, unaware even of my own identity, I simply saw this picture as a camera snaps it off from the world, a scene apart, with meaning only for those who knew the context:

The warm, soft thing I lay in was a bed—big, deep, comfortable; and the perfume came from flowers that stood beside it on a little table. It was in a stately, ancient chamber, with lofty ceiling and immense open fireplace of stone; old-fashioned pictures—familiar portraits and engravings I knew intimately—hung upon the walls; the floor was bare, with dignified, carved furniture of oak and mahogany, huge chairs and massive cupboards. And there were latticed windows set within deep embrasures of grey stone, where clambering roses patterned the sunshine that cast their moving shadows on the polished boards. With the perfume of the flowers there mingled, too, that delicate, elusive odour of age—of wood, of musty tapestries on spacious halls and corridors, and of chambers long unopened to the sun and air.

By the door that stood ajar far away at the end of the room—very far away it seemed—an old lady, wearing a little cap of silk embroidery, was whispering to a man of stern, uncompromising figure, who, as he listened, bent down to her with a grave and even solemn face. A wide stone corridor was just visible through the crack of the open door behind her.

The picture flashed, and vanished. The numerous details I took in because they were well known to me already. That I could not supply the context was merely a trick of the mind, the kind of trick that dreams play. Darkness swamped vision again. I sank back into the warm, soft, comfortable bed of delicious oblivion. There was not the slightest desire to know; sleep and soft forgetfulness were all I craved.

But a little later—or was it a very great deal later?—when I opened my eyes again, there was a thin trail of memory. I remembered my name and age. I remembered vaguely, as though from some unpleasant dream, that I was on the way to meet a climbing friend in the Alps of Haute Savoie, and that there was need to hurry and be very active. Something had gone wrong, it seemed. There had been a stupid, violent disaster, pain in it somewhere, an accident. Where were my belongings? Where, for instance, was my precious ice-axe—tried old instrument on which my life and safety depended? A rush of jumbled questions poured across my mind. The effort to sort them hurt atrociously....

A figure stood beside my bed. It was the same old lady I had seen a moment ago—or was it a month ago, even last year perhaps? And this time she was alone. Yet, though familiar to me as my own right hand, I could not for the life of me attract her name. Searching for it brought the pain again. Instead, I asked an easier question; it seemed the most important somehow, though a feeling of shame came with it, as though I knew I was talking nonsense:

'My ice-axe—is it safe? It should have stood any ordinary strain. It's ash....' My voice failed absurdly, caught away by a whisper half-way down my throat. What *was* I talking about? There was vile confusion somewhere.

She smiled tenderly, sweetly, as she placed her small, cool hand upon my forehead. Her touch calmed me as it always did, and the pain retreated a little.

'All your things are safe,' she answered, in a voice so soft beneath the distant ceiling it was like a bird's note singing in the sky. 'And *you* are also safe. There is no danger now. The bullet has been taken out and all is going well. Only you must be patient, and lie very still, and rest.' And then she added the morsel of delicious comfort she knew quite well I waited for: 'Marion is near you all day long, and most of the night besides. She rarely leaves you. She is in and out all day.'

I stared, thirsting for more. Memory put certain pieces in their place again. I heard them click together as they joined. But they only tried to join. There were several pieces missing They must have been lost in the disaster. The pattern was too ridiculous.

'I ought to tel—telegraph——' I began, seizing at a fragment that poked its end up, then plunged out of sight again before I could read more of it. The pieces fell apart; they would not hold together without these missing fragments. Anger flamed up in me.

'They're badly made,' I said, with a petulance I was secretly ashamed of; 'you have chosen the wrong pieces! I'm not a child—to be treated——' A shock of heat tore through me, led by a point of iron, with blasting pain.

'Sleep, my poor dear Félix, sleep,' she murmured soothingly, while her tiny hand stroked my forehead, just in time to prevent that pointed, hot thing entering my heart. 'Sleep again now, and a little later you shall tell me their names, and I will send on horseback quickly——'

'Telegraph——' I tried to say, but the word went lost before I could pronounce it. It was a nonsense word, caught up from dreams. Thought fluttered and went out.

'I will send,' she whispered, 'in the quickest possible way. You shall explain to Marion. Sleep first a little longer; promise me to lie quite still and sleep. When you wake again, she will come to you at once.'

She sat down gently on the edge of the enormous bed, so that I saw her outline against the window where the roses clambered to come in. She bent me—or was it a rose that bent in the wind across the stone embrasure? I saw her clear blue eyes—or was it two raindrops upon a withered rose-leaf that mirrored the summer sky?

'Thank you,' my voice murmured with intense relief, as everything sank away and the old-world garden seemed to enter by the latticed windows. For there was a power in her way that made obedience sweet, and her little hand, besides, cushioned the attack of that cruel iron so that I hardly felt its entrance. Before the fierce heat could reach me, darkness again put out the world....

Then, after a prodigious interval, my eyes once more opened to the stately, old-world chamber that I knew so well; and this time I found myself alone. In my brain was a stinging, splitting sensation, as though Memory shook her pieces together with angry violence, pieces, moreover, made of clashing metal. A degrading nausea almost vanquished me. Against my feet was a heated metal body, too heavy for me to move, and bandages were tight round my neck and the back of my head. Dimly, it came back to me that hands had been about me hours ago, soft, ministering hands that I loved. Their perfume lingered still. Faces and names fled in swift procession past me, yet without my making any attempt to bid them stay. I asked myself no questions. Effort of any sort was utterly beyond me. I lay and watched and waited, helpless and strangely weak.

One or two things alone were clear. They came, too, without the effort to think them:

There had been a disaster; they had carried me into the nearest house; and—the mountain heights, so keenly longed for, were suddenly denied me. I was being cared for by kind people somewhere far from the world's high routes. They were familiar people, yet for the moment I had lost the name. But it was the bitterness of losing my holiday climbing that chiefly savaged me, so that strong desire returned upon itself unfulfilled. And, knowing the danger of frustrated yearnings, and the curious states of mind they may engender, my tumbling brain registered a decision automatically:

'Keep careful watch upon yourself,' it whispered.

For I saw the peaks that towered above the world, and felt the wind rise from the hidden valleys. The perfume of lonely ridges came to me, and I saw the snow against the blue-black sky. Yet I could not reach them. I lay, instead, broken and useless upon my back, in a soft, deep, comfortable bed. And I loathed the thought. A dull and evil fury rose within me. Where was Haddon? He would get me out of it if any one could. And where was my dear, old trusted ice-axe? Above all, who were these gentle, old-world people who cared for me?... And, with this last thought, came some fairy touch of sweetness so delicious that I was conscious of sudden resignation—more, even of delight and joy.

This joy and anger ran races for possession of my mind, and I knew not which to follow: both seemed real, and both seemed true. The cruel confusion was an added torture. Two sets of places and people seemed to mingle.

'Keep a careful watch upon yourself,' repeated the automatic caution.

Then, with returning, blissful darkness, came another thing —a tiny point of wonder, where light entered in. I thought of a woman.... It was a vehement, commanding thought; and though at first it was very close and real—as much of To-day as Haddon and my precious ice-axe—the next second it was leagues away in another world somewhere. Yet, before the confusion twisted it all askew, I knew her; I remembered clearly even where she lived; that I knew her husband, too—had stayed with them in—in Scotland—yes, in Scotland. Yet no word in this life had ever crossed my lips, for she was not free to come. Neither of us, with eyes or lips or gesture, had ever betrayed a hint to the other of our deeply hidden secret. And although for me she was *the* woman, my great yearning—long, long ago it was, in early youth—had been sternly put aside and buried with all the vigour nature gave me. Her husband was my friend as well.

Only, now, the shock had somehow strained the prison bars, and the yearning escaped for a moment full-fledged, and vehement with passion long denied. The inhibition was destroyed. The knowledge swept deliciously upon me that we had the right to be together, because we always *were* together. I had the right to ask for her.

My mind was certainly a mere field of confused, ungoverned images. No thinking was possible, for it hurt too vilely. But this one memory stood out with violence. I distinctly remember that I called to her to come, and that she had the right to come because my need was so peremptory. To the one most loved of all this life had brought me, yet to whom I had never spoken because she was in another's keeping, I called for help, and called, I verily believe, aloud:

'Please come!' Then, close upon its heels, the automatic warning again: 'Keep close watch upon yourself....!'

It was as though one great yearning had loosed the other that was even greater, and had set it free.

Disappearing consciousness then followed the cry for an incalculable distance. Down into subterraneans within myself that were positively frightening it plunged away. But the cry was real; the yearning appeal held authority in it as of command. Love gave the right, supplied the power as well. For it seemed to me a tiny answer came, but from so far away that it was scarcely audible. And names were nowhere in it, either in answer or appeal.

'I am always here. I have never, never left you!'

The unconsciousness that followed was not complete, apparently. There was a memory of effort in it, of struggle, and, as it were, of searching. Some one was trying to get at me. I tossed in a troubled sea upon a piece of wreckage that another swimmer also fought to reach. Huge waves of transparent green now brought this figure nearer, now concealed it, but it came steadily on, holding out a rope. My exhaustion was too great for me to respond, yet this swimmer swept up nearer, brought by enormous rollers that threatened to engulf us both. The rope was for my safety, too. I saw hands outstretched. In the deep water I saw the outline of the body, and once I even saw the face. But for a second, merely. The wave that bore it crashed with a horrible roar that smothered us both and swept me from my piece of wreckage. In the violent flood of water the rope whipped against my feeble hands. I grasped it. A sense of divine security at once came over me —an intolerable sweetness of utter bliss and comfort, then blackness and suffocation as of the grave. The white-hot point of iron struck me. It beat audibly against my heart. I heard the knocking. The pain brought me up to the surface, and the knocking of my dreams was in reality a knocking on the door. Some one was gently tapping.

Such was the confusion of images in my painracked mind, that I expected to see the old lady enter, bringing ropes and ice-axes, and followed by Haddon, my mountaineering friend; for I thought that I had fallen down a deep crevasse and had waited hours for help in the cold, blue darkness of the ice. I was too weak to answer, and the knocking for that matter was not repeated. I did not even hear the opening of the door, so softly did she move into the room. I only knew that before I actually saw her, this wave of intolerable sweetness drenched me once again with bliss and peace and comfort, my pain retreated, and I closed my eyes, knowing I should feel that cool and soothing hand upon my forehead.

The same minute I did feel it. There was a perfume of old gardens in the air. I opened my eyes to look the gratitude I could not utter, and saw, close against me—not the old lady, but the young and lovely face my worship had long made familiar. With lips that smiled their yearning and eyes of brown that held tears of sympathy, she sat down beside me on the bed. The warmth and fragrance of her atmosphere enveloped me. I sank away into a garden where spring melts magically into summer. Her arms were round my neck. Her face dropped down, so that I felt her hair upon my cheek and eyes. And then, whispering my name twice over, she kissed me on the lips.

'Marion,' I murmured.

'Hush! Mother sends you this,' she answered softly. 'You are to take it all; she made it with her own hands. But *I* bring it to you. You must be quite obedient, please.'

She tried to rise, but I held her against my breast.

'Kiss me again and I'll promise obedience always,' I strove to say. But my voice refused so long a sentence, and anyhow her lips were on my own before I could have finished it. Slowly, very carefully, she disentangled herself, and my arms sank back upon the coverlet. I sighed in happiness. A moment longer she stood beside my bed, gazing down with love and deep anxiety into my face.

'And when all is eaten, all, mind, *all*,' she smiled, 'you are to sleep until the doctor comes this afternoon. You are much better. Soon you shall get up. Only, remember,' shaking her finger with a sweet pretence of looking stern, 'I shall exact complete obedience. You must yield your will utterly to mine. You are in my heart, and my heart must be kept very warm and happy.'

Her eyes were tender as her mother's and I loved the authority and strength that were so real in her. I remembered how it was this strength that had sealed the contract her beauty first drew up for me to sign. She bent down once more to arrange my pillows.

'What happened to—to the motor?' I asked hesitatingly, for my thoughts *would* not regulate themselves. The mind presented such incongruous fragments.

'The—what?' she asked, evidently puzzled. The word seemed strange to her. 'What is that?' she repeated, anxiety in her eyes.

I made an effort to tell her, but I could not. Explanation was suddenly impossible. The whole idea dived away out of sight. It utterly evaded me. I had again invented a word that was without meaning. I was talking nonsense. In its place my dream came up. I tried to tell her how I had dreamed of climbing dangerous heights with a stranger, and had spoken another language with him than my own—English, was it?—at any rate, not my native French.

'Darling,' she whispered close into my ear, 'the bad dreams will not come back. You are safe here, quite safe.' She put her little hand like a flower on my forehead and drew it softly down the cheek. 'Your wound is already healing. They took the bullet out four days ago. I have got it,' she added with a touch of shy embarrassment, and kissed me tenderly upon my eyes.

'How long have you been away from me?' I asked, feeling exhaustion coming back.

'Never once for more than ten minutes,' was the reply. 'I watched with you all night. Only this morning, while mother took my place, I slept a little. But, hush!' she said, with dear authority again; 'you are not to talk so much. You must eat what I have brought, then sleep again. You must rest and sleep. Good-bye, good-bye, my love. I shall come back in an hour, and I shall always be within reach of your dear voice.'

Her tall, slim figure, dressed in the grey I loved, crossed silently to the door. She gave me one more look—there was all the tenderness of passionate love in it—and then was gone.

I followed instructions meekly, and when a delicious sleep stole over me soon afterwards, I had forgotten utterly the ugly dream that I was climbing dangerous heights with another man, forgotten as well everything else, except that it seemed so many days since my love had come to me, and that my bullet wound would after all be healed in time for our wedding on the day so long, so eagerly waited for.

And when, several hours later, her mother came in with the doctor—his face less grave and solemn this time—the news that I might get up next day and lie a little in the garden, did more to heal me than a thousand bandages or twice that quantity of medical instructions.

I watched them as they stood a moment by the open door. They went out very slowly together, speaking in whispers. But the only thing I caught was the mother's voice, talking brokenly of the great wars. Napoleon, the doctor was saying in a low, hushed tone, was in full retreat from Moscow, though the news had only just come through. They passed into the corridor then, and there was a sound of weeping as the old lady murmured something about her son and the cruelty of Heaven. 'Both will be taken from me,' she was sobbing softly, while he stooped to comfort her; 'one in marriage, and the other in death.' They closed the door then, and I heard no more.

I

Convalescence seemed to follow very quickly then, for I was utterly obedient as I had promised, and never spoke of what could excite me to my own detriment—the wars and my own unfortunate part in them. We talked instead of our love, our already too-long engagement, and of the sweet dream of happines that life held waiting for us in the future. And, indeed, I was sufficiently weary of the world to prefer repose to much activity, for my body was almost incessantly in pain, and this old garden where we lay between high walls of stone, aloof from the busy world and very peaceful, was far more to my taste just then than wars and fighting.

The orchards were in blossom, and the winds of spring showered their rain of petals upon the long, new grass. We lay, half in sunshine, half in shade, beneath the poplars that lined the avenue towards the lake, and behind us rose the ancient grey stone towers where the jackdaws nested in the ivy and the pigeons cooed and fluttered from the woods beyond.

There was loveliness everywhere, but there was sadness too, for though we both knew that the wars had taken her brother whence there is no return, and that only her aged, failing mother's life stood between ourselves and the stately property, there hid a sadness yet deeper than either of these thoughts in both our hearts. And it was, I think, the sadness that comes with spring. For spring, with her lavish, short-lived promises of eternal beauty, is ever a symbol of passing human happiness, incomplete and always unfulfilled. Promises made on earth are playthings, after all, for children. Even while we make them so solemnly, we seem to know they are not meant to hold. They are made, as spring is made, with a glory of soft, radiant blossoms that pass away before there is time to realise them. And yet they come again with the return of spring, as unashamed and glorious as if Time had utterly forgotten.

And this sadness was in her too. I mean it was part of her and she was part of it. Not that our love could change to pass or die, but that its sweet, so-long-desired accomplishment must hold away, and, like the spring, must melt and vanish before it had been fully known. I did not speak of it. I well understood that the depression of a broken body can influence the spirit with its poisonous melancholy, but it must have betrayed itself in my words and gestures, even in my manner too. At any rate, she was aware of it. I think, if truth be told, she felt it too. It seemed so painfully inevitable.

My recovery, meanwhile, was rapid, and from spending an hour or two in the garden, I soon came to spend the entire day. For the spring came on with a rush, and the warmth increased deliciously. While the cuckoos called to one another in the great beech-woods behind the chateau, we sat and talked and sometimes had our simple meals or coffee there together, and I particularly recall the occasion when solid food was first permitted me and she gave me a delicate young *bondelle,* fresh caught that very morning in the lake. There were leaves of sweet, crisp lettuce with it, and she picked the bones out for me with her own white hands.

The day was radiant, with a sky of cloudless blue, soft airs stirred the poplar crests; the little waves fell on the pebbly beach not fifty metres away, and the orchard floor was carpeted with flowers that seemed to have caught from heaven's stars the patterns of their yellow blossoms. The bees droned peacefully among the fruit trees; the air was full of musical deep hummings. My former vigour stirred delightfully in blood, and I knew no pain, beyond occasional dull twinges in the head that came with a rush of temporary darkness over my mind. The scar was healed, however, and the hair had grown over it again. This temporary darkness alarmed her more than it alarmed me. There were grave complications, apparently, that I did not know of.

But the deep-lying sadness in me seemed independent of the glorious weather, due to causes so intangible, so far off that I never could dispel them by arguing them away. For I could not discover what they actually were. There was a vague, distressing sense of restlessness that I ought to have been elsewhere and otherwise, that we were together for a few days only, and that these few days I had snatched unlawfully from stern, imperative duties. These duties were immediate, but neglected. In a sense I had no right to this springtide of bliss her presence brought me. I was playing truant somehow, somewhere. It was *not* my absence from the regiment; that I know. It was infinitely deeper, set to some enormous scale that vaguely frightened me, while it deepened the sweetness of the stolen joy.

Like a child, I sought to pin the sunny hours against the sky and make them stay. They passed with such a mocking swiftness, snatched momentarily from some big oblivion. The twilights swallowed our days together before they had been properly tasted, and on looking back, each afternoon of happiness seemed to have been a mere moment in a flying dream. And I must have somehow betrayed the aching mood, for Marion turned of a sudden and gazed into my face with yearning and anxiety in the sweet brown eyes.

'What is it, dearest?' I asked, 'and why do your eyes bring questions?'

'You sighed,' she answered, smiling a little sadly; 'and sighed so deeply. You are in pain again. The darkness, perhaps, is over you?' And her hand stole out to meet my own. 'You are in pain?'

'Not physical pain,' I said, 'and not *the* darkness either. I see *you* clearly,' and would have told her more, as I carried her soft fingers to my lips, had I not divined from the expression in her eyes that she read my heart and knew all my strange, mysterious forebodings in herself.

'I know,' she whispered before I could find speech, 'for I feel it too. It is the shadow of separation that oppresses you—yet of no common, measurable separation you can understand. Is it not that?'

Leaning over then, I took her close into my arms, since words in that moment were mere foolishness. I held her so that she could not get away; but even while I did so it was like trying to hold the spring, or fasten the flying hour with a fierce desire. All slipped from me, and my arms caught at the sunshine and the wind.

'We have both felt it all these weeks,' she said bravely, as soon as I had released her, 'and we both have struggled to conceal it. But now——' she hesitated for a second, and with so exquisite a tenderness that I would have caught her to me again but for my anxiety to hear her further words—'now that you are well, we may speak plainly to each other, and so lessen our pain by sharing it.' And then she added, still more softly: 'You feel there is "something" that shall take you from me—yet what it is you cannot discover nor divine. Tell me, Félix—all your thought, that I in turn may tell you mine.'

Her voice floated about me in the sunny air. I stared at her, striving to focus the dear face more clearly for my sight. A shower of apple blossoms fell about us, and her words seemed floating past me like those passing petals of white. They drifted away. I followed them with difficulty and confusion. With the wind, I fancied, a veil of indefinable change slipped across her face and eyes.

'Yet nothing that could alter feeling,' I answered; for she had expressed my own thought completely. 'Nor anything that either of us can control. Only—perhaps, that everything must fade and pass away, just as this glory of the spring must fade and pass away——'

'Yet leaving its sweetness in us,' she caught me up passionately, 'and to come again, my beloved, to come again in every subsequent life, each time with an added sweetness in it too!' Her little face showed suddenly the courage of a lion in its eyes. Her heart was ever braver than my own, a vigorous, fighting soul. She spoke of lives, I prattled of days and hours merely.

A touch of shame stole over me. But that delicate, swift change in her spread too. With a thrill of ominous warning I noticed how it rose and grew about her. From within, outwards, it seemed to pass—like a shadow of great blue distance. Shadow was somewhere in it, so that she dimmed a little before my very eyes. The dreadful yearning searched and shook me, for I could not understand it, try as I would. She seemed going from me—drifting like her words and like the apple blossoms.

'But when we shall no longer be here to know it,' I made answer quickly, yet as calmly as I could, 'and when we shall have passed to some other place—to other conditions—where we shall not recognise the joy and wonder. When barriers of mist shall have rolled between us—our love and passion so made-over that we shall not know each other'—the words rushed out feverishly, half beyond control— 'and perhaps shall not even dare to speak to each other of our deep desire——'

I broke off abruptly, conscious that I was speaking out of some unfamiliar place where I floundered, helpless among strange conditions. I was saying things I hardly understood myself. Her bigger, deeper mood spoke through me, perhaps.

Her darling face came back again; she moved close within reach once more.

'Hush, hush!' she whispered, terror and love both battling in her eyes. 'It is the truth, perhaps, but you must not say such things. To speak them brings them closer. A chain is about our hearts, a chain of fashioning lives without number, but do not seek to draw upon it with anxiety or fear. To do so can only cause the pain of wrong entanglement, and interrupt the natural running of the iron links.' And she placed her hand swiftly upon my mouth, as though divining that the bleak attack of anguish was again upon me with its throbbing rush of darkness.

But for once I was disobedient and resisted. The physical pain, I realised vividly, was linked closely with this spiritual torture. One caused the other somehow. The disordered brain received, though brokenly, some hints of darker and unusual knowledge. It had stammered forth in me, but through her it flowed easily and clear. I saw the change move more swiftly then across her face. Some ancient look passed into both her eyes.

And it was inevitable; I must speak out, regardless of mere bodily well-being.

'We shall have to face them some day,' I cried, although the effort hurt abominably, 'then why not now?' And I drew her hand down and kissed it passionately over and over again. 'We are not children, to hide our faces among shadows and pretend we are invisible. At least we have the Present—the Moment that is here and now. We stand side by side in the heart of this deep spring day. This sunshine and these flowers, this wind across the lake, this sky of blue and this singing of the birds—all, all are ours *now*. Let us use the moment that Time gives, and so strengthen the chain you speak of that shall bring us again together times without number. We shall then, perhaps, remember. Oh, my heart, think what that would mean—to remember!'

Exhaustion caught me, and I sank back among my cushions. But Marion rose up suddenly and stood beside me. And as she did so, another Sky dropped softly down upon us both, and I smelt again the incense of old, old gardens that brought long-forgotten perfumes, incredibly sweet, but with it an ache of far-off, passionate remembrance that was pain. This great ache of distance swept over me like a wave.

I know not what grand change then was wrought upon her beauty, so that I saw her defiant and erect, commanding Fate because she understood it. She towered over me, but it was her soul that towered. The rush of internal darkness in me blotted out all else. The familiar, present sky grew dim, the sunshine faded, the lake and flowers and poplars dipped away. Conditions a thousand times more vivid took their place. She stood out, clear and shining in the glory of an undressed soul, brave and confident with an eternal love that separation strengthened but could never, never change. The deep sadness

I abruptly realised, was very little removed from joy—because, somehow, it was the condition of joy. I could not explain it more than that.

And her voice, when she spoke, was firm with a note of steel in it; intense, yet devoid of the wasting anger that passion brings. She was determined beyond Death itself, upon a foundation sure and lasting as the stars. The heart in her was calm, because she *knew*. She was magnificent.

'We are together—always,' she said, her voice rich with the knowledge of some unfathomable experience, 'for separation is temporary merely, forging new links in the ancient chain of lives that binds our hearts eternally together.' She looked like one who has conquered the adversity Time brings, by accepting it. 'You speak of the Present as though our souls were already fitted now to bid it stay, needing no further fashioning. Looking only to the Future, you forget our ample Past that has made us what we are. Yet our Past is here and now, beside us at this very moment. Into the hollow cups of weeks and months, of years and centuries, Time pours its flood beneath our eyes. Time is our schoolroom.... Are you so soon afraid? Does not separation achieve that which companionship never could accomplish? And how shall we dare eternity together of we cannot be strong in separation first?'

I listened while a flood of memories broke up through film upon film and layer upon layer that had long covered them. 'This Present that we seem to hold between our hands,' she went on in that earnest, distant voice, '*is* our moment of sweet remembrance that you speak of, of renewal, perhaps, too, of reconciliation—a fleeting instant when we may kiss again and say good-bye, but with strengthened hope and courage revived. But we may not stay together finally—we *cannot*—until long discipline and pain shall have perfected sympathy and schooled our love by searching, difficult tests, that it may last for ever.'

I stretched my arms out dumbly to take her in. Her face shone down upon me, bathed in an older, fiercer sunlight. The change in her seemed in an instant then complete. Some big, soft wind blew both of us ten thousand miles away. The centuries gathered us back together.

'Look, rather, to the Past,' she whispered grandly, 'where first we knew the sweet opening of our love. Remember, if you can, how the pain and separation have made it so worth while to continue. And be braver thence.'

She turned her eyes more fully upon my own, so that their light persuaded me utterly away with her. An immense new happiness broke over me. I listened, and with the stirrings of an ampler courage. It seemed I followed her down an interminable vista of remembrance till I was happy with her among the flowers and fields of our earliest pre-existence.

Her voice came to me with the singing of birds and the hum of summer insects.

'Have you so soon forgotten,' she sighed, 'when we knew together the perfume of the hanging Babylonian Gardens, or when the Hesperides were so soft, to us in the dawn of the world? And do you not remember,' with a little rise of passion in her voice, 'the sweet plantations of Chaldea, and how we tasted the odour of many a drooping flower in the gardens of Alcinous and Adonis, when the bees of olden time picked out the honey for our eating? It is the fragrance of those first hours we knew together that still lies in our hearts to-day, sweetening our love to this apparent suddenness. Hence comes the full, deep happiness we gather so easily To-day.... The breast of every ancient forest is torn with storms and lightning... that's why it is so soft and full of little gardens. You have forgotten too easily the glades of Lebanon, where we whispered our earliest secrets while the big winds drove their chariots down those earlier skies...'

There rose an indescribable tempest of remembrance in my heart as I strove to bring the pictures into focus; but words failed me, and the hand I eagerly stretched out to touch her own, met only sunshine and the rain of apple blossoms.

'The myrrh and frankincense,' she continued in a sighing voice that seemed to come with the wind from invisible caverns in the sky, 'the grapes and pomegranates—have they all passed from you, with the train of apes and peacocks, the tigers and the ibis, and the hordes of dark-faced slaves? And this little sun that plays so lightly here upon our woods of beech and pine—does it bring back nothing of the old-time scorching when the olive slopes, the figs and ripening cornfields heard our vows and watched our love mature?... Our spread encampment in the Desert—do not these sands upon our little beach revive its lonely majesty for you, and have you forgotten the gleaming towers of Semiramis ... or, in Sardis, those strange lilies that first tempted our souls to their divine disclosure...?'

Conscious of a violent struggle between pain and joy, both too deep for me to understand, I rose to seize her in my arms. But the effort dimmed the flying pictures. The wind that bore her voice down the stupendous vista fled back into the caverns whence it came. And the pain caught me in a vice of agony so searching that I could not move a muscle. My tongue lay dry against my lips. I could not frame a word of any sentence....

Her voice presently came back to me, but fainter, like a whisper from the stars. The light dimmed everywhere; I saw no more the vivid, shining scenery she had summoned. A mournful dusk instead crept down upon the world she had momentarily revived.

'... we may not stay together,' I heard her little whisper, 'until long discipline shall have perfected sympathy, and schooled our love to last. For this love of ours *is* for ever, and the pain that tries it is the furnace that fashions precious stones....'

Again I stretched my arms out. Her face shone a moment longer in that forgotten fiercer sunlight, then faded very swiftly. The change, like a veil, passed over it. From the place of prodigious distance where she had been, she swept down towards me with such dizzy speed. As she was To-day I saw her again, more and more.

'Pain and separation, then, are welcome,' I tried to stammer, 'and we will desire them'—but my thought got no further into expression than the first two words. Aching blotted out coherent utterance.

She bent down very close against my face. Her fragrance was about my lips. But her voice ran off like a faint thrill of music, far, far away. I caught the final words, dying away as wind dies in high branches of a wood. And they reached me this time through the droning of bees and of waves that murmured close at hand upon the shore.

'... for our love is of the soul and our souls are moulded in Eternity. It is not yet, it is not now, our perfect consummation. Nor shall our next time of meeting know it. We shall not even speak.... For I shall not be free....' was what I heard. She paused.

'You mean we shall not know each other?' I cried, in an anguish of spirit that mastered the lesser physical pain.

I barely caught her answer:

'My discipline then will be in another's keeping—yet only that I may come back to you ... more perfect ... in the end....'

The bees and waves then cushioned her whisper with their humming. The trail of a deeper silence led them far away. The rush of temporary darkness passed and lifted. I opened my eyes. My love sat close beside me in the shadow of the poplars. One hand held both my own, while with the other she arranged my pillows and stroked my aching head. The world dropped back into a tiny scale once more.

'You have had the pain again,' Marion murmured anxiously, 'but it is better now. It is passing.' She kissed my cheek. 'You must come in....'

But I would not let her go. I held her to me with all the strength that was in me. 'I had it, but it's gone again. An awful darkness came with it,' I whispered in the little ear that was so close against my mouth. 'I've been dreaming,' I told her, as memory dipped away, 'dreaming of you and me—together somewhere—in old gardens, or forests—where the sun was——'

But she would not let me finish. I think, in any case, I could not have said more, for thought evaded me, and any language of coherent description was in the same instant beyond my power. Exhaustion came upon me, that vile, compelling nausea with it.

'The sun here is too strong for you, dear love,' I heard her saying, 'and you must rest more. We have been doing too much these last few days. You must have more repose.' She rose to help me move indoors.

'I have been unconscious then?' I asked, in the feeble whisper that was all I could manage.

'For a little while. You slept, while I watched over you.'

'But I was away from you! Oh, how could you let me sleep, when our time together is so short?'

She soothed me instantly in the way she knew we both loved so. I clung to her until she released herself again.

'Not away from me,' she smiled, 'for I was with you in your dreaming.'

'Of course, of course you were'; but already I knew not exactly why I said it, nor caught the deep meaning that struggled up into my words from such unfathomable distance.

'Come,' she added, with her sweet authority again, 'we must go in now. Give me your arm, and I will send out for the cushions. Lean on me. I am going to put you back to bed.'

'But I shall sleep again,' I said petulantly, 'and we shall be separated.'

'We shall dream together,' she replied, as she helped me slowly and painfully towards the old grey walls of the château.

II

Half an hour later I slept deeply, peacefully, upon my bed in the big stately chamber where the roses watched beside the latticed windows.

And to say I dreamed again is not correct, for it can only be expressed by saying that I saw and knew. The figures round the bed were actual, and in life. Nothing could be more real than the whisper of the doctor's voice—that solemn, grave-faced man who was so tall—as he said, sternly yet brokenly, to some one: 'You must say good-bye; and you had better say it *now*.' Nor could anything be more definite and sure, more charged with the actuality of living, than the figure of Marion, as she stooped over me to obey the terrible command. For I saw her face float down towards me like a star, and a shower of pale spring blossoms rained upon me with her hair. The perfume of old, old gardens rose about me as she slipped to her knees beside the bed and kissed my lips—so softly it was like the breath of wind from lake and orchard, and so lingeringly it was as though the blossoms lay upon my mouth and grew into flowers that she planted there.

'Good-bye, my love; be brave. It is only separation.'

'It is death,' I tried to say, but could only feebly stir my lips against her own.

I drew her breath of flowers into my mouth ... and there came then the darkness which is final.

The voices grew louder. I heard a man struggling with an unfamiliar language. Turning restlessly, I opened my eyes—upon a little, stuffy room, with white walls whereon no pictures hung. It was very hot. A woman was standing beside the bed, and the bed was very short. I stretched, and my feet kicked against the boarding at the end.

'Yes, he *is* awake,' the woman said in French. 'Will you come in? The doctor said you might see him when he woke. I think he'll know you.' She spoke in French. I just knew enough to understand.

And of course I knew him. It was Haddon. I heard him thanking her for all her kindness, as he blundered in. His French, if anything, was worse than my own. I felt inclined to laugh. I did laugh.

'By Jove! old man, this is bad luck, isn't it? You've had a narrow shave. This good lady telegraphed——'

'Have you got my ice-axe? Is it all right?' I asked. I remembered clearly the motor accident—everything.

'The ice-axe is right enough,' he laughed, looking cheerfully at the woman, 'but what about yourself? Feel bad still? Any pain, I mean?'

'Oh, I feel all right,' I answered, searching for the pain of broken bones, but finding none. 'What happened? I was stunned, I suppose?'

'Bit stunned, yes,' said Haddon. 'You got a nasty knock on the head, it seems. The point of the axe ran into you, or something.'

'Was that all?'

He nodded. 'But I'm afraid it's knocked our climbing on the head. Shocking bad luck, isn't it?'

'I telegraphed last night,' the kind woman was explaining.

'But I couldn't get there till this morning,' Haddon said. 'The telegram didn't find me till midnight, you see.' And he turned to thank the woman in his voluble, dreadful French. She kept a little pension on the shores of the lake. It was the nearest house, and they had carried me in there and got the doctor to me all within the hour. It proved slight enough, apart from the shock. It was not even concussion. I had merely been stunned. Sleep had cured me, as it seemed.

'Jolly little place,' said Haddon, as he moved me that afternoon to Geneva, whence, after a few days' rest, we went on into the Alps of Haute Savoie, 'and lucky the old body was so kind and quick. Odd, wasn't it?' He glanced at me.

Something in his voice betrayed he hid another thought. I saw nothing 'odd' in it at all, only very tiresome.

'What's its name?' I asked, taking a shot at a venture.

He hesitated a second. Haddon, the climber, was not skilled in the delicacies of tact.

'Don't know its present name,' he answered, looking away from me across the lake, 'but it stands on the site of an old château—destroyed a hundred years ago—the Château de Bellerive.'

And then I understood my old friend's absurd confusion. For Bellerive chanced also to be the name of a married woman I knew in Scotland—at least, it was her maiden name, and she was of French extraction.

THE SEA FIT

THE sea that night sang rather than chanted; all along the far-running shore a rising tide dropped thick foam, and the waves, white-crested, came steadily in with the swing of a deliberate purpose. Overhead, in a cloudless sky, that ancient Enchantress, the full moon, watched their dance across the sheeted sands, guiding them carefully while she drew them up. For through that moonlight, through that roar of surf, there penetrated a singular note of earnestness and meaning—almost as though these common processes of Nature were instinct with the flush of an unusual activity that sought audaciously to cross the borderland into some subtle degree of conscious life. A gauze of light vapour clung upon the surface of the sea, far out—a transparent carpet through which the rollers drove shorewards in a moving pattern.

In the low-roofed bungalow among the sand-dunes the three men sat. Foregathered for Easter, they spent the day fishing and sailing, and at night told yarns of the days when life was younger. It was fortunate that there were three—and later four—because in the mouths of several witnesses an extraordinary thing shall be established—when they agree. And although whisky stood upon the rough table made of planks nailed to barrels, it is childish to pretend that a few drinks invalidate evidence, for alcohol, up to a certain point, intensifies the consciousness, focuses the intellectual powers, sharpens observation; and two healthy men, certainly three, must have imbibed an absurd amount before they all see, or omit to see, the same things.

The other bungalows still awaited their summer occupants. Only the lonely tufted sand-dunes watched the sea, shaking their hair of coarse white grass to the winds. The men had the whole spit to themselves—with the wind, the spray, the flying gusts of sand, and that great Easter full moon. There was Major Reese of the Gunners and his half-brother, Dr. Malcolm

Reese, and Captain Erricson, their host, all men whom the kaleidoscope of life had jostled together a decade ago in many adventures, then flung for years apart about the globe. There was also Erricson's body-servant, 'Sinbad,' sailor of big seas, and a man who had shared on many a ship all the lust of strange adventure that distinguished his great blonde-haired owner—an ideal servant and dog-faithful, divining his master's moods almost before they were born. On the present occasion, besides crew of the fishing-smack, he was cook, valet, and steward of the bungalow smoking-room as well.

'Big Erricson', Norwegian by extraction, student by adoption, wanderer by blood, a Viking reincarnated if ever there was one, belonged to that type of primitive man in whom burns an inborn love and passion for the sea that amounts to positive worship—devouring tide, a lust and fever in the soul. 'All genuine votaries of the old sea-gods have it,' he used to say, by way of explaining his carelessness of worldly ambitions. 'We're never at our best away from salt water—never quite right. I've got it bang in the heart myself. I'd do a bit before the mast sooner than make a million on shore. Simply can't help it, you see, and never could! It's our gods calling us to worship.' And he had never tried to 'help it', which explains why he owned nothing in the world on land except this tumble-down, one-storey bungalow—more like a ship's cabin than anything else, to which he sometimes asked his bravest and most faithful friends—and a store of curious reading gathered in long, becalmed days at the ends of the world. Heart and mind, that is, carried a queer cargo. 'I'm sorry if you poor devils are uncomfortable in her. You must ask Sinbad for anything you want and don't see, remember.' As though Sinbad could have supplied comforts that were miles away, or converted a draughty wreck into a snug, taut, brand-new vessel.

Neither of the Reeses had cause for grumbling on the score of comfort, however, for they knew the keen joys of roughing it, and both weather and sport besides had been glorious. It was on another score this particular evening that they found cause for uneasiness, if not for actual grumbling. Erricson had one of his queer sea fits on—the Doctor was responsible for the term—and was in the thick of it, plunging like a straining boat at anchor, talking in a way that made them both feel vaguely uncomfortable and distressed. Neither of them knew exactly perhaps why he should have felt this growing *malaise*, and each was secretly vexed with the other for confirming his own unholy instinct that something uncommon was astir. The loneliness of the sandspit and that melancholy singing of the sea before their very door may have had something to do with it, seeing that both were landsmen; for Imagination is ever Lord of the Lonely Places, and adventurous men remain children to the last. But, whatever it was that affected both men in different fashion, Malcolm Reese, the doctor, had not thought it necessary to mention to his brother that Sinbad had tugged his sleeve on entering and whispered in his ear significantly: 'Full moon, sir, please, and he's better without too much! These high spring tides get him all caught off his feet sometimes—clean sea-crazy'; and the man had contrived to let the doctor see the hilt of a small pistol he carried in his hippocket.

For Ericson had got upon his old subject: that the gods were not dead, but merely withdrawn, and that even a single true worshipper was enough to draw them down again into touch with the world, into the sphere of humanity, even into active and visible manifestation. He spoke of queer things he had seen in queerer places. He was serious, vehement, voluble; and the others had let it pour out unchecked, hoping thereby for its speedier exhaustion. They puffed their pipes in comparative silence, nodding from time to time, shrugging their shoulders, the soldier mystified and bewildered, the doctor alert and keenly watchful.

'And I like the old idea,' he had been saying, speaking of these departed pagan deities, 'that sacrifice and ritual feed their great beings, and that death is only the final sacrifice by which the worshipper becomes absorbed into them. The devout worshipper'—and there was a singular drive and power behind the words—'should go to his death singing, as to a wedding—

the wedding of his soul with the particular deity he has loved and served all his life.' He swept his tow-coloured beard with one hand, turning his shaggy head towards the window, where the moonlight lay upon the procession of shaking waves. 'It's playing the whole game, I always think, man-fashion.... I remember once, some years ago, down there off the coast by Yucatan——'

And then, before they could interfere, he told an extraordinary tale of something he had seen years ago, but told it with such a horrid earnestness of conviction—for it was dreadful, though fine, this adventure—that his listeners shifted in their wicker chairs, struck matches, unnecessarily, pulled at their long glasses, and exchanged glances that attempted a smile yet did not quite achieve it. For the tale had to do with sacrifice of human life and a rather haunting pagan ceremonial of the sea, and at its close the room had changed in some indefinable manner—was not exactly as it had been before perhaps—as though the savage earnestness of the language had introduced some new element that made it less cosy, less cheerful, even less warm. A secret lust in the man's heart, born of the sea, and of his intense admiration of the pagan gods called a light into his eye not altogether pleasant.

'They were great Powers, at any rate, those ancient fellows,' Erricson went on, refilling his huge pipe bowl; 'too great to disappear altogether, though to-day they may walk the earth in another manner. I swear they're still going it—especially the——' (he hesitated for a mere second) 'the old water Powers—the Sea Gods. Terrific beggars, every one of 'em.'

'Still move the tides and raise the winds, eh?' from the Doctor.

Erricson spoke again after a moment's silence, with impressive dignity. 'And I like, too, the way they manage to keep their names before us,' he went on, with a curious eagerness that did not escape the Doctor's observation, while it clearly puzzled the soldier. 'There's old Hu, the Druid god of justice, still alive in "Hue and Cry"; there's Typhon hammering his way against us in the typhoon; there's the mighty Hurakar, serpent god of the winds, you know, shouting to us in hurricane and *ouragan*; and there's——'

'Venus still at it as hard as ever,' interrupted the Major, facetiously, though his brother did not laugh because of their host's almost sacred earnestness of manner and uncanny grimness of face. Exactly how he managed to introduce that element of gravity—of conviction—into such talk neither of his listeners quite understood, for in discussing the affair later they were unable to pitch upon any definite detail that betrayed it. Yet there it was, alive and haunting, even distressingly so. All day he had been silent and morose, but since dusk, with the turn of the tide, in fact, these queer sentences, half mystical, half unintelligible, had begun to pour from him, till now that cabin-like room among the sand-dunes fairly vibrated with the man's emotion. And at last Major Reese, with blundering good intention, tried to shift the key from this portentous subject of sacrifice to something that might eventually lead towards comedy and laughter, and so relieve this growing pressure of melancholy and incredible things. The Viking fellow had just spoken of the possibility of the old gods manifesting themselves visibly, audibly, physically, and so the Major caught him up and made light mention of spiritualism and the so-called 'materialisation séances,' where physical bodies were alleged to be built up out of the emanations of the medium and the sitters. This crude aspect of the Supernatural was the only possible link the soldier's mind could manage. He caught his brother's eye too late, it seems, for Malcolm Reese realised by this time that something untoward was afoot, and no longer needed the memory of Sinbad's warning to keep him sharply on the look-out. It was not the first time he had seen Erricson 'caught' by the sea; but he had never known him quite so bad, nor seen his face so flushed and white alternately, nor his eyes so oddly shining. So that Major Reese's well-intentioned allusion only brought wind to fire.

The man of the sea, once Viking, roared with a rush of boisterous laughter at the comic suggestion, then dropped his voice to a sudden hard whisper, awfully earnest, awfully intense. Any one must have started at the abrupt change and the life-and-death manner of the big man. His listeners undeniably both did.

'Bunkum!' he shouted, 'bunkum, and be damned to it all! There's only one real materialisation of these immense Outer Beings possible, and that's when the great embodied emotions, which are their sphere of action'—his words became wildly incoherent, painfully struggling to get out—'derived, you see, from their honest worshippers the world over—constituting their Bodies, in fact—come down into matter and get condensed, crystallised into form—to claim that final sacrifice I spoke about just now, and to which any man might feel himself proud and honoured to be summoned.... No dying in bed or fading out from old age, but to plunge full-blooded and alive into the great Body of the god who has deigned to descend and fetch you——'

The actual speech may have been even more rambling and incoherent than that. It came out in a torrent at white heat. Dr. Reese kicked his brother beneath the table, just in time. The soldier looked thoroughly uncomfortable and amazed, utterly at a loss to know how he had produced the storm. It rather frightened him.

'I know it because I've seen it,' went on the sea man, his mind and speech slightly more under control. 'Seen the ceremonies that brought these whopping old Nature gods down into form—seen 'em carry off a worshipper into themselves—seen that worshipper, too, go off singing and happy to his death, proud and honoured to be chosen.'

'Have you really—by George!' the Major exclaimed. 'You tell us a queer thing, Erricson'; and it was then for the fifth time that Sinbad cautiously opened the door, peeped in and silently withdrew after giving a swiftly comprehensive glance round the room.

The night outside was windless and serene, only the growing thunder of the tide near the full woke muffled echoes among the sand-dunes.

'Rites and ceremonies,' continued the other, his voice booming with a singular enthusiasm, but ignoring the interruption, 'are simply means of losing one's self by temporary ecstasy in the God of one's choice—the God one has worshipped all one's life—of being partially absorbed into his being. And sacrifice completes the process——'

'At death, you said?' asked Malcolm Reese, watching him keenly.

'Or voluntary,' was the reply that came flash-like. 'The devotee becomes wedded to his Deity—goes bang into him, you see, by fire or water or air—as by a drop from a height—according to the nature of the particular God; at-one-ment, of course. A man's death that! Fine, you know!'

The man's inner soul was on fire now. He was talking at a fearful pace, his eyes alight, his voice turned somehow into a kind of sing-song that chimed well, singularly well, with the booming of waves outside, and from time to time he turned to the window to stare at the sea and the moon-blanched sands. And then a look of triumph would come into his face—that giant face framed by slow-moving wreaths of pipe smoke.

Sinbad entered for the sixth time without any obvious purpose, busied himself unnecessarily with the glasses and went out again, lingeringly. In the room he kept his eye hard upon his master. This time he contrived to push a chair and a heap of netting between him and the window. No one but Dr. Reese observed the manoeuvre. And he took the hint.

'The port-holes fit badly, Erricson,' he laughed, but with a touch of authority. 'There's a five-knot breeze coming through the cracks worse than an old wreck!' And he moved up to secure the fastening better.

'The room *is* confoundedly cold,' Major Reese put in; 'has been for the last half-hour, too.' The soldier looked what he felt—cold—distressed—creepy. 'But there's no wind really, you know,' he added.

Captain Erricson turned his great bearded visage from one to the other before he answered; there was a gleam of sudden suspicion in his blue eyes. 'The beggar's got that back door open again. If he's sent for any one, as he did once before, I swear I'll drown him in fresh water for his impudence—or perhaps—can it be already that he expects——?' He left the sentence incomplete and rang the bell, laughing with a boisterousness that was clearly feigned. 'Sinbad, what's this cold in the place? You've got the back door open. Not expecting any one, are you——?'

'Everything's shut tight, Captain. There's a bit of a breeze coming up from the east. And the tide's drawing in at a raging pace——'

'We can all hear *that*. But are you expecting any one? I asked,' repeated his master, suspiciously, yet still laughing. One might have said he was trying to give the idea that the man had some land flirtation on hand. They looked one another square in the eye for a moment, these two. It was the straight stare of equals who understood each other well.

'Some one—might be—on the way, as it were, Captain. Couldn't say for certain.'

The voice almost trembled. By a sharp twist of the eye, Sinbad managed to shoot a lightning and significant look at the Doctor.

'But this cold—this freezing, damp cold in the place? Are you sure no one's come—by the back ways?' insisted the master. He whispered it. 'Across the dunes, for instance?' His voice conveyed awe and delight, both kept hard under.

'It's all over the house, Captain, already,' replied the man, and moved across to put more sea-logs on the blazing fire. Even the soldier noticed then that their language was tight with allusion of another kind. To relieve the growing tension and uneasiness in his own mind he took up the word 'house' and made fun of it.

'As though it were a mansion,' he observed, with a forced chuckle, 'instead of a mere sea-shell!' Then, looking about him, he added: 'But, all the same, you know, there *is* a kind of fog getting into the room—from the sea, I suppose; coming up with the tide, or something, eh?' The air had certainly in the last twenty minutes turned thickish; it was not all tobacco smoke, and there was a moisture that began to precipitate on the objects in tiny, fine globules. The cold, too, fairly bit.

'I'll take a look round,' said Sinbad, significantly, and went out. Only the Doctor perhaps noticed that the man shook, and was white down to the gills. He said nothing, but moved his chair nearer to the window and to his host. It was really a little bit beyond comprehension how the wild words of this old sea-dog in the full sway of his 'sea fit' had altered the very air of the room as well as the personal equations of its occupants, for an extraordinary atmosphere of enthusiasm that was almost splendour pulsed about him, yet vilely close to something that suggested terror! Through the armour of every-day common sense that normally clothed the minds of these other two, had crept the faint wedges of a mood that made them vaguely wonder whether the incredible could perhaps sometimes—by way of bewildering exceptions—actually come to pass. The moods of their deepest life, that is to say, were already affected. An inner, and thoroughly unwelcome, change was in progress. And such psychic disturbances once started are hard to arrest. In this case it was well on the way before either the Army or Medicine had been willing to recognise the fact. There was something coming—coming from the sand-dunes or the sea. And it was invited, welcomed at any rate, by Erricson. His deep, volcanic enthusiasm and belief provided the channel. In lesser degree they, too, were caught in it. Moreover, it was terrific, irresistible.

And it was at this point—as the comparing of notes aferwards established—that Father Norden came in, Norden, the big man's nephew, having bicycled over from some point beyond Corfe Castle and raced along the hard Studland sand in the moonlight, and then hullood till a boat had ferried him across the narrow channel of Poole Harbour. Sinbad simply brought him in without any preliminary question or announcement. He could not resist the splendid night and the spring air, explained Norden. He felt sure his uncle could 'find a hammock' for him somewhere aft, as he put it. He did not add that Sinbad had telegraphed for him just before sundown from the coast-guard hut. Dr. Reese already knew him, but he was introduced to the Major. Norden was a member of the Society of Jesus, an ardent, not clever, and unselfish soul.

Erricson greeted him with obviously mixed feelings, and with an extraordinary sentence: 'It doesn't really matter,' he exclaimed, after a few commonplaces of talk, 'for all religions are the same if you go deep enough. All teach sacrifice, and, without exception, all seek final union by absorption into their Deity.' And then, under his breath, turning sideways to peer out of the window, he added a swift rush of half-smothered words that only Dr. Reese caught: 'The Army, the Church, the Medical Profession, and Labour—if they would only all come! What a fine result, what a grand offering! Alone—I seem so unworthy—insignificant...!'

But meanwhile young Norden was speaking before any one could stop him, although the Major did make one or two blundering attempts. For once the Jesuit's tact was at fault. He evidently hoped to introduce a new mood—to shift the current already established by the single force of his own personality. And he was not quite man enough to carry it off.

It was an error of judgment on his part. For the forces he found established in the room were too heavy to lift and alter, their impetus being already acquired. He did his best, anyhow. He began moving with the current—it was not the first sea fit he had combated in this extraordinary personality—then found, too late, that he was carried along with it himself like the rest of them.

'Odd—but couldn't find the bungalow at first,' he laughed, somewhat hardly. 'It's got a bit of seafog all to itself that hides it. I thought perhaps my pagan uncle——'

The Doctor interrupted him hastily, with great energy. 'The fog *does* lie caught in these sand hollows—like steam in a cup, you know,' he put in. But the other, intent on his own procedure, missed the cue.

THE SEA FIT

'——thought it was smoke at first, and that you were up to some heathen ceremony or other,' laughing in Erricson's face; 'sacrificing to the full moon or the sea, or the spirits of the desolate places that haunt sand-dunes, eh?'

No one spoke for a second, but Erricson's face turned quite radiant.

'My uncle's such a pagan, you know,' continued the priest, 'that as I flew along those deserted sands from Studland I almost expected to hear old Triton blow his wreathed horn... or see fair Thetis's tinsel-slippered feet....'

Erricson, suppressing violent gestures, highly excited, face happy as a boy's, was combing his great yellow beard with both hands, and the other two men had begun to speak at once, intent on stopping the flow of unwise allusion. Norden, swallowing a mouthful of cold soda-water, had put the glass down, spluttering over its bubbles, when the sound was first heard at the window. And in the back room the manservant ran, calling something aloud that sounded like 'It's coming, God save us, it's coming in...!' Though the Major swears some name was mentioned that he afterwards forgot—Glaucus —Proteus—Pontus—or some such word. The sound itself, however, was plain enough—a kind of imperious tappling on the window-panes as of a multitude of objects. Blown sand it might have been or heavy spray or, as Norden suggested later, a great water-soaked branch of giant seaweed. Every one started up, but Erricson was first upon his feet, and had the window wide open in a twinkling. His voice roared forth over those moonlit sand-dunes and out towards the line of heavy surf ten yards below.

'All along the shore of the Aegean,' he bellowed, with a kind of hoarse triumph that shook the heart, 'that ancient cry once rang. But it was a lie, a thumping and audacious lie. And He is not the only one. Another still lives—and, by Poseidon, He comes! He knows His own and His own know Him— and His own shall go to meet Him...!'

That reference to the Aegean 'cry'! It was so wonderful. Every one, of course, except the soldier, seized the allusion.

It was a comprehensive, yet subtle, way of suggesting the idea. And meanwhile all spoke at once, shouted rather, for the Invasion was somehow—monstrous.

'Damn it—that's a bit too much. Something's caught my throat!' The Major, like a man drowning, fought with the furniture in his amazement and dismay. Fighting was his first instinct, of course. 'Hurts so infernally—takes the breath,' he cried, by way of explaining the extraordinarily violent impetus that moved him, yet half ashamed of himself for seeing nothing he could strike. But Malcolm Reese struggled to get between his host and the open window, saying in tense voice something like 'Don't let him get out! Don't let him get out!' While the shouts of warning from Sinbad in the little cramped back offices added to the general confusion. Only Father Norden stood quiet—watching with a kind of admiring wonder the expression of magnificence that had flamed into the visage of Erricson.

'Hark, you fools! Hark!' boomed the Viking figure, standing erect and splendid.

And through that open window, along the far-drawn line of shore from Canford Cliffs to the chalk bluffs of Studland Bay, there certainly ran a sound that was no common roar of surf. It was articulate— message from the sea—an announcement—a thunderous warning of approach. No mere surf breaking on sand could have compassed so deep and multitudinous a voice of dreadful roaring—far out over the entering tide, yet at the same time close in along the entire sweep of shore, shaking all the ocean, both depth and surface, with its deep vibrations. Into the bungalow chamber came—the SEA!

Out of the night, from the moonlit spaces where it had been steadily accumulating, into that little cabined room so full of humanity and tobacco smoke, came invisibly—the Power of the Sea. Invisible, yes, but mighty, pressed forward by the huge draw of the moon, soft-coated with brine and moisture —the great Sea. And with it, into the minds of those three other men, leaped instantaneously, not to be denied, overwhelming suggestions of water-power, the tear and strain of thousand-mile currents, the irresistible pull and rush of tides, the suction of giant whirlpools—more, the massed and awful impetus of whole driven oceans. The air turned salt and briny, and a welter of seaweed clamped their very skins.

'Glaucus! I come to Thee, great God of the deep Waterways.... Father and Master!' Erricson cried aloud in a voice that most marvellously conveyed supreme joy.

The little bungalow trembled as from a blow at the foundations, and the same second the big man was through the window and running down the moonlit sands towards the foam.

'God in Heaven! Did you all see *that*?' shouted Major Reese, for the manner in which the great body slipped through the tiny window-frame was incredible. And then, first tottering with a sudden weakness, he recovered himself and rushed round by the door, followed by his brother. Sinbad, invisible, but not inaudible, was calling aloud from the passage at the back. Father Norden, slimmer than the others—well controlled, too—was through the little window before either of them reached the fringe of beach beyond the sand-dunes. They joined forces halfway down to the water's edge. The figure of Erricson, towering in the moonlight, flew before them, coasting rapidly along the wave-line.

No one of them said a word; they tore along side by side, Norden a trifle in advance. In front of them, head turned seawards, bounded Erricson in great flying leaps, singing as he ran, impossible to overtake.

Then, what they witnessed, all three witnessed; the weird grandeur of it in the moonshine was too splendid to allow the smaller emotions of personal alarm, it seems. At any rate, the divergence of opinion afterwards was unaccountably insignificant. For, on a sudden, that heavy roaring sound far out at sea came close in with a swift plunge of speed, followed simultaneously—accompanied, rather—by a dark line that was no mere wave moving: enormously, up and across, between the sea and sky it swept close in to shore. The moonlight caught it for a second as it passed, in a cliff of her bright silver.

And Erricson slowed down, bowed his great head and shoulders, spread his arms out and...

And what? For no one of those amazed witnesses could swear exactly what then came to pass. Upon this impossibility of telling it in language they all three agreed. Only those eyeless dunes of sand that watched, only the white and silent moon overhead, only that long, curved beach of empty and deserted shore retain the complete record, to be revealed some day perhaps when a later Science shall have learned to develop the photographs that Nature takes incessantly upon her secret plates. For Erricson's rough suit of tweed went out in ribbons across the air; his figure somehow turned dark like strips of tide-sucked seaweed; something enveloped and overcame him, half shrouding him from view. He stood for one instant upright, his hair wild in the moonshine, towering, with arms again outstretched; then bent forward, turned, drew out most curiously sideways, uttering the singing sound of tumbling waters. The next instant, curving over like a falling wave, he swept along the glistening surface of the sands—and was gone. In fluid form, wave-like, his being slipped away into the Being of the Sea. A violent tumult convulsed the surface of the tide near in, but at once, and with amazing speed, passed careering away into the deeper water—far out. To his singular death, as to a wedding, Erricson had gone, singing, and well content.

'May God, who holds the sea and all its powers in the hollow of His mighty hand, take them *both* into Himself!' Norden was on his knees, praying fervently.

The body was never recovered ... and the most curious thing of all was that the interior of the cabin, where they found Sinbad shaking with terror when they at length returned, was splashed and sprayed, almost soaked, with salt water. Up into the bigger dunes beside the bungalow, and far beyond the reach of normal tides, lay, too, a great streak and furrow as of a large invading wave, caking the dry sand. A hundred tufts of the coarse grass tussocks had been torn away.

THE SEA FIT

The high tide that night, drawn by the Easter full moon, of course, was known to have been exceptional, for it fairly flooded Poole Harbour, flushing all the coves and bays towards the mouth of the Frome. And the natives up at Arne Bay and Wych always declare that the noise of the sea was heard far inland even up to the nine Barrows of the Purbeck Hills—triumphantly singing.

THE ATTIC

The forest-girdled village upon the Jura slopes slept soundly, although it was not yet many minutes after ten o'clock. The clang of the *couvre-feu* had indeed just ceased, its notes swept far into the woods by a wind that shook the mountains. This wind now rushed down the deserted street. It howled about the old rambling building called La Citadelle, whose roof towered gaunt and humped above the smaller houses—Château left unfinished long ago by Lord Wemyss, the exiled Jacobite. The families who occupied the various apartments listened to the storm and felt the building tremble. 'It's the mountain wind. It will bring the snow,' the mother said, without looking up from her knitting. 'And how sad it sounds.'

But it was not the wind that brought sadness as we sat round the open fire of peat. It was the wind of memories. The lamplight slanted along the narrow room towards the table where breakfast things lay ready for the morning. The double windows were fastened. At the far end stood a door ajar, and on the other side of it the two elder children lay asleep in the big bed. But beside the window was a smaller unused bed, that had been empty now a year. And to-night was the anniversary....

And so the wind brought sadness and long thoughts. The little chap that used to lie there was already twelve months gone, far, far beyond the Hole where the Winds came from, as he called it; yet it seemed only yesterday that I went to tell him a tuck-up story, to stroke Riquette, the old motherly cat that cuddled against his back and laid a paw beside his pillow like a human being, and to hear his funny little earnest whisper say, 'Oncle, tu sais, j'ai prié pour Petavel.' For La Citadelle had its unhappy ghost—of Petavel, the usurer, who had hanged himself in the attic a century gone by, and was known to walk its dreary corridors in search of peace—and this wise Irish mother, calming the boys' fears with wisdom, had told him,

'If you pray for Petavel, you'll save his soul and make him happy, and he'll only love you.' And, thereafter, this little imaginative boy had done so every night. With a passionate seriousness he did it. He had wonderful, delicate ways like that. In all our hearts he made his fairy nests of wonder. In my own, I know, he lay closer than any joy imaginable, with his big blue eyes, his queer soft questionings, and his splendid child's unselfishness—a sun-kissed flower of innocence that, had he lived, might have sweetened half a world.

'Let's put more peat on,' the mother said, as a handful of rain like stones came flinging against the windows; 'that must be hail.' And she went on tiptoe to the inner room. 'They're sleeping like two puddings,' she whispered, coming presently back. But it struck me she had taken longer than to notice merely that; and her face wore an odd expression that made me uncomfortable. I thought she was somehow just about to laugh or cry. By the table a second she hesitated. I caught the flash of indecision as it passed. 'Pan,' she said suddenly—it was a nickname, stolen from my tuck-up stories, *he* had given me—'I wonder how Riquette got in.' She looked hard at me. 'It wasn't you, was it?' For we never let her come at night since he had gone. It was too poignant. The beastie always went cuddling and nestling into that empty bed. But this time it was not my doing, and I offered plausible explanations. 'But—she's on the bed. Pan, *would* you be so kind——' She left the sentence unfinished, but I easily understood, for a lump had somehow risen in my own throat too, and I remembered now that she had come out from the inner room so quickly—with a kind of hurried rush almost. I put 'mère Riquette' out into the corridor. A lamp stood on the chair outside the door of another occupant further down, and I urged her gently towards it. She turned and looked at me—straight up into my face; but, instead of going down as I suggested, she went slowly in the opposite direction. She stepped softly towards a door in the wall that led up broken stairs into the attics. There she sat down and waited. And so I left her, and came back hastily to the peat fire and companionship. The wind rushed in behind me and slammed the door.

And we talked then somewhat busily of cheerful things; of the children's future, the excellence of the cheap Swiss schools, of Christmas presents, ski-ing, snow, tobogganing. I led the talk away from mournfulness; and when these subjects were exhausted I told stories of my own adventures in distant parts of the world. But 'mother' listened the whole time—not to me. Her thoughts were all elsewhere. And her air of intently, secretly listening, bordered, I felt, upon the uncanny. For she often stopped her knitting and sat with her eyes fixed upon the air before her; she stared blankly at the wall, her head slightly on one side, her figure tense, attention strained—elsewhere. Or, when my talk positively demanded it, her nod was oddly mechanical and her eyes looked through and past me. The wind continued very loud and roaring; but the fire glowed, the room was warm and cosy. Yet she shivered, and when I drew attention to it, her reply, 'I do feel cold, but I didn't know I shivered,' was given as though she spoke across the air to some one else. But what impressed me even more uncomfortably were her repeated questions about Riquette. When a pause in my tales permitted, she would look up with 'I wonder where Riquette went?' or, thinking of the inclement night, 'I hope mère Riquette's not out of doors. Perhaps Madame Favre has taken her in?' I offered to go and see. Indeed I was already half-way across the room when there came the heavy bang at the door that rooted me to the ground where I stood. It was not wind. It was something alive that made it rattle. There was a second blow. A thud on the corridor boards followed, and then a high, odd voice that at first was as human as the cry of a child.

It is undeniable that we both started, and for myself I can answer truthfully that a chill ran down my spine; but what frightened me more than the sudden noise and the eerie cry was the way 'mother' supplied the immediate explanation. For behind the words 'It's only Riquette; she sometimes springs at the door like that; perhaps we'd better let her in,' was a certain touch of uncanny quiet that made me feel she had known the cat would come, and knew also *why* she came. One cannot explain such impressions further. They leave their vital touch, then go their way. Into the little room, however, in that moment there came between us this uncomfortable sense that the night held other purposes than our own—and that my companion was aware of them. There was something going on far, far removed from the routine of life as we were accustomed to it. Moreover, our usual routine was the eddy, while this was the main stream. It felt big, I mean.

And so it was that the entrance of the familiar, friendly creature brought this thing both itself and 'mother' *knew*, but whereof I as yet was ignorant. I held the door wide. The draught rushed through behind her, and sent a shower of sparks about the fireplace. The lamp flickered and gave a little gulp. And Riquette marched slowly past, with all the impressive dignity of her kind, towards the other door that stood ajar. Turning the corner like a shadow, she disappeared into the room where the two children slept. We heard the soft thud with which she leaped upon the bed. Then, in a lull of the wind, she came back again and sat on the oilcloth, staring into 'mother's' face. She mewed and put a paw out, drawing the black dress softly with half-opened claws. And it was all so horribly suggestive and pathetic, it revived such poignant memories, that I got up impulsively—I think I had actually said the words, 'We'd better put her out, mother, after all'— when my companion rose to her feet and forestalled me. She said another thing instead. It took my breath away to hear it. 'She wants us to go with her. Pan, will you come too?' The surprise on my face must have asked the question, for I do not remember saying anything. 'To the attic,' she said quietly.

She stood there by the table, a tall, grave figure dressed in black, and her face above the lamp-shade caught the full glare of light. Its expression positively stiffened me. She seemed so secure in her singular purpose. And her familiar appearance had so oddly given place to something wholly strange to me. She looked like another person—almost with the unwelcome transformation of the sleep-walker about her. Cold came over me as I watched her, for I remembered suddenly her Irish second-sight, her story years ago of meeting a figure on the attic stairs, the figure of Petavel. And the idea of this motherly, sedate, and wholesome woman, absorbed day and night in prosaic domestic duties, and yet 'seeing' things, touched the incongruous almost to the point of alarm. It was so distressingly convincing.

Yet she knew quite well that I would come. Indeed, following the excited animal, she was already by the door, and a moment later, still without answering or protesting, I was with them in the draughty corridor. There was something inevitable in her manner that made it impossible to refuse. She took the lamp from its nail on the wall, and following our four-footed guide, who ran with obvious pleasure just in front, she opened the door into the courtyard. The wind nearly put the lamp out, but a minute later we were safe inside the passage that led up flights of creaky wooden stairs towards the world of tenantless attics overhead.

And I shall never forget the way the excited Riquette first stood up and put her paws upon the various doors, trotted ahead, turned back to watch us coming, and then finally sat down and waited on the threshold of the empty, raftered space that occupied the entire length of the building underneath the roof. For her manner was more that of an intelligent dog than of a cat, and sometimes more like that of a human mind than either.

We had come up without a single word. The howling of the wind as we rose higher was like the roar of artillery. There were many broken stairs, and the narrow way was full of twists and turnings. It was a dreadful journey. I felt eyes watching us from all the yawning spaces of the darkness, and the noise of the storm smothered footsteps everywhere. Troops of shadows kept us company. But it was on the threshold of this big, chief attic, when 'mother' stopped abruptly

THE ATTIC

to put down the lamp, that real feat took hold of me. For Riquette marched steadily forward into the middle of the dusty flooring, picking her way among the fallen tiles and mortar, as though she went towards—some one. She purred loudly and uttered little cries of excited pleasure. Her tail went up into the air, and she lowered her head with the unmistakable intention of being stroked. Her lips opened and shut. Her green eyes smiled. She *was* being stroked.

It was an unforgettable performance. I would rather have witnessed an execution or a murder than watch that mysterious creature twist and turn about in the way she did. Her magnified shadow was as large as a pony on the floor and rafters. I wanted to hide the whole thing by extinguishing the lamp. For, even before the mysterious action began, I experienced the sudden rush of conviction that others besides ourselves were in this attic—and standing very close to us indeed. And, although there was ice in my blood, there was also a strange swelling of the heart that only love and tenderness could bring.

But, whatever it was, my human companion, still silent, knew and understood. She *saw*. And her soft whisper that ran with the wind among the rafters, 'Il a prié pour Petavel et le bon Dieu l'a entendu,' did not amaze me one quarter as much as the expression I then caught upon her radiant face. Tears ran down the cheeks, but they were tears of happiness. Her whole figure seemed lit up. She opened her arms—picture of great Motherhood, proud, blessed, and tender beyond words. I thought she was going to fall, for she took quick steps forward; but when I moved to catch her, she drew me aside instead with a sudden gesture that brought fear back in the place of wonder.

'Let them pass,' she whispered grandly. 'Pan, don't you see.... He's leading him into peace and safety ... by the hand!' And her joy seemed to kill the shadows and fill the entire attic with white light. Then, almost simultaneously with her words, she swayed. I was in time to catch her, but as I did so, across the very spot where we had just been standing—two figures, I swear, went past us like a flood of light.

There was a moment next of such confusion that I did not see what happened to Riquette, for the sight of my companion kneeling on the dusty boards and praying with a curious sort of passionate happiness, while tears pressed between her covering fingers—the strange wonder of this made me utterly oblivious to minor details....

We were sitting round the peat fire again, and 'mother' was saying to me in the gentlest, tenderest whisper I ever heard from human lips—'Pan, I think perhaps that's why God took him....'

And when a little later we went in to make Riquette cosy in the empty bed, ever since kept sacred to her use, the mournfulness had lifted; and in the place of resignation was proud peace and joy that knew no longer sad or selfish questionings.

THE HEATH FIRE

The men at luncheon in Rennie's Surrey cottage that September day were discussing, of course, the heat. All agreed it had been exceptional. But nothing unusual was said until O'Hara spoke of the heath fires. They had been rather terrific, several in a single day, devouring trees and bushes, endangering human life, and spreading with remarkable rapidity. The flames, too, had been extraordinarily high and vehement for heath fires. And O'Hara's tone had introduced into the commonplace talk something new—the element of mystery; it was nothing definite he said, but manner, eyes, hushed voice and the rest conveyed it. And it was genuine. What he *felt* reached the others rather than what he said. The atmosphere in the little room, with the honeysuckle trailing sweetly across the open windows, changed; the talk became of a sudden less casual, frank, familiar; and the men glanced at one another across the table, laughing still, yet with an odd touch of constraint marking little awkward, unfilled pauses. Being a group of normal Englishmen, they disliked mystery; it made them feel uncomfortable; for the things O'Hara hinted at had touched that kind of elemental terror that lurks secretly in all human beings. Guarded by 'culture', but never wholly concealed, the unwelcome thing made its presence known—the hint of primitive dread that, for instance, great thunder-storms, tidal waves, or violent conflagrations rouse.

And instinctively they fell at once to discussing the obvious causes of the fires. The stockbroker, scenting imagination, edged mentally away, sniffing. But the journalist was full of brisk information, 'simply given'.

'The sun starts them in Canada, using a dewdrop as a lens,' he said, 'and an engine's spark, remember, carries an immense distance without losing its heat.'

'But hardly miles,' said another, who had not been really listening.

'It's my belief,' put in the critic keenly, 'that a lot were done on purpose. Bits of live coal wrapped in cloth were found, you know.' He was a little, weasel-faced iconoclast, dropping the acid of doubt and disbelief wherever he went, but offering nothing in the place of what he destroyed. His head was turret-shaped, lips tight and thin, nose and chin running to points like gimlets, with which he bored into the unremunerative clays of life.

'The general unrest, yes,' the journalist supported him, and tried to draw the conversation on to labour questions. But their host preferred the fire talk. 'I must say,' he put in gravely, 'that some of the blazes hereabouts were uncommonly —er—queer. They started, I mean, so oddly. You remember, O'Hara, only last week that suspicious one over Kettlebury way——?'

It seemed he wished to draw the artist out, and that the artist, feeling the general opposition, declined.

'Why seek an unusual explanation at all?' the critic said at length, impatiently. 'It's all natural enough, if you ask me.'

'Natural! Oh yes!' broke in O'Hara, with a sudden vehemence that betrayed feeling none had as yet suspected; 'provided you don't limit the word to mean only what we understand. There's nothing anywhere—unnatural.'

A laugh cut short the threatened tirade, and the journalist expressed the general feeling with 'Oh *you*, Jim! You'd see a devil in a dust-storm, or a fairy in the tea-leaves of your cup!'

'And why not, pray? Devils and fairies are every bit as true as formulae.'

Some one tactfully guided them away from a profitless discussion, and they talked glibly of the damage done, the hideousness of the destroyed moors, the gaunt, black, ugly slopes, fifty-foot flames, roaring noises, and the splendour of the enormous smoke-clouds that had filled the skies. And Rennie, still hoping to coax O'Hara, repeated tales the beaters had brought in that crying, as though living things were caught, had been heard in places, and that some had seen tall shapes of fire passing headlong through the choking smoke. For the note O'Hara had struck refused to be ignored. It went on sounding underneath the commonest remark; and the atmosphere to the end retained that curious tinge that he had given to it—of the strange, the ominous, the mysterious and unexplained. Until, at last, the artist, having added nothing further to the talk, got up with some abruptness and left the room. He complained briefly that the fever he had suffered from still bothered him and he would go and lie down a bit. The heat, he said, oppressed him.

A silence followed his departure. The broker drew a sigh as though the market had gone up. But Rennie, old, comprehending friend, looked anxious. 'Excitement,' he said, 'not oppression, is the word he meant. He's always a bit strung up when that Black Sea fever gets him. He brought it with him from Batoum.' And another brief silence followed.

'Been with you most of the summer, hasn't he?' enquired the journalist, on the trail of a 'par', 'painting those wild things of his that no one understands.' And their host, weighing a moment how much he might in fairness tell, replied—among friends it was—'Yes; and this summer they have been more—er—wild and wonderful than usual—an extraordinary rush of colour——splendid schemes, "conceptions", I believe you critics call 'em, of fire, as though, in a way, the unusual heat had possessed him for interpretation.'

The group expressed its desultory interest by uninspired interjections.

'That was what he meant just now when he said the fires had been mysterious, required explanation, or something—the way they started, rather,' concluded Rennie.

Then he hesitated. He laughed a moment, and it was an uneasy, apologetic little laugh. How to continue he hardly knew. Also, he wished to protect his friend from the cheap jeering of miscomprehension. 'He is very imaginative, you know,' he went on, quietly, as no one spoke. 'You remember that glorious mad thing he did of the Fallen Lucifer—driving a star across the heavens till the heat of the descent set a light to half the planets, scorched the old moon to the white cinder that she now is, and passed close enough to earth to send our oceans up in a single jet of steam? Well, this time—he's been at something every bit as wild, only truer—finer. And what is it? Briefly, then, he's got the idea, it seems, that the unusual heat from the sun this year has penetrated deep enough— in places—especially on these unprotected heaths that retain their heat so cleverly—to reach another kindred expression— to waken a response—in sympathy, you see—from the central fires of the earth.'

He paused again a moment awkwardly, conscious how clumsily he expressed it. 'The parent getting into touch again with its lost child, eh? See the idea? Return of the Fire Prodigal, as it were?'

His listeners stared in silence, the broker looking his obvious relief that O'Hara was not on 'Change, the critic's eyes glancing sharply down that pointed, boring nose of his.

'And the central fires have felt it and risen in response,' continued Rennie in a lower voice. 'You see the idea? It's big, to say the least. The volcanoes have answered too— there's old Etna, the giant of 'em all, breaking out in fifty new mouths of flame. Heat is latent in everything, only waiting to be called out. That match you're striking, this coffee-pot, the warmth in our bodies, and so on—their heat comes first from the sun, and is therefore an actual part of the sun, the origin of all heat and life. And so O'Hara, you know, who sees the universe as a single homogeneous *One* and—and— well, I give it up. Can't explain it, you see. You must get him to do that. But somehow this year—cloudless—the protecting armour of water all gone too—the sun's rays managed to sink in and reach their kind buried deep below. Perhaps, later, we may get him to show us the studies that he's made —whew!—the most—er—amazing things you ever saw!'

The 'superiority' of unimaginative minds was inevitable, making Rennie regret that he had told so much. It was almost as if he had been untrue to his friend. But at length the group broke up for the afternoon. They left messages for O'Hara. Two motored, and the journalist took the train. The critic followed his sharp nose to London, where he might ferret out the failures that his mind delighted in. And when they were gone the host slipped quickly upstairs to find his friend. The heat was unbearable to suffocation, the little bedroom like an oven. But Jim O'Hara was not in it.

For, instead of lying down as he had said, a fierce revolt, stirred by the talk of those unvisioned minds below, had wakened, and the deep, sensitive, poet's soul in him had leaped suddenly to the acceptance of an impossible thing. He had escaped, driven forth by the secret call of wonder. He made full speed for the destroyed moors. Fever or no fever, he must see for himself. Did no one understand? Was he the only one?... Walking quickly, he passed the Frensham Ponds, came through that spot of loneliness and beauty, the Lion's Mouth, noting that even there the pool of water had dried up and the rushes waved in the hot air over a bed of hard, caked mud, and so reached within the hour the wide expanse of Thursley Common. On every side the world stretched dark and burnt, a cemetery of cinders. Great thrills rushed through his heart; and with the power of a tide that yet came at flashing speed the truth rose up in him... Half running now, he plunged forward another mile or two, and found himself, the only living thing, amid the great waste of heatherland. The blazing sunlight drenched it. It lay, a sheet of weird dark beauty, spreading like a black, enormous garden as far as the eye could reach.

Then, breathless, he paused and looked about him. Within his heart something, long smouldering, ran into sudden flame. Light blazed upon his inner world. For as the scorch of vehement passion may quicken tracts of human consciousness that lie ordinarily inert and unproductive, so here the surface of the earth had turned alive. He knew; he saw; he understood.

Here, in these open sun-traps that gathered and retained the heat, the fire of the Universe had dropped and lain, increasing week by week. These parched, dry months, the soil, free from rejecting and protective moisture, had let it all accumulate till at length it had sunk downwards, inwards, and the sister fires below, responding to the touch of their ancient parent source, too long unfelt, had answered with a swift uprising roar. They had come up with answering joy, and here and there had actually reached the surface, and had leaped out with dancing cry, wild to escape from an age-long prison back to their huge, eternal origin.

This sunshine, ah! what was it? These farthing dips of heat men complained about in their tiny, cage-like houses! It scorched the grass and fields, yes; but the surface never held it long enough to let it sink to union with its kindred of the darker fires beneath! These cried for it, but union was ever denied and stifled by the weight of cooled and cooling rock. And the ages of separation had almost cooled remembrance too—fire—the kiss and strength of fire—the flaming embrace and burning lips of the father sun himself.... He could have cried with the fierce delight of it all, and the picture he would paint rose there before him, burnt gloriously into the canvas of the entire heavens. Was not his own heat and life also from the sun?...

He stared about him in the deep silence of the afternoon. The world was still. It basked in the windless heat. No living thing stirred, for the common forms of life had fled away. Earth waited. He, too, waited. And then some touch of intuition, blown to white heat, supplied the link the pedestrian intellect missed, and he knew that what he waited for was on the way. For he would *see*. The message he should paint would come before his outer eye as well, though not, as he had first stupidly expected, on some grand, enormous scale. Rather would it be the equivalent of that still, small voice that once had inspired an entire nation....

The wind passed very softly across the unburnt patch of heather where he lay; he heard it rustling in the skeletons of scorched birch trees, and in the gorse and furze bushes that the flame had left so ghostly pale. Farther off it sang in the isolated pines, dying away like surf upon some far-off reef. He smelt the bitter perfume of burnt soil, the pungent, acrid odour of beaten ashes. The purple-black of the moors yawned like openings in the side of the earth. In all directions for miles stretched the deep emptiness of the heather-lands, an immense, dark, magic garden, still black with the feet of wonder that had flown across it and left it so beautifully scarred. The shadow of the terrible embrace still trailed and lingered as through Midnight had screened a time of passion with this curtain of her softest plumes.

And *they* had called it ugly, had spoken of its marred beauty, its hideousness! He laughed exultantly as he drank it in, for the weird and savage splendour everywhere broke loose and spread, passing from the earth into the receptive substance of his own mind. Even the roots of gorse and heather, like petrified, shadow-eating snakes, charged with the mystery of that eternal underworld whence they had risen, lay waiting for the return of the night of sleep whence Fire had wakened them. Lost ghosts of a salamander army that the flame had swept above the ground, they lay anguished and frightened in the glare of the unaccustomed sun....

And waiting, he stared about him in the deep silence of the afternoon. Hazy with distance he saw the peak of Crooksbury, dim in its sheet of pines, waving a blue-plumed crest into the sky for signal; and close about him rose the more sombre glory of the lesser knolls and boulders, still cloaked in the swarthy magic of the smoke. Amid pools of ashes in the nearer hollows he saw the blue beauty of the fire-weed that rushes instantly into life behind all conflagrations. It was ulowing softly in the wind. And here and there, set like emeralds bpon some dusky bosom, lay the brilliant spires of young bracken that rose to clap a thousand tiny hands in the heart of exquisite desolation. In a cloud of green they rustled in the wind above the sea of black.... And so within himself O'Hara realised the huge excitement of the flame this fragment of the earth had felt. For Fire, mysterious symbol of universal life, spirit that prodigally gives itself without itself diminishing, had passed in power across this ancient heather-land, leaving the soul of it all naked and unashamed. The sun had loved it. The fires below had risen up and answered. They had known that union with their source which some call death....

And the fires were rising still. The poet's heart in him became suddenly and awfully aware. Ye stars of fire! This patch of unburnt heather where he lay had been untouched as yet, but now the flame in his soul had brought the little needed link and he would *see*. The thing of wonder that the Universe should teach him how to paint was already on the way. Called by the sun, tremendous, splendid parent, the central fires were still rising.

And he turned, weakness and exultation racing for possession of him. The wind passed softly over his face, and with it came a faint, dry sound. It was distant and yet close beside him. At the stir of it there rose also in himself a strange vast thing that was bigger than the bulk of the moon and wide as the extension of swept forests, yet small and gentle as a blade of grass that pricks the lawn in spring. And he realised then that 'within' and 'without' had turned one, and that over the entire moorland arrived this thing that was happening too in a whitehot point of his own heart. He was linked with the sun and the farthest star, and in his little finger glowed the heat and fire of the universe itself. In sympathy *his own fires were rising too*.

The sound was born—a faint, light noise of crackling in the heather at his feet. He bent his head and searched, and among the obscure and tiny underways of the roots he saw a tip of curling smoke rise slowly upwards. It moved in a thin, blue spiral past his face. Then terror took him that was like a terror of the mountains, yet with it at the same time a realisation of beauty that made the heart leap within him into dazzling radiance. For the incense of this fairy column of thin smoke drew his soul with it—upwards towards its source. He rose to his feet, trembling....

He watched the line rise slowly to the sky and vanish into

blue. The whole expanse of blackened heather-land watched too. Wind sank away; the sunshine dropped to meet it. A sense of deep expectancy, profound and reverent, lay over all that sun-baked moor; and the entire sweep of burnt world about him knew with joy that what was taking place in that wee, isolated patch of Surrey heather was the thing the Hebrew mystic knew when the Soul of the Universe became manifest in the bush that burned, yet never was consumed. In that faint sound of crackling, as he stood aside to listen and to watch, O'Hara knew a form of the eternal Voice of Ages. There was no flame, but it seemed to him that all his inner being passed in fiery heat outwards towards its source.... He saw the little patch of dried-up heather sink to the level of the black surface all about it—a sifted pile of delicate, pale-blue ashes. The tiny spiral vanished; he watched it disappear, winding upwards out of sight in a little ghostly trail of beauty. So small and soft and simple was this wonder of the world. It was gone. And something in himself had broken, dropped in ashes, and passed also outwards like a tiny mounting flame.

But the picture O'Hara had thought himself designed to paint was never done. It was not even begun. The great canvas of 'The Fire Worshipper' stood empty on the easel, for the artist had not strength to lift a brush. Within two days the final breath passed slowly from his lips. The strange fever that so perplexed the doctor by its rapid development and its fury took him so easily. His temperature was extraordinary. The heat, as of an internal fire, fairly devoured him, and the smile upon his face at the last—so Rennie declared—was the most perplexingly wonderful thing he had ever seen. 'It was like a great, white flame,' he said.

THE RETURN

It was curious—that sense of dull uneasiness that came over him so suddenly, so stealthily at first he scarcely noticed it, but with such marked increase after a time that he presently got up and left the theatre. His seat was on the gangway of the dress circle, and he slipped out awkwardly in the middle of what seemed to be the best and jolliest song of the piece. The full house was shaking with laughter; so infectious was the gaiety that even strangers turned to one another as much as to say: 'Now, isn't *that* funny——?'

It was curious, too, the way the feeling first got into him at all, here in the full swing of laughter, music, light-heartedness, for it came as a vague suggestion: 'I've forgotten something—something I meant to do—something of importance. What in the world was it, now?' And he thought hard, searching vainly through his mind; then dismissed it as the dancing caught his attention. It came back a little later again, during a passage of long-winded talk that bored him and set his attention free once more, but came more strongly this time, insisting on an answer. What could it have been that he had overlooked, left undone, omitted to see to? It went on nibbling at the subconscious part of him. Several times this happened, this dismissal and return, till at last the thing declared itself more plainly—and he felt bothered, troubled, distinctly uneasy.

He was wanted somewhere. There was somewhere else he ought to be. That describes it best, perhaps. Some engagement of moment had entirely slipped his memory—an engagement that involved another person, too. But where, what, with whom? And at length, this vague uneasiness amounted to positive discomfort, so that he felt unable to enjoy the piece—and left abruptly. Like a man to whom comes suddenly the horrible idea that the match he lit his cigarette with and flung into the waste-paper basket on leaving was not really out—a sort of panic distress—he jumped into a taxi-cab and hurried to his flat: to find everything in order, of course; no smoke, no fire, no smell of burning.

But his evening was spoilt. He sat smoking in his armchair at home—this business man of forty, practical in mind, of character some called stolid—cursing himself for an imaginative fool. It was now too late to go back to the theatre; the club bored him; he spent an hour with the evening papers, dipping into books, sipping a long cool drink; doing odds and ends about the flat; 'I'll go to bed early for a change,' he laughed, but really all the time fighting—yes, deliberately fighting—this strange attack of uneasiness that so insidiously grew upwards, outwards from the buried depths of him that sought so strenuously to deny it. It never occurred to him that he was ill. He was *not* ill. His health was thunderingly good. He was robust as a coal-heaver.

The flat was roomy, high up on the top floor, yet in a busy part of town, so that the roar of traffic mounted round it like a sea. Through the open windows came the fresh night air of June. He had never noticed before how sweet the London night air could be, and that not all the smoke and dust could smother a certain touch of wild fragrance that tinctured it with perfume—yes, almost perfume—as of the country. He swallowed a draught of it as he stood there, staring out across the tangled world of roofs and chimney-pots. He saw the procession of the clouds; he saw the stars; he saw the moonlight falling in a shower of silver spears upon the slates and wires and steeples. And something in him quickened—something that had never stirred before.

He turned with a horrid start, for the uneasiness had of a sudden leaped within him like an animal. There was some one in the flat.

Instantly, with action, even this slight action, the fancy vanished; but, all the same, he switched on the electric lights and made a search. For it seemed to him that some one had crept up close behind him while he stood there watching the Night—some one, moreover, whose silent presence fingered with unerring touch both this new thing that had quickened in his hear *and* that sense of original deep uneasiness. He was amazed at himself, angry; indignant that he could be thus foolishly upset over nothing, yet at the same time profoundly distressed at this vehement growth of a new thing in his well-ordered personality. Growth? He dismissed the word the moment it occurred to him. But it had occurred to him. It stayed. While he searched the empty flat, the long passages, the gloomy bedroom at the end, the little hall where he kept his overcoats and golf sticks—it stayed. Growth! It was oddly disquieting. Growth, to him, involved—though he neither acknowledged nor recognised the truth perhaps—some kind of undesirable changeableness, instability, unbalance.

Yet, singular as it all was, he realised that the uneasiness and the sudden appreciation of Beauty that was so new to him had both entered by the same door into his being. When he came back to the front room he noticed that he was perspiring. There were little drops of moisture on his forehead. And down his spine ran positively chills—little, faint quivers of cold. He was shivering.

He lit his big meerschaum pipe, and left the lights all burning. The feeling that there was something he had overlooked, forgotten, left undone, had vanished. Whatever the original cause of this absurd uneasiness might be—he called it absurd on purpose, because he now realised in the depths of him that it was really more vital then he cared about—it was much nearer to discovery than before. It dodged about just below the threshold of discovery. It was as close as that. Any moment he would know what it was: he would remember. Yes, he would *remember*. Meanwhile, he was in the right place. No desire to go elsewhere afflicted him, as in the theatre. Here was the place, here in the flat.

And then it was, with a kind of sudden burst and rush—it seemed to him the only way to phrase it—memory gave up her dead.

At first he only caught her peeping round the corner at him, drawing aside a corner of an enormous curtain, as it were; striving for more complete entrance as though the mass of it were difficult to move. But he understood; he knew; he recognised. It was enough for that. An entrance into his being—heart, mind, soul—was being attempted, and the entrance, because of his stolid temperament, was difficult of accomplishment. There was effort, strain. Something in him had first to be opened up, widened, made soft and ready as by an operation, before full entrance could be effected. This much he grasped, though for the life of him he could not have put it into words. Also, he knew *who* it was that sought an entrance. Deliberately from himself he withheld the name. But he knew, as surely as though Straughan stood in the room and faced him with a knife, saying, 'Let me in, let me in. I wish you to know I'm here. I'm clearing a way...! You recall our promise...?'

He rose from his chair and went to the open window again, the strange fear slowly passing. The cool air fanned his cheeks. Beauty, till now, had scarcely ever brushed the surface of his soul. He had never troubled his head about it. It passed him by, indifferent; and he had ever loathed the mouthy prating of it on others' lips. He was practical; beauty was for dreamers, for women, for men who had means and leisure. He had not exactly scorned it; rather it had never touched his life, to sweeten, cheer, uplift. Artists for him were like monks—another sex almost, useless beings who never helped the world go round. He was for action always, work, activity, achievement—as he saw them. He remembered Straughan vaguely—Straughan, the ever impecunious, friend of his youth, always talking of colour, sound—mysterious, ineffective things. He even forgot what they had quarrelled about, if they *had* quarrelled at all even; or why they had gone apart all these years ago. And, certainly, he had forgotten any promise. Memory, as yet, only peeped round the corner of that huge curtain at him, tentatively, suggestively yet—he was obliged to admit it—somewhat winningly. He was conscious of this gentle, sweet seductiveness that now replaced his fear.

And, as he stood now at the open window, peering over huge London, Beauty came close and smote him between the eyes. She came blindingly, with her train of stars and clouds and perfumes. Night, mysterious, myriad-eyed, and flaming across her sea of haunted shadows, invaded his heart and shook him with her immemorial wonder and delight. He found no words, of course, to clothe the new, unwonted sensations. He only knew that all his former dread, uneasiness, distress, and with them this idea of 'growth' that had seemed so repugnant to him, were merged, swept up, and gathered magnificently home into a wave of Beauty that enveloped him. 'See it ... and understand,' ran a secret inner whisper across his mind. He saw. He understood....

He went back and turned the lights out. Then he took his place again at that open window, drinking in the night. He saw a new world; a species of intoxication held him. He sighed ... as his thoughts blundered for expression among words and sentences that knew him not. But the delight was there, the wonder, the mystery. He watched, with heart alternately tightening and expanding, the transfiguring play of moon and shadow over the sea of buildings. He saw the dance of the hurrying clouds, the open patches into outer space, the veiling and unveiling of that ancient silvery face; and he caught strange whispers of the hierophantic, sacerdotal Power that had echoed down the world since Time began and dropped strange magic phrases into every poet's heart since first 'God dawned on Chaos'—the Beauty of the Night....

A long time passed—it may have been one hour, it may have been three—when at length he turned away and went slowly to his bedroom. A deep peace lay over him. Something quite new and blessed had crept into his life and thought. He could not quite understand it all. He only knew that it uplifted. There was no longer the least sign of affliction or distress. Even the inevitable reaction that, of course, set in could not destroy that.

And then, as he lay in bed, nearing the borderland of sleep, suddenly and without any obvious suggestion to bring it, he remembered another thing. He remembered the promise. Memory got past the big curtain for an instant, and showed her face. She looked into his eyes. It must have been a dozen years ago when Straughan and he had made that foolish, solemn promise that whoever died first should show himself, if possible, to the other.

He had utterly forgotten it—till now. But Straughan had not forgotten it. The letter came three weeks later, from India. That very evening Straughan had died—at nine o'clock. And he had come back—in the Beauty that he loved.

THE TRANSFER

The child first began to cry in the early afternoon—about three o'clock, to be exact. I remember the hour, because I had been listening with secret relief to the sound of the departing carriage. Those wheels fading into distance down the gravel drive with Mrs. Frene, and her daughter Gladys to whom I was governess, meant for me some hours' welcome rest, and the June day was oppressively hot. Moreover, there was this excitement in the little country household that had told upon us all, but especially upon myself. This excitement, running delicately behind all the events of the morning, was due to some mystery, and the mystery was of course kept concealed from the governess. I had exhausted myself with guessing and keeping on the watch. For some deep and unexplained anxiety possessed me, so that I kept thinking of my sister's dictum that I was really much too sensitive to make a good governess, and that I should have done far better as a professional clairvoyante.

Mr. Frene, senior, 'Uncle Frank', was expected for an unusual visit from town about tea-time. That I knew. I also knew that his visit was concerned somehow with the future welfare of little Jamie, Gladys' seven-year-old brother. More than this, indeed, I never knew, and this missing link makes my story in a fashion incoherent—an important bit of the strange puzzle left out. I only gathered that the visit of Uncle Frank was of a condescending nature, that Jamie was told he must be upon his very best behaviour to make a good impression, and that Jamie, who had never seen his uncle, dreaded him horribly already in advance. Then, trailing thinly through the dying crunch of the carriage wheels this sultry afternoon, I heard the curious little wail of the child's crying, with the effect, wholly unaccountable, that every nerve in my body shot its bolt electrically, bringing me to my feet with a tingling of unequivocal alarm. Positively, the water ran into my eyes.

THE TRANSFER

I recalled his white distress that morning when told that Uncle Frank was motoring down for tea and that he was to be 'very nice indeed' to him. It had gone into me like a knife. All through the day, indeed, had run this nightmare quality of terror and vision.

'The man with the 'normous face?' he had asked in a little voice of awe, and then gone speechless from the room in tears that no amount of soothing management could calm. That was all I saw; and what he meant by 'the 'normous face' gave me only a sense of vague presentiment. But it came as anti-climax somehow—a sudden revelation of the mystery and excitement that pulsed beneath the quiet of the stifling summer day. I feared for him. For of all that commonplace household I loved Jamie best, though professionally I had nothing to do with him. He was a high-strung, ultra-sensitive child, and it seemed to me that no one understood him, least of all his honest, tender-hearted parents; so that his little wailing voice brought me from my bed to the window in a moment like a call for help.

The haze of June lay over that big garden like a blanket; the wonderful flowers, which were Mr. Frene's delight, hung motionless; the lawns, so soft and thick, cushioned all other sounds; only the limes and huge clumps of guelder roses hummed with bees. Through this muted atmosphere of heat and haze the sound of the child's crying floated faintly to my ears—from a distance. Indeed, I wonder now that I heard it at all, for the next moment I saw him down beyond the garden, standing in his white sailor suit alone, two hundred yards away. He was down by the ugly patch where nothing grew—the Forbidden Corner. A faintness then came over me at once, a faintness as of death, when I saw him *there* of all places—where he never was allowed to go, and where, moreover, he was usually too terrified to go. To see him standing solitary in that singular spot, above all to hear him crying there, bereft me momentarily of the power to act. Then, before I could recover my composure sufficiently to call him in, Mr. Frene came round the corner from the Lower Farm with the dogs, and, seeing his son, performed that office for me. In his loud, goodnatured, hearty voice he called him, and Jamie turned and ran as though some spell had broken just in time—ran into the open arms of his fond but uncomprehending father, who carried him indoors on his shoulder, while asking 'what all this hubbub was about?' And, at their heels, the tailless sheep-dogs followed, barking loudly, and performing what Jamie called their 'Gravel Dance', because they ploughed up the moist, rolled gravel with their feet.

I stepped back swiftly from the window lest I should be seen. Had I witnessed the saving of the child from fire or drowning the relief could hardly have been greater. Only Mr. Frene, I felt sure, would not say and do the right thing quite. He would protect the boy from his own vain imaginings, yet not with the explanation that could really heal. They disappeared behind the rose trees, making for the house. I saw no more till later, when Mr. Frene, senior, arrived.

To describe the ugly patch as 'singular' is hard to justify, perhaps, yet some such word is what the entire family sought, though never—oh, never!—used. To Jamie and myself, though equally we never mentioned it, that treeless, flowerless spot was more than singular. It stood at the far end of the magnificent rose garden, a bald, sore place, where the black earth showed uglily in winter, almost like a piece of dangerous bog, and in summer baked and cracked with fissures where green lizards shot their fire in passing. In contrast to the rich luxuriance of the whole amazing garden it was like a glimpse of death amid life, a centre of disease that cried for healing lest it spread. But it never did spread. Behind it stood the thick wood of silver birches and, glimmering beyond, the orchard meadow, where the lambs played.

The gardeners had a very simple explanation of its barrenness—that the water all drained off it owing to the lie of the slope immediately about it, holding no remnant to keep the soil alive. I cannot say. It was Jamie—Jamie who felt its spell and haunted it, who spent whole hours there, even while afraid, and for whom it was finally labelled 'strictly out of bounds' because it stimulated his already big imagination, not wisely but too darkly—it was Jamie who buried ogres there and heard it crying in an earthy voice, swore that it shook its surface sometimes while he watched it, and secretly gave it food in the form of birds or mice of rabbits he found dead upon his wanderings. And it was Jamie who put so extraordinarily into words the *feeling* that the horrid spot had given me from the moment I first saw it.

'It's bad, Miss Gould,' he told me.

'But Jamie, nothing in Nature is bad—exactly; only different from the rest sometimes.'

'Miss Gould, if you please, then it's empty. It's not fed. It's dying because it can't get the food it wants.'

And when I stared into the little pale face where the eyes shone so dark and wonderful, seeking within myself for the right thing to say to him, he added, with an emphasis and conviction that made me suddenly turn cold: 'Miss Gould'—he always used my name like this in all his sentences—'it's hungry, don't you see? But *I* know what would make it feel all right.'

Only the conviction of an earnest child, perhaps, could have made so outrageous a suggestion worth listening to for an instant; but for me, who felt that things an imaginative child believed were important, it came with a vast disquieting shock of reality. Jamie, in this exaggerated way, had caught at the edge of a shocking fact—a hint of dark, undiscovered truth had leaped into that sensitive imagination. Why there lay horror in the words I cannot say, but I think some power of darkness trooped across the suggestion of that sentence at the end, 'I know what would make it feel all right.' I remember that I shrank from asking explanation. Small groups of other words, veiled forunately by his silence, gave life to an unspeakable possibility that hitherto had lain at the back of my own consciousness. The way it sprang to life proves, I think, that my mind already contained it. The blood rushed from my heart as I listened. I remember that my knees shook. Jamie's idea was—had been all along—my own as well.

And now, as I lay down on my bed and thought about it all, I understood why the coming of his uncle involved somehow an experience that wrapped terror at its heart. With a sense of nightmare certainty that left me too weak to resist the preposterous idea, too shocked, indeed, to argue or reason it away, this certainty came with its full, black blast of conviction; and the only way I can put it into words, since nightmare horror really is not properly tellable at all, seems this: that there *was* something missing in that dying patch of garden; something lacking that it ever searched for; something, once found and taken, that would turn it rich and living as the rest; more—that there *was* some living person who could do this for it. Mr. Frene, senior, in a word, 'Uncle Frank,' was this person who out of his abundant life could supply the lack—unwittingly.

For this connection between the dying, empty patch and the person of this vigorous, wealthy, and successful man had already lodged itself in my subconsciousness before I was aware of it. Clearly it must have lain there all along, though hidden. Jamie's words, his sudden pallor, his vibrating emotion of fearful anticipation had developed the plate, but it was his weeping alone there in the Forbidden Corner that had printed it. The photograph shone framed before me in the air. I hid my eyes. But for the redness—the charm of my face goes to pieces unless my eyes are clear—I could have cried. Jamie's words that morning about the "'normous face' came back upon me like a battering-ram.

Mr. Frene, senior, had been so frequently the subject of conversation in the family since I came, I had so often heard him discussed, and had then read so much about him in the papers—his energy, his philanthropy, his success with everything he laid his hand to—that a picture of the man had grown complete within me. I knew him as he was—within; or, as my sister would have said—clairvoyantly. And the only time I saw him (when I took Gladys to a meeting where he was chairman, and later *felt* his atmosphere and presence while for a moment he patronisingly spoke with her) had justified the portrait I had drawn. The rest, you may say, was a woman's wild imagining; but I think rather it was that kind of divining intuition which women share with children. If souls could be made visible, I would stake my life upon the truth and accuracy of my portrait.

For this Mr. Frene was a man who drooped alone, but grew vital in a crowd—because he used their vitality. He was a supreme, unconscious artist in the science of taking the fruits of others' work and living—for his own advantage. He vampired, unknowingly no doubt, every one with whom he came in contact; left them exhausted, tired, listless. Others fed him, so that while in a full room he shone, alone by himself and with no life to draw upon he languished and declined. In the man's immediate neighbourhood you felt his presence draining you; he took your ideas, your strength, your very words, and later used them for his own benefit and aggrandisement. Not evilly, of course; the man was good enough; but you felt that he was dangerous owing to the facile way he absorbed into himself all loose vitality that was to be had. His eyes and voice and presence devitalised you. Life, it seemed, not highly organised enough to resist, must shrink from his too near approach and hide away for fear of being appropriated, for fear, that is, of—death.

Jamie, unknowingly, put in the finishing touch to my unconscious portrait. The man carried about with him some silent, compelling trick of drawing out all your reserves—then swiftly pocketing them. At first you would be conscious of taut resistance; this would slowly shade off into weariness; the will would become flaccid; then you either moved away or yielded—agreed to all he said with a sense of weakness pressing ever closer upon the edges to collapse. With a male antagonist it might be different, but even then the effort of resistance would generate force that *he* absorbed and not the other. He never gave out. Some instinct taught him how to protect himself from that. To human beings, I mean, he never gave out. This time it was a very different matter. He had no more chance than a fly before the wheels of a huge—what

Jamie used to call—'attraction' engine.

So this was how I saw him—a great human sponge, crammed and soaked with the life, or proceeds of life, absorbed from others—stolen. My idea of a human vampire was satisfied. He went about carrying these accumulations of the life of others. In this sense his 'life' was not really his own. For the same reason, I think, it was not so fully under his control as he imagined.

And in another hour this man would be here. I went to the window. My eye wandered to the empty patch, dull black there amid the rich luxuriance of the garden flowers. It struck me as a hideous bit of emptiness yawning to be filled and nourished. The idea of Jamie playing round its bare edge was loathsome. I watched the big summer clouds above, the stillness of the afternoon, the haze. The silence of the overheated garden was oppressive. I had never felt a day so stifling, motionless. It lay there waiting. The household, too, was waiting—waiting for the coming of Mr. Frene from London in his big motor-car.

And I shall never forget the sensation of icy shrinking and distress with which I heard the rumble of the car. He had arrived. Tea was all ready on the lawn beneath the lime trees, and Mrs. Frene and Gladys, back from their drive, were sitting in wicker chairs. Mr. Frene, junior, was in the hall to meet his brother, but Jamie, as I learned afterwards, had shown such hysterical alarm, offered such bold resistance, that it had been deemed wiser to keep him in his room. Perhaps, after all, his presence might not be necessary. The visit clearly had to do with something on the uglier side of life—money, settlements, or what not; I never knew exactly; only that his parents were anxious, and that Uncle Frank had to be propitiated. It does not matter. That has nothing to do with the affair. What has to do with it—or I should not be telling the story—is that Mrs. Frene sent for me to come down 'in my nice white dress, if I didn't mind,' and that I was terrified, yet pleased, because it meant that a pretty face would be considered a welcome addition to the visitor's landscape. Also, most odd it was, I felt my presence was somehow inevitable, that in some way it was intended that I should witness what I did witness. And the instant I came upon the lawn—I hesitate to set it down, it sounds so foolish, disconnected—I could have sworn, as my eyes met his, that a kind of sudden darkness came, taking the summer brilliance out of everything, and that it was caused by troops of small black horses that raced about us from his person—to attack.

After a first momentary approving glance he took no further notice of me. The tea and talk went smoothly; I helped to pass the plates and cups, filling in pauses with little under-talk to Gladys. Jamie was never mentioned. Outwardly all seemed well, bur inwardly everything was awful—skirting the edge of things unspeakable, and so charged with danger that I could not keep my voice from trembling when I spoke.

I watched his hard, bleak face; I noticed how thin he was, and the curious, oily brightness of his steady eyes. They did not glitter, but they drew you with a sort of soft, creamy shine like Eastern eyes. And everything he said or did announced what I may dare to call the *suction* of his presence. His nature achieved this result automatically. He dominated us all, yet so gently that until it was accomplished no one noticed it.

Before five minutes had passed, however, I was aware of one thing only. My mind focused exclusively upon it, and so vividly that I marvelled the others did not scream, or run, or do something violent to prevent it. And it was this: that, separated merely by some dozen yards of so, this man, vibrating with the acquired vitality of others, stood within easy reach of that spot of yawning emptiness, waiting and eager to be filled. Earth scented her prey.

These two active 'centres' were within fighting distance; he so thin, so hard, so keen, yet really spreading large with the loose 'surround' of others' life he had appropriated, so practised and triumphant; that other so patient, deep, with so mighty a draw of the whole earth behind it, and—ugh!—so obviously aware that its opportunity at last had come.

I saw it all as plainly as though I watched two great animals prepare for battle, both unconsciously; yet in some inexplicable way I saw it, of course, within me, and not externally. The conflict would be hideously unequal. Each side had already sent out emissaries, how long before I could not tell, for the first evidence *he* gave that something was going wrong with him was when his voice grew suddenly confused, he missed his words, and his lips trembled a moment and turned flabby. The next second his face betrayed that singular and horrid change, growing somehow loose about the bones of the cheek, and larger, so that I remembered Jamie's miserable phrase. The emissaries of the two kingdoms, the human and the vegetable, had met, I make it out, in that very second. For the first time in his long career of battening on others, Mr. Frene found himself pitted against a vaster kingdom than he knew and, so finding, shook inwardly in that little part that was his definite actual self. He felt the huge disaster coming.

'Yes, John,' he was saying, in his drawling, self-congratulating voice, 'Sir George gave me that car—gave it to me as a present. Wasn't it char——?' and then broke off abruptly, stammered, drew breath, stood up, and looked uneasily about him. For a second there was a gaping pause. It was like the click which starts some huge machinery moving—that instant's pause before it actually starts. The whole thing, indeed, then went with the rapidity of machinery running down and beyond control. I thought of a giant dynamo working silently and invisible.

'What's that?' he cried, in a soft voice charged with alarm. 'What's that horrid place? And some one's crying there—who is it?'

He pointed to the empty patch. Then, before any one could answer, he started across the lawn towards it, going every minute faster. Before any one could move he stood upon the edge. He leaned over—peering down into it.

It seemed a few hours passed, but really they were seconds, for time is measured by the quality and not the quantity of sensations it contains. I saw it all with merciless, photographic detail, sharply etched amid the general confusion. Each side was intensely active, but only one side, the human, exerted *all* its force—in resistance. The other merely stretched out a feeler, as it were, from its vast, potential strength; no more was necessary. It was such a soft and easy victory. Oh, it was rather pitiful! There was no bluster of great effort, on one side at least. Close by his side I witnessed it, for I, it seemed, alone had moved and followed him. No one else stirred, though Mrs. Frene clattered noisily with the cups, making some sudden impulsive gesture with her hands, and Gladys, I remember, gave a cry—it was like a litle scream—'Oh, mother, it's the heat, isn't it?' Mr. Frene, her father, was speechless, pale as ashes.

But the instant I reached his side, it became clear what had drawn me there thus instinctively. Upon the other side, among the silver birches, stood little Jamie. He was watching. I experienced—for him—one of those moments that shake the heart; a liquid fear ran all over me, the more effective because unintelligible really. Yet I felt that if I could know all, what lay actually behind, my fear would be more than justified; that the thing *was* awful, full of awe.

And then it happened—a truly wicked sight—like watching a universe in action, yet all contained within a small square foot of space. I think he understood vaguely that if some one could only take his place he might be saved, and that was why, discerning instinctively the easiest substitute within reach, he saw the child and called aloud to him across the empty patch, 'James, my boy, come here!'

His voice was like a thin report, but somehow flat and lifeless, as when a rifle misses fire, sharp, yet weak; it had no 'crack' in it. It was really supplication. And, with amazement, I heard my own ring out imperious and strong, though I was not conscious of saying it, 'Jamie, don't move. Stay where you are!' But Jamie, the little child, obeyed neither of us. Moving up nearer to the edge, he stood there—laughing! I heard that laughter, but could have sworn it did not come from him. The empty, yawning patch gave out that sound.

Mr. Frene turned sideways, throwing up his arms. I saw

his hard, bleak face grow somehow wider, spread through the air, and downwards. A similar thing, I saw, was happening at the same time to his entire person, for it drew out into the atmosphere in a stream of movement. The face for a second made me think of those toys of green indiarubber that children pull. It grew enormous. But this was an external impression only. What actually happened, I clearly understood, was that all this vitality and life he had transferred from others to himself for years was now in turn being taken from him and transferred—elsewhere.

One moment on the edge he wobbled horribly, then with that queer sideways motion, rapid yet ungainly, he stepped forward into the middle of the patch and fell heavily upon his face. His eyes, as he dropped, faded shockingly, and across the countenance was written plainly what I can only call an expression of destruction. He looked utterly destroyed. I caught a sound—from Jamie?—but this time not of laughter. It was like a gulp; it was deep and muffled and it dipped away into the earth. Again I thought of a troop of small black horses galloping away down a subterranean passage beneath my feet—plunging into the depths—their tramping growing fainter and fainter into buried distance. In my nostrils was a pungent smell of earth.

And then—all passed. I came back into myself. Mr. Frene, junior, was lifting his brother's head from the lawn where he had fallen from the heat, close beside the tea-table. He had never really moved from there. And Jamie, I learned afterwards, had been the whole time asleep upon his bed upstairs, worn out with his crying and unreasoning alarm. Gladys came running out with cold water, sponge and towel, brandy too—all kinds of things. 'Mother, it *was* the heat, wasn't it?' I heard her whisper, but I did not catch Mrs. Frene's reply. From her face it struck me that she was bordering on collapse herself. Then the butler followed, and they just picked him up and carried him into the house. He recovered even before the doctor came.

But the queer thing to me is that I was convinced the others all had seen what I saw, only that no one said a word about it; and to this day no one *has* said a word. And that was, perhaps, the most horrid part of all.

From that day to this I have scarcely heard a mention of Mr. Frene, senior. It seemed as if he dropped suddenly out of life. The papers never mentioned him. His activities ceased, as it were. His after-life, at any rate, became singularly ineffective. Certainly he achieved nothing worth public mention. But it may be only that, having left the employ of Mrs. Frene, there was no particular occasion for me to hear anything.

The after-life of that empty patch of garden, however, was quite otherwise. Nothing, so far as I know, was done to it by gardeners, or in the way of draining it or bringing in new earth, but even before I left in the following summer it had changed. It lay untouched, full of great, luscious, driving weeds and creepers, very strong, full-fed, and bursting thick with life.

CLAIRVOYANCE

In the darkest corner, where the firelight could not reach him, he sat listening to the stories. His young hostess occupied the corner on the other side; she was also screened by shadows; and between them stretched the horse-shoe of eager, frightened faces that seemed all eyes. Behind yawned the blackness of the big room, running as it were without a break into the night.

Some one crossed on tiptoe and drew a blind up with a rattle, and at the sound all started: through the window, opened at the top, came a rustle of the poplar leaves that stirred like footsteps in the wind. 'There's a strange man walking past the shrubberies,' whispered a nervous girl; 'I saw him crouch and hide. I saw his eyes!' 'Nonsense! came sharply from a male member of the group; 'it's far too dark to see. You heard the wind.' For mist had risen from the river just below the lawn, pressing close against the windows of the old house like a soft grey hand, and through it the stir of leaves was faintly audible.... Then, while several called for lights, others remembered that hop-pickers were still about in the lanes, and the tramps this autumn overbold and insolent. All, perhaps, wished secretly for the sun. Only the elderly man in the corner sat quiet and unmoved, contributing nothing. He had told no fearsome story. He had evaded, indeed, many openings expressly made for him, though fully aware that to his well-known interest in psychical things was partly due his presence in the week-end party. 'I never have experiences—that way,' he said shortly when some one asked him point blank for a tale; 'I have no unusual powers.' There was perhaps the merest hint of contempt in his tone, but the hostess from her darkened corner quickly and tactfully covered his retreat. And he wondered. For he knew why she invited him. The haunted room, he was well aware, had been specially allotted to him.

CLAIRVOYANCE

And then, most opportunely, the door opened noisily and the host came in. He sniffed at the dakrness, rang at once for lamps, puffed at his big curved pipe, and generally, by his mere presence, made the group feel rather foblish. Light streamed past him from the corridor. His white hair shone like silver. And with him came the atmosphere of common sense, of shooting, agriculture, motors, and the rest. Age entered at that door. And his young wife sprang up instantly to greet him, as though his disapproval of this kind of entertainment might need humouring.

It may have been the light—that witchery of half-lights from the fire and the corridor, or it may have been the abrupt entrance of the Practical upon the soft Imaginative that traced the outline with such pitiless, sharp conviction. At any rate, the contrast—for those who had this inner clairvoyant sight all had been prating of so glibly!—was unmistakably revealed. It was poignantly dramatic, pain somewhere in it—naked pain. For, as she paused a moment there beside him in the light, this childless wife of three years' standing, picture of youth and beauty, there stood upon the threshold of that room the presence of a true ghost story.

And most marevellously she changed—her lineaments, her very figure, her whole presentment. Etched against the gloom, the delicate, unmarked face shone suddenly keen and anguished, and a rich maturity, deeper than any mere age, flushed all her little person with its secret grandeur. Lines started into being upon the pale skin of the girlish face, lines of pleading, pity, and love the daylight did not show, and with them an air of magic tenderness that betrayed, though for a second only, the full soft glory of a motherhood denied, yet somehow mysteriously enjoyed. About her slenderness rose all the deep-bosomed sweetness of maternity, a potential mother of the world, and a mother, though she might know no dear fulfilment, who yet yearned to sweep into her immense embrace all the little helpless things that ever lived.

Light, like emotion, can play strangest tricks. The change pressed almost upon the edge of revelation.... Yet, when a moment later lamps were brought, it is doubtful if any but the silent guest who had told no marvellous tale, knew no psychical experience, and disclaimed the smallest clairvoyant faculty, had received and registered the vivid, poignant picture. For an instant it had flashed there, mercilessly clear for all to see who were not blind to subtle spiritual wonder thick with pain. And it was not so much mere picture of youth and age ill-matched, as of youth that yearned with the oldest craving in the world, and of age that had slipped beyond the power of sympathetically divining it.... It passed, and all was as before.

The husband laughed with genial good-nature, not one whit annoyed. 'They've been frightening you with stories, child,' he said in his jolly way, and put a protective arm about her. 'Haven't they now? Tell me the truth. Much better,' he added, 'have joined me instead at billiards, or for a game of Patience, eh?' She looked up shyly into his face, and he kissed her on the forehead. 'Perhaps they have—a little, dear,' she said, 'but now that you've come, I feel all right again.' 'Another night of this,' he added in a graver tone, 'and you'd be at your old trick of putting guests to sleep in the haunted room. I was right after all, you see, to make it out of bounds.' He glanced fondly, paternally down upon her. Then he went over and poked the fire into a blaze. Some one struck up a waltz on the piano, and couples danced. All trace of nervousness vanished, and the butler presently brought in the tray with drinks and biscuits. And slowly the group dispersed. Candles were lit. They passed down the passage into the big hall, talking in lowered voices of to-morrow's plans. The laughter died away as they went up the stairs to bed, the silent guest and the young wife lingering a moment over the embers.

'You have not, after all then, put me in your haunted room?' he asked quietly. 'You mentioned, you remember, in your letter——'

'I admit,' she replied at once, her manner gracious beyond her years, her voice quite different, 'that I wanted you to sleep there—some one, I mean, who really knows, and is not merely curious. But—forgive my saying so—when I *saw* you'—she laughed very slowly—'and when you told no marvellous story like the others, I somehow felt——'

'But I never *see* anything——' he put in hurriedly.

'You *feel*, though,' she interrupted swiftly, the passionate tenderness in her voice but half suppressed. 'I can tell it from your——'

'Others, then,' he interrupted abruptly, almost bluntly, 'have slept there—sat up, rather?'

'Not recently. My husband stopped it.' She paused a second, then added, 'I had that room — for a year—when first we married.'

The other's anguished look flew back upon her little face like a shadow and was gone, while at the sight of it there rose in himself a sudden deep rush of wonderful amazement beckoning almost towards worship. He did not speak, for his voice would tremble.

'I had to give it up,' she finished, very low.

'Was it so terrible?' after a pause he ventured.

She bowed her head. 'I had to change,' she repeated softly.

'And since then—*now*—you see nothing?' he asked.

Her reply was singular. 'Because I will not, not because it's gone.' ... He followed her in silence to the door, and as they passed along the passage, again that curious great pain of emptiness, of loneliness, of yearning rose upon him, as of a sea that never, never can swim beyond the shore to reach the flowers that it loves ...

'Hurry up, child, or a ghost will catch you,' cried her husband, leaning over the banisters, as the pair moved slowly up the stairs towards him. There was a moment's silence when they met. The guest took his lighted candle and went down the corridor. Good-nights were said again. They moved away, she to her loneliness, he to his unhaunted room. And at his door he turned. At the far end of the passage, silhouetted against the candle-light, he watched them—the fine old man with his silvered hair and heavy shoulders, and the slim young wife with that amazing air as of some great bountiful mother of the world for whom the years yet passed hungry and unharvested. They turned the corner, and he went in and closed his door.

Sleep took him very quickly, and while the mist rose up and veiled the countryside, something else, veiled equally for all other sleepers in that house but two, drew on towards its climax.... Some hours later he awoke; the world was still, and it seemed the whole house listened; for with that clear vision which some bring out of sleep, he remembered that there had been no direct denial, and of a sudden realised that this big, gaunt chamber where he lay was after all the haunted room. For him, however, the entire world, not merely separate rooms in it, was ever haunted; and he knew no terror to find the space about him charged with thronging life quite other than his own.... He rose and lit the candle, crossed over to the window where the mist shone grey, knowing that no barriers of walls or door or ceiling could keep out this host of Presences that poured so thickly everywhere about him. It was like a wall of being, with peering eyes, small hands stretched out, a thousand pattering wee feet, and tiny voices crying in a chorus very faintly and beseeching.... The haunted room! Was it not, rather, a temple vestibule, prepared and sanctified by yearning rites few men might ever guess, for all the childless women of the world? How could she know that *he* would understand—this woman he had seen but twice in all his life? And how entrust to him so great a mystery that was her secret? Had she so easily divined in him a similar yearning to which, long years ago, death had denied fulfilment? Was she clairvoyant in the true sense, and did all faces bear on them so legibly this great map that sorrow traced?...

And then, with awful suddenness, mere feelings dipped away, and something concrete happened. The handle of the door had faintly rattled. He turned. The round brass knob was slowly moving. And first, at the sight, something of common fear did grip him, as though his heart had missed a beat, but on the instant he heard the voice of his own mother, now long beyond the stars, calling to him to go softly yet with speed. He watched a moment the feeble efforts to undo the door, yet never afterwards could swear that he saw actual movement, for something in him, tragic as blindness, rose through a mist of tears and darkened vision utterly....

He went towards the door. He took the handle very gently, and very softly then he opened it. Beyond was darkness. He saw the empty passage, the edge of the banisters where the great hall yawned below, and, dimly, the outline of the Alpine photograph and the stuffed deer's head upon the wall. And then he dropped upon his knees and opened wide his arms to something that came in upon uncertain, viewless feet. All the young winds and flowers and dews of dawn passed with it ... filling him to the brim ... covering closely his breast and eyes and lips. There clung to him all the small beginnings of life that cannot stand alone ... the little helpless hands and arms that have no confidence ... and when the wealth of tears and love that flooded his heart seemed to break upon the frontiers of some mysterious yet impossible fulfilment, he rose and went with curious small steps towards the window to taste the cooling, misty air of that other dark Emptiness that waited so patiently there above the entire world. He drew the sash up. The air felt soft and tender as though there were somewhere children in it too—children of stars and flowers, of mists and wings and music, all that the Universe contains unborn and tiny.... And when at length he turned again the door was closed. The room was empty of any life but that which lay so wonderfully blessed within himself. And this, he felt, had marvellously increased and multiplied....

Sleep then came back to him, and in the morning he left the house before the others were astir, pleading some overlooked engagement. For he had seen Ghosts indeed, but yet no ghost that he could talk about with others round an open fire.

THE GOLDEN FLY

It fell upon him out of a clear sky just when existence seemed on its very best behaviour, and he savagely resented the undeserved affliction of it. Involving him in an atrocious scandal that reflected directly upon his honour, it destroyed in a moment the erection his entire life had so laboriously built up—his reputation. In the eyes of the world he was a broken, discredited man, at the very moment, moreover, when his most cherished ambitions touched fulfilment. And the cruelty of it appalled his sense of justice, for it was impossible to vindicate himself without inculpating others who were dearer to him than life. It seemed more than he could bear; and the grim course he contemplated—decision itself as yet hung darkly waiting in the background—appeared the only way of escape that offered.

He had discussed the matter with friends until his brain whirled. Their sympathy maddened him, with hints of *qui s'excuse s'accuse*, and he turned at last in desperation to something that could not answer back. For the first time in his life he turned to Nature—to that dead, inanimate Nature he had left to poets and rhapsodising women: 'I must face it alone,' he put it. For the Finger of God was a phrase without meaning to him, and his entire being contained no trace of the religious instinct. He was a business man, honest, selfish, and ambitious; and the collapse of his worldly position was paramount to the collapse of the universe itself—his universe, at any rate. This 'crumbling of the universe' was the thought he took out with him. He left the house by the path that led into solitude, and reached the heathery expanse that formed one of the breathing-places of the New Forest. There he flung himself down wearily in the shadow of a little pine-copse. And his crumbled universe lay down with him, for he could not escape it.

Taking the pistol from the hip-pocket where it hurt him, he lay upon his back and watched the clouds. Half stunned, half dazed, he stared into the sky. The perfumed wind played softly on his eyes; he smelt the heather-honey; golden flies hung motionless in the air, like coloured pins fastening the sunshine against the blue curtain of the summer, while dragon-flies, like darting shuttles, wove across its pattern their threads of gleaming bronze. He heard the petulant crying of the peewits, and watched their tumbling flight. Below him tinkled a rivulet, its brown water rippling between banks of peaty earth. Everywhere was singing, peace, and careless unconcern.

And this lordly indifference of Nature calmed and soothed him. Neither human pain nor the injustice of man could shift the key of the water, alter the peewits' cry a single tone, nor influence one fraction of an inch those cloudy frigates of vapour that sailed the sky. The earth bulged sunwards as she had bulged for centuries. The power of her steady gait, superbly calm, breathed everywhere with grandeur—undismayed, unhasting, and supremely confident.... And, like the flash of those golden flies, there leaped suddenly upon him this vivid thought: that his world of agony lay neatly buttoned up within the tiny space of his own brain. Outside himself it had no existence at all. His mind contained it—the minute interior he called his heart. From this vaster world about him it lay utterly apart, like deeds in the black boxes of japanned tin he kept at the office, shut off from the universe, huddled in an overcrowded space within his skull.

How this commonplace thought reached him, garbed in such startling novelty, was odd enough; for it seemed as though the fierceness of his pain had burned away something. His thoughts it merely enflamed; but this other thing it consumed. Something that had obscured clear vision shrivelled before it as a piece of paper, eaten up by fire, dwindles down into a thimbleful of unimportant ashes. The thicket of his mind grew half transparent. At the farther end he saw, for the first time—light. The perspective of his inner life, hitherto so enormous, telescoped into the proportions of a miniature. Just as momentous and significant as before, it was somehow abruptly different—seen from another point of view. The suffering had burned up rubbish he himself had piled over the head of a little Fact. Like a point of metal that glows yet will not burn, he discerned in the depths of him the essential shining fact that not all this ruinous conflagration could destroy. And this brilliant, indestructible kernel was—his Innocence. The rest was self-reared rubbish: opinion of the world. He had magnified an atom into a universe....

Pain, as it seemed, had cleared a way for the sublimity of Nature to approach him. The calm old Universe rolled past. The deep, majestic Day gave him a push, as though the shoulder of some star had brushed his own. He had thought his feelings were the world: instead, they were merely his way of looking at it. The actual 'world' was some glorious, unchanging thing he never saw direct. His attitude of mind was but a peephole into it. The choice of his particular peephole, moreover, lay surely within the power of his individual will. The anguish, centred upon so small a point, had seemed to affect the entire spread universe around him, whereas in reality it affected nothing but his attitude of mind towards it. The truism struck him like a blow between the eyes, that a man is what he thinks or feels himself to be. It leaped the barrier between words and meaning. The intellectual concept became a hard-edged fact, because he realised it—for the first time in his very circumscribed life. And this dreadful pain that had made even suicide seem desirable was entirely a fabrication of his own mind. The universe about him rolled on just the same in the majesty of its eternal purpose. His tiny inner world was clouded, but the glory of this stupendous world about him was undimmed, untroubled, unaffected. Even death itself....

With a swift smash of the hand he crushed the golden fly that settled on his knee. The murder was done impulsively, utterly without intention. He watched the little point of gold quiver for a moment among the hairs of the rough tweed; then lie still for ever ... but the scent of heather-honey filled the air as before; the wind passed sighing through the pines; the clouds still sailed their uncharted sea of blue. There lay the whole spread surface of the Forest in the sun. Only the attitude of the golden fly towards it all was gone. A single, tiny point of view had disappeared. Nature passed on calmly and unhasting; she took no note.

Then, with a rush of awe, another thought flashed through him: Nature *had* taken note. There was a difference everywhere. Not a sparrow falleth, he remembered, without God knowing. God was certainly in Nature somewhere. His clumsy senses could not register this difference, yet it was there. His own small world, fed by these senses, was after all the merest little corner of Existence. To the whole of Existence, that included himself, the golden fly, the sun, and all the stars, he must somehow answer for his crime. It was a wanton interference with a sublime and sovereign Purpose that he now divined for the first time. He looked at the wee point of gold lying still and silent in the forest of hairs. He realised the enormity of his act. It could not have been graver had he put out the sun, or the little, insignificant flame of his own existence. He had done a criminal, evil thing, for he had put an end to a certain point of view; had wiped it out; made it impossible. Had the fly been quicker, less easily overwhelmed, or more tenacious of the scrap of universal life it used, Nature would at this instant be richer for its little contribution to the whole of things—to which he himself also belonged. And wherein, he asked himself, did he differ from that fly in the importance, the significance of his contribution to the universe? The soul ...? He had never given the question a single thought; but if the scrap of life he owned was called a soul, why should that point of golden glory not comprise one too? Its minute size, its trivial purpose, its few hours of apparently futile existence ... these formed no true criterion ...!

Similarly, the thought rushed over him, a Hand was being stretched out to crush himself. His pain was the shadow of its approach; anger in his heart, the warning. Unless he were quick enough, adroit and skilled enough, he also would be wiped out, while Nature continued her slow, unhasting way without him. His attitude towards the personal pain was really the test of his ability, of his merit—of his right to survive. Pain teaches, pain develops, pain brings growth: he had heard it since his copybook days. But now he realised it, as again thought leaped the barrier between familiar words and meaning. In his attitude of mind to his catastrophe lay his salvation or his ... death.

In some such confused and blundering fashion, because along unaccustomed channels, the truth charged into him to overwhelm, yet bringing with it an unwonted sense of joy that seemed to break a crust which long had held back—life. Thus tapped, these sources gushed forth and bubbled over, spread about his being, flooded him with hope and courage, above all with—calmness. Nature held forces just as real and living as human sympathy, and equally able to modify the soul. And Nature was always accessible. A sense of huge companionship, denied him by the littleness of his fellow-men, stole sweetly over him It was amazingly uplifting, yet fear came close behind it, as he realised the presumption of his former attitude of cynical indifference. These Powers were aware of his petty insolence, yet had not crushed him.... It was, of course, the awakening of the religious instinct in a man who hitherto had worshipped merely a rather low-grade form of intellect.

And, while the enormous confusion of it shook him, this sense of incommunicable sweetness remained. Bright haunting eyes, with love in them, gazed at him from the blue; and this thing that came so close, stood also far away upon the line of the horizon. It was everywhere. It filled the hollows, but towered over him as well towards the pinnaces of cloud. It was in the sharpness of the peewits' cry, and in the water's murmur. It whispered in the pine-boughs, and blazed in every patch of sunlight. And it was glory, pure and simple. It filled him with a sense of strength for which he could find but one description—Triumph.

And so, first, the anger faded from his mind and crept away. Resentment then slunk after it. Revolt and disappointment also melted, and bitterness gave place to the most marvellous peace the man had ever known. Then came resignation to fill the empty places. Pain, as a means and not an end, had cleared the way, though the accomplishment was like a miracle. But Conversion *is* a miracle. No ordinary pain can bring it. This anguish he understood now in a new relation to life—as something to be taken willingly into himself and dealt with, all regardless of public opinion. What people said and thought was in their world, not in his. It was less than nothing. The pain cultivated dormant tracts. The terror also purged. It disclosed....

He watched the wind, and even the wind brought revelation; for without obstacles in its path it would be silent. He watched the sunshine, and the sunshine taught him too; for without obstacles to fling it back against his eye, he could never see it. He would neither hear the tinkling water nor feel the summer heat unless both one and other overcame some reluctant medium in their pathways. And, similarly with his moral being—his pain resulted from the friction of his personal ambitions against the stress of some noble Power that sought to lift him higher. That Power he could not know direct, but he recognised its strain against him by the resistance it generated in the inertia of his selfishness. His attitude of mind had switched completely round. It was what the preachers termed development through suffering.

Moreover, he had acquired this energy of resistance somehow from the wind and sun and the beauty of a common summer's day. Their peace and strength had passed into himself. Unconsciously on his way home he drew upon it steadily. He tossed the pistol into a pool of water. Nature had healed him; and Nature, should he turn weak again, was always there. It was very wonderful. He wanted to sing....

SPECIAL DELIVERY

Meiklejohn the curate, was walking through the Jura when this thing happened to him. There is only his word to vouch for it, for the inn and its proprietor are now both of the past, and the local record of the occurrence has long since assumed the proportions of a picturesque but inaccurate legend. As a true story, however, it stands out from those of its kidney by the fact that there seems to have been a deliberate intention in it. It saved a life—a life the world had need of. And this singular rescue of a man of value to the best order of things makes one feel that there was some sense, even logic, in the affair.

Moreover, Meiklejohn asserts that it was the only psychic experience he ever knew. Things of the sort were not a 'habit' with him. His rescue, thus was not one of those meaningless interventions that puzzle the man in the street while they exhilarate the psychologist. It was a deliberate and very determined affair.

Meiklejohn found himself that hot August night in one of the valleys that slip like blue shadows hidden among pine-woods between the Swiss frontier and France. He had passed Ste. Croix earlier in the day; Les Rasses had been left behind about four o'clock; Buttes, and the Val de Travers, where the cement of many a London street comes from, was his goal. But the light failed long before he reached it, and he stopped at an inn that appeared unexpectedly round a corner of the dusty road, built literally against the great cliffs that formed one wall of the valley. He was so footsore, and his knapsack so heavy, that he turned in without more ado.

Le Guillaume Tell was the name of the inn—dirty white walls, with thin, almost mangy vines scrambling over the door, and the stream brawling beneath shuttered windows with green and white stripes all patched by sun and rain. His room was sevenpence, his dinner of soup, omelette, fruit, cheese, and coffee, a franc. The prices suited his pocket and made him feel comfortable and at home. Immediately behind the hotel—the only house visible, except the sawmill across the road, rose the ever-crumbling ridges and precipices that formed the flanks of Chasseront and ran on past La Sagne towards the grey Aiguilles de Baulmes. He was in the Jura fastnesses where tourists rarely penetrate.

Through the low doorway of the inn he carried with him the strong atmosphere of thoughts that had accompanied him all day—dreams of how he intended to spend his life, plans of sacrifice and effort. For his hopes of great achievement, even then at twenty-five, were a veritable passion in him, and his desire to spend himself for humanity a devouring flame. So occupied, indeed, was his mind with the emotions belonging to this line of thinking, that he hardly noticed the singular, though exceedingly faint, sense of alarm that stirred somewhere in the depths of his being as he passed within that doorway where the dropping vine-leaves clutched at his hat. He remembered it a little later. The sense of danger had been touched in him. He felt at the moment only a hint of discomfort, too vague to claim definite recognition. Yet it was there—the instant he stepped within the threshold—and afterwards he distinctly recalled its sudden and unaccountable advent.

His bedroom, though stuffy, as from windows long unopened, was clean; carpetless, of course, and primitive, with white pine floor and walls, and the short bed, smothered under its duvet, very creaky. And very short! For Meiklejohn was well over six feet.

'I shall have to curl up, as usual, in a knot,' was his reflection as he measured the bed with his eye; 'though to-night I think—after my twenty miles in this air——'

The thought refused to complete itself. He was going to add that he was tired enough to have slept on a stone floor, but for some undefined reason the same sense of alarm that had tapped him on the shoulder as he entered the inn returned now when he contemplated the bed. A sharp repugnance for that bed, as sudden and unaccountable as it was curious, swept into him—and was gone again before he had time to seize it wholly. It was in reality so slight that he dismissed it immediately as the merest fancy; yet, at the same time, he was aware that he would rather have slept on another bed, had there been one in the room—and then the queer feeling that, after all, perhaps, he would *not* sleep there in the end at all. How this idea came to him he never knew. He records it, however, as part of the occurrence.

After eight o'clock a few peasants, and workmen from the sawmill, came in to drink their *demi-litre* of red wine in the common room downstairs, to stare at the unexpected guest, and to smoke their vile tobacco. They were neither picturesque nor amusing—simply dirty and slightly malodorous. At nine o'clock Meiklejohn knocked the ashes from his briar pipe upon the limestone window-ledge, and went upstairs, overpowered with sleep. The sense of alarm had utterly disappeared; his mind was busy once more with his great dreams of the future—dreams that materialised themselves, as all the world knows, in the famous Meiklejohn Institutes....

Berthoud, the proprietor, short and sturdy, with his faded brown coat and no collar, slightly confused with red wine and a 'tourist' guest, showed him the way up. For, of course, there was no *femme de chambre*.

'You have the corridor all to yourself,' the man said; showed him the best corner of the landing to shout from in case he wanted anything—there being no bell—eyed his boots, knapsack, and flask with considerable curiosity, wished him goodnight, and was gone. He went downstairs with a noise like a horse, thought the curate, as he locked the door after him.

The windows had been open now for a couple of hours, and the room smelt sweet with the odours of sawn wood and shavings, the resinous perfume of the surrounding hosts of pines, and the sharp, delicate touch of a lonely mountain valley where civilisation has not yet tainted the air. Whiffs of coarse tobacco, pungent without being offensive, came invisibly through the cracks of the floor. Primitive and simple it all was—a—sort of vigorous 'backwoods' atmosphere. Yet, once again, as he turned to examine the room after Berthoud's steps had blundered down below into the passage, something rose faintly within him to set his nerves mysteriously a-quiver.

Out of these perfectly simple conditions, without the least apparent cause, the odd feeling again came over him that he was—in danger.

The curate was not much given to analysis. He was a man of action pure and simple, as a rule. But to-night, in spite of himself, his thoughts went plunging, searching, asking. For this singular message of dread that emanated as it were from the room, or from some article of furniture in the room perhaps—that bed still touched his mind with a peculiar repugnance—demanded somewhat insistently for an explanation. And the only explanation that suggested itself to his unimaginative mind was that the forces of nature hereabouts were—overpowering; that, after the slum streets and factory chimneys of the last twelve months, these towering cliffs and smothering pine-forests communicated to his soul a word of grandeur that amounted to awe. Inadequate and far-fetched as the explanation seems, it was the only one that occurred to him; and its value in this remarkable adventure lies in the fact that he connected his sense of danger partly with the bed and partly with the mountains.

'I felt once or twice,' he said afterwards, 'as though some powerful agency of a spiritual kind were all the time trying to beat into my stupid brain a message of warning.' And this way of expressing it is more true and graphic than many paragraphs of attempted analysis.

Meiklejohn hung his clothes by the open window to air, washed, read his Bible, looked several times over his shoulder without apparent cause, and then knelt down to pray. He was a simple and devout soul; his Self lost in the yearning, young but sincere, to live for humanity. He prayed, as usual, with intense earnestness that his life might be preserved for use in the world, when in the middle of his prayer—there came a knocking at the door.

Hastily rising from his knees, he opened. The sound of rushing water filled the corridor. He heard the voices of the workmen below in the drinking-room. But only darkness stood in the passages, filling the house to the very brim. No one was there. He returned to his interrupted devotions.

'I imagined it,' he said to himself. He continued his prayers, however, longer than usual. At the back of his thoughts, dim, vague, half-defined only, lay this lurking sense of uneasiness—that he was in danger. He prayed earnestly and simply, as a child might pray, for the preservation of his life....

Again, just as he prepared to get into bed, struggling to make the heaped-up duvet spread all over, came that knocking at the bedroom door. It was soft, wonderfully soft, and something within him thrilled curiously in response. He crossed the floor to open—then hesitated. Suddenly he understood that that knocking at the door was connected with the sense of danger in his heart. In the region of subtle intuitions the two were linked. With this realisation there came over him, he declares, a singular mood in which, as in a revelation, he knew that Nature held forces that might somehow communicate directly and positively with—human beings. This thought rushed upon him out of the night, as it were. It arrested his movements. He stood there upon the bare pine boards, hesitating to open the door.

The delay thus described lasted actually only a few seconds, but in those few seconds these thoughts tore rapidly and like fire through his mind. The beauty of this lost and mysterious valley was certainly in his veins. He felt the strange presence of the encircling forests, soft and splendid, their million branches sighing in the night airs. The crying of the falling water touched him. He longed to transfer their peace and power to the hearts of suffering thousands of men and women and children. The towering precipices that literally dropped their pale walls over the roof of the inn lifted his thoughts to their own wind-swept heights; he longed to convey their message of inflexible strength to the weak-kneed folk in the slums where he worked. He was peculiarly conscious of the presence of these forces of Nature—the irresistible powers that regenerate as easily as they destroy.

All this, and far more, swept his soul like a huge wind as he stood there, waiting to open the door in answer to that mysterious soft knocking.

And there, when at length he opened, stood the figure of a man—staring at him and smiling.

Disappointment seized him instantly. He had expected, almost believed, that he would see something un-ordinary; and instead, there stood a man who had merely mistaken the door of his room, and was now bowing his apology for the interruption. Then, to his amazement, he saw that the man beckoned: the figure was some one who sought to draw him out.

'Come with me,' it seemed to say.

But Meiklejohn only realised this afterwards, he says, when it was too late and he had already shut the door in the stranger's face. For the man had withdrawn into the darkness a little, and the curate had taken the movement for a mere acknowledgment of his mistake instead of—as he afterwards felt—a sign that he should follow.

'And the moment the door was shut,' he says, 'I felt that it would have been better for me to have gone out into the passage to see what he wanted. It came over me that the man had something important to say to me. I had missed it.'

For some seconds, it seemed, he resisted the inclination to go after him. He argued with himself; then turned to his bed, pulled back the sheets and heavy duvet, and was met sharply again with the sense of repugnance, almost of fear, as before. It leaped out upon him—as though the drawing back of the blankets had set free some cold blast of wind that struck him across the face and made him shiver.

At the same moment a shadow fell from behind his shoulder and dropped across the pillow and upper half of the bed. It may, of course, have been the magnified shadow of the moth that buzzed about the pale-yellow electric light in the ceiling. He does not pretend to know. It passed swiftly, however, and was gone; and Meiklejohn, feeling less sure of himself than ever before in his life, crossed the floor quickly, almost running, and opened the door to go after the man who had knocked—twice. For in reality less than half a minute had passed since the shutting of the door and its reopening.

But the corridor was empty. He marched down the pine-board floor for some considerable distance. Below he saw the glimmer of the hall, and heard the voices of the peasants and workmen from the sawmill as they still talked and drank their red wine in the public room. That sound of falling water, as before, filled the air. Darkness reigned. But the person—the *messenger*—who had twice knocked at his door was gone utterly.... Presently a door opened downstairs, and the peasants clattered out noisily. He turned and went back to bed. The electric light was switched off below. Silence fell. Conquering his strange repugnance, Meiklejohn, with a prayer on his lips, got into bed, and in less than ten minutes was sound asleep.

'I admit,' he says, in telling the story, 'that what happened afterwards came so swiftly and so confusingly, yet with such a storm of overwhelming conviction of its reality, that its sequence may be somewhat blurred in my memory, while, at the same time, I see it after all these years as though it was a thing of yesterday. But in my sleep, first of all, I again heard that soft, mysterious tapping—not in the course of a dream of any sort, but sudden and alone out of the dark blank of forgetfulness. I tried to wake. At first, however, the bonds of unconsciousness held me tight. I had to struggle in order to return to the waking world. There was a distinct effort before I opened my eyes; and in that slight interval I became aware that the person who had knocked at the door had meanwhile opened it and passed into the room. I had left the lock unturned. The person was close beside me in the darkness— not in utter darkness, however, for a rising three-quarter moon shed its faint silver upon the floor in patches, and as I sprang swiftly from the bed, I noticed something alive moving towards me across the carpetless boards. Upon the edges of a patch of moonlight, where the fringe of silver and shadow mingled, it stopped. Three feet away from it I, too, stopped, shaking in every muscle. It lay there crouching at my very feet, staring up at me. But was it man or was it animal? For at first I took it certainly for a human being on all fours; but the next moment, with a spasm of genuine terror that half stopped my breath, it was borne in upon me that the creature was—nothing human. Only in this way can I describe it. It was identical with the human figure who had knocked before and beckoned to me to follow, but it was another presentation of that figure.

'And it held (or brought, if you will) some tremendous message for me—some message of tremendous importance, I mean. The first time I had argued, resisted, refused to listen. Now it had returned in a form that ensured obedience. Some quite terrific power emanated from it—a power that I understood instinctively belonged to the mountains and the forests and the untamed elemental forces of Nature. Amazing as it may sound in cold blood, I can only say that I felt as though the towering precipices outside had sent me a direct warning—that my life was in immediate danger.

'For a space that seemed minutes, but was probably less than a few seconds, I stood there trembling on the bare boards, my eyes riveted upon the dark, uncouth shape that covered all the floor beyond. I saw no limbs or features, no suggestion of outline that I could connect with any living form I know, animate or inanimate. Yet it moved and stirred all the time—*whirled within itself*, describes it best; and into my mind sprang a picture of an immense dark wheel, turning, spinning, whizzing so rapidly that it appears motionless, and uttering that low and ominous thunder that fills a great machinery-room of a factory. Then I thought of Ezekiel's vision of the Living Wheels....

'And it must have been at this instant, I think, that the muttering and deep note that issued from it formed itself into words within me. At any rate, I heard a voice that spoke with unmistakable intelligence:

'"Come!" it said. "Come out—at once!" And the sense of power that accompanied the Voice was so splendid that my fear vanished and I obeyed instantly without thinking more. I followed; it led. It altered in shape. The door *was* open. It ran silently in a form that was more like a stream of deep black water than anything else I can think of—out of the room, down the stairs, across the hall, and up to the deep shadows that lay against the door leading into the road. There I lost sight of it.'

Meiklejohn's only desire, he says, then was to rush after it—to escape. This he did. He understood that somehow it had passed through the door into the open air. Ten seconds later, perhaps even less, he, too, was in the open air. He acted almost automatically; reason, reflection, logic all swept away. Nowhere, however, in the soft moonlight about him was any sign of the extraordinary apparition that had succeeded in drawing him out of the inn, out of his bedroom, out of his—bed. He stared in a dazed way at everything—just beginning to get control of his faculties a bit—wondering what in the world it all meant. That huge spinning form, he felt convinced, lay hidden somewhere close beside him, waiting for the end. The danger it had enabled him to avoid was close at hand.... He *knew* that, he says....

There lay the meadows, touched here and there with wisps of floating mist; the stream roared and tumbled down its rocky bed to his left; across the road the sawmill lifted its skeleton-like outline, moonlight shining on the dew-covered shingles of the roof, its lower part hidden in shadow. The cold air of the valley was exquisitely scented.

To the right, where his eye next wandered, he saw the thick black woods rising round the base of the precipices that soared into the sky, sheeted with silvery moonlight. His gaze ran up them to the far ridges that seemed to push the very stars farther into the heavens. Then, as he saw those stars crowding the night, he staggered suddenly backwards, seizing the wall of the road for support, and catching his breath. For the top of the cliff, he fancied, moved. A group of stars was for a fraction of a second—hidden. The earth—the scenery of the valley, at least—turned about him. Something prodigious was happening to the solid structure of the world. The precipices seemed to bend over upon the valley. The far, uppermost ridge of those beetling cliffs shifted downwards. Meiklejohn declares that the way its movement hid momentarily a group of stars was the most startling—for some reason horrible—thing he had ever witnessed.

Then came the roar and crash and thunder as the mass toppled, slid, and finally—took the frightful plunge. How long the forces of rain and frost had been chiselling out the slow detachment of the giant slabs that fell, or whence came the particular extra little push that drove the entire mass out from the parent rock, no one can know. Only one thing is certain: that it was due to no chance, but to the nicely and exactly calculated results of balanced cause and effect. From the beginning of time it had been known—it might have been accurately calculated, rather—that this particular thousand tons of rock would break away from the crumbling tops of the precipices and crash downwards with the roar of many tempests into the lost and mysterious mountain valley where Meiklejohn the curate spent such and such a night of such and such a holiday. It was just as sure as the return of Halley's comet.

'I watched it,' he says, 'because I couldn't do anything else. I would far rather have run—I was so frightfully close to it all—but I couldn't move a muscle. And in a few seconds it was over. A terrific wind knocked me backwards against the stone wall; there was a vast clattering of smaller stones, set rolling down the neighbouring couloirs; a steady roll of echoes ran thundering up and down the valley; and then all was still again exactly as it had been before. And the curious thing was—ascertained a little later, as you may imagine, and not at once—that the inn, being so closely built up against the cliffs, had almost entirely escaped. The great mass of rock and trees had taken a leap farther out, and filled the meadows, blocked the road, crushed the sawmill like a matchbox, and dammed up the stream; but the inn itself was almost untouched.

'*Almost*—for a single block of limestone, about the size

of a grand piano, had dropped straight upon one corner of the roof and smashed its way through my bedroom, carrying everything it contained down to the level of the cellar, so terrific was the momentum of its crushing journey. Not a stick of the furniture was afterwards discoverable—as such. The bed seems to have been caught by the very middle of the fallen mass.'

The confusion in Meiklejohn's mind may be imagined— the rush of feeling and emotion that swept over him. Berthoud and the peasants mustered in less than a dozen minutes, talking, crying, praying. Then the stream, dammed up by the accumulation of rock, carried off the debris of the broken roof and walls in less than half an hour. The rock, however, that swept the room and the *empty* bed of Meiklejohn the curate into dust, still lies in the valley where it fell.

'The only other thing that I remember,' he says, in telling the story, 'is that, as I stood there, shaking with excitement and the painful terror of it all, before Berthoud and the peasants had come to count over their number and learn that no one was missing—while I stood there, leaning against the wall of the road, something rose out of the white dust at my feet, and, with a noise like the whirring of some immense projectile, passed swiftly and invisibly away up into space—so far as I could judge, towards the distant ridges that reared their motionless outline in moonlight beneath the stars.'

THE DESTRUCTION OF SMITH

TEN years ago, in the western States of America, I once met Smith. But he was no ordinary member of the clan: he was Ezekiel B. Smith of Smithville. He *was* Smithville, for he founded it and made it live.

It was in the oil region, where towns spring up on the map in a few days like mushrooms, and may be destroyed again in a single night by fire and earthquake. On a hunting expedition Smith stumbled upon a natural oil well, and instantly staked his claim; a few months later he was rich, grown into affluence as rapidly as that patch of wilderness grew into streets and houses where you could buy anything from an evening's gambling to a tin of Boston baked pork-and-beans. Smith was really a tremendous fellow, a sort of human dynamo of energy and pluck, with rare judgment in his great square head—the kind of judgment that in higher walks of life makes statesmen. His personality cut through the difficulties of life with the clean easy force of putting his whole life into anything he touched. 'God's own luck,' his comrades called it; but really it was sheer ability and character and personality. The man had power.

From the moment of that 'oil find' his rise was very rapid, but while his brains went into a dozen other big enterprises, his heart remained in little Smithville, the flimsy mushroom town he had created. His own life was in it. It was his baby. He spoke tenderly of its hideousness. Smithville was an intimate expression of his very self.

Ezekiel B. Smith I saw once only, for a few minutes; but I have never forgotten him. It was the moment of his death. And we came across him on a shooting trip where the forests melt away towards the vast plains of the Arizona desert. The personality of the man was singularly impressive. I caught myself thinking of a mountain, or of some elemental force of Nature so sure of itself that hurry is never necessary. And his gentleness was like the gentleness of women. Great strength often—the greatest always—has tenderness in it, a depth of tenderness unknown to pettier life.

Our meeting was coincidence, for we were hunting in a region where distances are measured by hours and the chance of running across white men very rare. For many days our nightly camps were pitched in spots of beauty where the loneliness is akin to the loneliness of the Egyptian Desert. On one side the mountain slopes were smothered with dense forest, hiding wee meadows of sweet grass like English lawns; and on the other side, stretching for more miles than a man can count, ran the desolate alkali plains of Arizona where tufts of sage-brush are the only vegetation till you reach the lips of the Colorado Canyons. Our horses were tethered for the night beneath the stars. Two backwoodsmen were cooking dinner. The smell of bacon over a wood fire mingled with the keen and fragrant air—when, suddenly, the horses neighed, signalling the approach of one of their own kind. Indians, white men—probably another hunting party—were within scenting distance, though it was long before my city ears caught any sound, and still longer before the cause itself entered the circle of our firelight.

I saw a square-faced man, tanned like a redskin, in a hunting shirt and a big sombrero, climb down slowly from his horse and move towards us keenly searching with his eyes; and at the same moment Hank, looking up from the frying-pan where the bacon and venison spluttered in a pool of pork-fat, exclaimed, 'Why, it's Ezekiel B.!' The next words, addressed to Jake, who held the kettle, were below his breath: 'And if he ain't all broke up! Jest look at the eyes on him!' I saw what he meant—the face of a human being distraught by some extraordinary emotion, a soul in violent distress, yet betrayal well kept under. Once, as a newspaper man, I had seen a murderer walk to the electric chair. The expression was similar. Death was *behind* the eyes, not in them. Smith brought in with him—terror.

In a dozen words we learned he had been hunting for some

weeks, but was now heading for Tranter, a 'stop-off' station where you could flag the daily train 140 miles south-west. He was making for Smithville, the little town that was the apple of his eye. Something 'was wrong' with Smithville. No one asked him what—it is the custom to wait till information is volunteered. But Hank, helping him presently to venison (which he hardly touched), said casually, 'Good hunting, Boss, your way?'; and the brief reply told much, and proved how eager he was to relieve his mind by speech. 'I'm glad to locate your camp, boys,' he said. 'That's luck. There's something going wrong'—and a catch came into his voice—'with Smithville.' Behind the laconic statement emerged somehow the terror the man experienced. For Smith to confess cowardice and in the same breath admit mere 'luck', was equivalent to the hysteria that makes city people laugh or cry. It was genuinely dramatic. I have seen nothing more impressive by way of human tragedy—though hard to explain why—than this square-jawed, dauntless man, sitting there with the firelight on his rugged features, and saying this simple thing. For how in the world could he know it——?

In the pause that followed, his Indians came gliding in, tethered the horses, and sat down without a word to eat what Hank distributed. But nothing was to be read on their impassive faces. Redskins, whatever they may feel, show little. Then Smith gave us another pregnant sentence. '*They* heard it too,' he said, in a lower voice, indicating his three men; 'they saw it jest as I did.' He looked up into the starry sky a second. 'It's hard upon our trail right now,' he added, as though he expected something to drop upon us from the heavens. And from that moment I swear we all felt creepy. The darkness round our lonely camp hid terror in its folds; the wind that whispered through the dry sage-brush brought whispers and the shuffle of watching figures; and when the Indians went softly out to pitch the tents and get more wood for the fire, I remember feeling glad the duty was not mine. Yet this feeling of uneasiness is something one rarely experiences in the open. It belongs to houses, overwrought imaginations, and the presence of evil men. Nature gives peace and security. That we all felt it proves how real it was. And Smith, who felt it most, of course, had brought it.

'There's something gone wrong with Smithville' was an ominous statement of disaster. He said it just as a man in civilised lands might say, 'My wife is dying; a telegram's just come. I must take the train.' But how he felt so sure of it, a thousand miles away in this uninhabited corner of the wilderness, made us feel curiously uneasy. For it was an incredible thing—yet true. We all felt *that*. Smith did not imagine things. A sense of gloomy apprehension settled over our lonely camp, as though things were about to happen. Already they stalked across the great black night, watching us with many eyes. The wind had risen, and there were sounds among the trees. I, for one, felt no desire to go to bed. The way Smith sat there, watching the sky and peering into the sheet of darkness that veiled the Desert, set my nerves all jangling. He expected something—but what? It was following him. Across this tractless wilderness, apparently above him against the brilliant stars, Something was 'hard upon his trail.'

Then, in the middle of painful silences, Smith suddenly turned loquacious—further sign with him of deep mental disturbance. He asked questions like a schoolboy—asked them of me too, as being 'an edicated man.' But there were such queer things to talk about round an Arizona camp-fire that Hank clearly wondered for his sanity. He knew about the 'wilderness madness' that attacks some folks. He let his green cigar go out and flashed me signals to be cautious. He listened intently, with the eyes of a puzzled child, half cynical, half touched with superstitious dread. For, briefly, Smith asked me what I knew about stories of dying men appearing at a distance to those who loved them much. He had read such tales, 'heard tell of 'em,' but 'are they dead true, or are they jest little feery tales?' I satisfied him as best I could with one or two authentic stories. Whether he believed or not I cannot say; but his swift mind jumped in a flash to the point. 'Then, if that kind o' stuff is true,' he asked, simply, 'it looks as though a feller had a dooplicate of himself—sperrit maybe—that gits loose and active at the time of death, and heads straight for the party it loves best. Ain't that so, Boss?' I admitted the theory was correct. And then he startled us with a final question that made Hank drop an oath below his breath—sure evidence of uneasy excitement in the old backwoodsman. Smith whispered it, looking over his shoulder into the night: 'Ain't it jest possible then,' he asked, 'seeing that men an' Nature is all made of a piece like, that places too have this dooplicate appearance of theirselves that gits loose when they go under?'

It was difficult, under the circumstances, to explain that such a theory *had* been held to account for visions of scenery people sometimes have, and that a city may have a definite personality made up of all its inhabitants—moods, thoughts, feelings, and passions of the multitude who go to compose its life and atmosphere, and that hence is due the odd changes in man's individuality when he goes from one city to another. Nor was there any time to do so, for hardly had he asked his singular question when the horses whinnied, the Indians leaped to their feet as if ready for an attack, and Smith himself turned the colour of the ashes theat lay in a circle of whitish-grey about the burning wood. There was an expression in his face of death, or, as the Irish peasants say, 'destroyed.'

'That's Smithville,' he cried, springing to his feet, then tottering so that I thought he must fall into the flame; 'that's my baby town—got loose and huntin' for me, who made it, and love it better'n anything on Gawd's green earth!' And then he added with a kind of gulp in his throat as of a man who wanted to cry but couldn't: 'And it's going to bits—it's dying—and I'm not thar to save it——!'

He staggered and I caught his arm. The sound of his frightened, anguished voice, and the shuffling of our many feet among the stones, died away into the night. We all stood, staring. The darkness came up closer. The horses ceased their whinnying. For a moment nothing happened. Then Smith turned slowly round and raised his head towards the stars as though he saw something. 'Hear that?' he whispered. 'It's coming up close. That's what I've bin hearing now, on and off, two days and nights. Listen!' His whispering voice broke horribly; the man was suffering atrociously. For a moment he became vastly, horribly animated—then stood still as death.

But in the hollow silence, broken only by the sighing of the wind among the spruces, we at first heard nothing. Then most curiously, something like rapid driven mist came trooping down the sky, and veiled a group of stars. With it, as from an enormous distance, but growing swiftly nearer, came noises that were beyond all question the noises of a city rushing through the heavens. From all sides they came; and with them there shot a reddish, streaked appearance across the misty veil that swung so rapidly and softly between the stars and our eyes. Lurid it was, and in some way terrible. A sense of helpless bewilderment came over me, scattering my faculties as in scenes of fire, when the mind struggles violently to possess itself and act for the best. Hank, holding his rifle ready to shoot, moved stupidly round the group, equally at a loss, and swearing incessantly below his breath. For this overwhelming certainty that Something living had come upon us from the sky possessed us all, and I, personally, felt as if a gigantic Being swept against me through the night, destructive and enveloping, and yet that it was not one, but many. Power of action left me. I could not even observe with accuracy what was going on. I stared, dizzy and bewildered, in all directions; but my power of movement was gone, and my feet refused to stir. Only I remember that the Redskins stood like figures of stone, unmoved.

And the sounds about us grew into a roar. The distant murmur came past us like a sea. There was a babel of shouting. Here, in the deep old wilderness that knew no living human beings for hundreds of leagues, there was a tempest of voices calling, crying, shrieking; men's hoarse clamouring, and the high screaming of women and children. Behind it ran a booming sound like thunder. Yet all of it, while apparently so close above our heads, seemed in some inexplicable way far off in the distance—muted, faint, thinning out among the quiet stars. More like a *memory* of turmoil and tumult it seemed than the actual uproar heard at first hand. And through it ran the crash of big things tumbling, breaking, falling in destruction with an awful detonating thunder of collapse. I thought the hills were toppling down upon us. A shrieking city, it seemed, fled past us through the sky.

How long it lasted it is impossible to say, for my power of measuring time had utterly vanished. A dreadful wild anguish summed up all the feelings I can remember. It seemed I watched, or read, or dreamed some desolating scene of disaster in which human life went overboard wholesale, as though one threw a hatful of insects into a blazing fire. This idea of burning, of thick suffocating smoke and savage flame, coloured the entire experience. And the next thing I knew was that it had passed away as completely as though it had never been at all; the stars shone down from an air of limpid clearness, and—there was a smell of burning leather in my nostrils. I just stepped back in time to save my feet. I had moved in my excitement against the circle of hot ashes. Hank pushed me back roughly with the barrel of his rifle.

But, strangest of all, I understood, as by some flash of divine intuition, the reason of this abrupt cessation of the horrible tumult. The Personality of the town, set free and loosened in the moment of death, had returned to him who gave it birth, who loved it, and of whose life it was actually an expression. The Being of Smithville was literally a projection, an emanation of the dynamic, vital personality of its puissant creator. And, in death, it had returned on him with the shock of an accumulated power impossible for a human being to resist. For years he had provided it with life—but *gradually*. It now rushed back to its source, thus concentrated, in a single terrific moment.

'That's him,' I heard a voice saying from a great distance as it seemed. 'He's fired his last shot—!' and saw Hank turning the body over with his riflebutt. And, though the face itself was calm beneath the stars, there was an attitude of limbs and body that suggested the bursting of an enormous shell that had twisted every fibre by its awful force yet somehow left the body as a whole intact.

We carried 'it' to Tranter, and at the first real station along the line we got the news by telegraph: 'Smithville wiped out by fire. Burned two days and nights. Loss of life, 3000.' And all the way in my dreams I seemed still to hear that curious, dreadful cry of Smithville, the shrieking city rushing headlong through the sky.

THE TRYST

As he got out of the train at the little wayside station he remembered the conversation as if it had been yesterday, instead of fifteen years ago—and his heart went thumping against his ribs so violently that he almost heard it. The original thrill came over him again with all its infinite yearning. He felt it as he had felt it *then*—not with that tragic lessening the interval had brought to each repetition of its memory. Here, in the familiar scenery of its birth, he realised with mingled pain and wonder that the subsequent years had not destroyed, but only dimmed it. The forgotten rapture flamed back with all the fierce beauty of its genesis, desire at white heat. And the shock of the abrupt discovery shattered time. Fifteen years became a negligible moment; the crowded experiences that had intervened seemed but a dream. The farewell scene, the conversation on the steamer's deck, were clear as of the day before. He saw the hand holding her big hat that fluttered in the wind, saw the flowers on the dress where the long coat was blown open a moment, recalled the face of a hurrying steward who had jostled them; he even heard the voices—his own and hers:

'Yes,' she said simply; 'I promise you. You have my word. I'll wait——'

'Till I come back,' he interrupted.

Steadfastly she repeated his actual words, then added: 'Here; at home—that is.'

'I'll come to the garden gate as usual,' he told her, trying to smile. 'I'll knock. You'll open the gate—as usual—and come out to me.'

These words, too, she attempted to repeat, but her voice failed, her eyes filled suddenly with tears; she looked into his face and smiled. It was just then that her little hand went up to hold the hat on—he saw the very gesture still. He remembered that he was vehemently tempted to tear his ticket up there and then, to go ashore with her, to stay in England, to brave all opposition—when the siren roared its third horrible warning ... and the ship put out to sea.

Fifteen years, thick with various incident, had passed between them since that moment. His life had risen, fallen, crashed, then risen again. He had come back at last, fortune won by a lucky coup—at thirty-five; had come back to find her, come back, above all, to keep his word. Once every three months they had exchanged the brief letter agreed upon: 'I am well; I am waiting; I am happy; I am unmarried. Yours——.' For his youthful wisdom had insisted that no 'man' had the right to keep 'any woman' too long waiting; and she, thinking that letter brave and splendid, had insisted likewise that he was free—if freedom called him. They had laughed over this last phrase in their agreement. They put five years as the possible limit of separation. By then he would have won success, and obstinate parents would have nothing more to say.

But when five years ended he was 'on his uppers' in a western mining town, and with the end of ten in sight those uppers, though changed, were little better, apparently, than patched and mended. It was just then, too, that the change which had been stealing over him first betrayed itself. He realised it abruptly, a sense of shame and horror in him. The discovery was made unconsciously: it disclosed itself. He was reading her letter as a labourer on a Californian fruit farm: 'Funny she doesn't marry—someone else!' he heard himself say. The words were out before he knew it, and certainly before he could suppress them. They just slipped out, startling him into the truth; and he knew instantly that the thought was fathered in him by a hidden wish.... He was older. He had lived. It was a memory he loved.

Despising himself in a contradictory fashion—both vaguely and fiercely—he yet held true to his boyhood's promise. He did not write and offer to release her as he knew they did in stories; he persuaded himself that he meant to keep his word. There was this fine, stupid, selfish obstinacy in his character. In any case, she would misunderstand and think he wanted to set free—himself. 'Besides—I'm still—awfully fond of her,' he asserted. And it was true; only the love, it seemed, had gone its way. Not that another woman took it; he kept himself clean, held firm as steel. The love, apparently, just faded of its own accord; her image dimmed, her letters had ceased to thrill, then ceased to interest him.

Subsequent reflection made him realise other details about himself. In the interval he had suffered hardships, had learned the uncertainty of life that depends for its continuance on a little food, but that food often hard to come by, and had seen so many others go under that he held it more cheaply than of old. The wandering instinct, too, had caught him, slowly killing the domestic impulse; he lost his desire for a settled place of abode, the desire for children of his own, lost the desire to marry at all. Also—he reminded himself with a smile—he had lost other things: the expression of youth *she* was accustomed to and held always in her thoughts of him, two fingers of one hand, his hair! He wore glasses, too. The gentlemen-adventurers of life get scarred in those wild places where he lived. He saw himself a rather battered specimen well on the way to middle age.

There was confusion in his mind, however, *and* in his heart: a struggling complex of emotions that made it difficult to know exactly what he did feel. The dominant clue concealed itself. Feelings shifted. A single, clear determinant did not offer. He was an honest fellow. 'I can't quite make it out,' he said. 'What is it I really feel? And why?' His motive seemed obscured. To keep the flame alight for the long buffeting years was no small achievement; better men had succumbed in half the time. Yet something in him still held fast to the girl as with a band of steel that *would* not let her go entirely. Occasionally there came strong reversions, when he ached with longing, yearning, hope; when he loved her again; remembered passionately each detail of the far-off courtship days in the forbidden rectory garden beyond the small, white garden gate. Or was it merely the image and the memory he loved 'again'? He hardly knew himself. He could not tell.

That 'again' puzzled him. It was the wrong word surely....
He still wrote the promised letter, however; it was so easy;
those short sentences could not betray the dead or dying fires.
One day, besides, he would return and claim her. He meant
to keep his word.

And he had kept it. Here he was, this calm September
afternoon, within three miles of the village where he first
had kissed her, where the marvel of first love had come to
both; three short miles between him and the little white garden
gate of which at this very moment she was intently thinking,
and behind which some fifty minutes later she would be standing, waiting for him....

He had purposely left the train at an earlier station; he would
walk the three miles in the dusk, climb the familiar steps,
knock at the white gate in the wall as of old, utter the promised
words, 'I have come back to find you,' enter, and—keep his
word. He had written from Mexico a week before he sailed;
he had made careful, even accurate calculations: 'In the dusk,
on the sixteenth of September, I shall come and knock,' he
added to the usual sentences. The knowledge of his coming,
therefore, had been in her possession seven days. Just before
sailing, moreover, he had heard from her—though not in
answer, naturally. She was well; she was happy; she was
unmarried; she was waiting.

And now, as by some magical process of restoration—possible
to deep hearts only, perhaps, though even to them quite
inexplicable—the state of first love had blazed up again in
him. In all its radiant beauty it lit his heart, burned unextinguished in his soul, set body and mind on fire. The years had merely
veiled it. It burst upon him, captured, overwhelmed him
with the suddenness of a dream. He stepped from the
train. He met it in the face. It took him prisoner. The familiar
trees and hedges, the unchanged countryside, the 'fields-smells
known in infancy,' all these, with something subtly added
to them, rolled back the passion of his youth upon him in
a flood. No longer was he bound upon what he deemed,
perhaps, an act of honourable duty; it was love that drove

him, as it drove him fifteen years before. And it drove him with the accumulated passion of desire long forcibly repressed; almost as if, out of some fancied notion of fairness to the girl, he had deliberately, yet still unconsciously, said 'No' to it; that *she* had not faded, but that he had decided, '*I* must forget her.' That sentence: 'Why dosen't she marry—someone else?' had not betrayed change in himself. It surprised another motive: 'It's not fair to—her!'

His mind worked with a curious rapidity, but worked within one circle only. The stress of sudden emotion was extraordinary. He remembered a thousand things; yet, chief among them, those occasional reversions when he had felt he 'loved her again.' Had he not, after all, deceived himself? Had she ever really 'faded' at all? Had he not felt he ought to let her fade—release her that way? And the change in himself?—that sentence on the Californian fruit-farm—what did they mean? Which had been true, the fading or the love?

The confusion in his mind was hopeless, but, as a matter of fact, he did not think at all: he only felt. The momentum, besides, was irresistible, and before the shattering onset of the sweet revival he did not stop to analyse the strange result. He knew certain things, and cared to know no others: that his heart was leaping, his blood running with the heat of twenty, that joy recaptured him, that he must see, hear, touch her, hold her in his arms—and marry her. For the fifteen years had crumbled to a little thing, and at thirty-five he felt himself but twenty, rapturously, deliciously in love.

He went quickly, eagerly, down the little street to the inn, still feeling only, not thinking anything. The vehement uprush of the old emotion made reflection of any kind impossible. He gave no further thought to those long years 'out there,' when her name, her letters, the very image of her in his mind had found him, if not cold, at least without keen response. All that was forgotten as though it had not been. The steadfast thing in him, this strong holding to a promise which had never wilted, ousted the recollection of fading and decay that, whatever caused them, certainly had existed. And this steadfast thing now took command. This enduring quality in his character led him. It was only towards the end of the hurried tea he first received the singular impression—vague, indeed, but undeniably persistent—that he was *being* led.

Yet, though aware of this, he did not pause to argue or reflect. The emotional displacement in him, of course, had been more than considerable: there had been upheaval, a change whose abruptness was even dislocating, fundamental in a sense he could not estimate—shock. Yet he took no count of anything but the one mastering desire to get to her as soon as possible, knock at the small, white garden gate, hear her answering voice, see the low wooden door swing open—take her. There was joy and glory in his heart, and a yearning sweet delight. At this very moment she was expecting him. And he—had come.

Behind these positive emotions, however, there lay concealed all the time others that were of a negative character. Consciously, he was not aware of them, but they were there; they revealed their presence in various little ways that puzzled him. He recognised them absent-mindedly, as it were; did not analyse or investigate them. For, through the confusion upon his faculties, rose also a certain hint of insecurity that betrayed itself by a slight hesitancy or miscalculation in one or two unimportant actions. There was a touch of melancholy, too, a sense of something lost. It lay, perhaps, in that tinge of sadness which accompanies the twilight of an autumn day, when a gentler, mournful beauty veils a greater beauty that is past. Some trick of memory connected it with a scene of early boyhood, when, meaning to see the sunrise, he overslept, and, by a brief half-hour, was just—too late. He noted it merely, then passed on; he did not understand it; he hurried all the more, this hurry the only sign that it *was* noted. 'I must be quick,' flashed up across his strongly positive emotions.

And, due to this hurry, possibly, were the slight miscalculations that he made. They were very trivial. He rang for sugar, though the bowl stood just before his eyes, yet when the girl

THE TRYST

came in he forgot completely what he rang for—and inquired instead about the late trains back to London. And, when the time-table was laid before him, he examined it without intelligence, then looked up suddenly into the maid's face with a question about flowers. Were there flowers to be had in the village anywhere? What kind of flowers? 'Oh, a bouquet or a'—he hesitated, searching for a word that tried to present itself, yet was not the word *he* wanted to make use of—'or a wreath—of some sort?' he finished. He took the very word he did not want to take. In several things he did and said, this hesitancy and miscalculation betrayed themselves—such trivial things, yet significant in and elusive way that he disliked. There was sadness, insecurity somewhere in them. And he resented them, though aware of their existence only because they qualified his joy. There was a whispered 'No' floating somewhere in the dusk. Almost—he felt disquiet. He hurried, more and more eager to be off upon his journey—the final part of it.

Moreover, there were other signs of an odd miscalculation—dislocation, perhaps, properly speaking—in him. Though the inn was familiar from his boyhood days, kept by the same old couple, too, he volunteered no information about himself, nor asked a single question about the village he was bound for. He did not even inquire if the rector—her father—still were living. And when he left he entirely neglected the gilt-framed mirror above the mantelpiece of plush, dusty pampas-grass in waterless vases on either side. It did not matter, apparently, whether he looked well or ill, tidy or untidy. He forgot that when his cap was off the absence of thick, accustomed hair must alter him considerably, forgot also that two fingers were missing from one hand, the right hand, the hand that she would presently clasp. Nor did it occur to him that he wore glasses, which must change his expression and add to the appearance of the years he bore. None of these obvious and natural things seemed to come into his thoughts at all. He was in a hurry to be off. He did not think. But though his mind may not have noted these slight betrayals with actual sentences, his attitude, nevertheless, expressed them. This was, it seemed, the feeling in him: 'What could such details matter to her *now*? Why, indeed, should he give to them a single thought? It was himself she loved and waited for, not separate items of his external, physical image.' As well think of the fact that she, too, must have altered—outwardly. It never once occurred to him. Such details were of To-day.... He was only impatient to come to her quickly, very quickly, instantly, if possible. He hurried.

There was a flood of boyhood's joy in him. He paid for his tea, giving a tip that was twice the price of the meal, and set out gaily and impetuously along the winding lane. Charged to the brim with a sweet picture of a small, white garden gate, the loved face close behind it, he went forward at a headlong pace, singing 'Nancy Lee' as he used to sing it fifteen years before.

With action, then, the negative sensations hid themselves, obliterated by the positive ones that took command. The former, however, merely lay concealed; they waited. Thus, perhaps, does vital emotion, overlong restrained, denied, indeed, of its blossoming altogether, take revenge. Repressed element in his psychic life asserted themselves, selecting, as though naturally a dramatic form.

The dusk fell rapidly, mist rose in floating strips along the meadows by the stream; the old, familiar details beckoned him forwards, then drove him from behind as he went swiftly past them. He recognised others rising through the thickening air beyond; they nodded, peered, and whispered, sometimes they almost sang. And each added to his inner happiness; each brought its sweet and precious contribution, and built it into the reconstructed picture of the earlier, long-forgotten rapture. It was an enticing and enchanted journey that he made, something impossibly blissful in it, something, too, that seemed curiously irresistible.

For the scenery had not altered all these years, the details of the country were unchanged, everything he saw was rich with dear and precious association, increasing the momentum of the tide that carried him along. Yonder was the stile over whose broken step he had helped her yesterday, and there the slippery plank across the stream where she looked above her shoulder to ask for his support; he saw the very bramble bushes where she scratched her hand, a-blackberrying, the day before ... and, finally, the weather-stained signpost, 'To the Rectory.' It pointed to the path through the dangerous field where Farmer Sparrow's bull provided such a sweet excuse for holding, leading—protecting her. From the entire landscape rose a stream of recent memory, each incident alive, each little detail brimmed with its cargo of fond association.

He read the rough black lettering on the crooked arm—it was rather faded, but he knew it too well to miss a single letter—and hurried forward along the muddy track; he looked about him for a sign of Farmer Sparrow's bull; he even felt in the misty air for the little hand, that he might take and lead her into safety. The thought of her drew him on with such irresistible anticipation that it seemed as if the cumulative drive of vanished and unsated years evoked the tangible phantom almost. He actually felt it, soft and warm and clinging in his own, that was no longer incomplete and mutilated.

Yet it was not he who led and guided now, but, more and more, he who was being led. The hint had first betrayed its presence at the inn; it now openly declared itself. It had crossed the frontier into a positive sensation. Its growth, swiftly increasing all this time, had accomplished itself; he had ignored, somehow, both its genesis and quick development; the result he plainly recognised. She was expecting him, indeed, but it was more than expectation; there was calling in it—she summoned him. Her thought and longing reached him along that old, invisible track love builds so easily between true, faithful hearts. All the forces of her being, her very voice, came towards him through the deepening autumn twilight. He had not noticed the curious physical restoration in his hand, but he was vividly aware of this more magical alteration—that *she* led and guided him, drawing him ever more swiftly towards the little, white garden gate where she stood at this very moment, waiting. Her sweet strength compelled him; there was this new touch of something irresistible about the familiar journey, where formerly had been delicious yielding only, shy, tentative advance.

His footsteps hurried, faster and ever faster; so deep was the allurement in his blood, he almost ran. He reached the narrow, winding lane, and raced along it. He knew each bend, each angle of the holly hedge, each separate incident of ditch and stone. He could have plunged blindfold down it at top speed. The familiar perfumes rushed at him—dead leaves and mossy earth and ferns and dock leaves, bringing the bewildering currents of strong emotion in him all together as in a rising wave. He saw, then, the crumbling wall, the cedars topping it with spreading branches, the chimneys of the rectory. On his right bulked the outline of the old, grey church; the twisted, ancient yews, the company of gravestones, upright and leaning, dotting the ground like listening figures. But he looked at none of these. For, a little beyond, he already saw the five rough steps of stone that led from the lane towards a small, white garden gate. That gate at last shone before him, rising through the misty air. He reached it.

He stopped dead a moment. His heart, it seemed, stopped too, then took to violent hammering in his brain. There was a roaring in his mind, and yet a marvellous silence—just behind it. Then the roar of emotion died away. There was utter stillness. This stillness, silence, was all about him. The world seemed preternaturally quiet.

But the pause was too brief to measure. For the tide of emotion had receded only to come on again with redoubled power. He turned, leaped forward, clambered impetuously up the rough stone steps, and flung himself, breathless and exhausted, against the trivial barrier that stood between his eyes and—hers. In his wild, half violent impatience, however, he stumbled. That roaring, too, confused him. He fell forward, it seemed, for twilight had merged in darkenss, and he misjudged the steps, the distances he yet knew so well. For a moment, certainly, he lay at full length upon the uneven ground against the wall; the steps had tripped him. And then he raised himself and knocked. His right hand struck upon the small, white garden gate. Upon the two lost fingers he felt the impact. 'I am here,' he cried, with a deep sound in his throat as though utterance was choked and difficult. 'I have come back.'

For a fraction of a second he waited, while the world stood still and waited with him. But there was no delay. Her answer came at once: 'I am well.... I am happy.... I am waiting.'

And the voice was dear and marvellous as of old. Though the words were strange, reminding him of something dreamed, forgotten, lost, it seemed, he did not take special note of them. He only wondered that she did not open instantly that he might see her. Speech could follow, but sight came surely first! There was this lightning-flash of disappointment in him. Ah, she was lengthening out the marvellous moment, as often and often she had done before. It was to tease him that she made him wait. He knocked again; he pushed against the unyielding surface. For he noticed that it was unyielding; and there was a depth in the tender voice that he could not understand.

'Open!' he cried again, but louder than before. 'I have come back!' And, as he said it, the mist struck cold against his face.

But her answer froze his blood.

'I cannot open.'

And a sudden anguish of despair rose over him; the sound of her voice was strange; in it was faintness, distance as well as depth. It seemed to echo. Something frantic seized him then—the panic sense.

'Open, open! Come out to me!' he tried to shout. His voice failed oddly; there was no power in it. Something appalling struck him between the eyes. 'For God's sake, open. I'm waiting here! Open, and come out to me!'

The reply was muffled by distance that already seemed increasing; he was conscious of freezing cold about him—in his heart:

'I cannot. You must come in to me.'

He knew not exactly then what happened, for the cold grew dreadful and the icy mist was in his throat. No words would come. He rose to his knees, and from his knees to his feet. He stooped. With all his force he knocked again; in a blind frenzy of despair he hammered and beat against the unyielding barrier of the small, white garden gate. He battered it till the skin of his knuckles was torn and bleeding—the first two fingers of a hand already mutilated. He remembered the torn and broken skin, for he noticed in the gloom that stains upon the gate bore witness to his violence; it was not till afterwards that he remembered the other fact—that the hand had already suffered mutilation, long, long years ago. The power of sound was feebly in him; he called aloud; there was no answer. He tried to scream, but the scream was muffled in his throat before it issued properly; it was a nightmare scream. As a last resort he flung himself bodily upon the unyielding gate, with such precipitate violence, moreover, that his face struck against its surface.

From the friction, then, along the whole length of his cheek he knew that the surface was not smooth. Cold and rough that surface was; but also—it was not of wood. Moreover, there was writing on it he had not seen before. How he deciphered it in the gloom, he never knew. The lettering was deeply cut. Perhaps he traced it with his fingers; his right hand certainly lay stretched upon it. He made out a name, a date, a broken verse from the Bible, and strange words: '*Je suis la première au rendez-vous. Je vous attends.*' The lettering way sharply cut with edges that were new. For the date was of a week ago; the broken verse ran, 'When the shadows flee away ...' and the small, white garden gate was unyielding because it was of— stone.

At the inn he found himself staring at a table from which the tea things had not been cleared away. There was a railway time-table in his hands, and his head was bent forwards over it, trying to decipher the lettering in the growing twilight.

THE TRYST

Beside him, still fingering a florin, stood the serving-girl; her other hand held a brown tray with a running dog painted upon its dented surface. It swung to and fro a little as she spoke, evidently continuing a conversation her customer had begun. For she was giving information—in the colourless, disinterested voice such persons use:

'We all went to the funeral, sir, all the country people went. The grave was her father's—the family grave....' Then, seeing that her customer was too absorbed in the time-table to listen further, she said no more but began to pile the tea things on to the tray with noisy clatter.

Ten minutes later, in the road, he stood hesitating. The signal at the station just opposite was already down. The autumn mist was rising. He looked along the winding road that melted away into the distance, then slowly turned and reached the platform just as the London train came in. He felt very old—too old to walk three miles....

THE WINGS OF HORUS

Binovitch had the bird in him somewhere: in his features, certainly, with his piercing eye and hawk-like nose; in his movements, with his quick way of flitting, hopping, darting; in the way he perched on the edge of a chair; in the manner he pecked at his food; in his twittering, high-pitched voice as well; and, above all, in his airy, flashing mind. He skimmed all subjects and picked their heart out neatly, as a bird skims lawn or air to snatch its prey. He had the bird's-eye view of everything. He loved birds and understood them instinctively; could imitate their whistling notes with astonishing accuracy. Their one quality he had not was poise and balance. He was a nervous little man; he was neurasthenic. And he was in Egypt by doctor's orders.

Such imaginative, unnecessary ideas he had! Such uncommon beliefs!

'The old Egyptians,' he said laughingly yet with a touch of solemn conviction in his manner, 'were a great people. Their consciousness was different from ours. The bird idea, for instance, conveyed a sense of deity to them—of bird deity, that is: they had sacred birds—hawks, ibis, and so forth—and worshipped them.' And he put his tongue out as though to say with challenge, 'Ha, ha!'

'They also worshipped cats and crocodiles and cows,' grinned Palazov. Binovitch seemed to dart across the table at his adversary. His eyes flashed; his nose pecked the air. Almost one could imagine the beating of his angry wings.

'Because everything alive,' he half screamed, 'was a symbol of some spiritual power to them. Your mind is as literal as a dictionary and as incoherent. Pages of ink without connected meaning! Verb always in the infinitive! If you were an old Egyptian, you—you'—he flashed and spluttered, his tongue shot out again, his keen eyes blazed—'you would take all those words and spin them into a great interpretation of life, a cosmic romance, as they did. Instead, you get the bitter, dead taste of ink in your mouth, and spit it over us—like that'—he made a quick movement of his whole body as a bird that shakes itself—'in empty phrases.'

Khilkoff ordered another bottle of champagne, while Vera, his sister, said half nervously, 'Let's go for a drive: it's moonlight.' There was enthusiasm at once. Another of the party called the head waiter and told him to pack food and drink in baskets. It was only eleven o'clock. They would drive out into the desert, have a meal at two in the morning, tell stories, sing, and see the dawn.

It was in one of those cosmopolitan hotels in Egypt which attract the ordinary tourists as well as those who are doing a 'cure,' and all these Russians were ill with one thing or another. All were ordered out for their health, and all were the despair of their doctors. They were as unmanageable as a bazaar and as incoherent. Excess and bed were their routine. They lived, but none of them got better. Equally, none of them got angry. They talked in this strange personal way without a shred of malice or offence. The English, French, and Germans in the hotel watched them with remote amazement, referring to them as 'that Russian lot'. Their energy was elemental. They never stopped. They merely disappeared when the pace became too fast, then reappeared after a day or two, and resumed their 'living' as before. Binovitch, despite his neurasthenia, was the life of the party. He was also a special patient of Dr. Plitzinger, the famous psychiatrist, who took a peculiar interest in his case. It was not surprising. Binovitch was a man of unusual ability and of genuine, deep culture. But there was something more about him that stimulated curiosity. There was this striking originality. He said and did surprising things.

'I could fly if I wanted to,' he said once when the airmen came to astonish the natives with their biplanes over the desert, 'but without all that machinery and noise. It's only a question of believing and understanding——'

'Show us!' they cried. 'Let's see you fly!'

'He's got it! He's off again! One of his impossible, delightful moments!'

These occasions when Binovitch let himself go always proved wildly entertaining. He said monstrously incredible things as though he really believed them. They loved his madness, for it gave them new sensations.

'It's only levitation, after all, this flying,' he exclaimed, shooting out his tongue between the words, as his habit was when excited; 'and what is levitation but a power of the air? None of you can hang an orange in space for a second, with all your scientific knowledge; but the moon is always levitated perfectly. And the stars. D'you think they swing on wires? What raised the enormous stones of ancient Egypt? D'you really believe it was heaped-up sand and ropes and clumsy leverage and all our weary and laborious mechanical contrivances? Bah! It was levitation. It was the powers of the air. Believe in those powers, and gravity becomes a mere nursery trick—true where it is, but true nowhere else. To know the fourth dimension is to step out of a locked room and appear instantly on the roof or in another country altogether. To know the powers of the air, similarly, is to annihilate what you call weight—and fly.'

'Show us, show us!' thy cried, roaring with delighted laughter.

'It's a question of belief,' he repeated, his tongue appearing and disappearing like a pointed shadow. 'It's in the heart; the power of the air gets into your whole being. Why should I show you? Why should I ask my deity to persuade your scoffing little minds by any miracle? For it is deity, I tell you, and nothing else. I know it. Follow *one* idea like that, as I follow my bird-idea—follow it with the impetus and undeviating concentration of a projectile—and you arrive at power. You know deity—the bird-idea of deity, that is. *They* knew that. The old Egyptians knew it.'

'Oh show us, show us!' they shouted impatiently, wearied of his nonsense-talk. 'Get up and fly! Levitate yourself, as they did! Become a star!'

THE WINGS OF HORUS

Binovitch turned suddenly very pale, and an odd light shone in his keen brown eyes. He rose slowly from the edge of the chair where he was perched. Something about him changed. There was silence instantly.

'I *will* show you,' he said calmly, to their intense amazement; 'not to convince your disbelief, but to prove it to myself. For the powers of the air are with me here. I believe. And Horus, great falcon-headed symbol, is my patron god.'

The suppressed energy in his voice and manner was indescribable. There was a sense of lifting, upheaving power about him. He raised his arms; his face turned upward; he inflated his lungs with a deep, long breath, and his voice broke into a kind of singing cry, half prayer, half chant:

> 'O Horus,
> Bright-eyed deity of wind,
> [1]Feather my soul
> Through earth's thick air,
> To know thy awful swiftness—'

He broke off suddenly. He climbed lightly and swiftly upon the nearest table—it was in a deserted card-room, after a game in which he had lost more pounds than there are days in the year—and leaped into the air. He hovered a second, spread his arms and legs in space, appeared to float a moment —then buckled, rushed down and forward, and dropped in a heap upon the floor, while everyone roared with laughter.

But the laughter died out quickly, for there was something in his wild performance that was peculiar and unusual. It was uncanny, not quite natural. His body had seemed, as with Mordkin and Nijinski, literally to hang upon the air a moment. For a second he gave the distressing impression of overcoming gravity. There was a touch in it of that faint horror which appals by its very vagueness. He picked himself up unhurt, and his face was as grave as a portrait in the Academy, but with a new expression in it that everybody noticed with this strange, half-shocked amazement. And it was this

[1]The original is untraslatable. The phrase means, 'Give my life wings.'

expression that extinguished the claps of laughter as wind takes away the sound of bells. Like many ugly men, he was an inimitable actor, and his facial repertory was endless and incredible. But this was neither acting nor clever manipulation of expressive features. There was something in his curious Russian physiognomy that made the heart beat slower. And that was why the laughter died away so suddenly.

'You ought to have flown farther,' cried someone. It expressed what all had felt.

'Icarus didn't drink champagne,' another replied, with a laugh; but nobody laughed with him.

'You went too near to Vera,' said Palazov, 'and passion melted the wax.' But his face twitched oddly as he said it. There was something he did not understand, and so heartily disliked.

The strange expression on the features deepened. It was arresting in a disagreeable, almost in a horrible way. The talk stopped dead; all stared; there was a feeling of dismay in everybody's heart, yet unexplained. Some lowered their eyes, or else looked stupidly elsewhere; but the women of the party felt a kind of fascination. Vera, in particular, could not move her sight away. The joking reference to his passionate admiration for her passed unnoticed. There was a general and individual sense of shock. And a chorus of whispers rose instantly:

'Look at Binovitch! What's happened to his face?'

'He's changed—he's changing!'

'God! Why he looks like a—bird!'

But no one laughed. Instead, they chose the names of birds —hawk, eagle, even owl. The figure of a man leaning against the edge of the door, watching them closely, they did not notice. He had been passing down the corridor, had looked in unobserved, and then had paused. He had seen the whole performance. He watched Binovitch narrowly now with calm, discerning eyes. It was Dr. Plitzinger, the great psychiatrist.

For Binovitch had picked himself up from the floor in a way that was oddly self-possessed, and precluded the least possibility of the ludicrous. He looked neither foolish nor abashed. He looked surprised, but also he looked half angry and half frightened. As someone had said, he 'ought to have flown farther.' That was the incredible impression his acrobatics had produced—incredible, yet somehow actual. This uncanny idea prevailed, as at a séance where nothing genuine is expected to happen, and something genuine, after all, does happen. There was no pretence in this: Binovitch had flown.

And now he stood there, white in the face—with terror and with anger white. He looked extraordinary, this little, neurasthenic Russian, but he looked at the same time half terrific. Another thing, not commonly experienced by men, was in him, breaking out of him, affecting *directly* the minds of his companions. His mouth opened; blood and fury shone in his blazing eyes; his tongue shot out like an ant-eater's, though even in this the comic had no place. His arms were spread like flapping wings, and his voice rose poignantly:

'He failed me, he failed me!' he tried to shout. 'Horus, my falcon-headed deity, my power of the air, deserted me! Hell take him! Hell burn his wings and blast his piercing sight! Hell scorch him into dust for his false prophecies! I curse him—I curse Horus!'

The voice that should have roared across the silent room emitted, instead, this high-pitched, bird-like scream. The added touch of sound, the reality it lent, was ghastly. Yet it was marvellously done and acted. The entire thing was a bit of instantaneous inspiration—his voice, his words, his gestures, his whole wild appearance. Only—here was the reality that caused the sense of shock—the expression on his altered features was genuine. *That* was not assumed. There was something new and alien in him, something cold and difficult to human life, something alert and swift and cruel, of another element than earth. A strange, rapacious grandeur had leaped upon the struggling features. The face looked hawk-like.

And he came forward suddenly and sharply toward Vera, whose fixed, staring eyes had never once ceased to watch him with a kind of anxious yet eager fascination. She was both drawn and beaten back. Binovitch advanced on tiptoe. No doubt he still was acting, still pretending this mad nonsense that he worshipped Horus, the falcon-headed deity of forgotten days, and that Horus had failed him in his hour of need; but somehow there was just a hint of too much reality in the way he moved and looked. The girl, a little creature, with fluffy golden hair, opened her lips; her cigarette fell to the floor; she shrank back; she looked for a moment like some smaller, coloured bird trying to escape from a great pursuing hawk; she screamed. Binovitch, his arms wide, his bird-like face thrust forward, had swooped upon her. He leaped. Almost he caught her.

No one could say exactly what happened. Play, become suddenly and unexpectedly too real, confuses the emotions. The change of key was swift. From fun to terror is a dislocating jolt upon the mind. Someone—it was Khilkoff, the brother—upset a chair; everybody spoke at once; everybody stood up. An unaccountable feeling of disaster was in the air, as with those drinkers' quarrels that blaze out from nothing, and end in a pistol-shot and death, no one able to explain clearly how it came about. It was the silent, watching figure in the doorway who saved the situation. Before anyone had noticed his approach, there he was among the group, laughing, talking, applauding—between Binovitch and Vera. He was vigorously patting his patient on the back, and his voice rose easily above the general clamour. He was a strong, quiet personality; even in his laughter there was authority. And his laughter now was the only sound in the room, as though by his mere presence peace and harmony were restored. Confidence came with him. The noise subsided; Vera was in her chair again. Khilkoff poured out a glass of wine for the great man.

'The Czar!' said Plitzinger, sipping his champagne, while all stood up, delighted with his compliment and tact. 'And to your opening night with the Russian ballet,' he added quickly a second toast, 'or to your first performance at the Moscow Théâtre des Arts!' Smiling significantly, he glanced at Binovitch; he clinked glasses with him. Their arms were already linked, but it was Palazov who noticed that the doctor's fingers seemed rather tight upon the creased black coat. All drank, looking with laughter, yet with a touch of respect, toward Binovitch, who stood there dwarfed beside the stalwart Austrian, and suddenly as meek and subdued as any mole. Apparently the abrupt change of key had taken his mind successfully off something else.

'Of course—"The Fire-Bird."' exclaimed the little man, mentioning the famous Russian ballet. 'The very thing!' he exclaimed. 'For *us*,' he added, looking with devouring eyes at Vera. He was greatly pleased. He began talking vociferously about dancing and the rationale of dancing. They told him he was an undiscovered master. He was delighted. He winked at Vera and touched her glass again with his. 'We'll make our début together,' he cried. 'We'll begin at Covent Garden, in London. I'll design the dresses and the posters "The Hawk and the Dove!" *Magnifique!* I in dark grey, and you in blue and gold! Ah, dancing, you know, is sacred. The little self is lost, absorbed. It is ecstasy, it is divine. And dancing in air— the passion of the birds and stars—ah! they are the movements of the gods. You know deity that way—by living it.'

He went on and on. His entire being had shifted with a leap upon this new subject. The idea of realising divinity by dancing it absorbed him. The party discussed it with him as though nothing else existed in the world, all sitting now and talking eagerly together. Vera took the cigarette he offered her, lighting it from her own; their fingers touched; he was as harmless and normal as a retired diplomat in a drawing room. But it was Plitzinger whose subtle manoeuvring had accomplished the change so cleverly, and it was Plitzinger who presently suggested a game of billiards, and led him off, full now of a fresh enthusiasm for cannons, balls, and pockets, into another room. They departed arm in arm, laughing and talking together.

Their departure, it seemed, made no great difference at first. Vera's eyes watched him out of sight, then turned to listen to Baron Minski, who was describing with gusto how he caught wolves alive for coursing purposes. The speed and power of the wolf, he said, was impossible to realise; the force of their awful leap, the strength of their teeth, which could bite through metal stirrup-fastenings. He showed a scar on his arm and another on his lip. He was telling truth, and everybody listened with deep interest. The narrative lasted perhaps the minutes or more, when Minski abruptly stopped. He had come to an end; he looked about him; he saw his glass, and emptied it. There was a general pause. Another subject did not at once present itself. Sighs were heard; several fidgeted; fresh cigarettes were lighted. But there was no sign of boredom, for where one or two Russians are gathered together there is always life. They produce gaiety and enthusiasm as wind produces waves. Like great children, they plunge wholeheartedly into whatever interest presents itself at the moment. There is a kind of uncouth gambolling in their way of taking life. It seems as if they are always fighting that deep, underlying, national sadness which creeps into their very blood.

'Midnight!' then exclaimed Palazov, abruptly, looking at his watch; and the others fell instantly to talking about that watch, admiring it and asking questions. For the moment that very ordinary timepiece became the centre of observation. Palazov mentioned the price. 'It never stops,' he said proudly, 'not even under water'. He looked up at everybody, challenging admiration. And he told how, at a country house, he made a bet that he would swim to a certain island in the lake, and won the bet. He and a girl were the winners, but as it was a horse they had bet, he got nothing out of it for himself, giving the horse to her. It was a genuine grievance in him. One felt he could have cried as he spoke of it. 'But the watch went all the time,' he said delightedly, holding the gunmetal object in his hand to show, 'and I was twelve minutes in the water with my clothes on.'

Yet this fragmentary talk was nothing but pretence. The sound of clicking billiard-balls was audible from the room at the end of the corridor. There was another pause. The pause, however, was intentional. It was not vacuity of mind or absence of ideas that caused it. There was another subject, an unfinished subject, that each member of the group was still considering. Only no one cared to begin about it, till at last, unable to resist the strain any longer, Palazov turned to Khilkoff, who was saying he would take a 'whisky-soda,' as the champagne was too sweet, and whispered something beneath his breath; whereupon Khilkoff, forgetting his drink, glanced at his sister, shrugged his shoulders, and made a curious grimace. 'He's all right now'—his reply was just audible—'he's with Plitzinger.' He cocked his head sidewise to indicate that the clicking of the billiard-balls still was going on.

The subject was out: all turned their heads; voices hummed and buzzed; questions were asked and answered or half answered; eyebrows were raised, shoulders shrugged, hands spread out expressively. There came into the atmosphere a feeling of presentiment, of mystery, of things half understood; primitive, buried instinct stirred a little, the kind of racial dread of vague emotions that might gain the upper had if encouraged. They shrank from looking something in the face, while yet this unwelcome influence drew closer round them all. They discussed Binovitch and his astonishing performance. Pretty little Vera listened with large and troubled eyes, though saying nothing. The Arab waiter had put out the lights in the corridor, and only a solitary cluster burned now above their heads, leaving their faces in shadow. In the distance the clicking of the billiard-balls still continued.

'It was not play; it was real,' exclaimed Minski vehemently. 'I can catch wolves,' he blurted; 'but birds—ugh!—and human birds!' He was half inarticulate. He had witnessed something he could not understand, and it had touched instinctive terror in him. 'It was the way he leaped that put the wolf first into my mind, only it was not a wolf at all.' The others agreed and disagreed. 'It was play at first, but it was reality at the end,' another whispered; 'and it was no animal he mimicked, but a bird, and a bird of prey at that!'

Vera thrilled. In the Russian woman hides that touch of savagery which loves to be caught, mastered, swept helplessly away, captured utterly and deliciously by the one strong enough to do it thoroughly. She left her chair and sat down beside an older woman in the party, who took her arm quietly at once. Her little face wore a perplexed expression, mournful, yet somehow wild. It was clear that Binovitch was not indifferent to her.

'It's become an *idée fixe* with him,' this older woman said. 'The bird-idea lives in his mind. He lives it in his imagination. Ever since that time at Edfu, when he pretended to worship the great stone flacons ouside the temple—the Horus figures—he's been full of it.' She stopped. The way Binovitch had behaved at Edfu was better lefet unmentioned at the moment, perhaps. A slight shiver ran round the listening group, each one waiting for someone else to focus their emotion, and so explain it by saying the convincing thing. Only no one ventured. Then Vera abruptly gave a little jump.

'Hark!' she exclaimed, in a staccato whisper, speaking for the first time. She sat bolt upright. She was listening. 'Hark!' she repeated. 'There it is again, but nearer than before. It's coming closer. I hear it.' She trembled. Her voice, her manner, above all her great staring eyes, startled everybody. No one spoke for several seconds; all listened. The halls and corridors lay in darkness, and gloom was over the big hotel. Everybody was in bed. But the clicking of the billiard-balls had ceased.

'Hear what?' asked the older woman soothingly, yet with a perceptible quaver in her voice, too. She was aware that the girl's hand tightened upon her arm.

'Do you not hear it, too?' the girl whispered.

All listened without speaking. All watched her paling face. Something wonderful, yet half incomprehensible, seemed in the air about them. There was a dull murmur, audible, faint, remote, its direction hard to tell. It had come suddenly from nowhere. They shivered. That strange racial thrill again passed into the group, unwelcome, unexplained. It was aboriginal; it belonged to the unconscious primitive mind, half childish, half terrifying.

'*What* do you hear?' her brother asked angrily—the irritable anger of nervous fear.

'When he came at me,' she answered very low, 'I heard it first. I hear it now again. Listen! He's coming.'

And at that minute, out of the dark mouth of the corridor, emerged two human figures, Plitzinger and Binovitch. Their game was over; they were going up to bed. They passed the open door of the card-room. But Binovitch was being half dragged, half restrained, for he was apparently attempting to run down the passage with flying, dancing leaps. He bounded. It was like a huge bird trying to rise for flight, while his companion kept him down by force upon the earth. As they entered the strip of light, Plitzinger changed his own position, placing himself swiftly between his companion and the group in the dark corner of the room. He hurried Binovitch along as though he sheltered him from view. They passed into the shadows down the passage. They disappeared. And everyone looked significantly, questioningly at his neighbour, though at first saying no word. It seemed that a curious disturbance of the air had followed them audibly.

Vera was the first to open her lips. 'You heard it *then*,' she said breathlessly, her face whiter than the ceiling.

'Damn!' exclaimed her brother furiously. 'It was wind against the outside walls—wind in the desert. The sand is driving.'

Vera looked at him. She shrank closer against the side of the older woman, whose arm was tight about her.

'It was *not* wind,' she whispered simply.

She paused. All waited uneasily for the completion of her sentence. They stared into her face like peasants who expected a miracle.

'Wings,' she whispered. 'It was the sound of wings.'

And at four o'clock in the morning, when they all returned exhausted from their excursion into the desert, little Binovitch was sleeping soundly and peacefully in his bed. They passed his door on tiptoe. But he did not hear them. He was dreaming. His spirit was at Edfu, experiencing with that ancient diety who was master of all flying life those strange enjoyments upon which his own troubled human heart was passionately set. Safe with that mighty falcon whose powers his lips had scorned a few hours before, his soul, released in vivid dream, went sweetly flying. It was amazing, it was gorgeous. He shimmed the Nile at lightning speed. Dashing down headlong from the height of the great Pyramid, he chased with faultless accuracy a little dove that sought vainly to hide from his terrific pursuit beneath the palm trees. For what he loved must worship where he worshipped, and the majesty of those tremendous effigies had fired his imagination to the creative point where expression was imperative.

Then suddenly, at the very moment of delicious capture, the dream turned horrible, becoming awful with the nightmare touch. The sky lost all its blue and sunshine. Far, far below him the little dove enticed him into nameless depths, so that he flew faster and faster, yet never fast enough to overtake it. Behind him came a great thing down the air, black, hovering, with gigantic wings outstretched. It had terrific eyes, and the beating of its feathers stole his wind away. It followed him, crowding space. He was aware of a colossal beak, curved like a scimitar and pointed wickedly like a troth of steel. He dropped. He faltered. He tried to scream.

Through empty space he fell, caught by the neck. The huge spectral falcon was upon him. The talons were in his heart. And in sleep he remembered then that he had cursed. He recalled his reckless language. The curse of the ignorant is meaningless; that of the worshipper is real. This attack was on his soul. He had invoked it. He realised next, with a shock of ghastly horror, that the dove he chased was, after all, the bait that had lured him purposely to destruction ... and awoke with a suffocating terror upon him, and his entire body bathed in icy perspiration. Outside the open window he heard a sound of wings retreating with powerful strokes into the surrounding darkness of the sky.

The nightmare made its impression upon Binovitch's impressionable and dramatic temperament. It aggravated his tendencies. He related it next day to Mme. de Drühn, the friend of Vera, telling it with that somewhat boisterous laughter some minds use to disguise less kind emotions. But he received no encouragement. The mood of the previous night was not recoverable; it was already ancient hitory. Russians never make the banal mistake of repeating a sensation till it is exhausted; they hurry on to novelties. Life flashes and rushes with them, never standing still for exposure before the cameras of their minds. Mme. de Drühn, however, took the trouble to mention the matter to Plitzinger, for Plitzinger, like Freud of Vienna, held that dreams revealed subconscious tendencies which sooner or later must betray themselves in action.

'Thank you for telling me,' he smiled politely; 'but I have already heard it from him.' He watched her eyes a moment, really examining her soul. 'Binovitch, you see,' he continued, apparently satisfied with what he saw, 'I regard as that rare phenomenon—a genius without an outlet. His spirit, intensely creative, finds no adequate expression. His power of production is enormous and prolific; yet he accomplishes nothing.' He paused an instant. 'Binovitch, therefore, is in danger of poisoning—himself.' He looked steadily into her face, as a man who weighs how much he may confide. 'Now,' he continued, '*if* we can find an outlet for him, a field wherein his bursting imaginative genius can produce results—above all, *visible* results'—he shrugged his shoulders—'the man is saved. Otherwise'—he looked extraordinarily impressive—'there is bound to be sooner or later——'

'Madness?' she asked very quietly.

'An explosion, let us say,' he replied gravely. 'For instance, take this Horus obsession of his, quite wrong archaeologically though it is. *Au fond* it is megalomania of a most unusual kind. His passionate interet, his love, his worship of birds, wholesome enough in themselves, find no satisfying outlet. A man who really loves birds neither keeps them in cages, nor shoots, nor stuffs them. What, then can, he do? The commonplace bird-lover observes them through glasses, studies their habits, then writes a book about them. But a man like Binovitch, overflowing with this intense creative power of mind and imagination, is not content with that. He wants to know them from within. He wants to feel what they feel, to live their life. He wants to *become* them.... You follow me? Not quite. Well, he seeks to be identified with the object of his sacred, passionate adoration. All genius seeks to know the thing-itself from its own point of view. It desires union. That tendency, unrecognised by himself, perhaps, and therefore subconscious, hides in his very soul.' He paused a moment. 'And the sudden sight of those majestic figures at Edfu—that crystallisation of his *idée fixe* in granite—took hold of this excess in him, so to speak—and is now focusing it toward some definite act. Binovitch sometimes—feels himself a bird! You noticed what occurred last night?'

She nodded; a slight shiver passed over her.

'A most curious performance,' she murmured; 'an exhibition I never want to see again.'

'The most curious part,' replied the doctor coolly, 'was its truth.'

'Its truth!' she exclaimed beneath her breath. She was frightened by something in his voice and by the uncommon gravity in his eyes. It seemed to arrest her intelligence. She felt upon the edge of things beyond her. 'You mean that Binovitch did for a moment—hang—in the air?' The other verb, the right one, she could not bring herself to use.

The great man's face was enigmatical. He talked to her sympathy, perhaps, rather than to her mind.

'Real genius,' he said smilingly, 'is as rare as talent, even great talent, is common. It means that the personality, if only for one second, becomes everything; becomes the universe; becomes the soul of the world. It gets the flash. It is identified with the universal life. Being everything and everywhere, all is possible to it—in that second of vivid realisation. It can brood with the crystal, grow with the plant, leap with the animal and fly with the bird: genius unifies all three. That is the meaning of 'creative.' It is faith. Knowing it, you can pass through fire and not be burned, walk on water and not sink, move a mountain, fly. Because you *are* fire, water, earth, air. Genius, you see, is madness in the magnificent sense of being superhuman. Binovitch has it.'

He broke off abruptly, seeing he was not understood. Some great enthusiasm in him he deliberately suppressed.

'The point is,' he resumed, speaking more carefully, 'that we must try to lead this passionately constructive genius of the man into some human channel that will absorb it, and therefore render it harmless.'

'He loves Vera,' the woman said, bewildered, yet seizing this point correctly.

'But would he marry her?' asked Plitzinger at once.

'He is already married.'

The doctor looked steadily at her a moment, hesitating whether he should utter all his thought.

'In that case,' he said slowly after a pause, 'it is better he or she should leave.'

His tone and manner were exceedingly impressive.

'You mean there's danger?' she asked.

'I mean, rather,' he replied earnestly, 'that this great creative flood in him, so curiously focused now upon his Horus falcon-bird idea, may result in some act of violence——'

'Which would be madness,' she said, looking hard at him.

'Which would be disastrous,' he corrected her. And then he added slowly: 'Because in the mental moment of creation he might overlook material laws.'

The costume ball two nights later was a great success. Palazov was a Bedouin, and Khilkoff an Apache; Mme. de Drühn wore a national headdress; Minski looked almost natural as Don Quixote; and the entire Russian 'set' was cleverly, if somewhat extravagantly, dressed. But Binovitch and Vera were the most successful of all the two hundred dancers who took part. Another figure, a big man dressed as a Pierrot, also claimed exceptional attention, for though the costume was commonplace enough, there was something of dignity in his appearance that drew the eyes of all upon him. But he wore a mask, and his identity was not discoverable.

It was Binovitch and Vera, however, who must have won the prize, if prize there had been, for they not only looked their parts, but acted them as well. The former in his dark grey feather tunic, and his falcon mask, complete even to the brown hooked beak and tufted talons, looked fierce and splendid. The disguise was so admirable, yet so entirely natural, that it was uncommonly seductive. Vera, in blue and gold, a charming head-dress of a dove upon her loosened hair, and a pair of little dove-pale wings fluttering from her shoulders, her tiny twinkling feet and slender ankles well visible, too, was equally successful and admired. Her large and timid eyes, her flitting movements, her light and dainty way of dancing—all added touches that made the picture perfect.

How Binovitch contrived his dress remained a mystery, for the layers of wings upon his back were real; the large black kites that haunt the Nile, soaring in their hundreds over Cairo and the bleak Mokattam Hills, had furnished them. He had procured them none knew how. They measured five feet across from tip to tip; they swished and rustled as he swept along; they were true falcons' wings. He danced with nautch girls and Egyptian princesses and Rumanian gipsies; he danced well, with beauty, grace, and lightness. But with Vera he did not dance at all; with her he simply flew. A kind of passionate abandon was in him as he skimmed the floor with her in a way that made everybody turn to watch them. They seemed to leave the ground together. It was delightful, an amazing sight; but it was peculiar. The strangeness of it was on many lips. Somehow its queer extravagance communicated itself to the entire ball-room. They became the centre of observation. There were whispers.

'There's that extraordinary bird-man! Look! He goes by like a hawk. And he's always after that dove-girl. How marvellously he does it! It's rather awful. Who is he? I don't envy *her*.'

People stood aside when he rushed past. They got out of his way. He seemed for ever pursuing Vera, even when dancing with another partner. Word passed from mouth to mouth.

A kind of telepathic interest was established everywhere. It was a shade too real sometimes, something unduly earnest in the chasing wildness, something unpleasant. There was even alarm.

'It's rowdy; I'd rather not see it; it's quite disgraceful,' was heard. '*I* think it's horrible; you can see she's terrified.'

And once there was a little scene, trivial enough, yet betraying this reality that many noticed and disliked. Binovitch came up to claim a dance, programme clutched in his great tufted claws, and at the same moment the big Pierrot appeared abruptly round the corner with a similar claim. Those who saw it assert he had been waiting, and came on purpose, and that there was something protective and authoritative in his bearing. The misunderstanding was ordinary enough—both men had written her name against the dance but 'No. 13, Tango' also included the supper interval, and neither Hawk nor Pierrot would give way. They were very obstinate. Both men wanted her. It was awkward.

'The Dove shall decide between us,' smiled the Hawk politely, yet his taloned fingers working nervously. Pierrot, however, more experienced in the ways of dealing with women, or more bold, said suavely:

'I am ready to abide by her decision'—his voice poorly cloaked this aggravating authority, as though he had the right to her—'only I engaged this dance before His Majesty Horus appeared upon the scene at all, and therefore it is clear that Pierrot has the right of way.'

At once, with a masterful air, he took her off. There was no withstanding him. He meant to have her and he got her. Both yielding and resisting, she was swept away. They vanished among the maze of coloured dancers, leaving the Hawk, disconsolate and vanquished, amid the titters of the onlookers His swiftness, as against this steady power, was of no avail.

It was then that the singular phenomenon was witnessed first. Those who saw it affirm that he changed absolutely into the part he played. It was dreadful; it was not possible. A frightened whisper ran about the rooms and corridors:

'An extraordinary thing is in the air!'

Some shrank away, while others flocked to see. There were those who swore that a curious, rushing sound was audible, the atmosphere visibly disturbed and shaken; that a shadow fell upon the spot the couple had vacated; that a cry was heard, a high, wild, searching cry: 'Horus! bright deity of wind,' it began, then died away. One man was positive that the windows had been opened and that something had flown in. It was the obvious explanation. The thing spread rapidly. As in a fire panic, there was consternation and excitement. Confusion caught the feet of all the dancers. The music fumbled and lost time. The leading pair of tango dancers halted and looked round. It seemed that everybody pressed back, hiding, shuffling, eager to see, yet more eager not to be seen, as though something unusual, dangerous, terrible, had broken loose. In rows against the wall they stood. For a great space had made itself in the middle of the ball-room, and into this empty space reappeared suddenly the Pierrot and the Dove.

It was like a challenge. A sound of applause, half voices, half clapping of gloved hands, was heard. The couple danced exquisitely into the arena. All stared. There was an impression that a set piece had been prepared, and that this was its beginning. The music again took heart. Pierrot was strong and dignified, no whit nonplussed by this abrupt publicity. The Dove, though faltering, seemed deliciously obedient. They danced together like a single outline. She was captured utterly. And to the man who needed her the sight was naturally agonising—the protective way the Pierrot held her, the right and strength of it, the mastery the complete possession.

'He's still got her!' someone breathed too loud, uttering the thought of all. 'Good thing it's not the Hawk!'

And, to the absolute amazement of the throng, this sight was then apparent. A figure dropped through space. That high, shrill cry again was heard:

'Feather my soul ... to know thy awful swiftness!'

Its singing loveliness touched the heart, its appealing, passionate sweetness was marvellous, as from an upper gallery this figure of a man, dressed as a strong, dark bird, shot down with splendid grace and ease. The feathers swept; the wings spread out as sails that take the wind. Like a hawk that darts with unerring power and aim upon its prey, this thing of mighty wings rushed down into the empty space where the couple danced. Observed by all, he entered, swooping beautifully, stretching his wings like any eagle. He dropped. He fixed his point of landing with consummate skill close beside the astonished dancers. He landed.

It happened with such swiftness that it brought the dazzle and blindness as when lighting strikes. People in different parts of the room saw different details; a few saw nothing at all after the first startling shock, closing their eyes, or holding their arms before their faces as in self-protection. The touch of panic fear caught the entire room. The nameless thing that all the evening had been vaguely felt was come. It had suddenly materialised.

For this incredible thing occurred in the full blaze of light upon the open floor. Binovitch, grown in some sense formidable, opened his dark, big wings about the girl. He drew her to him. The long grey feathers moved, causing powerful draughts of wind that made a rushing sound. An aspect of the terrible was about him, like an emanation. The great beaked head was poised to strike, the tufted claws were raised like fingers that shut and opened, and the whole presentiment of his amazing figure focused in an attitude of attack that was magnificent and terrible. No one who saw it doubted. Yet there were those who swore that it was not Binovitch at all, but that another outline monstrous and shadowy, towered above him, draping his lesser proportions with two colossal wings of darkness. That some touch of strange divinity lay in it may be claimed, however confused the wild descriptions afterward. For many lowered their heads and bowed their shoulders. There was terror. There was also awe. The onlookers swayed as though some power passed over them across the air.

A sound of wings was certainly in the room.

Then someone screamed; a shriek broke high and clear; and emotion, ordinary, human emotion, unaccustomed to terrific things, swept loose. The Hawk and Vera flew—the girl with willing happiness, the man with power. Beaten back against the wall as by a stroke of whirlwind, the Pierrot staggered. He watched them go. Out of the lighted room they flew, out of the crowded human atmosphere, out of the heat and artificial light, the walled-in, airless halls that were a cage. All this they left behind. They seemed things of wind and air, made free happily of another element. Earth held them not. Toward the open night they raced with this extraordinary lightness as of birds, down the long corridor and on to the southern terrace, where great coloured curtains were hung suspended from the columns. A moment they were visible. Then the fringe of one huge curtain, lifted by the wind, showed their dark outline for a second against the starry sky. There was a cry, a leap. The curtain flapped again and closed. They vanished. And into the ball-room swept the cold draught of night air from the desert.

But three figures instantly were close upon their heels. The throng of half dazed, half stupefied onlookers, it seemed, projected them as though by some explosive force. The general mass held back, but, like projectiles, these three flung themselves after the fugitives down the corridor at high speed—the Apache, Don Quixote, and, last of them, the Pierrot. For Khilkoff, the brother, and Baron Minski, the man who caught wolves alive, had been for some time keenly on the watch, while Dr. Plitzinger, reading the symptoms clearly, never far away, had been faithfully observant of every movement. His mask tossed aside, the great psychiatrist was now recognised by all. They reached the parapet just as the curtain flapped back heavily into place; the next second all three were out of sight behind it. Khilkoff was first, however, urged forward at frantic speed by the warning words the doctor had whispered as they ran. Some thirty yards beyond the terrace was the brink of the crumbling cliff on which the great hotel was built, and there was a drop of sixty feet to the desert floor below. Only a low stone wall marked the edge.

Accounts varied. Khilkoff, it seems, arrived in time—in the nick of time—to seize his sister, virtually hovering on the brink. He heard the loose stones strike the sand below. There was a moment's violent struggle. She resisted the interference passionately and with all her strength at first. In a sence she was beside—outside—herself. And he did a characteristic thing; he not only brought her back into the ball-room, but he *danced* her back. It was admirable. Nothing could have calmed the general excitement better. The pair of them danced in together as though nothing was amiss. Accustomed to the strenuous practice of his Cossack regiment, this young cavalry officer's muscles were equal to the semi-dead weight in his arms. At most the onlookers thought her tired, perhaps. Confidence was restored—such is the psychology of a crowd—and in the middle of a thrilling Viennese waltz he easily smuggled her out of the room, administered brandy, and got her up to bed.... The absence of the Hawk, meanwhile, was hardly noticed; comments were made and then forgotten; it was Vera in whom the strange, anxious sympathy had centred. And, with her obvious safety, the moment of primitive, childish panic passed away. Don Quixote, too, was presently seen dancing gaily as though nothing untoward had happened; supper intervened; the incident was over; it had melted into the general wildness of the evening's irresponsibility. The fact that Pierrot did not appear again was noticed by no single person.

But Dr. Plitzinger was otherwise engaged, his heart and mind and soul all deeply exercised. A death-certificate is not always made out quite so simply as the public thinks. That Binovitch had died of suffocation in his swift descent through merely sixty feet of air was not conceivable; yet that his body lay so neatly placed upon the desert after such a fall was stranger still. It was not crumpled, it was not torn; no single bone was broken, no muscle wrenched; there was no bruise. There was no indenture in the sand. The figure lay sidewise as though in sleep, no sign of violence visible anywhere, the dark wings folded as a great bird folds them when it creeps away to die in loneliness. Beneath the Horus mask the face was smiling. It seemed he had floated into death upon the element he loved. And only Vera had seen the enormous wings that, hovering invitingly above the dark abyss, bore him so softly into another world. Plitzinger, that is, saw them, too, but he said firmly that they belonged to the big black falcons that haunt the Mokattam Hills and roost upon these ridges, close beside the hotel, at night. Both he and Vera, however, agreed on one thing: the high, sharp cry in the air above them, wild and plaintive, was certainly the black kite's cry—the note of the falcon that passionately seeks its mate. It was the pause of a second, when she stood to listen, that made her rescue possible. A moment later and she, too, would have flown to death with Binovitch.

INITIATION

A FEW years ago, on a Black Sea steamer heading for the Caucasus, I fell into conversation with an American. He mentioned that he was on his way to the Baku oil-fields, and I replied that I was going up into the mountains. He looked at me questioningly a moment. 'Your first trip?' he asked with interest. I said it was. A conversation followed; it was continued the next day, and renewed the following day, until we parted company at Batoum. I don't know why he talked so freely to me in particular. Normally, he was a taciturn, silent man. We had been fellow travellers from Marseilles, but after Constantinople we had the boat pretty much to ourselves. What struck me about him was his vehement, almost passionate, love of natural beauty—in seas and woods and sky, but above all in mountains. It was like a religion in him. His taciturn manner hid deep poetic feeling.

And he told me it had not always been so with him. A kind of friendship sprang up between us. He was a New York business man—buying and selling exchange between banks—but was English born. He had gone out forty years before, and become naturalised. His talk was exceedingly 'American', slangy, and almost Western. He said he had roughed it in the West for several years first. But what he chiefly talked about was mountains. He said it was in the mountains an unusual experience had come to him that had opened his eyes to many things, but principally to the beauty that was now everything to him, and to the—insignificance of death.

He knew the Caucasus well where I was going. I think that was why he was interested in me and my journey. 'Up there,' he said, 'you'll feel things—and maybe find out things you never knew before.'

'What kind of things?' I asked.

'Why, for one,' he replied with emotion and enthusiasm in his voice, 'that living and dying ain't either of them of much account. That if you know Beauty, I mean, and Beauty is in your life, you live on in it and with it for others—even when you're dead.'

The conversation that followed is too long to give here, but it led to his telling me the experience in his own life that had opened his eyes to the truth of what he said. 'Beauty is imperishable,' he declared, 'and if you live with it, why, you're imperishable too!'

The story, as he told it verbally in his curious language, remains vividly in my memory. But he had written it down, too, he said. And he gave me the written account, with the remark that I was free to hand it on to others if I 'felt that way'. He called it 'Initiation'. It runs as follows:

1

In my own family this happened, for Arthur was my nephew. And a remote Alpine valley was the place. It didn't seem to me in the least suitable for such occurrences, except that it was Catholic, and the 'Church', I understand—at least, scholars who ought to know have told me so—has subtle Pagana origins incorporated unwittingly in its observations of certain Saints' Days, as well as in certain ceremonials. All this kind of thing is Dutch to me, a form of poetry or superstition, for I am interested chiefly in the buying and selling of exchange, with an office in New Yok City, just off Wall Street, and only come to Europe now occasionally for a holiday. I like to see the dear old musty cities, and go to the Opera, and take a motor run through Shakespeare's country or round the Lakes, get in touch again with London and Paris at the Ritz Hotels—and then back again to the greatest city on earth, where for years now I've been making a good thing out of it. Repton and Cambridge, long since forgotten, had their uses. They were all right enough at the time. But I'm now 'on the make,' with a good fat partnership, and have left all that truck behind me.

My half-brother, however—he was my senior and got the

cream of the family wholesale chemical works—has stuck to the trade in the Old Country, and is making probably as much as I am. He approved my taking the chance that offered, and is only sore now because his son, Arthur, is on the stupid side. He agreed that finance suited my temperament far better than drugs and chemicals, though he warned me that all American finance was speculative and therefore dangerous. 'Arthur is getting on,' he said in his last letter, 'and will some day take the director's place you would be in now had you cared to stay. But he's a plodder, rather.' That meant, I knew, that Arthur was a fool. Business, at any rate, was not suited to his temperament. Some years ago, when I came home with a month's holiday to be used in working up connections in English banking circles, I saw the boy. He was fifteen years of age at the time, a delicate youth, with an artist's dreams in his big blue eyes, if my memory goes for anything, but with a tangle of yellow hair and features of classical beauty that would have made half the young girls of my New York set in love with him, and a choice of heiresses at his disposal when he wanted them.

I have a clear recollection of my nephew then. He struck me as having grit and character, but as being wrongly placed. He had his grandfather's tastes. He ought to have been, like him, a great scholar, a poet, and editor of marvellous old writings in new editions. I couldn't get much out of the boy, except that he 'liked the chemical business fairly', and meant to please his father by 'knowing it thoroughly' so as to qualify later for his directorship. But I have never forgotten the evening when I caught him in the hall, staring up at his grandfather's picture, with a kind of light about his face, and the big blue eyes all rapt and tender (moist, too, as if from tears), and replying, when I asked him what was up: '*That* was worth living for. He brought Beauty back into the world!'

'Yes,' I said, 'I guess that's right enough. He did. But there was no money in it to speak of.'

The boy looked at me and smiled. He twigged somehow or other that deep down in me, somewhere below the money-making instinct, a poet, but a dumb poet, lay in hiding. 'You know what I mean,' he said. 'It's in you too.'

The picture was a copy—my father had it made—of the presentation portrait given to Balliol, and 'the grandfather' was celebrated in his day for the translations he made of Anacreon and Sappho, of Homer, too, if I remember rightly, as well as for a number of classical studies and essays that he wrote. A lot of stuff like that he did, and made a name at it too. His 'Lives of the Gods' went into six editions. They said—the big critics of his day—that he was 'a poet who wrote no poetry, yet lived it passionately in the spirit of old-world, classical Beauty', and I know he was a wonderful felllow in his way and made the dons and schoolmasters all sit up. We're proud of him all right. After thirty years of successful 'exchange' in New York City, I confess I am unable to appreciate all that, feeling more in touch with the commercial and financial spirit of the age, progress, development and the rest. But, still, I'm not ashamed of the classical old boy, who seems to have been a good deal of a Pagan, judging by the records we have kept. However, Arthur peering up at that picture in the dusk, his eyes half moist with emotion, and his voice gone positively shaky, is a thing I never have forgotten. He stimulated my curiosity uncommonly. It stirred something deep down in me that I hardly cared to acknowledge on Wall Street—something burning.

And the next time I saw him was in the summer of 1910, when I came to Europe for a two months' look around—my wife at Newport with the children—and hearing that he was in Switzerland, learning a bit of French to help him in the business, I made a point of dropping in upon him just to see how he was shaping generally and what new kinks his mind had taken on. There was something in Arthur I never could quite forget. Whenever his face came into my mind I began to think. A kind of longing came over me — a desire for Beauty, I guess, it was. It made me dream.

I found him at an English tutor's—a lively old dog, with a fondness for the cheap native wines and a financial interest in

INITIATION

the tourist development of the village. The boys learnt French in the mornings, possibly, but for the rest of the day were free to amuse themselves exactly as they pleased and without a trace of supervision—provided the parents footed the bills without demur.

This suited everybody all round; and as long as the boys came home with an accent and a vocabulary, all was well. For myself, having learned in New York to attend strictly to my own business—exchange between different countries with a profit—I did not deem it necessary to exchange letters and opinions with my brother—with no chance of profit anywhere. But I got to know Arthur, and had a queer experience of my own into the bargain. Oh, there was profit in it for me. I'm drawing big dividends to this day on the investment.

I put up at the best hotel in the village, a one-horse show, differing from the other inns only in the prices charged for a lot of cheap decoration in the dining-room, and went up to surprise my nephew with a call the first thing after dinner. The tutor's house stood some way back from the narrow street, among fields where there were more flowers than grass, and backed by a forest of fine old timber that stretched up several thousand feet to the snow. The snow at least was visible, peeping out far overhead just where the dark line of forest stopped; but in reality, I suppose, that was an effect of foreshortening, and big slopes and pastures intervened between the trees and the snow-fields. The sunset, long since out of the valley, still shone on those white ridges, where the peaks stuck up like the teeth of a gigantic saw. I guess it meant five or six hours' good climbing to get up to them—and nothing to do when you got there. Switzerland, anyway, seemed a poor country, with its little bit of watch-making, sour wines, and every square yard hanging upstairs at an angle of 60 degrees used for hay. Picture post cards, chocolate and cheap tourists kept it going apparently, but I dare say it was all right enough to learn French in—and cheap as Hoboken to live in.

Arthur was out; I just left a card and wrote on it that I would be very pleased if he cared to step down to take luncheon with me at my hotel next day. Having nothing better to do, I strolled homewards by way of the forest.

Now what came over me in that bit of dark pine forest is more than I can quite explain, but I think it must have been due to the height—the village was 4,000 feet above sea-level—and the effect of the rarefied air upon my circulation. The nearest thing to it in my experience is rye whisky, the queer touch of wildness, of self-confidence, a kind of whooping rapture and the reckless sensation of being a tin god of sorts that comes from a lot of alcohol—a memory, please understand, of years before, when I thought it a grand thing to own the earth and paint the old town red. I seemed to walk on air, and there was a smell about those trees that made me suddenly—well, that took my mind clean out of its accustomed rut. It was just too lovely and wonderful for me to describe it. I had got well into the forest and lost my way a bit. The smell of an old-world garden wasn't in it. It smelt to me as if someone had just that minute turned out the earth all fresh and new. There was moss and tannin, a hint of burning, something between smoke and incense, say, and a fine clean odour or pitch-pine bark when the sun gets on it after rain—and a flavour of the sea thrown in for luck. That was the first I noticed, for I had never smelt anything half so good since my camping days on the coast of Maine. And I stood still to enjoy it. I threw away my cigar for fear of mixing things and spoiling it. 'If that could be bottled,' I said to myself, 'it'd sell for two dollars a pint in every city in the Union!'

And it was just then, while standing and breathing it in, that I got the queer feeling of someone watching me. I kept quite still. Someone was moving near me. The sweat went trickling down my back. A kind of childhood thrill got hold of me.

It was very dark. I was not afraid exactly, but I was a stranger in these parts and knew nothing about the habits of the mountain peasants. There might be tough customers lurking around after dark on the chance of striking some guy of a tourist with money in his pockets. Yet, somehow, that wasn't the kind of feeling that came to me at all, for, though I had a pocket Browning at my hip, the notion of getting at it did not even occur to me. The sensation was new—a kind of lifting, exciting sensation that made my heart swell out with exhilaration. There was happiness in it. A cloud that *weighed* seemed to roll off my mind, same as that light-hearted mood when the office door is locked and I'm off on a two months' holiday—with gaiety and irresponsibility at the back of it. It was invigorating. I felt youth sweep over me.

I stood there, wondering what on earth was coming on me, and half expecting that any moment someone would come out of the darkness and show himself; and as I held my breath and made no movement at all the queer sensation grew stronger. I believe I even resisted a temptation to kick up my heels and dance, to let out a flying shout as a man with liquor in him does. Instead of this, however, I just kept dead still. The wood was black as ink all round me, too black to see the tree-trunks separately, except far below where the village lights came up twinkling between them, and the only way I kept the path was by the soft feel of the pine-needles that were thicker than a Brussels carpet. But nothing happened, and no one stirred. The idea that I was being watched remained, only there was no sound anywhere except the roar of falling water that filled the entire valley. Yet someone was very close to me in the darkness.

I can't say how long I might have stood there, but I guess it was the best part of ten minutes, and I remember it struck me that I had run up against a pocket of extra-rarefied air that had a lot of oxygen in it—oxygen or something similar—and that was the cause of my elation. The idea was nonsense, I have no doubt; but for the moment it half explained the thing to me. I realised it was all *natural* enough, at any rate—and so moved on. It took a longish time to reach the edge of the wood, and a footpath led me—oh, it was quite a walk, I tell you—into the village street again. I was both glad and sorry to get there. I kept myself busy thinking the whole thing over again. What caught me all of a heap was that million-dollar sense of beauty, youth, and happiness. Never in my born days had I felt anything to touch it. And it hadn't cost a cent!

Well, I was sitting there enjoying my smoke and trying to puzzle it all out, and the hall was pretty full of people smoking and talking and reading papers, and so forth, when all of a sudden I looked up and caught my breath with such a jerk that I actually bit my tongue. There was grandfather in front of my chair! I looked into his eyes. I saw him as clear and solid as the porter standing behind his desk across the lounge, and it gave me a touch of cold all down the back that I needn't forget unless I want to. He was looking into my face, and he had a cap in his hand, and he was speaking to me. It was my grandfather's picture come to life, only much thinner and younger and a kind of light in his eyes like fire.

'I beg your pardon, but you *are*—Uncle Jim, aren't you?'

And then, with another jump of my nerves, I understood.

'You, Arthur! Well, I'm jiggered. So it is. Take a chair, boy. I'm right glad you found me. Shake! Sit down.' And I took his hand and pushed a chair up for him. I was never so surprised in my life. The last time I set eyes on him he was a boy. Now he was a young man, and the very image of his ancestor.

He sat down, fingering his cap. He wouldn't have a drink and he wouldn't smoke. 'All right,' I said, 'let's talk then. I've lots to tell you and I've lots to hear. How are you, boy?'

He didn't answer at first. He eyed me up and down. He hesitated. He was as handsome as a young Greek god.

'I say, Uncle Jim,' he began presently, 'it *was* you—just now—in the wood—wasn't it?' It made me start, that question put so quietly.

'I *have* just come through that wood up there,' I answered, pointing in the direction as well as I could remember, 'if that's what you mean. But why? *You* weren't there, were you?' It gave me a queer sort of feeling to hear him say it. What in the name of heaven did he mean?

He sat back in his chair with a sigh of relief.

INITIATION

'Oh, that's all right then,' he said, 'if it *was* you. Did you see,' he asked suddenly, 'did you see—anything?'

'Not a thing,' I told him honestly. 'It was far too dark.' I laughed. I fancied I twigged his meaning. But I was not the sort of uncle to come prying on him. Life must be dull enough, I remembered, in this mountain village.

But he didn't understand my laugh. He didn't mean what I meant.

And there came a pause between us. I discovered that we were talking different lingoes. I leaned over towards him.

'Look here, Arthur,' I said in a lower voice, 'what is it, and what do you mean? I'm all right, you know, and you needn't be afraid of telling me. What d'you mean by—did I see anything?'

We looked at each other squarely in the eye. He saw he could trust me, and I saw—well, a whole lot of things, perhaps, but I felt chiefly that he liked me and would tell me things later, all in his own good time. I liked him all the better for that too.

'I only meant' he answered slowly, 'whether you really *saw*—anything?'

'No,' I said straight, 'I didn't see a thing, but, by the gods, I *felt* something.'

He started. I started too. An astonishing big look came swimming over his fair, handsome face. His eyes seemed all lit up. He looked as if he'd just made a cool million in wheat or cotton.

'I knew—you were that sort,' he whispered. 'Though I hardly remembered what you looked like.'

'Then what on earth was it?' I asked.

His reply staggered me a bit. 'It was just that,' he said—'the Earth!'

And then, just when things were getting interesting and promising a dividend, he shut up like a clam. He wouldn't say another word. He asked after my family and business, my health, what kind of crossing I'd had, and all the rest of the common stock. It fairly bowled me over. And I couldn't change him either.

I suppose in America we get pretty free and easy, and don't quite understand reserve. But this young man of half my age kept me in my place as easily as I might have kept a nervous customer quiet in my own office. He just refused to take me on. He was polite and cool and distant as you please, and when I got pressing sometimes he simply pretended he didn't understand. I could no more get him back again to the subject of the wood than a customer could have gotten me to tell him about the prospects of exchange being cheap or dear—when I didn't know myself but wouldn't let him see I didn't know. He was charming, he was delightful, enthusiastic and even affectionate; downright glad to see me, too, and to chin with me—but I couldn't draw him worth a cent. And in the end I gave up trying.

And the moment I gave up trying he let down a little—but only a very little.

'You'll stay here some time, Uncle Jim, won't you?'

'That's my idea,' I said, 'if I can see you, and you can show me round some.'

He laughed with pleasure. 'Oh, rather. I've got lots of time. After three in the afternoon I'm free till—any time you like. There's a lot to see,' he added.

'Come along to-morrow then,' I said. 'If you can't take lunch, perhaps you can come just afterwards. You'll find me waiting for you—right here.'

'I'll come at three,' he replied, and we said good night.

2

HE turned up sharp on time, and I liked his punctuality. I saw him come swinging down the dusty road; tall, deep-chested, his broad shoulders a trifle high, and his head set proudly. He looked like a young chap in training, a thoroughbred, every inch of him. At the same time there was a touch of something a little too refined and delicate for a man, I thought. That was the poetic, scholarly vein in him, I guess—grandfather cropping out. This time he wore no cap. His thick light hair, not brushed back like the London shop-boys, but parted on the side, yet untidy for all that, suited him exactly and gave him a touch of wildness.

'Well,' he asked, 'what would you like to do, Uncle Jim? I'm at your service, and I've got the whole afternoon till supper at seven-thirty.' I told him I'd like to go through that wood. 'All right,' he said, 'come along. I'll show you.' He gave me one quick glance, but said no more. 'I'd like to see if I feel anything this time,' I explained. 'We'll locate the very spot, maybe.' He nodded. 'You know where I mean, don't you?' I asked, 'because you saw me there?' He just said yes, and then we started.

It was hot, and air was scarce. I remember that we went uphill, and that I realised there was considerable difference in our ages. We crossed some fields first—smothered in flowers so thick that I wondered how much grass the cows got out of it!—and then came to a sprinkling of fine young larches that looked as soft as velvet. There was no path, just a wild mountain side. I had very little breath on the steep zigzags, but Arthur talked easily—and talked mighty well, too: the light and shade, the colouring, and the effect of all this wilderness of lonely beauty on the mind. He kept all this suppressed at home in business. It was safety valves. I twigged *that*. It was the artist in him talking. He seemed to think there was nothing in the world but Beauty—with a big B all the time. And the odd thing was he took for granted that I felt the same. It was cute of him to flatter me that way. 'Daulis and the lone Cephissian vale,' I heard; and a few moments later—with a sort of reverence in his voice like worship—he called out a great singing name: '*Astarte!*'

> 'Day is her face, and midnight is her hair,
> And morning hours are but the golden stair
> By which she climbs to Night.'

'Steady on, boy! I've forgotten all my classics ages ago,' I cried.

He turned and gazed down on me, his big eyes glowing,

and not a sign of perspiration on his skin.

'That's nothing,' he exclaimed in his musical, deep voice. 'You know it, or you'd never have felt things in this wood last night; and you wouldn't have wanted to come out with me now!'

'How?' I gasped. 'How's that?'

'You've come,' he continued quietly, 'to the only valley in this artificial country that has atmosphere. This valley is *alive*—especially this end of it. There's superstition here, thank God! Even the peasants know things.'

It was here first that a queer change began to grow upon me too.

I stared at him. 'See here, Arthur,' I objected. 'I'm not a Cath. And I don't know a thing—at least it's all dead in me and forgotten—about poetry or classics or your gods and pan—pantheism—in spite of grandfather——'

His face turned like a dream face.

'Hush!' he said quickly. 'Don't mention *him*. There's a bit of him in you as well as in me, and it was here, you know, he wrote——'

I didn't hear the rest of what he said. A creep came over me. I remembered that this ancestor of ours lived for years in the isolation of some mountain forest where he claimed—he used that setting for his writing—to have found the exiled gods, their ghosts, their beauty, their eternal essence—or something astonishing of that sort. I had clean forgotten it till this moment. It all rushed back upon me, a memory of my boyhood.

And, as I say, a creep came over me—something as near to awe as ever could be. The sunshine on the field of yellow daisies and blue forget-me-nots turned paler. The warm valley wind had a touch of snow in it. And, ashamed and frightened of my baby mood, I looked at Arthur, meaning to choke him off with all this rubbish—and then saw something in his eyes that fairly scared me stiff.

I admit it. What's the use? There was an expression on his face that made my blood go curdled. I got cold feet right there. It mastered me. In him, behind him, near him—blest if I know which, *through* him probably—came an ernormous thing that turned me insignificant. It downed me utterly.

It was over in a second, the flash of a wing. I recovered instantly. No mere boy should come these muzzy tricks on me, scholar or no scholar. For the change in me was on the increase, and I shrank.

'See here, Arthur,' I said plainly once again, 'I don't know what your game is, but—there's something queer up here I don't quite get at. I'm only a business man, with classics and poetry all gone dry in me twenty years ago and more——'

He looked at me so strangely that I stopped, confused.

'But, Uncle Jim,' he said as quietly as though we talked tobacco brands, 'you needn't be alarmed. It's natural you should feel the place. You and I belong to it. We've both got *him* in us. You're just as proud of him as I am, only in a different way.' And then he added, with a touch of disappointment: 'I thought you'd like it. You weren't afraid last night. You felt the beauty *then*.'

Flattery is a darned subtle thing at any time. To see him standing over me in that superior way and talking down at my poor business mind—well, it just came over me that I was laying my cards on the table a bit too early. After so many years of city life——!

Anyway, I pulled myself together. 'I was only kidding you, boy,' I laughed. 'I feel this beauty just as much as you do. Only, I guess, you're more accustomed to it than I am. Come on now,' I added with energy, getting upon my feet, 'let's push on and see the wood. I want to find that place again.'

He pulled me with a hand of iron, laughing as he did so. Gee! I wished I had his teeth, as well as the muscles in his arm. Yet I, too, felt younger, somehow—youth flowed more and more into my veins. I had forgotten how sweet the winds and woods and flowers could be. Something melted in me. For it was Spring, and the whole world was singing like a dream. Beauty was creeping over me. I don't know. I began to feel all big and tender and open to a thousand wonderful sensations.

The thought of streets and houses seemed like death....

We went on again, not talking much; my breath got shorter and shorter, and he kept looking about him as though he expected something. But we passed no living soul, not even a peasant; there were no chalets, no cattle, no cattle-shelters even. And then I realised that the valley lay at our feet in haze and that we had been climbing at least a couple of hours. 'Why, last night I got home in twenty minutes at the outside,' I said. He shook his head, smiling. 'It seemed like that,' he replied, 'but you really took much longer. It was long after ten when I found you in the hall.' I reflected a moment. 'Now I come to think of it, you're right, Arthur. Seems curious, though, somehow.' He looked closely at me. 'I followed you all the way,' he said.

'You followed me!'

'And you went at a good pace too. It was your feelings that made it seem so short—you were singing to yourself and happy as a dancing faun. We kept close behind you for a long way.'

I think it was 'we' he said, but for some reason or other I didn't care to ask.

'Maybe,' I answered shortly, trying uncomfortably to recall what particular capers I had cut. 'I guess that's right.' And then I added something about the loneliness, and how deserted all this slope of mountain was. And he explained that the peasants were afraid of it and called it No Man's Land. From one year's end to another no human foot went up or down it; the hay was never cut; no cattle grazed along the splendid pastures; no chalet had even been built within a mile of the wood we slowly made for. 'They're superstitious,' he told me. 'It was just the same a hundred years ago when *he* discovered it—there was a little natural cave on the edge of the forest where he used to sleep sometimes—I'll show it to you presently —but for generations this entire mountain-side has been undisturbed. You'll never meet a living soul in any part of it.' He stopped and pointed above us to where the pine wood hung in mid-air, like a dim blue carpet. 'It's just the place for

INITIATION

Them, you see.'

And a thrill of power went smashing through me. I can't describe it. It drenched me like a waterfall. I thought of Greece—Mount Ida and a thousand songs! Something in me—it was like the click of a shutter—announced that the 'change' was suddenly complete. I was another man; or rather a deeper part of me had come on top. My very language showed it.

The calm of halcyon weather lay over all. Overhead the peaks rose clear as crystal; below us the village lay in a bluish smudge of smoke and haze, as though a great finger had rubbed them softly into the earth. Absolute loneliness fell upon me like a clap. From the world of human beings we seemed quite shut off. And there began to steal over me again the strange elation of the night before.... We found ourselves almost at once against the edge of the wood.

It rose in front of us, a big wall of splendid trees, motionless as if cut out of dark green metal, the branches hanging stiff, and the crowd of trunks lost in the blue dimness underneath. I shaded my eyes with one hand, trying to peer into the solemn gloom. The contrast between the brilliant sunshine on the pastures and this region of heavy shadows blurred my sight.

'It's like the entrance to another world,' I whispered.

'It is,' said Arthur, watching me. 'We will go in. You shall pluck asphodel....'

And, before I knew it, he had me by the hand. We were advancing. We left the light behind us. The cool air dropped upon me like a sheet. There was a temple silence. The sun ran down behind the sky, leaving a marvellous blue radiance everywhere. Nothing stirred. But through the stillness there rose power, power that has no name, power that hides at the foundations somewhere—foundations that are changeless, invisible, everlasting. What do I mean? My mind grew to the dimensions of a planet. We were among the roots of life—whence issues that *one thing* in infinite guise that seeks so many temporary names from the protean minds of men.

'You shall pluck asphodel in the meadows this side of Erebus,'

Arthur was chanting. 'Hermes himself, the Psychopomp, shall lead, and Malahide shall welcome us.'

Malahide...!

To hear him use that name, the name of our scholar-ancestor, now dead and buried close upon a century—the way he half chanted it—gave me the goose-flesh. I stopped against a tree-stem, thinking of escape. No words came to me at the moment, for I didn't know what to say; but, on turning to find the bright green slopes just left behind, I saw only a crowd of trees and shadows hanging thick as a curtain—as though we had walked a mile. And it was a shock. The way out was lost. The trees closed up behind us like a tide.

'It's all right,' said Arthur; 'just keep an open mind and a heart alive with love. It has a shattering effect at first, but that will pass.' He saw I was afraid, for I shrank visibly enough. He stood beside me in his grey flannel suit, with his brilliant eyes and his great shock of hair, looking more like a column of light than a human being. 'It's all quite right and natural,' he repeated; 'we have passed the gateway, and Hecate, who presides over gateways, will let us out again. Do not make discord by feeling fear. This is a pine wood, and pines are the oldest, simplest trees; they are true primitives. They are an open channel; and in a pine wood where no human life has ever been you shall often find gateways where Hecate is kind to such as us.'

He took my hand—he must have felt mine trembling, but his own was cool and strong and felt like silver—and led me forward into the depths of a wood that seemed to me quite endless. It felt endless, that is to say. I don't know what came over me. Fear slipped away, and elation took its place.... As we advanced over ground that seemed level, or slightly undulating, I saw bright pools of sunshine here and there upon the forest floor. Great shafts of light dropped in slantingly between the trunks. There was movement everywhere, though I never could see what moved. A delicious, scented air stirred through the lower branches. Running water sang not very far away. Figures I did not actually see; yet there were limbs and flowing draperies and flying hair from time to time, ever just beyond the pools of sunlight. Surprise went from me too. I was on air. The atmosphere of dream came round me, but a dream of something just hovering outside the world I knew—a dream wrought in gold and silver, with shining eyes, with graceful beckoning hands, and with voices that rang like bells of music ... And the pools of light grew larger, merging one into another, until a delicate soft light shone equably throughout the entire forest. Into this zone of light we passed together. Then something fell abruptly at our feet, as though thrown down... two marvellous, shining sprays of blossom such as I had never seen in all my days before!

'Asphodel!' cried my companion, stooping to pick them up and handing one to me. I took it from him with a delight I could not understand. 'Keep it,' he murmured; 'it is the sign that we are welcome. For Malahide has dropped these on our path.'

And at the use of that ancestral name it seemed that a spirit passed before my face and the hair of my head stood up. There was a sense of violent, unhappy contrast. A composite picture presented itself, then rushed away. What was it? My youth in England, music and poetry at Cambridge and my passionate love of Greek that lasted two terms at most, when Malahide's great books formed part of the curriculum. Over against this, then, the drag and smother of solid worldly business, the sordid weight of modern ugliness, the bitterness of an ambitious, over-striving life. And abruptly—beyond both pictures—a shining, marvellous Beauty that scattered stars beneath my feet and scarved the universe with gold.

All this flashed before me with the utterance of that old family name. An alternative sprang up. There seemed some radical, elemental choice presented to me—to what I used to call my soul. My soul could take it or leave it as it pleased....

I looked at Arthur moving beside me like a shaft of light. What had come over me? How had our walk and talk and mood, our quite recent everyday and ordinary view, our normal relationship with the things of the world—how had it all slipped into this? So insensibly, so easily, so naturally!

'Was it worth while?'

The question—*I* didn't ask it—jumped up in me of its own accord. Was 'what' worth while? Why, my present life of commonplace and grubbing toil, of course; my city existence, with its meagre, unremunerative ambitions. Ah, it was this new Beauty calling me, this shining dream that lay beyond the two pictures I have mentioned.... I did not argue it, even to myself. But I understood. There was a radical change in me. The buried poet, too long hidden, rushed into the air like some great singing bird.

I glanced again at Arthur moving along lightly by my side, half dancing almost in his brimming happiness. 'Wait till you see Them,' I heard him singing. 'Wait till you hear the call of Artemis and the footsteps of her flying nymphs. Wait till Orion thunders overhead and Selene, crowned with the crescent moon, drives up the zenith in her white-horsed chariot. The choice will be beyond all question then...!'

A great silent bird, with soft brown plumage, whirred across our path, pausing an instant as though to peep, then disappearing with a muted sound into an eddy of the wind it made. The big trees hid it. It was an owl. The same moment I heard a rush of liquid song come pouring through the forest with a gush of almost human notes, and another pair of glossy wings flashed past us, swerving upwards to find the open sky—blue-black, pointed wings.

'His favourites!' exclaimed my companion with clear joy in his voice. 'They all are here! Athene's bird, Procne and Philomela too! The owl—the swallow—and the nightingale! Tereus and Itys are not far away.' And the entire forest, as he said it, stirred with movement, as though that great bird's quiet wings had waked the sea of ancient shadows. There were voices too—ringing, laughing voices, as though his words woke echoes that had been listening for it. For I heard sweet singing in the distance. The names he had used perplexed me. Yet even I, stranger as I was to such refined delights, could not mistake the passion of the nightingale and the dart

INITIATION

of the eager swallow. That wild burst of music, that curve of swift escape, were unmistakable.

And I struck a stalwart tree-stem with my open hand, feeling the need of hearing, touching, sensing it. My link with known, remembered things was breaking. I craved the satisfaction of the commonplace. I got that satisfaction; but I got something more as well. For the trunk was round and smooth and comely. It was no dead thing I struck. Somehow it brushed me into intercourse with inanimate Nature. And next the desire came to hear my voice—my own familiar, high-pitched voice with the twang and accent the New World climate brings, so-called American:

'Exchange Place, Noo York City. I'm in that business, buying and selling of exchange between the banks of two civilised countries, one of them stoopid and old-fashioned, the other leading all creation...!'

It was an effort, but I made it firmly. Only it sounded odd, remote, unreal.

'Sunlit woods and a wind among the branches,' followed close and sweet upon my words. But who, in the name of Wall Street, said it?

'England's buying gold,' I tried again. 'We've had a private wire. Cut in quick. First National is selling!'

Great-faced Hephaestus, how ridiculous! It was like saying, 'I'll take your scalp unless you give me meat.' It was barbaric, savage, centuries ago. Again there came another voice that caught up my own and turned it into common syntax. Some heady beauty of the Earth rose about me like a cloud.

'Hark! Night comes, with the dusk upon her eyelids. She brings those dreams that every dew-drop holds at dawn. Daughter of Thanatos and Hypnos...!'

But again—who said the words? It surely was not Arthur, my nephew Arthur, of To-day, learning French in a Swiss mountain village! I felt—well, what did I feel? In the name of the Stock Exchange and Wall Street, what was the cash surrender of my amazing feelings?

3

AND, turning to look at him, I made a discovery. I don't know how to tell it quite; such shadowy marvels have never been my line of goods. He looked several things at once—taller, slighter, sweeter, but chiefly—it sounds so crazy when I write it down—grander is the word, I think. And radiating with some power that flowed like Spring when it pours upon a landscape. Eternally young and glorious—young, J mean, in the sense that a field of flowers in the Spring looks young; and glorious in the sense the sky looks glorious at dawn or sunset. Something big shone through him like a storm, something that would go on for ever just as the Earth goes on, always renewing itself; something of gigantic life that in the human sense could never age at all—something the old gods had. But the figure, so far as there was any figure at all, was that old family picture come to life. Our great ancestor and Arthur were one being, and that one being was vaster than a million people. Yet it was Malahide I saw....

'They laid me in the earth I loved,' he said in a low, penetrating voice like running wind and water, 'and I found eternal life. I live now for ever in Their divine existence. I share the life that changes yet can never pass away.'

I felt myself rising like a cloud as he said it. A rising beauty captured me completely. If I could tell it in honest newspaper language—the common language used in flats and offices—why, I guess I could patent a new meaning in ordinary words, a new power of expression, the thing that all the churches and poets and thinkers have been trying to say since the world began. I caught on to a fact so fine and simple that it knocked me silly to think I'd never realised it before. I had read about it, yes; but now I *knew* it. The Earth, the whole bustling universe, was nothing after all but a visible production of eternal, living Powers—spiritual powers, mind you—that just happened to include the particular little type of strutting creature we called mankind. And these Powers, as seen in Nature, were the gods. It was our refusal of their grand appeal, so wild and sweet

INITIATION

and beautiful, that caused 'evil'. It was this barrier between ourselves and the rest of....

My thoughts and feelings swept away upon the rising flood as the 'figure' came upon me like a shaft of moonlight, melting the last remnant of opposition that was in me. I took my brain, my reason, chucking them aside for the futile little mechanism I suddenly saw them to be. In place of them came—oh, God, I hate to say it, for only nursery talk can get within a mile of it, and yet what I need is something simpler even than the words that children use. Under one arm I carried a whole forest breathing in the wind, and beneath the other a hundred meadows full of singing streams with golden marigolds and blue forget-me-nots along their banks. Upon my back and shoulders lay the clouded hills with dew and moonlight in their brimmed, capacious hollows. Thick in my hair hung the unaging powers that are stars and sunlight; though the sun was far away, it sweetened the currents of my blood with liquid gold. Breast and throat and face, as I advanced, met all the rivers of the world and all the winds of heaven, their strength and swiftness melting into me as light melts into everything it touches. And into my eyes passed all the radiant colours that weave the cloth of Nature as she takes the sun. I mean that the beauty of the world which never dies was one with the beauty in my soul—imperishable.

And this 'figure', pouring upon me like a burst of moonlight, spoke:

'They all are in you—air, and fire, and water....'

'And I—my feet stand—on the *Earth*,' my own voice interrupted, power lifting through the sound of it.

'The Earth! He laughed gigantically. He spread. He seemed everywhere about me. He seemed a race of men. My life swam forth in waves of some immense sensation that issued from the mountain and the forest, then returned to them again. I reeled. I became afraid. I clutched at something in me that was slipping beyond control, slipping down a bank towards a deep, dark river flowing at my feet. A shadowy boat appeared, a still more shadowy outline at the helm. I was in the act of stepping into it. For the tree I caught at to save myself was only air. I couldn't stop. I tried to scream.

'You have plucked asphodel,' sang the voice beside me, 'and you shall pluck more....'

I slipped and slipped, the speed increasing horribly. Then something caught, as though a cog held fast and stopped me—I remembered my business in New York City.

'Arthur!' I yelled. 'Arthur!' I shouted again as hard as I could shout. There was frantic terror in me. I felt as though I should never get back to myself again. Death!

The answer came in his normal voice: 'Keep close to me. I know the way....'

The scenery dwindled suddenly; the trees came back. I was walking in the forest beside my nephew, and the moonlight lay in patches and little shafts of silver. The crests of the pines just murmured in a wind that scarcely stirred, and through an opening on our right I saw the deep valley clasped about the twinkling village lights. Towering in splendour the spectral snowfields hung upon the sky, huge summits guarding them. And Arthur took my arm—oh, solidly enough this time. Thank heaven, he asked no questions of me.

'There's a smell of myrrh,' he whispered, 'and we are very near the undying, ancient things.'

I said something about the resin from the trees, but he took no notice.

'It enclosed its body in an egg of myrrh,' he went on, smiling down at me; 'then, setting it on fire, rose from the ashes with its life renewed. Once every five hundred years, you see——'

'What did?' I cried, feeling that loss of self stealing over me again. And his answer came like a blow between the eyes:

'The Phœnix. They called it a bird, though, of course, the true...'

'But my life's insured in that,' I cried, for he had named the company that took large yearly premiums from me; 'and I pay...'

'Your life's insured in *this*,' he said quietly, waving his arms to indicate the Earth. 'Your love of Nature and your sympathy with it make you safe.' He gazed at me. There was a marvellous expression in his eyes. I understood why poets talked of stars and flowers in a human face. But behind the face crept back another look as well. There grew about his figure an indeterminate extension. The outline of Malahide again stirred through his own. A pale, delicate hand reached out to take my own. And something broke in me.

I was conscious of two things—a burst of joy that meant losing myself entirely, and a rush of terror that meant staying as I was, a small, painful, struggling item of individual life. Another spray of that awful asphodel fell fluttering through the air in front of my face. It rested on the earth against my feet. And Arthur—this weirdly changing Arthur—stooped to pick it up for me. I kicked it with my foot beyond his reach... then turned and ran as though the Furies of that ancient world were after me. I ran for what I called my 'very life'. How I escaped from that thick wood without banging my body to bits against the trees I can't explain. I ran from something I desired yet feared. I leaped along in a succession of flying bounds. Each tree I passed turned of its own accord and flung after me until the entire forest followed. But I got out. I reached the open. Upon the sloping field in the full, clear light of the moon I collapsed in a panting heap. The Earth drew back with a great shuddering sigh behind me. There was this strange, tumultuous sound upon the night. I lay beneath the open heavens that were full of moonlight. I was myself—but there were tears in me. Beauty too high for understanding had slipped between my fingers. I had lost Malahide. I had lost the gods of Earth.... Yet I had seen... and felt. I had not lost all. Something remained that I could never lose again....

I don't know how it happened exactly, but presently I heard Arthur saying: 'You'll catch your death of cold if you lie on that soaking grass,' and felt his hand seize mine to pull me to my feet.

'I feel safer on earth,' I believed I answered. And then he said: 'Yes, but it's such a stupid way to die—a chill!'

4

I GOT up then, and we went downhill together towards the village lights. I danced—oh, I admit it—I sang as well. There was a flood of joy and power about me that beat anything I'd ever felt before. I didn't think or hesitate, there was no self-consciousness; I just let it rip for all there was, and if there had been ten thousand people there in front of me, I could have made them feel it too. That was the kind of feeling—power and confidence and a sort of raging happiness. I think I know what it was too. I say this soberly, with reverence... all wool and no fading. There was a bit of God in me, God's power that drives the Earth and pours through Nature—the imperishable Beauty expressed in those old-world nature-deities!

And the fear I'd felt was nothing but the little tickling pain of losing my ordinary two-cent self, the dread of letting go, the shrinking before the plunge—what a fellow feels when he's falling in love, and hesitates, and tries to think it out and hold back, and is afraid to let the enormous tide flow in and drown him.

Oh, yes, I began to think it over a bit as we raced down the mountain-side that glorious night. I've read some in my day; my brain's all right; I've heard of dual personality and subliminal uprush and conversion—no new line of goods, all that. But somehow these stunts of the psychologists and philosophers didn't cut any ice with me just then, because I'd *experienced* what they merely *explained*. And explanation was just a bargain sale. The best things can't be explained at all. There's no real value in a bargain sale.

Arthur had trouble to keep up with me. We were running due east, and the Earth was turning, therefore, with us. We all three ran together at her own pace—terrific! The moonlight danced along the summits, and the snowfields flew like spreading robes, and the forests everywhere, far and near, hung watching us and booming like a thousand organs. There were uncaged winds about; you could hear them whistling among the precipices. But the one great thing I knew was—Beauty, a beauty of the common old familiar Earth, and a beauty that's stayed with me ever since, and given me joy and strength and a source of power and delight I'd never guessed existed before.

As we dropped lower into the thicker air of the valley I sobered down. Gradually the ecstasy passed from me. We slowed up a bit. The lights and the houses and the sight of the hotel where people were dancing in a stuffy ballroom, all this put blotting-paper on something that had been flowing.

Now you'll think this an odd thing too—but when we reached the village street, I just took Arthur's hand and shook it and said good-night and went up to bed and slept like a two-year-old till morning. And from that day to this I've never set eyes on the boy again.

Perhaps it's difficult to explain, and perhaps it isn't. I can explain it to myself in two lines—I was afraid to see him. I was afraid he might explain. I was afraid he might explain away. I just left a note—he never replied to it—and went off by a morning train. Can you understand that? Because if you can't you haven't understood this account I've tried to give of the experience Arthur gave me. Well—anyway—I'll just let it go at that.

Arthur's a director now in his father's wholesale chemical business, and I—well, I'm doing better than ever in the buying and selling of exchange between banks in New York City as before.

But when I said I was still drawing dividends on my Swiss investment, I meant it. And it's not 'scenery.' Everybody gets a thrill from 'scenery.' It's a darned sight more than that. It's those little wayward patches of blue on a cloudy day; those blue pools in the sky just above Trinity Church steeple when I pass out of Wall Street into Lower Broadway; it's the rustle of the sea-wind among the Battery trees; the wash of the waves when the Ferry's starting for Staten Island, and the glint of the sun far down the Bay, or dropping a bit of pearl into the old East River. And sometimes it's the strip of cloud in the west above the Jersey shore of the Hudson, the first star, the sickle of the new moon behind the masts and shipping. But usually it's something nearer, bigger, simpler than all or any of these. It's just the certainty that, when I hurry along the hard stone pavements from bank to bank, I'm walking on the —Earth. It's just that—*the Earth!*

A DESERT EPISODE

1

'BETTER put wraps on now. The sun's getting low,' a girl said.

It was the end of a day's expedition in the Arabian Desert, and they were having tea. A few yards away the donkeys munched their *barsim*; beside them in the sand the boys lay finishing bread and jam. Immense, with gliding tread, the sun's rays slid from crest to crest of the limestone ridges that broke the huge expanse towards the Red Sea. By the time the tea-things were packed the sun hovered, a giant ball of red, above the Pyramids. It stood in the western sky a moment, looking out of its majestic hood across the sand. With a movement almost visible it leaped, paused, then leaped again. It seemed to bound towards the horizon; then, suddenly, was gone.

'It *is* cold, yes,' said the painter, Rivers. And all who heard looked up at him because of the way he said it. A hurried movement ran through the merry party, and the girls were on their donkeys quickly, not wishing to be left to bring up the rear. They clattered off. The boys cried; the thud of sticks was heard; hoofs shuffled through the sand and stones. In single file the picnickers headed for Helouan, some five miles distant. And the desert closed up behind them ast they went, following in a shadowy wave that never broke, noiseless, foamless, unstreaked, driven by no wind, and of a volume undiscoverable. Against the orange sunset the Pyramids turned deep purple. The strip of silvery Nile among its palm trees looked like rising mist. In the incredible Egyptian after-glow the enormous horizons burned a little longer, then went out. The ball of the earth—a huge round globe that bulged—curved visibly as at sea. It was no longer a flat espanse; it turned. Its splendid curves were realised.

'Better put wraps on; it's cold and the sun is low'—and

then the curious hurry to get back among the houses and the haunts of men. No more was said, perhaps, than this, yet, the time and place being what they were, the mind became suddenly aware of that quality which ever brings a certain shrinking with it—vastness; and more than vastness: that which is endless because it is also beginningless—eternity. A colossal splendour stole upon the heart; and the senses, unaccustomed to the unusual stretch, reeled a little, as though the wonder was more than could be faced with comfort. Not all, doubtless, realised it, though to two, at least, it came with a staggering impact there was no withstanding. For, while the luminous greys and purples crept round them from the sand wastes, the hearts of these two became aware of certain common things whose simple majesty is usually dulled by mere familiarity. Neither the man nor the girl knew for certain that the other felt it, as they brought up the rear together; yet the fact that each *did* feel it set them side by side in the same strange circle—and made them silent. They realised the immensity of a moment: the dizzy stretch of time that led up to the casual pinning of a veil, to the tightening of a stirrup strap, to the little speech with a companion, to the roar of the vanished centuries that have ground mountains into sand and spread them over the floor of Africa; above all, to the little truth that they themselves existed amid the whirl of stupendous systems all delicately balanced as a spider's web—that they were *alive*.

For a moment this vast scale of reality revealed itself, then hid swiftly again behind the debris of the obvious. The universe, containing their two tiny yet important selves, stood still for an instant before their eyes. They looked at it—realised that they belonged to it. Everything moved and had its being, *lived*—here in this silent, empty desert even more actively than in a city of crowded houses. The quiet Nile, sighing with age, passed down towards the sea; there loomed the menacing Pyramids across the twilight; beneath them, in monstrous dignity, crouched that Shadow from whose eyes of battered stone proceeds the nameless thing that contracts the heart, then opens it again to terror; and everywhere, from towering monoliths as from secret tombs, rose that strange, long whisper which, defying time and distance, laughs at death. The spell of Egypt, which is the spell of immortality, touched their hearts.

Already, as the group of picnickers rode homewards now, the first stars twinkled overhead, and the peerless Egyptian night was on the way. There was hurry in the passing of the dusk. And the cold sensibly increased.

'So you did no painting after all,' said Rivers to the girl who rode a little in front of him, 'for I never saw you touch your sketch-book once.'

They were some distance now behind the others; the line straggled; and when no answer came he quickened his pace, drew up alongside and saw that her eyes, in the reflection of the sunset, shone with moisture. But she turned her head a little, smiling into his face, so that the human and the non-human beauty came over him with an onset that was almost shock. Neither one nor other, he knew, were long for him, and the realisation fell upon him with a pant of actual physical pain. The acuteness, the hopelessness of the realisation, for a moment, were more than he could bear, stern of temper though he was, and he tried to pass in front of her, urging his donkey with resounding strokes. Her own animal, however, following the lead, at once came up with him.

'You felt it, perhaps, as I did,' he said some moments later, his voice quite steady again. 'The stupendous, everlasting thing—the—*life* behind it all.' He hesitated a little in his speech, unable to find the substantive that could compass even a fragment of his thought. She paused, too, similarly inarticulate before the surge of incomprehensible feelings.

'It's—awful,' she said, half laughing, yet the tone hushed and a little quaver in it somewhere. And her voice to him was like the first sound he had ever heard in the world, for the first sound a full-grown man heard in the world would be beyond all telling—magical. 'I shall not try again,' she continued, leaving out the laughter this time; 'my sketch-book is a farce. For, to tell the truth'—and the next three words she said below her breath—'I dare not.'

He turned and looked at her for a second. It seemed to him that the following wave had caught them up, and was about to break above her too. But the big-brimmed hat and the streaming veil shrouded her features. He saw, instead, the Universe. He felt as though he and she had always, always been together, and always, always would be. Separation was inconceivable.

'It came so close,' she whispered. 'It—shook me!'

They were cut off from their companions, whose voices sounded far ahead. Her words might have been spoken by the darkness, or by someone who peered at them from within that following wave. Yet the fanciful phrase was better than any he could find. From the immeasurable space of time and distance men's hearts vainly seek to plumb, it drew into closer perspective a certain meaning that words may hardly compass, a formidable truth that belongs to that deep place where hope and doubt fight their incessant battle. The awe she spoke of was the awe of immortality, of belonging to something that is endless and beginningless.

And he understood that the tears and laughter were one—caused by that spell which takes a little human life and shakes it, as an animal shakes its prey that later shall feed its blood and increase its power of growth. His other thoughts—really but a single thought—he had not the right to utter. Pain this time easily routed hope as the wave came nearer. For it was the wave of death that would shortly break, he knew, over him, but not over her. Him it would sweep with its huge withdrawal into the desert whence it came: her it would leave high upon the shores of life—alone. And yet the separation would somehow not be real. They were together in eternity even now. They were endless as this desert, beginningless as this sky ... immortal. The realisation overwhelmed....

The lights of Helouan seemed to come no nearer as they rode on in silence for the rest of the way. Against the dark background of the Mokattam Hills these fairy lights twinkled brightly, hanging in mid-air, but after an hour they were no closer than before. It was like riding towards the stars. It would take centuries to reach them. There were centuries in which to do so. Hurry has no place in the desert; it is born in streets. The desert stands still; to go fast in it is to go backwards.

Now, in particular, its enormous, uncanny leisure was everywhere—in keeping with that mighty scale the sunset had made visible. His thoughts, like the steps of the weary animal that bore him, had no progress in them. The serpent of eternity, holding its tail in its own mouth, rose from the sand, enclosing himself, the stars—and her. Behind him, in the hollows of that shadowy wave, the procession of dynasties and conquests, the great series of gorgeous civilisations the mind calls Past, stood still, crowded with shining eyes and beckoning faces, still waiting to arrive. There is no death in Egypt. His own death stood so close that he could touch it by stretching out his hand, yet it seemed as much behind him as in front. What man called a beginning was a trick. There was no such thing. He was with this girl—*now*, when Death waited so close for him—yet he had never really begun. Their lives ran always parallel. The hand he stretched to clasp approaching death caught instead in this girl's shadowy hair, drawing her in with him to the centre where he breathed the eternity of the desert. Yet expression of any sort was as futile as it was unnecessary. To paint, to speak, to sing, even the slightest gesture of the soul, became a crude and foolish thing. Silence was here the truth. And they rode in silence towards the fairy lights.

Then suddenly the rocky ground rose up close before them; boulders stood out vividly with black shadows and shining heads; a flatroofed house slid by; three palm trees rattled in the evening wind; beyond, a mosque and minaret sailed upwards, like the spars and rigging of some phantom craft; and the colonnades of the great modern hotel, standing upon its dome of limestone ridge, loomed over them. Helouan was about them before they knew it. The desert lay behind with its huge, arrested billow. Slowly, owing to its prodigious volume, yet with a speed that merged it instantly with the far horizon behind the night, this wave now withdrew a little. There was no hurry. It came, for the moment, no farther. Rivers knew. For he was in it to the throat. Only his head was above the surface. He still could breathe—and speak—and see. Deepening with every hour into an incalculable splendour, it waited.

2

IN the street the foremost riders drew rein, and, two and two abreast, the long line clattered past the shops and cafés, the railway station and hotels, stared at by the natives from the busy pavements. The donkeys stumbled, blinded by the electric light. Girls in white dresses flitted here and there, arabîyehs rattled past with people hurrying home to dress for dinner, and the evening train, just in from Cairo, disgorged its stream of passengers. There were dances in several of the hotels that night. Voices rose on all sides. Questions and answers, engagements and appointments were made, little plans and plots and intrigues for seizing happiness on the wing—before the wave rolled in and caught the lot. They chattered gaily:

'You *are* going, aren't you? You promised——'

'Of course I am.'

'Then I'll drive you over. May I call for you?'

'All right. Come at ten.'

'We shan't have finished our bridge by then. Say ten-thirty.'

And eyes exchanged their meaning signals. The group dismounted and dispersed. Arabs standing under the lebbekh trees, or squatting on the pavements before their dim-lit booths, watched them with faces of gleaming bronze. Rivers gave his bridle to a donkey-boy, and moved across stiffly after the long ride to help the girl dismount. 'You feel tired?' he asked gently. 'It's been a long day.' For her face was white as chalk, though the eyes shone brilliantly.

'Tired, perhaps,' she answered, 'but exhilarated too. I

should like to be there now. I should like to go back this minute—if someone would take me.' And, though she said it lightly, there was a meaning in her voice he apparently chose to disregard. It was as if she knew his secret. 'Will you take me—some day soon?'

The direct question, spoken by those determined little lips, was impossible to ignore. He looked close into her face as he helped her from the saddle with a spring that brought her a moment half into his arms. 'Some day—soon,' I will, he said with emphasis; 'when you are—ready.' The pallor in her face, and a certain expression in it he had not known before, startled him. 'I think you have been overdoing it, he added, with a tone in which authority and love were oddly mingled, neither of them disguised.

'Like yourself,' she smiled, shaking her skirts out and looking down at her dusty shoes. 'I've only a few days more—before I sail. We're both in such a hurry, but you are the worse of the two.'

'Because my time is even shorter,' ran his horrified thought—for he said no word.

She raised her eyes suddenly to his, with an expression that for an instant almost convinced him she had guessed—and the soul in him stood rigidly at attention, urging back the rising fires. The hair dropped loosely round the sun-burned neck. Her face was level with his shoulder. Even the glare of the street lights could not make her undesirable. But behind the gaze of the deep brown eyes another thing looked forth imperatively into his own. And he recognised it with a rush of terror, yet of singular exultation.

'It followed us all the way,' she whispered. 'It came after us from the desert—where it *lives*.'

'At the houses,' he said equally low, 'it stopped,'. He gladly adopted her syncopated speech, for it helped him in his struggle to subdue those rising fires.

For a second she hesitated. 'You mean, if we had not left so soon—when it turned cold. If we had not hurried—if we had remained a little longer——'

He caught at her hand, unable to control himself, but dropped it again the same second, while she made as though she had not noticed, forgiving him with her eyes. 'Or a great deal longer,' she added slowly—'for ever?'

And then he was certain that she *had* guessed—not that he loved her above all else in the world, for that was so obvious that a child might know it, but that his silence was due to his other, lesser secret: that the great Executioner stood waiting to drop the hood about his eyes. He was already pinioned. Something in her gaze and in her manner persuaded him suddenly that she understood.

His exhilaration increased extraordinarily. 'I mean,' he said very quietly, 'that the spell weakens here among the houses and among the—so-called living.' There was masterfulness, triumph, in his voice. Very wonderfully he saw her smile change; she drew slightly closer to his side, as though unable to resist. 'Mingled with lesser things we should not understand completely,' he added softly.

'And that might be a mistake, you mean?' she asked quickly, her face grave again.

It was his turn to hesitate a moment. The breeze stirred the hair about her neck, bringing its faint perfume—perfume of young life—to his nostrils. He drew his breath in deeply, smothering back the torrent of rising words he knew were unpermissible. 'Misunderstanding,' he said briefly. 'If the eye be single——' He broke off, shaken by a paroxysm of coughing. 'You know my meaning,' he continued, as soon as the attack had passed; 'you feel the difference *here*,' pointing round him to the hotels, the shops, the busy stream of people; 'the hurry, the excitement, the feverish, blinding child's play which pretends to be alive, but does not know it——' And again the coughing stopped him. This time she took his hand in her own, pressed it very slightly, then released it. He felt it as the touch of that desert wave upon his soul. 'The reception must be in complete and utter resignation. Tainted by lesser things, the disharmony might be——' he began stammeringly.

Again there came interruption, as the rest of the party called impatiently to know if they were coming up to the hotel. He had not time to find the completing adjective. Perhaps he could not find it ever. Perhaps it does not exist in any modern language. Eternity is not realised to-day; men have no time to know they are alive for ever; they are too busy....

They all moved in a chattering, merry group towards the big hotel. Rivers and the girl were separated.

3

THERE was a dance that evening, but neither of these took part in it. In the great dining-room their tables were far apart. He could not even see her across the sea of intervening heads and shoulders. The long meal over, he went to his room, feeling it imperative to be alone. He did not read, he did not write; but, leaving the light unlit, he wrapped himself up and leaned out upon the broad window-sill into the great Egyptian night. His deep-sunken thoughts, like to the crowding stars, stood still, yet for ever took new shapes. He tried to see behind them, as, when a boy, he had tried so see behind the constellations—out into space—where there is nothing.

Below him the lights of Helouan twinkled like the Pleiades reflected in a pool of water; a hum of queer soft noises rose to his ears; but just beyond the houses the desert stood at attention, the vastest thing he had ever known, very stern, yet very comforting, with its peace beyond all comprehension, its delicate, wild terror, and its awful message of immortality. And the attitude of his mind, though he did not know it, was one of prayer.... From time to time he went to lie on the bed with paroxysms of coughing. He had overtaxed his strength —his swiftly fading strength. The wave had risen to his lips.

Nearer forty than thirty-five, Paul Rivers had come out to Egypt, plainly understanding that with the greatest care he might last a few weeks longer than if he stayed in England. A few more times to see the sunset and the sunrise, to watch the stars, feel the soft airs of earth upon his cheeks; a few more days of intercourse wtih his kind, asking and answering questions, wearing the old, familiar clothes he loved, reading his favourite pages, and then—out into the big spaces—where there is nothing.

Yet no one, from his stalwart, energetic figure, would have guessed—no one but the expert mind, not to be deceived, to whom in the first attack of overwhelming despair and desolation he went for final advice. He left that house, as many had left it before, knowing that soon he would need no earthly protection of roof and walls, and that his soul, if it existed, would be shelterless in the space behind all manifested life. He had looked forward to fame and position in this world; had, indeed, already achieved the first step towards his end; and now, with the vanity of all earthly aims so mercilessly clear before him, he had turned, in somewhat of a nervous, concentrated hurry, to make terms with the Infinite while still the brain was there. And had, of course, found nothing. For it takes a lifetime crowded with experiment and effort to learn even the alphabet of genuine faith; and what could come of a few weeks' wild questioning but confusion and bewilderment of mind? It was inevitable. He came out to Egypt wondering, thinking, questioning, but chiefly wondering. He had grown, that is, more childlike, abandoning the futile tool of Reason, which hitherto had seemed to him the perfect instrument. Its foolishness stood naked before him in the pitiless light of the specialist's decision; for 'Who can by searching find out God?'

To be exceedingly careful of over-exertion was the final warning he brought with him, and within a few hours of his arrival, three weeks ago, he had met this girl and utterly disregarded it. He took it somewhat thus: 'Instead of lingering I'll enjoy myself and go out—a little sooner. I'll *live*. The time is very short.' His was not a nature, anyhow, that could heed a warning. He could not kneel. Upright and unflinching, he went to meet things as they came, reckless, unwise, but certainly not afraid. And this characteristic operated now. He ran to meet Death full tilt in the uncharted spaces that lay behind the stars. With love for a companion, he raced, his speed increasing from day to day, she, as he thought, knowing merely that he sought her, but had not guessed his darker secret that was now his *lesser* secret.

And in the desert, this afternoon of the picnic, the great thing he sped to meet had shown itself with its familiar touch of appalling cold and shadow: familiar, because all minds know of and accept it; appalling, because, until realised close and with the mental power at the full, it remains but a name the heart refuses to believe in. And he had discovered that its name was—Life.

Rivers had seen the wave that sweeps incessant, tireless, but as a rule invisible, round the great curve of the bulging earth, brushing the nations into the deeps behind. It had followed him home to the streets and houses of Helouan. He saw it now, as he leaned from his window, dim and immense, too huge to break. Its beauty was nameless, undecipherable. His coughing echoed back from the wall of its great sides.... And the music floated up at the same time from the ball-room in the opposite wing. The two sounds mingled. Life, which is love, and Death, which is their unchanging partner, held hands beneath the stars.

He leaned out farther to drink in the cool, sweet air. Soon, on this air, his body would be dust, driven, perhaps, against her very cheek, trodden on possibly by her little foot—until, in turn, she joined him too, blown by the same wind loose about the desert. True. Yet at the same time they would always be together, always somewhere side by side, continuing in the vast universe, alive. This new, absolute conviction was in him now. He remembered the curious, sweet perfume in the desert, as of flowers, where yet no flowers are. It was the perfume of life. But in the desert there is no life. Living things that grow and move and utter, are but a protest against death. In the desert they are unnecessary, because death there *is* not. Its overwhelming vitality needs no insolent, visible proof, no protest, no challenge, no little signs of life. The message of the desert is immortality....

He went finally to bed, just before midnight. Hovering magnificently just outside his window, Death watched him while he slept. The wave crept to the level of his eyes. He called her name....

And downstairs, meanwhile, the girl, knowing nothing, wondered where he was, wondered unhappily and restlessly; more—though this she did not understand—wondered motheringly. Until to-day, on the ride home, and from their singular conversation together, she had guessed nothing of his reason for being at Helouan, where so many come in order to find life. She only knew her own. And she was but twenty-five....

Then, in the desert, when that touch of unearthly chill had stolen out of the sand towards sunset, she had realised clearly, astonished she had not seen it long ago, that this man loved her, yet that something prevented his obeying the great impulse. In the life of Paul Rivers, whose presence had profoundly stirred her heart the first time she saw him, there was some obstacle that held him back, a barrier his honour must respect. He could never tell her of his love. It could lead to nothing. Knowing that he was not married, her intuition failed her utterly at first. Then, in their silence on the homeward ride, the truth had somehow pressed up and touched her with its hand of ice. In that disjointed conversation at the end, which reads as it sounded, as though no coherent meaning lay behind the words, and as though both sought to conceal by speech what yet both burned to utter, she had divined his darker secret, and knew that it was the same as her own. She understood then it was Death that had tracked them from the desert, following with its gigantic shadow from the sandy wastes. The cold, the darkness, the silence which cannot answer, the stupendous mystery which is the spell of its inscrutable Presence, had risen about them in the dusk, and kept them company at a little distance, until the lights of Helouan had bade it halt. Life which may not, cannot end, had frightened her.

His time, perhaps, was even shorter than her own. None knew his secret, since he was alone in Egypt and was caring for himself. Similarly, since she bravely kept her terror to herself her companions had no inkling of her own, aware merely that the disease was in her system and that her orders were to be extremely cautious. This couple, therefore, shared secretly together the two clearest glimpses of eternity life has to offer to the soul. Side by side they looked into the splenid eyes of Love and Death. Life, moreover, with its instinct for simple and terrific drama, had produced this majestic climax, breaking with pathos, at the very moment when it could not be developed—this side of the stars. They stood together upon the stage, a stage emptied of other human players; the audience had gone home and the lights were being lowered; no music sounded; the critics were a-bed. In this great game of Consequences it was known where he met her, what he said and what she answered, possibly what they did and even what the world thought. But 'what the consequence was' would remain unknown, untold. That would happen in the big spaces of which the desert in its silence, its motionless serenity, its shelterless, intolerable vastness, is the perfect symbol. And the desert gives no answer. It sounds no challenge, for it is complete. Life in the desert makes no sign. It *is*.

4

IN the hotel that night there arrived by chance a famous International dancer, whise dahabiyeh lay anchored at San Giovanni, in the Nile below Heoluan; and this woman, with her party, had come to dine and take part in the festivities. The news spread. After twelve the lights were lowered, and while the moonlight flooded the terraces, streaming past pillar and colonnade, she rendered in the shadowed halls the music of the Masters, interpreting with an instinctive genius messages which ternal and divine.

Among the crowd of enthralled and delighted guests, the girl sat on the steps and watched her. The rhythmical interpretation held a power that seemed, in a sense, inspired; there lay in it a certain unconscious something that was pure, unearthly; something that the stars, wheeling in stately movements over the sea and desert, know; something the great winds bring to mountains where they play together; something the forests capture and fix magically into their gathering of big and little branches. It was both passionate and spiritual, wild and tender, intensely human and seductively non-human. For it was original, taught of Nature, a revelation of naked, unhampered life. It comforted, as the desert comforts. It brought the desert awe into the stuffy corridors of the hotel, with the moonlight and the whispering of stars, yet behind it ever the silence of those grey, mysterious, interminable spaces which utter to themselves the wordless song of life. For it was the same dim thing, she felt, that had followed her from the desert several hours before, halting just outside the streets and houses as though blocked from further advance; the thing that had stopped her foolish painting, skilled thought she was, because it hides behind colour and not in it; the thing that veiled the meaning in the cryptic sentences she and he had stammered out together; the thing, in a word, as near as she could approach it by any means of interior expression, that the realisation of death for the first time makes comprehensible—Immortality. It was unutterable, but it *was*. He and she were indissolubly together. Death was no separation. There was no death... It was terrible. It was—she had already used the word—awful, full of awe.

'In the desert,' thought whispered, as she watched spellbound, 'it is impossible even to conceive of death. The idea is meaningless. It simply is not.'

The music and the movement filled the air with life which, being there, must continue always, and continuing always can have never had a beginning. Death, therefore, was the great revealer of life. Without it none could realise that they are alive. Others had discovered this before her, but she did not know it. In the desert no one can realise death: it is hope and life that are the only certainty. The entire conception of the Egyptian system was based on this—the conviction, sure and glorious, of life's endless continuation. Their tombs and temples, their pyramids and sphinxes surviving after thousands of years, defy the passage of time and laugh at death; the very bodies of their priests and kings, of their animals even, their fish, their insects, stand to-day as symbols of their stalwart knowledge.

And this girl, as she listened to the music and watched the inspired dancing, remembered it. The message poured into her from many sides, though the desert brought it clearest. With death peering into her face a few short weeks ahead, she thought instead of—life. The desert, as it were, became for her a little fragment of eternity, focused into an intelligible point for her mind to rest upon with comfort and comprehension. Her steady, thoughtful nature stirred towards an objective far beyond the small enclosure of one narrow lifetime. The scale of the desert stretched her to the grandeur of its own imperial meaning, its divine repose, its unassailable and everlasting majesty. She looked beyond the wall.

Eternity! That which is endless; without pause, without beginning, without divisions or boundaries. The fluttering of her brave yet frightened spirit ceased, aware with awe of its own everlastingness. The swiftest motion produces the effect of immobility; excessive light is darkness; size, run loose into enormity, is the same as the minutely tiny. Similarly, in the desert, life, too overwhelming and terrific to know limit or confinement, lies undetailed and stupendous, still as deity, a revelation of nothingness because it is all. Turned golden beneath its spell that the music and the rhythm made even more comprehensible, the soul in her, already lying beneath the shadow of the great wave, sank into rest and peace, too certain of itself to fear. And panic fled away. 'I am immortal... because I *am*. And what I love is not apart from me. It is myself. We are together endlessly because we *are*.'

Yet in reality, though the big desert brought this, it was Love, which, being of similar parentage, interpreted its vast meaning to her little heart—that sudden love which, without a word of preface or explanation, had come to her a short three weeks before.... She went up to her room soon after midnight, abruptly, unexpectedly stricken. Someone, it seemed, had called her name. She passed his door.

The lights had been turned up. The clamour of praise was loud round the figure of the weary dancer as she left in a carriage for her dahabiyeh on the Nile. A low wind whistled round the walls of the great hotel, blowing chill and bitter between the pillars of the colonnades. The girl heard the voices float up to her through the night, and once more, behind the confused sound of the many, she heard her own name called, but more faintly than before, and from very far away. It came through the spaces beyond her open window; it died away again; then—but for the sighing of that bitter wind—silence, the deep silence of the desert.

And these two, Paul Rivers and the girl, between them merely a floor of that stone that built the Pyramids, lay a few moments before the Wave of Sleep engulfed them. And, while they slept, two shadowy forms hovered above the roof of the quiet hotel, melting presently into one, as dreams stole down from the desert and the stars. Immortality whispered to them. On either side rose Life and Death, towering in splendour. Love, joining their spreading wings, fused the gigantic outlines into one. The figures grew smaller, comprehensible. They entered the little windows. Above the beds they paused a moment, watching, waiting, and then, like a wave that is just about to break, they stooped....

And in the brilliant Egyptian sunlight of the morning, as she went downstairs, she passed his door again. She had awakened, but he slept on. He had preceded her. It was next day she learned his room was vacant.... Within the month she joined him, and within the year the cool north wind that sweetens Lower Egypt from the sea blew the dust across the desert as before. It is the dust of kings, of queens, of priests, princesses, lovers. It is the dust no earthly power can annihilate. It, too, lasts for ever. There was a little more of it... the desert's message slightly added to: Immortality.

TRANSITION

John Mudbury was on his way home from the shops, his arms full of Christmas Presents. It was after six o'clock and the streets were very crowded. He was an ordinary man, lived in an ordinary suburban flat, with an ordinary wife and ordinary children. *He* did not think them ordinary, but everybody else did. He had ordinary presents for each one, a cheap blotter for his wife, a cheap air-gun for the boy, and so forth. He was over fifty, bald, in an office, decent in mind and habits, of uncertain opinions, uncertain politics, and uncertain religion. Yet he considered himself a decided, positive gentleman, quite unaware that the morning newspaper determined his opinions for the day. He just lived—from day to day. Physically, he was fit enough, except for a weak heart (which never troubled him); and his summer holiday was bad golf, while the children bathed and his wife read Garvice on the sands. Like the majority of men, he dreamed idly of the past, muddled away the present, and guessed vaguely—after imaginative reading on occasions—at the future.

'I'd like to survive all right,' he said, 'provided it's better than this,' surveying his wife and children, and thinking of his daily toil. 'Otherwise——!' and he shrugged his shoulders as a brave man should.

He went to church regularly. But nothing in church convinced him that he did survive, just as nothing in church enticed him into hoping that he would. On the other hand, nothing in life persuaded him that he didn't, wouldn't, couldn't. 'I'm an Evolutionist,' he loved to say to thoughtful cronies (over a glass), having never heard that Darwinism had been questioned.

And so he came home gaily, happily, with his bunch of Christmas Presents 'for the wife and little ones,' stroking himself upon their keen enjoyment and excitement. The night before he had taken 'the wife' to see *Magic* at a select

London theatre where the Intellectuals went—and had been extraordinarily stirred. He had gone questioningly, yet expecting something out of the common. 'It's *not* musical,' he warned her, 'nor farce, nor comedy, so to speak'; and in answer to her question as to what the critics had said, he had wriggled, sighed, and put his gaudy neck-tie straight four times in quick succession. For no Man in the Street, with any claim to self-respect, could be expected to understand what the critics had said, even if he understood the Play. And John had answered truthfully: 'Oh, they just said things. But the theatre's always full—and that's the only test.'

And just now, as he crossed the crowded Circus to catch his 'bus, it chanced that his mind (having glimpsed an advertisement) was full of this particular Play, or rather, of the effect it had produced upon him at the time. For it had thrilled him—inexplicably: with its marvellous speculative hint, its big audacity, its alert and spiritual beauty.... Thought plunged to find something—plunged after this bizarre suggestion of a bigger universe, after this quasi-jocular suggestion that man is not the only—then dashed full-tilt against a sentence that memory thrust beneath his nose: 'Science does *not* exhaust the Universe'—and at the same time dashed full-tilt against destruction of another kind as well...!

How it happened he never exactly knew. He saw a Monster glaring at him with eyes of blazing fire. It was horrible! It rushed upon him. He dodged.... Another Monster met him round the corner. Both came at him simultaneously. He dodged again—a leap that might have cleared a hurdle easily, but was too late. Between the pair of them—his heart literally in his gullet—he was mercilessly caught. Bones crunched.... There was a soft sensation, icy cold and hot as fire. Horns and voices roared. Battering-rams he saw, and a carapace of iron.... Then dazzling light.... 'Always *face* the traffic!' he remembered with a frantic yell—and, by some extraordinary luck, escaped miraculously on to the opposite pavement.

There was no doubt about it. By the skin of his teeth he had dodged a rather ugly death. First... he felt for his Presents

—all were safe. And then, instead of congratulating himself and taking breath, he hurried homewards—on foot, which proved that his mind had lost control a bit!—thinking only how disappointed the wife and children would have been if—well, if anything had happened. Another thing he realised, oddly enough, was that he no longer really loved his wife, but had only great affection for her. What made him think of that, Heaven only knows, but he *did* think of it. He was an honest man without pretence. This came as a discovery somehow. He turned a moment, and saw the crowd gathered about the entangled taxi-cabs, policemen's helmets gleaming in the lights of the shop windows ... then hurried on again, his thoughts full of the joy his Presents would give... of the scampering children... and of his wife—bless her silly heart!—eyeing the mysterious parcels....

And, though he never could explain how, he presently stood at the door of the jail-like building that contained his flat, having walked the whole three miles. His thoughts had been so busy and absorbed that he had hardly noticed the length of weary trudge. 'Besides,' he reflected, thinking of the narrow escape, 'I've had a nasty shock. It was a d——d near thing, now I come to think of it....' He still felt a bit shaky and bewildered. Yet, at the same time, he felt extraordinarily jolly and lighthearted.

He counted his Christmas parcels... hugged himself in anticipatory joy ... and let himself in swiftly with his latchkey. 'I'm late,' he realised, 'but when she sees the brown-paper parcels, she'll forget to say a word. God bless the old faithful soul.' And he softly used the key a second time and entered his flat on tiptoe.... In his mind was the master impulse of that afternoon—the pleasure these Christmas Presents would give his wife and children....

He heard a noise. He hung up hat and coat in the poky vestibule (they never called it 'hall') and moved softly towards the parlour door, holding the packages behind him. Only of them he thought, not of himself—of his family, that is, not of the packages. Pushing the door cunningly ajar, he peeped

in slyly. To his amazement the room was full of people. He
withdrew quickly, wondering what it meant. A party? And
without his knowing about it! Extraordinary!... Keen
disappointment came over him. But, as he stepped back, the
vestibule, he saw, was full of people too.

He was uncommonly surprised, yet somehow not surprised
at all. People were congratulating him. There was a perfect
mob of them. Moreover, he knew them all—vaguely remembered them, at least. And they all knew him.

'Isn't it a game?' laughed someone, patting him on the back.
'*They* haven't the least idea...!'

And the speaker—it was old John Palmer, the book-keeper
at the office—emphasised the 'they'.

'Not the least idea,' he answered with a smile, saying something he didn't understand, yet knew was right.

His face, apparently, showed the utter bewilderment he
felt. The shock of the collision had been greater than he realised
evidently. His mind was wandering.... Possibly! Only the
odd thing was—he had never felt so clear-headed in his life.
Ten thousand things grew simple suddenly. But, how thickly
these people pressed about him, and how—familiarly!

'My parcels,' he said, joyously pushing his way across the
throng. 'These are Chistmas Presents I've bought for them.'
He nodded toward the room. 'I've saved for weeks—stopped
cigars and billiards and—and several other good things—to
buy them.'

'Good man!' said Palmer with a happy laugh. 'It's the heart
that counts.'

Mudbury looked at him. Palmer had said an amazing truth,
only—people would hardly understand and believe him....
Would they?

'Eh?' he asked, feeling stuffed and stupid, muddled somewhere between two meanings, one of which was gorgeous
and the other stupid beyond belief.

'If you *please*, Mr. Mudbury, step inside. They are expecting
you,' said a kindly, pompous voice. And, turning sharply,
he met the gentle, foolish eyes of Sir James Epiphany, a director

of the Bank where he worked.

The effect of the voice was instantaneous from long habit. 'They are,' he smiled from his heart, and advanced as from the custom of many years. Oh, how happy and gay he felt! His affection for his wife was real. Romance, indeed, had gone, but he needed her—and she needed him. And the children—Milly, Bill, and Jean—he deeply loved them. Life was worth living indeed!

In the room was a crowd, but—an astounding silence. John Mudbury looked round him. He advanced towards his wife, who sat in the corner arm-chair with Milly on her knee. A lot of people talked and moved about. Momentarily the crowd increased. He stood in front of them—in front of Milly and his wife. And he spoke—holding out his packages. 'It's Christmas Eve,' he whispered shyly, 'and I've—brought you something—something for everybody. Look!' He held the packages before their eyes.

'Of course, of course,' said a voice behind him, 'but you may hold them out like that for a century. They'll *never* see them!'

'Of course they won't. But I love to do the old, sweet thing,' replied John Mudbury—then wondered with a gasp of stark amazement why he said it.

'*I* think——' whispered Milly, staring round her.

'Well, what do you think?' her mother asked sharply. 'You're always thinking something queer.'

'I think,' the girl continued dreamily, 'that Daddy's already here.' She paused, then added with a child's impossible conviction, 'I'm sure he is. I *feel* him.'

There was an extraordinary laugh. Sir James Epiphany laughed. The others—the whole crowd of them—also turned their heads and smiled. But the mother, thrusting the child away from her, rose up suddenly with a violent start. Her face had turned to chalk. She stretched her arms out—into the air before her. She gasped and shivered. There was anguish in her eyes.

'Look' repeated John, 'these are the Presents that I brought.' But his voice apparently was soundless. And, with a spasm of icy pain, he remembered that Palmer and Sir James—some years ago—had died.

'It's magic,' he cried, 'but—I love you, Jinny—I love you—and—and I have always been true to you—as true as steel. We need each other—oh, can't you see—we go on together—you and I—for ever and ever——'

'*Think*,' interrupted an exquisitely tender voice, 'don't shout! They can't *hear* you—now.' And, turning, John Mudbury met the eyes of Everard Minturn, their President of the year before. Minturn had gone down with the *Titanic*.

He dropped his parcels then. His heart gave an enormous leap of joy.

He saw her face—the face of his wife—look through him. But the child gazed straight into his eyes. She *saw* him.

The next thing he knew was that he heard something tinkling ... far, far away. It sounded miles below him—inside him—he was sounding himself—all utterly bewildering—like a bell. It *was* a bell.

Milly stooped down and picked the parcels up. Her face shone with happiness and laughter....

But a man came in soon after, a man with a ridiculous, solemn face, a pencil, and a notebook. He wore a dark blue helmet. Behind him came a string of other men. They carried something ... something ... he could not see exactly what it was. But, when he pressed forward through the laughing throng to gaze upon it, he dimly made out two eyes, a nose, a chin, a deep red smear, and a pair of folded hands upon and overcoat. A woman's form fell down upon them then, and he heard soft sounds of children weeping strangely ... and other sounds ... as of familiar voices laughing ... laughing gaily.

'They'll join us presently. It goes like a flash....'

And, turning with great happiness in his heart, he saw that Sir James had said it, holding Palmer by the arm as with some natural yet unexpected love of sympathetic friendship.

'Come on,' said Palmer, smiling like a man who accepts a gift in universal fellowship, 'let's help 'em. They'll never understand.... Still, we can always try.'

The entire throng moved up with laughter and amusement. It was a moment of hearty, genuine life at last. Delight and Joy and Peace were everywhere.

Then John Mudbury realised the truth—that he was dead.

THE OTHER WING

1

It used to puzzle him that, after dark, someone *would* look in round the edge of the bedroom door, and withdraw again too rapidly for him to see the face. When the nurse had gone away with the candle this happened: 'Good night, Master Tim,' she said usually, shading the light with one hand to protect his eyes; 'dream of me and I'll dream of you.' She went out slowly. The sharp-edged shadow of the door ran across the ceiling like a train. There came a whispered colloquy in the corridor outside, about himself, of course, and—he was alone. He heard her steps going deeper and deeper into the bosom of the old country house; they were audible for a moment on the stone flooring of the hall; and sometimes the dull thump of the baize door into the servants' quarters just reached him, too—then silence. But it was only when the last sound as well as the last sign of her had vanished that the face emerged from its hiding-place and flashed in upon him round the corner. As a rule, too, it came just as he was saying, 'Now I'll go to sleep. I won't think any longer. Good night, Master Tim, and happy dreams.' He loved to say this to himself; it brought a sense of companionship, as though there were two persons speaking.

The room was on the top of the old house, a big, high--ceilinged room, and his bed against the wall had an iron railing round it; he felt very safe and protected in it. The curtains at the other end of the room were drawn. He lay watching the firelight dancing on the heavy folds, and their pattern, showing a spaniel chasing a long-tailed bird towards a bushy tree, interested and amused him. It was repeated over and over again. He counted the number of dogs, and the number of birds, and the number of trees, but could never make them agree. There was a plan somewhere in that pattern;

if only he could discover it, the dogs and birds and trees would 'come out right.' Hundreds and hundreds of times he had played this game, for the plan in the pattern made it possible to take sides, and the bird and dog were against him. They always won, however; Tim usually fell asleep just when the advantage was on his own side. The curtains hung steadily enough most of the time, but it seemed to him once or twice that they stirred—hiding a dog or bird on purpose to prevent his winning. For instance, he had eleven birds and eleven trees, and, fixing them in his mind by saying, 'that's eleven birds and eleven trees, but only ten dogs', his eyes darted back to find the eleventh dog, when—the curtain moved and threw all his calculations into confusion again. The eleventh dog was hidden. He did not quite like the movement; it gave him questionable feelings, rather, for the curtain did not move of itself. Yet, usually, he was too intent upon counting the dogs to feel positive alarm.

Opposite to him was the fireplace, full of red and yellow coals; and, lying with his head sideways on the pillow, he could see directly in between the bars. When the coals settled with a soft and powdery crash, he turned his eyes from the curtains to the grate, trying to discover exactly which bits had fallen. So long as the glow was there the sound seemed pleasant enough, but sometimes he awoke later in the night, the room huge with darkness, the fire almost out—and the sound was not so pleasant then. It startled him. The coals did not fall of themselves. It seemed that someone poked them cautiously. The shadows were very thick before the bars. As with the curtains, moreover, the morning aspect of the extinguished fire, the ice-cold cinders that made a clinking sound like tin, caused no emotion whatever in his soul.

And it was usually while he lay waiting for sleep, tired both of the curtain and the coal games, on the point, indeed, of saying, 'I'll go to sleep now,' that the puzzling thing took place. He would be staring drowsily at the dying fire, perhaps counting the stockings and flannel garments that hung along the high fender rail when, suddenly, a person looked in with lightning swiftness through the door and vanished again before he could possibly turn his head to see. The appearance and disappearance were accomplished with amazing rapidity always.

It was a head and shoulders that looked in, and the movement combined the speed, the lightness and the silence of a shadow. Only it was not a shadow. A hand held the edge of the door. The face shot round, saw him, and withdrew like lightning. It was utterly beyond him to imagine anything more quick and clever. It darted. He heard no sound. It went. But—it had seen him, looked him all over, examined him, noted what he was doing with that lightning glance. It wanted to know if he were awake still, or asleep. And though it went off, it still watched him from a distance; it waited somewhere; it knew all about him. *Where* it waited no one could ever guess. It came probably, he felt, from beyond the house, possibly from the roof, but most likely from the garden or the sky. Yet, though strange, it was not terrible. It was a kindly and protective figure, he felt. And when it happened he never called for help, because the occurrence simply took his voice away.

'It comes from the Nightmare Passage,' he decided; 'but it's *not* a nightmare.' It puzzled him.

Sometimes, moreover, it came more than once in a single night. He was pretty sure—not *quite* positive—that it occupied his room as soon as he was properly asleep. It took possession, sitting perhaps before the dying fire, standing upright behind the heavy curtains, or even lying down in the empty bed his brother used when he was home from school. Perhaps it played the curtain game, perhaps it poked the coals; it knew, at any rate, where the eleventh dog had lain concealed. It certainly came in and out; certainly, too, it did not wish to be seen. For, more than once, on waking suddenly in the midnight blackness, Tim knew it was standing close beside his bed and bending over him. He felt, rather than heard, its presence. It glided quietly away. It moved with marvellous softness, yet he was positive it moved. He felt the difference, so to speak: it had been near him, now it was gone. It came back, too—just as he was falling into sleep again. Its midnight coming and going, however, stood out sharply different from its first shy, tentative approach. For in the firelight it came alone; whereas in the black and silent hours, it had with it—others.

And it was then he made up his mind that its swift and quiet movements were due to the fact that it had wings. It flew. And the others that came with it in the darkness were 'its little ones.' He also made up his mind that all were friendly, comforting, protective, and that while positively *not* a Nightmare, it yet came somehow along the Nightmare Passage before it reached him. 'You see, it's like this,' he explained to the nurse: 'The big one comes to visit me alone, but it only brings its little ones when I'm *quite* asleep.'

'Then the quicker you get to sleep the better, isn't it, Master Tim?'

He replied: 'Rather! I always do. Only I wonder where they come *from!*' He spoke, however, as though he had an inkling.

But the nurse was so dull about it that he gave her up and tried his father. 'Of course,' replied this busy but affectionate parent, 'it's either nobody at all, or else it's Sleep coming to carry you away to the land of dreams.' He made the statement kindly but somewhat briskly, for he was worried just then about the extra taxes on his land, and the effort to fix his mind on Tim's fanciful world was beyond him at the moment. He lifted the boy on to his knee, kissed and patted him as though he were a favourite dog, and planted him on the rug again with a flying sweep. 'Run and ask your mother,' he added; 'she knows all that kind of thing. Then come back and tell me all about it—another time.'

Tim found his mother in an arm-chair before the fire of another room; she was knitting and reading at the same time—a wonderful thing the boy could never understand. She raised her head as he came in, pushed her glasses on to her forehead, and held her arms out. He told her everything, ending up with what his father said.

'You see, it's *not* Jackman, or Thompson, or anyone like

that,' he exclaimed. 'It's someone real.'

'But nice,' she assured him, 'someone who comes to take care of you and see that you're all safe and cosy.'

'Oh, yes, I know that. But——'

'I think your father's right,' she added quickly. 'It's Sleep, I'm sure, who pops in round the door like that. Sleep *has* got wings, I've always heard.'

'Then the other thing—the little ones?' he asked. 'Are they just sorts of dozes, you think?'

Mother did not answer for a moment. She turned down the page of her book, closed it slowly, and put it on the table beside her. More slowly still she put her knitting away, arranging the wool and needles with some deliberation.

'Perhaps,' she said, drawing the boy closer to her and looking into his big eyes of wonder, 'they're dreams!'

Tim felt a thrill run through him as she said it. He stepped back a foot or so and clapped his hands softly. 'Dreams!' he whispered with enthusiasm and belief; 'of course! I never thought of that.'

His mother, having proved her sagacity, then made a mistake. She noted her success, but instead of leaving it there, she elaborated and explained. As Tim expressed it she 'went on about it.' Therefore he did not listen. He followed his train of thought alone. And presently, he interrupted her long sentences with a conclusion of his own:

'Then I know where She hides,' he announced with a touch of awe. 'Where She lives, I mean.' And without waiting to be aked, he imparted the information: 'It's in the Other Wing.'

'Ah!' said his mother, taken by surprise. 'How clever of you, Tim!'—and thus confirmed it.

Thenceforward this was established in his life—that Sleep and her attendant Dreams hid during the daytime in that unused portion of the great Elizabethan mansion called the Other Wing. This other wing was unoccupied, its corridors untrodden, its windows shuttered and its rooms all closed. At various places green baize doors led into it, but no one ever opened them. For many years this part had been shut up; and for the children, properly speaking, it was out of bounds. They never mentioned it as a possible place, at any rate; in hide-and-seek it was not considered, even; there was a hint of the inaccessible about the Other Wing. Shadows, dust, and silence had it to themselves.

But Tim, having ideas of his own about everything, possessed special information about the Other Wing. He believed it *was* inhabited. Who occupied the immense series of empty rooms, who trod the spacious corridors, who passed to and fro behind the shuttered windows, he had not known exactly. He had called these occupants, 'they', and the most important among them was 'The Ruler.' The Ruler of the Other Wing was a kind of deity, powerful, far away, ever present yet never seen.

And about this Ruler he had a wonderful conception for a little boy; he connected her, somehow, with deep thoughts of his own, the deepest of all. When he made up adventures to the moon, to the stars, or to the bottom of the sea, adventures that he lived inside himself, as it were—to reach them he must invariably pass through the chambers of the Other Wing. Those corridors and halls, the Nightmare Passage among them, lay along the route; they were the first stage of the journey. Once the green baize doors swung to behind him and the long dim passage stretched ahead, he was well on his way into the adventure of the moment; the Nightmare Passage once passed, he was safe from capture; but once the shutters of a window had been flung open, he was free of the gigantic world that lay beyond. For then light poured in and he could see his way.

The conception, for a child, was curious. It established a correspondence between the mysterious chambers of the Other Wing and the occupied, but unguessed chambers of his Inner Being. Through these chambers, through these darkened corridors, along a passage, sometimes dangerous, or at least of questionable repute, he must pass to find all adventures that were *real*. The light—when he pierced far enough to take the shutters down—was discovery. Tim did not actually think, much less say, all this. He was aware of it, however. He felt it. The Other Wing was inside himself as well as through the green baize doors. His inner map of wonder included both of them.

But now, for the first time in his life, he knew who lived there and who the Ruler was. A shutter had fallen of its own accord; light poured in; he made a guess, and Mother had confirmed it. Sleep and her Little Ones, the host of dreams, were the daylight occupants. They stole out when the darkness fell. All adventures in life began and ended by a dream —discoverable by first passing through the Other Wing.

2

AND, having settled this, his one desire now was to travel over the map upon journeys of exploration and discovery. The map inside himself he knew already, but the map of the Other Wing he had not seen. His imagination knew it, he had a clear mental picture of rooms and halls and passages, but his feet had never trod the silent floors where dust and shadows hid the flock of dreams by day. The mighty chambers where Sleep ruled he longed to stand in, to see the Ruler face to face. He made up his mind to get into the Other Wing.

To accomplish this was difficult; but Tim was a determined youngster, and he meant to try; he meant, also, to succeed. He deliberated. At night he could not possibly manage it; in any case, the Ruler and her host all left it after dark to fly about the world; the Wing would be empty, and the emptiness would frighten him. Therefore he must make a daylight visit; and it was a daylight visit he decided on. He deliberated more. There were rules and risks involved: it meant going out of bounds, the danger of being seen, the certainty of being questioned by some idle and inquisitive grown-up: 'Where in the world have you been all this time?'—and so forth. These things he thought out carefully, and though he arrived at no solution, he felt satisfied that it would be all right. That is, he recognised the risks. To be thus prepared was half the battle, for nothing then could take him by surprise.

The notion that he might slip in from the garden was soon abandoned; the red bricks showed no openings; there was no door; from the courtyard, also, entrance was impracticable: even on tiptoe he could barely reach the broad window-sills of stone. When playing alone, or walking with the French governess, he examined every outside possibility. None offered. The shutters, supposing he could reach them, were thick and solid.

Meanwhile, when opportunity offered, he stood against the tight red bricks; the towers and gables of the Wing rose overhead; he heard the wind go whispering along the eaves; he imagined tiptoe movements and a sound of wings inside. Sleep and her Little Ones were busily preparing for their journeys after dark; they hid, but they did not sleep; in this unused Wing, vaster alone than any other country house he had ever seen, Sleep taught and trained her flock of feathered Dreams. It was very wonderful. They probably supplied the entire County. But more wonderful still was the thought that the Ruler herself should take the trouble to come to his particular room and personally watch over him all night long. That was amazing. And it flashed across his imaginative inquiring mind: 'Perhaps they take me with them! The moment I'm asleep! That's why she comes to see me!'

Yet his chief preoccupation was, how Sleep got out. Through the green baize doors, of course! By a process of elimination he arrived at a conclusion: he, too, must enter through a green baize door and risk detection.

Of late, the lightning visits had ceased. The silent, darting figure had not peeped in and vanished as it used to do. He fell asleep too quickly now, almost before Jackman reached the hall, and long before the fire began to die. Also, the dogs and birds upon the curtains always matched the trees exactly, and he won the curtain game quite easily; there was never a dog or bird too many; the curtain never stirred. It had been thus ever since his talk with Mother and Father. And so he came to make a second discovery: His parents did not really believe in his Figure. She kept away on that account. They doubted her; she hid. Here was still another incentive to go and find her out. He ached for her, she was so kind, she gave herself so much trouble—just for his little self in the big and lonely bedroom. Yet his parents spoke of her as though she were of no account. He longed to see hear, face to face, and tell her that *he* believed in her and loved her. For he was positive she would like to hear it. She cared. Though he had fallen asleep of late too quickly for him to see her flash in at the door, he had known nicer dreams than in his life before—travelling dreams. And it was she who sent them. More—he was sure she took him out with her.

One evening, in the dusk of a March day, his opportunity came; and only just in time, for his brother, Jack, was expected home from school on the morrow, and with Jack in the other bed, no Figure would ever care to show itself. Also it was Easter, and after Easter, though Tim was not aware of it at the time, he was to say good-bye finally to governesses and become a day-boarder at a preparatory school for Wellington. The opportunity offered itself so naturally, moreover, that Tim took it without hesitation. It never occurred to him to question, much less to refuse it. The thing was obviously meant to be. For he found himself unexpectedly in front of a green baize door; and the green baize door was—swinging! Somebody, therefore, had just passed through it.

It had come about in this wise. Father, away in Scotland, at Inglemuir, the shooting place, was expected back next morning; Mother had driven over to the church upon some Easter business or other; and the governess had been allowed her holiday at home in France. Tim, therefore, had the run of the house, and in the hour between tea and bed-time he made good use of it. Fully able to defy such second-rate obstacles as nurses and butlers, he explored all manner of forbidden places with ardent thoroughness, arriving finally in the sacred precincts of his father's study. This wonderful room was the very heart and centre of the whole big house; he had been birched here long ago; here, too, his father had told him with a grave yet smiling face: 'You've got a new companion, Tim, a little sister; you must be very kind to her.' Also, it was the place where all the money was kept. What he called 'father's jolly smell' was strong in it—papers, tobacco, books, flavoured by hunting crops and gunpowder.

At first he felt awed, standing motionless just inside the door; but presently, recovering equilibrium, he moved cautiously on tiptoe towards the gigantic desk where important papers were piled in untidy patches. These he did not touch; but beside them his quick eye noted the jagged piece of iron shell his father brought home from his Crimean campaign and now used as a letter-weight. It was difficult to lift, however. He climbed into the comfortable chair and swung round and round. It was a swivel-chair, and he sank down among the cushions in it, staring at the strange things on the great desk before him, as if fascinated. Next he turned away and saw the stick-rack in the corner—this, he knew, he was allowed to touch. He had played with these sticks before. There were twenty, perhaps, all told, with curious carved handles, brought from every corner of the world; many of them cut by his father's own hand in queer and distant places. And, among them, Tim fixed his eye upon a cane with an ivory handle, a slender, polished cane that he had always coveted tremendously. It was the kind he meant to use when he became a man. It bent, it quivered, and when he swished it through the air it trembled like a riding-whip, and made a whistling noise. Yet it was very strong in spite of its elastic qualities. A family treasure, it was also an old-fashioned relic; it had been his great-grandfather's walking stick. Something of another century clung visibly about it still. It had dignity and grace and leisure in its very aspect. And it suddenly occurred to him. 'How great-grandpapa must miss it! Wouldn't he just love to have it back again!'

How it happened exactly, Tim did not know, but a few minutes later he found himself walking about the deserted halls and passages of the house with the air of an elderly gentleman of a hundred years ago, proud as a courtier, flourishing the stick like an Eighteenth Century dandy in the Mall. That the cane reached to his shoulder made no difference; he held it accordingly, swaggering on his way. He was off upon an adventure. He dived down through the byways of the Other Wing inside himself, as though the stick transported him to the days of the old gentleman who had used it in another century.

It may seem strange to those who dwell in smaller houses, but in this rambling Elizabethan mansion there were whole sections that, even to Tim, were strange and unfamiliar. In his mind the map of the Other Wing was clearer by far than the geography of the part he travelled daily. He came to passages and dim-lit halls, long corridors of stone beyond the Picture Gallery; narrow, wainscoted connecting-channels with four steps down and a little later two steps up; deserted chambers with arches guarding them—all hung with the soft March twilight and all bewilderingly unrecognised. With a sense of adventure born of naughtiness he went carelessly along, farther and farther into the heart of this unfamiliar country, swinging the cane, one thumb stuck into the arm-pit of his blue serge suit, whistling softly to himself, excited yet keenly on the alert —and suddenly found himself opposite a door that checked all further advance. It was a green baize door. And it was swinging.

He stopped abruptly, facing it. He stared, he gripped his cane more tightly, he held his breath. 'The Other Wing!' he gasped in a swallowed whisper.

It was an entrance, but an entrance he had never seen before. He thought he knew every door by heart; but this one was new. He stood motionless for several minutes, watching it; the door had two halves, but one half only was swinging, each swing shorter than the one before; he heard the little puffs of air it made; it settled finally, the last movements very short and rapid; it stopped. And the boy's heart, after similar rapid strokes, stopped also—for a moment.

'Someone's just gone through,' he gulped. And even as he said it he knew who the someone was. The conviction just dropped into him. 'It's great-grandpapa; he knows I've got his stick. He wants it!' On the heels of this flashed instantly another amazing certainty. 'He sleeps in there. He's having dreams. That's what being dead means.'

His first impulse, then, took the form of, 'I must let Father know; it'll make him burst for joy!' but his second was for himself—to finish his adventure. And it was this, naturally enough, that gained the day. He could tell his father later. His first duty was plainly to go through the door into the Other Wing. He must give the stick back to its owner. He must *hand* it back.

The test of will and character came now. Tim had imagination, and so knew the meaning of fear; but there was nothing craven in him. He could howl and scream and stamp like any other person of his age when the occasion called for such behaviour, but such occasions were due to temper roused by a thwarted will, and the histrionics were half 'pretended' to produce a calculated effect. There was no one to thwart his will at present. He also knew how to be afraid of Nothing, to be afraid without ostensible cause that is—which was merely 'nerves'. He could have 'the shudders' with the best of them.

But, when a real thing faced him, Tim's character emerged to meet it. He would clench his hands, brace his muscles, set his teeth—and wish to heaven he was bigger. But he would not flinch. Being imaginative, he lived the worst a dozen times before it happened, yet in the final crash he stood up like a man. He had that highest pluck—the courage of a sensitive temperament. And at this particular juncture, somewhat ticklish for a boy of eight or nine, it did not fail him. He lifted the cane and pushed the swinging door wide open. Then he walked through it—into the Other Wing.

3

The green baize door swung to behind him; he was even sufficiently master of himself to turn and close it with a steady hand, because he did not care to hear the series of muffled thuds its lessening swings would cause. But he realised clearly his position, knew he was doing a tremendous thing.

Holding the cane between fingers very tightly clenched, he

advanced bravely along the corridor that stretched before him. And all fear left him from that moment, replaced, it seemed, by a mild and exquisite surprise. His footsteps made no sound, he walked on air; instead of darkness, or the twilight he expected, a diffused and gentle light that seemed like the silver on the lawn when a half-moon sails a cloudless sky, lay everywhere. He knew his way, moreover, knew exactly where he was and whither he was going. The corridor was as familiar to him as the floor of his own bedroom; he recognised the shape and length of it; it agreed exactly with the map he had constructed long ago. Though he had never, to the best of his knowledge, entered it before, he knew with intimacy its every detail.

And thus the surprise he felt was mild and far from disconcerting. 'I'm here again!' was the kind of thought he had. It was *how* he got here that caused the faint surprise, apparently. He no longer swaggered, however, but walked carefully, and half on tiptoe, holding the ivory handle of the cane with a kind of affectionate respect. And as he advanced, the light closed softly up behind him, obliterating the way by which he had come. But this he did not know, because he did not look behind him. He only looked in front, where the corridor stretched its silvery length towards the great chamber where he knew the cane must be surrendered. The person who had preceded him down this ancient corridor, passing through the green baize door just before he reached it, this person, his father's grandfather, now stood in that great chamber, waiting to receive his own. Tim knew it as surely as he knew he breathed. At the far end he even made out the larger patch of silvery light which marked its gaping doorway.

There was another thing he knew as well—that this corridor he moved along between rooms with fast-closed doors, was the Nightmare Corridor; often and often he had traversed it; each room was occupied. 'This is the Nightmare Passage,' he whispered to himself, 'but I know the Ruler—it doesn't matter. None of the Nightmares can get out or do anything.' He heard them, none the less, inside, as he passed by; he heard them scratching to get out. The feeling of security made him reckless; he took unnecessary risks; he brushed the panels as he passed. And the love of keen sensation for its own sake, the desire to feel 'an awful thrill', temped him once so sharply that he suddenly raised his stick and poked a fast-shut door with it!

He was not prepared for the result, but he gained the sensation and the thrill. For the door opened with instant swiftness half and inch, a hand emerged, caught the stick and tried to draw it in. Tim sprang back as if he had been struck. He pulled at the ivory handle with all his strength, but his strength was less than nothing. He tried to shout, but his voice had gone. A terror of the moon came over him, for he was unable to loosen his hold of the handle; his fingers had become a part of it. An appalling weakness turned him helpless. He was dragged inch by inch towards the fearful door. The end of the stick was already through the narrow crack. He could not see the hand that pulled, but he knew it was gigantic. He understood now why the world was strange, why horses galloped furiously, and why trains whistled as they raced through stations. All the comedy and terror of nightmare gripped his heart with pincers made of ice. The disproportion was abominable. The final collapse rushed over him when, without a sign of warning, the door slammed silently, and between the jamb and the wall the cane was crushed as flat as if it were a bulrush. So irresistible was the force behind the door that the solid stick just went flat as the stalk of a bulrush.

He looked at it. It *was* a bulrush.

He did not laugh; the absurdity was so distressingly unnatural. The horror of finding a bulrush where he had expected a polished cane—this hideous and appalling detail held the nameless horror of the nightmare. It betrayed him utterly. Why had he not always known really that the stick was not a stick, but a thin and hollow reed...?

Then the cane was safely in his hand, unbroken. He stood looking at it. The Nightmare was in full swing. He heard another door opening behind his back, a door he had not touched. There was just time to see a hand thrusting and waving dreadfully, horribly, at him through the narrow crack—just time to realise that this was another Nightmare acting in atrocious concert with the first, when he saw closely beside him, towering to the ceiling, the protective, kindly Figure that visited his bedroom. In the turning movement he made to meet the attack, he became aware of her. And his terror passed. It was a nightmare terror merely. The infinite horror vanished. Only the comedy remained. He smiled.

He saw her dimly only, she was so vast, but he saw her, the Ruler of the Other Wing at last, and knew that he was safe again. He gazed with a tremendous love and wonder, trying to see her clearly; but the face was hidden far aloft and seemed to melt into the sky beyond the roof. He discerned that she was larger than the Night, only far, far softer, with wings that folded above him more tenderly even than his mother's arms; that there were points of light like stars among the feathers, and that she was vast enough to cover millions and millions of people all at once. Moreover, she did not fade or go, so far as he could see, but spread herself in such a way that he lost sight of her. She spread over the entire Wing...

And Tim remembered that this was all quite natural really. He had often and often been down this corridor before; the Nightmare Corridor was no new experience; it had to be faced as usual. Once knowing what hid inside the rooms, he was bound to tempt them out. They drew, enticed, attracted him; this was their power. It was their special strength that they could suck him helplessly towards them, and that he was obliged to go. He understood exactly why he was tempted to tap with the cane upon their awful doors, but, having done so, he had accepted the challenge and could now continue his journey quietly and safely. The Ruler of the Other Wing had taken him in charge.

A delicious sense of carelessness came on him. There was softness as of water in the solid things about him, nothing that could hurt or bruise. Holding the cane firmly by its ivory handle, he went forward along the corridor, walking as on air.

The end was quickly reached: He stood upon the threshold

of the mighty chamber where he knew the owner of the cane was waiting; the long corridor lay behind him, in front he saw the spacious dimensions of a lofty hall that gave him the feeling of being in the Crystal Palace, Euston Station, or St. Paul's. High, narrow windows, cut deeply into the wall, stood in a row upon the other side; an enormous open fireplace of burning logs was on his right; thick tapestries hung from the ceiling to the floor of stone; and in the centre of the chamber was a massive table of dark, shining wood, great chairs with carved stiff backs set here and there beside it. And in the biggest of these thronelike chairs there sat a figure looking at him gravely—the figure of an old, old man.

Yet there was no surprise in the boy's fast-beating heart; there was a thrill of pleasure and excitement only, a feeling of satisfaction. He had known quite well the figure would be there, known also it would look like this exactly. He stepped forward on to the floor of stone without a trace of fear or trembling, holding the precious cane in two hands now before him, as though to present it to its owner. He felt proud and pleased. He had run risks for this.

And the figure rose quietly to meet him, advancing in a stately manner over the hard stone floor. The eyes looked gravely, sweetly down at him, the aquiline nose stood out. Tim knew him perfectly: the knee-breeches of shining satin, the gleaming buckles on the shoes, the neat dark stockings, the lace and ruffles about neck and wrists, the coloured waistcoat opening so widely—all the details of the picture over father's mantelpiece, where it hung between two Crimean bayonets, were reproduced in life before his eyes as last. Only the polished cane with the ivory handle was not there.

Tim went three steps nearer to the advancing figure and held out both his hands with the cane laid crosswise on them.

'I've brought it, great-grandpapa,' he said, in a faint but clear and steady tone; 'here it is.'

And the other stooped a little, put out three fingers half concealed by falling lace, and took it by the ivory handle. He made a courtly bow to Tim. He smiled, but though there was pleasure, it was a grave, sad smile. He spoke then: the voice was slow and very deep. There was a delicate softness in it, the suave politeness of an older day.

'Thank you,' he said; 'I value it. It was given to me by my grandfather. I forgot it when I——' His voice grew indistinct a little.

'Yes?' said Tim.

'When I—left,' the old gentleman repeated.

'Oh,' said Tim, thinking how beautiful and kind the gracious figure was.

The old man ran his slender fingers carefully along the cane, feeling the polished surface with satisfaction. He lingered specially over the smoothness of the ivory handle. He was evidently very pleased.

'I was not quite myself—er—at the moment,' he went on gently; 'my memory failed me somewhat.' He sighed, as though an immense relief was in him.

'*I* forget things, too—sometimes,' Tim mentioned sympathetically. He simply loved his great-grandfather. He hoped—for a moment—he would be lifted up and kissed. 'I'm *awfully* glad I brought it,' he added— 'that you've got it again.'

The other turned his kind grey eyes upon him; the smile on his face was full of gratitude as he looked down.

'Thank you, my boy. I am truly and deeply indebted to you. You courted danger for my sake. Others have tried before, but the Nightmare Passage—er——' He broke off. He tapped the stick firmly on the stone flooring, as thought to test it. Bending a trifle, he put his weight upon it. 'Ah!' he exclaimed with a short sigh of relief, 'I can now——'

His voice again grew indistinct; Tim did not catch the words.

'Yes?' he asked again, aware for the first time that a touch of awe was in his heart.

'—get about again,' the other continued very low. 'Without my cane,' he added, the voice failing with each word the old lips uttered, 'I could not... possibly... allow myself... to be seen. It was indeed... deplorable... unpardonable of me... to forget in such a way. Zounds, sir...! I—I...'

THE OTHER WING

His voice sank away suddenly into a sound of wind. He straightened up, tapping the iron ferrule of his cane on the stones in a series of loud knocks. Tim felt a strange sensation creep into his legs. The queer words frightened him a little.

The old man took a step towards him. He still smiled, but there was a new meaning in the smile. A sudden earnestness had replaced the courtly, leisurely manner. The next words seemed to blow down upon the boy from above, as though a cold wind brought them from the sky outside.

Yet the words, he knew, were kindly meant, and very sensible. It was only the abrupt change that startled him. Great-grandpapa, after all, was but a man! This distant sound recalled something in him to that outside world from which the cold wind blew.

'My eternal thanks to you,' he heard, while the voice and face and figure seemed to withdraw deeper and deeper into the heart of the mighty chamber. 'I shall not forget your kindness and your courage. It is a debt I can, fortunately, one day repay.... But now you had best return, and with dispatch. For your head and arm lie heavily on the table, the documents are scattered, there is a cushion fallen... and my son's son is in the house.... Farewell! You had best leave me quickly. See! *She* stands behind you, waiting. Go with her! Go now...!'

The entire scene had vanished even before the final words were uttered. Tim felt empty space about him. A vast, shadowy Figure bore him through it as with mighty wings. He flew, he rushed, he remembered nothing more—until he heard another voice and felt a heavy hand upon his shoulder.

'Tim, you rascal! What are you doing in my study? And in the dark, like this!'

He looked up into his father's face without a word. He felt dazed. The next minute his father had caught him up and kissed him.

'Ragamuffin! How did you guess I was coming back tonight?' He shook him playfully and kissed his tumbling hair. 'And you've been asleep, too, into the bargain. Well—how's everything et home—eh? Jack's coming back from school to-morrow, you know, and...'

4

JACK came home, indeed, the following day, and when the Easter holidays were over, the governess stayed abroad and Tim went off to adventures of another kind in the preparatory school for Wellington. Life slipped rapidly along with him; he grew into a man; his mother and his father died; Jack followed them within a little space; Tim inherited, married, settled down into his great possessions—and opened up the Other Wing. The dreams of imaginative boyhood all had faded; perhaps he had merely put them away, or perhaps he had forgotten them. At any rate, he never spoke of such things now, and when his Irish wife mentioned her belief that the old country house possessed a family ghost, even declaring that she had met an Eighteenth Century figure of a man in the corridors, 'an old, old man who bends down upon a stick'—Tim only laughed and said:

'That's as it ought to be! And if these awful land taxes force us to sell some day, a respectable ghost will increase the market value.'

But one night he woke and heard a tapping on the floor. He sat up in bed and listened. There was a chilly feeling down his back. Belief had long since gone out of him; he felt uncannily afraid. The sound came nearer and nearer; there were light footsteps with it. The door opened—it opened a little wider, that is, for it already stood ajar—and there upon the threshold stood a figure that it seemed he knew. He saw the face as with all the vivid sharpness of reality. There was a smile upon it, but a smile of warning and alarm. The arm was raised. Tim saw the slender hand, lace falling down upon the long, thin fingers, and in them, tightly gripped, a polished cane. Shaking the cane twice to and fro in the air, the face thrust forward, spoke certain words, and—vanished. But the words were inaudible; for, though the lips distinctly moved, no sound, apparently, came from them.

And Tim sprang out of bed. The room was full of darkness. He turned the light on. The door, he saw, was shut as usual.

He had, of course, been dreaming. But he noticed a curious odour in the air. He sniffed it once or twice—then grasped the truth. It was a smell of burning!

Fortunately, he awoke just in time....

He was acclaimed a hero for his promptitude. After many days, when the damage was repaired, and nerves had settled down once more into the calm routine of country life, he told the story to his wife—the entire story. He told the adventure of his imaginative boyhood with it. She asked to see the old family cane. And it was this request of hers that brought back to memory a detail Tim had entirely forgotten all these years. He remembered it suddenly again—the loss of the cane, the hubbub his father kicked up about it, the endless, futile search. For the stick had never been found, and Tim, who was questioned very closely concerning it, swore with all his might that he had not the smallest notion where it was. Which was, of course, the truth.